# P. G. Wodehouse

'The ultimate in comfort reading because nothing bad ever happens in P.G. Wodehouse land. Or even if it does, it's always sorted out by the end of the book. For as long as I'm immersed in a P.G. Wodehouse book, it's possible to keep the real world at bay and live in a far, far nicer, funnier one where happy endings are the order of the day' *Marian Keyes*

'You should read Wodehouse when you're well and when you're poorly; when you're travelling, and when you're not; when you're feeling clever, and when you're feeling utterly dim. Wodehouse always lifts your spirits, no matter how high they happen to be already' *Lynne Truss*

'P.G. Wodehouse remains the greatest chronicler of a certain kind of Englishness, that no one else has ever captured quite so sharply, or with quite as much wit and affection' *Julian Fellowes*

'Not only the funniest English novelist who ever wrote but one of our finest stylists. His world is perfect, his stories are perfect, his writing is perfect. What more is there to be said?' *Susan Hill*

'One of my (few) proud boasts is that I once spent a day interviewing P.G. Wodehouse at his home in America. He was exactly as I'd expected: a lovely, modest man. He could have walked out of one of his own novels. It's dangerous to use the word genius to describe a writer, but I'll risk it with him' *John Humphrys*

'The incomparable and timeless genius — perfect for readers of all ages, shapes and sizes!' *Kate Mosse*

'A genius . . . Elusive, delicate but lasting. He created such a credible world that, sadly, I suppose, never really existed but what a delight it always is to enter it and the temptation to linger there is sometimes almost overwhelming' *Alan Ayckbourn*

'Wodehouse was quite simply the Bee's Knees. And then some' *Joseph Connolly*

'Compulsory reading for anyone who has a pig, an aunt – or a sense of humour!' *Lindsey Davis*

'I constantly find myself drooling with admiration at the sublime way Wodehouse plays with the English language' *Simon Brett*

'I've recorded all the Jeeves books, and I can tell you this: it's like singing Mozart. The perfection of the phrasing is a physical pleasure. I doubt if any writer in the English language has more perfect music' *Simon Callow*

'Quite simply, the master of comic writing at work' *Jane Moore*

'To pick up a Wodehouse novel is to find oneself in the presence of genius – no writer has ever given me so much pure enjoyment' *John Julius Norwich*

'P.G. Wodehouse is the gold standard of English wit' *Christopher Hitchens*

'Wodehouse is so utterly, properly, simply funny' *Adele Parks*

'To dive into a Wodehouse novel is to swim in some of the most elegantly turned phrases in the English language' *Ben Schott*

'P.G. Wodehouse should be prescribed to treat depression. Cheaper, more effective than valium and far, far more addictive' *Olivia Williams*

'My only problem with Wodehouse is deciding which of his enchanting books to take to my desert island' *Ruth Dudley Edwards*

The author of almost a hundred books and the creator of Jeeves, Blandings Castle, Psmith, Ukridge, Uncle Fred and Mr Mulliner, P.G. Wodehouse was born in 1881 and educated at Dulwich College. After two years with the Hong Kong and Shanghai Bank he became a full-time writer, contributing to a variety of periodicals including *Punch* and the *Globe*. He married in 1914. As well as his novels and short stories, he wrote lyrics for musical comedies with Guy Bolton and Jerome Kern, and at one time had five musicals running simultaneously on Broadway. His time in Hollywood also provided much source material for fiction.

At the age of 93, in the New Year's Honours List of 1975, he received a long-overdue knighthood, only to die on St Valentine's Day some 45 days later.

# P. G. WODEHOUSE

# The World of Blandings

arrow books

Published by Arrow Books 2008

10

This collection first published in the United Kingdom in 1976 by Barrie & Jenkins Ltd

Arrow Books
The Random House Group Limited
20 Vauxhall Bridge Road
London SW1V 2SA

www.rbooks.co.uk

www.wodehouse.co.uk

Addresses for companies within The Random House Group Limited can be found at: www.randomhouse.co.uk/offices.htm

The Random House Group Limited Reg. No. 954009

A CIP catalogue record for this book is available from the British Library

ISBN 9780099514244

The Random House Group Limited supports The Forest Stewardship Council® (FSC®), the leading international forest-certification organisation. Our books carrying the FSC label are printed on FSC®-certified paper. FSC is the only forest-certification scheme supported by the leading environmental organisations, including Greenpeace. Our paper procurement policy can be found at www.randomhouse.co.uk/environment

Typeset by SX Composing DTP, Rayleigh, Essex
Printed and bound in the United Kingdom by Clays Ltd, St Ives PLC

# The World of Blandings

# CONTENTS

SOMETHING FRESH

CHAPTER ONE

I

The sunshine of a fair Spring morning fell graciously upon London town. Out in Piccadilly its heartening warmth seemed to infuse into traffic and pedestrians alike a novel jauntiness, so that bus-drivers jested and even the lips of chauffeurs uncurled into not unkindly smiles. Policemen whistled at their posts, clerks on their way to work, beggars approached the task of trying to persuade perfect strangers to bear the burden of their maintenance with that optimistic vim which makes all the difference. It was one of those happy mornings.

At nine o'clock precisely the door of No. 7A, Arundell Street, Leicester Square, opened, and a young man stepped out.

Of all the spots in London which may fairly be described as back-waters, there is none that answers so completely to the description as Arundell Street, Leicester Square. Passing along the north pavement of the Square, just where it joins Piccadilly, you hardly notice the bottle-neck opening of the tiny *cul-de-sac*.

Day and night the human flood roars past, ignoring it. Arundell Street is less than forty yards in length, and, though there are two hotels in it, they are not fashionable hotels. It is just a back-water.

In shape Arundell Street is exactly like one of those flat stone jars in which Italian wine of the cheaper sort is stored. The narrow neck which leads off Leicester Square opens abruptly into a small court. Two sides of this hotels occupy; the third is at present given up to furnished lodgings for the impecunious. These are always just going to be pulled down in the name of Progress, to make room for another hotel, but they never do meet with that fate, and as they stand now so will they, in all probability stand for generations to come.

They provide single rooms of moderate size, the bed modestly hidden during the day behind a battered screen. They contain a table, an easy-chair, a hard chair, a bureau, and a round tin bath, which, like the bed, goes into hiding after its useful work is performed. And you may rent one of these rooms, with breakfast thrown in, for five dollars a week.

Ashe Marson had done so. He had rented the second-floor front of No. 7A.

Twenty-six years before this story opens there had been born to the Reverend Joseph Marson, minister, and Sarah his wife, of Much Middleford, Salop, a son. This son, christened Ashe after a wealthy uncle who subsequently double-crossed them by leaving his money to charities, in due course proceeded to Oxford to read for the Church. So far as can be ascertained from contemporary records, he did not read a great deal for the Church, but he did succeed in running the mile in four and a half minutes and the half mile at a correspondingly rapid speed, and his researches in the art of long-jumping won him the respect of all.

He secured his Blue for Athletics, and gladdened thousands by winning the mile and the half-mile two years in succession against Cambridge at Queen's Club. But, owing to the pressure of other engagements, he unfortunately omitted to do any work, and, when the hour of parting arrived, he was peculiarly unfitted for any of the learned professions. Having, however, managed to obtain a sort of degree, enough to enable him to call himself a Bachelor of Arts, and realizing that you can fool some of the people some of the time, he applied for and secured a series of private tutorships. Having saved a little money at this dreadful trade, Ashe came to London and tried newspaper work. After two years of moderate success, he got in touch with the Mammoth Publishing Company.

The Mammoth Publishing Company, which controls several important newspapers, a few weekly journals, and a number of other things, does not disdain the pennies of the office-boy and the junior clerk. One of its many profitable ventures is a series of paper-covered tales of crime and adventure. It was here that Ashe found his niche. Those 'Adventures of Gridley Quayle, Investigator', which are so popular with a certain section of the reading public, were his work. Until the advent of Ashe and Mr. Quayle, the 'British Pluck Library' had been written by many hands and had included the adventures of many heroes; but in Gridley Quayle the proprietors held that the ideal had been reached, and Ashe received a commission to conduct the entire 'British Pluck Library' (monthly) himself. On the meagre salary paid him for these labours he had been supporting himself ever since.

That was how Ashe came to be in Arundell Street, Leicester Square, on this May morning.

He was a tall, well-built, fit-looking young man, with a clear eye and a strong chin; and he was dressed, as he closed the front door behind him, in a sweater, flannel trousers, and rubber-soled gymnasium shoes. In one hand he bore a pair of Indian clubs, in the other a skipping-rope.

Having drawn in and expelled the morning air in a measured and solemn fashion which the initiated observer would have recognized as that 'scientific deep breathing' which is so popular nowadays, he laid down his clubs, adjusted his rope, and began to skip.

When one considers how keenly London, like all large cities, resents physical exercise, unless taken with some practical and immediately utilitarian object in view, this young man's calm, as he did this peculiar thing, was amazing. The rules governing exercise in London are clearly defined. You may run, if you are running after a hat, or an omnibus; you may jump, if you do so with the idea of avoiding a taxi-cab or because you have stepped on a banana-skin. But, if you run because you wish to develop your lungs or jump because jumping is good for the liver, London punishes you with its mockery. It rallies round and points the finger of scorn.

Yet this morning, Arundell Street bore the spectacle absolutely unmoved. Due West, the proprietor of the Hotel Previtali leaned against his hostelry, his mind an obvious blank; due North, the proprietor of the Hotel Mathis propped up his caravanserai, manifestly thinking of nothing. In various windows of the two hotels the upper portions of employees appeared, and not a single employee ceased his task for a moment to fling a jibe. Even the little children who infested the court forbore to scoff, and the customary cat rubbing itself against the railings rubbed on without a glance.

The whole thing affords a remarkable object-lesson of what a young man can achieve with patience and perseverance.

When he had taken the second-floor front of No. 7A three months before, Ashe Marson had realized that he must forget those morning exercises which had become a second nature to him, or else defy London's unwritten law and brave London's mockery. He had not hesitated long. Physical fitness was his gospel. On the subject of exercise he was confessedly a crank. He decided to defy London.

The first time he appeared in Arundell Street in his sweater and flannels, he had barely whirled his Indian clubs once round his head before he had attracted the following audience:

(a)  Two cabmen (one intoxicated);
(b)  Four waiters from the Hotel Mathis;
(c)  Six waiters from the Hotel Previtali;
(d)  Six chambermaids from the Hotel Mathis;
(e)  Five chambermaids from the Hotel Previtali;
(f)  The proprietor of the Hotel Mathis;
(g)  The proprietor of the Hotel Previtali;
(h)  A street-cleaner;
(i)  Eleven nondescript loafers;
(j)  Twenty-seven children;
(k)  A cat.

They all laughed, even the cat, and kept on laughing. The intoxicated cabman called Ashe 'Bill Bailey!' And Ashe kept on swinging his clubs.

A month later, such is the magic of perseverance, his audience had narrowed down to the twenty-seven children. They still laughed, but without that ringing conviction which the sympathetic support of their elders had lent them.

And now, after three months, the neighbourhood having accepted Ashe and his morning exercises as a natural phenomenon, paid him no further attention.

On this particular morning, Ashe Marson skipped with even more than his usual vigour. This was because he wished to expel by means of physical fatigue a small devil of discontent of whose presence within him he had been aware ever since getting out of bed. It is in the Spring that the ache for the Larger Life comes upon us, and this was a particularly mellow Spring morning. It was the sort of morning when the air gives us a feeling of anticipation, a feeling that, on a day like this, things surely cannot go joggling along in the same dull old groove, a premonition that something romantic and exciting is about to happen to us. On such a morning you will see stout old gentlemen make sudden rollicking swings with their umbrellas; and a note of shrill optimism thrills in the errand-boy's whistle, as he sees life opening before him, large and splendid.

But the south-west wind of Spring brings also remorse. We catch the vague spirit of unrest in the air, and we regret our misspent youth.

Ashe was doing this. Even as he skipped, he was conscious of a wish that he had worked harder at Oxford, and was now in a position to be doing something better than hack-work for a soulless publishing company. Never before had he been so completely certain that he was sick to death of the rut into which he had fallen. The thought that after breakfast he must sit down and hammer out another Gridley Quayle adventure numbed him like a blow from what the papers always call 'some blunt instrument'. The mere thought of Gridley Quayle was loathsome on a morning like this, with all creation shouting at him that Summer was on its way and that there were brave doings afoot just around the corner.

Skipping brought no balm. He threw down his rope, and took up the Indian clubs.

Indian clubs left him still unsatisfied. The thought came to him that it was a long time since he had done his Larsen Exercises. Perhaps they would heal him.

A gentleman named Lieutenant Larsen, of the Danish Army, as the result of much study of the human anatomy, some time ago evolved a series of Exercises. All over the world at the present moment his apostles are twisting themselves into knots in accordance with the dotted lines in the illustrative plates of his admirable book. From Peebles to Baffin's Bay arms and legs are being swung in daily thousands from point A to point B, and flaccid muscles are gaining the consistency of india-rubber. Larsen's Exercises are the last word in exercises. They bring into play every sinew of the body. They promote a brisk circulation. They enable you, if you persevere, to fell oxen, if desired, with a single blow.

But they are not dignified. Indeed, to one seeing them suddenly and without warning for the first time, they are markedly humorous. The only reason why King Henry of England, whose son sank with the White Ship, never smiled again, was because Lieutenant Larsen had not then invented his admirable Exercises.

So complacent, so insolently unselfconscious had Ashe become in the course of three months, owing to his success in inducing the populace to look on anything he did with the indulgent eye of understanding, that it simply did not occur to him, when he abruptly twisted his body into the shape of a corkscrew in accordance with the directions in the Lieutenant's book for the consummation of Exercise One, that he was doing anything funny. And the behaviour of those present seemed to justify his confidence. The proprietor of the Hotel Mathis regarded him without a smile. The proprietor of the Hotel Previtali might have been in a trance for all the interest he displayed. The hotel employees continued their tasks impassively. The children were blind and dumb. The cat across the way stropped its backbone against the railings unheeding.

But, even as he unscrambled himself and resumed a normal posture, from his immediate rear there rent the quiet morning air a clear and musical laugh. It floated out upon the breeze, and hit him like a bullet.

Three months ago Ashe would have accepted the laugh as inevitable, and would have refused to allow it to embarrass him. But long immunity from ridicule had sapped his resolution. He spun round with a jump, flushed and self-conscious.

From the window of the first floor of No. 7A a girl was leaning. The Spring sunshine played on her golden hair and lit up her bright blue eyes, fixed on his flannelled and sweatered person with a fascinated amusement. Even as he turned, the laugh smote him afresh.

For the space of perhaps two seconds they stared at each other, eye to eye. Then she vanished into the room.

Ashe was beaten. Three months ago a million girls could have laughed at his morning exercises without turning him from his purpose. Today this one scoffer, alone and unaided, was sufficient for his undoing. The depression which exercise had begun to dispel surged back upon him. He had no heart to continue. Sadly gathering up his belongings, he returned to his room, and found a cold bath tame and uninspiring.

The breakfasts (included in rent) provided by Mrs. Bell, the landlady of No. 7A, were not exhilarating feasts. By the time Ashe had done his best with the dishevelled fried egg, the chicory, blasphemously called coffee, and the charred bacon, Misery had him firmly in its grip. And when he forced himself to the table, and began to try to concoct the latest of the adventures of Gridley Quayle, Investigator, his spirit groaned within him.

With that musical laugh ringing in his ears, he found himself wishing that he had never thought of Gridley Quayle, that the baser elements of the British reading public had never taken him for their hero, and that he personally was dead.

The unholy alliance had been in progress now for more than two years, and it seemed to Ashe that Gridley grew less human each month. He was so complacent and so maddeningly blind to the fact that only the most amazing luck enabled him to detect anything. To depend on Gridley Quayle for one's income was like being chained to some horrible monster.

This morning, as he sat and chewed his pen, his loathing for Gridley seemed to have reached its climax. It was his habit, in writing these stories, to think of a good title first, and then fit an adventure to it.

And overnight, in a moment of inspiration, he had jotted down on an envelope the words:

## THE ADVENTURE OF THE WAND OF DEATH

It was with the sullen repulsion of a vegetarian who finds a caterpillar in his salad that he now sat glaring at them.

The title had seemed so promising overnight, so full of strenuous possibilities. It was still speciously attractive, but, now that the moment had arrived for writing the story, its flaws became manifest.

What was a Wand of Death? It sounded good, but, coming down to hard facts, what *was* it? You cannot write a story about a wand of death without knowing what a wand of death is; and, conversely, if you have thought of such a splendid title, you cannot jettison it offhand.

Ashe rumpled his hair, and gnawed his pen.

There came a knock at the door.

Ashe spun round in his chair. This was the last straw. If he had told Mrs. Bell once that he was never to be disturbed in the morning on any pretext whatsoever, he had told her twenty times. It was simply too infernal to be endured if his work-time was to be cut into like this. He ran over in his mind a few opening remarks.

'Come in,' he shouted, and braced himself for battle.

A girl walked in, the girl of the first-floor front, the girl with the blue eyes who had laughed at his Larsen Exercises.

## II

Various circumstances contributed to the poorness of the figure which Ashe cut in the opening moments of this interview. In the first place, he was expecting to see his landlady, whose height was about four feet six, and the sudden entry of some one who was about five feet seven threw the universe temporarily out of focus. In the second place, in anticipation of Mrs. Bell's entry, he had twisted his face into a forbidding scowl and it was no slight matter to change this on the spur of the moment into a pleasant smile. Finally a man who has been sitting for half an hour in front of a sheet of paper bearing the words:

## THE ADVENTURE OF THE WAND OF DEATH

and trying to decide what a wand of death may be, has not his mind under proper control.

The net result of these things was that, for perhaps half a minute, Ashe behaved absurdly. He goggled and he yammered. A lunacy commissioner, had one been present, would have made up his mind about him without further investigation. It was not for an appreciable time that he thought of rising from his seat. When he did, the combined leap and twist which he executed practically amounted to a Larsen Exercise.

Nor was the girl unembarrassed. If Ashe had been calmer, he would have observed upon her cheek the flush that told that she too was finding the situation trying. But, women being ever better equipped with poise than men, it was she who spoke first.

'I'm afraid I'm disturbing you.'

'No, no,' said Ashe. 'Oh, no, not at all, not at all, no, oh no, not at all, no,' and would have continued to play upon the theme indefinitely, had not the girl spoken again.

'I wanted to apologize,' she said, 'for my abominable rudeness in laughing at you just now. It was idiotic of me, and I don't know why I did it. I'm sorry.'

Science, with a thousand triumphs to her credit, has not yet succeeded in discovering the correct reply for a young man to make who finds himself in the appalling position of being apologized to by a pretty girl. If he says nothing, he seems sullen and unforgiving. If he says anything, he makes a fool of himself. Ashe, hesitating between these two courses, suddenly caught sight of the sheet of paper over which he had been poring so long.

'What is a wand of death?' he asked.

'I beg your pardon?'

'A wand of death.'

'I don't understand.'

The delirium of the conversation was too much for Ashe. He burst out laughing. A moment later the girl did the same. And simultaneously embarrassment ceased to be.

'I suppose you think I'm mad?' said Ashe.

'Certainly,' said the girl.

'Well, I should have been if you hadn't come in.'

'Why was that?'

'I was trying to write a detective story.'

'I was wondering if you were a writer.'

'Do *you* write?'

'Yes. Do you ever read *Home Gossip*?'

'Never.'

'I congratulate you. It's a horrid little paper, all brown-paper patterns and advice to the love-lorn. I do a short story for it every week, under various names. A duke or an earl goes with each story. I loathe it intensely.'

'I am sorry for your troubles,' said Ashe firmly, 'but we are wandering from the point. What is a wand of death?'

'A wand of death?'

'A wand of death.'

The girl frowned reflectively.

'Why, of course it's the sacred ebony stick stolen from the Indian temple which is supposed to bring death to whoever possesses it. The hero gets hold of it, and the priests dog him and send him threatening messages. What else could it be?'

Ashe could not restrain his admiration.

'This is genius!'

'Oh, no.'

'Absolute genius. I see it all. The hero calls in Gridley Quayle, and that patronizing ass, by the aid of a series of wicked coincidences, solves the mystery, and there am I with another month's work done.'

She looked at him with interest.

'Are you the author of "Gridley Quayle"?'

'Don't tell me you read him!'

'I do *not* read him. But he is published by the same firm that publishes *Home Gossip*, and I can't help seeing his cover sometimes while I am waiting in the waiting-room to see the editress.'

Ashe felt like one who meets a boyhood's chum on a desert island. Here was a real bond between them.

'Do the Mammoth publish you too? Why, we are comrades in misfortune – fellow-serfs. We should be friends. Shall we be friends?'

'I should be delighted.'

'Shall we shake hands, sit down, and talk about ourselves a little?'

'But I am keeping you from your work.'

'An errand of mercy.'

She sat down. It is a simple act, this of sitting down, but like everything else it may be an index to character. There was something wholly satisfactory to Ashe in the manner in which this girl did it. She neither seated herself on the extreme edge of the easy-chair, as one braced for instant flight; nor did she wallow in the easy-chair, as one come to stay for the week-end. She carried herself in an unconventional situation with an unstudied self-confidence which he could not sufficiently admire. Etiquette is not rigid in Arundell Street, but, nevertheless, a girl in a first-floor front may be excused for showing surprise and hesitation when invited to a confidential chat with a second-floor front young man whom she has only known five minutes. But there is a Free Masonry among those who live in large cities on small earnings.

'Shall we introduce ourselves?' said Ashe. 'Or did Mrs. Bell tell you my name? By the way, you have not been here long, have you?'

'I took my room the day before yesterday. But your name, if you are the author of Gridley Quayle, is Felix Clovelly, isn't it?'

'Good Heavens, no! Surely you don't think any one's name could really be Felix Clovelly? That is only the cloak under which I hide my shame. My real name is Marson, Ashe Marson. And yours?'

'Valentine. Joan Valentine.'

'Will you tell me the story of your life, or shall I tell mine first?'

'I don't know that I have any particular story.'

'Come, come!'

'Well, I haven't.'

'Think again. Let us thrash this thing out. You were born!'

'I was.'

'Where?'

'In London.'

'Now we seem to be started. I was born in Much Middleford.'

'I'm afraid I never heard of it.'

'Strange! I know your birth-place quite well. But I have not yet made Much Middleford famous. In fact, I doubt if I ever shall. I am beginning to realize that I am one of the failures.'

'How old are you?'

'Twenty-six.'

'You are twenty-six, and you call yourself a failure? I think that is a shameful thing to say.'

'What would you call a man of twenty-six whose only means of making a living was the writing of Gridley Quayle stories? An empire builder?'

'How do you know it's your only means of making a living? Why don't you try something new?'

'Such as—?'

'How should I know? Anything that comes along. Good gracious, Mr. Marson, here you are in the biggest city in the world, with chance of adventure simply shrieking to you on every side—'

'I must be deaf. The only thing I have heard shrieking to me on every side has been Mrs. Bell – for the week's rent.'

'Read the papers. Read the advertisement columns. I'm sure you will find something sooner or later. Don't get into a groove. Be an adventurer. Snatch at the next chance, whatever it is.'

Ashe nodded.

'Continue,' he said. 'Proceed. You are stimulating me.'

'But why should you want a girl like me to stimulate you? Surely London is enough to do it without my help? You can always find *something* new, surely? Listen, Mr. Marson. I was thrown on my own resources about five years ago. Never mind how. Since then I have worked in a shop, done typewriting, been on the stage, had a position as governess, been a lady's maid—'

'A *what*? A lady's maid?'

'Why not? It was all experience, and I can assure you I would much rather be a lady's maid than a governess.'

'I think I know what you mean. I was a private tutor once. I suppose a governess is the female equivalent. I have often wondered what General Sherman would have said about private tutoring, if he expressed himself so breezily about mere War. Was it fun being a lady's maid?'

'It was pretty good fun, and it gave me an opportunity of studying the aristocracy in its native haunts, which has made me *Home Gossip*'s established authority on dukes and earls.'

Ashe drew a deep breath – not a scientific deep breath, but one of admiration.

'You are perfectly splendid?'

'Splendid?'

'I mean, you have such pluck!'

'Oh, well, I keep on trying. I'm twenty-three, and I haven't achieved anything much yet, but I certainly don't feel like sitting back and calling myself a failure.'

Ashe made a grimace.

'All right,' he said. 'I got it!'

'I meant you to,' said Joan placidly. 'I hope I haven't bored you with my autobiography, Mr. Marson? I'm not setting myself up as a shining example, but I do like action and hate stagnation.'

'You are absolutely wonderful,' said Ashe. 'You are a human correspondence course in Efficiency – one of the ones you see in the back pages of the magazines, beginning, "Young man are you earning enough?" with a picture showing the dead-beat gazing wistfully at the boss's chair. You would galvanize a jellyfish.'

'If I have really stimulated you—'

'I think,' said Ashe pensively, 'that that was another insult. Well, I deserve it. Yes, you *have* stimulated me. I feel a new man. It's queer that you should have come to me right on top of everything else. I don't remember when I have felt so restless and discontented as this morning.'

'It's the Spring.'

'I suppose it is. I feel like doing something big and adventurous.'

'Well, do it then. You have a *Morning Post* on the table. Have you read it yet?'

'I glanced at it.'

'But you haven't read the advertisement pages? Read them. They may contain just the opening you want.'

'Well, I'll do it, but my experience of advertisement pages is that they are monopolized by philanthropists who want to lend you any sum from ten to a hundred thousand pounds on your note of hand only. However, I will scan them.'

Joan rose, and held out her hand.

'Goodbye, Mr. Marson. You've got your detective story to write, and I have to think out something with a duke in it by tonight, so I must be going.' She smiled. 'We have travelled a good way from the point we started at, but I may as well go back to it before I leave you. I'm sorry I laughed at you this morning.'

Ashe clasped her hand in a fervent grip.

'I'm not. Come and laugh at me whenever you feel like it. I like being laughed at. Why, when I started my morning exercises, half London used to come and roll about the pavements in convulsions. I'm not an attraction any longer, and it makes me feel lonely. There are twenty-nine of those Larsen Exercises, and you only saw part of the first. You have done so much for me that, if I can be of any use to you in helping you to greet the day with a smile, I shall be only too proud. Exercise Six is funny without being vulgar. I'll start with it tomorrow morning. I can also recommend Exercise Eleven. Don't miss it.'

'Very well. Well, goodbye for the present.'

'Goodbye.'

She was gone; and Ashe, thrilling with new emotions, stared at the door which had been closed behind her. He felt as if he had been awakened from sleep by a powerful electric shock.

A wonderful girl . . . An astounding girl . . . An amazing girl. . . .

Close behind the sheet of paper on which he had inscribed the now luminous and suggestive title of his new Gridley Quayle story lay the *Morning Post*, whose advertisement columns he had promised her to explore. The least he could do was to begin at once.

His spirits sank as he did so. It was the same old game. A Mr. Brian MacNeill, though doing no business with minors, was willing, even anxious, to part with his vast fortune to anyone over the age of twenty-one whose means happened to be a trifle straitened. This good man required no security whatever. Nor did his rivals in generosity, the Messrs. Angus Bruce, Duncan Macfarlane, Wallace Mackintosh and Donald MacNab. They, too, showed a curious distaste for dealing with minors, but any one of maturer years could simply come round to the office and help himself.

Beneath these was the heart-cry of Young Man (Christian) who wanted a thousand pounds at once to enable him to complete his education with the Grand Tour.

Ashe threw the paper down wearily. He had known all along that it was no good. Romance was dead, and the Unexpected no longer happened.

He picked up his pen, and began to write the Adventure of the Wand of Death.

## CHAPTER TWO

I

In a bedroom on the fourth floor of the Hotel Guelph in Piccadilly, the Hon. Frederick Threepwood sat in bed with his knees drawn up to his chin and glared at the day with a glare of mental anguish. He had very little mind, but what he had was suffering.

He had just remembered.

It is like that in this life. You wake up, feeling as fit as a fiddle; you look at the window and see the sun and thank Heaven for a fine day; you begin to plan a perfectly corking luncheon-party with some of the chappies you met last night at the National Sporting Club, and then – you remember.

'Oh, dash it!' said the Hon. Freddie. And after a moment's pause, 'And I was feeling so dashed happy!'

For the space of some minutes he remained plunged in sad meditation. Then, picking up the telephone on the table at his side, he asked for a number.

'Hello?'

'Hello?' responded a rich voice at the other end of the wire.

'Oh, I say, is that you, Dickie?'

'Who is that?'

29

'This is Freddie Threepwood. I say, Dickie, old top, I want to see you about something devilish important. Will you be in at twelve?'

'Certainly. What's the trouble?'

'I can't explain over the wire, but it's deuced serious.'

'Very well. By the way, Freddie, congratulations on the engagement.'

'Thanks, old man. Thanks very much, and so forth, but you won't forget to be in at twelve, will you? Goodbye.'

He replaced the receiver quickly, and sprang out of bed, for he had heard the door-handle turn. When the door opened he was giving a correct representation of a young man wasting no time in beginning his toilet for the day.

An elderly, thin-faced, bald-headed, amiably vacant man entered. He regarded the Hon. Freddie with a certain disfavour.

'Are you only just getting up, Frederick?'

'Hullo, gov'nor. Good morning. I shan't be two ticks now.'

'You should have been out and about two hours ago. The day is glorious.'

'Shan't be more than a minute, gov'nor, now. Just got to have a tub and chuck on a few clothes.'

He disappeared into the bathroom. His father, taking a chair, placed the tips of his fingers together and in this attitude remained motionless, a figure of disapproval and suppressed annoyance.

Like many fathers in his rank of life, the Earl of Emsworth had suffered much through that problem which – with the exception of Mr. Lloyd George – is practically the only fly in the British aristocratic amber – the problem of What To Do With The Younger Sons. It is useless to try to gloss over the fact, the Younger Son is not required. You might reason with a British peer by the hour – you might point out to him how, on the one hand, he is far better off than the male codfish, who may at any moment find itself in the distressing position of being called on to provide for a family of over a million; and remind him, on the other, that every additional child he acquires means a corresponding rise for him in the estimation of ex-President Roosevelt; but you would not cheer him up in the least. He does not want the Younger Son.

Apart, however, from the fact that he was a younger son, and, as such a nuisance in any case, the Honourable Freddie had always annoyed his father in a variety of ways. The Earl of Emsworth was so constituted that no man or thing really had the power to trouble him deeply, but Freddie had come nearer to doing it than anybody else in the world. There had been a consistency, a perseverance, about his irritating performances which had acted on the placid peer as dripping water on a stone. Isolated acts of annoyance would have been powerless to ruffle his calm; but Freddie had been exploding bombs under his nose since he went to Eton.

He had been expelled from Eton for breaking out at night and roaming the streets of Windsor in a false moustache. He had been sent down from Oxford for pouring ink from a second-storey window on to the Junior Dean of his college. He had spent two years at an expensive London crammer's and failed to pass into the Army. He had also accumulated an almost record series of racing debts, besides as shady a gang of friends, for the most part vaguely connected with the turf, as any young man of his age ever contrived to collect.

These things try the most placid of parents, and finally Lord Emsworth had put his foot down. It was the only occasion in his life when he had acted with decision, and he did it with the accumulated energy of years. He stopped his son's allowance, haled him home to Blandings Castle, and kept him there so relentlessly that, until the previous night, when they had come up together by an afternoon train, Freddie had not seen London for nearly a year.

It was possibly the reflection that, whatever his secret troubles, he was at any rate once more in his beloved metropolis that caused Freddie at this point to burst into discordant song. He splashed and warbled simultaneously.

Lord Emsworth's frown deepened, and he began to tap his fingers together irritably. Then his brow cleared, and a pleased smile flickered over his face. He, too, had remembered.

What Lord Emsworth had remembered was this. Late in the previous Autumn, the next estate to Blandings had been rented by an American, a Mr. Peters, a man with many millions, chronic dyspepsia, and one fair daughter, Aline. The two families had met. Freddie and Aline had been thrown together. And, only a few days before, the engagement had been announced, and for Lord Emsworth the only flaw in this best of all possible worlds had been removed.

The singing in the bathroom was increasing in volume, but Lord Emsworth heard it now without wincing. It was amazing what a difference it made to a man's comfort, this fair prospect of getting his younger son off his hands. For nearly a year Freddie, a prisoner at Blandings, had afflicted his father's nerves with a never-failing discomfort. Blandings was a large house, but not so large that father and son did not occasionally meet; and on these occasions it had maddened Lord Emsworth to perceive the martyred aspect of the young man. To Lord Emsworth the park and gardens of Blandings were the nearest earthly approach to Paradise. Freddie, chafing at captivity, had mooned about them with an air of crushed gloom which would have caused comment in Siberia.

Yes, he was glad Freddie was engaged to be married to Aline Peters. He liked Aline. He liked Mr. Peters. Such was the relief he experienced that he found himself feeling almost affectionate towards Freddie, who emerged from the bathroom at this moment clad in a pink bath-robe, to find the paternal wrath evaporated and all, so to speak, right with the world.

Nevertheless, he wasted no time about his dressing. He was always ill at ease in his father's presence, and he wished to be elsewhere with all possible speed. He sprang into his trousers with such energy that he nearly tripped himself up.

As he disentangled himself, he recollected something which had slipped his memory.

'By the way, guv'nor, I met an old pal of mine last night, and asked him down to Blandings this week. That's all right, isn't it, what?'

For a moment Lord Emsworth's geniality faltered. He had had experience of Freddie's old pals.

'Who is he? Kindly remember that Mr. Peters and Aline and nearly all your relations will be at Blandings this week. If he is one of—'

'Oh, no, that's all right. Honour bright. He isn't one of the old crowd. He's a man named Emerson. Most respectable chap. Policeman or something in Hong Kong. He knows Aline quite well, he says. Met her on the boat coming over.'

'I do not remember any friend of yours named Emerson.'

'Well, as a matter of fact I met him last night for the first time. But it's all right. He's a good chap, don't you know, and all that sort of rot.'

Lord Emsworth was feeling too benevolent to raise the

objections which he would certainly have raised, had his mood been less sunny.

'Certainly, let him come, if he wishes.'

'Thanks, guv'nor.'

Freddie completed his toilet.

'Doing anything special this morning, guv'nor? I rather thought of getting a bit of breakfast and then strolling round a bit. Have you had breakfast?'

'Two hours ago. I trust that, in the course of your strolling, you will find time to call at Mr. Peters' and see Aline. I shall be going there directly after lunch. Mr. Peters wishes to show me his collection of – I think scarabs was the word he used.'

'Oh, I'll look in all right. Don't you worry. Or, if I don't, I'll call the old boy up on the 'phone and pass the time of day. Well, I rather think I'll be popping off now and getting that bit of breakfast, what?'

Several comments on this speech suggested themselves to Lord Emsworth. In the first place, he did not approve of Freddie's allusion to one of America's merchant-princes as 'the old boy'. Secondly, his son's attitude did not strike him as the ideal attitude of a young man towards his betrothed. There seemed a lack of warmth. But, he reflected, possibly this was simply another manifestation of the Modern Spirit, and in any case it was not worth bothering about, so he offered no criticism; and presently, Freddie having given his shoes a flick with a silk handkerchief and thrust the latter carefully up his sleeve, they passed out and down into the main lobby of the hotel, where they parted, Freddie to his bit of breakfast, his father to potter about the streets and kill time till lunch. London was always a trial to the Earl of Emsworth. His heart was in the country, and the city held no fascinations for him.

## II

On one of the floors in one of the buildings in one of the streets which slope precipitously from the Strand to the Thames Embankment, there is a door, which would be all the better for a lick of paint, which bears what is perhaps the most modest and unostentatious announcement of its kind in London.

The grimly ground-glass displays the words:

R. JONES,

simply that, and nothing more.

Situated between a door profusely illustrated with the legend, 'Sarawak and New Guinea Rubber Estates Exploitation Company. General Manager, Jno. Bradbury-Eggleston' and a door belonging to the Bhangaloo Ruby Mines Incorporated, it has a touch of the woodland violet nestling among orchids.

R. JONES.

It is rugged in its simplicity. You wonder, as you look at it, if you have time to look at and wonder about these things, who this Jones may be and what is the business which he conducts with such a coy reticence.

As a matter of fact, these speculations had passed through suspicious minds at Scotland Yard, which had for some time taken not a little interest in R. Jones. But, beyond ascertaining that he bought and sold curios, did a certain amount of book-making during the flat-racing season, and had been known to lend money, Scotland Yard did not find out much about Mr. Jones, and presently dismissed him from its thoughts. Not that Scotland Yard was satisfied. To a certain extent, baffled would be a better description of its attitude. The suspicion that R. Jones was, among other things, a receiver of stolen goods still lingered, but proof was not forthcoming.

R. Jones saw to that. He did a great many things, for he was one of the busiest men in London; but what he did best was seeing to it that proof was not forthcoming.

On the theory, given to the world by my brother-author, William Shakespeare, that it is the lean and hungry-looking men who are dangerous and that the fat, the sleek-headed men and such as sleep o' nights, are harmless, R. Jones should have been above suspicion. He was infinitely the fattest man in the west-central postal district of London. He was a round ball of a man, who wheezed when he walked upstairs, which was seldom, and shook like a jelly if some tactless friend, wishing to attract his attention, tapped him unexpectedly on the shoulder. But this occurred still less frequently than his walking upstairs, for in R. Jones' circle it was recognized that nothing is a greater breach of etiquette and worse form than to tap people unexpectedly on the shoulder. That, it was felt, should be left to those who are paid by the Government to do it.

R. Jones was about fifty years old, grey-haired, of a mauve complexion, jovial among his friends, and perhaps even more jovial with chance acquaintances. It was estimated by envious intimates that his joviality with chance acquaintances, especially with young men of the upper classes with large purses and small foreheads, was worth hundreds of pounds a year to him. There was something about his comfortable appearance and his jolly manner which irresistibly attracted a certain type of young man. It was his good fortune that this type of young man should be the type, financially, most worth attracting.

Freddie Threepwood had fallen under his spell during his

short but crowded life in London. They had met for the first time at the Derby, and ever since R. Jones had held, in Freddie's estimation, that position of guide, philosopher and friend, which he held in the estimation of so many young men of Freddie's type.

That was why, at twelve o'clock punctually on this Spring morning, he tapped with his cane on R. Jones' ground-glass, and showed such satisfaction and relief when the door was opened by the proprietor in person.

'Well, well, well!' said R. Jones, rollickingly. 'Whom have we here? The dashing bridegroom-to-be, and no other!'

R. Jones, like Lord Emsworth, was delighted that Freddie was about to marry a nice girl with plenty of money. The sudden turning-off of the tap from which Freddie's allowance had flowed had hit him hard. He had other sources of income, of course, but few so easy and unfailing as Freddie's had been in the days of his prosperity.

'The prodigal son, by George! Creeping back into the fold after all this weary time! It seems years since I saw you, Freddie. The old guv'nor put his foot down, didn't he, and stopped the funds? Damned shame! I take it that things have loosened up a bit since the engagement was announced, eh?'

Freddie sat down, and chewed the knob of his cane unhappily.

'Well, as a matter of fact, Dickie, old top,' he said, 'not so that you could notice it, don't you know. Things are still pretty much the same. I managed to get away from Blandings for a night, because the governor had to come to London, but I've got to go back with him on the three o'clock train. And, as for money, I can't get a quid out of him. As a matter of fact, I'm in the deuce of a hole, and that's why I've come to you.'

Even fat, jovial men have their moments of depression. R. Jones' face clouded, and jerky remarks about the hardness of times and losses on the Stock Exchange began to proceed from him. As Scotland Yard had discovered, he lent money on occasion, but he did not lend it to youths in Freddie's unfortunate position.

'Oh, I don't want to make a touch, you know,' Freddie hastened to explain. 'It isn't that. As a matter of fact, I managed to raise five hundred of the best this morning. That ought to be enough.'

'Depends what you want it for,' said R. Jones, magically genial once more. The thought entered his mind, as it had so often done, that the world was full of easy marks. He wished he could meet the money-lender who had been rash enough to advance the Honourable Freddie five hundred pounds. These philanthropists cross our path too seldom.

Freddie felt in his pocket, produced a cigarette-case, and from it extracted a newspaper-clipping.

'Did you read about poor old Percy in the papers? The case, you know?'

'Percy?'

'Lord Stockheath, you know.'

'Oh, the Stockheath breach-of-promise case? I did more than that. I was in court all three days.' R. Jones emitted a cosy chuckle. 'Is he a pal of yours? A cousin, eh? I wish you had seen him in the witness-box, with Jellicoe-Smith cross-examining him! The funniest thing I ever heard. And his letters to the girl! They read them out in court, and all of the—'

'Don't, old man! Dickie, old top, please! I know all about it. I read the reports. They made poor old Percy look an absolute ass.'

'Well, Nature had done that already, but I'm bound to say they improved on Nature's work. I should think your cousin Percy must have felt like a plucked chicken.'

A spasm of pain passed over the Honourable Freddie's vacant face. He wriggled in his chair.

'Dickie, old man, I wish you wouldn't talk like that. It makes me feel ill.'

'Why, is he such a pal of yours as all that?'

'It's not that. It's – the fact is, Dickie, old top, I'm in exactly the same bally hole as poor old Percy was, myself.'

'What! You have been sued for breach of promise?'

'Not absolutely that – yet. Look here, I'll tell you the whole thing. Do you remember a show at the Piccadilly about a year ago, called, *The Girl from Dublin?* There was a girl in the chorus.'

'Several. I remember noticing.'

'No. I mean one particular girl – a girl called Joan Valentine. The rotten part is that I never met her.'

'Pull yourself together, Freddie. What exactly is the trouble?'

'Well, don't you see, I used to go to the show every other night, and I fell frightfully in love with this girl—'

'Without having met her?'

'Yes. You see, I was rather an ass in those days.'

'No, no,' said R. Jones, handsomely.

'I must have been, or I wouldn't have been such an ass, don't you know. Well, as I was saying, I used to write this girl letters, saying how much I was in love with her, and – and—'

'Specifically proposing marriage?'

'Eh?'

'I say, specifically proposing marriage?'

'I can't remember. I expect I did. I was awfully in love.'

'How was it that you never met her?'

'She wouldn't meet me. She wouldn't even come out to lunch. She didn't even answer my letters – just sent word down by the Johnnie at the stage-door. And then—'

Freddie's voice died away. He thrust the knob of his cane into his mouth in a sort of frenzy.

'What then?' inquired R. Jones.

A scarlet blush manifested itself on Freddie's young face. His eyes wandered sideways. After a long pause a single word escaped him, almost inaudible.

'Poetry!'

R. Jones trembled as if an electric current had been passed through his plump frame. His little eyes sparkled with merriment.

'You wrote her poetry!'

'Yards of it, old boy, yards of it!' groaned Freddie.

Panic filled him with speech.

'You see the frightful hole I'm in? This girl is bound to have kept the letters. I don't remember if I actually proposed to her or not, but anyway she's got enough material to make it worthwhile to have a dash at an action, especially after poor old Percy has just got soaked for such a pile of money, and made breach-of-promise cases the fashion, so to speak. And now that the announcement of my engagement is out, she's certain to get busy. Probably she has been waiting for something of the sort. Don't you see that all the cards are in her hands? We couldn't afford to let the thing come into court. That poetry would dish my marriage for a certainty. I'd have to emigrate or something! Goodness knows what would happen at home. My old governor would murder me. So you see what a frightful hole I'm in, don't you, Dickie, old man?'

'And what do you want me to do?'

'Why, to get hold of this girl and get back the letters, don't you see? I can't do it myself, cooped up miles away in the country. And besides I shouldn't know how to handle a thing like that. It wants a chappie with a lot of sense and a persuasive sort of way with him.'

'Thanks for the compliment, Freddie, but I should imagine that something a little more solid than a persuasive way would be required in a case like this. You said something a while ago about five hundred pounds?'

'Here it is, old man, in notes. I brought it on purpose. Will you really take the thing on? Do you think you can work it for five hundred?'

'I can have a try.'

Freddie rose with an expression approximating to happiness on his face. Some men have the power of inspiring confidence in some of their fellows, while filling others with distrust. Scotland Yard might look askance at R. Jones, but to Freddie he was all that was helpful and reliable. He shook R. Jones' hand several times in his emotion.

'That's absolutely topping of you, old man,' he said. 'Then I'll leave the whole thing to you. Write me the moment you have done anything, won't you. Goodbye, old top, and thanks ever so much.'

The door closed. R. Jones remained where he sat, his fingers straying luxuriously among the crackling paper. A feeling of complete happiness warmed R. Jones' bosom. He was not certain whether or not his mission would be successful, and, to be truthful, he was not letting this worry him much. What he was certain of, was the fact that the Heavens had opened unexpectedly and dropped five hundred pounds into his lap.

## CHAPTER THREE

I

The Earl of Emsworth stood in the doorway of the Senior Conservative Club's vast dining-room, and beamed with a vague sweetness upon the two hundred or so Senior Conservatives, who, with much clattering of knife and fork, were keeping body and soul together by means of the coffee-room luncheon. He might have been posing for a Statue of Amiability. His pale blue eyes shone with a friendly light through their protecting glasses; the smile of a man at peace with all men curved his weak mouth; his bald head, reflecting the sunlight, seemed almost to wear a halo.

Nobody appeared to notice him. He so seldom came to London these days that he was practically a stranger in the club; and in any case your Senior Conservative, when at lunch, has little leisure for observing anything not immediately on the table in front of him. To attract attention in the dining-room of the Senior Conservative Club between the hours of one and two-thirty, you have to be a mutton-chop, not an earl.

It is possible that, lacking the initiative to make his way down the long aisle and find a table for himself, he might have stood there indefinitely, but for the restless activity of Adams, the head steward. It was Adams' mission in life to flit to and fro, hauling would-be lunchers to their destinations, as a St. Bernard dog hauls travellers out of Alpine snow-drifts.

He sighted Lord Emsworth, and secured him with a genteel pounce.

'A table, your lordship? This way, your lordship.'

Adams remembered him, of course. Adams remembered everybody.

Lord Emsworth followed him beamingly, and presently came to anchor at a table at the further end of the room. Adams handed him the bill of fare, and stood brooding over him like a Providence.

'Don't often see your lordship in the club,' he opened chattily. It was his business to know the tastes and dispositions of all the five thousand or so members of the Senior Conservative Club and to suit his demeanour to them. To some he would hand the bill of fare swiftly, silently, almost brusquely, as one who realizes that there are moments in life too serious for talk. Others, he knew, liked conversation, and to these he introduced the subject of food almost as a sub-motive.

Lord Emsworth, having examined the bill of fare with a mild curiosity, laid it down and became conversational.

'No, Adams, I seldom visit London nowadays. London does not attract me. The country . . . the fields . . . the woods . . . the birds . . .'

Something across the room seemed to attract his attention, and his voice trailed off. He inspected this for some time with bland interest, then turned to Adams once more.

'What was I saying, Adams?'

'The birds, your lordship.'

'Birds? What birds? What about birds?'

'You were speaking of the attractions of life in the country, your lordship. You included the birds in your remarks.'

'Oh, yes, yes, yes. Oh, yes, yes. Oh yes, to be sure. Do you ever go to the country, Adams?'

'Generally to the seashore, your lordship, when I take my annual vacation.'

Whatever was the attraction across the room once more exercised its spell. His lordship concentrated himself upon it to the exclusion of all other mundane affairs. Presently he came out of his trance again.

'What were you saying, Adams?'

'I said that I generally went to the seashore, your lordship.'

'Eh? When?'

'For my annual vacation, your lordship.'

'Your what?'

'My annual vacation, your lordship.'

'What about it?'

Adams never smiled during business hours, unless professionally, as it were, when a member made a joke, but he was storing up in the recesses of his highly respectable body, a large laugh, to be shared with his wife when he reached home that night. Mrs. Adams never wearied of hearing of the eccentricities of the members of the club. It occurred to Adams that he was in luck today. He was expecting a little party of friends to supper that night, and he was a man who loved an audience. You would never have thought it, to look at him when engaged on his professional duties, but Adams had built up a substantial reputation as a humorist in his circle by his imitations of certain members of the club, and it was a matter of regret to him that he got so few opportunities nowadays of studying the absent-minded Lord Emsworth. It was rare luck, his lordship coming in today evidently in his best form.

'Adams, who is the gentleman over by the window? The gentleman in the brown suit?'

'That is a Mr. Simmonds, your lordship. He joined us last year.'

'I never saw a man take such large mouthfuls. Did *you* ever see a man take such large mouthfuls, Adams?'

Adams refrained from expressing an opinion, but inwardly he was thrilling with artistic fervour. Mr. Simmonds, eating, was one of his best imitations, though Mrs. Adams was inclined to object to it on the score that it was a bad example for the children. To be privileged to witness Lord Emsworth watching and criticizing Mr. Simmonds was to collect material for a double-barrelled character-study which would assuredly make the hit of the evening.

'That man,' went on Lord Emsworth, 'is digging his grave with his teeth. Digging his grave with his teeth, Adams. Do *you* take large mouthfuls, Adams?'

'No, your lordship.'

'Quite right. Very sensible of you, Adams. Very sensible of you. Very sen . . . What was I saying, Adams?'

'About my not taking large mouthfuls, your lordship.'

'Quite right. Quite right. Never take large mouthfuls, Adams. Never gobble. Have you any children, Adams?'

'Two, your lordship.'

'I hope you teach them not to gobble. They pay for it in later life. Americans gobble when young, and ruin their digestions. My American friend, Mr. Peters, suffers terribly from his digestion.'

Adams lowered his voice to a confidential murmur.

'If you will pardon the liberty, your lordship – I saw it in the paper—'

'About Mr. Peters' digestion?'

'About Miss Peters, your lordship, and the Honourable Frederick. May I be permitted to offer my congratulations?'

'Eh? Oh, yes, the engagement. Yes, yes, yes. Yes, to be sure. Yes, very satisfactory in every respect. High time he settled down and got a little sense. I put it to him straight. I cut off his allowance, and made him stay at home. That made him think, lazy young devil. I—'

Lord Emsworth had his lucid moments, and in the one that occurred now it came home to him that he was not talking to himself, as he had imagined, but confiding intimate family secrets to the head steward of his club's dining-room. He checked himself abruptly, and with a slight decrease of amiability fixed his gaze on the bill of fare, and ordered clear soup. For an instant he felt resentful against Adams for luring him on to soliloquize, but the next moment his whole mind was gripped by the fascinating spectacle of Mr. Simmonds dealing with a wedge of Stilton cheese, and Adams was forgotten.

The clear soup had the effect of restoring his lordship to complete amiability, and, when Adams in the course of his wanderings again found himself at the table, he was once more disposed for light conversation.

'So you saw the news of the engagement in the paper, did you, Adams?'

'Yes, your lordship, in the *Mail*. It had quite a long piece about it. And the Honourable Frederick's photograph and the young lady's were in the *Mirror*. Mrs. Adams clipped them out and put them in an album knowing that your lordship was a member of ours. If I may say so, your lordship, a beautiful young lady.'

'Devilish attractive, Adams, and devilish rich. Mr. Peters is a millionaire, Adams.'

'So I read in the paper, your lordship.'

'Damme, they all seem millionaires in America. Wish I knew how they managed it. Honestly, I hope. Mr. Peters is an honest man, but his digestion is bad. He used to bolt his food. *You* don't bolt your food, I hope, Adams?'

'No, your lordship, I am most careful.'

'The late Mr. Gladstone used to chew each mouthful thirty-three times. Deuced good notion, if you aren't in a hurry. What cheese would you recommend, Adams?'

'The gentlemen are speaking well of the gorgonzola.'

'All right, bring me some. You know, Adams, what I admire about Americans is their resource. Mr. Peters tells me that, as a boy of eleven, he earned twenty dollars a week selling mint to saloon-keepers, as they call publicans over there. Why they wanted mint I cannot recollect. Mr. Peters explained the reason to me, and it seemed highly plausible at the time, but I have forgotten it. Possibly for mint-sauce. It impressed me, Adams. Twenty dollars is four pounds. *I* never earned four pounds a week when I was a boy of eleven. In fact, I don't think I ever earned four pounds a week. His story impressed me, Adams. Every man ought to have an earning capacity. . . . Tell me, Adams, have I eaten my cheese?'

'Not yet, your lordship. I was about to send the waiter for it.'

'Never mind. Tell him to bring the bill instead. I remember that I have an appointment. I must not be late.'

'Shall I take the fork, your lordship?'

'The fork?'

'Your lordship has inadvertently put a fork in your coat-pocket.'

Lord Emsworth felt in the pocket indicated, and, with the air of an inexpert conjuror whose trick has succeeded contrary to his expectations, produced a silver-plated fork. He regarded it with surprise, then he looked wonderingly at Adams.

'Adams, I'm getting absent-minded. Have you ever noticed any traces of absent-mindedness in me before?'

'Oh, no, your lordship.'

'Well, it's deuced peculiar. I have no recollection whatsoever of placing that fork in my pocket. . . . Adams, I want a taxi-cab.'

He glanced round the room, as if expecting to locate one by the fireplace.

'The hall-porter will whistle one for you, your lordship.'

'So he will, by George, so he will. Good day, Adams.'

'Good day, your lordship.'

The Earl of Emsworth ambled benevolently to the door, leaving Adams with the feeling that his day had not been ill-spent. He gazed almost with reverence after the slow-moving figure.

'What a nut!' said Adams to his immortal soul.

Wafted through the sun-lit streets in his taxi-cab, the Earl of Emsworth smiled benevolently upon London's teeming millions. He was as completely happy as only a fluffy-minded old man with excellent health and a large income can be. Other people worried about all sorts of things – strikes, wars, suffragettes, diminishing birth-rates, the growing materialism of the age, and a score of similar subjects. Worrying, indeed, seemed to be the twentieth century's speciality. Lord Emsworth never worried. Nature had equipped him with a mind so admirably constructed for withstanding the disagreeableness of life that, if an unpleasant thought entered it, it passed out again a moment later. Except for a few of Life's fundamental facts, such as that his cheque-book was in the right-hand top drawer of his desk, that the Honourable Freddie Threepwood was a young idiot who required perpetual restraint, and that, when in doubt about anything, he had merely to apply to his secretary, Rupert Baxter – except for these basic things, he never remembered anything for more than a few minutes.

At Eton, in the sixties, they had called him Fathead.

His was a life which lacked, perhaps, the sublimer emotions which raised Man to the level of the gods, but it was undeniably an extremely happy one. He never experienced the thrill of ambition fulfilled, but, on the other hand, he never knew the agony of ambition frustrated. His name, when he died, would not live for ever in England's annals; he was spared the pain of worrying about this by the fact that he had no desire to live for ever in England's annals. He was possibly as nearly contented as a human being can be in this century of alarms and excursions. Indeed, as he bowled along in his cab, and reflected that a really charming girl, not in the chorus of any West End theatre, a girl with plenty of money and excellent breeding had – in a moment, doubtless of mental aberration – become engaged to be married to the Honourable Freddie, he told himself that life was at last absolutely without a crumpled rose-leaf.

The cab drew up before a house gay with flowered window-boxes. Lord Emsworth paid the driver, and stood on the sidewalk looking up at this cheerful house, trying to remember why on earth he had told the man to drive there.

A few moments' steady thought gave him the answer to the riddle. This was Mr. Peters' town house, and he had come to it by invitation to look at Mr. Peters' collection of scarabs.

To be sure. He remembered now. His collection of scarabs.

Or was it Arabs?

He smiled. Scarabs, of course. You couldn't collect Arabs. He wondered idly, as he rang the bell, what scarabs might be. But he was interested in a fluffy kind of way in all forms of collecting, and he was very pleased to have the opportunity of examining these objects, whatever they were.

He rather thought they were a kind of fish.

## II

There are men in this world who cannot rest, who are so constituted that they can only take their leisure in the shape of a change of work. To this fairly numerous class belonged Mr. J. Preston Peters, father of Freddie's Aline. And to this merit – or defect – is to be attributed his almost maniacal devotion to that rather unattractive species of curio – the Egyptian scarab.

Five years before, a nervous breakdown had sent Mr. Peters to a New York specialist.

The specialist had grown rich on similar cases, and his advice was always the same. He insisted on Mr. Peters taking up a hobby.

'What sort of a hobby?' inquired Mr. Peters irritably. His digestion had just begun to trouble him at the time, and his temper was not of the best.

The very word hobby seemed futile and ridiculous to him. His hobby was avoiding hobbies and attending to business. Which, the specialist pointed out, was precisely the reason why he had just written a hundred-dollar cheque for his advice. This impressed Mr. Peters. He disliked writing unnecessary cheques, and, if the only way to avoid doing so was to have a hobby, a hobby he must have.

'Any sort of hobby,' said the specialist. 'There must be something outside of business in which you are interested?'

Mr. Peters could not think of anything. Even his meals were beginning to interest him less.

'Now my hobby,' said the specialist, 'is the collecting of scarabs. Why should you not collect scarabs?'

'Because,' said Mr. Peters, 'I shouldn't know one if you brought it to me on a plate. What *are* scarabs?'

'Scarabs,' said the specialist, warming to his subject, 'are Egyptian hieroglyphs.'

'And what,' inquired Mr. Peters, 'are Egyptian hieroglyphs?'

The specialist began to wonder whether it would not have been better to advise Mr. Peters to collect postage stamps.

'A scarab,' he said, 'derived from the Latin *scarabeus*, is literally a beetle.'

'I will *not* collect beetles,' said Mr. Peters definitely. 'I despise beetles. Beetles give me that pain.'

'Scarabs are Egyptian symbols in the form of beetles,' the specialist hurried on. 'The most common form of scarab is in the shape of a ring. Scarabs were used for seals. They were also employed as beads or ornaments. Some scarabei bear inscriptions having reference to places, as, for instance, "Memphis is mighty for ever".'

Mr. Peters' scorn changed suddenly to active interest.

'Have you got one like that?'

'Like—?'

'A scarab boosting Memphis. It's my home town.'

'I think it possible that some other Memphis was alluded to.'

'There isn't any other except the one in Tennessee,' said Mr. Peters patriotically.

The specialist owed the fact that he was a nerve doctor instead of a nerve patient to his habit of never arguing with his visitors.

'Perhaps,' he said, 'You would care to glance at my collection? It is in the next room.'

That was the beginning of Mr. Peters' devotion to scarabs. At first he did his collecting without any love of it, partly because he had to collect something or suffer, but principally because of a remark the specialist made as he was leaving the room.

'How long would it take me to get together that number of the things?' he inquired, when, having looked his fill upon the dullest assortment of objects which he remembered ever to have seen, he was preparing to take his leave.

The specialist was proud of his collection.

'How long? To make a collection as large as mine? Many years, Mr. Peters. Oh, many, many years.'

'I'll bet you a hundred dollars I do it in six months.'

And from that moment Mr. Peters had brought to the collecting of scarabs the same furious energy which had given him so many dollars and so much indigestion. He went after scarabs like a dog after rats. He scooped in scarabs from all the four corners of the earth, until, at the end of a year, he found himself possessed of what, purely as regarded quantity, was a record collection.

This marked the end of the first phase of, so to speak, the scarabean side of his life. Collecting had become a habit with him, but he was not yet a real enthusiast. It occurred to him that the time had arrived for a certain amount of pruning and elimination. He called in an expert, and bade him go through the collection and weed out what he felicitously termed the 'dead ones'. The expert did his job thoroughly. When he had finished, the collection was reduced to a mere dozen specimens.

'The rest,' he explained, 'are practically valueless. If you are thinking of making a collection that will have any value in the eyes of archaeologists, I should advise you to throw them away. The remaining twelve are good.'

'How do you mean "good"? Why is one of these things valuable and another so much junk? They all look alike to me.'

And then the expert had talked to Mr. Peters for nearly two hours about the New Kingdom, the Middle Kingdom, Osiris, Ammon, Mut, Bubastis, Dynasties, Cheops, the Hyksos kings, cylinders, bezels, Amenophis III, Queen Taia, the Princess Gilukhipa of Mitanni, the Lake of Zarukhe, Naucratis, and the Book of the Dead. He did it with a relish. He liked doing it.

When he had finished, Mr. Peters thanked him and went to the bathroom, where he bathed his temples with eau de Cologne.

That talk changed J. Preston Peters from a supercilious scooper-up of random scarabs to a genuine scarab maniac. It does not matter what a man collects; if Nature has given him the collector's mind, he will become a fanatic on the subject of whatever collection he sets out to make. Mr. Peters had collected dollars, he began to collect scarabs with precisely the same enthusiasm. He would have become just as enthusiastic about butterflies, or old china, if he had turned his thoughts to them, but it chanced that what he had taken up was the collecting of the scarab, and it gripped him more and more as the years went on. Gradually he came to love his scarabs with that love passing the love of women which only collectors know. He became an expert on these curious relics of a dead civilization. For a time they ran neck and neck in his thoughts with business. When he retired from business, he was free to make them the master passion of his life. He treasured each individual scarab in his collection as a miser treasures gold.

Collecting, as Mr. Peters did it, resembles the drink habit. It begins as an amusement, and ends as an obsession.

He was gloating over his treasures when the maid announced Lord Emsworth.

A curious species of mutual toleration – it could hardly be dignified by the title of friendship – had sprung up between these two men, so opposite in practically every respect. Each regarded the other with that feeling of perpetual amazement with which we encounter those whose whole view-point and mode of life is foreign to our own. The American's force and nervous energy fascinated Lord Emsworth. In a purely detached way Lord Emsworth liked force and nervous energy. They interested him. He was glad he did not possess them himself, but he enjoyed them as a spectacle, just as a man who would not like to be a purple cow may have no objection to seeing one. As for Mr. Peters, nothing like the earl had ever happened to him before in a long and varied life. He had seen men and cities, but Lord Emsworth was something new. Each, in fact, was to the other a perpetual freak-show with no charge for admission. And, if anything had been needed to cement the alliance, it would have been supplied by the fact that they were both collectors.

They differed in collecting as they did in everything else. Mr. Peters' collecting, as has been shown, was keen, furious, concentrated; Lord Emsworth's had the amiable dodderingness which marked every branch of his life. In the museum at Blandings Castle you might find every manner of valuable and valueless curio. There was no central motive, the place was simply an amateur junk-shop. Side by side with a Gutenberg Bible for which rival collectors would have bidden without a limit, you would come upon a bullet from the field of Waterloo, one of a consignment of ten thousand shipped there for the use of tourists by a Birmingham firm. Each was equally attractive to its owner.

'My dear Mr. Peters,' said Lord Emsworth sunnily, advancing into the room, 'I trust I am not unpunctual. I have been lunching at my club.'

'I'd have asked you to lunch here,' said Mr. Peters, 'but you know how it is with me. I've promised the doctor I'll give those nuts and grasses of his a fair trial, and I can do it pretty well when I'm alone or with Aline. But to have to sit by and see some one else eating real food would be trying me too high.'

Lord Emsworth murmured sympathetically. The other's digestive tribulations touched a ready chord. An excellent trencherman himself, he understood what Mr. Peters must suffer.

'Too bad,' he said.

Mr. Peters turned the conversation into other channels.

'These are my scarabs,' he said.

Lord Emsworth adjusted his glasses, and the mild smile disappeared from his face, to be succeeded by a set look. A stage director of a moving-picture firm would have recognized the look; Lord Emsworth was 'registering' interest – interest which, he perceived from the first instant, would have to be completely simulated; for instinct told him as Mr. Peters began to talk, that he was about to be bored as he had seldom been bored in his life.

We may say what we will against the aristocracy of England; we may wear red ties and attend Socialist meetings; but we cannot deny that in certain crises blood will tell. An English peer of the right sort can be bored nearer to the point where mortification sets in, without showing it, than anyone else in the world. From early youth he has been accustomed to staying at English country-houses, where, though horses bored him intensely, he has had to accompany his host round the stables every morning and pretend to enjoy it, and this Spartan upbringing stands him in good stead in after years.

It was pleasant, then, to see the resolute, if painful, politeness with which Lord Emsworth accepted the trying role of the man who listens to a monomaniac discoursing on his pet subject. His mind was elsewhere, but early in the proceedings he began to make use of a musical 'Ah!' which, emitted at regular intervals, seemed to be all that Mr. Peters demanded of him.

Mr. Peters, in his character of showman, threw himself into his work with even more than his customary energy. He was both exhaustive and exhausting. His flow of speech never faltered. He spoke of the New Kingdom, the Middle Kingdom, Osiris, and Ammon; waxed eloquent concerning Mut, Bubastis, Cheops, the Hyksos kings, cylinders, bezels, and Amenophis III; and became at times almost lyrical when touching on Queen Taia, the Princess Gilukhipa of Mitanni, the Lake of Zarukhe, and the Book of the Dead.

Time slid by . . .

'Take a look at this, Lord Emsworth.'

As one who, brooding on love or running over business projects in his mind, walks briskly into a lamp-post and comes back to the realities of life with a sense of jarring shock, Lord Emsworth started, blinked and returned to consciousness. Far away his mind had been, seventy miles away, in the pleasant hot-houses and shady garden-walks of Blandings Castle. He came back to London to find that his host, with a mingled air of pride and reverence, was extending towards him a small, dingy-looking something.

He took it and looked at it. That, apparently, was what he was meant to do. So far, all was well.

'Ah!' he said.

That blessed word, covering everything. He repeated it, pleased at his ready resource.

'A Cheops of the Fourth Dynasty,' said Mr. Peters fervently.

'I beg your pardon?'

'A Cheops! Of the Fourth Dynasty!'

Lord Emsworth began to feel like a hunted stag. He could not go on saying 'Ah!' indefinitely, yet what else was there to say to this curious little beastly sort of a beetle kind of thing?

'Dear me! A Cheops!'

'Of the Fourth Dynasty!'

'Bless my soul! The Fourth Dynasty!'

'What do you think of that, eh?'

Strictly speaking, Lord Emsworth thought nothing of it, and he was wondering how to veil this opinion in diplomatic words, when the providence which looks after all good men saved him by causing a knock at the door to occur.

In response to Mr. Peters' irritated cry, a maid entered.

'If you please, sir. Mr. Threepwood wishes to speak to you on the telephone.'

Mr. Peters turned to his guest.

'Excuse me for one moment.'

'Certainly,' said Lord Emsworth gratefully. 'Certainly, certainly, certainly. By all means.'

The door closed behind Mr. Peters. Lord Emsworth was alone.

For some moments he stood where he had been left, a figure

with small signs of alertness about it. But Mr. Peters did not return immediately. The booming of his voice came faintly from some distant region. Lord Emsworth strolled to the window and looked out.

The sun still shone brightly on the quiet street. Across the road were trees. Lord Emsworth was fond of trees; he looked at these approvingly. Then round the corner came a vagrant man, wheeling flowers in a barrow.

Flowers! Lord Emsworth's mind shot back to Blandings like a homing pigeon. Flowers! Had he or had he not given head-gardener Thorne adequate instructions as to what to do with those hydrangeas? Assuming that he had not, was Thorne to be depended on to do the right thing by them by the light of his own intelligence?

Lord Emsworth began to brood upon head-gardener Thorne.

He was aware of some curious little object in his hand; he accorded it a momentary inspection. It had no message for him. It was probably something, but he couldn't remember what.

He put it in his pocket, and returned to his meditation.

III

At about the hour when the Earl of Emsworth was driving to keep his appointment with Mr. Peters, a party of two sat at a corner table at Simpson's Restaurant in the Strand. One of the two was a small, pretty, good-natured looking girl of about twenty, the other a sturdy young man with a small moustache, a wiry crop of red-brown hair and an expression of mingled devotion and determination. The girl was Aline Peters, the young man's name was George Emerson. He was, as Freddie had said, a policeman or something in Hong Kong. That is to say, he was second-in-command of the police force in that distant spot. At present, he was home on leave. He had a strong, square face, with a dogged and persevering chin.

There is every kind of restaurant in London, from the restaurant which makes you fancy you are in Paris to the restaurant which makes you wish you were. There are palaces in Piccadilly, quaint lethal chambers in Soho, and strange food factories in Oxford Street and the Tottenham Court Road. There are restaurants which specialize in ptomaine, and restaurants which specialize in sinister vegetable-messes. But there is only one Simpson's.

Simpson's in the Strand is unique. Here if he wishes, the Briton may, for the small sum of half a dollar, stupefy himself with food. The God of Fatted Plenty has the place under his protection. Its keynote is solid comfort. County clergymen, visiting London for the Annual Clerical Congress, come here to get the one square meal which will last them till next year's Clerical Congress. Fathers and uncles with sons or nephews on their hands rally to Simpson's with silent blessings on the head of the genius who founded the place, for here only can the young boa-constrictor really fill himself at moderate expense. Militant suffragettes come to it to make up leeway after their last hunger-strike.

A pleasant, soothing hearty place. A restful Temple of Food. No strident orchestra forces the diner to bolt beef in ragtime. No long, central aisle distracts his attention with its stream of new arrivals. There he sits, alone with his food, while white-robed priests, wheeling their smoking trucks, move to and fro, ever ready with fresh supplies.

All round the room, some at small tables, some at large tables, the worshippers sit, in their eyes that resolute, concentrated look which is the peculiar property of the British luncher, ex-President Roosevelt's man-eating fish, and the American army-worm.

Conversation does not flourish at Simpson's. Only two of all those present on this occasion showed any disposition towards chattiness. They were Aline Peters and her escort.

'The girl you ought to marry,' Aline was saying, 'is Joan Valentine.'

'The girl I am going to marry,' said George Emerson, 'is Aline Peters.'

For answer Aline picked up from the floor beside her an illustrated paper, and, having opened it at a page towards the end, handed it across the table.

George Emerson glanced at it disdainfully. There were two photographs on the page. One was of Aline, the other of a heavy, loutish-looking youth, who wore that peculiar expression of pained glassiness which Young England always adopts in the face of a camera.

Under one photograph were printed the words, 'Miss Aline Peters, who is to marry the Hon. Frederick Threepwood in June.' Under the other, 'The Hon. Frederick Threepwood, who is to marry Miss Aline Peters in June.' Above the photographs was the legend, 'Forthcoming International Wedding. Son of the Earl of Emsworth to marry American heiress.' In one corner of the picture a Cupid draped in the Stars and Stripes aimed his bow at the gentleman; in the other another Cupid, clad in a natty Union Jack, was drawing a bead on the lady.

The sub-editor had done his work well. He had not been ambiguous. What he intended to convey to the reader was that

Miss Aline Peters of America was going to marry the Hon. Frederick Threepwood, son of the Earl of Emsworth; and that was exactly the impression the average reader got.

George Emerson, however, was not an average reader. The sub-editor's work did not impress him.

'You mustn't believe everything you see in the papers,' he said. 'What are the stout children in the bathing-suits supposed to be doing?'

'Those are Cupids, George, aiming at us with their little bows – a pretty and original idea.'

'Why Cupids?'

'Cupid is the God of Love. I can see that *you* never went to night-school.'

'What has the God of Love got to do with it?'

Aline placidly devoured a fried potato.

'You're simply trying to make me angry,' she said, 'and I call it very mean of you. You know perfectly well how fatal it is to get angry at meals. It was eating while he was in a bad temper that ruined Father's digestion. George, that nice, fat carver is wheeling his truck this way. Flag him, and make him give me some more of that mutton.'

George looked round him morosely.

'Why is it,' he said, 'that every one in London looks exactly the same as every one else? They used to tell me that I should find that all Chinamen looked alike. There isn't a Chinaman in Hong Kong that I would have the least difficulty in recognizing. But these blighters—' His eye roamed about the room. It returned to a stout young man at a neighbouring table, who had been the original cause of this homily, owing to the fact that he had reminded him of the Hon. Freddie Threepwood. He scowled at this harmless youth, who was browsing contentedly on fish-pie. 'Do you see the fellow in the grey suit?' he said. 'Look at the stodgy face. Mark the glassy eye. If that man sandbagged your Freddie and tied him up somewhere and turned up at the church instead of him, can you honestly tell me that you would know the difference? Come now, wouldn't you simply say, "Why, Freddie, how natural you look," and go through the ceremony without a suspicion?'

'He isn't a bit like Freddie. And you oughtn't to speak of him as Freddie. You don't know him.'

'Yes, I do. And what is more he expressly asked me to call him Freddie. "Oh, dash it, old top, don't keep on calling me Threepwood. Freddie to pals." Those were his very words.'

'George, you're making this up.'

'Not at all. We met last night at the National Sporting Club. Porky Jones was going twenty rounds with Eddie Flynn. I offered to give three to one on Eddie. Freddie, who was sitting next to me, took me in fivers. And if you want any further proof of your young man's fat-headedness, mark that. A child could have seen that Eddie had him going. Afterwards Threepwood chummed up with me, and told me that to real pals like me he was Freddie. I was a real pal, as I understood it, because I would have to wait for my money. The fact was, he explained, that his old governor had cut off his bally allowance.'

'You're simply trying to poison my mind against him, and I don't think it's very nice of you, George.'

'What do you mean, poison your mind? I'm not poisoning your mind, I'm simply telling you a few things about him. You know perfectly well that you don't love him, and that you aren't going to marry him, and that you are going to marry me.'

'How do you know I don't love my Freddie?'

'If you can look me straight in the eyes and tell me that you do, I will drop the whole thing and put on a little page's dress and carry your train up the aisle! Now then?'

'And all the while you're talking you're letting my carver get away,' said Aline.

George signalled to the willing priest, who steered his truck towards them. Aline directed his dissection of the shoulder of mutton with word and gesture.

'Enjoy yourself,' said Emerson coldly.

'So I do, George, so I do. What excellent meat they have in England.'

'I wish you would be a bit more spiritual. I don't want to sit here discussing food-products.'

'If you were in my position, George, you wouldn't want to talk about anything else. It's doing him a world of good, poor dear, but there are times when I'm sorry father ever started this food-reform thing. You don't know what it means for a healthy young girl to try and support life on nuts and grasses.'

'And why should you?' broke out Emerson. 'I'll tell you what it is, Aline, you are perfectly absurd about your father. I don't want to say anything against him to you, naturally, but—'

'Go ahead, George. Why this diffidence? Say what you like.'

'Very well, then, I will. I'll give it to you straight. You know quite well that you let your father bully you. I don't say it is your fault or his fault or anybody's fault, I just state it as a fact. It's temperament, I suppose. You are yielding, and he is aggressive, and he has taken advantage of it. Take this food business, for a start. Your father's digestion has gone wrong, and as a result he has to live on nuts and bananas and things. Why should you let him make you do the same?'

'It isn't a question of making. He doesn't make me, I do it to encourage him, to show him that it can be done. If I weakened he would lose all his resolution in a moment, and rush out and start a regular debauch of *pâté de fois gras* and lobster. And then he would suffer agonies. What a terrible thing it is, George, that father should combine a schoolboy appetite with a Rockefeller digestion. Either by itself wouldn't be so bad, but the combination is awful.'

George, baffled, but determined, resumed the attack.

'All right, then, if you really are starving yourself of your own free will, there is no more to say.'

'But you are going to say it, aren't you, George?'

'We now come to this idiotic Freddie marriage business. Your father has forced you into that. It's all very well to say that you are a free agent, and that fathers don't coerce their daughters nowadays. The trouble is that your father does. You let him do what he likes with you. And you won't break away from this Freddie foolishness because you can't find the pluck. I'm going to help you find it. I'm coming down to Blandings Castle when you go there on Friday.'

'Coming to Blandings?'

'Freddie invited me last night. I think it was done by way of interest on the money he owed me, but he did it, and I accepted.'

'But, George, my dear, dear boy, do you *never* read the Etiquette Books and the hints in the papers on how to be the Perfect Gentleman? Don't you know that you can't be a man's guest and take advantage of his hospitality to try to steal his fiancée away from him?'

'Watch me!'

A dreamy look came into Aline's eyes.

'I wonder what it feels like being a countess,' she said.

'You will never know,' George looked at her pityingly. 'My

poor girl,' he said, 'have you been lured into this engagement in the belief that Freddie, the Idiot Child, is going to be an earl some day? They were ragging you. Freddie is not the heir. His elder brother, Lord Bosham, is as fit as a prize-fighter and has three healthy sons. Freddie has about as much chance of getting the title as I have.'

'George, your education has been sadly neglected. Don't you know that the heir to the title always goes for a yachting cruise with his whole family and gets drowned, and the children too? It happens in every English novel you read.'

'Listen, Aline, let us get this thing straight. I have been in love with you ever since we met on the *Olympic*. I proposed to you twice on the voyage and once in the train on the way to London. That was eight months ago, and I have been proposing to you at intervals ever since. I go to Scotland for a few weeks to see my people, and when I come back, what do I find? I find you engaged to be married to this Freddie excrescence.'

'I like your chivalrous attitude towards Freddie. So many men in your position might say horrid things about him.'

'Oh, I've nothing against Freddie. He is practically an imbecile and I don't like his face, but apart from that he's all right. But you will be glad later that you did not marry him. You are much too real a person. What a wife you will make for a hard-working man!'

'What does Freddie work hard at?'

'I am alluding at the moment not to Freddie but to myself. I shall come home tired out. Things will have gone wrong at my office: I shall be fagged, disheartened. And then you will come with cool, white hands, and placing them gently on my forehead—'

Aline shook her head.

'It's no good, George. Really, you had better realize it. I'm very fond of you, but we are not suited.'

'Why not?'

'You are too overwhelming, too much like a bomb. I think you must be one of these Supermen one reads about. You would want your own way and nothing but your own way. I expect it's through having to be constantly moving people on out in Hong Kong, and all that sort of thing. Now Freddie will roll through hoops and sham dead, and we shall be the happiest pair in the world. I am much too placid and mild to make you happy. You want someone who would stand up to you. Somebody like Joan Valentine.'

'That's the second time you have mentioned this Joan Valentine. Who *is* she?'

'She is a girl who was at school with me. I was at school in England, you know – Mother wanted me to get the tone, or something. We were the greatest chums. At least, I worshipped her and would have done anything for her, and I think she liked me. Then I went back to America and we lost touch with one another. I met her on the street yesterday, and she is just the same. She has been through the most awful times. Her father was quite rich, and he died suddenly, and she found that he hadn't left a penny. He had been living right up to his income all the time. His life wasn't even insured. She came to London, and, as far as I could make out from the short talk we had, she had done pretty nearly everything since we last met. She worked in a shop and went on the stage, and all sorts of things. Isn't it awful, George?'

'Frightful,' said Emerson. He was but faintly interested in Miss Valentine.

'She is so plucky and full of life. She would stand up to you.'

'Thanks! My idea of marriage is not a perpetual fight. My notion of a wife is something cosy and sympathetic and soothing. That is why I love you. We shall be the happiest—'

Aline laughed.

'Dear old George! And now pay the bill, and get me a taxi. I've endless things to do at home. If Freddie is in town, I suppose he will be calling to see me. Who is Freddie, do you ask? Freddie is my fiancée, George. My betrothed. The young man I'm going to marry.'

Emerson shook his head resignedly.

'Curious how you cling to that Freddie idea. Never mind. I'll come down to Blandings on Friday, and we will see what happens. Bear in mind the broad fact that you and I are going to get married and that nothing on earth is going to stop us.'

## IV

The reason why all we novelists with bulging foreheads and expensive educations are abandoning novels and taking to writing motion-picture scenarii is because the latter are so infinitely the more simple and pleasant.

If this narrative, for instance, were a film-drama, the operator at this point would flash on the screen the words:

## MR. PETERS DISCOVERS THE LOSS OF THE SCARAB,

and for a brief moment the audience would see an interior set, in which a little angry man with a sharp face and starting eyes would register first, Discovery; next Dismay. The whole thing would be over in an instant.

The printed word demands a greater elaboration.

It was Aline who had to bear the brunt of her father's mental agony when he discovered, shortly after his guest had left him, that the gem of his collection of scarabs had done the same. It is always the innocent bystander who suffers.

'The darned old sneak-thief!' said Mr. Peters.

'Father!'

'Don't just sit there saying "Father!" What's the use of saying, "Father"? Do you think it is going to help, your saying "Father!"? I'd rather the old pirate had taken the house and lot than that scarab. He knows what's what! Trust him to walk off with the pick of the whole bunch. I did think I could trust the father of the man who's going to marry my daughter for a second alone with the things. There's no morality among collectors, none. I'd trust a syndicate of Jesse James, Captain Kidd and Dick Turpin sooner than I would a collector. My Cheops of the Fourth Dynasty! I wouldn't have lost it for five thousand dollars.'

'But, father, couldn't you write him a letter, asking for it back? He's such a nice old man; I'm sure he didn't mean to steal the scarab.'

Mr. Peters' overwrought soul blew off steam in the shape of a passionate snort.

'Didn't mean to steal it! What do you think he meant to do – take it away and keep it safe for me in case I should lose it? Didn't mean to steal it! I bet you he's well known in Society as a kleptomaniac. I bet you that, when his name is announced, his friends lock up their spoons and send in a hurry-call to police headquarters for a squad to come and see that he doesn't sneak the front door. Of course, he meant to steal it. He has a museum of his own down in the country. My Cheops is going to lend tone to that. I'd give five thousand dollars to get it back. If there's a burglar in this country with the spirit to break into the Castle and steal that scarab and hand it back to me, there's five thousand waiting for him right here, and, if he wants to, he can knock that old pirate on the head with a jemmy into the bargain.'

'But father, why can't you simply go to him and say it's yours and that you must have it back?'

'And have him come back at me by calling off this engagement of yours! Not if I know it. You can't go about the place charging a man with theft and expect him to go on being willing to have his son marry your daughter, can you? The slightest suggestion that I thought he had stolen this scarab, and he would do the Proud Old English Aristocrat and end everything. He's in the strongest position a thief has ever been in. You can't get at him.'

'I didn't think of that.'

'You don't think at all. That's the trouble with you,' said Mr. Peters.

You see now why we prefer writing motion-picture scenarii. It is painful to a refined and sensitive young novelist to have to set down such a scene between father and child. But what is one to do? Years of indigestion had made Mr. Peters' temper, even when in a normal mood, perfectly impossible; in a crisis like this it ran amuck. He vented it on Aline because he had always vented his irritabilities on Aline, because the fact of her sweet, gentle disposition, combined with the fact of their relationship, made her the ideal person to receive the overflow of his black moods. While his wife had lived, he had bullied her. On her death, Aline had stepped into the vacant position.

Aline did not cry, because she was not a girl who was given to tears, but for all her placid good-temper, she was wounded. She was a girl who liked everything in the world to run smoothly and easily, and these scenes with her father always depressed her. She took advantage of a lull in Mr. Peters' flow of words and slipped from the room.

Her cheerfulness had received a shock. She wanted sympathy. She wanted comforting. For a moment she considered George Emerson in the role of comforter. But there were objections to George in this character. Aline was accustomed to tease and chaff George, but at heart she was a little afraid of him, and instinct told her that, as comforter, he would be too volcanic and Super manly for a girl who was engaged to marry another man in June. George as comforter would be far too prone to trust to action rather than to the soothing power of the spoken word. George's idea of healing the wound, she felt, would be to push her into a cab and drive to the nearest registrar's.

No, she would not go to George; to whom, then?

The vision of Joan Valentine came to her – of Joan as she had seen her yesterday, strong, cheerful, self-reliant, bearing herself in spite of adversity with a valiant jauntiness. Yes, she would go and see Joan.

She put on her hat and stole from the house.

Curiously enough, only a quarter of an hour before, R. Jones had set out with exactly the same object in view.

V

How pleasant it is, after assisting at a scene of violence and recrimination, to be transferred to one of peace and goodwill. It is with a sense of relief that I find that the snipe-like flight of this story takes us next, far from Mr. Peters and his angry outpourings, to the cosy smoking-room of Blandings Castle.

At almost exactly the hour when Aline Peters set off to visit her friend Miss Valentine, three men sat in the cosy smoking-room of Blandings Castle.

They were variously occupied. In the long chair nearest the door, the Hon. Frederick Threepwood – Freddie to pals – was reading. Next to him sat a young man whose eyes, glittering through rimless spectacles, were concentrated on the upturned faces of several neat rows of playing-cards. (Rupert Baxter, Lord Emsworth's invaluable secretary, had no vices, but he sometimes relaxed his busy brain with a game of solitaire.) Beyond Baxter, a cigar in his mouth and a weak high-ball at his side, the Earl of Emsworth took his ease. After the scene we have just been through it does one good merely to contemplate such a picture.

The book which the Hon. Freddie was reading was a small, paper-covered book. Its cover was decorated with a colour-scheme in red, black and yellow, depicting a tense moment in the lives of a man with a black beard, a man with a yellow beard, a man without any beard at all, and a young woman, who, at first sight, appeared to be all eyes and hair. The man with the black beard, to gain some private end, had tied this young woman with ropes to a complicated system of machinery, mostly wheels and pulleys. The man with the yellow beard was in the act of pushing or pulling a lever. The beardless man, protruding through a trap-door in the floor, was pointing a large revolver at the parties of the second part.

Beneath this picture were the words, 'Hands up, you scoundrels!' Above it, in a meandering scroll across the page, 'Gridley Quayle, Investigator. The Adventure of the Secret Six. By Felix Clovelly.'

The Hon. Freddie did not so much read as gulp the adventure

of the Secret Six. His face was crimson with excitement; his hair was rumpled; his eyes bulged. He was absorbed.

This is peculiarly an age in which each one of us may, if he does but search diligently, find the literature suited to his mental powers. Grave and earnest men, at Eton and elsewhere, had tried Freddie Threepwood with Greek, with Latin, and with English, and the sheeplike stolidity with which he declined to be interested in the masterpiece of all three tongues had left them with the conviction that he would never read anything.

And then, years afterwards, he had suddenly blossomed out as a student. Only, it is true, a student of the Adventures of Gridley Quayle, but still a student. His was a dull life, and Gridley Quayle was the only person who brought romance into it. Existence for the Hon. Freddie was simply a sort of desert punctuated with monthly oases in the shape of new Quayle adventures. It was his ambition to meet the man who wrote them.

Lord Emsworth sat and smoked and sipped and smoked again, at peace with all the world. His mind was as nearly a blank as it is possible for the human mind to be.

The hand which had not the task of holding the cigar was at rest in his trouser-pocket. The fingers of it fumbled idly with a small, hard object.

Gradually it filtered into his lordship's mind that this small hard object was not familiar. It was something new – something that was neither his keys, his pencil, nor his small change.

He yielded to a growing curiosity, and drew it out.

He examined it.

It was a little something, rather like a fossilized beetle. It touched no chord in him. He looked at it with an amiable distaste.

'Now, how in the world did that get there?' he said.

The Hon. Freddie paid no attention to the remark. He was now at the very crest of his story, when every line intensified the thrill. Incident was succeeding incident. The Secret Six were here, there and everywhere, like so many malignant June bugs. Annabel, the heroine, was having a perfectly rotten time, kidnapped and imprisoned every few minutes. Gridley Quayle, hot on the scent, was covering someone or other with his revolver almost continuously. The Hon. Freddie had no time for chatting with his father.

Not so Rupert Baxter. Chatting with Lord Emsworth was one of the things for which he received his salary. He looked up from his cards.

'Lord Emsworth?'

'I have found a curious object in my pocket, Baxter. I was wondering how it got there.'

He handed the thing to his secretary. Rupert Baxter's eyes lit up with a sudden enthusiasm. He gasped.

'Magnificent!' he cried. 'Superb!'

Lord Emsworth looked at him inquiringly.

'It is a scarab, Lord Emsworth, and, unless I am mistaken – and I think I may claim to be something of an expert – a Cheops of the Fourth Dynasty. A wonderful addition to your museum.'

'Is it, by gad! You don't say so, Baxter!'

'It is indeed. If it is not a rude question, how much did you give for it, Lord Emsworth? It must have been the gem of someone's collection. Was there a sale at Christie's this afternoon?'

Lord Emsworth shook his head.

'I did not get it at Christie's for I recollect that I had an important engagement which prevented my going to Christie's. I had – to be sure, yes. I had promised to call on Mr. Peters and examine his collection of – now I wonder what it was that Mr. Peters said he collected?'

'Mr. Peters is one of the best-known living collectors of scarabs.'

'Scarabs! You are quite right, Baxter. And now that I recall the episode, this is a scarab, and Mr. Peters gave it to me.'

'*Gave* it to you, Lord Emsworth!'

'Yes. The whole scene comes back to me. Mr. Peters, after telling me a great many exceedingly interesting things about scarabs, which I regret to say I cannot remember, gave me this. And you say it is really valuable, Baxter?'

'It is, from a collector's point of view, of extraordinary value.'

'Bless my soul!' Lord Emsworth beamed. 'This is extremely interesting, Baxter. One has heard so much of the princely hospitality of Americans. How exceedingly kind of Mr. Peters. I shall certainly treasure it, though I must confess that, from a purely spectacular standpoint, it leaves me a little cold. However, I must not look a gift horse in the mouth, eh, Baxter?'

From afar came the silver booming of a gong. Lord Emsworth rose.

'Time to dress for dinner? I had no idea it was so late. Baxter, you will be going past the museum door. Will you be a good fellow and place this among the exhibits? You will know what to do with it better than I. I always think of you as the curator of my little collection. Baxter; ha, ha! Mind how you step when you are in the museum. I was painting a chair there yesterday, and I think I left the paint-pot on the floor.'

He cast a less amiable glance at his studious son.

'Get *up*, Frederick, and go and dress for dinner. What is that trash you are reading?'

The Hon. Freddie came out of his book much as a

sleepwalker awakes, with a sense of having been violently assaulted. He looked up with a kind of stunned plaintiveness.

'Eh, governor?'

'Make haste. Beach rang the gong five minutes ago. What is that you are reading?'

'Oh, nothing, governor. Just a book.'

'I wonder how you can waste your time on such trash. Make haste.'

He turned to the door, and the benevolent expression once more wandered athwart his face.

'*Extremely* kind of Mr. Peters!' he said. 'Really, there is something almost oriental in the lavish generosity of our American cousins.'

## VI

It had taken R. Jones just six hours to discover Joan Valentine's address. That it had not taken him longer is a proof of his energy and of the excellence of his system of obtaining information. But R. Jones, when he considered it worth his while, could be extremely energetic, and he was a past master at the art of finding out things.

He poured himself out of his cab, and rang the bell of No. 7A. A dishevelled maid answered the ring.

'Miss Valentine in?'

'Yes, sir.'

R. Jones produced his card.

'On important business, tell her. Half a minute, I'll write it.'

He wrote the words on the card, and devoted the brief period of waiting to a careful scrutiny of his surroundings. He looked out into the court and he looked as far he could down the dingy

75

passage, and the conclusions he drew from what he saw were complimentary to Miss Valentine.

'If this girl is the sort of girl who would hold up Freddie's letters,' he mused, 'she wouldn't be living in a place like this. If she were on the make, she would have more money than she evidently possesses. Therefore, she is not on the make, and I should be prepared to bet that she destroyed the letters as fast as she got them.'

Those were, roughly, the thoughts of R. Jones, as he stood in the doorway of No. 7A, and they were important thoughts, inasmuch as they determined his attitude towards Joan in the approaching interview. He perceived that this matter must be handled delicately, that he must be very much the gentleman. It would be a strain, but he must do it.

The maid returned and directed him to Joan's room with a brief word and a sweeping gesture.

'Eh?' said R. Jones. 'First floor?'

'Front,' said the maid.

R. Jones trudged laboriously up the short flight of stairs. It was very dark on the stairs, and he stumbled. Eventually, however, light came to him through an open door. Looking in, he saw a girl standing at the table. She had an air of expectation, so he deduced that he had reached his journey's end.

'Miss Valentine?'

'Please come in.'

R. Jones waddled in.

'Not much light on your stairs.'

'No. Will you take a seat?'

'Thanks.'

One glance at the girl convinced R. Jones that he had been right. Circumstances had made him a rapid judge of character, for in the profession of living by one's wits in a large city, the first principle of offence and defence is to sum people up at first sight. This girl was not on the make.

Joan Valentine was a tall girl, with wheat-gold hair and eyes as brightly-blue as a November sky when the sun is shining on a frosty world. There was in them a little of November's cold glitter, too, for Joan had been through much in the last few years, and experience, even if it does not harden, erects a defensive barrier between its children and the world. Her eyes were eyes that looked straight and challenged. They could thaw to the satin blue of the Mediterranean Sea where it purrs about the little villages of Southern France, but they did not thaw for everyone. She looked what she was – a girl of action, a girl whom Life had made both reckless and wary, wary of friendly advances, reckless when there was a venture afoot.

Her eyes, as they met R. Jones' now, were cold and challenging. She, too, had learned the trick of swift diagnosis of character, and what she saw of R. Jones' in that first glance did not impress her very favourably.

'You wished to see me on business?'

'Yes,' said R. Jones. 'Yes . . . Miss Valentine, may I begin by begging you to realize that I have no intention of insulting you?'

Joan's eyebrows rose. For an instant she did her visitor the injustice of suspecting that he had been dining too well.

'I don't understand.'

'Let me explain. I have come here,' R. Jones went on, getting more gentlemanly every moment, 'on a very distasteful errand, to oblige a friend. Will you bear in mind that, whatever I say, is said entirely on his behalf?'

By this time Joan had abandoned the idea that this stout

person was a life-insurance tout, and was inclining to the view that he was collecting funds for a charity.

'I came here at the request of the Hon. Frederick Threepwood.'

'I don't quite understand.'

'You never met him, Miss Valentine, but, when you were in the chorus at the Piccadilly Theatre, I believe he wrote you some very foolish letters. Possibly you have forgotten them?'

'I certainly have.'

'You have probably destroyed them, eh?'

'Certainly. I don't often keep letters. Why do you ask?'

'Well, you see, Miss Valentine, the Hon. Frederick Threepwood is about to be married, and he thought that possibly, on the whole, it would be better that the letters – and poetry – which he wrote you were non-existent.'

Not all R. Jones' gentlemanliness – and during this speech he diffused it like a powerful scent in waves about him – could hide the unpleasant meaning of the words.

'He was afraid I might try and blackmail him?' said Joan with formidable calm.

R. Jones raised and waved a fat hand deprecatingly.

'My dear Miss Valentine!'

Joan rose and R. Jones followed her example. The interview was plainly at an end.

'Please tell Mr. Threepwood to make his mind quite easy. He is in no danger.'

'Exactly, exactly, precisely. I assured Threepwood that my visit here would be a mere formality. I was quite sure you had no intention whatever of worrying him. I will tell him definitely then, that you have destroyed the letters?'

'Yes. Good evening.'

'Good evening, Miss Valentine.'

The closing of the door behind him left him in total darkness, but he hardly liked to return and ask Joan to reopen it in order to light him on his way. He was glad to be out of her presence. He was used to being looked at in an unfriendly way by his fellows, but there had been something in Joan's eyes which had curiously discomfited him. He groped his way down, relieved that all was over and had ended well. He believed what she had told him, and he could conscientiously assure Freddie that the prospect of his sharing the fate of poor old Percy was non-existent. It is true that he proposed to add in his report that the destruction of the letters had been purchased with difficulty, at a cost of just five hundred pounds, but that was a mere business formality.

He had almost reached the last step when there was a ring at the front door. With what he was afterwards wont to call an inspiration, he retreated with unusual nimbleness till he had almost reached Joan's door again. Then he leaned over the banisters and listened.

The dishevelled maid opened the door. A girl's voice spoke.

'Is Miss Valentine in?'

'She's in, but she's engaged.'

'I wish you would go up and tell her that I want to see her. Say it's Miss Peters. Miss Aline Peters.'

The banisters shook beneath R. Jones' sudden clutch. For a moment he had felt almost faint. Then he began to think swiftly. A great light had dawned upon him, and the thought outstanding in his mind was that never again would he trust a man or woman on the evidence of his senses. He could have sworn that this Valentine girl was on the level. He had been perfectly satisfied with her statement that she had destroyed the letters. And all the while she had been playing as deep a game as he had ever come across in the whole course of his professional career. He almost admired her. How she had taken him in! It was obvious now what her game was. Previous to his visit she had arranged a meeting with Freddie's fiancée, with the view of opening negotiations for the sale of the letters. She had held him, Jones, at arm's length, because she was going to sell the letters to whoever would pay the best price. But for the accident of his happening to be here when Miss Peters arrived, Freddie and his fiancée would have been bidding against each other, and raising each other's price. He had worked the same game himself a dozen times, and he resented the entry of female competition into what he regarded as essentially a male field of enterprise.

As the maid stumped up the stairs, he continued his retreat. He heard Joan's door open, and the stream of light showed him the dishevelled maid standing in the doorway.

'Ow, I thought there was a gentleman with you, miss.'

'He left a moment ago. Why?'

'There's a lady wants to see you. Miss Peters her name is.'

'Will you ask her to come up?'

The dishevelled maid was no polished mistress of ceremonies. She leaned down into the void, and hailed Aline.

'She says, will you come up.'

Aline's feet became audible on the staircase. There were greetings.

'Whatever brings you here, Aline?'

'Am I interrupting you, Joan, dear?'

'No. Do come in. I was only surprised to see you so late. I didn't know you paid calls at this hour. Is anything wrong? Come in.'

The door closed, the maid retired to the depths, and R. Jones stole cautiously down again. He was feeling absolutely bewildered. Apparently his deductions, his second thoughts, had been all wrong, and Joan was, after all, the honest person he had imagined at first sight. These two girls had talked to each other as if they were old friends, as if they had known each other all their lives. That was the thing that perplexed R. Jones.

With the tread of a Red Indian he approached the door, and put his ear to it. He found that he could hear quite comfortably.

Aline meanwhile, inside the room, had begun to draw comfort from Joan's very appearance. She looked so capable.

Joan's eyes had changed the expression they had contained during the recent interview. They were soft now, with a softness that was half compassionate, half contemptuous. It is the compensation which Life gives to those whom it has handled roughly that they shall be able to regard with a certain contempt the small troubles of the sheltered. Joan remembered Aline of old, and knew her for a perennial victim of small troubles. Even in their school days she had always needed to be looked after and comforted. Her sweet temper had seemed to invite the minor slings and arrows of fortune. Aline was a girl who inspired protectiveness in a certain type of her fellow human beings. It was this quality in her which kept George Emerson awake at nights; and it appealed to Joan now. Joan, for whom life was a constant struggle to keep the wolf within a reasonable distance from the door, and who counted that day happy on which she saw her way clear to paying her weekly rent and possibly having a trifle over for some coveted hat or pair of shoes, could not help feeling, as she looked at Aline, that her own troubles were as nothing, and that the immediate need of the moment was to pet and comfort her friend. Her knowledge of Aline told her that the probable tragedy was that she had lost a brooch or had been spoken to crossly by somebody, but it also told her that such tragedies bulked very large on Aline's horizon. Trouble, after all, like beauty, is in the eye of the beholder, and Aline was far less able to endure with fortitude the loss of a brooch than she herself the loss of a position whose emoluments meant the difference between having just enough to eat and starving.

'You're worried about something,' she said. 'Sit down and tell me about it.'

Aline sat down, and looked about her at the shabby room. By that curious process of the human mind which makes the spectacle of another's misfortune a palliative for one's own, she was feeling oddly comforted already. Her thoughts were not definite, and she could not analyse them, but what they amounted to was that, while it was an unpleasant thing to be bullied by a dispeptic father, the world manifestly held worse tribulations which her father's other outstanding quality besides dyspepsia – wealth, to wit – enabled her to avoid. It was at this point that the dim beginnings of a philosophy began to invade her mind. The thing resolved itself almost into an equation. If father had not had indigestion, he would not have bullied her. But, if father had not made a fortune, he would not have had indigestion. Therefore, if father had not made a fortune, he would not have bullied her. Practically, in fact, if father did not bully her, he would not be rich. And, if he were not rich. . . . She took in the faded carpet, the stained wallpaper and the soiled curtains, in a comprehensive glance. . . . It certainly cut both ways. She began to be a little ashamed of her misery.

'It's nothing at all, really,' she said. 'I think I've been making rather a fuss about very little.'

Joan was relieved. The struggling life breeds moods of depression, and such a mood had come to her just before Aline's arrival. Life, at that moment, had seemed to stretch before her like a dusty, weary road, without hope. She was sick of fighting. She wanted money and ease and a surcease from this perpetual race with weekly bills. The mood had been the outcome partly of R. Jones' gentlemanly-veiled insinuations, but still more, though she did not realize it, of her yesterday's meeting with Aline. Mr. Peters might be unguarded in his speech, when conversing with his daughter, he might play the tyrant towards her in many ways, but he did not stint her in the matter of dress allowance, and on the occasion when she met Joan, Aline had been wearing so Parisian a hat and a tailor-made suit of such obviously expensive simplicity that green-eyed envy had almost spoiled Joan's pleasure at meeting this friend of her opulent days. She had suppressed the envy, and it had revenged itself by assaulting her afresh in the form of the worst fit of blues which she had had in two years. She had been loyally ready to sink her depression in order to alleviate Aline's, but it was a distinct relief to find that the feat would not be necessary.

'Never mind,' she said, 'tell me what the very little thing was.'

'It was only father,' said Aline simply.

'Was he angry with you about something?'

'Not exactly angry with me. But – well, I was there.'

Joan's depression lifted slightly. She had forgotten, in the stunning anguish of the sudden spectacle of that hat and that tailor-made suit, that Paris hats and twenty-five pound suits not infrequently had their accompanying disadvantages. After all, she was independent. She might have to murder her beauty with hats and frocks which had never been nearer Paris than the

Tottenham Court Road, but at least no one bullied her because she happened to be at hand when tempers were short.

'What a shame!' she said. 'Tell me all about it.'

With a prefatory remark that it was all so ridiculous really, Aline embarked upon the narrative of the afternoon's events.

Joan heard her out, checking a strong disposition to giggle. Her view-point was that of the Average Person, and the Average Person cannot see the importance of the scarab in the scheme of things. The opinion she formed of Mr. Peters was of an eccentric old gentleman making a great to-do about nothing at all. Losses had to have a concrete value before they could impress Joan. It was beyond her to grasp that Mr. Peters would sooner have lost a diamond necklace, if he had happened to possess one, than his Cheops of the Fourth Dynasty.

It was not until Aline, having concluded her tale, added one more strand to it that she found herself treating the matter seriously.

'Father says he would give a thousand pounds to anyone who would get it back for him.'

'What!'

The whole story took on a different complexion for Joan. Money talks. Mr. Peters' words might have been merely the rhetorical outburst of a heated moment, but, even discounting them, there seemed to remain a certain exciting substratum. A man who shouts that he will give a thousand pounds for a thing may very well mean that he will give a hundred, and Joan's finances were perpetually in a condition which makes a hundred pounds a sum to be gasped at.

'He wasn't serious, surely?'

'I think he was,' said Aline.

'But a thousand pounds!'

'It isn't really very much to father, you know. He gives away a hundred thousand dollars a year to a University.'

'But for a grubby little scarab!'

'You don't understand how father loves his scarabs. Since he retired from business, he has been simply wrapped up in them. You know, collectors are like that. You read in the papers about men giving all sorts of money for funny things.'

Outside the door, R. Jones, his ear close to the panel, drank in all these things greedily. He would have been willing to remain in that attitude indefinitely in return for this kind of special information, but, just as Aline said these words, a door opened on the floor above and somebody came out, whistling, and began to descend the stairs.

R. Jones stood not upon the order of his going. He was down in the hall and fumbling with the handle of the front door with an agility of which few casual observers of his dimensions would have deemed him capable.

The next moment he was out in the street, walking calmly towards Leicester Square, pondering over what he had heard.

Much of R. Jones' substantial annual income was derived from pondering over what he had heard.

In the room, Joan was looking at Aline with the distended eyes of one who sees visions or has inspirations. She got up. There are occasions when one must speak standing.

'Then you mean to say that your father would really give a thousand pounds to anyone who got this thing back for him?'

'I am sure he would. But who could do it?'

'I could,' said Joan. 'And what is more, I'm going to.'

Aline stared at her helplessly. In their schooldays, Joan had always swept her off her feet. Then, she had always had the feeling that with Joan nothing was impossible. Heroine-worship, like hero-worship, dies hard. She looked at Joan now with the stricken sensation of one who has inadvertently set powerful machinery in motion.

'But, Joan!'

It was all she could say.

'My dear child, it's perfectly simple. This earl of yours has taken the thing off to his castle, like a brigand. You say you are going down there on Friday for a visit. All you have to do is to take me along with you.'

'But, Joan!'

'Where's the difficulty?'

'I don't see how I could take you down very well.'

'Why not?'

'Oh, I don't know.'

'But, what is your objection?'

'Well, don't you see. . . . If you come down there as a friend of mine, and were caught stealing the scarab, there would be . . . just the trouble father wants to avoid. About my engagement, you see, and so on.'

It was an aspect of the matter which had escaped Joan. She frowned thoughtfully.

'I see. Yes, there is that. But there must be a way.'

'You mustn't, Joan, really. Don't think any more about it.'

'Not think any more about it! My child, do you even faintly realize what a thousand pounds, or a quarter of a thousand pounds, means to me? I would do anything for it, *anything*. And there's the fun of it. I don't suppose you can realize that either. I want a change. I want something new. I've been grubbing away here on nothing a week for years, and it's time I had a vacation.

There must be a way by which you could get me down . . . .
Why, of course! Why didn't I think of it before! You shall take
me on Friday as your lady's maid!'

'But, Joan, I couldn't.'

'Why not?'

'I – I couldn't.'

'Why not?'

'Oh, well!'

Joan advanced upon her where she sat, and grasped her firmly
by the shoulders. Her face was inflexible.

'Aline, my pet, it's no good arguing. You might just as well
argue with a wolf on the trail of a fat Russian peasant. I need that
money. I need it in my business. I need it worse than anybody
has ever needed anything. And I'm going to have it. Frow now
on till further notice, I am your lady's maid. You can give your
present one a holiday.'

Aline met her eyes waveringly. The spirit of the old schooldays, when nothing was impossible where Joan was concerned,
had her in its grip. Moreover, the excitement of the scheme
began to attract her.

'But, Joan,' she said, 'You know it's simply ridiculous. You
could never pass as a lady's maid. The other servants would find
you out. I expect there are all sorts of things a lady's maid has got
to do and not do.'

'My dear Aline, I know them all. You can't stump me on
below-stairs etiquette. I have *been* a lady's maid!'

'Joan!'

'It's quite true. Three years ago, when I was more than usually
impecunious. The wolf was glued to the door like a postage
stamp, so I answered an advertisement and became a lady's maid.'

'You seem to have done everything.'

'I have – pretty nearly. It's all right for you Idle Rich, Aline, you can sit still and contemplate Life, but we of the submerged tenth have got to work.'

Aline laughed.

'You know, you always could make me do anything you wanted, in the old days, Joan. I suppose I have got to look on this as quite settled now?'

'Absolutely settled. Oh, Aline, there's one thing you must remember. Don't call me Joan when I'm down at the Castle. You must call me Valentine.' She paused. The recollection of the Hon. Freddie had come to her. No. Valentine would not do. 'No, not Valentine,' she went on. 'It's too jaunty. I used it three years ago, but it never sounded just right. I want something more respectable, more suited to my position. Can't you suggest something?'

Aline pondered.

'Simpson?'

'Simpson! It's exactly right. You must practise it. Simpson! Say it kindly and yet distantly, as if I were a worm, but a worm for whom you felt a mild liking. Roll it round your tongue.'

'Simpson.'

'Splendid! No, once again – a little more haughtily.'

'Simpson . . . Simpson . . . Simpson . . .'

Joan regarded her with affectionate approval.

'It's wonderful,' she said. 'You might have been doing it all your life.'

'What are you laughing at?' asked Aline.

'Nothing,' said Joan. 'I was just thinking of something. There's a young man who lives on the floor above this, and I was lecturing him yesterday on Enterprise. I told him to go and find something exciting to do. I wonder what he would say if he knew how thoroughly I am going to practise what I preach.'

## CHAPTER FOUR

I

On the morning following Aline's visit to Joan Valentine, Ashe sat in his room, the *Morning Post* on the table before him. The heady influence of Joan had not yet ceased to work within him, and he proposed, in pursuance of his promise to her, to go carefully through the column of advertisements however pessimistic he might feel concerning the utility of that action.

His first glance assured him that the vast fortunes of the philanthropists whose acquaintance he had already made in print were not yet exhausted. Brian MacNeill still dangled his gold before the public. So did Angus Bruce. So did Duncan Macfarlane. So, likewise, Wallace Mackintosh and Donald MacNab. They still had the money and they still wanted to give it away.

The young Christian still wanted that thousand. . . .

He was reading listlessly down the column, when, from the mass of advertisements, one of an unusual sort detached itself:

WANTED – Young Man of Good Appearance, who is poor and reckless, to undertake delicate and dangerous enterprise. Good pay for the right man. Apply between the

hours of ten and twelve at offices of Mainprice, Mainprice
& Boole, 3 Denvers Street, Strand.

And, as he read it, half-past ten struck on the little clock on his
mantelpiece.

It was probably this fact that decided Ashe. If he had been
compelled to postpone his visit to the offices of Messrs.
Mainprice, Mainprice & Boole until the afternoon, it is possible
that barriers of laziness might have reared themselves in the
path of adventure, for Ashe, an adventurer at heart, was also
uncommonly lazy. But as it was, he could make an immediate
start.

Pausing but to put on his shoes, and having satisfied himself
by a glance at the mirror that his appearance was reasonably
good, he seized his hat, shot out of the narrow mouth of
Arundell Street like a shell, and scrambled into a taxi-cab with
the feeling that, short of murder, they couldn't make it too
delicate and dangerous for him.

He was conscious of strange thrills. This, he told himself, was
the only possible mode of life with Spring in the air. He had
always been partial to those historical novels in which the
characters are perpetually vaulting on to chargers and riding
across country on perilous errands. This leaping into taxi-cabs to
answer stimulating advertisements in the *Morning Post* was very
much the same sort of thing. It was with a fine fervour
animating him that he entered the gloomy offices of Mainprice,
Mainprice & Boole. His brain was afire, and he felt ready for
anything.

'I have come in answ—' he began to the diminutive office-
boy, who seemed to be the nearest thing visible to a Mainprice
or a Boole.

'Siddown. Gottatakeyerturn,' said the office-boy, and for the first time Ashe perceived that the ante-room in which he stood was crowded to overflowing.

This, in the circumstances, was something of a damper. He had pictured himself, during the ride in the cab, striding into the office and saying, 'The delicate and dangerous enterprise. Lead me to it.' He had not realized till now that he was not the only man in London who read the advertisement columns in the *Morning Post*, and for an instant his heart sank at the sight of all this competition.

A second and more comprehensive glance at his rivals gave him confidence.

The 'Wanted' column of the morning paper is a sort of dredger which churns up strange creatures from the mud of London's under-world. Only in response to the dredger's operations do they come to the surface in such numbers as to be noticeable, for as a rule they are of a solitary habit and shun company: but when they do come they bring with them something of the horror of the depths. It is the saddest spectacle in the world, that of the crowd collected by a 'Wanted' advertisement. They are so palpably not wanted by anyone for any purpose whatsoever: yet every time they gather together with a sort of hopeful hopelessness. What they were originally, the units of these collections, Heaven knows. Fate has battered out of them every trace of individuality. Each now is exactly like his neighbour, no worse, no better.

Ashe, as he sat and watched them, was filled with conflicting emotions. One half of him, thrilled with the glamour of adventure, was chafing at the delay and resentful of these poor creatures as of so many obstacles to the beginning of all the brisk and exciting things which lay behind the mysterious brevity of the advertisement. The other, pitifully alive to the tragedy of the occasion, was grateful for the delay. On the whole he was glad to feel that if one of these derelicts did not secure the 'good pay for the right man', it would not be his fault. He had been the last to arrive, and he would be the last to pass through that door which was the gateway of adventure, the door with 'Mr. Boole' inscribed on its ground-glass, beyond which sat the author of the mysterious request for assistance, interviewing applicants. It would be through their own shortcomings, not because of his superior attractions, if they failed to please that unseen arbiter.

That they were so failing was plain. Scarcely had one scarred victim of London's unkindness passed through, than the bell would ring, the office-boy who, in the intervals of frowning sternly on the throng as much as to say that he would stand no nonsense, would cry 'Next!' and another dull-eyed wreck would drift through, to be followed a moment later by yet another. The one fact at present ascertainable concerning the unknown searcher for reckless young men of good appearance was that he appeared to be possessed of considerable decision of character, a man who did not take long to make up his mind. He was rejecting applicants now at the rate of two a minute.

Expeditious as he was, however, he kept Ashe waiting for a considerable time. It was not till the hands of the fat clock over the door pointed to twenty minutes past eleven that the office-boy's 'Next!' found him the only survivor. He gave his clothes a hasty smack with the palm of his hand and his hair a fleeting dab, to accentuate his good appearance, and turned the handle of the door of fate.

The room assigned by the firm to their Mr. Boole for his personal use was a small and dingy compartment, redolent of that atmosphere of desolation which lawyers alone know how to achieve. It gave the impression of not having been swept since the foundation of the firm in the year 1786. There was one small window, covered with grime. It was one of those windows which you see only in lawyers' offices. Possibly, some reckless Mainprice or hairbrained Boole had opened it, in a fit of mad excitement induced by the news of the Battle of Waterloo, in 1815, and had been instantly expelled from the firm. Since then no one had dared to tamper with it.

Looking out of this window, or rather, looking at it, for X-rays could hardly have succeeded in actually penetrating the alluvial deposits upon the glass, was a little man. As Ashe entered, he turned, and looked at him as if he hurt him rather badly in some tender spot.

Ashe was obliged to own to himself that he felt a little nervous. It is not every day that a young man of good appearance, who has led a quiet life, meets face to face one who is prepared to pay him well for doing something delicate and dangerous. To Ashe the sensation was entirely novel. The most delicate and dangerous act he had performed to date had been the daily mastication of Mrs. Bell's breakfasts (included in rent). Yes, he had to admit it, he was nervous: and the fact that he was nervous made him hot and uncomfortable.

To judge him by his appearance, the man at the window was also hot and uncomfortable. He was a little, truculent-looking man, and his face at present was red with a flush which sat unnaturally on a normally leaden-coloured face. His eyes looked out from under thick grey eyebrows with an almost tortured expression. This was partly owing to the strain of interviewing Ashe's preposterous predecessors, but principally to the fact that the little man had suddenly become seized with acute indigestion, a malady to which he was peculiarly subject.

He removed from his mouth a black cigar which he was smoking, inserted a digestive tabloid, and replaced the cigar. Then he concentrated his attention upon Ashe. As he did so, the hostile expression of his face became modified. He looked surprised and – grudgingly – pleased.

'Well, what do *you* want?' he said.

'I came in answer to—'

'In answer to my advertisement? I had given up hope of seeing anything part-human. I thought you must be one of the clerks. You're certainly more like what I advertised for. Of all the seedy bunches of dead-beats I ever struck, the aggregation I've just been interviewing was the seediest. When I spend good money advertising for a young man of good appearance, then I want a young man of good appearance, not a tramp of fifty-five.'

Ashe was sorry for his predecessors, but he was bound to admit that they certainly had corresponded somewhat faithfully to the description just given. The comparative cordiality of his own reception removed the slight nervousness which had been troubling him. He began to feel confident, almost jaunty.

'I'm through,' said the little man wearily. 'I've had enough of interviewing applicants. You're the last one I'll see. Are there any more hoodoos outside?'

'Not when I came in.'

'Then we'll get down to business. I'll tell you what I want done, and, if you are willing, you can do it: if you are not willing, you can leave it and go to the devil. Sit down.'

Ashe sat down. He resented the little man's tone, but this was not the moment for saying so.

His companion scrutinized him narrowly.

'As far as appearance goes,' he said, 'You are what I want.'

Ashe felt inclined to bow.

'Whoever takes on this job has got to act as my valet, and you look like a valet.' Ashe felt less inclined to bow. 'You're tall and thin and ordinary-looking. Yes, as far as appearance goes, you fill the bill.'

It seemed to Ashe that it was time to correct an impression which the little man appeared to have formed.

'I am afraid,' he said, 'that, if all you want is a valet, you will have to look elsewhere. I got the idea from your advertisement that something rather more exciting than that was in the air. I can recommend you to several good employment agencies, if you wish.'

He rose. 'Good morning,' he said. He would have liked to fling the massive pewter ink-pot at this little creature who had so keenly disappointed him.

'Sit down!' snapped the other.

Ashe resumed his seat. The hope of adventure dies hard on a Spring morning, when one is twenty-six, and he had the feeling that there was more to come.

'Don't be a damned fool,' said the little man. 'Of course I'm not asking you to be a valet and nothing else.'

'You would want me to do some cooking and plain sewing on the side, perhaps?'

Their eyes met in a hostile glare. The flush on the little man's face deepened.

'Are you trying to get gay with me?' he demanded dangerously.

'Yes,' said Ashe.

The answer seemed to disconcert his adversary. He was silent for a moment.

'Well,' he said at last, 'maybe it's all for the best. If you weren't full of gall, probably you wouldn't have come here at all, and whoever takes on this job of mine has got to have gall, if he has nothing else. I think we shall suit each other.'

'What is the job?'

The little man's face showed doubt and perplexity.

'It's awkward. If I'm to make the thing clear to you, I've got to trust you. And I don't know a thing about you. I wish I had thought of that before I inserted the advertisement.'

Ashe appreciated the difficulty.

'Wouldn't you make an A B case out of it?'

'Maybe I could, if I knew what an A B case was.'

'Call the people mixed up in it A and B.'

'And forget half-way through who was which! No, I guess I'll have to trust you.'

'I'll play square.'

The little man fastened his eyes on Ashe's in a piercing stare. Ashe met them smilingly. His spirits, always fairly cheerful, had risen high by now. There was something about the little man, in spite of his brusqueness and ill-temper, which made him feel flippant.

'Pure white,' he said.

'Eh?'

'My soul. And this' – he thumped the left section of his waistcoat – 'solid gold. Proceed.'

'I don't know where to begin.'

'Without presuming to dictate, why not at the beginning?'

'It's all so darned complicated that I don't rightly know which *is* the beginning. Well, see here. I collect scarabs. I'm crazy about scarabs. Ever since I quit business, you might say that I have practically lived for scarabs.'

'Though it sounds an unkind thing to say of any one,' said Ashe, 'incidentally, what *are* scarabs?' He held up his hand.

'Wait! It all comes back to me. Expensive Classical education now bearing belated fruit. Scarabaeus – Latin-noun, nominative – a beetle. Scarabeum, accusative, the beetle. Scarabei, of the beetle. Scarabeo, to or for the beetle. I remember now. Egypt – Rameses – Pyramids – sacred scarabs. Right!'

'Well, I guess I've gotten together the best collection of scarabs outside the British Museum, and some of them are worth what you like to me. I don't reckon money when it comes to a question of my scarabs. Do you understand?'

'I take you, laddie.'

Displeasure clouded the little man's face.

'Don't call me "laddie"!'

'I used the word figuratively, as it were.'

'Well, don't do it again. My name is J. Preston Peters, and "Mr. Peters" will do as anything else when you want to attract my attention.'

'Mine is Marson. You were saying, Mr. Peters?'

'Well, it's this way,' said the little man.

Shakespeare and Pope have both emphasized the tediousness of a twice-told tale, so the episode of the stolen scarab need not be repeated at this point, though it must be admitted that Mr. Peters' version of it differed considerably from the calm, dispassionate description which the author, in his capacity of official historian, has given earlier in the story. In Mr. Peters' version, the Earl of Emsworth appeared as a smooth and purposeful robber, a sort of elderly Raffles, worming his way into the homes of the innocent and only sparing that portion of their property which was too heavy for him to carry away. Mr. Peters, indeed, specifically described the Earl of Emsworth as an oily old plug-ugly.

It took Ashe some little time to get a thorough grasp of the tangled situation, but he did it at last. Only one point perplexed him.

'You want to employ somebody to go to the Castle and get this scarab back for you. I follow that. But why must he go as your valet?'

'That's simple enough. You don't think I'm asking him to buy a black mask and break in, do you? I'm making it as easy for him as possible. I can't take a secretary down to the Castle, for everybody knows that, now I've retired, I haven't got a secretary; and, if I engaged a new one and he was caught trying to steal my scarab from the Earl's collection, it would look suspicious. But a valet is different. Anyone can get fooled by a crook valet with bogus references.'

'I see. There's just one other point. Suppose your accomplice does get caught. What then?'

'That,' said Mr. Peters, 'is the catch, and it's just because of that that I am offering good pay to my man. We'll suppose for the sake of argument that you accept the contract, and get caught. Well, if that happens, you've got to look after yourself. I couldn't say a word. If I did, it would all come out, and, as far as the breaking-off of my daughter's engagement to young Threepwood was concerned, it would be just as bad as if I had tried to get the thing back myself. You've got to bear that in mind. You've got to remember it if you forget everything else. I don't appear in this business in any way whatsoever. If you get caught, you take what's coming to you without a word. You don't turn round and say, "I am innocent. Mr. Peters will explain all," because Mr. Peters certainly won't. Mr. Peters won't utter a syllable of protest if they want to hang you. No, if you go into this, young man, you go into it with your eyes open. You go into it with a full understanding of the risks, because you think the reward, if you are successful, makes the taking of those risks worth while. You and I know that what you are doing isn't really stealing; it's simply a tactful way of getting back my own property. But the judge and jury will have different views.'

'I am beginning to understand,' said Ashe thoughtfully, 'why you called the job "delicate and dangerous".'

Certainly it had been no over-statement. As a writer of detective-stories for the British office-boy, he had imagined in his time many undertakings which might be so described, but few to which the description was more admirably suited.

'It is,' said Mr. Peters, 'and this is why I'm offering good pay. Whoever carries this job through gets five thousand dollars cash.'

Ashe started.

'Five thousand dollars! A thousand pounds?'

'Yes.'

'When do I begin?'

'You'll do it?'

'For a thousand pounds I certainly will.'

'With your eyes open?'

'Wide open.'

A look of positive geniality illuminated Mr. Peters' pinched features. He even went so far as to pat Ashe on the shoulder.

'Good boy!' he said. 'Meet me at Paddington Station at four o'clock on Friday. And if there's anything more you want to know, come round to this address.'

II

There remained the telling of Joan Valentine. For it was obviously impossible not to tell her. When you have revolutionized your life at the bidding of another, you cannot well conceal the fact, as if nothing had happened.

Ashe had not the slightest desire to conceal the fact. On the contrary, he was glad to have such a capital excuse for renewing the acquaintance.

He could not tell her, of course, the secret details of the thing. Naturally, those must remain hidden. No, he would just go airily in and say, 'You know what you told me about doing something new? Well, I've just got a job as a valet.'

So he went airily in and said it.

'To whom?' said Joan.

'To a man named Peters. An American.'

Women are trained from infancy up to conceal their feelings. Joan did not start or otherwise express emotion.

'Not Mr. Preston Peters?'

'Yes. Do you know him? What a remarkable thing.'

'His daughter,' said Joan, 'has just engaged me as a lady's maid.'

'What!'

'It will not be quite the same thing as three years ago,' Joan explained. 'It is just a cheap way of getting a holiday. I used to know Miss Peters very well, you see. It will be more like travelling as her guest.'

Ashe had not yet overcome his amazement.

'But – but—'

'Yes?'

'But what an extraordinary coincidence.'

'Yes. By the way, how did you get the situation? And what put it into your head to be a valet at all? It seems such a curious thing for you to think of doing.'

Ashe was embarrassed.

'I – I – well, you see, the experience will be useful to me, of course, in my writing.'

'Oh! Are you now thinking of taking up my line of work, Dukes?'

'No, no. Not exactly that.'

'It seems so odd. How did you happen to get in touch with Mr. Peters?'

'Oh, I answered an advertisement.'

'I see.'

Ashe was becoming conscious of an undercurrent of something not altogether agreeable in the conversation. It lacked the gay ease of their first interview. He was not apprehensive lest she might have guessed his secret. There was, he felt, no possible means by which she could have done that. Yet the fact remained that those keen blue eyes of hers were looking at him in a peculiar and penetrating manner. He felt dampened.

'It will be nice being together,' he said feebly.

'Very,' said Joan.

There was a pause.

'I thought I would come and tell you.'

'Quite so.'

There was another pause.

'It seems so funny that you should be going out as a lady's maid.'

'Yes?'

'But of course you have done it before.'

'Yes.'

'The really extraordinary thing is that we should be going to the same people.'

'Yes.'

'It – it's remarkable, isn't it?'

'Yes.'

Ashe reflected. No, he did not appear to have any further remarks to make.

'Goodbye for the present,' he said.

'Goodbye.'

Ashe drifted out. He was conscious of a wish that he understood girls. Girls, in his opinion, were odd.

When he had gone, Joan Valentine hurried to the door, and having opened it an inch, stood listening. When the sound of his door closing came to her, she ran down the stairs and out into Arundell Street.

She went to the Hotel Mathis.

'I wonder,' she said to the sad-eyed waiter, 'if you have a copy of the *Morning Post*?'

The waiter, a child of romantic Italy, was only too anxious to oblige Youth and Beauty. He disappeared, and presently returned with a crumpled copy. Joan thanked him with a bright smile.

Back in her room she turned to the advertisement page. She knew that life was full of what the unthinking call coincidences, but the miracle of Ashe having selected by chance the father of Aline Peters as an employer was too much of a coincidence for her. Suspicion furrowed her brow.

It did not take her long to discover the advertisement which had sent Ashe hurrying in a taxi-cab to the offices of Messrs. Mainprice, Mainprice & Boole. She had been looking for something of the kind.

She read it through twice and smiled. Everything was very clear to her. She looked at the ceiling above her, and shook her head.

'You are quite a nice young man, Mr. Marson,' she said softly, 'but you mustn't try and jump my claim. I dare say you need that money too, but I'm afraid you must go without. I am going to have it, and nobody else.'

CHAPTER FIVE

I

The four-fifteen express slid softly out of Paddington
Station, and Ashe settled himself in the corner seat of his
second-class compartment. Opposite him, Joan Valentine had
begun to read a magazine. Along the corridor, in a first-class
smoking compartment, Mr. Peters was lighting a big black
cigar. Still farther along the corridor, in a first-class, non-
smoking compartment, Aline Peters looked out of the window
and thought of many things.

Ashe was feeling remarkably light-hearted. He wished that
he had not bought Joan that magazine and thus deprived
himself temporarily of the pleasure of her conversation: but that
was the only flaw in his happiness. With the starting of the train,
which might be considered the formal and official beginning of
the delicate and dangerous enterprise on which he had
embarked, he had definitely come to the conclusion that the life
adventurous was the life for him. He had frequently suspected
this to be the case, but it had required the actual experiment to
bring certainty.

Almost more than physical courage the ideal adventurer
needs a certain lively inquisitiveness, the quality of not being

content to mind his own affairs: and in Ashe this quality was highly developed. From boyhood up he had always been interested in things which were none of his business. And it is just that attribute which the modern young man, as a rule, so sadly lacks.

The modern young man may do adventurous things if they are thrust upon him, but, left to himself, he will edge away uncomfortably and look in the other direction when the Goddess of Adventure smiles at him. Training and tradition alike pluck at his sleeve and urge him not to risk making himself ridiculous. And from sheer horror of laying himself open to the charge of not minding his own business he falls into a stolid disregard of all that is out of the ordinary and exciting. He tells himself that the shriek from the lonely house he passed just now was only the high note of some amateur songstress, and that the maiden in distress whom he saw pursued by the ruffian with a knife was merely earning the salary paid her by some motion-picture firm. And he proceeds on his way, looking neither to left nor right.

Ashe had none of this degenerate coyness towards adventure. It is true that it had needed the eloquence of Joan Valentine to stir him from his groove, but that was because he was also lazy. He loved new sights and new experiences.

Yes, he was happy. The rattle of the train shaped itself into a lively march. He told himself that he had found the right occupation for a young man in the Spring.

Joan, meanwhile, entrenched behind her magazine, was also busy with her thoughts. She was not reading the magazine: she held it before her as a protection, knowing that, if she laid it down, Ashe would begin to talk. And just at present she had no desire for conversation. She, like Ashe, was contemplating the immediate future, but unlike him was not doing so with much pleasure. She was regretting heartily that she had not resisted the temptation to uplift this young man, and wishing that she had left him to wallow in the slothful peace in which she had found him. It is curious how frequently in this world our attempts to stimulate and uplift swoop back on us and smite us like boomerangs. Ashe's presence was the direct outcome of her lecture on Enterprise, and it added a complication to an already complicated venture.

She did her best to be fair to Ashe. It was not his fault that he was about to try to deprive her of five thousand dollars which she looked upon as her personal property. But, illogically, she found herself feeling a little hostile.

She glanced furtively at him over the magazine, choosing by ill chance a moment when he had just directed his gaze at her. Their eyes met, and there was nothing for it but to talk. So she tucked away her hostility in a corner of her mind where she could find it again when she wanted it, and prepared for the time being to be friendly. After all, except for the fact that he was her rival, this was a pleasant and amusing young man, and one for whom, till he made the announcement which had changed her whole attitude towards him, she had entertained a distinct feeling of friendship.

Nothing warmer. There was something about him which made her feel that she would have liked to stroke his hair in a motherly way and straighten his tie and have cosy chats with him in darkened rooms by the light of open fires, and make him tell her his inmost thoughts and stimulate him to do something really worthwhile with his life: but this, she held, was merely the instinct of a generous nature to be kind and helpful even to a comparative stranger.

'Well, Mr. Marson,' she said. 'Here we are!'

'Exactly what I was thinking,' said Ashe.

He was conscious of a marked increase in the exhilaration which the starting of the expedition had brought to him. At the back of his mind, he realized, there had been all along a kind of wistful resentment at the change in this girl's manner towards him. During the brief conversation when he had told her of his having secured his present situation, and later, only a few minutes back, on the platform of Paddington Station, he had sensed a coldness, a certain hostility, so different from her pleasant friendliness at their first meeting.

She had returned now to her earlier manner, and he was surprised at the difference it made. He felt somehow younger, more alive. The lilt of the train's rattle changed to a gay ragtime.

This was curious, because Joan was nothing more than a friend. He was not in love with her. One does not fall in love with a girl whom one has met only three times. One is attracted, yes; but one does not fall in love.

A moment's reflection enabled him to diagnose his sensations correctly. This odd impulse to leap across the compartment and kiss Joan was not love. It was merely the natural desire of a good-hearted young man to be decently chummy with his species.

'Well, what do you think of it all, Mr. Marson?' said Joan. 'Are you sorry or glad that you let me persuade you to do this perfectly mad thing? I feel responsible for you, you know. If it had not been for me, you would have been comfortably at Arundell Street, writing your "Wand of Death".'

'I'm glad.'

'You don't feel any misgivings now that you are actually committed to domestic service?'

'Not one.'

Joan, against her will, smiled approval on this uncompromising attitude. This young man might be her rival, but his demeanour on the eve of perilous times appealed to her. That was the spirit she liked and admired, that reckless acceptance of whatever might come. It was the spirit in which she herself had gone into the affair, and she was pleased to find that it animated Ashe also. Though, to be sure, it had its drawbacks. It made his rivalry the more dangerous.

This reflection injected a touch of the old hostility into her manner.

'I wonder if you will continue to feel so brave.'

'What do you mean?'

Joan perceived that she was in danger of going too far. She had no wish to unmask Ashe at the expense of revealing her own secret. She must resist the temptation to hint that she had discovered his.

'I meant,' she said quickly, 'that from what I have seen of him, Mr. Peters seems likely to be a rather trying man to work for.'

Ashe's face cleared. For a moment he had almost suspected that she had guessed his errand.

'Yes. I imagine he will be. He is what you might call quick-tempered. He has dyspepsia, you know.'

'I know.'

'What he wants is plenty of fresh air and no cigars, and a regular course of Larsen Exercises which amused you so much.' Joan laughed.

'Are you going to try and persuade Mr. Peters to twist himself about like that? Do let me see it if you do.'

'I wish I could.'

'Do suggest it to him.'

'Don't you think he would resent it from a valet?'

'I keep forgetting that you are a valet. You look so unlike one.'

'Old Peters didn't think so. He rather complimented me on my appearance. He said I was ordinary looking.'

'I shouldn't have called you that. You look so very strong and fit.'

'Surely there are muscular valets?'

'Well, yes, I suppose there are.'

Ashe looked at her. He was thinking that never in his life had he seen a girl so amazingly pretty. What it was that she had done to herself was beyond him, but something, some trick of dress, had given her a touch of the demure which made her irresistible. She was dressed in sober black, the ideal background for her fairness.

'While on the subject,' he said, 'I suppose you know you don't look in the least like a lady's maid. You look like a disguised princess.'

She laughed.

'That's very nice of you, Mr. Marson, but you're quite wrong. Anyone could tell I was a lady's maid a mile away. You aren't criticizing the dress, surely?'

'The dress is all right. It's the general effect. I don't think your expression is right. It's – it's – there's too much *attack in* it. You aren't meek enough.' Joan's eyes opened wide.

'*Meek!* Have you ever seen a lady's maid, Mr. Marson?'

'Why, no, now that I come to think of it, I don't believe I have.'

'Well, let me tell you that meekness is her last quality. Why should she be meek? Doesn't she go in after the Groom of the Chambers?'

'Go in? Go in where?'

'Into dinner.'

She smiled at the sight of his bewildered face.

'I'm afraid you don't know much about the etiquette of the new world you have entered so rashly. Didn't you know that the rules of precedence among the servants of a big house are more rigid and complicated than in Society?'

'You're joking.'

'I'm not joking. You try going into dinner out of your proper place when we get to Blandings, and see what happens. A public rebuke from the butler is the least that you could expect.'

A bead of perspiration appeared on Ashe's forehead.

'My God!' he whispered. 'If a butler publicly rebuked me I think I should commit suicide. I couldn't survive it.'

He stared with fallen jaw into the abyss of horror into which he had leaped so light-heartedly. The Servant Problem, on this large scale, had been non-existent for him till now. In the days of his youth at Much Middleford, Salop, his needs had been ministered to by a muscular Irishwoman. Later, at Oxford, there had been his 'scout' and his bedmaker, harmless persons both, provided you locked up your whisky. And in London, his last phase, a succession of servitors of the type of the dishevelled maid at No. 7A, had tended him. That, dotted about the land, there were houses in which larger staffs of domestics were maintained, he had been vaguely aware. Indeed, in 'Gridley Quayle, Investigator, The Adventure of the Missing Marquess' (number four of the series) he had drawn a picture of the home-life of a Duke, in which a butler and two powdered footmen had played their parts. But he had had no idea that rigid and complicated rules of etiquette swayed the private lives of these individuals. If he had given the matter a thought, he had supposed that, when the dinner-hour arrived, the butler and the two footmen would troop into the kitchen and squash in at the table wherever they found room.

'Tell me,' he said, 'tell me all you know. I feel as if I had escaped a frightful disaster.'

'You probably have. I don't suppose there is anything so terrible as a snub from a butler.'

'If there is I can't think of it. When I was at Oxford, I used to go and stay with a friend of mine who had a butler who looked like a Roman emperor in swallow-tails. He terrified me. I used to grovel to the man. Please give me all the tips you can.'

'Well, as Mr. Peters' valet, I suppose you will be rather a big man.'

'I shan't feel it.'

'However large the house-party is, Mr. Peters is sure to be the principal guest, so your standing will be correspondingly magnificent. You come after the butler, the housekeeper, the groom of the chambers, Lord Emsworth's valet, Lady Ann Warblington's lady's maid—'

'Who is she?'

'Lady Ann? Lord Emsworth's sister. She has lived with him since his wife died. What was I saying? Oh yes. After them come the Hon. Frederick Threepwood's valet and myself, and then you.'

'I'm not so high up then, after all?'

'Yes, you are. There's a whole crowd who come after you. It all depends on how many other guests there are besides Mr. Peters.'

'I suppose I charge in at the head of a drove of housemaids and scullery-maids?'

'My dear Mr. Marson, if a housemaid or a scullery-maid tried to get into the Steward's Room and have her meals with us, she would be—'

'Rebuked by the butler?'

'Lynched, I should think. Kitchen-maids and scullery-maids eat in the kitchen. Chauffeurs, footmen, under-butler, pantry-boys, hall-boys, odd man and steward's room footman take their meals in the Servants' Hall, waited on by the hall-boy. The still-room maids have breakfast and tea in the still-room and dinner and supper in the Hall. The housemaids and nursery-maids have breakfast and tea in the housemaid's sitting-room and dinner and supper in the Hall. The head-housemaid ranks next to the head still-room maid. The laundry-maids have a place of their own near the laundry, and the head laundry-maid ranks above the head housemaid. The chef has his meals in a room of his own near the kitchen. . . . Is there anything else I can tell you, Mr. Marson?'

Ashe was staring at her with vacant eyes. He shook his head dumbly.

'We stop at Swindon in half an hour,' said Joan softly. 'Don't you think you would be wise to get out there and go straight back to London, Mr. Marson? Think of all you would avoid.'

Ashe found speech.

'It's a nightmare.'

'You would be far happier in Arundell Street. Why don't you get out at Swindon and go back?'

Ashe shook his head.

'I can't. There's — there's a reason.'

Joan picked up her magazine again. Hostility had come out from the corner into which she had tucked it away, and was once more filling her mind. She knew that it was illogical, but she could not help it. For a moment during her revelations of Servants' Etiquette she had allowed herself to hope that she had frightened her rival out of the field, and the disappointment made her feel irritable. She buried herself in a short story, and countered Ashe's attempts at renewing the conversation with cold mono-syllables, till he ceased his efforts and fell into a moody silence.

He was feeling hurt and angry. Her sudden coldness, following on the friendliness with which she had talked for so long, puzzled and infuriated him. He felt as if he had been snubbed, and for no reason.

He resented the defensive magazine, though he had bought it for her himself. He resented her attitude of having ceased to recognize his existence. A sadness, a filmy melancholy crept over him. He brooded on the unutterable silliness of humanity, especially the female portion of it, in erecting artificial barriers to friendship.

It was so unreasonable. At their first meeting, when she might have been excused for showing defensiveness, she had treated him with unaffected ease. When that meeting had ended, there was a tacit understanding between them that all the preliminary awkwardnesses of the first stages of acquaintance-ship were to be considered as having been passed, and that when they met again, if they ever did, it would be as friends. And here she was, luring him on with apparent friendliness, and then withdrawing into herself as if he had presumed.

A rebellious spirit took possession of him. *He* didn't care! Let her be cold and distant. He would show her that she had no monopoly of those qualities. He would not speak to her until she spoke to him, and when she spoke to him, he would freeze her with his courteous but bleakly aloof indifference. . . .

The train rattled on. Joan read her magazine. Silence reigned in the second-class compartment.

Swindon was reached and passed. Darkness fell on the land. The journey began to seem interminable to Ashe.

But presently there came a creaking of brakes, and the train jerked itself to another stop.

A voice on the platform made itself heard, calling, 'Market Blandings. Market Blandings Station.'

## II

The village of Market Blandings is one of those sleepy hamlets which modern progress has failed to touch, except by the addition of a railroad station and a room over the grocer's shop where moving-pictures are on view on Tuesdays and Fridays. The church is Norman, and the intelligence of the majority of the natives palaeozoic. To alight at Market Blandings Station in the dusk of a rather chilly Spring day, when the south-west wind has shifted to due east, and the thrifty inhabitants have not yet lit their windows, is to be smitten with the feeling that one is at the edge of the world with no friends near.

Ashe, as he stood beside Mr. Peters' luggage and raked the unsympathetic darkness with a dreary eye, gave himself up to melancholy. Above him an oil lamp shed a meagre light. Along the platform a small but sturdy porter was juggling with a milk-can. The east wind explored his system with chilly fingers.

Somewhere out in the darkness, into which Mr. Peters and Aline had already vanished in a large automobile, lay the Castle with its butler, and its fearful code of etiquette. Soon the cart which was to convey him and the trunks thither would be arriving. He shivered.

Out of the gloom and into the feeble rays of the oil lamp came Joan Valentine. She had been away tucking Aline into the car. She looked warm and cheerful. She was smiling in the old friendly way.

If girls realized their responsibilities, they would be so careful when they smiled that they would probably abandon the practice altogether. There are moments in a man's life when a girl's smile can have as important results as an explosion of dynamite. In the course of their brief acquaintance Joan had smiled at Ashe many times, but the conditions governing those occasions had not been such as to permit him to be seriously affected. He had been pleased on such occasions; he had admired her smile in a detached and critical spirit; but he had not been overwhelmed by it. The frame of mind necessary for that result had been lacking. But now, after five minutes of solitude on the depressing platform of Market Blandings Station, he was what the spiritualists call a sensitive subject. He had reached that depth of gloom and bodily discomfort when a sudden smile has all the effect of strong liquor and good news administered simultaneously, warming the blood and comforting the soul and generally turning the world from a bleak desert into a land flowing with milk and honey.

It is not too much to say that he reeled before Joan's smile. It was so entirely unexpected. He clutched Mr. Peters' steamertrunk in his emotion.

All his resolutions to be cold and distant were swept away. He had the feeling that in a friendless universe here was someone who was fond of him and glad to see him.

A smile of such importance demands analysis, and in this case repays it; for many things lay behind this smile of Joan Valentine's on the platform of Market Blandings Station.

In the first place, she had had another of her swift changes of mood, and had once again tucked away hostility into its corner. She had thought it over, and had come to the conclusion that as she had no logical grievance against Ashe for anything he had done, to be distant to him was the behaviour of a cat. Consequently, she resolved, when they should meet again, to resume her attitude of good-fellowship. That in itself would have been enough to make her smile.

But there was another reason, which had nothing to do with Ashe. While she had been tucking Aline into the automobile, she had met the eye of the driver of that vehicle and had perceived a curious look in it, a look of amazement and sheer terror. A moment later, when Aline called the driver Freddie, she had understood. No wonder the Hon. Freddie had looked as if he had seen a ghost. It would be a relief to the poor fellow when, as he undoubtedly would do in the course of the drive, he inquired of Aline the name of her maid and was told it was Simpson. He would mutter something about, 'Reminds me of a girl I used to know,' and would brood on the remarkable way in which Nature produces doubles. But he had had a bad moment, and it was partly at the recollection of his face that Joan smiled.

A third reason was that the sight of the Hon. Freddie had reminded her that R. Jones had said that he had written her poetry. That thought too had contributed towards the smile that so dazzled Ashe.

Ashe, not being miraculously intuitive, accepted the easier explanation that she smiled because she was glad to be in his company, and this thought, coming on top of his mood of despair and general dissatisfaction with everything mundane, acted on him like some powerful chemical.

In every man's life there is generally one moment to which in later years he can look back and say, 'In this moment I fell in love.' Such a moment came to Ashe now.

> *Betwixt the stirrup and the ground*
> *Mercy I asked, mercy I found.*

So sings the poet, and so it was with Ashe.

In the almost incredibly brief time which it took the small but sturdy porter to roll a milk-can across the platform and bump it with a clang against other milk-cans similarly treated a moment before, Ashe fell in love.

The word is so loosely used to cover a thousand varying shades of emotion – from the volcanic passion of an Antony for a Cleopatra to the tepid preference of a grocer's assistant for the housemaid at the second house in the High Street as opposed to the cook at the first house past the post-office – that the mere statement that Ashe fell in love is not a sufficient description of his feelings as he stood grasping Mr. Peters' steamer-trunk. We must expand. We must analyse.

From his fourteenth year onward Ashe had been in love many times. His sensations in the case of Joan were neither the terrific upheaval which had caused him in his fifteenth year to collect twenty-eight photographs of the principal girl of the Theatre Royal, Birmingham, pantomime, nor the milder flame which had caused him, when at Oxford, to give up smoking for a week and try to learn by heart the Sonnets from the Portuguese. His love was something that lay between these two poles. He did not wish the station platform of Market Blandings to become suddenly congested with Red Indians, so that he might save Joan's life, and he did not wish to give up anything at all. But he was conscious, to the very depths of his being, that a future in which Joan did not figure would be so insupportable as not to bear considering, and in the immediate present, he very strongly favoured the idea of clasping Joan in his arms and kissing her till further notice. Mingled with these feelings was an excited gratitude to her for coming to him like this with that electric smile on her face; a stunned realization that she was a thousand times prettier than he had ever imagined: and a humility which threatened to make him loose his clutch on the steamer-trunk and roll about at her feet, yapping like a dog.

Gratitude, as far as he could dissect his tangled emotions, was the predominating ingredient of his mood. Only once in his life had he felt so passionately grateful to any human being. On that occasion, too, the object of his gratitude had been feminine.

Years before, when a boy in his father's home in distant Much Middleford, Salop, those in authority had commanded that he, in his eleventh year and shy as one can be only at that interesting age, rise in the presence of a room full of strangers, adult guests, and recite, 'The Wreck of the Hesperus'.

He had risen. He had blushed. He had stammered. He had contrived to whisper, 'It was the schooner Hesperus.' And then, in a corner of the room, a little girl, for no properly explained reason, had burst out crying. She had yelled, she had bellowed, and would not be comforted, and in the ensuing confusion Ashe had escaped to the woodshed at the bottom of the garden, saved by a miracle.

All his life he had remembered the gratitude he had felt for that timely girl, and never till now had he experienced any other similar spasm.

But, as he looked at Joan, he found himself renewing that emotion of fifteen years ago.

She was about to speak. In a sort of trance he watched her lips part. He waited almost reverently for the first words which she should speak to him in her new role of the only authentic goddess.

'Isn't it a shame,' she said, 'I've just put a penny in the chocolate slot machine, and it's empty. I've a good mind to write to the company.'

Ashe felt as if he were listening to the strains of some grand, sweet anthem.

The small but sturdy porter, weary of his work amongst the milk-cans, or perhaps – let us do him an injustice, even in thought – having finished it, approached them.

'The cart from the Castle's here.'

In the gloom beyond him there gleamed a light which had not been there before. The meditative snort of a horse supported his statement. He began to deal as authoritatively with Mr. Peters' steamer-trunk as he had dealt with the milk-cans.

'At last,' said Joan. 'I hope it's a covered cart. I'm frozen. Let's go and see.'

Ashe followed her with the rigid gait of an automaton.

### III

Cold is the ogre which drives all beautiful things into hiding. Below the surface of a frost-bound garden there lurk hidden bulbs which are only biding their time to burst forth in a riot of laughing colour (unless the gardener has planted them upside down) but shivering Nature dare not put forth her flowers till the ogre has gone. Not otherwise does cold suppress love. A man in an open cart on an English Spring night may continue to be in love, but love is not the emotion uppermost in his bosom. It shrinks within him and waits for better times.

For the cart was not a covered cart. It was open to the four winds of heaven, of which the one at present active proceeded from the bleak east. To this fact may be attributed Ashe's swift recovery from the exalted mood into which Joan's smile had thrown him, his almost instant emergence from the trance. Deep down in him he was aware that his attitude towards Joan had not changed, but his conscious self was too fully occupied with the almost hopeless task of keeping his blood circulating to permit of thoughts of love. Before the cart had travelled twenty yards he was a mere chunk of frozen misery.

After an eternity of winding roads, darkened cottages and black fields and hedges, the cart turned in at a massive iron gate which stood open, giving entrance to a smooth gravel drive. Here the way ran for nearly a mile through an open park of great trees, and was then swallowed in the darkness of dense shrubberies. Presently to the left appeared lights, at first in ones and twos, shining out and vanishing again, then as the shrubberies ended and the smooth lawns and terraces began, blazing down on the travellers from a score of windows with the heartening effect of fires on a winter night. Against the pale grey sky Blandings Castle stood out like a mountain.

It was a noble pile, of early Tudor building. Its history is recorded in England's history books and Violett-le-Duc has written of its architecture. It dominated the surrounding country.

The feature of it which impressed Ashe most at this moment, however, was the fact that it looked warm, and for the first time since the drive began he found himself in a mood that approximated to cheerfulness. It was a little early to begin feeling cheerful, he discovered, for the journey was by no means over. Arrived within sight of the Castle, the cart began a detour,

SOMETHING FRESH

which, ten minutes later, brought it under an arch and over cobble-stones to the rear of the buildings, where it eventually pulled up in front of a great door.

Ashe descended painfully, and beat his feet against the cobbles. He helped Joan to climb down. Joan was apparently in a gentle glow. Women seem impervious to cold.

The door opened. Warm, kitcheny scents came through it. Strong men hurried out to take down the trunks, while fair women, in the shape of two nervous scullery-maids, approached Joan and Ashe and bobbed curtseys. This, under more normal conditions, would have been enough to unman Ashe, but in his frozen state a mere curtseying scullery-maid expended herself harmlessly upon him. He even acknowledged the greeting with a kindly nod.

The scullery-maids, it seemed, were acting in much the same capacity as the *attachés* of Royalty. One was there to conduct Joan to the presence of Mrs. Twemlow the housekeeper, the other to lead Ashe to where Beach the butler waited to do honour to the valet of the Castle's most important guest.

After a short walk down a stone-flagged passage, Joan and her escort turned to the right. Ashe's objective appeared to be located to the left. He parted from Joan with regret. Her moral support would have been welcome.

Presently his scullery-maid stopped at a door and tapped thereon. A fruity voice, like old tawny port made audible, said, 'Come in.' Ashe's guide opened the door.

'The gentleman, Mr. Beach,' said she, and scuttled away to the less rarified atmosphere of the kitchen.

Ashe's first impression of Beach the butler was one of tension. Other people, confronted for the first time with Beach, had felt the same. He had that strained air of being on the very

121

point of bursting which one sees in frogs and toy balloons. Nervous and imaginative men, meeting Beach, braced themselves involuntarily, stiffening their muscles for the explosion. Those who had the pleasure of more intimate acquaintance with him soon passed this stage, just as people whose homes are on the slopes of Mount Vesuvius become immune to fear of eruptions. As far back as they could remember, Beach had always looked as if an apoplectic fit were a matter of minutes, but he never had apoplexy, and in time they came to ignore the possibility of it. Ashe, however, approaching him with a fresh eye, had the feeling that this strain could not possibly continue, and that within a very short space of time the worst must happen. The prospect of this did much to arouse him from the coma into which he had been frozen by the rigours of the journey.

Butlers as a class seem to grow less and less like anything human in proportion to the magnificence of their surroundings. There is a type of butler, employed in the comparatively modest homes of small country gentlemen, who is practically a man and a brother, who hob-nobs with the local tradesmen, sings a good comic song at the village inn, and in times of crisis will even turn to and work the pump when the water supply suddenly fails. The greater the house, the more does the butler diverge from this type. Blandings Castle was one of the more important of England's show-places, and Beach, accordingly, had acquired a dignified inertia which almost qualified him for inclusion in the vegetable kingdom. He moved, when he moved at all, slowly. He distilled speech with the air of one measuring out drops of some precious drug. His heavy-lidded eyes had the fixed expression of a statue's.

With an almost imperceptible wave of a fat white hand he

conveyed to Ashe that he desired him to sit down. With a stately movement of his other hand he picked up a kettle which simmered on the hob. With an inclination of his head he called Ashe's attention to a decanter on the table.

In another moment Ashe was sipping a whisky toddy with the feeling that he had been privileged to assist at some mystic rite.

Mr. Beach, posting himself before the fire and placing his hands behind his back, permitted speech to drip from him.

'I have not the advantage of your name, Mr.—'

Ashe introduced himself. Beach acknowledged the information with a half bow.

'You must have had a cold ride, Mr. Marson. The wind is in the east.'

Ashe said yes, the ride had been cold.

'When the wind is in the east,' continued Mr. Beach, letting each syllable escape with apparent reluctance, 'I Suffer From My Feet.'

'I beg your pardon?'

'I Suffer From My Feet,' repeated the butler, measuring out the drops. 'You are a young man, Mr. Marson. Probably you do not know what it is to Suffer From Your Feet.'

He surveyed Ashe, his whisky toddy and the wall beyond with his heavy-lidded inscrutability.

'Corns,' he said.

Ashe said that he was sorry.

'I Suffer Extremely From My Feet. Not only corns. I have but recently recovered from an Ingrowing Toe-Nail. I Suffered Greatly From My Ingrowing Toe-Nail. I Suffer From Swollen Joints.'

Ashe regarded this martyr with increasing disfavour. It is the flaw in the character of many excessively healthy young men that, while kind-hearted enough in most respects, they listen with a regrettable feeling of impatience to the confessions of those less happily situated as regards the ills of the flesh. Rightly or wrongly they hold that these statements should be reserved for the ear of the medical profession and other and more general topics selected for conversation with laymen.

'I'm sorry,' he said hastily. 'You must have a bad time. Is there a large house-party here just now?'

'We are expecting,' said Mr. Beach, 'a Number of Guests. We shall in all probability sit down thirty or more to dinner.'

'A responsibility for you,' said Ashe ingratiatingly, well pleased to be quit of the feet topic.

Mr. Beach nodded.

'You are right, Marson. Few persons realize the responsibilities of a man in my position. Sometimes, I can assure you, it preys upon my mind, and I Suffer From Nervous Headaches.'

Ashe began to feel like a man trying to put out a fire which, as fast as he checks it at one point, breaks out at another.

'Sometimes, when I come off duty, everything gets Blurred. The outlines of objects grow misty. I have to sit down in a chair. The Pain Is Excruciating.'

'But it helps you to forget the pain in your feet.'

'No. No. I Suffer From My Feet simultaneously.'

Ashe gave up the struggle.

'Tell me about your feet,' he said.

Mr. Beach told him all about his feet.

The pleasantest functions must come to an end, and the moment arrived when the final word on the subject of swollen joints was spoken. Ashe, who had resigned himself to a permanent contemplation of the subject, could hardly believe that he heard correctly when, at the end of some ten minutes, his companion changed the conversation.

'You have been with Mr. Peters some time, Mr. Marson?'

'Eh? Oh! Oh no, only since last Wednesday.'

'Indeed! Might I inquire whom you assisted before that?'

For a moment Ashe did what he would not have believed himself capable of doing – regretted that the topic of feet was no longer under discussion. The question placed him in an awkward position. If he lied, and credited himself with a lengthy experience as a valet, he risked exposing himself. If he told the truth, and confessed that this was his maiden effort in the capacity of gentleman's gentleman, what would the butler think? There were objections to each course, but to tell the truth was the easier of the two, so he told it.

'Your first situation?' said Mr. Beach. 'Indeed!'

'I was – er – doing something else before I met Mr. Peters,' said Ashe.

Mr. Beach was too well bred to be inquisitive, but his eyebrows were not.

'Ah!' he said.

'?' cried his eyebrows. '? ? ?'

Ashe ignored the eyebrows.

'Something different,' he said.

There was an awkward silence. Ashe appreciated its awkwardness. He was conscious of a grievance against Mr. Peters. Why could not Mr. Peters have brought him down here as his secretary? To be sure, he had advanced some objection to that course in their conversation at the offices of Mainprice, Mainprice & Boole, but merely some silly, far-fetched objection. He wished that he had had the sense to fight the point while there was time; but, at the moment when they were arranging plans, he had been rather tickled by the thought of becoming a valet. The notion had a pleasing musical-comedy touch about it. Why had he not foreseen the complications which must ensue? He could tell by the look on his face that this confounded butler was waiting for him to give a full explanation. What would he think if he withheld it? He would probably suppose that Ashe had been in prison.

Well, there was nothing to be done about it. If Beach was suspicious, he must remain suspicious. Fortunately, the suspicions of a butler do not matter much.

Mr. Beach's eyebrows were still mutely urging him to reveal all, but Ashe directed his gaze at that portion of the room which Mr. Beach did not fill. He was hanged if he was going to let himself be hypnotized by a pair of eyebrows into incriminating himself. He glared stolidly at the pattern of the wall-paper, which represented a number of birds of an unknown species seated on a corresponding number of exotic shrubs.

The silence was growing oppressive. Somebody had to break it soon. And, as Mr. Beach was still confining himself to the language of the eyebrow and apparently intended to fight it out on these lines if it took all summer, Ashe broke it himself.

It seemed to him, as he reconstructed the scene in bed that night, that Providence must have suggested the subject of Mr. Peters' indigestion, for the mere mention of his employer's sufferings acted like magic on the butler.

'I might have had better luck, while I was looking for a place,' said Ashe. 'I dare say you know how bad-tempered Mr. Peters is? He is dyspeptic.'

'So,' responded Mr. Beach, 'I have been informed.' He brooded for a space. 'I, too,' he proceeded, 'Suffer From My Stomach. I have a Weak Stomach. The Lining Of My Stomach is not what I could wish the Lining Of My Stomach to be.'

'Tell me,' said Ashe gratefully, 'all about the lining of your stomach.'

It was a quarter of an hour later that Mr. Beach was checked in his discourse by the chiming of the little clock on the mantel-piece. He turned round and gazed at it with surprise not unmixed with displeasure.

'So late!' he said. 'I shall have to be going about my duties. And you also, Mr. Marson, if I may make the suggestion. No doubt Mr. Peters will be wishing to have your assistance in preparing for dinner. If you go along the passage outside you will come to the door which separates our portion of the house from the other. I must beg you to excuse me. I have to go to the cellar.'

Following his directions, Ashe came, after a walk of a few yards, to a green baize door, which, swinging at his push, gave him a view of what he took correctly to be the main hall of the Castle, a wide, comfortable space, ringed with settees and warmed by a log fire burning in a mammoth fireplace. To the right a broad staircase led to upper regions.

It was at this point that Ashe realized the incompleteness of Mr. Beach's directions. Doubtless the broad staircase would take him to the floor on which were the bedrooms, but how was he to ascertain without the tedious process of knocking and inquiring at each door which was the one assigned to Mr. Peters? It was too late to go back and ask the butler for further guidance. Already he was on his way to the cellar in quest of the evening's wine.

As he stood irresolute, a door across the hall opened, and a man of his own age came out. Through the door which the young man held open for an instant while he answered a question from someone still within, Ashe had a glimpse of glass-topped cases.

Could this be the museum, his goal? The next moment the door, opening another few inches, revealed the outlying portions of an Egyptian mummy, and brought certainty.

It flashed across Ashe's mind that the sooner he explored the museum and located Mr. Peters' scarab the better. He decided to ask Beach to take him there as soon as he had leisure.

Meanwhile the young man had closed the museum door, and was crossing the hall. He was a wiry-haired, severe-looking young man, with a sharp nose and eyes that gleamed through rimless spectacles. None other, in fact, than Lord Emsworth's private secretary, the Efficient Baxter.

Ashe hailed him.

'I say, old man, would you mind telling me how I get to Mr. Peters' room? I've lost my bearings.'

He did not reflect that this was hardly the way in which valets in the best society addressed the Upper Classes. That is the worst of adopting what might be called a 'character' part. One can manage the business well enough; it is the dialogue which provides the pitfalls.

Mr. Baxter would have accorded a hearty agreement to the statement that this was not the way in which a valet should have spoken to him. But at the moment he was not aware that Ashe was a valet. From his easy mode of address he assumed that he was one of the numerous guests who had been arriving at the Castle all day. As he had asked for Mr. Peters he fancied that Ashe must be the Hon. Freddie's friend, George Emerson, whom he had not yet met.

Consequently, he replied with much cordiality that Mr. Peters' room was the second to the left on the second floor.

He said that Ashe couldn't miss it. Ashe said that he was much obliged.

'Awfully good of you,' said Ashe.

'Not at all,' said Mr. Baxter.

'You lose your way in a place like this,' said Ashe.

'Yes, don't you!' said Mr. Baxter.

And Ashe went on his upward path, and in a few moments was knocking at the door indicated.

And sure enough it was Mr. Peters' voice that invited him to enter.

IV

Mr. Peters, partially arrayed in the correct garb for gentlemen to dine, was standing in front of the mirror, wrestling with his evening tie. As Ashe entered, he removed his fingers and anxiously examined his handiwork. It proved unsatisfactory. With a yelp and an oath he tore the offending linen from his neck.

'Damn the thing!'

It was plain to Ashe that his employer was in no sunny mood. There are few things less calculated to engender sunniness in a naturally bad-tempered man than a dress-tie which will not let itself be pulled and twisted into the right shape. Even when things went well, Mr. Peters hated dressing for dinner. Words cannot describe his feelings when they went wrong.

There is something to be said in excuse for this impatience. It is a hollow mockery to be obliged to deck one's person as for a feast, when that feast is to consist of a little asparagus and a few nuts.

His eyes met Ashe's in the mirror.

'Oh, it's you, it it? Come in then. Don't stand staring. Close that door quick. Hustle! Don't scrape your feet on the floor. Try to look intelligent. Don't gape. Where have you been all this while? Why didn't you come before? Can you tie a tie? All right then, do it.'

Somewhat calmed by the snow-white butterfly-shaped creation which grew under Ashe's fingers he permitted himself to be helped into his coat. He picked up the remnant of a black cigar from the dressing-table and relit it.

'I've been thinking about you,' he said.

'Yes?' said Ashe.

'Have you located the scarab yet?'

'No.'

'What the devil have you been doing with yourself then? You've had time to grab it a dozen times.'

'I have been talking to the butler.'

'What the devil do you waste time talking to butlers for? I suppose you haven't even located the museum yet?'

'Yes, I've done that.'

'Oh, you have, have you? Well, that's something. And how do you propose setting about the job?'

'The best plan would be to go there very late at night.'

'Well, you didn't propose to stroll in in the afternoon, did you? How are you going to find the scarab when you do get in?'

Ashe had not thought of that. The deeper he went into this business, the more things did there seem to be in it of which he had not thought.

'I don't know,' he confessed.

'You don't know! Tell me, young man, are you considered pretty bright, as Englishmen go?'

'I really couldn't say.'

'Oh, you couldn't, couldn't you, you blanked bone-headed boob!' cried Mr. Peters, frothing over quite unexpectedly and waving his arms in a sudden burst of fury. 'What's the matter with you? Why don't you show a little more enterprise? Why don't you put something over? Why do you loaf about the place as if you were supposed to be an ornament? I want results, and I want them quick! I'll tell you how you can recognize my scarab when you get into the museum. That shameless old crook who sneaked it away from me has had the impudence to put it all by itself with a notice as big as a circus-poster alongside it saying that it is a Cheops of the Fourth Dynasty, presented' – Mr. Peters choked – '*presented* by J. Preston Peters, Esq. That's how you're going to recognize it.'

Ashe did not laugh, but he nearly dislocated a rib in his effort to abstain. To rob a man of his choicest possession and then thank him publicly for letting you have it appealed to Ashe as excellent comedy.

'The thing isn't even in a glass case,' continued Mr. Peters. 'It's lying on an open tray on top of a cabinet of Roman coins. Anybody who was left alone for two minutes in the place could take it. It's criminal carelessness to leave a valuable scarab lying about like that. If he was going to steal my Cheops, he might at least have had the decency to treat it as if it was worth something.'

'But it makes it easier for me to get it,' said Ashe consolingly.

'It's got to be made easy if you are to get it,' snapped Mr. Peters. 'Here's another thing. You are going to try for it late at night. Well, what are going to say if anyone catches you prowling around at that time? Have you considered that?'

'No.'

'You would have to say something, wouldn't you? You

wouldn't discuss the latest play? You would have to think up some mighty good reason for being out of bed at that time, wouldn't you?'

'I suppose so.'

'Oh, you do admit that, do you? Well, what you would say is this. You would explain that I had rung for you to come and read me to sleep. Do you understand?'

'You think that would be a satisfactory explanation of my being in the museum?'

'Idiot! I don't mean that you're to say it if you're caught actually in the museum. If you're caught in the museum, the best thing you can do is to say nothing and hope that the judge will let you off lightly because it's your first offence. You're to say it if you're found wandering about on your way there.'

'It sounds thin to me.'

'Does it! Well let me tell you that it isn't so thin as you suppose, for it's what you will actually have to do most nights. Two nights out of three I have to be read to sleep. My indigestion gives me insomnia.'

As if to push this fact home, Mr. Peters suddenly bent double.

'Oof!' he said. 'Wow!'

He removed the cigar from his mouth, and inserted a digestive tabloid.

'The lining of my stomach is all wrong,' he added.

It is curious how trivial are the immediate causes which produce revolutions. If Mr. Peters had worded his complaint differently, Ashe would, in all probability, have borne it without active protest. He had been growing more and more annoyed with this little person who buzzed and barked and bit at him, but the idea of definite revolt had not occurred to him. But his sufferings at the hands of Beach the butler had reduced him to a state where he could endure no further mention of stomachic linings. There comes a time when our capacity for listening to data about the linings of other people's stomachs is exhausted.

He looked at Mr. Peters sternly. He had ceased to be intimidated by the fiery little man, and regarded him simply as a hypochondriac who needed to be told a few useful facts.

'How do you expect not to have indigestion? You take no exercise and you smoke all day long.'

The novel sensation of being criticized, and by a beardless youth at that, held Mr. Peters silent. He started convulsively, but he did not speak.

Ashe, on his pet subject, became eloquent. In his opinion dyspeptics cumbered the earth. To his mind, they had the choice between health and sickness, and they deliberately chose the latter.

'Your sort of man makes me sick. I know your type inside out. You overwork and shirk exercise and let your temper run away with you and smoke strong cigars on an empty stomach, and when you get indigestion as a natural result, you look on yourself as a martyr, and make the lives of everybody you meet miserable. If you would put yourself into my hands for a month I would have you eating bricks and thriving on them. Up in the morning, Larsen Exercises, cold bath, brisk rub down, sharp walk. . . .'

'Who the devil asked your opinion, you impertinent young hound?' inquired Mr. Peters.

'Don't interrupt, confound you,' shouted Ashe. 'Now you have made me forget what I was going to say.'

There was a tense silence. Then Mr. Peters began to speak.

'You – infernal – impudent—'

'Don't talk to me like that.'

'I'll talk to you how—'

Ashe took a step towards the door.

'Very well, then,' he said, 'I resign. I give notice. You can get somebody else to do this job for you.'

The sudden sagging of Mr. Peters' jaw, the look of consternation which flashed upon his face, told him that he had found the right weapon, that the game was in his hands. He continued with a feeling of confidence.

'If I had known what being your valet involved, I wouldn't have undertaken the thing for a hundred thousand pounds. Just because you had some idiotic prejudice against letting me come down here as your secretary, which would have been the simple and obvious thing, I find myself in a position where at any moment I may be publicly rebuked by the butler and have the head still-room maid looking at me as if I were something the cat had brought in.' His voice trembled with self-pity. 'Do you realize a fraction of the awful things you have let me in for? How on earth am I to remember whether I go in before the chef or after the third footman? I shan't have a peaceful minute while I'm in this place. I've got to sit and listen by the hour to a bore of a butler who seems to be a sort of walking hospital. I've got to steer my way through a complicated system of etiquette. And on top of all that you have the nerve, the insolence, to imagine that you can use me as a punching-bag to work your bad temper off! You have the immortal rind to suppose that I will stand being nagged and bullied by you whenever your suicidal way of living brings on an attack of indigestion! You have the supreme cheek to fancy that you can talk as you please to me! Very well! I've had enough of it. If you want this scarab of yours recovered, let somebody else do it. I've retired from business.'

134

He took another step towards the door. A shaking hand clutched at his sleeve.

'My boy, my dear boy, be reasonable!'

Ashe was intoxicated with his own oratory. The sensation of bully-ragging a genuine millionaire was new and exhilarating. He expanded his chest, and spread his feet like a Colossus.

'That's all very well,' he said, coldly disentangling himself from the hand. 'You can't get out of it like that. We have got to come to an understanding. The point is that, if I am to be subjected to your – your senile malevolence every time you have a twinge of indigestion, no amount of money could pay me to stop on.'

'My dear boy, it shall not occur again. I was hasty.'

Mr. Peters with agitated fingers relit the stump of his cigar.

'Throw away that cigar!'

'My boy!'

'Throw it away! You say you were hasty. Of course you were hasty. And as long as you abuse your digestion you will go on being hasty. I want something better than apologies. If I am to stop here, we must get to the root of things. You must put yourself in my hands as if I were your doctor. No more cigars. Every morning regular exercises.'

'No, no.'

'Very well.'

'No, stop, stop! What sort of exercises?'

'I'll show you tomorrow morning. Brisk walks.'

'I hate walking.'

'Cold baths.'

'No, no.'

'Very well.'

'No, stop. A cold bath would kill me at my age.'

'It would put new life into you. Do you consent to cold baths? No? Very well.'

'Yes, yes, yes.'

'You promise?'

'Yes, yes.'

'All right then.'

The distant sound of the dinner-gong floated in.

'We settled that just in time,' said Ashe.

Mr. Peters regarded him fixedly.

'Young man,' he said slowly, 'if after all this you fail to recover my Cheops for me, I'll – I'll – by George, I'll skin you.'

'Don't talk like that,' said Ashe. 'That's another thing you have got to remember. If my treatment is to be successful, you must not let yourself think in that way. You must exercise self-control mentally. You must think beautiful thoughts.'

'The idea of skinning you *is* a beautiful thought,' said Mr. Peters wistfully.

## V

In order that their gaiety might not be diminished and the food turned to ashes in their mouths by the absence from the festive board of Mr. Beach, it was the custom for the upper servants at Blandings to postpone the start of their evening meal until dinner was nearly over above stairs. This enabled the butler to take his place at the head of the table without fear of interruption except for a few moments when coffee was being served.

Every night, shortly before half-past eight, at which hour Mr. Beach felt that he might safely withdraw from the dining-room and leave Lord Emsworth and his guests to the care of Merridew, the under-butler, and James and Alfred, the footmen, returning only for a few minutes to lend tone and distinction to the distribution of cigars and liqueurs, those whose rank entitled them to do so made their way to the Housekeeper's Room, to pass in desultory conversation the interval before Mr. Beach should arrive and a kitchen-maid, with all the appearance of one who has been straining at the leash and has at last managed to get free, opened the door with the announcement, 'Mr. Beach, if you please, dinner is served.' Upon which Mr. Beach, extending a crooked elbow towards the housekeeper, would say, 'Mrs. Twemlow,' and lead the way high and disposedly down the passage, followed in order of rank by the rest of the company in couples, to the Steward's Room. For Blandings was not one of those houses – or shall we say hovels? – where the upper servants are expected not only to feed but to congregate before feeding in the Steward's Room. Under the auspices of Mr. Beach and of Mrs. Twemlow, who saw eye to eye with him in these matters, things were done properly at the Castle, with the right solemnity. To Mr. Beach and to Mrs. Twemlow the suggestion that they and their peers should gather together in the same room in which they were to dine would have been as repellent as an announcement from Lady Ann Warblington, the chatelaine, that the house-party would eat in the drawing-room.

When Ashe, returning from his interview with Mr. Peters, was intercepted by a respectful small boy and conducted to the Housekeeper's Room, he was conscious of a sensation of shrinking inferiority akin to his emotions on his first day at school. The room was full and apparently on very cordial terms with itself. Everybody seemed to know everybody, and conversation was proceeding in the liveliest manner. As a matter of fact, the house-party at Blandings being in the main a gathering together of the Emsworth clan by way of honour and as a means of introduction to Mr. Peters and his daughter, the bride-of-the-house-to-be, most of the occupants of the Housekeeper's Room were old acquaintances, and were renewing interrupted friendships at the top of their voices.

A lull followed Ashe's arrival, and all eyes, to his great discomfort, were turned in his direction. His embarrassment was relieved by Mrs. Twemlow, who advanced to do the honours. Of Mrs. Twemlow little need be attempted in the way of pen-portraiture beyond the statement that she went as harmoniously with Mr. Beach as one of a pair of vases or one of a brace of pheasants goes with its fellow. She had the same appearance of imminent apoplexy, the same air of belonging to some dignified and haughty branch of the vegetable kingdom.

'Mr. Marson, welcome to Blandings Castle.'

Ashe had been waiting for somebody to say that, and had been a little surprised that Mr. Beach had not done so. He was also surprised at the housekeeper's ready recognition of his identity, until he saw Joan in the throng and deduced that she must have been the source of information. He envied Joan. In some amazing way she contrived to look not out of place in this gathering. He himself, he felt, had imposter stamped in large characters all over him.

Mrs. Twemlow began to make the introductions – a long and tedious process which she performed relentlessly, without haste and without scamping her work. With each member of the aristocracy of his new profession Ashe shook hands, and on each member he smiled, until his facial and dorsal muscles were like to crack under the strain. It was amazing that so many high-class domestics could be collected into one moderate-sized room.

'Miss Simpson you know,' said Mrs. Twemlow, and Ashe

was about to deny the charge when he perceived that Joan was the individual referred to. 'Mr. Judson, Mr. Marson. Mr. Judson is the Honourable Frederick's gentleman.'

'You have not the pleasure of our Freddie's acquaintance as yet, I take it, Mr. Marson?' observed Mr. Judson genially, a smooth-faced, lazy-looking young man. 'Freddie repays inspection.'

'Mr. Marson, permit me to introduce you to Mr. Ferris, Lord Stockheath's gentleman.'

Mr. Ferris, a dark, cynical man with a high forehead, shook Ashe by the hand.

'Happy to meet you, Mr. Marson.'

'Miss Willoughby, this is Mr. Marson, who will take you in to dinner. Miss Willoughby is Lady Mildred Mant's lady. As of course you are aware, Lady Mildred, our eldest daughter, married Colonel Horace Mant.'

Ashe was not aware, and he was rather surprised that Mrs. Twemlow should have a daughter whose name was Lady Mildred, but Reason, coming to his rescue, suggested that by 'our' she meant the offspring of the Earl of Emsworth and his late countess. Miss Willoughby was a light-hearted damsel with a smiling face and chestnut hair done low over her forehead. Since Etiquette forbade that he should take Joan in to dinner, Ashe was glad that at least an apparently pleasant substitute had been provided. He had just been introduced to an appallingly statuesque lady of the name of Chester, Lady Ann Warblington's own maid, and his somewhat hazy recollections of Joan's lecture on Below Stairs precedence had left him with the impression that this was his destined partner. He had frankly quailed at the prospect of being linked to so much aristocratic hauteur.

When the final introduction had been made, conversation

broke out again. It dealt almost exclusively as far as Ashe could follow it, with the idiosyncrasies of the employers of those present. He took it that this happened all down the social scale below stairs. Probably the lower servants in the Servants' Hall discussed the upper servants in the Steward's Room, and the still lower servants in the housemaids' sitting-room discussed their superiors of the Servants' Hall, and the still-room gossiped about the housemaids' sitting-room. He wondered which was the bottom circle of all, and came to the conclusion that it was probably represented by the small respectful boy who had acted as his guide a short while before. This boy, having nobody to discuss anybody with, presumably sat in solitary meditation, brooding on the odd-job man.

He thought of mentioning this theory to Miss Willoughby, but decided that it was too abstruse for her, and contented himself with speaking of some of the plays he had seen before leaving London. Miss Willoughby was an enthusiast on the drama, and, Colonel Mant's devotion to his various clubs keeping him much in town, she had had wide opportunities of indulging her tastes. Miss Willoughby did not like the country. She thought it dull.

'Don't you think the country dull, Mr. Marson.'

'I shan't find it dull here,' said Ashe, and was surprised to discover through the medium of a pleased giggle that he was considered to have perpetrated a compliment.

Mr. Beach appeared in due season, a little distrait as becomes a man who has just been engaged on important and responsible duties.

'Alfred spilled the 'ock!' Ashe heard him announce to Mrs. Twemlow in a bitter undertone. 'Within 'alf an inch of 'is lordship's arm he spilled it.'

Mrs. Twemlow murmured condolences. Mr. Beach's set expression was that of one who is wondering how long the strain of existence can be supported.

'Mr. Beach, if you please, dinner is served.'

The butler crushed down sad thoughts, and crooked his elbow.

'Mrs. Twemlow.'

Ashe, miscalculating degrees of rank in spite of all his caution, was within a step of leaving the room out of his proper turn, but the startled pressure of Miss Willoughby's hand on his arm warned him in time. He stopped to allow the statuesque Miss Chester to sail out under escort of a wizened little man with a horseshoe pin in his tie, whose name, in company with nearly all the others which had been spoken to him since he came into the room, had escaped Ashe's memory.

'You *were* nearly making a bloomer,' said Miss Willoughby brightly. 'You must be absent-minded, Mr. Marson, like his lordship.'

'Is Lord Emsworth absent-minded?'

Miss Willoughby laughed.

'Why, he forgets his own name sometimes. If it wasn't for Mr. Baxter, goodness knows what would happen to him.'

'I don't think I know Mr. Baxter.'

'You will if you stay here long. You can't get away from him if you're in the same house. Don't tell anyone I said so, but he's the real master here. His lordship's secretary he calls himself, but he's really everything rolled into one like the man in the play.'

Ashe, searching in his dramatic memories for such a person in a play, inquired if Miss Willoughby meant Pooh Bah in *The Mikado*, of which there had been a revival in London recently. Miss Willoughby did mean Pooh Bah.

'But Nosey Parker is what *I* call him,' she said. 'He minds everybody's business as well as his own.'

The last of the procession trickled into the Steward's Room. Mr. Beach said grace somewhat patronizingly. The meal began.

'You've seen Miss Peters, of course, Mr. Marson?' said Miss Willoughby, resuming conversation with the soup.

'Just for a few minutes at Paddington.'

'Oh! You haven't been with Mr. Peters long then?'

Ashe began to wonder if everybody he met was going to ask him this dangerous question.

'Only a day or so.'

'Where were you before that?'

Ashe was conscious of a prickly sensation. A little more of this and he might as well reveal his true mission at the Castle and have done with it.

'Oh, I was – that is to say—'

'How are you feeling after the journey, Mr. Marson?' said a voice from the other side of the table, and Ashe, looking up gratefully, found Joan's eyes looking into his with a curiously amused expression. He was too grateful for the interruption to try to account for this. He replied that he was feeling very well, which was not the case. Miss Willoughby's interest was diverted to a discussion of the defects of the various railroad systems of Great Britain.

At the end of the table, Mr. Beach had started an intimate conversation with Mr. Ferris, the valet of Lord Stockheath, the Hon. Freddie's 'poor old Percy' – a cousin, Ashe had gathered, of Aline Peters' husband-to-be. The butler spoke in more measured tones even than usual, for he was speaking of tragedy.

'We were all extremely sorry, Mr. Ferris, to read of your misfortune.'

Ashe wondered what had been happening to Mr. Ferris.

'Yes, Mr. Beach,' replied the valet, 'it's a fact we made a pretty poor show.' He took a sip from his glass. 'There is no concealing the fact – I have tried to conceal it – that poor Percy is *not* bright.'

Miss Chester entered the conversation.

'I couldn't see where the girl, what's her name, was so very pretty. All the papers had pieces where it said that she was attractive and what not, but she didn't look anything special to *me* from her photograph in the *Daily Sketch*. What his lordship could see in her I can't understand.'

'The photo didn't quite do her justice, Miss Chester. I was present in court, and I must admit she was *svelte*, decidedly *svelte*. And you must recollect that Percy, from childhood up, has always been a highly susceptible young nut. I speak as one who knows him.'

Mr. Beach turned to Joan.

'We are speaking of the Stockheath breach-of-promise case, Miss Simpson, of which you doubtless read in the newspapers. Lord Stockheath is a nephew of ours. I fancy his lordship was greatly shocked at the occurrence.'

'He was,' chimed in Mr. Judson from down the table. 'I happened to overhear him speaking of it to young Freddie. It was in the library on the morning when the judge made his final summing up and slipped into Lord Stockheath so crisp. "If ever anything of this sort happens to you, you young scallywag," he says to Freddie—'

Mr. Beach coughed.

'Mr. Judson!'

'Oh, it's all right, Mr. Beach, we're all in the family here, in a manner of speaking. It isn't as if I was telling it to a lot of outsiders. I'm sure none of these ladies or gentlemen will let it go beyond this room?'

The company murmured virtuous acquiescence.

'He says to Freddie, "You young scallywag, if ever anything of this sort happens to you, you can pack up and go off to Canada, for I'll have nothing more to do with you," or words to that effect. And Freddie says, "Oh, dash it all, guv'nor, you know what?"'

However short Mr. Judson's imitation of his master's voice may have fallen of histrionic perfection, it pleased the company. The room shook with mirth.

Mr. Beach thought it expedient to deflect the conversation. By the unwritten laws of the room every individual had the right to speak as freely as he wished about his own personal employer, but Judson, in his opinion, sometimes went a trifle too far.

'Tell me, Mr. Ferris,' he said, 'does his lordship seem to bear it well?'

'Oh, Percy is bearing it well enough.' Ashe noted as a curious fact that while the actual valet of any person under discussion spoke of him almost affectionately by his Christian name, the rest of the company used the greatest ceremony and gave him his title with all respect. Lord Stockheath was Percy to Mr. Ferris, and the Hon. Frederick Threepwood was Freddie to Mr. Judson; but to Ferris Mr. Judson's Freddie was the Hon. Frederick, and to Judson Mr. Ferris' Percy was Lord Stockheath. It was rather a pleasant form of etiquette, and struck Ashe as somehow vaguely feudal.

'Percy,' went on Mr. Ferris, 'is bearing it like a little Briton. The damages not having come out of *his* pocket. It's his old father, who had to pay them, that's taking it to heart. You might say he's doing himself proud. He says it's brought on his gout again, and that's why he's gone to Droitwich instead of coming here. I dare say Percy isn't sorry.'

'It has been,' said Mr. Beach, summing up, 'a Most Unfortunate Occurrence. The modern tendency of the Lower Classes to get above themselves is becoming more marked every day. The young female in this case was, I understand, a barmaid. It is Deplorable that our young men should allow themselves to get into Such Entanglements.'

'The wonder to me,' said the irrepressible Mr. Judson, 'is that more of these young chaps don't get put through it. His lordship wasn't so wide of the mark when he spoke like that to Freddie in the library that time. I give you my word it's a mercy young Freddie *hasn't* been up against it. When we was in London, Freddie and I,' he went on, cutting through Mr. Beach's disapproving cough, 'before what you might call the crash, when his lordship cut off supplies and had him come back and live here, Freddie was asking for it, believe me. Fell in love with a girl in the chorus of one of the theatres. Used to send me to the stagedoor with notes and flowers every night as regular as clockwork for weeks. What was her name? It's on the tip of my tongue. Funny how you forget these things. Freddie was pretty far gone. I recollect once, happening to be looking round his room in his absence, coming on a poem he had written to her. It was hot stuff, very hot. If that girl has kept those letters, it's my belief we shall see Freddie following in Lord Stockheath's footsteps.'

There was a hush of delighted horror round the table.

'Goo!' said Miss Chester's escort, with unction. 'You don't say so, Mr. Judson! It wouldn't half make them look silly if the Honourable Freddie was sued for breach just now with the wedding coming on.'

'There is no danger of that.'

It was Joan's voice, and she had spoken with such decision that she had the ear of the table immediately. All eyes looked in her direction. Ashe was struck with her expression. Her eyes were shining, as if she were angry, and there was a flush on her face. A phrase he had used in the train came back to him. She looked like a princess in disguise.

'What makes you say that, Miss Simpson?' inquired Judson, annoyed. He had been at pains to make the company's flesh creep, and it appeared to be Joan's aim to undo his work.

It seemed to Ashe that Joan made an effort of some sort, as if she were pulling herself together and remembering where she was.

'Well,' she said, almost lamely, 'I don't think it at all likely that he proposed marriage to this girl.'

'You never can tell,' said Judson. 'My impression is that Freddie did. It's my belief that there's something on his mind these days. Before he went to London with his lordship the other day, he was behaving very strange. And since he came back it's my belief that he has been brooding. And I happen to know that he followed the affair of Lord Stockheath pretty close, for he clipped the clippings out of the paper. I found them myself one day when I happened to be going through his things.'

Beach cleared his throat – his mode of indicating that he was about to monopolize the conversation.

'And in any case, Miss Simpson,' he said solemnly, 'with things come to the pass they have come to, and with juries – drawn from the lower classes – in the Nasty Mood they're in, it don't seem hardly necessary in these affairs for there to have been any definite promise of marriage. What with all this Socialism rampant, they seem so 'appy at the idea of being able to do one

of Us an injury that they give 'eavy damages without it. A few
Ardent Expressions, and that's enough for them. You recollect
the Havant case, and when young Lord Mount Anville was sued.
What it comes to is that Anarchy is getting the Upper Hand, and
the Lower Classes are getting above themselves. It's all these here
cheap newspapers that does it. They tempt the Lower Classes to
get Above Themselves. Only this morning, I had to speak severe
to that young fellow James, the footman. He was a good fellow
once, and did his work well, and 'ad a proper respect for people;
but now he's gone all to pieces. And why? Because six months
ago he had the rheumatism, and had the audacity to send his
picture and a testimonial saying that it had cured him of Awful
Agonies to Walkinshaw's Supreme Ointment, and they printed
it in half a dozen papers, and it has been the ruin of James. He
has got Above Himself and don't care for nobody.'

'Well, all I can say is,' resumed Judson, 'that I 'ope to
goodness nothing won't happen to Freddie of that kind, for it's
not every girl that would have him.'

There was a murmur of assent to this truth.

'Now your Miss Peters,' said Judson, tolerantly, 'she seems a
nice little thing.'

'She would be pleased to hear you say so,' said Joan.

'Joan Valentine!' cried Judson, bringing his hands down on
the tablecloth with a bang. 'I've just remembered it. That was
the name of the girl Freddie used to write the letters and poems
to. And that's who it is I've been trying all along to think who
you reminded me of, Miss Simpson. You're the living image of
Freddie's Miss Joan Valentine.'

Ashe was not normally a young man of particularly ready wit,
but on this occasion it may have been that the shock of this
revelation, added to the fact that something must be done

speedily if Joan's discomposure was not to become obvious to all present, quickened his intelligence. Joan, usually so sure of herself, so ready of resource, had gone temporarily to pieces. She was quite white, and her eyes met Ashe's with almost a hunted expression.

If the attention of the company was to be diverted, something drastic must be done. A mere verbal attempt to change the conversation would be useless.

Inspiration descended upon Ashe.

In the days of his childhood in Much Middleford, Salop, he had played truant from Sunday School again and again in order to frequent the society of one Eddie Waffles, the official Bad Boy of the locality. It was not so much Eddie's charm of conversation that had attracted him – though that had been great – as the fact that Eddie, among his other accomplishments, could give a life-like imitation of two cats fighting in a back-yard, and Ashe felt that he could never be happy until he had acquired this gift from the master. In course of time he had done so. It might be that his absences from Sunday School in the cause of Art had left him in later years a trifle shaky on the subject of the Kings of Judah, but his hard-won accomplishment had made him in request at every smoking-concert at Oxford, and it saved the situation now.

'Have you ever heard two cats fighting in a back-yard?' he inquired casually of his neighbour Miss Willoughby.

The next moment the performance was in full swing.

Young Master Waffles, who had devoted considerable study to his subject, had conceived the combat of his imaginary cats in a broad, almost a Homeric vein. The unpleasantness opened with a low gurgling sound, answered by another a shade louder and possibly a little more querulous. A momentary silence was followed by a long-drawn note like rising wind cut off abruptly and succeeded by a grumbling mutter. The response to this was a couple of sharp howls. Both parties to the contest then indulged in a discontented whining, growing louder and louder till the air was full of electric menace. And then, after another sharp silence, came War, noisy and overwhelming. Standing at Master Waffles' side, you could almost follow every movement of that intricate fray, and mark how now one, now the other of the battlers gained a short-lived advantage. It was a great fight. Shrewd blows were taken and given, and in the eye of the imagination you could see the air thick with flying fur. Louder and louder grew the din, and then, at its height, it ceased in one crescendo of tumult, and all was still save for a faint, angry moaning.

Such was the cat fight of Master Eddie Waffles, and Ashe, though falling short of the master, as a pupil must, rendered it faithfully and with energy.

To say that the attention of the company was diverted from Mr. Judson and his remarks by the extraordinary noises which proceeded from Ashe's lips would be to offer a mere shadowy suggestion of the sensation caused by his efforts. At first stunned surprise, then consternation greeted him. Beach the butler was staring as one watching a miracle, nearer apparently to apoplexy than ever. On the faces of the others every shade of emotion was to be seen. That this should be happening in the Steward's Room at Blandings Castle was scarcely less amazing than if it had taken place in a cathedral. The upper servants, rigid in their seats, looked at each other, like Cortes' soldiers, 'with a wild surmise'.

The last faint moan of feline defiance died away, and silence fell upon the room.

Ashe turned to Miss Willoughby.

'Just like that,' he said. 'I was telling Miss Willoughby,' he added apologetically to Mrs. Twemlow, 'about the cats in London. They were a great trial.'

For perhaps three seconds his social reputation swayed to and fro in the balance, while the company pondered on what he had done. It was new – but was it humorous or was it vulgar? There is nothing your upper servants so abhor as vulgarity. That was what the Steward's Room was trying to make up its mind about.

And then Miss Willoughby threw her shapely head back, and the squeal of her laughter smote the ceiling. And at that the company made its decision. Everybody laughed. Everybody urged Ashe to give an encore. Everybody was his friend and admirer.

Everybody but Beach the butler. Beach the butler was shocked to his very core. His heavy-lidded eyes rested on Ashe with disapproval.

It seemed to Beach the butler that this young man Marson had Got Above Himself.

Ashe found Joan at his side. Dinner was over, and the diners were making for the Housekeeper's Room.

'Thank you, Mr. Marson. That was very good of you, and very clever.' Her eyes twinkled. 'But what a terrible chance you took. You have made yourself a popular success, but you might just as easily have become a social outcast. As it is, I am afraid Mr. Beach did not approve.'

'I'm afraid he didn't. In a minute or so I'm going to fawn upon him and make all well.'

Joan lowered her voice.

'It was quite true what that odious little man said. He did

write me letters. Of course I destroyed them long ago.'

'But weren't you running the risk in coming here that he might recognize you? Wouldn't that make it rather unpleasant for you?'

'I never met him, you see. He only wrote to me. When he came to the station to meet us this evening, he looked startled to see me, so I suppose he remembers my appearance. But Aline will have told him that my name is Simpson.'

'That fellow Judson said that he was brooding. I think you ought to put him out of his misery.'

'Mr. Judson must have been letting his imagination run away with him. He is out of his misery. He sent a horrid fat man named Jones to see me in London about the letters, and I told him that I had destroyed them. He must have let him know that by this time.'

'I see.'

They went into the housekeeper's room. Mr. Beach was standing before the fire. Ashe went up to him.

It was not an easy matter to mollify Mr. Beach. Ashe tried the most tempting topics. He mentioned swollen feet, he dangled the lining of Mr. Beach's stomach temptingly before his eyes, but the butler was not to be softened. Only when Ashe turned the conversation to the subject of the museum did a flicker of animation stir him.

Mr. Beach was fond and proud of the Blandings Castle museum. It had been the means of getting him into print for the first and only time in his life. A year ago a representative of the *Intelligencer and Echo* from the neighbouring town of Blatchford had come to visit the Castle on behalf of his paper, and he had begun one section of his article with the words: 'Under the auspices of Mr. Beach, my genial cicerone, I then visited his lordship's museum. . . .' Mr. Beach treasured the clipping in a special writing desk.

He responded almost amiably to Ashe's questions. Yes, he had seen the scarab – he pronounced it 'scayrub' – which Mr. Peters had presented to 'is lordship. He understood that 'is lordship thought very highly of Mr. Peters' scayrub. He had overheard Mr. Baxter telling his lordship that it was extremely valuable.

'Mr. Beach,' said Ashe, 'I wonder if you would take me to see Lord Emsworth's museum?'

Mr. Beach regarded him heavily.

'I shall be pleased to take you to see 'is lordship's museum,' he replied.

## VI

One can only attribute to the nervous mental condition following on the interview which he had had with Ashe in his bedroom the rash act which Mr. Peters attempted shortly after dinner.

Mr. Peters, shortly after dinner, was in a dangerous and reckless mood. He had had a wretched time all through the meal. The Blandings *chef* had extended himself in honour of the house-party, and had produced a succession of dishes which, in happier days, Mr. Peters would have devoured eagerly. To be compelled by considerations of health to pass these by was enough to damp the liveliest optimist. Mr. Peters had suffered terribly. Occasions of feasting and revelry like the present were for him so many battlefields on which Greed fought with Prudence.

All through dinner he brooded upon Ashe's defiance and the

horrors which were to result from that defiance. One of Mr. Peters' most painful memories was of a two weeks' visit which he had once paid to Mr. William Muldoon at his celebrated health-restoring establishment at White Plains in the State of New York. He had been persuaded to go there by a brother-millionaire whom till then he had always regarded as a friend. The memory of Mr. Muldoon's cold shower-baths and brisk system of physical exercise still lingered.

The thought that under Ashe's rule he was to go through privately very much what he had gone through in the company of a gang of other unfortunates at Muldoon's froze him with horror. He knew these health-cranks who believed that all mortal ailments could be cured by cold showers and brisk walks. They were all alike, and they nearly killed you. His worst nightmare was the one where he dreamed that he was back at Muldoon's leading his horse up that infernal hill outside the village, your only reward when you reached the summit, being the distant prospect of Sing-Sing prison.

He wouldn't stand it. He would be hanged if he would stand it. He would defy Ashe.

But if he defied Ashe, Ashe would go away, and then whom could he find to recover his lost scarab?

Mr. Peters began to appreciate the true meaning of the phrase about the horns of a dilemma.

The horns of this dilemma occupied his attention until the end of dinner. He shifted uneasily from one to the other and back again. He rose from the table in a thoroughly overwrought condition of mind.

And then, somehow, in the course of the evening, he found himself alone in the Hall, not a dozen feet from the unlocked museum door.

It was not immediately that he appreciated the significance of this fact. He had come to the Hall because its solitude suited his mood. It was only after he had finished a cigar – Ashe could not stop him smoking after dinner – that it suddenly flashed upon him that he had ready to hand a solution of all his troubles. A brief minute's resolute action, and the scarab would be his again and the menace of Ashe a thing of the past.

He glanced about him. Yes, he was alone.

Not once, since the removal of the scarab had begun to exercise his mind, had Mr. Peters contemplated for an instant the possibility of recovering it for himself. The prospect of the unpleasantness which would ensue had been enough to make him regard such an action as out of the question. The risk was too great to be considered for a moment.

But here he was in a position where the risk was neglible. Like Ashe, he had always visualized the recovery of his scarab as a thing of the small hours, a daring act to be performed when sleep held the Castle in its grip. That an opportunity would be presented to him of walking in quite calmly and walking out again with the Cheops in his pocket had never occurred to him as a possibility.

Yet now this chance was presenting itself in all its simplicity, and all he had to do was to grasp it. The door of the museum was not even closed. He could see from where he stood that it was ajar.

He moved cautiously in its direction – not in a straight line, as one going to a museum, but circuitously, as one strolling without an aim. From time to time he glanced over his shoulder.

He reached the door, hesitated, and passed it. He turned, reached the door again, and again passed it. He stood for a moment darting his eyes about the Hall, then, in a burst of resolution, dashed for the door and shot in like a rabbit.

At the same moment the Efficient Baxter, who from the shelter of a pillar on the gallery that ran round two-thirds of the Hall had been eyeing the peculiar movements of the distinguished guest with considerable interest for some minutes, began to descend the stairs.

Rupert Baxter, the Earl of Emsworth's indefatigable private secretary, was one of those men whose chief characteristic is a vague suspicion of their fellow human beings. He did not suspect them of this or that definite crime: he simply suspected them. He prowled through life as we are told that the Hosts of Midian prowled. His powers in this respect were well known at Blandings Castle. The Earl of Emsworth said: 'Baxter is invaluable, positively invaluable.' The Hon. Freddie said: 'A chappie can't take a step in this bally house without stumbling over that damn feller Baxter.' The man-servant and the maid-servant within the gates, employing, like Miss Willoughby, that crisp gift for characterisation which is the property of the English lower orders, described him as a Nosey Parker.

Peering over the railings of the balcony and observing the curious movements of Mr. Peters, who, as a matter of fact, while making up his mind to approach the door, had been backing and filling about the Hall in a quaint serpentine manner like a man trying to invent a new variety of the Tango, the Efficient Baxter had found himself in some way – why, he did not know – of what, he could not say – but in some nebulous way, suspicious.

He had not definitely accused Mr. Peters in his mind of any specific tort or malfeasance. He had merely felt that something fishy was toward.

He had a sixth sense in such matters.

But when Mr. Peters, making up his mind, leaped into the

P.G. WODEHOUSE

museum, Baxter's suspicions lost their vagueness and became crystallized. Certainty descended on him like a bolt from the skies.

On oath, before a solicitor, the Efficient Baxter would have declared that J. Preston Peters was about to try to purloin the scarab.

Lest we should seem to be attributing too miraculous powers of intuition to Lord Emsworth's secretary, it should be explained that the mystery which hung about that curio had exercised his mind not a little since his employer had given it to him to place in the museum. He knew Lord Emsworth's powers of forgetting, and he did not believe his account of the transaction. Scarab-maniacs like Mr. Peters did not give away specimens from their collections as presents. But he had not divined the truth, of what had happened in London. The conclusion at which he had arrived was that Lord Emsworth had bought the scarab, and had forgotten all about it. To support this theory was the fact that the latter had taken his cheque-book to London with him. Baxter's long acquaintance with the earl had left him with the conviction that there was no saying what he might not do if let loose in London with a cheque-book.

As to Mr. Peters' motive for entering the museum, that too seemed completely clear to the secretary. He was a curio enthusiast himself and he had served collectors in a secretarial capacity, and he knew both from experience and observation that strange madness which may at any moment afflict the collector, blotting out morality and the nice distinction between *meum* and *tuum* as with a sponge. He knew that collectors who would not steal a loaf if they were starving might, and did, fall before the temptation of a coveted curio.

156

He descended the stairs three at a time, and entered the museum at the very instant when Mr. Peters' twitching fingers were about to close on his treasure.

He handled the delicate situation with eminent tact. Mr. Peters, at the sound of his step, had executed a backward leap which was as good as a confession of guilt, and his face was rigid with dismay, but the Efficient Baxter affected not to notice these phenomena. His manner, when he spoke, was easy and unembarrassed.

'Ah! Taking a look at our little collection, Mr. Peters? You will see that we have given the place of honour to your Cheops. It is certainly a fine specimen, a wonderful fine specimen.'

Mr. Peters was recovering slowly. Baxter talked on to give him time. He spoke of Mut and Bubastis, of Ammon and the Book of the Dead. He directed the other's attention to the Roman coins.

He was touching on some aspects of the Princess Gilukhipa of Mitanni, in whom his hearer could scarcely fail to be interested, when the door opened and Beach the butler came in, accompanied by Ashe. In the bustle of the interruption Mr. Peters escaped, glad to be elsewhere and questioning for the first time in his life the dictum that, if you want a thing well done, you must do it yourself.

'I was not aware, sir,' said Beach the butler, 'that you were in occupation of the museum. I would not have intruded. But this young man expressed a desire to examine the exhibits, and I took the liberty of conducting him.'

'Come in, Beach, come in,' said Baxter.

The light fell on Ashe's face, and he recognized him as the cheerful young man who had inquired the way to Mr. Peters' room before dinner, and who, he had by this time discovered, was not the Hon. Freddie's friend George Emerson, nor indeed any other of the guests of the house.

He felt suspicious.

'Oh, Beach.'

'Sir.'

'Just a moment.'

He drew the butler into the Hall out of earshot.

'Beach, who is that man?'

'Mr. Peters' valet, sir.'

'Mr. Peters' valet?'

'Yes, sir.'

'Has he been in service long?' asked Baxter, remembering that a mere menial had addressed him as 'old man'.

Beach lowered his voice. He and the Efficient Baxter were old allies, and it seemed right to Beach to confide in him.

'He has only just joined Mr. Peters, sir, and he has never been in service before. He told me so himself, and I was unable to elicit from him any information as to his antecedents. His manner struck me, sir, as peculiar. It crossed my mind to wonder whether Mr. Peters happened to be aware of this. I should dislike to do any young man an injury, but, if you think that Mr. Peters should be informed. . . . It might be anyone coming to a gentleman without a character like this young man. Mr. Peters might have been Deceived, sir.'

The Efficient Baxter's manner became distrait. His mind was working rapidly.

'Should he be Informed, sir?'

'Eh? Who?'

'Mr. Peters, sir. In case he should have been Deceived!'

'No, no. Mr. Peters knows his own business.'

'Far from me be it to appear officious, sir, but. . . .'

'Mr. Peters probably knows all about him. Tell me, Beach, who was it suggested this visit to the museum? Did you?'

'It was at the young man's express desire that I conducted him, sir.'

The Efficient Baxter returned to the museum without a word. Ashe, standing in the middle of the room, was impressing the geography of the place on his memory. He was unaware of the piercing stare of suspicion which was being directed at him from behind.

He did not see Baxter. He was not even thinking of Baxter. But Baxter was on the alert. Baxter was on the war-path.

Baxter *knew*.

CHAPTER SIX

I

Among the compensations of advancing age is a wholesome pessimism, which, while it takes the fine edge off whatever triumphs may come to us, has the admirable effect of preventing Fate from working off on us any of those gold bricks, coins with strings attached, and unhatched chickens at which Ardent Youth snatches with such enthusiasm, to its subsequent disappointment. As we emerge from the twenties we grow into a habit of mind, which looks askance at Fate bearing gifts. We miss, perhaps, the occasional prize, but we also avoid leaping light-heartedly into traps.

Ashe Marson had yet to reach the age of tranquil mistrust, and, when Fate seemed to be treating him kindly, he was still young enough to accept such kindnesses on their face value and rejoice at them.

As he sat on his bed, at the end of his first night at Blandings Castle, he was conscious to a remarkable degree that Fortune was treating him well. He had survived, not merely without discredit, but with positive triumph, the initiatory plunge into the etiquette-maelstrom of life below stairs. So far from doing the wrong thing and drawing down on himself the just scorn of the Steward's Room, he had been the life and soul of the party. Even if tomorrow in an absent-minded fit, he should anticipate the groom of the chambers in the march to the table, it would be forgiven him, for the humorist has his privileges.

So much for that. But that was only a part of Fortune's kindnesses. To have discovered on the first day of their association the correct method of handling and reducing to subjection his irascible employer was an even greater boon. A prolonged association with Mr. Peters on the lines of which their acquaintance had begun would have been extremely trying. Now, by virtue of a fortunate stand at the outset, he had spiked the millionaire's guns.

Thirdly, and most important than all, he had not only made himself familiar with the locality and surroundings of the scarab, but he had seen beyond the possibility of doubt that the removal of it and the earning of the thousand pounds would be the simplest possible task. Already he was spending the money in his mind, and to such lengths had optimism led him that, as he sat on his bed reviewing the events of the day, his only doubt was whether to get the scarab at once or to let it remain where it was until he had the opportunity of doing Mr. Peters' interior good on the lines which he had mapped out in their conversation. For, of course, directly he had restored the scarab to its rightful owner and pocketed the reward, his position as healer and trainer to the millionaire would cease automatically.

He was sorry for that, for it troubled him to think that a sick man should not be made well. But, on the whole, looking at it from every aspect, it would be best to get the scarab as soon as possible and leave Mr. Peters' digestion to look after itself.

Being twenty-six and an optimist, he had no suspicion that Fate might be playing with him, that Fate might have unpleasant surprises in store, that Fate even now was preparing to smite him in his hour of joy with that powerful weapon, the Efficient Baxter.

He looked at his watch. It was five minutes to one. He had no idea whether they kept early hours at Blandings Castle or not, but he deemed it prudent to give the household another hour in which to settle down. After which he would just trot down and collect the scarab.

The novel which he had brought down with him from London fortunately proved interesting. Two o'clock came before he was ready for it. He slipped the book in his pocket, and opened the door.

All was still – still and uncommonly dark. Along the corridor in which his room was situated the snores of sleeping domestics exploded, growled, and twittered in the air. Every menial on the list seemed to be snoring, some in one key, some in another, some defiantly, some plaintively; but the main fact was that they were all snoring, somehow thus intimating that, as far as this side of the house was concerned, the coast might be considered clear and interruption of his plans a negligible risk.

Researches made at an earlier hour had familiarized him with the geography of the place. He found his way to the green baize door without difficulty, and, stepping through, was in the Hall where the remains of the log fire still glowed a fitful red. This, however, was the only illumination, and it was fortunate that he did not require light to guide him to the museum.

He knew the direction and had measured the distance. It was precisely seventeen steps from where he stood. Cautiously, and with avoidance of noise, he began making the seventeen steps. He was beginning the eleventh when he bumped into somebody.

Somebody soft.

Somebody whose hand, as it touched his, felt small and feminine.

The fragment of a log fell on the ashes, and the fire gave a dying spurt. Darkness succeeded the sudden glow. The fire was out. That little flame had been its last effort before expiring. But it had been enough to enable him to recognize Joan Valentine.

'Good Lord!' he gasped.

His astonishment was short-lived. Next moment the only thing that surprised him was the fact that he was not more surprised. There was something about this girl that made the most bizarre happenings seem right and natural. Ever since he had met her his life had changed from an orderly succession of uninteresting days to a strange carnival of the unexpected, and use was accustoming him to it. Life had taken on the quality of a dream in which anything might happen, and in which everything which did happen was to be accepted with the calmness natural in dreams. It was strange that she should be here in the pitch-dark Hall in the middle of the night, but – after all – no stranger than that he should be. In this dream-world in which he now moved it had to be taken for granted that people did all sorts of odd things from all sorts of odd motives.

'Hallo!' he said.

'Don't be alarmed.'

'No, no.'

'I think we are both here for the same reason.'

'You don't mean to say—'

'Yes, I have come to earn the thousand pounds too, Mr. Marson. We are rivals.'

In his present frame of mind it seemed so simple and intelligible to Ashe that he wondered if he was really hearing it for the first time. He had an odd feeling that he had known this all along.

'You are here to get the scarab?'

'Exactly.'

Ashe was dimly conscious of some objection to this, but at first it eluded him. Then he pinned it down.

'But you aren't a young man of good appearance,' he said.

'I don't know what you mean. But Aline Peters is an old friend of mine. She told me that her father would give a large reward to whoever recovered the scarab, so I—'

'Look out!' whispered Ashe. 'Run! There's someone coming!'

There was a soft footfall on the stairs, a click, and above Ashe's head a light flashed out. He looked around. He was alone, and the green baize door was swaying gently to and fro.

'Who's that? Who's there?' said a voice.

The Efficient Baxter was coming down the broad staircase.

A general suspicion of mankind and a definite and particular suspicion of one individual made a bad opiate. For over an hour sleep had avoided the Efficient Baxter with an unconquerable coyness. He had tried all the known ways of wooing slumber, but they had failed him, from the counting of sheep downwards. The events of the night had whipped his mind to a restless activity. Try as he might to lose consciousness, the recollection of the plot which he had discovered surged up and kept him wakeful. It is the penalty of the suspicious type of mind that it suffers from its own activity. From the moment when he detected Mr. Peters in the act of rifling the museum and marked down Ashe as an accomplice, Baxter's repose was doomed. Nor poppy nor mandragora nor all the drowsy syrups of the world could ever medicine him to that sweet sleep that he owed yesterday.

But it was the recollection that, on previous occasions of

wakefulness, hot whisky and water had done the trick, which had now brought him from his bed and downstairs. His objective was the decanter on the table of the smoking-room, which was one of the rooms opening off the gallery which looked down on the Hall. Hot water he could achieve in his bedroom by means of his Etna stove.

So out of bed he had climbed, and downstairs he had come, and here he was, to all appearances, just in time to foil the very plot on which he had been brooding. Mr. Peters might be in bed, but there in the Hall below him stood the Accomplice, not ten paces from the museum door.

He arrived on the spot at racing speed, and confronted Ashe. 'What are you doing here?'

And then, from the Baxter view-point, things began to go wrong. By all the rules of the game Ashe, caught as it were red-handed, should have wilted, stammered, and confessed all. But Ashe was fortified by that philosophic calm which comes to us in dreams, and moreover he had his story ready.

'Mr. Peters rang for me, sir.'

He had never expected to feel grateful to the little firebrand who employed him, but he had to admit that the millionaire, in their last conversation, had shown forethought. The thought struck him that, but for Mr. Peters' advice, he might by now be in an extremely awkward position, for his was not a swiftly inventive mind.

'Rang for you? At half-past two in the morning?'

'To read to him, sir.'

'To read to him at this hour?'

'Mr. Peters suffers from insomnia, sir. He has a weak digestion, and the pain sometimes prevents him from sleeping. The lining of his stomach is not at all what it should be.'

'I don't believe a word of it.'

With that meekness which makes the good man wronged so impressive a spectacle, Ashe produced and exhibited his novel.

'Here is the book, which I was about to read to him. I think, sir, if you will excuse me, I had better be going to his room. Good-night, sir.'

And he proceeded to mount the stairs. He was sorry for Mr. Peters, so shortly about to be aroused from a refreshing slumber, but these were Life's tragedies and must be borne bravely.

The Efficient Baxter dogged him the whole way, springing silently in his wake, and dodging into the shadows whenever the light of an occasional electric bulb made it inadvisable to keep in the open. Then, abruptly, he gave up the pursuit. For the first time his comparative impotence in this silent conflict on which he had embarked was made manifest to him, and he perceived that on mere suspicion, however strong, he could do nothing. To accuse Mr. Peters of theft or to accuse him of being accessory to a theft was out of the question. Yet his whole being revolted at the thought of allowing the sanctity of the museum to be violated. Officially its contents belonged to Lord Emsworth, but ever since his connexion with the Castle he had been in charge of them, and he had come to look on them as his own property. If he was only a collector by proxy, he had nevertheless the collector's devotion to his curios, beside which the lioness's attachment to her cubs is tepid, and he was prepared to do anything to retain in his possession a scarab towards which he already entertained the feelings of a life-proprietor.

No, not quite anything. He stopped short at the idea of causing unpleasantness between the father of the Hon. Freddie and the father of the Hon. Freddie's fiancée. His secretarial position at the Castle was a valuable one, and he was loath to jeopardize it.

There was only one way in which this delicate affair could be brought to a satisfactory conclusion. It was obvious, from what he had seen that night, that Mr. Peters' connexion with the attempt on the scarab was to be merely sympathetic, and that the actual theft was to be accomplished by Ashe. His only course, then, was to catch Ashe actually in the museum. Then Mr. Peters need not appear in the matter at all. Mr. Peters' position in those circumstances would be simply that of a man who had happened to employ through no fault of his own a valet who happened to be a thief.

He had made a mistake, he perceived, in locking the door of the museum. In future he must leave it open, as a trap is open. And he must stay up at nights and keep watch.

With these reflections, the Efficient Baxter returned to his room.

Ashe, meanwhile, had entered Mr. Peters' bedroom and switched on the light. Mr. Peters, who had just succeeded in dropping off to sleep, sat up with a start.

'I've come to read to you,' said Ashe.

Mr. Peters emitted a stifled howl, in which wrath and self-pity were nicely blended.

'You fool, do you know that I have just managed to get to sleep.'

'And now you're awake again,' said Ashe soothingly. 'Such is life. A little rest, a little folding of the hands in sleep, and then, bing! off we go again. I hope you will like this novel. I dipped into it and it seems good.'

'What do you mean by coming in here at this time of night? Are you crazy?'

'It was your suggestion, and, by the way, I must thank you for it. I apologize for calling it thin. It worked like a charm. I don't think he believed it – in fact, I know he didn't – but it held him. I couldn't have thought up anything half so good in an emergency.'

Mr. Peters' wrath changed to excitement.

'Did you get it? Have you been after my Cheops?'

'I have been after your Cheops, but I didn't get it. Bad men were abroad. That fellow with the spectacles who was in the museum when I met you there this evening swooped down from nowhere, and I had to tell him that you had rung for me to read to you. Fortunately I had this novel on me. I think he followed me upstairs to see that I really did come to your room.'

Mr. Peters groaned miserably.

'Baxter,' he said. 'He's a man named Baxter, Lord Emsworth's private secretary, and he suspects us. He's the man we – I mean you – have got to look out for.'

'Well, never mind. Let's be happy while we can. Make yourself comfortable, and I'll start reading. After all, what could be pleasanter than a little literature in the small hours? Shall I begin?'

II

Ashe found Joan in the stable-yard after breakfast next morning, playing with a retriever puppy.

'Can you spare me a moment of your valuable time?'

'Certainly, Mr. Marson.'

'Shall we walk out into the open somewhere where we can't be overheard?'

'Perhaps it would be better.'

They moved off.

'Request your canine friend to withdraw,' said Ashe. 'He prevents me marshalling my thoughts.'

'I'm afraid he won't withdraw.'

'Never mind. I'll do my best in spite of him. Tell me, was I dreaming, or did I really meet you in the Hall this morning at about twenty minutes after two?'

'You did.'

'And did you really tell me that you had come to the Castle to steal—'

'Recover.'

'Recover Mr. Peters' scarab?'

'I did.'

'Then it's true?'

'It is.'

Ashe scraped the ground with a meditative toe.

'This,' he said, 'seems to me to complicate matters somewhat.'

'It complicates them abominably.'

'I suppose you were surprised when you found that I was on the same game as yourself?'

'Not in the least.'

'You weren't!'

'I knew directly I saw the advertisement in the *Morning Post*. And I hunted up the *Morning Post* directly you had told me that you had become Mr. Peters' valet.'

'You have known all along?'

'I have.'

Ashe regarded her admiringly.

'You're wonderful!'

'Because I saw through you?'

'Partly that. But chiefly because you had the pluck to undertake a thing like this.'

'*You* undertook it.'

'But I'm a man.'

'And I'm a woman! And my theory is, Mr. Marson, that a woman can do nearly everything better than a man. What a splendid test-case this would make to settle the Votes for Women question once and for all! Here we are, you and I, a man and a woman, each trying for the same thing, and each starting with equal chances. Suppose I beat you? How about the inferiority of women then?'

'I never said that women were inferior.'

'You did with your eye.'

'Besides you're an exceptional woman.'

'You can't get out of it with a compliment. I'm a very ordinary woman, and I'm going to beat a real man.' Ashe frowned.

'I don't like to think of us working against each other.'

'Why not?'

'Because I like you.'

'I like you, Mr. Marson, but we must not let sentiment interfere with business. You want Mr. Peters' thousand pounds. So do I.'

'I hate the thought of being the instrument to prevent you getting the money.'

'You won't be. I shall be the instrument to prevent you getting it. I don't like that thought either, but one has got to face it.'

'It makes me feel mean.'

'That's simply your old-fashioned masculine attitude towards the female, Mr. Marson. You look on woman as a weak creature to be shielded and petted. We aren't anything of the sort. We're terrors. You mustn't let my sex interfere with your trying to get this reward. Think of me as if I were another man. We're up against each other in a fair fight, and I don't want any special privileges. If you don't do your best from now onwards, I shall never forgive you. Do you understand?'

'I suppose so.'

'And we shall need to do our best. That little man with the glasses is on his guard. I was listening to you last night from behind the door. By the way, you shouldn't have told me to run away, and then have stayed yourself to be caught. That is an example of the sort of thing I mean. It was chivalry, not business.'

'I had a story ready to account for my being there. You had not.'

'And what a capital story it was! I shall borrow it for my own use. If I am caught, I shall say that I had to read Aline to sleep because she suffers from insomnia. And I shouldn't wonder if she did, poor girl. She doesn't get enough to eat. She is being starved, poor child. I heard one of the footmen say that she refused everything at dinner last night. And though she vows it isn't, my belief is that it's all because she is afraid to make a stand against her old father. It's a shame.'

'She is a weak creature to be shielded and petted,' said Ashe solemnly.

Joan laughed.

'Well, yes, you caught me there. I admit that poor Aline is not a shining example of the formidable modern woman, but—' She stopped. 'Oh, bother, I've just thought of what I ought to have said – the good repartee which would have crushed you. I suppose it's too late now?'

'Not at all. I'm like that myself. Only it is generally next day that I hit the right answer. Shall we go back? . . . She is a weak creature, to be shielded and petted.'

'Thank you so much,' said Joan gratefully. 'And why is she a weak creature? Because she has *allowed* herself to be shielded and petted. Because she has permitted Man to give her special privileges and generally – No, it isn't so good as I thought it was going to be.'

'It should be crisper,' said Ashe critically. 'It lacks the punch.'

'But it brings me back to my point, which is that I am not going to imitate her and forfeit my independence of action in return for chivalry. Try to look at it from my point of view, Mr. Marson. I know that you need the money just as much as I do. Well, don't you think that I should feel a little mean if I thought you weren't trying your hardest to get it, simply because you didn't think it would be fair to try your hardest against a woman? It would cripple me. I should not feel as if I had the right to do anything. It's too important a matter for you to treat me like a child and let me win to avoid disappointing me. I want the money, but I don't want it handed to me.'

'Believe me,' said Ashe earnestly, 'it will not be handed to you. I have studied the Baxter question more deeply than you, and I can assure you that Baxter is a menace. What has put him so firmly on the right scent I don't know, but he seems to have divined the exact state of affairs in its entirety. As far as I am concerned, that is to say. Of course he has no idea that you are mixed up in the business, but I am afraid that his suspicion of me will hit you as well. What I mean is that for some time to come I fancy that that man proposes to camp out on the rug in front of the museum door. It would be madness for either of us to attempt to go there at present.'

'It is being made very hard for us, isn't it? And I thought it was going to be so simple!'

'I think we should give him at least a week to simmer down.'

'Fully that.'

'Let us look on the bright side. We are in no hurry. Blandings Castle is quite as comfortable as No. 7A Arundell Street, and the commissariat department is a revelation to me. I had no idea that servants did themselves so well. And as for the social side, I love it. I revel in it. For the first time in my life I feel as if I were somebody. Did you observe my manner towards the kitchen-maid who waited on us at dinner last night? A touch of the old *noblesse* about it, I fancy? Dignified, but not unkind, I think? And I can keep it up. As far as I'm concerned let this life continue indefinitely.'

'But what about Mr. Peters? Don't you think there is a danger that he may change his mind about that thousand pounds if we keep him waiting too long?'

'Not a chance of it. Being almost within touch of his scarab has had the worst effects on him. It has intensified the craving. By the way, have you seen the scarab?'

'Yes, I got Mrs. Twemlow to take me to the museum while you were talking to the butler. It was dreadful to feel that it was lying there in the open, waiting for someone to take it, and not be able to do anything.'

'I felt exactly the same. It isn't much to look at, is it? If it hadn't been for the label, I wouldn't have believed that it was the thing for which Peters was offering a thousand pounds reward. But that's his affair. A thing is worth what somebody will give for it. Ours not to reason why. Ours but to elude Baxter, and gather it in.'

'"Ours", indeed! You speak as if we were partners, instead of rivals.'

Ashe uttered an exclamation.

'You've hit it! Why not? Why any cut-throat competition? Why shouldn't we form a company? It would solve everything.'

Joan looked thoughtful.

'You mean, divide the reward?'

'Exactly. Into two equal parts.'

'And the labour?'

'The labour?'

'How shall we divide that?'

Ashe hesitated.

'My idea,' he said, 'was that I should do the – what I might call the *rough* work, and—'

'You mean that you should do the actual taking of the scarab?'

'Exactly. I would look after that end of it.'

'And what would *my* duties be?'

'Well, you – you would, as it were – how shall I put it? You would, so to speak, lend moral support.'

'By lying snugly in bed, fast asleep?'

Ashe avoided her eyes.

'Well, yes – er – something on those lines.'

'While you ran all the risks.'

'No, no. The risks are practically non-existent.'

'I thought you said just now that it would be madness for either of us to attempt to go to the museum at present?'

Joan laughed.

'It won't do, Mr. Marson. You remind me of an old cat I once had. Whenever he killed a mouse, he would bring it into the drawing-room and lay it affectionately at my feet. I would reject the corpse with horror and turn him out, but back he would come with his loathsome gift. I simply couldn't make him understand that he was not doing me a kindness. He thought highly of his mouse, and it was beyond him to realize that I did not want it. You are just the same with your chivalry. It's very kind of you to keep offering me your dead mouse, but, honestly, I have no use for it. I *won't* take favours just because I happen to be a female. If we are going to form this partnership, I insist on doing my fair share of the work, and running my fair share of the risks – the "practically non-existent" risks.'

'You're very – resolute.'

'Say pig-headed. I shan't mind. Certainly I am. A girl has got to be, even nowadays, if she wants to play fair. Listen, Mr. Marson, I will not have the dead mouse. I do not like dead mice. If you attempt to work off your dead mouse on me, this partnership ceases before it has begun. If we are to work together, we are going to make alternate attempts to get the scarab. No other arrangement will satisfy me.'

'Then I claim the right to make the first one.'

'You don't do anything of the sort. We toss for a first chance like little ladies and gentlemen. Have you a coin? I will spin, and you call.'

Ashe made a last stand.

'This is perfectly—'

'Mr. Marson!'

Ashe gave in. He produced a coin, and handed it to her gloomily.

'Under protest,' he said.

'Heads or tails?' said Joan, unmoved.

Ashe watched the coin gyrating in the sunshine.

'Tails,' he cried.

The coin stopped rolling.

'Tails it is,' said Joan. 'What a nuisance! Well, never mind. I get my chance if you fail.'

'I shan't fail,' said Ashe fervently. 'If I have to pull the museum down, I won't fail. Thank Heaven there's no chance now of your doing anything foolish.'

'Don't be too sure. Well, good luck, Mr. Marson.'

'Thank you, partner.'

They shook hands.

As they parted at the door Joan made one further remark: 'There's just one thing, Mr. Marson.'

'Yes?'

'If I could have accepted the mouse from anyone, I would certainly have accepted it from you.'

## CHAPTER SEVEN

I

It is worthy of record, in the light of after events, that at the beginning of their visit, it was the general opinion of the guests gathered together at Blandings Castle that the place was dull. The house-party had that air of torpor which one sees in the saloon passengers of an Atlantic liner, that appearance of resignation to an enforced idleness and a monotony only to be broken by meals. Lord Emsworth's guests gave the impression, collectively, of being just about to yawn and look at their watches.

This was partly the fault of the time of year, for most house-parties are dull if they happen to fall between the hunting and the shooting seasons, but must be attributed chiefly to Lord Emsworth's extremely sketchy notions of the duties of a host.

A host has no right to intern a regiment of his relations in his house unless he also invites lively and agreeable outsiders to meet them. If he does commit this solecism, the least he can do is to work himself to the bone in the effort to invent amusements and diversions for his victims. Lord Emsworth had failed badly in both these matters. With the exception of Mr. Peters, his daughter Aline, and George Emerson, there was nobody in the house who did not belong to the clan; and as for his exerting himself to entertain, the company was lucky if it caught a glimpse of its host at meals. Lord Emsworth belonged to the people-like-to-be-left-alone-to-amuse-themselves-when-they-come-to-a-place school of hosts. He pottered about the garden in an old coat, now uprooting a weed, now wrangling with the autocrat from Scotland who was – theoretically – in his service as head-gardener; dreamily satisfied, when he thought of them at all, that his guests were as perfectly happy as he was. Apart from his son Freddie, whom he had long since dismissed as a youth of abnormal tastes from whom nothing reasonable was to be expected, he could not imagine anyone not being content merely to be at Blandings when the buds were bursting on the trees.

A resolute hostess might have saved the situation, but Lady Ann Warblington's abilities in that direction stopped short at leaving everything to Mrs. Twemlow and writing letters in her bedroom. When Lady Ann Warblington was not writing letters in her bedroom – which was seldom, for she had an apparently inexhaustible correspondence – she was nursing sick headaches in it. She was one of those hostesses whom a guest never sees except when he goes into the library and espies the tail of her skirt vanishing through the other door.

As for the ordinary reactions of the country-house, the guests could frequent the billiard-room, where they were sure to find Lord Stockheath playing a hundred up with his cousin, Algernon Wooster – a spectacle of the liveliest interest; or they could, if fond of the game, console themselves for the absence of a links in the neighbourhood with the exhilarating pastime of clock-golf; or they could stroll about the terraces with such of their relations as they happened to be on speaking terms with at the moment and abuse their host and the rest of their relations.

This was the favourite amusement, and after breakfast on a morning ten days after Joan and Ashe had formed their compact, the terraces were full of perambulating couples. Here, Colonel Horace Mant, walking with the Bishop of Godalming, was soothing that dignitary by clothing in soldierly words thoughts which the latter had not been able to crush down but which his holy office scarcely permitted him to utter. There, Lady Mildred Mant, linked to Mrs. Jack Hale, of the collateral branch of the family, was saying things about her father in his capacity of host and entertainer which were making her companion feel another woman. Farther on, stopping occasionally to gesticulate, could be seen other Emsworth relatives and connexions. It was a typical scene of quiet, peaceful English family life.

Leaning on the broad stone balustrade of the upper terrace, Aline Peters and George Emerson surveyed the malcontents.

Aline gave a little sigh, almost inaudible. But George's hearing was good.

'I was wondering when you were going to admit it,' he said, shifting his position so that he faced her.

'Admit what?'

'That you couldn't stand the prospect. That the idea of being stuck for life with this crowd, like a fly on fly-paper, was too much for you. That you were ready to break off your engagement to Freddie and come away and marry me and live happily ever after.'

'George!'

'Well, wasn't that what it meant? Be honest.'

'What what meant?'

'That sigh.'

'I didn't sigh. I was just breathing.'

'Then you *can* breathe in this atmosphere? You surprise me.' He raked the terraces with hostile eyes. 'Look at them! Look at them crawling around like doped beetles. My dear girl, it's no use your pretending that this sort of thing wouldn't kill you. You're pining away already. You're thinner and paler since you came here. Heavens! How we shall look back at this and thank our stars that we're out of it, when we're settled down happily in Hong Kong. You'll like Hong Kong. It's a most picturesque place. Something going on all the time.'

'George, you mustn't really!'

'Why mustn't I?'

'It's wrong. You can't talk like that when we are both enjoying the hospitality—'

A wild laugh, almost a howl, disturbed the talk of the more adjacent of the perambulating relatives. Colonel Horace Mant, checked in mid-sentence, looked up resentfully at the cause of the interruption.

'I wish someone would tell me whether it's that fellow Emerson or young Freddie who's supposed to be engaged to Miss Peters. Hanged if you ever see her and Freddie together, but she and Emerson are never to be found apart. If my respected father-in-law had any sense, I should have thought he would have had sense enough to stop that. If that girl isn't in love with Emerson I'll be – I'll eat my hat.'

'No, no,' said the Bishop. 'No, no. Surely not, Horace. What were you saying when you broke off?'

'I was saying that if a man wanted his relations never to speak to each other again for the rest of their lives, the best thing he could do would be to herd them all together in a dashed barrack of a house a hundred miles from anywhere and then go off and spend all his time prodding dashed flower-beds with a spud, dash it!'

'Just so, just so. So you were. Go on, Horace. I find a curious comfort in your words.'

On the terrace above them, Aline was looking at George with startled eyes.

'George!'

'I'm sorry. But you shouldn't spring these jokes on me so suddenly. You said *enjoying*. Yes. Revelling in it, aren't we?'

'It's a lovely old place,' said Aline, defensively.

'And when you've said that, you've said everything. You can't live on scenery and architecture for the rest of your life. There's the human element to be thought of. And you're beginning—'

'There goes father,' interrupted Aline. 'How fast he is walking. George, have you noticed a sort of difference in father these last few days?'

'I haven't. My speciality is keeping an eye on the rest of the Peters family.'

'He seems better somehow. He seems to have almost stopped smoking – and I'm very glad, for those cigars were awfully bad for him. The doctor expressly told him he must stop them, but he wouldn't pay any attention to him. And he seems to take so much more exercise. My bedroom is next to his, you know, and every morning I can hear things going on through the wall. Father dancing about and purring a good deal. And one morning I met his valet going in with a pair of Indian clubs and some boxing-gloves. I believe father is really taking himself in hand at last.'

George Emerson exploded.

'And about time, too! How much longer are you to go on

starving yourself to death just to give him the resolution to stick to his dieting? It maddens me to see you at dinner. And it's killing you. You're getting pale and thin. You can't go on like this.'

A wistful look came over Aline's face.

'I do get a little hungry sometimes. Late at night generally.'

'You want someone to take care of you and look after you. I'm the man. You may think you can deceive me, but I can tell. I *know*, I tell you. You're weakening. You're beginning to see that it won't do. One of these days you're going to come to me, and say, "George, you were right. Let's sneak off to the station without anybody knowing and leg it for London and get married at a registrar's." Oh, *I* know! I couldn't have loved you all this time and not know. You're weakening.'

The trouble with these Supermen is that they lack reticence. They do not know how to omit. They expand their chests and whoop. And a girl, even a girl like Aline Peters, cannot help resenting the note of triumph. But Supermen despise tact. As far as one can gather, that is the chief difference between them and the ordinary man.

A little frown appeared on Aline's forehead, and she set her mouth mutinously.

'I'm not weakening at all,' she said, and her voice was, for her, quite acid. 'You – you take too much for granted.'

George was contemplating the landscape with a conqueror's eye.

'You are beginning to see that it is impossible, this Freddie foolery.'

'It is not foolery,' said Aline pettishly, tears of annoyance in her eyes. 'And I wish you wouldn't call him Freddie.'

'He asked me to. He *asked* me to.'

Aline stamped her foot.

'Well, never mind. Please don't do it.'

'Very well, little girl,' said George softly. 'I wouldn't do anything to hurt you.'

The fact that it never even occurred to George Emerson that he was being offensively patronizing shows the stern stuff of which these Supermen are made.

## II

The Efficient Baxter bicycled broodingly to Market Blandings for tobacco. He brooded for several reasons. He had just seen Aline Peters and George Emerson in confidential talk on the upper terrace, and that was one thing that exercised his mind, for he suspected George Emerson. He suspected him nebulously as a snake in the grass, as an influence working against the orderly progress of events concerning the marriage which had been arranged and would shortly take place between Miss Peters and the Hon. Frederick Threepwood. It would be too much to say that he had any idea that George was putting in such hard and consistent work in his serpentine role, indeed, if he could have overheard the conversation just recorded, it is probable that Rupert Baxter would have had heart-failure; but he had observed the intimacy between the two, as he observed most things in his immediate neighbourhood, and he disapproved of it. He blamed the Hon. Freddie. If the Hon. Freddie had been a more ardent lover, he would have spent his time with Aline, and George Emerson would have taken his proper place as one of the crowd at the back of the stage. But Freddie's view of the matter seemed to be that he had done all that could be expected of a chappie in getting engaged to the girl, and that now he might consider himself at liberty to drop her for a while.

So Baxter, as he bicycled to Market Blandings for tobacco, brooded on Freddie, Aline Peters and George Emerson.

He also brooded on Mr. Peters and Ashe Marson.

Finally he brooded in a general way because he had had very little sleep for the past week.

The spectacle of a young man doing his duty and enduring considerable discomforts while doing it is painful, but it affords so excellent a moral picture that I cannot omit a short description of the manner in which Rupert Baxter had spent the nine nights which had elapsed since his meeting with Ashe in the small hours in the Hall.

In the gallery which ran above the Hall, there was a large chair, situated a few paces from the great staircase. On this, in an overcoat – for the nights were chilly – and rubber-soled shoes, the Efficient Baxter had sat, without missing a single night, from one in the morning till daybreak, waiting, waiting, waiting, waiting. It had been an ordeal to try the stoutest determination. Nature had never intended Baxter for a night-bird. He loved his bed. He knew that doctors held that insufficient sleep made a man pale and sallow, and he had always aimed at the peach-bloom complexion which comes from a sensible eight hours between the sheets. One of the Georges – I forget which – once said that a certain number of hours' sleep each night – I cannot recall at the moment how many – made a man something, which for the time being has slipped my memory. Baxter agreed with him. It went against all his instincts to sit up in this fashion, but it was his duty and he did it.

It troubled him that, as night after night went by, and Ashe, the suspect, did not walk into the trap so carefully laid for him, he found an increasing difficulty in keeping awake. The first two or three of his series of vigils he had passed in an unimpeachable wakefulness, his chin resting on the rail of the gallery and his ears alert for the slightest sound. But he had not been able to maintain this standard of excellence. On several occasions he had caught himself in the act of dropping off, and last night he had actually woken with a start to find it quite light. As his last recollection before that was of an inky darkness, impenetrable to the eye, dismay gripped him with a sudden clutch, and he ran swiftly down to the museum. His relief on finding that the scarab was still there had been tempered by thoughts of what might have been.

Baxter, then, as he bicycled to Market Blandings for tobacco, had good reason to brood.

Having bought his tobacco and observed the life and thought of the town for half an hour – it was market-day and the normal stagnation of the place was temporarily relieved and brightened by pigs that eluded their keepers and a bull-calf which caught a stout farmer at the psychological moment when he was tying his shoe-lace and lifted him six feet – he made his way to the Emsworth Arms, the most respectable of the eleven inns which the citizens of Market Blandings contrived in some miraculous way to support. In most English country towns, if the public-houses do not actually outnumber the inhabitants, they all do an excellent trade. It is only when they are two to one that hard times hit them and set the innkeepers blaming the Government.

It was not the busy bar, full to overflowing with honest British yeomen, many of them in the same condition, that Baxter sought. His goal was the genteel dining-room on the first floor, where a bald and shuffling waiter, own cousin to a tortoise, served luncheon to those desiring it. Lack of sleep had reduced Baxter to a condition where the presence and chatter of the house-party were unsupportable. It was his purpose to lunch at the Emsworth Arms and take a nap in an armchair afterwards.

He had relied on having the room to himself, for Market Blandings did not lunch to a great extent; but to his annoyance and disappointment the room was already occupied by a man in brown tweeds.

Occupied is the correct word, for at first sight, this man seemed to fill the room. Never since almost forgotten days when he used to frequent circuses and side-shows had Baxter seen a fellow human being so extraordinarily obese.

He was a man about fifty years old, grey-haired, of a mauve complexion, and his general appearance suggested joviality.

To Baxter's chagrin this person engaged him in conversation directly he took his seat at the table. There was only one table in the room, and it had the disadvantage that it collected those seated at it into one party. It was impossible for Baxter to withdraw into himself and ignore this person's advances.

It is doubtful if he could have done, however, had they been separated by yards of floor, for the fat man was not only naturally talkative, but as it appeared from his opening remarks, speech had been dammed up within him for some time by lack of a suitable victim.

'Morning,' he began. 'Nice day. Good for the farmers. I'll move up to your end of the table if I may, sir. Waiter, bring my beef to this gentleman's end of the table.'

He creaked into a chair at Baxter's side, and resumed.

'Infernally quiet place, this, sir. I haven't found a soul to speak to since I arrived yesterday afternoon except deaf and dumb rustics. Are you making a long stay here?'

'I live outside the town.'

'I pity you. Wouldn't care to do it myself. Had to come here on business, and shan't be sorry when it's finished. I give you my word I couldn't sleep a wink last night because of the quiet. I was just dropping off when a beast of a bird outside the window gave a chirrup, and it brought me up with a jerk as if somebody had fired a gun off. There's a damned cat somewhere near my room which mews. I lie in bed waiting for the next mew, all worked up. Heaven save me from the country. It may be all right for you, if you've got a comfortable home and a pal or two to chat with after dinner, but you've no conception what it's like in this infernal town – I suppose it calls itself a town. A man told me there was a moving-picture place here, and I hurried off to it, and found that it was the wrong day. Only open Tuesdays and Fridays. What a hole! There's a church down the street. I'm told it's Norman or something. Anyway it's old. I'm not much of a man for churches as a rule, but I went and took a look at it. And then somebody told me that there was a fine view from the end of the High Street. So I went and took a look at that, and now, as far as I can make out, I've done the sights and exhausted every possibility of entertainment the town has to provide. Unless there's another church. I'm so reduced that I'll go and see the Methodist chapel, if there is one.'

Fresh air, want of sleep and the closeness of the dining-room combined to make Baxter drowsy. He ate his lunch in a torpor, hardly replying to his companion's remarks, who, for his part, did not seem to wish for or to expect replies. It was enough for him to be talking.

'What do people *do* with themselves in a place like this? When they want amusement, I mean. I suppose it's different if you've been brought up to it. Like being born colour-blind or

something. You don't notice it. It's the visitors who suffer.
They've no enterprise in this sort of place. There's a bit of land
just outside here which would make a sweet steeplechase course.
Natural barriers. Everything. It hasn't occurred to them to do
anything with it. It makes you despair of your species, that sort
of thing. Now, if I—'

Baxter dozed. With his fork still impaling a piece of cold beef
he dropped into that half-awake, half-asleep state which is
Nature's daytime substitute for the true slumber of the night.
The fat man, either not noticing or not caring, talked on. His
voice was a steady drone, lulling Baxter to rest.

Suddenly there was a break. Baxter sat up, blinking. He had
a curious impression that his companion had said, 'Hallo,
Freddie!' and that the door had just opened and closed again.

'Eh?' he said.

'Yes?' said the fat man.

'What did you say?'

'I was speaking of—'

'I thought you said, "Hallo, Freddie!"'

His companion eyed him indulgently.

'I thought you were dropping off when I looked at you.
You've been dreaming. What should I say, "Hallo, Freddie!"
for?'

The conundrum was unanswerable. Baxter did not attempt to
answer it. But there remained at the back of his mind a quaint
idea that he had caught sight as he woke of the Hon. Frederick
Threepwood, his face warningly contorted, vanishing through
the door.

Yet what would the Hon. Freddie be doing at the Emsworth
Arms?

A solution of the difficulty occurred to him. He had dreamed that he had seen Freddie, and that had suggested the words which, Reason pointed out, his companion could hardly have spoken. Even if the Hon. Freddie should enter the room, this fat man, who was apparently a drummer of some kind, would certainly not know who he was, nor would he address him so familiarly. Yes, that must be the explanation. After all the quaintest things happened in dreams. Last night, when he had fallen asleep in his chair, he had dreamed that he was sitting in a glass case in the museum making faces at Lord Emsworth, Mr. Peters and Beach, the butler, who were trying to steal him under the impression that he was a scarab of the reign of the Cheops of the Fourth Dynasty – a thing which he would never have done when awake.

Yes, he must certainly have been dreaming.

In the bedroom into which he had dashed to hide himself on discovering that the dining-room was in the possession of the Efficient Baxter, the Hon. Freddie sat on a rickety chair, scowling.

He elaborated a favourite dictum of his.

'You can't take a step *anywhere* without stumbling over that damn feller Baxter!'

He wondered if Baxter had seen him. He wondered if Baxter had recognized him. He wondered if Baxter had heard R. Jones say, 'Hullo, Freddie!'

He wondered, if such should be the case, whether R. Jones' presence of mind and native resource would be equal to explaining away the remark.

## CHAPTER EIGHT

I

'"Put the butter or dripping in a kettle on the range, and when hot add the onions and fry them; add the veal and cook till brown. Add the water, cover closely, and cook very slowly until the meat is tender, then add the seasonings and place the potatoes on top of the meat. Cover and cook until the potatoes are tender, but not falling to pieces."'

'Sure,' said Mr. Peters. '*Not* falling to pieces. That's right. Go on.'

'"Then add the cream and cook five minutes longer,"' read Ashe.

'Is that all?'

'That's all of that one.'

Mr. Peters settled himself more comfortably in bed.

'Read me the piece where it says about Curried Lobster.'

Ashe cleared his throat.

'"Curried Lobster,"' he read. '"Materials: two two-pound lobsters, two teaspoonfuls lemon juice, half teaspoonful curry powder, two tablespoonfuls butter, one tablespoonful flour, one cup scalded milk, one cup cracker crumbs, half teaspoonful salt, quarter teaspoonful pepper."'

'Go on.'

'"Way of Preparing: cream the butter and flour and add the scalded milk, then add the lemon juice, curry powder, salt and pepper. Remove the lobster meat from the shells and cut into half-inch cubes."'

'"Half-inch cubes,"' sighed Mr. Peters wistfully. 'Yes?'

'"Add the latter to the sauce."'

'You didn't say anything about the latter. Oh, I see, it means the half-inch cubes. Yes?'

'"Refill the lobster shells, cover with buttered crumbs, and bake until the crumbs are brown. This will serve six persons."'

'And make them feel an hour afterwards as if they had swallowed a live wild-cat,' said Mr. Peters ruefully.

'Not necessarily,' said Ashe. 'I could eat two portions of that at this very minute and go off to bed and sleep like a little child.'

Mr. Peters raised himself on his elbow, and stared at him. They were in the millionaire's bedroom, the time being one in the morning, and Mr. Peters had expressed a wish that Ashe would read him to sleep. He had voted against Ashe's novel and produced from the recesses of his suit-case a much-thumbed cookery-book. He explained that since his digestive misfortune had come upon him, he had derived a certain solace from its perusal. It may be that to some men a sorrow's crown of sorrow is remembering happier things, but Mr. Peters had not found that to be the case. In his hour of affliction it soothed him to read of Hungarian Goulash and Escalloped Brains and to remember that he, too, the nut-and-grass eater of today, had once dwelt in Arcadia.

The passage of the days, which had so sapped the stamina of the Efficient Baxter, had had the opposite effect on Mr. Peters. His was one of those natures which cannot deal in half-measures. Whatever he did he did with the same driving energy. After the first passionate burst of resistance, he had settled down into a model pupil in Ashe's one-man school of physical culture. It had been the same, now that he came to look back on it, at Muldoon's. Now that he remembered, he had come away from White Plains, hoping indeed never to see the place again, but undeniably a different man physically. It is not the habit of Professor Muldoon to let his patients loaf, but Mr. Peters, after the initial plunge, had needed no driving. He had worked hard at his cure then, because it was the job in hand. He worked hard now, under Ashe's guidance, because, once he had begun, the thing interested and gripped him. Ashe, who had expected continued reluctance, had been astonished and delighted at the way in which the millionaire had behaved. Nature had really intended Ashe for a trainer. He identified himself so thoroughly with his man and rejoiced at the least signs of improvement.

In Mr. Peters' case there had been distinct improvement already. Miracles do not happen nowadays, and it was too much to expect one who had maltreated his body so consistently for so many years to become whole in a day, but to an optimist like Ashe signs were not wanting that in due season Mr. Peters would rise on stepping-stones of his dead self to higher things, and while never soaring into the class which devours curried lobster and smiles after it, might yet prove himself a devil of a fellow among the mutton cutlets.

'You're a wonder,' said Mr. Peters. 'You're sassy and you have no respect for your elders and betters, but you deliver the goods. That's the point. Why, I'm beginning to feel great. Say, do you know, I felt a new muscle in the small of my back this morning! They are coming out on me like a rash.'

'That's the Larsen Exercises. They develop the whole body.'

'Well, you're a pretty good advertisement for them, if they need one. What were you before you came to me – a prize-fighter?'

'That's the question everybody I have met since I arrived here has asked me. I believe it made the butler think I was some sort of a crook when I couldn't answer it. I used to write stories, detective stories.'

'What you ought to be doing is running a place over here in England like Muldoon has back home. But you will be able to write one more story out of this business here, if you want to. When are you going to have another try for my scarab?'

'Tonight.'

'Tonight? How about Baxter?'

'I shall have to risk Baxter.'

Mr. Peters hesitated. He had fallen out of the habit of being magnanimous during the past few years, for dyspepsia brooks no divided allegiance and magnanimity has to take a back seat when it has its grip on a man.

'See here,' he said awkwardly, 'I've been thinking it over lately, and what's the use? It's a queer thing, and if anybody had told me a week ago that I should be saying it I wouldn't have believed them, but I am beginning to like you. I don't want to get you into trouble. Let the old scarab go. What's a scarab anyway? Forget about it, and stick on here as my private Muldoon. If it's the money that's worrying you, forget that too. I'll give it you as your fee.'

Ashe was astounded. That it could really be his peppery employer who spoke was almost unbelievable. Ashe's was a friendly nature, and he could never be long associated with anyone without trying to establish pleasant relations, but he had resigned himself in the present case to perpetual warfare.

He was touched, and if he had ever contemplated abandoning his venture, this, he felt, would have spurred him on to see it through. This sudden revelation of the human in Mr. Peters was like a trumpet-call.

'I wouldn't think of it,' he said. 'It's great of you to suggest such a thing, but I know just how you feel about the thing, and I'm going to get it for you if I have to wring Baxter's neck. Probably Baxter will have given up waiting as a bad job by now, if he has been watching all this while. We've given him ten nights to cool off. I expect he is in bed, dreaming pleasant dreams. It's nearly two o'clock. I'll wait another ten minutes and then go down.'

He picked up the cookery book.

'Lie back, and make yourself comfortable, and I'll read you to sleep first.'

'You're a good boy,' said Peters drowsily.

'Are you ready? "Pork Tenderloin Larded. Half pound fat pork."'

A faint smile curved Mr. Peters' lips. His eyes were closed and he breathed softly. Ashe went on in a low voice.

'"Four large pork tenderloins, one cup cracker crumbs, one cup boiling water, two tablespoonfuls butter, one teaspoonful salt, half teaspoonful pepper, one teaspoonful poultry seasoning."'

A little sigh came from the bed.

'"Way of Preparing: wipe the tenderloins with a damp cloth. With a sharp knife make a deep pocket lengthwise in each tenderloin. Cut your pork into long thin strips, and with a needle lard each tenderloin. Melt the butter in the water, add the seasoning and the cracker crumbs, combining all thoroughly. Now fill each pocket in the tenderloin with this stuffing, place the tenderloins—?"'

A snore sounded from the pillows, punctuating the recital like a mark of exclamation. Ashe laid down the book and peered into the darkness beyond the rays of the bed-lamp. His employer slept.

Ashe switched off the light and crept to the door. Out in the passage he stopped and listened. All was still.

He stole downstairs.

## II

George Emerson sat in his bedroom smoking a cigarette. A light of resolution was in his eyes. He glanced at the table beside his bed and at what was on that table, and the light of resolution flamed into a glare of fanatic determination. So might a mediaeval knight have looked on the eve of setting forth to rescue a maiden from a dragon.

His cigarette burned down. He looked at his watch, put it back, and lit another cigarette. His aspect was the aspect of one waiting for the appointed hour.

Smoking his second cigarette, he resumed his meditations. They had to do with Aline Peters.

George Emerson was troubled about Aline Peters. Watching over her as he did with a lover's eye, he had perceived that about her which distressed him. On the terrace that morning she had been abrupt to him – what, in a girl of a less angelic disposition, one might have called snappy. Yes, to be just, she had snapped at him. That meant something. It meant that Aline was not well. It meant what her pallor and tired eyes meant that the life she was leading was doing her no good.

Eleven nights had George dined at Blandings Castle, and on each of the eleven nights he had been distressed to see the manner in which Aline, declining the baked meats, had restricted herself to the miserable vegetable messes which were all that doctor's orders permitted to her suffering father. George's pity had its limits. His heart did not bleed for Mr. Peters. Mr. Peters' diet was his own affair. But that Aline should starve herself in this fashion, purely by way of moral support of her parent, was another matter.

George was perhaps a shade material. Himself a robust young man and taking what might be called an out-size in meals, he attached perhaps too much importance to food as an adjunct to the perfect life. In his survey of Aline, he took a line through his own requirements, and, believing that eleven such dinners as he had seen Aline partake of would have killed him, he decided that his loved one was on the point of starvation. No human being, he held, could exist on such Barmecide feasts. That Mr. Peters continued to do so did not occur to him as a flaw in his reasoning. He looked on Mr. Peters as a sort of machine. Successful business men often give that impression to the young. If George had been told that Mr. Peters went along on petrol like a motor-car, he would not have been much surprised. But that Aline, his Aline, should have to deny herself the exercise of that mastication of rich meats which, together with the gift of speech, raises Man above the beasts of the field! That was what tortured George.

He had devoted the day to thinking out a solution of the problem. Such was the overflowing goodness of Aline's heart that not even he could persuade her to withdraw her moral support from her father and devote herself to the keeping up of her strength as she should do. It was necessary to think of some other plan.

And then a speech of hers had come back to him.

She had said – poor child! – 'I do get a little hungry sometimes. Late at night, generally.'

The problem was solved. Food should be brought to her late at night.

On the table by his bed was a stout sheet of packing-paper. On this lay, like one of those pictures in still-life which one sees on suburban parlour-walls, a tongue, some bread, a knife, a fork, salt, a corkscrew and a small bottle of white wine.

It is a pleasure, when one has been able hitherto to portray George's devotion only through the medium of his speeches, to produce these comestibles as Exhibit A to show that he loved Aline with no common love. For it had not been an easy task to get them there. In a house of smaller dimensions he would have raided the larder without shame, but at Blandings Castle there was no saying where the larder might be. All he knew was that it lay somewhere beyond that green baize door opening on the Hall, past which he was wont to go on his way to bed. To prowl through the maze of the servants' quarters in search of it was impossible. The only thing to be done was to go to Market Blandings and buy the things.

Fortune had helped him at the start by arranging that the Hon. Freddie also should be going into Market Blandings in the little runabout which seated two. He had acquiesced in George's suggestion that he, George, should occupy the other seat, but with a certain lack, it seemed to George, of enthusiasm. He had not volunteered any reason why he was going to Market Blandings in the little runabout, and on arrival there had betrayed an unmistakable desire to get rid of George at the earliest opportunity. As this had suited George to perfection, he being desirous of getting rid of the Hon. Freddie at the earliest opportunity, he had not been inquisitive, and they had parted at the outskirts of the town without mutual confidences. George had then proceeded to the grocer's, and after that to another of the Market Blanding inns, not the Emsworth Arms, where he had bought the white wine. He did not believe in the white wine, for he was a young man with a palate and mistrusted country cellars, but he assumed that, whatever its quality, it would cheer Aline in the small hours.

He had then tramped the whole five miles back to the Castle with his purchases.

It was here that his real troubles began, and the quality of his love was wasted. The walk, to a heavily-laden man, was bad enough, but as nothing compared with the ordeal of smuggling the cargo up to his bedroom. Superman as he was, George was alive to the delicacy of the situation. One cannot convey food and drink to one's room at a strange house without, if detected, seeming to cast a slur on the table of the host. It was as one who carries despatches through an enemy's lines that George took cover, emerged from cover, dodged, ducked, and ran; and the moment when he sank, down on his bed, the door locked behind him, was one of the happiest of his life.

The recollection of that ordeal made the one he proposed to embark on now seem light in comparison. All he had to do was to go to Aline's room, knock softly on the door till signs of wakefulness made themselves heard from within, and then dart away into the shadows whence he had come, and so back to bed. He gave Aline credit for the intelligence which would enable her to finding a tongue, some bread, a knife, a fork, salt, a corkscrew and a bottle of white wine on the mat, to know what to do with them and, perhaps to guess whose was the loving hand which had laid them there.

The second clause, however, was not important, for he

proposed to tell her whose was the hand next morning. Other people might hide their light under a bushel, not George Emerson.

It only remained now to allow time to pass until the hour should be sufficiently advanced to ensure safety for the expedition. He looked at his watch again. It was nearly two. By this time the house must be asleep.

He gathered up the tongue, the bread, the knife, the fork, the salt, the corkscrew, and the bottle of white wine, and left the room.

All was still. He stole downstairs.

### III

On his chair on the gallery that ran round the Hall, swathed in an overcoat and wearing rubber-soled shoes, the Efficient Baxter sat and gazed into the darkness. He had lost the first fine careless rapture, as it were, which had helped him to endure these vigils, and a great weariness was upon him. He found a difficulty in keeping his eyes open, and when they were open the darkness seemed to press upon them painfully. Take him for all in all, the Efficient Baxter had had about enough of it.

Time stood still.

Baxter's thoughts began to wander. He knew that this was fatal, and exerted himself to drag them back. He tried to concentrate his mind on one definite thing. He selected the scarab as a suitable object, but it played him false. He had hardly concentrated on the scarab before his mind was straying off to ancient Egypt, to Mr. Peters' dyspepsia, and on a dozen other branch lines of thought.

He blamed the fat man at the inn for this. If the fat man had not thrust his presence and conversation upon him, he would have been able to enjoy a sound sleep in the afternoon, and would have come fresh to his nocturnal task. He began to muse upon the fat man.

And, by a curious coincidence, whom should he meet a few moments later but this same man.

It happened in a somewhat singular manner, though it all seemed perfectly logical and consecutive to Baxter. He was climbing up the outer wall of Westminster Abbey in his pyjamas and a tall hat, when the fat man, suddenly thrusting his head out of a window which Baxter had not noticed till that moment, said, 'Hallo, Freddie!' Baxter was about to explain that his name was not Freddie, when he found himself walking down Piccadilly with Ashe Mason. Ashe said to him, 'Nobody loves me!' and the pathos of it cut the Efficient Baxter like a knife. He was on the point of replying, but Ashe vanished and Baxter discovered that he was not in Piccadilly, as he had supposed, but in an aeroplane with Mr. Peters, hovering over the Castle. Mr. Peters had a bomb in his hand, which he was fondling with loving care. He explained to Baxter that he had stolen it from the Earl of Emsworth's museum. 'I did it with a slice of cold beef and a pickle,' he explained, and Baxter found himself realizing that that was the only way.

'Now watch me drop it,' said Mr. Peters, closing one eye and taking aim at the Castle. 'I have to do this by the doctor's orders.' He loosed the bomb, and immediately Baxter was in bed watching it drop. He was frightened, but the idea of moving did not occur to him. The bomb fell very slowly, dipping and fluttering like a feather. It came closer and closer. Then it struck with a roar and a sheet of flame. . . .

Baxter awoke to a sound of tumult and crashing. For a

moment he hovered between dreaming and waking, and then sleep passed from him, and he was aware that something noisy and exciting was in progress in the Hall below.

## IV

Coming down to first causes, the only reason why collisions of any kind occur is because two bodies defy Nature's law that a given spot on a given plane shall at a given moment of time be occupied by only one body. There was a certain spot near the foot of the great staircase which Ashe, coming downstairs, and George Emerson coming up, had to pass on their respective routes. George reached it at one minute and three seconds after two a.m., moving silently but swiftly, and Ashe, also maintaining a good rate of speed, arrived there at one minute and four seconds after the hour, when he ceased to walk and began to fly, accompanied by George Emerson, now going down. His arms were round George's neck, and George was clinging to his waist. In due season they reached the foot of the stairs and a small table covered with occasional china and photographs in frames which lay adjacent to the foot of the stairs.

That, especially the occasional china, was what Baxter had heard.

George Emerson thought it was a burglar. Ashe did not know what it was, but he knew he wanted to shake it off, so he insinuated a hand beneath George's chin and pushed upwards. George, by this time parted for ever from the tongue, the bread, the knife, the fork, the salt, the corkscrew, and the bottle of white wine, and having both hands free for the work of the moment, held Ashe with the left and punched him in the ribs with the right. Ashe, removing his left arm from George's neck, brought it up as a reinforcement to his right, and used both as a means of throttling George. This led George, now permanently underneath, to grasp Ashe's ears firmly and twist them, relieving the pressure on his throat and causing Ashe to utter the first vocal sound of the evening, other than the explosive 'Ugh' which both had emitted at the instant of impact. Ashe dislodged George's hands from his ears, and hit George in the ribs with his elbow. George kicked Ashe on the left ankle. Ashe rediscovered George's throat and began to squeeze it afresh, and a pleasant time was being had by all, when the Efficient Baxter, whizzing down the stairs, tripped over Ashe's legs, shot forward, and cannoned into another table, also covered with occasional china and photographs in frames. The Hall at Blandings Castle was more an extra drawing-room than a hall, and, when not nursing a sick headache in her bedroom, Lady Ann Warblington would dispense afternoon tea there to her guests. Consequently it was dotted pretty freely with small tables. There were indeed, no fewer than five or more in various spots waiting to be bumped into and smashed.

But the bumping into and smashing of small tables is a task that calls for plenty of time, a leisured pursuit, and neither George nor Ashe, a third party having added to their little affair, felt a desire to stay on and do the thing properly. Ashe was strongly opposed to being discovered and called upon the account for his presence there at that hour, and George, conscious of the tongue and its adjuncts now strewn about the Hall, had a similar prejudice against the tedious explanations which detection must involve. As if by mutual consent each relaxed his grip. They stood panting for an instant, then, Ashe in the direction where he supposed the green baize door of the servant's quarters to be, George to the staircase which led to his bedroom, they went away from that place.

They had hardly done so, when Baxter, having dissociated himself from the contents of the table which he had upset, began to grope his way towards the electric light switch, the same being situated near the foot of the main staircase. He went on all fours, as a safer method of locomotion, if slower, than the one which he had attempted before.

Noises began to make themselves heard on the floors above. Roused by the merry crackle of occasional china, the house-party was bestirring itself to investigate. Voices sounded, muffled and inquiring.

Baxter meanwhile crawled steadily on his hands and knees towards the light switch. He was in much the same condition as one White Hope of the ring is after he has put his chin in the way of the fist of a rival member of the Truck-drivers' Union. He knew that he was still alive. More he could not say. The mists of sleep which still shrouded his brain and the shaking-up he had had from his encounter with the table, a corner of which he had rammed with the top of his head, combined to produce a dream-like state.

And so the Efficient Baxter crawled on, and as he crawled his hand, advancing cautiously, fell on a Something – a something that was not alive, something clammy and icy-cold, the touch of which filled him with a nameless horror.

To say that Baxter's heart stood still would be medically inexact. The heart does not stand still. Whatever the emotions of its owner, it goes on beating. It would be more accurate to say that Baxter felt like a man taking his first ride in an express elevator who has outstripped his vital organs by several floors and sees no immediate prospect of their ever catching up with him again. There was a great cold void where the more intimate parts of his body should have been. His throat was dry and contracted. The flesh of his back crawled. For he knew what it was that he had touched.

Painful and absorbing as had been his encounter with the table, Baxter had never lost sight of the fact that close beside him a furious battle between unseen forces was in progress. He had heard the bumping and the thumping and the tense breathing even as he picked occasional china from his person. Such a combat, he had felt, could hardly fail to result in personal injury to either the party of the first part or the party of the second part, or both. He knew now that worse than mere injury had happened, and that he knelt in the presence of death.

There was no doubt that the man was dead. Insensibility alone could never have produced this icy chill.

He raised his head in the darkness, and cried aloud, to those approaching.

He meant to cry, 'Help! Murder!' but fear prevented clear articulation.

What he shouted was, 'Heh! Mer!'

Upon which from the neighbourhood of the staircase, someone began to fire off a revolver.

The Earl of Emsworth had been sleeping a sound and peaceful sleep when the imbroglio began downstairs. He sat up and listened. Yes, undoubtedly burglars. He switched on his light and jumped out of bed. He took a pistol from the drawer, and thus armed, went to look into the matter. The dreamy peer was no poltroon.

It was quite dark when he arrived on the scene of conflict in the van of a mixed bevy of pyjamaed and dressing-gowned relations. He was in the van because meeting those relations in the passage above, he had said to them, 'Let me go first. I have a pistol.' And they let him go first. They were, indeed, awfully nice about it, not thrusting themselves forward or jostling or anything, but behaving in a modest and self-effacing manner which was pretty to watch. When Lord Emsworth said, 'Let me go first,' young Algernon Wooster, who was on the very point of leaping to the fore, said, 'Yes, by Jove, sound scheme, by Gad!' and withdrew into the background, and the Bishop of Godalming said, 'By all means, Clarence, undoubtedly, most certainly precede us.'

When his sense of touch told him that he had reached the foot of the stairs, Lord Emsworth paused. The Hall was very dark, and the burglars seemed to have suspended activities. And then one of them, a man with a ruffianly grating voice, spoke. What it was he said, Lord Emsworth could not understand. It sounded like 'Heh! Mer!' Probably some secret signal to his confederate. Lord Emsworth raised his revolver and emptied it in the direction of the sound.

Extremely fortunate for him, the Efficient Baxter had not changed his all-fours attitude. This undoubtedly saved Lord Emsworth the worry of engaging a new secretary. The shots sang above Baxter's head, one after the other, six in all, and found themselves billets other than his person. They disposed themselves as follows. The first shot broke a window and whistled out into the night. The second shot hit the dinner-gong and made a perfectly extraordinary noise like the Last Trump. The third, fourth and fifth shots embedded themselves in the wall. The sixth and final shot hit a life-size picture of his lordship's maternal grandmother in the face and improved it out of all knowledge. One thinks no worse of Lord Emsworth's maternal grandmother because she looked like George Robey, and had allowed herself to be painted, after the heavy Classical manner of some of the portraits of a hundred years ago, in the character of Venus (suitably draped, of course) rising from the sea; but it was beyond the possibility of denial that her grandson's bullet permanently removed one of Blanding Castle's most prominent eyesores.

Having emptied his revolver, Lord Emsworth said, 'Who is there! Speak?' in rather an aggrieved tone, as if he felt he had done his part in breaking the ice and it was now for the intruder to exert himself and bear his share of the social amenities.

The Efficient Baxter did not reply. Nothing in the world would have induced him to speak at that moment or to make any sound whatsoever that might betray his position to a dangerous maniac who might at any instant reload his pistol and resume the fusillade. Explanations, in his opinion, could be deferred till somebody had the presence of mind to switch on the lights. He flattened himself on the carpet, and hoped for better things. His cheek touched the corpse beside him, but, though he winced and shuddered, he made no outcry. After those six shots he was through with outcries.

A voice from above – the Bishop's voice – said, 'I think you have killed him, Clarence.'

Another voice – that of Colonel Horace Mant – said, 'Switch on those dashed lights, why doesn't someone, dash it?'

The whole strength of the company began to demand light. When the lights came it was from the other side of the Hall. Six revolver shots, fired at a quarter-past two in the morning, will rouse even sleeping domestics. The servants' quarters were buzzing like a hive. Shrill feminine screams were puncturing the air. Mr. Beach, the butler, in a suit of pink silk pyjamas of which no one would have suspected him, was leading a party of men-servants down the stairs, not so much because he wanted to lead them as because they pushed him. The passage beyond the green baize door became congested, and there were cries for Mr. Beach to open it, and look through and see what was the matter, but Mr. Beach was smarter than that, and wriggled back so that he no longer headed the procession.

This done, he shouted, 'Open the door there, open that door. Look and see what the matter is.'

Ashe opened the door. Since his escape from the Hall he had been lurking in the neighbourhood of the green baize, and had been engulfed by the swirling throng. Finding himself with elbow-room for the first time, he pushed through, swung the door open, and switched on the lights.

They shone on a collection of semi-dressed figures, crowding the staircase, on a hall littered with china and glass, on a dented dinner-gong, on an edited and improved portrait of the late Countess of Emsworth and on the Efficient Baxter, in an overcoat and rubber-soled shoes, lying beside a cold tongue.

At no great distance lay a number of other objects – a knife, a fork, some bread, salt, a corkscrew, and a bottle of white wine.

Using the word in the sense of saying something coherent, the Earl of Emsworth was the first to speak. He peered down at his recumbent secretary and said, 'Baxter! My dear fellow, what the devil?'

The feeling of the company was one of profound disappointment. They were disgusted at the anti-climax. For an instant, when the Efficient one did not move, hope began to stir, but as soon as it was seen that he was not even injured, gloom reigned. One of two things would have satisfied them – either a burglar or a corpse. A burglar would have been welcome, dead or alive, but if Baxter proposed to fill the part adequately, it was imperative that he be dead. He had disappointed them deeply by turning out to be the object of their quest. That he should not have been even grazed was too much.

There was a cold silence as he slowly raised himself from the floor.

As his eyes fell on the tongue, he started, and remained gazing fixedly at it. Surprise paralysed him.

Lord Emsworth was also looking at the tongue, and he leaped to a not unreasonable conclusion. He spoke coldly and haughtily, for he was not only annoyed like the others at the anti-climax, but offended. He knew that he was not one of your energetic hosts who exert themselves unceasingly to supply their guests with entertainment, but there was one thing on which, as a host, he did pride himself. In the material matters of life he did his guests well. He kept an admirable table.

'My dear Baxter,' he said in the tones which usually he reserved for the correction of his son Freddie, 'if your hunger is so great that you are unable to wait for breakfast and have to raid my larder in the middle of the night, I wish to goodness you would contrive to make less noise about it. I do not grudge you the food – help yourself when you please – but do remember that people who have not such keen appetites as yourself, like to sleep during the night. A far better plan, my dear fellow, would be to have sandwiches – or buns – whatever you consider most sustaining sent up to your bedroom.'

Not even the bullets had disordered Baxter's faculties so much as this monstrous accusation. Explanations pushed and jostled one another in his fermenting brain, but he could not utter them. On every side he met gravely reproachful eyes. George Emerson was looking at him in pained disgust. Ashe Marson's face was the face of one who could never have believed this had he not seen it with his own eyes. The scrutiny of the knife-and-shoe boy was unendurable.

He stammered. Words began to proceed from him, tripping and stumbling over each other.

Lord Emsworth's frigid disapproval did not relax.

'Pray do not apologize, Baxter. The desire for food is human. It is your boisterous mode of securing and conveying it that I deprecate. Let us all go to bed.'

'But, Lord Emsworth—!'

'To bed,' repeated his lordship firmly.

The company began to stream moodily upstairs. The lights were switched off. The Efficient Baxter dragged himself away.

From the darkness in the direction of the servants' door a voice spoke.

'Greedy pig!' said the voice scornfully.

It sounded like the fresh young voice of the knife-and-shoe boy, but Baxter was too broken to investigate. He continued his retreat without pausing. 'Stuffin' of 'isself at all hours!' said the voice. There was a murmur of approval from the unseen throng of domestics.

## CHAPTER NINE

### I

As we grow older and realize more clearly the limitations of human happiness, we come to see that the only real and abiding pleasure in life is to give pleasure to other people. One must assume that the Efficient Baxter had not reached the age when this comes home to a man, for the fact that he had given genuine pleasure to some dozens of his fellow-men brought him no balm.

There was no doubt about the pleasure which he had given. Once they had got over their disappointment at finding that he was not a dead burglar, the house-party rejoiced whole-heartedly at the break in the monotony of life at Blandings Castle. Relations who had not been on speaking terms for years forgot their quarrels, and strolled about the grounds in perfect harmony, abusing Baxter. The general verdict was that he was insane.

'Don't tell me that young fellow's all there,' said Colonel Horace Mant, 'because I know better. Have you noticed his eye? Furtive! Shifty! Nasty gleam in it. Besides, dash it, did you happen to take a look at the Hall last night after he had been there? It was in ruins, my dear sir, absolute dashed ruins. It was positively littered with broken china and tables which had been bowled over. Don't tell me that was just an accidental collision in the dark. My dear sir, the man must have been thrashing about, absolutely *thrashing* about, like a dashed salmon on a dashed hook. He must have had a paroxysm of some kind. Some kind of dashed fit. A doctor could give you the name for it. It's a well-known form of insanity. Paranoia – isn't that what they call it? Rush of blood to the head, followed by a general running amuck. I've heard fellows who have been in India talk of it. Natives get it. Don't know what they're doing, and charge through the streets taking cracks at people with dashed whacking great knives. Same with this young man, probably in a modified form at present. He ought to be in a Home. One of these nights, if the thing grows on him, he will be massacring Emsworth in his bed.'

'My dear Horace!'

The Bishop of Godalming's voice was properly horror-stricken, but there was a certain unctuous relish in it.

'Take my word for it. Though, mind you, I don't say they aren't well suited. Every one knows that Emsworth has been to all practical intents and purposes a dashed lunatic for years.'

'My dear Horace! Your father-in-law. The head of the family.'

'A dashed lunatic, my dear sir, head of the family or no head of the family. A man as absent-minded as he is has no right to call himself sane.'

The Efficient Baxter, who had just left his presence, was feeling much the same about his noble employer. After a sleepless night he had begun at an early hour to try and corner Lord Emsworth in order to explain to him the true inwardness of last night's happenings. Eventually he had tracked him to the museum where he had found him happily engaged in painting a cabinet of birds' eggs. He was seated on a small stool, a large pot of red paint on the floor beside him, dabbing at the cabinet with a dripping brush. He was absorbed, and made no attempt whatever to follow his secretary's remarks.

For ten minutes Baxter gave a vivid picture of his vigil and the manner in which it had been interrupted.

'Just so, just so, my dear fellow,' said the earl, when he had finished. 'I quite understand. All I say is, if you do require additional food in the night, let one of the servants bring it to your room, before bed-time, then there will be no danger of these disturbances. There is no possible objection to your eating a hundred meals a day, my good Baxter, provided you do not rouse the whole house over them. Some of us like to sleep during the night.'

'But Lord Emsworth! I have just explained . . . It was not . . . I was not . . . !'

'Never mind, my dear fellow, never mind. Why make such an important thing of it? Many people like a light snack before actually retiring. Doctors, I believe, sometimes recommend it. Tell me, Baxter, how do you think the museum looks now? A little brighter? Better for the dash of colour? I think so. Museums are generally such gloomy places.'

'Lord Emsworth, may I explain once again?'

The earl looked annoyed.

'My dear Baxter, I have told you that there is nothing to explain. You are getting a little tedious. . . . What a deep, rich red this is, and how clean new paint smells! Do you know, Baxter, I have been longing to mess about with paint ever since I was a boy. I recollect my old father beating me with a walking stick. That would be before your time, of course. By the way, if you see Freddie, will you tell him I want to speak to him? He is probably in the smoking-room. Send him to me here.'

It was an overwrought Baxter, who delivered the message to the Hon. Freddie, who, as predicted, was in the smoking-room, lounging in a deep arm-chair.

There are times when Life presses hard upon a man, and it pressed hard on Baxter now. Fate had played him a sorry trick. It had put him in a position where he had to choose between two courses, each as disagreeable as the other. He must either face a possible fiasco like that of last night, or else he must abandon his post and cease to mount guard over his threatened treasure.

His imagination quailed at the thought of a repetition of last night's horrors. He had been badly shaken by his collision with the table and even more so by the events which had followed it. Those revolver shots still rang in his ears.

It was probably the memory of those shots which turned the scale. It was unlikely that he would again become entangled with a man bearing a tongue and the other things – he had given up in despair the attempt to unravel the mystery of the tongue; it completely baffled him; but it was by no means unlikely that, if he spent another night in the gallery looking on the Hall, he might again become a target for Lord Emsworth's irresponsible fire-arm. Nothing, in fact, was more likely, for in the disturbed state of the public mind the slightest sound after nightfall would be sufficient cause for a fusillade. He had actually overheard young Algernon Wooster telling Lord Stockheath that he had a jolly good mind to sit upon the stairs that night with a shot-gun, because it was his opinion that there was a jolly sight more in this business than there seemed to be, and that what he thought of the bally affair was that there was a gang of some kind at work and that that feller, what's-his-name, that feller Baxter, was some sort of an accomplice.

With these things in his mind, Baxter decided to remain that night in the security of his bedroom. He had lost his nerve.

He formed this decision with the utmost reluctance, for the thought of leaving the road to the museum clear for marauders was bitter in the extreme.

If he could have overheard a conversation between Joan Valentine and Ashe Marson, it is probable that he would have risked Lord Emsworth's revolver and the shot-gun of the Honourable Algernon Wooster.

Ashe, when he met Joan and recounted the events of the past night, at which Joan, who was a sound sleeper, had not been present, was inclined to blame himself as a failure. True, fate had been against him but the fact remained that he had achieved nothing.

Joan, however, was not of this opinion.

'You have done wonders,' she said. 'You have cleared the way for me. That is my ideal of real team-work. I'm so glad now that we formed our partnership. It would have been too bad if I had got all the advantage of your work and had jumped in and deprived you of the reward. As it is, I shall go down and finish the thing off tonight with a clear conscience.'

'You can't mean that you dream of going down to the museum tonight?'

'Of course I do.'

'But it's madness.'

'On the contrary, tonight is the one night where there ought to be no risk at all.'

'After what happened last night?'

'Because of what happened last night. Do you imagine that Mr. Baxter will dare to stir from his bed after that? If ever there was a chance of getting this thing finished, it will be tonight.'

'You're quite right. I never looked at it in that way. Baxter wouldn't risk a second disaster. I'll certainly make a success of it this time.'

Joan raised her eyebrows.

'I don't quite understand you, Mr. Marson. Do you propose to try and get the scarab again tonight?'

'Yes. It will be as easy as——'

'Are you forgetting that, by the terms of our agreement, it is my turn?'

'You surely don't intend to hold me to that?'

'Certainly I do.'

'But good heavens, consider my position! Do you seriously expect me to lie in bed while you do all the work, and then to take a half share in the reward?'

'I do.'

'It's ridiculous.'

'It's no more ridiculous than that I should do the same. Mr. Marson, it's no use our going over all this again. We settled it long ago.'

And she refused to discuss the matter further, leaving Ashe in a condition of anxious misery comparable only to that which, as night began to draw near, gnawed the vitals of the Efficient Baxter.

II

Breakfast at Blandings Castle was an informal meal. There was food and drink in the long dining-hall for such as were energetic enough to come down and get it, but the majority of the house-party breakfasted in their rooms, Lord Emsworth, whom nothing in the world would have induced to begin the day in the company of a crowd of his relations, most of whom he disliked, setting them the example.

When, therefore, Baxter, yielding to Nature after having remained awake till the early morning, fell asleep at nine o'clock, nobody came to rouse him. He did not ring his bell, so he was not disturbed, and he slept on until half-past eleven, by which time, it being Sunday morning and the house-party including one bishop and several of the minor clergy, most of the occupants of the place had gone off to church.

Baxter shaved and dressed hastily, for he was in a state of nervous apprehension. He blamed himself for having laid in bed so long. When every minute he was away might mean the loss of the scarab, he had passed several hours in dreamy sloth.

He had woken with a presentiment. Something told him that the scarab had been stolen in the night, and he wished now that he had risked all and kept guard.

The house was very quiet as he made his way rapidly to the Hall. As he passed a window, he perceived Lord Emsworth, in an un-Sabbatarian suit of tweeds and bearing a gardening-fork which must have pained the Bishop, bending earnestly over a flower-bed; but he was the only occupant of the grounds, and indoors there was a feeling of emptiness. The Hall had that Sunday morning air of wanting to be left to itself and disapproving of the entry of anything human till lunch-time, which can only be felt by a guest in a large house who remains at home when his fellows have gone to church.

The portraits on the walls, especially the one of the late Countess of Emsworth in the character of Venus rising from the sea, stared at Baxter, as he entered, with cold reproof. The very chairs seemed distant and unfriendly. But Baxter was in no mood to appreciate their attitude. His conscience slept. His mind was occupied to the exclusion of all other things, by the scarab and its probable fate. How disastrously remiss it had been of him not to keep guard last night! Long before he opened the museum door he was feeling the absolute certainty that the worst had happened.

His premonition was correct. The museum was still there; the card announcing that here was a scarab of the reign of Cheops of the Fourth Dynasty, presented by Mr. J. Preston Peters, was still there; the mummies, birds' eggs, tapestry, missals, and all the rest of Lord Emsworth's treasure were still there.

But the scarab was gone.

III

For all that this was precisely what he had expected, it was an appreciable time before the Efficient Baxter rallied from the blow. He stood transfixed, goggling at the empty place.

He was still goggling when the Earl of Emsworth pottered in. The Earl of Emsworth was one of the world's leading potterers, and Sunday morning was his favourite time for pottering. Since breakfast he had pottered about the garden, pottered round the stables, and pottered about the library. He now pottered into the museum.

'Lord Emsworth!'

By the time Baxter sighted him and gave tongue, the earl had pottered to within a foot or so of where the secretary stood. A whisper would have reached him, but such was the Efficient Baxter's emotion that he emitted the words in a sharp roar which would have been noticeably stentorian in a sea-captain exchanging remarks with one of his men who happened at the moment to be working in the crow's-nest. Lord Emsworth sprang six feet, and, having disentangled himself from a piece of old tapestry, put one hand to his ear and, massaging it tenderly, glared at his young assistant.

'What do you mean by barking at me like that, Baxter? Really, you exceed all bounds. You are becoming a perfect pest.'

'Lord Emsworth, it has gone. The scarab has gone.'

'You have broken my ear-drum.'

'Somebody has stolen the scarab which Mr. Peters gave you, Lord Emsworth.'

The probable fate of his ear-drum ceased to grip the earl's undivided attention. He followed the secretary's pointing finger with a startled eye, and examined the spot where the tragedy had occurred.

'Bless my soul. You're perfectly right, my dear fellow. Somebody has stolen the scarab. This is extremely annoying. Mr. Peters may be offended. I should dislike intensely to wound Mr. Peters' feelings. He may think that I ought to have taken more care of it. Now, who in the world could have stolen that scarab?'

Baxter was about to reply, when there came from the direction of the Hall, slightly muffled by the intervening door and passage-way, a sound like the delivery of a ton of coal. A heavy body bumped down the stairs, and a voice which both recognized as that of the Hon. Freddie Threepwood uttered an oath that lost itself in a final crash and a musical splintering sound which Baxter for one had no difficulty in diagnosing as the dissolution of occasional china.

Neither Lord Emsworth nor Baxter had any difficulty in deducing from the evidence what had happened. The Hon. Freddie had fallen downstairs.

With a little ingenuity this portion of the story of Mr. Peters' scarab could be converted into an excellent tract, driving home the perils, even in this world, of absenting oneself from church on Sunday morning. If the Hon. Freddie had gone to church, he would not have been running down the great staircase of the Castle at this hour; and, if he had not been running down the great staircase of the Castle at that hour, he would not have encountered Muriel.

Muriel was a Persian cat belonging to Lady Ann Warblington. Lady Ann had breakfasted in her room and lain in bed late, as she rather fancied that she had one of her sick headaches coming on. Muriel had left the room in the wake of the breakfast tray, being anxious to be present at the obsequies of a fried sole which had formed Lady Ann's simple meal, and had followed the maid who bore it until she had reached the Hall. At this point, the maid, who disliked Muriel, stopped and made a noise like an exploding ginger-beer bottle, at the same time taking a little run in Muriel's direction and kicking at her with a menacing foot. Muriel, wounded and startled, turned in her tracks and sprinted back up the stairs, at the exact moment when the Hon. Freddie, who for some reason was in a great hurry, ran lightly down them.

There was an instant when Freddie could have saved himself at the expense of planting a number ten boot on Muriel's spine, but even in that crisis he bethought him that he hardly stood solid enough with the authorities to risk adding to his misdeeds the slaughter of his aunt's favourite cat, and he executed a rapid swerve. The scared cat proceeded on her journey upstairs, while Freddie, touching the staircase at intervals, went on down.

Having reached the bottom, he sat amidst the occasional china like Marius among the ruins of Carthage, and endeavoured to ascertain the extent of his injuries. He had a growing suspicion that he was irretrievably fractured in a dozen places.

When his father and the Efficient Baxter arrived, they found him being helped to his feet by Ashe Marson.

Ashe had been near at hand when the secretary made the discovery that the museum had been robbed in the night. He had, indeed, anticipated Baxter in that discovery by a matter of minutes. For some little time he had been in waiting behind the green baize door, hoping for an opportunity of finding whether Joan had carried out her threat of stealing the scarab, and he had contrived to pop in and out of the museum while the Hall was empty. It was not until he heard Baxter's voice raised in anguish that he realized how nearly he had been discovered. He had waited in his place of hiding during the conversation between the secretary and Lord Emsworth, and, like them, had been drawn to the stairs by the noise of Freddie's downfall.

He gave the victim a tentative pull, but Freddie sat down again with a sharp howl. He was still seated when the others arrived. He gazed up at them with silent pathos.

'It was that bally cat of Aunt Ann's, gov'nor. It came legging it up the stairs. I think I've broken my ankle.'

'You certainly have broken everything else,' said his father unsympathetically. 'Between you and Baxter I wonder there's a stick of furniture standing in the house.'

'Thanks, old chap,' said Freddie, gratefully, as Ashe once more assisted him to his feet. 'I wish you would give me a hand up to my room.'

'And, Baxter, my dear fellow,' said Lord Emsworth, 'You might telephone to Doctor Bird in Market Blandings and ask him to be good enough to drive out. I am sorry, Freddie,' he added, 'that you should have met with this accident, but – but –

everything is so disturbing nowadays that I feel – I feel most disturbed.'

Ashe and Freddie began to move across the Hall, Freddie hopping, Ashe advancing with a sort of polka-step. Baxter stood looking after them wistfully. The sight of Ashe, coming on top of the discovery of the loss of the scarab, made him feel more clearly than ever that he had been out manoeuvred. He was quite certain in his mind that Ashe was the thief, and the impossibility of denouncing him made life for the moment very bitter.

There was a sound of wheels outside, and the vanguard of the party, returned from church, entered the house.

'It's all very well to give it out officially that Freddie fell downstairs and sprained his ankle,' said Colonel Mant, discussing the affair with the Bishop of Godalming later in the day, 'but it's my firm belief that that fellow Baxter did precisely as I said he would – ran amuck and inflicted dashed frightful injuries on young Freddie. When I got into the house, there was Freddie being helped up the stairs, while Baxter was looking after him with a sort of evil glare. The whole thing is dashed fishy and mysterious, and the sooner I can get Mildred safely out of the place, the better I shall be pleased. The fellow's as mad as a hatter.'

IV

When Lord Emsworth, sighting Mr. Peters in the group of returned churchgoers, drew him aside and broke the news that the valuable scarab so kindly presented by him to the Castle museum had been stolen in the night by some person unknown, he thought that the millionaire took it exceedingly well.

Although the stolen object no longer belonged to him, Mr. Peters no doubt still continued to take an affectionate interest in it, and might have been excused had he shown annoyance that his gift had been so carelessly guarded.

He was, however, thoroughly magnanimous about the matter. He depreciated the notion that the earl could possibly have prevented this unfortunate occurrence. He quite understood. He was not in the least hurt. Nobody could have foreseen such a calamity. These things happened, and one had to accept them. He himself had once suffered in much the same way, the gem of his collection having been removed almost beneath his eyes in the smoothest possible fashion. Altogether, he relieved Lord Emsworth's mind very much; and, when he had finished doing so, he departed swiftly and rang for Ashe.

When Ashe arrived he bubbled over with enthusiasm. He was lyrical in his praise. He went so far as to slap Ashe on the back. It was only when the latter disclaimed all credit for what had occurred that he checked the flow of approbation.

'It wasn't you who got it? Who was it then?'

'It was Miss Peters' maid. It's a long story, but we were working in partnership. I tried for the thing and failed, and she succeeded.'

It was with mixed feelings that Ashe listened while Mr. Peters transferred his adjectives of commendation to Joan. He admired Joan's courage, he was relieved that her venture had ended without disaster, and he knew that she deserved whatever anyone could find to say in praise of her enterprise; but at first, though he tried to crush it down, he could not help feeling a certain amount of chagrin that a girl should have succeeded where he, though having the advantage of first chance, had failed. The terms of his partnership with Joan had jarred on him from the beginning. A man may be in sympathy with the modern movement for the emancipation of Women, and yet feel aggrieved when a mere girl proves herself a more efficient thief than he. Woman is invading Man's sphere more successfully every day, but there are still certain fields in which Man may consider that he is rightfully entitled to a monopoly, and the purloining of scarabs in the watches of the night is surely one of them. Joan, in Ashe's opinion, should have played a meeker and less active part.

These unworthy emotions did not last long. Whatever his shortcomings, Ashe possessed a just mind. By the time he had found Joan, after Mr. Peters had said his say and dispatched him below stairs for that purpose, he had purged himself of petty regrets and was prepared to congratulate her wholeheartedly. He was, however, resolved that nothing should induce him to share in the reward. On that point, he resolved, he would refuse to be shaken.

'I have just left Mr. Peters,' he began. 'All is well. His cheque-book lies before him on the table, and he is trying to make his fountain-pen work long enough to write a cheque. But there is just one thing I want to say.'

She interrupted him. To his surprise, she was eyeing him coldly and with disapproval.

'And there is just one thing I want to say,' she said. 'And that is that, if you imagine that I shall consent to accept a penny of the reward—'

'Exactly what I was going to say. Of course, I couldn't dream of taking any of it.'

'I don't understand you. You are certainly going to have it all. I told you when we made our agreement that I would only take my share if you let me do my share of the work. Now that you have broken that agreement, nothing would induce me to take it. I know you meant it kindly, Mr. Marson, but I simply can't feel grateful. I told you that ours was a business contract, and that I wouldn't have any chivalry, and I thought that, after you had given me your promise—'

'One moment,' said Ashe, bewildered. 'I can't follow this. What do you mean?'

'What do I mean? Why, that you went down to the museum last night before me and took the scarab, although you had promised to stay away and give me my chance.'

'But I didn't do anything of the sort.'

It was Joan's turn to look bewildered.

'But you have got the scarab, Mr. Marson?'

'Why, you have got it.'

'No.'

'But – but it has gone.'

'I know. I went down to the museum last night, as we had arranged, and, when I got there, there was no scarab. It had disappeared.'

They looked at each other in consternation. Ashe was the first to speak.

'It was gone when you got to the museum?'

'There wasn't a trace of it. I took it for granted that you had been down before me. I was furious.'

'But this is ridiculous,' said Ashe. 'Who can have taken it? There was nobody beside ourselves who knew that Peters was offering the reward. What exactly happened last night?'

'I waited till one o'clock. Then I slipped down, got into the museum, struck a match, and looked for the scarab. It wasn't there. I couldn't believe it at first. I struck some more matches, quite a number, but it was no good. The scarab had gone, so I went back to bed, and thought hard thoughts about you. It was silly of me. I ought to have known that you would not break your word. But there didn't seem any other solution of the thing's disappearance. Well, somebody must have taken it, and the question is, What are we to do?' She laughed. 'It seems to me that we were a little premature in quarrelling about how we were to divide that reward. It looks as if there wasn't going to be any reward.'

'Meanwhile,' said Ashe gloomily, 'I suppose I have got to go back and tell Peters. I expect it will break his heart.'

## CHAPTER TEN

I

Blandings Castle dozed in the calm of Sunday afternoon. All was peace. Freddie was in bed, with orders from the doctor to stay there till further notice. Lord Emsworth had returned to his gardening-fork. The rest of the house-party strolled about the grounds or sat in them, for the day was one of those late Spring days which are warm with a premature suggestion of midsummer.

Aline Peters was sitting at the open window of her bedroom, which commanded an extensive view of the terraces. A pile of letters lay on the table beside her. The postman came late to the Castle on Sundays, and she had not been able to read them until lunch was over.

Aline was puzzled. She was conscious of a fit of depression, for which she could in no way account. As a rule something had to go very definitely wrong to make her depressed, for she was not a girl who brooded easily on the vague undercurrent of sadness in Life. As a rule she found nothing tragic in the fact that she was alive. She liked being alive.

But this afternoon she had a feeling that all was not well with the world, which was the more remarkable in that she was usually keenly susceptible to weather conditions and revelled in sunshine like a kitten. Yet here was a day nearly as fine as an American day and she found no solace in it.

She looked down on the terrace, and as she looked the figure of George Emerson appeared, walking swiftly. And at the sight of him something seemed to tell her that she had found the key to her gloom.

There are many kinds of walk. George Emerson's was the walk of mental unrest. His hands were clasped behind his back, his eyes stared straight in front of him from beneath lowering brows, and between his teeth was an unlighted cigar. No man holds an unlighted cigar in his mouth unless unpleasant meditations have caused him to forget that he has it there. Plainly, then, all was not well with George Emerson.

Aline had suspected as much at lunch, and, looking back, she realized that it was at lunch that her depression had begun. The discovery startled her a little. She had not been aware, or she had refused to admit to herself, that George's troubles bulked so large on her horizon. She had always told herself that she liked George, that George was a dear old friend, that George amused and stimulated her; but she would have denied that she was so wrapped up in George that the sight of him in trouble would be enough to spoil for her the finest day she had seen since she left America. There was something not only startling but shocking in the thought, for she was honest enough with herself to recognize that Freddie, her official loved one, might have paced the Castle grounds chewing an unlighted cigar by the hour without stirring any emotion in her at all.

And she was to marry Freddie next month. This was surely a matter that called for thought. She proceeded, gazing down the while to the perambulating George, to give it thought.

Aline's was not a deep nature. She had never pretended to herself that she loved the Hon. Freddie in the sense in which the word is used in books. She liked him, and she liked the idea, and she liked her father, and the combination of these likings had caused her to reply, 'Yes' when, last Autumn, Freddie, swelling himself out like an embarrassed frog and gulping, had uttered that memorable speech, beginning, 'I say, you know, it's like this, don't you know,' and ending, 'What I mean is, will you marry me, what?' She had looked forward to being placidly happy as the Hon. Mrs. Frederick Threepwood. And then, George Emerson had reappeared in her life, a disturbing element.

Until today she would have resented the suggestion that she was in love with George. She liked to be with him, partly because he was so easy to talk to, and partly because it was exciting to be continually resisting the will-power which he made no secret of trying to exercise.

But today there was a difference. She had suspected it at lunch, and she realized it now. As she looked down at him from behind the curtain and marked his air of gloom, she could no longer disguise it from herself.

She felt maternal, horribly maternal. George was in trouble, and she wanted to comfort him.

Freddie too was in trouble. But did she want to comfort Freddie? No. On the contrary, she was already regretting her promise, so lightly given before lunch, to come and sit with him that afternoon. A well-marked feeling of annoyance that he should have been so silly as to tumble downstairs and sprain his ankle was her chief sentiment respecting Freddie.

George Emerson continued to perambulate, and Aline continued to watch him. At last she could endure it no longer.

She gathered up her letters, stacked them in a corner of the dressing-table, and left the room.

George had reached the end of the terrace and turned when she began to descend the stone steps outside the front door. He quickened his pace as he caught sight of her. He halted before her and surveyed her morosely.

'I have been looking for you,' he said.

'And here I am. Cheer up, George. Whatever is the matter? I've been sitting in my room looking at you, and you have been simply prowling. What has gone wrong?'

'Everything.'

'How do you mean, everything?'

'Exactly what I say. I'm done for. Read this.'

Aline took the yellow slip of paper.

'A cable,' said George. 'I got it this morning, mailed on from my rooms in London. Read it.'

'I'm trying to. It doesn't seem to make sense.'

George laughed grimly.

'It makes sense all right.'

'I don't see how you can say that. "Meredith elephant kangaroo. . . ."'

'Official cypher. I was forgetting. "Elephant" means "seriously ill and unable to attend to duty". Meredith is the man who was doing my work while I was on leave.'

'Oh, I'm so sorry. Do you think he is very bad? Are you very fond of Mr. Meredith?'

'Meredith is a good fellow, and I like him, but if it was simply a matter of his being ill I'm afraid I could manage to bear up. Unfortunately "kangaroo" means "return without fail by the next boat".'

'You must return by the next boat?'

Aline looked at him, in her eyes slow-growing comprehension of the situation.

'Oh,' she said at length.

'I put it stronger than that,' said George.

'But . . . the next boat . . . when is that?'

'Wednesday morning. I shall have to leave here tomorrow.'

Aline's eyes were fixed on the blue hills across the valley, but she did not see them. There was a mist between. She was feeling crushed and ill-treated and lonely. It was as if George was already gone and she was left alone in an alien land.

'But, George,' she said.

She could find no other words for her protest against the inevitable.

'It's bad luck,' said Emerson quietly. 'But I shouldn't wonder if it is not the best thing really that could have happened. It finishes me cleanly, instead of letting me drag on and make both of us miserable. If this cable hadn't come, I suppose I should have gone on bothering you up to the day of your wedding. I should have fancied to the last moment that there was a chance for me. But this ends me with one punch. Even I haven't the nerve to imagine that I can work a miracle in the few hours before the train leaves tomorrow. I must just make the best of it. If we ever meet again, and I don't see why we should, you will be married. My particular brand of mental suggestion doesn't work at long range. I shan't hope to influence you by telepathy.'

He leaned on the balustrade at her side, and spoke in a low, level voice.

'This thing,' he said, 'coming as a shock, coming out of the blue sky without warning – Meredith is the last man in the world you would expect to crack up; he looked as fit as a drayhorse last time I saw him – somehow seems to have hammered a certain amount of sense into me. Odd it never struck me before, but I suppose I have been about the most bumptious, conceited fool that ever happened. Why I should have imagined that there was a sort of irresistible fascination in me which was bound to make you break off your engagement and upset the whole universe simply to win the wonderful reward of marrying me, is more than I can understand. I suppose it takes a shock to make a fellow see exactly what he really amounts to. I couldn't think any more of you than I do, but, if I could, the way you have put up with my mouthing and swaggering and posing as a sort of Superman would make me do it. You have been wonderful.'

Aline could not speak. She felt as if her whole world had been turned upside down in the last quarter of an hour. This was a new George Emerson, a George at whom it was impossible to laugh, an insidiously attractive George. Her heart beat quickly. Her mind was not clear, but dimly she realized that he had pulled down her chief barrier of defence, and that she was more open to attack than she had ever been. Obstinacy, the automatic desire to resist the pressure of a will that attempted to overcome her own, had kept her cool and level-headed in the past. With masterfulness she had been able to cope. Humility was another thing altogether.

Soft-heartedness was Aline's weakness. She had never clearly recognized it, but it had been partly pity which had induced her to accept Freddie. He had seemed so downtrodden and sorry for himself during those Autumn days when they had first met. Prudence warned her that strange things might happen if once she allowed herself to pity George Emerson.

The silence lengthened. Aline could find nothing to say. In her present mood there was danger in speech.

'We have known each other so long,' said Emerson, 'and I have told you so often that I love you that we have come to make almost a joke of it, as if we were playing some game. It just happens that that is our way, to laugh at things. But I am going to say it once again, even if it has come to be a sort of catchphrase. I love you. I'm reconciled to the fact that I am done for, out of the running, and that you are going to marry somebody else; but I am not going to stop loving you. It isn't a question of whether I should be happier if I forgot you. I can't do it. It's just an impossibility, and that's all there is to it. Whatever I may be to you, you are part of me, and you always will be part of me. I might just as well try to go on living without breathing as living without loving you.'

He stopped, and straightened himself.

'That's all. I don't want to spoil a perfectly good Spring afternoon for you by pulling out the tragic stop. I had to say all that, but it's the last time. It shan't occur again. There will be no tragedy when I step into the train tomorrow. Is there any chance that you might come and see me off?'

Aline nodded.

'You will? That will be splendid. Now I'll go and pack and break it to my host that I must leave him. I expect it will be news to him to learn that I am here. I doubt if he knows me by sight.'

Aline stood where he had left her, leaning on the balustrade.

In the fulness of time there came to her the recollection that she had promised Freddie that shortly after lunch she would come and sit with him.

The Hon. Freddie, draped in purple pyjamas and propped up with many pillows, was lying in bed, reading 'Gridley Quayle, Investigator'. Aline's entrance occurred at a peculiarly poignant moment in the story, and gave him a feeling of having been brought violently to earth from a flight in the clouds. It is not often that an author has the good fortune to grip a reader as the author of Gridley Quayle gripped Freddie.

One of the results of his absorbed mood was that he greeted Aline with a stare of an even glassier quality than usual. His eyes were by nature a trifle prominent, and to Aline, in the overstrung condition in which her talk with George Emerson had left her, they seemed to bulge at her like a snail's. A man seldom looks at his best in bed, and to Aline, seeing him for the first time at this disadvantage, the Hon. Freddie seemed quite repulsive. It was with a feeling of positive panic that she wondered whether he would want her to kiss him.

Freddie made no such demand. He was not one of your demonstrative lovers. He contented himself with rolling over in bed and dropping his lower jaw.

'Hello, Aline.'

Aline sat down on the edge of the bed.

'Well, Freddie.'

Her betrothed improved his appearance a little by hitching up his lower jaw. As if feeling that that would be too extreme a measure, he did not close his mouth altogether, but he diminished the abyss. The Hon. Freddie belonged to the class of persons who move through life with their mouths always restfully open.

It seemed to Aline that on this particular afternoon a strange dumbness had descended upon her. She had been unable to speak to George, and now she could not think of anything to say to Freddie. She looked at him, and he looked at her, and the clock on the mantelpiece went on ticking.

'It was that bally cat of Aunt Ann's,' said Freddie at length, essaying light conversation. 'It came legging it up the stairs, and

I took the most frightful toss. I hate cats. Do you hate cats? I knew a fellow in London who couldn't stand cats.'

Aline began to wonder if there was not something permanently wrong with her organs of speech. It should have been a simple matter to develop the cat theme, but she found herself unable to do so. Her mind was concentrated, to the exclusion of all else, on the repellent nature of the spectacle provided by her loved one in pyjamas.

Freddie resumed the conversation.

'I was just reading a corking book. Have you ever read these things? They come out every month, and they're corking. The fellow who writes them must be a corker. It beats me how he thinks of these things. They are about a detective, a chap called Gridley Quayle. Frightfully exciting.'

An obvious remedy for dumbness struck Aline.

'Shall I read to you, Freddie?'

'Right-ho! Good scheme. I've got to the top of this page.'

Aline took the paper-covered book.

' "Seven guns covered him with deadly precision." Did you get as far as that?'

'Yes, just beyond. It's a bit thick, don't you know. This chappie Quayle has been trapped in a lonely house, thinking he was going to see a pal in distress, and instead of the pal there pop out a whole squad of masked blighters with guns. I don't see how he's going to get out of it myself, but I bet he does. He's a corker.'

If anybody could have pitied Aline more than she pitied herself, as she waded through the adventures of Mr. Quayle, it would have been Ashe Marson. He had writhed as he wrote the words, and she writhed as she read them. The Hon. Freddie also writhed, but with intense excitement.

'What's the matter? Don't stop,' he cried, as Aline's voice ceased.

'I'm getting hoarse, Freddie.'

Freddie hesitated. The desire to remain on the trial with Gridley struggled with rudimentary politeness.

'How would it be. . . . Would you mind if I just took a look at the rest of it myself? We could talk afterwards, don't you know. I shan't be long.'

'Of course. Do read if you want to. But do you really like this sort of thing, Freddie?'

'Me! Rather. Why, don't you?'

'I don't know. It seems a little . . . I don't know.'

Freddie had become absorbed in his story. Aline did not attempt further analysis of her attitude towards Mr. Quayle. She relapsed into silence.

It was a silence pregnant with thought. For the first time in their relations, she was trying to visualize to herself exactly what marriage with this young man would mean. Hitherto, it struck her, she had really seen so little of Freddie that she had scarcely had a chance of examining him. In the crowded world outside he had always seemed a tolerable enough person. Today, somehow, he was different. Everything was different today.

This, she took it, was a fair sample of what she might expect after marriage. Marriage meant, to come to essentials, that two people were very often and for lengthy periods alone together, dependent on each other for mutual entertainment. What exactly would it be like being alone often for lengthy periods with Freddie?

Well, it would, she assumed, be like this.

'It's all right,' said Freddie without looking up. 'He *did* get out. He had a bomb on him, and he threatened to drop it and blow the place to pieces unless the blighters let him go. So they cheesed it. I knew he had something up his sleeve.'

Like this. . . .

Aline drew a deep breath. It would be like this – for ever and ever and ever, till she died.

She bent forward, and stared at him.

'Freddie,' she said, 'do you love me?'

There was no reply.

'Freddie, do you love me? Am I a part of you? If you hadn't me, would it be like trying to go on living without breathing?'

The Hon. Freddie raised a flushed face, and gazed at her with an absent eye.

'Eh, what?' he said. 'Do I . . . ? Oh, yes. Rather. I say, one of the blighters has just loosed a rattlesnake into Gridley Quayle's bedroom through the transom.'

Aline rose from her seat and left the room softly. The Hon. Freddie read on, unheeding.

## II

Ashe had not fallen far short of the truth in his estimate of the probable effect on Mr. Peters of the information that his precious scarab had once more been removed by alien hands and was now farther from his grasp than ever. A drawback to success in life is that failure, when it does come, acquires an exaggerated importance. Success had made Mr. Peters, in certain aspects of his character, a spoiled child. At the moment when Ashe broke the news, he would have parted with half his fortune to recover the scarab. Its recovery had become a point of honour. He saw it as the prize of a contest between his will and that of whatever malignant powers there might be, ranged against him in the effort to show him that there were limits to what he could achieve. He felt as he had felt in the old days when people sneaked up behind him in Wall Street and tried to loosen his grip on a railway or a pet stock. He was suffering from that form of paranoia which makes men multimillionaires. Nobody would be foolish enough to become a multimillionaire, if it were not for the desire to prove himself irresistible.

He obtained a small relief for his feelings by doubling the existing reward, and Ashe went off in search of Joan, hoping that this new stimulus, acting on their joint brains, might develop inspiration.

'Have any fresh ideas been vouchsafed to you?' he asked. 'You may look on me as baffled.'

Joan shook her head.

'Don't give it up,' she urged. 'Think again. Try to realize what this means, Mr. Marson. Between us we have lost ten thousand dollars, in a single night. I can't afford it. It is like losing a legacy. I absolutely refuse to give in without an effort and go back to writing duke-and-earl stories for *Home Gossip*.'

'The prospect of tackling Gridley Quayle again—'

'Why, I was forgetting that you were a writer of detective stories. You ought to be able to solve this mystery in a moment. Ask yourself, what would Gridley Quayle have done?'

'I can answer that. Gridley Quayle would have waited helplessly for some coincidence to happen to help him out.'

'Had he no methods?'

'He was full of methods. But they never led him anywhere without a coincidence. However, we might try to figure it out. What time did you get to the museum?'

'One o'clock.'

'And you found the scarab gone. What does that suggest to you?'

'Absolutely nothing. Let us try again. Whoever took the scarab must have had special information that Peters was offering the reward.'

'Then why hasn't he been to Mr. Peters and claimed it?'

'True. That would seem to be a flaw in the reasoning. Once again. Whoever took it must have been in urgent and immediate need of money.'

'And how are we going to find out who was in urgent and immediate need of money?'

'Exactly. How indeed?'

There was a pause.

'I should think your Mr. Quayle must have been a great comfort to his clients, wasn't he?' said Joan.

'Inductive reasoning, I admit, seems to have fallen down to a certain extent,' said Ashe. 'We must wait for the coincidence. I have a feeling that it will come.' He paused. 'I am very fortunate in the way of coincidences.'

'Are you?'

Ashe looked about him, and was relieved to find that they appeared to be out of earshot of their species. It was not easy to achieve this position at the Castle, if you happened to be there as a domestic servant. The space provided for the ladies and gentlemen attached to the guests was limited, and it was rarely that you could enjoy a stroll without bumping into a maid, a valet or a footman. But now they appeared to be alone. The drive leading to the back regions of the Castle was empty. As far as the eye could reach, there were no signs of servants, upper or lower.

Nevertheless, Ashe lowered his voice.

'Was it not a strange coincidence,' he said, 'that you should have come into my life at all?'

'Not very,' said Joan prosaically. 'It was quite likely that we should meet, sooner or later, as we lived on different floors of the same house.'

'It was a coincidence that you should have taken that room.'

'Why?'

Ashe felt damped. Logically, no doubt, she was right, but surely she might have helped him out a little in this difficult situation. Surely her woman's intuition might have told her that a man who has been speaking in a loud and cheerful voice does not lower it to a husky whisper without some reason. The hopelessness of his task began to weigh upon him. Ever since that evening at Market Blandings Station, when he had realized that he had loved her, he had been trying to find an opportunity to tell her so; and every time they had met the talk had seemed to be drawn irresistibly into practical and unsentimental channels. And now, when he was doing his best to reason it out that they were twin souls who had been brought together by a destiny which it would be foolish to struggle against, when he was trying to convey the impression that fate had designed them for each other, she said, 'Why?' It was hard.

He was about to go deeper into the matter, when, from the direction of the Castle, he perceived the Hon. Freddie's valet, Mr. Judson, approaching. That it was this repellent young man's object to break in upon them and rob him of his one small chance of inducing Joan to appreciate as he did the mysterious workings of Providence as they affected herself and him was obvious. There was no mistaking the valet's desire for conversation. He had the air of one brimming over with speech. His wonted indolence was cast aside, and as he drew nearer, he positively ran. He was talking before he reached them.

'Miss Simpson, Mr. Marson, it's true. What I said that night. It's a fact.'

Ashe regarded this intruder with a malevolent eye. Never fond of Mr. Judson, he looked on him now with positive loathing. It had not been easy for him to work himself up to the point where he could discuss with Joan the mysterious ways of Providence, for there was that about her which made it hard to achieve sentiment. That indefinable something in Joan Valentine which made for nocturnal raids on other people's museums also rendered her a somewhat difficult person to talk to about twin souls and destiny. The qualities that Ashe loved in her, her strength, her capability, her valiant self-sufficingness, were the very qualities which seemed to check him when he tried to tell her that he loved them.

Mr. Judson was still babbling.

'It's true. There ain't a doubt of it now. It's been and happened just as I said that night.'

'What did you say – which night?' inquired Ashe.

'That night at dinner, the first night you two came here. Don't you remember me talking about Freddie and the girl he used to write letters to in London, the girl I said was so like you, Miss Simpson? What was her name again? Joan Valentine. That was it. The girl at the theatre that Freddie used to send me with letters to pretty nearly every evening. Well, she's been and done it, same as I told you all that night that she was jolly likely to go and do. She's sticking young Freddie up for his letters, just as he ought to have known she would do if he hadn't been a young fat-head. They're all alike these girls, every one of them.'

Mr. Judson paused, subjected the surrounding scenery to a cautious scrutiny, and resumed.

'I took a suit of Freddie's clothes away to brush just now, and happening' – Mr. Judson paused and gave a little cough – 'happening to glance at the contents of his pockets, I came across a letter. I took a sort of look at it before setting it aside, and it was from a fellow named Jones, and it said that this girl Valentine was sticking on to young Freddie's letters what he'd written her and would see him blowed if she parted with them under another thousand. And, as I made it out, Freddie had already given her five hundred. Where he got it is more than I can understand, but that's what the letter said. This fellow Jones said that he had passed it to her with his own hands, but she wasn't satisfied, and if she didn't get the other thousand she was going to bring an action for breach. And now Freddie has given me a note to take to this Jones, who is stopping in Market Blandings.'

Joan had listened to this remarkable speech with a stunned amazement. At this point she made her first comment.

'But that can't be true.'

'Saw the letter with my own eyes, Miss Simpson.'

'But—'

She looked at Ashe helplessly. Their eyes met, hers wide with perplexity, his bright with the light of comprehension.

'It shows,' said Ashe slowly, 'that he was in immediate and urgent need of money.'

'You bet it does,' said Mr. Judson with relish. 'It looks to me as if young Freddie had about reached the end of his tether this time. My word, there won't half be a kick-up if she does sue him for breach. I'm off to tell Mr. Beach and the rest. They'll jump out of their skins.' His face fell. 'Oh, Lord, I was forgetting this note. He told me to take it at once.'

'I'll take it for you,' said Ashe. 'I'm not doing anything.'

Mr. Judson's gratitude was effusive.

'You're a good feller, Marson,' he said. 'I'll do as much for you another time. I couldn't hardly bear not to tell a bit of news like this right away. I should burst or something.'

And Mr. Judson, with shining face, hurried off to the house-keeper's room.

'I simply can't understand it,' said Joan at length. 'My head's going round.'

'Can't understand it? Why, it's perfectly clear. This is the coincidence for which, in my capacity of Gridley Quayle, I was waiting. I can now resume inductive reasoning. Weighing the evidence, what do we find? That young sweep Freddie is the man. *He* has the scarab.'

'But it's all such a muddle. I'm not holding his letters.'

'For Jones' purposes you are. Let's get this Jones element in the affair straightened out. What do you know of him?'

'He was an enormously fat man who came to see me one night and said that he had been sent to get back some letters. I told him I had destroyed them ages ago, and he went away.'

'Well, that part of it is clear, then. He is working a simple but ingenious game on Freddie. It wouldn't succeed with every one, I suppose, but, from what I have seen and heard of him, Freddie isn't strong on intellect. He seems to have accepted the story without a murmur. What does he do? He has to raise a thousand pounds immediately, and the raising of the first five hundred has exhausted his credit. He gets the idea of stealing the scarab.'

'But why? Why should he have thought of the scarab at all? That is what I can't understand. He couldn't have meant to give it to Mr. Peters and claim the reward. He couldn't have known that Mr. Peters was offering a reward. He couldn't have known that Lord Emsworth had not got the scarab quite properly. He couldn't have known – he couldn't have known anything.'

Ashe's enthusiasm was a trifle damped.

'There's something in that. But – I have it. Jones must have known about the scarab and told him.'

'But how could he have known?'

'Yes, there's something in that, too. How could Jones have known?'

'He couldn't. He had gone by the time Aline came that night.'

'I don't quite understand. Which night?'

'It was the night of the day I first met you. I was wondering for a moment whether he could by any chance have overheard Aline telling me about the scarab and the reward Mr. Peters was offering for it.'

'Overheard! That word is like a bugle-blast to me. Nine out of ten of Gridley Quayle's triumphs were due to his having overheard something. I think we are now on the right track.'

'I don't. How could he have overheard us? The door was closed, and he was in the street by that time.'

'How do you know he was in the street? Did you see him out?'

'No, but he went.'

'He might have waited on the stairs – you remember how dark they were at No. 7A – and listened.'

'Why?'

Ashe reflected.

'Why? Why? What a beast of a word that is. The detective's bugbear. I thought I had got it till you said – Great Scott. I'll bet you why. I see it all. I have him with the goods. His object in coming to you about the letters was because Freddie wanted them back owing to his approaching marriage with Miss Peters, wasn't it?'

'Yes.'

'You tell him you have destroyed the letters. He goes off. Am I right?'

'Yes.'

'Before he is out of the house Miss Peters is giving her name at the front door. Put yourself in Jones' place. What does he think? He is suspicious. He thinks there is some game on. He skips upstairs again, waits till Miss Peters has gone into your room, then stands outside and listens. How about that?'

'I do believe you are right. He might quite easily have done that.'

'He did do exactly that. I know it as if I had been there. In fact, it is highly probable that I was there. You say all this happened on the night of the day we first met? I remember coming downstairs that night – I was going out to a music-hall – and hearing voices in your room. I remember it distinctly. In all probability I nearly ran into Jones.'

'It does all seem to fit in, doesn't it?'

'It's a clear case. There isn't a flaw in it. The only question is, can I, on the evidence, go to young Freddie and choke the scarab out of him? On the whole I think I had better take this note to Jones, as I promised Judson, and see if I can't work something through him. Yes, that's the best plan. I'll be starting at once.'

## III

Perhaps the greatest hardship in being an invalid is the fact that people come and see you and keep your spirits up. The Hon. Freddie Threepwood suffered extremely from this. His was not a gregarious nature, and it fatigued his limited brain-powers to have to find conversation for his numerous visitors. All he wanted was to be left alone to read the Adventures of Gridley Quayle and when tired of doing that, to lie on his back, and look at the ceiling and think of nothing. It is your dynamic person, your energetic World's Worker, who chafes at being laid up with a sprained ankle. The Hon. Freddie enjoyed it. From boyhood up, he had loved lying in bed, and now that fate had allowed him to do this without incurring rebuke, he objected to having his reveries broken in upon by officious relatives.

He spent his rare intervals of solitude in trying to decide in his mind which of his cousins, uncles and aunts was, all things considered, the greatest nuisance. Sometimes he would give the palm to Colonel Horace Mant, who struck the soldierly note ('I recollect in a hill campaign in the Winter of the year '93 giving my ankle the deuce of a twist'); anon the more spiritual attitude of the Bishop of Godalming seemed to annoy him more keenly. Sometimes he would head the list with the name of his cousin Percy, Lord Stockheath, who refused to talk of anything except his late breach-of-promise case and the effect the verdict had had on his old governor. Freddie was in no mood just now to be sympathetic with others on their breach-of-promise cases.

As he lay in bed reading on the Monday morning, the only flaw in his enjoyment of this unaccustomed solitude was the thought that presently the door was bound to open, and some kind inquirer insinuate himself into the room.

His apprehensions proved well-founded. Scarcely had he got well into the details of an ingenious plot on the part of a secret society to eliminate Gridley Quayle by bribing his cook (a bad lot) to sprinkle chopped-up horse-hair in his chicken fricassee, when the handle turned, and Ashe Marson came in.

Freddie was not the only person who had found the influx of visitors into the sick-room a source of irritation. The fact that the invalid seemed unable to get a moment to himself had annoyed Ashe considerably. For some little time he had hung about the passage in which Freddie's room was situated, full of enterprise but unable to make a forward move owing to the throng of sympathizers. What he had to say to the sufferer could not be said in the presence of a third party.

Freddie's sensation, on perceiving him, was one of relief. He had been half afraid that it was the Bishop. He recognized Ashe as the valet chappie who had helped him to bed on the occasion of his accident. It might be that he had come in a respectful way to make inquiries but he was not likely to stop long. He nodded, and went on reading.

And then, glancing up, he perceived Ashe standing beside the bed, fixing him with a piercing stare.

The Hon. Freddie hated piercing stares. One of the reasons why he objected to being left alone with his future father-in-law, Mr. Preston Peters, was that Nature had given the millionaire a penetrating pair of eyes, and the stress of business life in New York had developed in him a habit of boring holes in people with them. A young man had to have a stronger nerve and a clearer conscience than the Hon. Freddie to enjoy a *tête-à-tête* with Mr. Peters.

But, while he accepted Aline's father as a necessary evil and recognized that his position entitled him to look at people as sharply as he liked, whatever their feelings, he was hanged if he was going to extend this privilege to Mr. Peters' valet. This man standing beside him was giving him a look which seemed to his sensitive imagination to have been fired red-hot from a gun; and this annoyed and exasperated Freddie.

'What do you want?' he said querulously. 'What are you staring at me like that for?'

Ashe sat down, leaned his elbows on the bed, and applied the look again, from a lower elevation.

'Ah!' he said.

Whatever may have been Ashe's defects as far as the handling of the inductive-reasoning side of Gridley Quayle's character was concerned, there was one scene in each of his stories in which he never failed. That was the scene in the last chapter where Quayle, confronting his quarry, unmasked him. Quayle might have floundered in the earlier part of the story, but in his big scene he was exactly right. He was curt, brisk and mercilessly compelling. Ashe, rehearsing this interview in the passage before his entry, had decided that he could hardly do better than model himself on the detective. So he began to be curt, crisp and mercilessly compelling to Freddie; and after the first few sentences he had that youth gasping for air.

'I will tell you,' he said. 'If you can spare me a few moments of your valuable time, I will put the facts before you. Yes, press that bell, if you wish, and I will put them before witnesses. Lord Emsworth will no doubt be pleased to learn that his son, whom he trusted, is – a thief.'

Freddie's hand fell limply. The bell remained untouched. His mouth opened to its fullest extent. In the midst of his panic he had a curious feeling that he had heard or read that last sentence somewhere before. Then he remembered, those very words occurred in *Gridley Quayle, Investigator. The Adventure of the Blue Ruby.*

'What – what do you mean?' he stammered.

'I will tell you what I mean. On Saturday night a valuable

scarab was stolen from Lord Emsworth's private museum. The case was put into my hands—'

'Great Scott! Are you a detective?'

'Ah!' said Ashe.

Life, as many a worthy writer has pointed out, is full of ironies. It seemed to Freddie that here was a supreme example of this fact. All these years he had wanted to meet a detective, and now that his wish had been gratified the detective was detecting *him*.

'The case,' continued Ashe severely, 'was placed in my hands. I investigated it. I discovered that you were in urgent and immediate need of money.'

'How on earth did you do that?'

'Ah!' said Ashe. 'I further discovered that you were in communication with an individual named Jones.'

'Good lord! How?'

Ashe smiled quietly.

'Yesterday I had a talk with this man Jones, who is staying in Market Blandings. Why is he staying in Market Blandings? Because he had a reason for keeping in touch with you. Because you were about to transfer to his care something which you could get possession of but which only he could dispose of. The scarab.'

The Hon. Freddie was beyond speech. He made no comment on this statement. Ashe continued.

'I interviewed this man Jones. I said to him, "I am in the Hon. Frederick Threepwood's confidence, I know everything. Have you any instruction for me?" He replied, "What do you know?" I answered, "I know that the Hon. Frederick Threepwood has something which he wishes to hand to you, but which he has been unable to hand to you owing to having had an accident and being confined to his room." He then told me to tell you to let him have the scarab by messenger.'

Freddie pulled himself together with an effort. He was in sore straits, but he saw one last chance. His researches in detective fiction had given him the knowledge that detectives occasionally relaxed their austerity when dealing with a deserving case. Even Gridley Quayle could sometimes be softened by a pathetic story. Freddie could recall half a dozen times when a detected criminal had been spared by him because he had done it all from the best motives. He determined to throw himself on Ashe's mercy.

'I say, you know,' he said ingratiatingly, 'I think it's bally marvellous the way you've deduced everything and so forth.'

'Well?'

'But I believe you would chuck it, if you heard my side of the case.'

'I know your side of the case. You think you are being blackmailed by a Miss Valentine for some letters you once wrote her. You are not. Miss Valentine has destroyed the letters. She told the man Jones so when he went to see her in London. He kept your five hundred pounds, and is trying to get another thousand out of you under false pretences!'

'What! You can't be right.'

'I am always right.'

'You must be mistaken.'

'I am never mistaken.'

'But how do you know?'

'I have my sources of information.'

'She isn't going to sue me for breach?'

'She never had any intention of doing so.'

The Hon. Frederick sank back on the pillows.

'Good egg!' he said with fervour. He beamed happily. 'This,' he observed, 'is a bit of all right.'

'Never mind that,' said Ashe. 'Give me the scarab. Where is it?'

'What are you going to do with it?'

'Restore it to its rightful owner.'

'Are you going to give me away to the governor?'

'I am not.'

'It strikes me,' said Freddie gratefully, 'that you are a dashed good sort. You seem to me to have the makings of an absolute topper! It's under the mattress. I had it on me when I fell downstairs, and I had to shove it in there.'

Ashe drew it out. He stood looking at it, absorbed. He could hardly believe that his quest was at an end, and that a small fortune lay in the palm of his hand.

Freddie was eyeing him admiringly.

'You know,' he said, 'I've always wanted to meet a detective. What beats me is how you chappies find out things.'

'We have our methods.'

'I believe you. You're a blooming marvel! What first put you on my track?'

'That,' said Ashe, 'would take too long to explain. Of course I had to do some tense inductive reasoning. But I could not trace every link in the chain for you. It would be tedious.'

'Not to me.'

'Some other time.'

'I say, I wonder if you've ever read any of these things, these Gridley Quayle stories? I know them by heart.'

With the scarab safely in his pocket, Ashe could contemplate the brightly-coloured volume which the other extended towards him without active repulsion. Already he was beginning to feel a sort of sentiment for the depressing Quayle, as for something that had once formed part of his life.

'Do you read these things?'

'I should say I did.'

'I write them.'

There are certain supreme moments which cannot be adequately described. Freddie's appreciation of the fact that such a moment had occurred in his life expressed itself in a startled cry and a convulsive movement of all his limbs. He shot up from the pillows and gaped at Ashe.

'You write them? You don't mean *write* them?'

'Yes.'

'Great Scott!'

He would have gone on, doubtless, to say more, but at this moment voices made themselves heard outside the door. There was a movement of feet. Then the door opened, and a small procession entered.

It was headed by the Earl of Emsworth. Following him, came Mr. Peters. And in the wake of the millionaire Colonel Horace Mant and the Efficient Baxter. They filed into the room, and stood by the bedside. Ashe seized the opportunity to slip out.

Freddie glanced at the deputation without interest. His mind was occupied with other matters. He supposed that they had come to inquire after his ankle, and he was mildly thankful that they had come in a body instead of one by one. The deputation grouped itself about the bed, and shuffled its feet. There was an atmosphere of awkwardness.

'Er, Frederick,' said Lord Emsworth. 'Freddie, my boy.'

Mr. Peters fiddled dumbly with the coverlet, Colonel Mant cleared his throat. The Efficient Baxter scowled.

'Er, Freddie, my dear boy, I fear that we have a painful – ah – duty to perform.'

The words struck straight home at the Hon. Freddie's guilty

conscience. Had they, too, tracked him down, and was he now to be accused of having stolen that infernal scarab! A wave of relief swept over him as he realized that he had got rid of the thing. A decent chappie like that detective would not give him away. All he had to do was to keep his head and stick to stout denial. That was the game. Stout denial.

'I don't know what you mean,' he said defensively.

'Of course you don't, dash it,' said Colonel Mant. 'We're coming to that. And I should like to begin by saying that, though in a sense it was my fault, I fail to see how I could have acted—'

'Horace.'

'Oh, very well. I was only trying to explain.'

Lord Emsworth adjusted his pince-nez, and sought inspiration from the wallpaper.

'Freddie, my boy,' he began, 'we have a somewhat unpleasant – a somewhat – ah – disturbing. . . . We are compelled to break it to you. . . . We are all most pained and astounded and . . .'

The Efficient Baxter spoke. It was plain that he was in a bad temper.

'Miss Peters,' he snapped, 'has eloped with your friend Emerson.'

Lord Emsworth breathed a sigh of relief.

'Exactly, Baxter. Precisely. You have put the thing in a nut-shell. Really, my dear fellow, you are invaluable.'

All eyes searched Freddie's face for signs of uncontrollable emotion. The deputation waited anxiously for his first grief-stricken cry.

'Eh, what?' said Freddie.

'It is quite true, Freddie, my dear boy. She went to London with him on the ten-fifty.'

'And, if I had not been forcibly restrained,' said Baxter acidly, casting a vindictive look at Colonel Mant, 'I could have prevented it.'

Colonel Mant cleared his throat again, and put a hand to his moustache.

'I'm afraid that is true, Freddie. It was a most unfortunate misunderstanding. I'll tell you how it happened. I chanced to be at the station bookstall when the train came in. Mr. Baxter was also in the station. The train pulled up, and this young fellow Emerson got in. Said goodbye to us, don't you know, and got in. Just as the train was about to start, Miss Peters, exclaiming, "George, dear, I'm coming with you, dash it," or some such speech, proceeded to go hell for leather for the door of young Emerson's compartment. Upon which—'

'Upon which,' interrupted Baxter, 'I made a spring to try and catch her. Apart from any other consideration, the train was already moving, and Miss Peters ran a considerable risk of injury. I had hardly moved when I felt a violent perk at my ankle and fell to the ground. After I had recovered from the shock, which was not immediately, I found—'

'The fact is, Freddie, my boy, I acted under a misapprehension. Nobody can be sorrier for the mistake than I, but recent events in this house had left me with the impression that Mr. Baxter here was not quite responsible for his actions. Overwork or something, I imagined. I have seen it happen so often in India, don't you know, where fellows run amuck and kick up the deuce's own delight. I am bound to admit that I have been watching Mr. Baxter rather closely lately, in the expectation that something of this very kind might happen. Of course, I now realize my mistake, and I have apologized – apologized humbly, dash it. But at the moment I was firmly under the impression that our friend here had had an attack of some kind, and was about to inflict injuries on Miss Peters. If I've seen it happen once in India, I've seen it happen a dozen times. I recollect in the hot weather of the year '92 – or was it '93? – I think '93 – one of my native bearers. . . . However, I sprang forward and caught the crook of my walking stick in Mr. Baxter's ankle and brought him down. And by the time the explanations were made, it was too late. The train had gone, with Miss Peters in it.'

'And a telegram has just arrived,' said Lord Emsworth, 'to say that they are being married this afternoon at a registrar's. The whole occurrence is most disturbing.'

'Bear it like a man, my boy,' urged Colonel Mant.

To all appearances, Freddie was bearing it magnificently. Not a single exclamation, either of wrath or pain, had escaped his lips. One would have said that the shock had stunned him or that he had not heard, for his face expressed no emotion whatsoever.

The fact was that the story had made very little impression on the Hon. Freddie of any sort. His relief at Ashe's news about Joan Valentine, the stunning joy of having met in the flesh the author of the Adventures of Gridley Quayle, the general feeling that all was now right with the world – these things deprived him of the ability to be greatly distressed.

And there was a distinct feeling of relief, actual relief, that now it would not be necessary for him to get married. He had liked Aline, but, whenever he had really thought of it, the prospect of getting married had rather appalled him. A chappie looked such an ass getting married. . . .

It appeared, however, that some verbal comment on the state of affairs was required of him. He searched in his mind for something adequate.

'You mean to say Aline has bolted with Emerson?'

The deputation nodded painful nods. Freddie searched in his mind again. The deputation held its breath.

'Well, I'm blowed,' said Freddie. 'Fancy that!'

## IV

Mr. Peters walked heavily into his room. Ashe Marson was waiting for him there. He eyed Ashe dully.

'Pack,' he said.

'Pack?'

'Pack. We're getting out of here by the afternoon train.'

'Has anything happened?'

'My daughter has eloped with Emerson.'

'What!'

'Don't stand there saying "What!" Pack.'

Ashe put his hand in his pocket.

'Where shall I put this?' he asked.

For a moment Mr. Peters looked without comprehension at what he was holding out, then his whole demeanour altered. His eyes lit up. He uttered a howl of pure rapture.

'You got it!'

'I got it.'

'Where was it? Who had taken it? How did you choke it out of them? How did you find it? Who had it?'

'I don't know whether I ought to say. I don't want to start anything. You won't tell anyone?'

'Tell anyone? What do you take me for? Do you think I am going about advertising this? If I can sneak out without that fellow Baxter jumping on my back, I shall be satisfied. You can take it from me that there won't be any sensational exposures if I can help it. Who had it?'

'Young Threepwood.'

'Threepwood? What did he want it for?'

'He needed money, and he was going to raise it on this.'

Mr. Peters exploded.

'And I have been kicking because Aline can't marry him, and has gone off with a regular fellow like young Emerson. He's a good boy, young Emerson. He'll make a name for himself one of these days. He's got get-up in him. And I have been wanting to shoot him because he has taken Aline away from that goggle-eyed chump up in bed there. Why, if she had married Threepwood, I should have had grandchildren who would have sneaked my watch while I was dancing them on my knee. There is a taint of some sort in the whole family. Father sneaks my Cheops, and sonny sneaks it from father. What a gang! And the best blood in England. If that's England's idea of good blood, give me Kalamazoo. This settles it, I was a chump ever to come to a country like this. Property isn't safe over here. I'm going back to America on the next boat.

'Where's my cheque-book? I'm going to write you out that cheque right away. You've earned it. Listen, young man, I don't know what your ideas are, but if you aren't chained to this country, I'd make it worth your while to stay on with me. They say no one's indispensible, but you come mighty near it. If I had you at my elbow for a few years, I'd get right back into shape. I'm feeling better now than I felt in years, and you've only just started in on me. How about it? You can call yourself what you like – secretary or trainer or whatever suits you best. What you will be is the fellow who makes me take exercise and stop smoking cigars and generally looks after me. How do you feel about it?'

It was a proposition which appealed both to Ashe's commercial and to his missionary instincts. His only regret had been that, the scarab recovered, he and Mr. Peters would now, he supposed, part company. He had not liked the idea of sending the millionaire back to the world a half-cured man. Already he had begun to look upon him in the light of a piece of creative work, to which he had just set his hand.

But the thought of Joan gave him pause. If this meant separation from Joan, it was not to be considered.

'Let me think it over,' he said.

'Well, think quick,' said Mr. Peters.

## V

It is said by those who have been through fires, earthquakes and shipwrecks, that in such times of stress the social barriers are temporarily broken down, and the spectacle may be seen of persons of the highest social standing speaking quite freely to persons who are not in Society at all, and of quite nice people addressing others to whom they have never been introduced. The news of Aline Peters' elopement with George Emerson, carried beyond the green baize door by Slingsby, the chauffeur, produced very much the same state of affairs in the servants' quarters at Blandings Castle.

It was not only that Slingsby was permitted to penetrate into the housekeeper's room and tell his story to his social superiors there, though that was an absolutely unprecedented occurrence; what was really extraordinary was that mere menials discussed the affair with the personal ladies and gentlemen of the Castle guests, and were allowed to do so uncrushed. James, the footman, that pushing individual, actually shoved his way into the room, and was heard by witnesses to remark to no less a person than Mr. Beach that it was a bit thick. And it is on record that his fellow-footman, Alfred, meeting the Groom of the Chambers in the passage outside, positively prodded him in the lower ribs, winked, and said, 'What a day we're having.' One has to go back to the worst excesses of the French Revolution to parallel these outrages.

It was held by Mr. Beach and Mrs. Twemlow afterwards that the social fabric of the Castle never fully recovered from this upheaval. It may be that they took an extreme view of the matter, but it cannot be denied that it wrought changes. The rise of Slingsby is a case in point. Until this affair took place, the chauffeur's standing had never been satisfactorily settled. Mr. Beach and Mrs. Twemlow led the party which considered that he was merely a species of coachman, but there was another smaller group which, dazzled by Slingsby's personality, openly declared that it was not right that he should take his meals in the Servants' Hall with such admitted plebians as the odd man and the Steward's Room footman. The Aline-George elopement settled the point once and for all. Slingsby had carried George's bag to the train. Slingsby had been standing a few yards from the spot where Aline began her dash for the carriage door. Slingsby was able to exhibit the actual half-sovereign which George had tipped him, only five minutes before the great event. To send such a public man back to the Servants' Hall was impossible. By unspoken consent the chauffeur dined that night in the Steward's Room, from which he was never again dislodged.

Mr. Judson alone stood apart from the throng which clustered about the chauffeur. He was suffering the bitterness of the supplanted. A brief while before, and he had been the central figure with his story of the letter which he had found in the Hon. Freddie's coat pocket. Now the importance of his story had been engulfed in that of this later and greater sensation, and Mr. Judson was learning for the first time on what unstable foundations popularity stands.

Joan was nowhere to be seen. In none of the spots where she might have been expected to be at such a time was she to be found. Ashe had almost given up the search when, going to the back door and looking out as a last chance, he perceived her walking slowly on the gravel drive.

She greeted Ashe with a smile, but something was plainly troubling her. She did not speak for a moment, and they walked side by side.

'What is it?' said Ashe at length. 'What is the matter?'

She looked at him gravely.

'Gloom,' she said. 'Despondency, Mr. Marson. A sort of flat feeling. Don't you hate things happening?'

'I don't quite understand!'

'Well, this affair of Aline, for instance. It's so big. It makes you feel as if the whole world had altered. I should like nothing to happen, ever, and life just to jog peacefully along. That's not the gospel I preached to you in Arundell Street, it is? I thought I was an advanced apostle of action. But I seem to have changed. I'm afraid I should never be able to make it clear what I do mean. I only know what I feel as if I had grown suddenly old. These things are such milestones. Already I am beginning to look on the time before Aline behaved so sensationally as terribly remote. Tomorrow it will be worse, and the day after that worse still. I can see that you don't in the least understand what I mean.'

'Yes, I do. Or I think I do. What it comes to, in a few words, is that somebody you were fond of has gone out of your life. Is that it?'

Joan nodded.

'Yes. At least, that is partly it. I didn't really know Aline particularly well, beyond having been at school with her, but you're right. It's not so much what has happened as what it represents that matters. This elopement has marked the end of a phase of my life. I think I have it now. My life has been such a series of jerks. I dash along, then something happens which stops that bit of my life with a jerk, and then I have to start over again – a new bit. I think I'm getting tired of jerks. I want something stodgy and continuous. I'm like one of the old bus horses who could go on for ever if people got off without making them stop. It's the having to get the bus moving again that wears one out. This little section of my life since we came here is over, and it is finished for good. I've got to start the bus going again on a new road and with a new set of passengers. I wonder if the old horses used to be sorry when they dropped one set of passengers and took on a lot of strangers?'

A sudden dryness invaded Ashe's throat. He tried to speak, but found no words. Joan went on.

'Do you ever get moods when life seems absolutely meaning-less? It's like a badly-constructed story, with all sorts of characters moving in and out who have nothing to do with the plot. And, when somebody comes along who you think really has something to do with the plot, he suddenly drops out. After a while you begin to wonder what the story is about, and you feel that it's about nothing – just a jumble.'

'There is one thing,' said Ashe, 'that knits it together.'

'What is that?'

'The love interest.'

Their eyes met, and suddenly there descended upon Ashe confidence. He felt cool and alert, sure of himself, as in the old days he had felt when he ran races and, the nerve-racking hours of waiting past, he listened for the starter's gun. Subconsciously he was aware that he had always been a little afraid of Joan, and that now he was no longer afraid.

'Joan, will you marry me?'

Her eyes wandered from his face. He waited.

'I wonder,' she said softly. 'You think that is the solution?'

'Yes.'

'How can you tell?' she broke out. 'We scarcely know each other. I shan't always be in this mood. I may get restless again. I may find that it is the jerks that I really like.'

'You won't.'

'You're very confident.'

'I am absolutely confident.'

'"She travels the fastest who travels alone,"' misquoted Joan.

'What is the good,' said Ashe, 'of travelling fast if you're going round in a circle? I know how you feel. I've felt the same myself. You are an individualist. You think that there is something tremendous just round the corner, and that you can get it if you try hard enough. There isn't. Or, if there is, it isn't worth getting. Life is nothing but a mutual aid association. I am going to help old Peters; you are going to help me; I am going to help you.'

'Help me to do what?'

'Make life coherent instead of a jumble.'

'Mr. Marson——'

'Don't call me Mr. Marson.'

'Ashe, you don't know what you are doing. You don't know me. I've been knocking about the world for five years, and I'm hard – hard right through. I should make you wretched.'

'You are not in the least hard, and you know it. Listen to me,

Joan. Where's your sense of fairness? You crash into my life, turn it upside down, dig me out of my quiet groove, revolutionize my whole existence, and now you propose to drop me and pay no further attention to me. Is it fair?'

'But I don't. We shall always be the best of friends.'

'We shall. But we will get married first.'

'You are determined?'

'I am.'

Joan laughed happily.

'How perfectly splendid. I was terrified lest I might have made you change your mind. I had to say all I did, to preserve my self-respect after proposing to you. Yes, I did. But strange it is that men never seem to understand a woman, however plainly she talks. You don't think I was really worrying because I had lost Aline, do you? I thought I was going to lose you, and it made me miserable. You couldn't expect me to say so in so many words, but I thought you guessed. I practically said it. Ashe! What are you doing?'

Ashe paused for a moment to reply.

'I am kissing you,' he said.

'But you mustn't. There's a scullery-maid or something looking out of the kitchen window. She will see us.'

Ashe drew her to him.

'Scullery-maids have few pleasures,' he said. 'Theirs is a dull life. Let her see us.'

## THE END

The morning sunshine descended like an amber shower-bath on Blandings Castle, lighting up with a heartening glow its ivied walls, its rolling parks, its gardens, outhouses, and messuages, and such of its inhabitants as chanced at the moment to be taking the air. It fell on green lawns and wide terraces, on noble trees and bright flower-beds. It fell on the baggy trousers-seat of Angus McAllister, head-gardener to the ninth Earl of Emsworth, as he bent with dour Scottish determination to pluck a slug from its reverie beneath the leaf of a lettuce. It fell on the white flannels of the Hon. Freddie Threepwood, Lord Emsworth's second son, hurrying across the water-meadows. It also fell on Lord Emsworth himself and on Beach, his faithful butler. They were standing on the turret above the west wing, the former with his eye to a powerful telescope, the latter holding the hat which he had been sent to fetch.

'Beach,' said Lord Emsworth.

'M'lord?'

'I've been swindled. This dashed thing doesn't work.'

'Your lordship cannot see clearly?'

'I can't see at all, dash it. It's all black.'

The butler was an observant man.

'Perhaps if I were to remove the cap at the extremity of the instrument, m'lord, more satisfactory results might be obtained.'

'Eh? Cap? Is there a cap? So there is. Take it off, Beach.'

'Very good, m'lord.'

'Ah!' There was satisfaction in Lord Emsworth's voice. He twiddled and adjusted, and the satisfaction deepened. 'Yes, that's better. That's capital. Beach, I can see a cow.'

'Indeed, m'lord?'

'Down in the water-meadows. Remarkable. Might be two yards away. All right, Beach. Shan't want you any longer.'

'Your hat, m'lord?'

'Put it on my head.'

'Very good, m'lord.'

The butler, this kindly act performed, withdrew. Lord Emsworth continued gazing at the cow.

The ninth Earl of Emsworth was a fluffy-minded and amiable old gentleman with a fondness for new toys. Although the main interest of his life was his garden, he was always ready to try a side line, and the latest of these side lines was this telescope of his. Ordered from London in a burst of enthusiasm consequent upon the reading of an article on astronomy in a monthly magazine, it had been placed in position on the previous evening. What was now in progress was its trial trip.

Presently, the cow's audience-appeal began to wane. It was a fine cow, as cows go, but, like so many cows, it lacked sustained dramatic interest. Surfeited after awhile by the spectacle of it chewing the cud and staring glassily at nothing, Lord Emsworth decided to swivel the apparatus round in the hope of picking up something a trifle more sensational. And he was just about to do so, when into the range of his vision there came the Hon. Freddie. White and shining, he tripped along over the turf like a Theocritan shepherd hastening to keep an appointment with a nymph, and a sudden frown marred the serenity of Lord Emsworth's brow. He generally frowned when he saw Freddie, for with the passage of the years that youth had become more and more of a problem to an anxious father.

Unlike the male codfish, which, suddenly finding itself the parent of three million five hundred thousand little codfish, cheerfully resolves to love them all, the British aristocracy is apt to look with a somewhat jaundiced eye on its younger sons. And Freddie Threepwood was one of those younger sons who rather invite the jaundiced eye. It seemed to the head of the family that there was no way of coping with the boy. If he was allowed to live in London, he piled up debts and got into mischief; and when you jerked him back into the purer surroundings of Blandings Castle, he just mooned about the place, moping broodingly. Hamlet's society at Elsinore must have had much the same effect on his stepfather as did that of Freddie Threepwood at Blandings on Lord Emsworth. And it is probable that what induced the latter to keep a telescopic eye on him at this moment was the fact that his demeanour was so mysteriously jaunty, his bearing so intriguingly free from its customary crushed misery. Some inner voice whispered to Lord Emsworth that this smiling, prancing youth was up to no good and would bear watching.

The inner voice was absolutely correct. Within thirty seconds its case had been proved up to the hilt. Scarcely had his lordship had time to wish, as he invariably wished on seeing his offspring, that Freddie had been something entirely different in manners, morals and appearance, and had been the son of somebody else living a considerable distance away, when out of a small spinney near the end of the meadow there bounded a girl. And Freddie, after a cautious glance over his shoulder, immediately proceeded to fold this female in a warm embrace.

Lord Emsworth had seen enough. He tottered away from the telescope, a shattered man. One of his favourite dreams was of some nice, eligible girl, belonging to a good family, and possessing a bit of money of her own, coming along some day and taking Freddie off his hands; but that inner voice, more confident now than ever, told him that this was not she. Freddie would not sneak off in this furtive fashion to meet eligible girls, nor could he imagine any eligible girl, in her right senses, rushing into Freddie's arms in that enthusiastic way. No, there was only one explanation. In the cloistral seclusion of Blandings, far from the Metropolis with all its conveniences for that sort of thing, Freddie had managed to get himself entangled. Seething with anguish and fury, Lord Emsworth hurried down the stairs and out on to the terrace. Here he prowled like an elderly leopard waiting for feeding-time, until in due season there was a flicker of white among the trees that flanked the drive and a cheerful whistling announced the culprit's approach.

It was with a sour and hostile eye that Lord Emsworth watched his son draw near. He adjusted his pince-nez, and with their assistance was able to perceive that a fatuous smile of self-satisfaction illumined the young man's face, giving him the appearance of a beaming sheep. In the young man's buttonhole there shone a nosegay of simple meadow flowers, which, as he walked, he patted from time to time with a loving hand.

'Frederick!' bellowed his lordship.

The villain of the piece halted abruptly. Sunk in a roseate trance, he had not observed his father. But such was the sunniness of his mood that even this encounter could not damp him. He gambolled happily up.

'Hullo, guv'nor!' he carolled. He searched in his mind for a pleasant topic of conversation – always a matter of some little difficulty on these occasions. 'Lovely day, what?'

His lordship was not to be diverted into a discussion of the weather. He drew a step nearer, looking like the man who smothered the young princes in the Tower.

'Frederick,' he demanded, 'who was that girl?'

The Hon. Freddie started convulsively. He appeared to be swallowing with difficulty something large and jagged.

'Girl?' he quavered. 'Girl? Girl, guv'nor?'

'That girl I saw you kissing ten minutes ago down in the water-meadows.'

'Oh!' said Hon. Freddie. He paused. 'Oh, ah!' He paused again. 'Oh, ah, yes! I've been meaning to tell you about that, guv'nor.'

'You have, have you?'

'All perfectly correct, you know. Oh, yes, indeed! All most absolutely correct-o! Nothing fishy, I mean to say, or anything like that. She's my *fiancée*.'

A sharp howl escaped Lord Emsworth, as if one of the bees humming in the lavender-beds had taken time off to sting him in the neck.

'Who is she?' he boomed. 'Who is this woman?'

'Her name's Donaldson.'

'Who is she?'

'Aggie Donaldson. Aggie's short for Niagara. Her people spent their honeymoon at the Falls, she tells me. She's American and all that. Rummy names they give kids in America,' proceeded Freddie, with hollow chattiness. 'I mean to say! Niagara! I ask you!'

'Who is she?'

'She's most awfully bright, you know. Full of beans. You'll love her.'

'Who is she?'

'And can play the saxophone.'

'Who,' demanded Lord Emsworth for the sixth time, 'is she? And where did you meet her?'

Freddie coughed. The information, he perceived, could no longer be withheld, and he was keenly alive to the fact that it scarcely fell into the class of tidings of great joy.

'Well, as a matter of fact, guv'nor, she's a sort of cousin of Angus McAllister's. She's come over to England for a visit, don't you know, and is staying with the old boy. That's how I happened to run across her.'

Lord Emsworth's eyes bulged and he gargled faintly. He had had many unpleasant visions of his son's future, but they had never included one of him walking down the aisle with a sort of cousin of his head-gardener.

'Oh!' he said. 'Oh, indeed?'

'That's the strength of it, guv'nor.'

Lord Emsworth threw his arms up, as if calling on Heaven to witness a good man's persecution, and shot off along the terrace at a rapid trot. Having ranged the grounds for some minutes, he ran his quarry to earth at the entrance to the yew valley.

The head-gardener turned at the sound of his footsteps. He was a sturdy man of medium height, with eyebrows that would have fitted a bigger forehead. These, added to a red and wiry beard, gave him a formidable and uncompromising expression. Honesty Angus McAllister's face had in full measure, and also intelligence; but it was a bit short on sweetness and light.

'McAllister,' said his lordship, plunging without preamble into the matter of his discourse. 'That girl. You must send her away.'

A look of bewilderment clouded such of Mr. McAllister's features as were not concealed behind his beard and eyebrows.

'Gurrul?'

'That girl who is staying with you. She must go!'

'Gae where?'

Lord Emsworth was not in the mood to be finicky about details.

'Anywhere,' he said. 'I won't have her here a day longer.'

'Why?' inquired Mr. McAllister, who liked to thresh these things out.

'Never mind why. You must send her away immediately.'

Mr. McAllister mentioned an insuperable objection.

'She's payin' me twa poon' a week,' he said simply.

Lord Emsworth did not grind his teeth, for he was not given to that form of displaying emotion; but he leaped some ten inches into the air and dropped his pince-nez. And, though normally a fair-minded and reasonable man, well aware that modern earls must think twice before pulling the feudal stuff on their *employés*, he took on the forthright truculence of a large landowner of the early Norman period ticking off a serf.

'Listen, McAllister! Listen to me! Either you send that girl away to-day or you can go yourself. I mean it!'

A curious expression came into Angus McAllister's face – always excepting the occupied territories. It was the look of a man who has not forgotten Bannockburn, a man conscious of belonging to the country of William Wallace and Robert the Bruce. He made Scotch noises at the back of his throat.

'Y'r lorrudsheep will accept ma notis,' he said, with formal dignity.

'I'll pay you a month's wages in lieu of notice and you will leave this afternoon,' retorted Lord Emsworth with spirit.

'Mphm!' said Mr. McAllister.

Lord Emsworth left the battle-field with a feeling of pure exhilaration, still in the grip of the animal fury of conflict. No twinge of remorse did he feel at the thought that Angus McAllister had served him faithfully for ten years. Nor did it cross his mind that he might miss McAllister.

But that night, as he sat smoking his after-dinner cigarette, Reason, so violently expelled, came stealing timidly back to her throne, and a cold hand seemed suddenly placed upon his heart.

With Angus McAllister gone, how would the pumpkin fare?

The importance of this pumpkin in the Earl of Emsworth's life requires, perhaps, a word of explanation. Every ancient family in England has some little gap in its scroll of honour, and that of Lord Emsworth was no exception. For generations back his ancestors had been doing notable deeds; they had sent out from Blandings Castle statesmen and warriors, governors and leaders of the people: but they had not – in the opinion of the present holder of the title – achieved a full hand. However splendid the family record might appear at first sight, the fact remained that no Earl of Emsworth had ever won a first prize for pumpkins at the Shrewsbury Show. For roses, yes. For tulips, true. For spring onions, granted. But not for pumpkins; and Lord Emsworth felt it deeply.

For many a summer past he had been striving indefatigably to remove this blot on the family escutcheon, only to see his hopes go tumbling down. But this year at last victory had seemed in sight, for there had been vouchsafed to Blandings a competitor of such amazing parts that his lordship, who had watched it grow practically from a pip, could not envisage failure. Surely, he told himself as he gazed on its golden roundness, even Sir

Gregory Parsloe-Parsloe, of Matchingham Hall, winner for three successive years, would never be able to produce anything to challenge this superb vegetable.

And it was this supreme pumpkin whose welfare he feared he had jeopardized by dismissing Angus McAllister. For Angus was its official trainer. He understood the pumpkin. Indeed, in his reserved Scottish way, he even seemed to love it. With Angus gone, what would the harvest be?

Such were the meditations of Lord Emsworth as he reviewed the position of affairs. And though, as the days went by, he tried to tell himself that Angus McAllister was not the only man in the world who understood pumpkins, and that he had every confidence, the most complete and unswerving confidence, in Robert Barker, recently Angus's second-in-command, now promoted to the post of head-gardener and custodian of the Blandings Hope, he knew that this was but shallow bravado. When you are a pumpkin-owner with a big winner in your stable, you judge men by hard standards, and every day it became plainer that Robert Barker was only a makeshift. Within a week Lord Emsworth was pining for Angus McAllister.

It might be purely imagination, but to his excited fancy the pumpkin seemed to be pining for Angus too. It appeared to be drooping and losing weight. Lord Emsworth could not rid himself of the horrible idea that it was shrinking. And on the tenth night after McAllister's departure he dreamed a strange dream. He had gone with King George to show his Gracious Majesty the pumpkin, promising him the treat of a lifetime; and, when they arrived, there in the corner of the frame was a shrivelled thing the size of a pea. He woke, sweating, with his sovereign's disappointed screams ringing in his ears; and Pride

P.G. WODEHOUSE

gave its last quiver and collapsed. To reinstate Angus would be a surrender, but it must be done.

'Beach,' he said that morning at breakfast, 'do you happen to – er – to have McAllister's address?'

'Yes, your lordship,' replied the butler. 'He is in London, residing at number eleven Buxton Crescent.'

'Buxton Crescent? Never heard of it.'

'It is, I fancy, your lordship, a boarding-house or some such establishment off the Cromwell Road. McAllister was accustomed to make it his headquarters whenever he visited the Metropolis on account of its handiness for Kensington Gardens. He liked,' said Beach with respectful reproach, for Angus had been a friend of his for nine years, 'to be near the flowers, your lordship.'

Two telegrams, passing through it in the course of the next twelve hours, caused some gossip at the post-office of the little town of Market Blandings.

The first ran:

> McAllister,
> 11, Buxton Crescent,
> Cromwell Road,
> London.
> Return immediately. – Emsworth.

The second:

> Lord Emsworth,
> Blandings Castle,
> Shropshire.
> I will not. – McAllister.

272

Lord Emsworth had one of those minds capable of accommodating but one thought at a time – if that; and the possibility that Angus McAllister might decline to return had not occurred to him. It was difficult to adjust himself to this new problem, but he managed it at last. Before nightfall he had made up his mind. Robert Barker, that broken reed, could remain in charge for another day or so, and meanwhile he would go up to London and engage a real head-gardener, the finest head-gardener that money could buy.

It was the opinion of Dr. Johnson that there is in London all that life can afford. A man, he held, who is tired of London is tired of life itself. Lord Emsworth, had he been aware of this statement, would have contested it warmly. He hated London. He loathed its crowds, its smells, its noises; its omnibuses, its taxis, and its hard pavements. And, in addition to all its other defects, the miserable town did not seem able to produce a single decent head-gardener. He went from agency to agency, interviewing candidates, and not one of them came within a mile of meeting his requirements. He disliked their faces, he distrusted their references. It was a harsh thing to say of any man, but he was dashed if the best of them was even as good as Robert Barker.

It was, therefore, in a black and soured mood that his lordship, having lunched frugally at the Senior Conservative Club on the third day of his visit, stood on the steps in the sunshine, wondering how on earth he was to get through the afternoon. He had spent the morning rejecting head-gardeners, and the next batch was not due until the morrow. And what – besides rejecting head-gardeners – was there for a man of reasonable tastes to do with his time in this hopeless town?

And then there came into his mind a remark which Beach the butler had made at the breakfast-table about flowers in Kensington Gardens. He could go to Kensington Gardens and look at the flowers.

He was about to hail a taxi-cab from the rank down the street when there suddenly emerged from the Hotel Magnificent over the way a young man. This young man proceeded to cross the road, and, as he drew near, it seemed to Lord Emsworth that there was about his appearance something oddly familiar. He started for a long instant before he could believe his eyes, then with a wordless cry bounded down the steps just as the other started to mount them.

'Oh, hullo, guv'nor!' ejaculated the Hon. Freddie, plainly startled.

'What – what are you doing here?' demanded Lord Emsworth.

He spoke with heat, and justly so. London, as the result of several spirited escapades which still rankled in the mind of a father who had had to foot the bills, was forbidden ground to Freddie.

The young man was plainly not at his ease. He had the air of one who is being pushed towards dangerous machinery in which he is loath to become entangled. He shuffled his feet for a moment, then raised his left shoe and rubbed the back of his right calf with it.

'The fact is, guv'nor—'

'You know you are forbidden to come to London.'

'Absolutely, guv'nor, but the fact is—'

'And why anybody but an imbecile should want to come to London when he could be at Blandings—'

'I know, guv'nor, but the fact is—' Here Freddie, having replaced his wandering foot on the pavement, raised the other, and rubbed the back of his left calf. 'I wanted to see you,' he said. 'Yes. Particularly wanted to see you.'

This was not strictly accurate. The last thing in the world which the Hon. Freddie wanted was to see his parent. He had come to the Senior Conservative Club to leave a carefully written note. Having delivered which, it had been his intention to bolt like a rabbit. This unforeseen meeting had upset his plans.

'To see me?' said Lord Emsworth. 'Why?'

'Got – er – something to tell you. Bit of news.'

'I trust it is of sufficient importance to justify your coming to London against my express wishes.'

'Oh, yes. Oh, yes, yes yes. Oh, rather. It's dashed important. Yes – not to put too fine a point upon it – most dashed important. I say, guv'nor, are you in fairly good form to stand a bit of a shock?'

A ghastly thought rushed into Lord Emsworth's mind. Freddie's mysterious arrival – his strange manner – his odd hesitation and uneasiness – could it mean—? He clutched the young man's arm feverishly.

'Frederick! Speak! Tell me! Have the cats got at it?'

It was a fixed idea of Lord Emsworth, which no argument would have induced him to abandon, that cats had the power to work some dreadful mischief on his pumpkin and were continually lying in wait for the opportunity of doing so; and his behaviour on the occasion when one of the fast sporting set from the stables, wandering into the kitchen garden and finding him gazing at the Blandings Hope, had rubbed itself sociably against his leg, lingered long in that animal's memory.

Freddie stared.

'Cats? Why? Where? Which? What cats?'

'Frederick! Is anything wrong with the pumpkin?'

In a crass and materialistic world there must inevitably be a scattered few here and there in whom pumpkins touch no chord. The Hon. Freddie Threepwood was one of these. He was accustomed to speak in mockery of all pumpkins, and had even gone so far as to allude to the Hope of Blandings as 'Percy'. His father's anxiety, therefore, merely caused him to giggle.

'Not that I know of,' he said.

'Then what do you mean?' thundered Lord Emsworth, stung by the giggle. 'What do you mean, sir, by coming here and alarming me – scaring me out of my wits, by Gad! – with your nonsense about giving me shocks?'

The Hon. Freddie looked carefully at his fermenting parent. His fingers, sliding into his pocket, closed on the note which nestled there. He drew it forth.

'Look here, guv'nor,' he said nervously. 'I think the best thing would be for you to read this. Meant to leave it for you with the hall-porter. It's – well, you just cast your eye over it. Goodbye, guv'nor. Got to see a man.'

And, thrusting the note into his father's hand, the Hon. Freddie turned and was gone. Lord Emsworth, perplexed and annoyed, watched him skim up the road and leap into a cab. He seethed impotently. Practically any behaviour on the part of his son Frederick had the power to irritate him, but it was when he was vague and mysterious and incoherent that the young man irritated him most.

He looked at the letter in his hand, turned it over, felt it. Then – for it had suddenly occurred to him that if he wished to ascertain its contents he had better read it – he tore open the envelope.

The note was brief, but full of good reading matter.

*Dear Guv'nor,*

*Awfully sorry and all that, but couldn't hold out any longer. I've popped up to London in the two-seater and Aggie and I were spliced this morning. There looked like being a bit of a hitch at one time, but Aggie's guv'nor, who has come over from America, managed to wangle it all right by getting a special licence or something of that order. A most capable Johnny. He's coming to see you. He wants to have a good long talk with you about the whole binge. Lush him up hospitably and all that, would you mind, because he's a really sound egg, and you'll like him. Well, cheerio!*

*Your affectionate son,*
*Freddie.*

*P.S. – You won't mind if I freeze on to the two-seater for the nonce, what? It may come in useful for the honeymoon.*

The Senior Conservative Club is a solid and massive building, but, as Lord Emsworth raised his eyes dumbly from the perusal of this letter, it seemed to him that it was performing a kind of whirling dance. The whole of the immediate neighbourhood, indeed, appeared to be shimmying in the middle of a thick mist. He was profoundly stirred. It is not too much to say that he was shaken to the core of his being. No father enjoys being flouted and defied by his own son; nor is it reasonable to expect a man to take a cheery view of life who is faced with the prospect of supporting for the remainder of his years a younger son, a younger son's wife, and possibly younger grandchildren.

For an appreciable space of time he stood in the middle of the pavement, rooted to the spot. Passers-by bumped into him or grumblingly made *détours* to avoid a collision. Dogs sniffed at his ankles. Seedy-looking individuals tried to arrest his attention in order to speak of their financial affairs. Lord Emsworth heeded none of them. He remained where he was, gaping like a fish, until suddenly his faculties seemed to return to him.

An imperative need for flowers and green trees swept upon Lord Emsworth. The noise of the traffic and the heat of the sun on the stone pavement were afflicting him like a nightmare. He signalled energetically to a passing cab.

'Kensington Gardens,' he said, and sank back on the cushioned seat.

Something dimly resembling peace crept into his lordship's soul as he paid off his cab and entered the cool shade of the gardens. Even from the road he had caught a glimpse of stimulating reds and yellows; and as he ambled up the asphalt path and plunged round the corner the flower-beds burst upon his sight in all their consoling glory.

'Ah!' breathed Lord Emsworth, rapturously, and came to a halt before a glowing carpet of tulips. A man of official aspect, wearing a peaked cap and a uniform, stopped as he heard the exclamation and looked at him with approval and even affection.

'Nice weather we're 'aving,' he observed.

Lord Emsworth did not reply. He had not heard. There is that about a well-set-out bed of flowers which acts on men who love their gardens like a drug, and he was in a sort of trance. Already he had completely forgotten where he was, and seemed to himself to be back in his paradise of Blandings. He drew a step nearer to the flower-bed, pointing like a setter.

The official-looking man's approval deepened. This man with the peaked cap was the park-keeper, who held the rights of the high, the low and the middle justice over that section of the gardens. He, too, loved these flower-beds, and he seemed to see in Lord Emsworth a kindred soul. The general public was too apt to pass by, engrossed in its own affairs, and this often wounded the park-keeper. In Lord Emsworth he thought that he recognized one of the right sort.

'Nice—' he began.

He broke off with a sharp cry. If he had not seen it with his own eyes, he would not have believed it. But, alas, there was no possibility of a mistake. With a ghastly shock he realized that he had been deceived in this attractive stranger. Decently, if untidily, dressed; clean; respectable to the outward eye; the stranger was in reality a dangerous criminal, the blackest type of evil-doer on the park-keeper's index. He was a Kensington Gardens flower-picker.

For, even as he uttered the word 'Nice', the man had stepped lightly over the low railing, had shambled across the strip of turf, and before you could say 'weather' was busy on his dark work. In the brief instant in which the park-keeper's vocal cords refused to obey him, he was two tulips ahead of the game and reaching out to scoop in a third.

'Hi! ! !' roared the park-keeper, suddenly finding speech. 'I there! ! !'

Lord Emsworth turned with a start.

'Bless my soul,' he murmured reproachfully.

He was in full possession of his senses now, such as they were, and understood the enormity of his conduct. He shuffled back on to the asphalt, contrite.

'My dear fellow—' he began remorsefully.

The park-keeper began to speak rapidly and at length. From time to time Lord Emsworth moved his lips and made deprecating gestures, but he could not stem the flood. Louder and more rhetorical grew the park-keeper and denser and more interested the rapidly assembling crowd of spectators. And then through the stream of words another voice spoke.

'Wot's all this?'

The Force had materialized in the shape of a large solid constable.

The park-keeper seemed to understand that he had been superseded. He still spoke, but no longer like a father rebuking an erring son. His attitude now was more that of an elder brother appealing for justice against a delinquent junior. In a moving passage he stated his case.

"E Says,' observed the constable judicially, speaking slowly and in capitals, as if addressing an untutored foreigner, "E Says You Was Pickin' The Flowers.'

'I saw 'im. I was standin' as close as I am to you.'

"E Saw You,' interpreted the constable. "E Was Standing At Your Side.'

Lord Emsworth was feeling weak and bewildered. Without a thought of annoying or doing harm to anybody, he seemed to have unchained the fearful passions of a French Revolution; and there came over him a sense of how unjust it was that this sort of thing should be happening to him, of all people – a man already staggering beneath the troubles of a Job.

'I'll 'ave to ask you for your name and address,' said the constable, more briskly. A stubby pencil popped for an instant into his stern mouth and hovered, well and truly moistened, over the virgin page of his notebook – that dreadful notebook before which taxi-drivers shrink and hardened bus-conductors quail.

'I – I – why, my dear fellow – I mean, officer – I am the Earl of Emsworth.'

Much has been written of the psychology of crowds, designed to show how extraordinary and inexplicable it is, but most of such writing is exaggeration. A crowd generally behaves in a perfectly natural and intelligible fashion. When, for instance, it sees a man in a badly-fitting tweed suit and a hat he ought to be ashamed of getting put through it for pinching flowers in the Park, and the man says he is an earl, it laughs. This crowd laughed.

'Ho?' The constable did not stoop to join in the merriment of the rabble, but his lip twitched sardonically. 'Have you a card, your lordship?'

Nobody intimate with Lord Emsworth would have asked such a foolish question. His card-case was the thing he always lost second when visiting London – immediately after losing his umbrella.

'I – er – I'm afraid—'

'R!' said the constable. And the crowd uttered another happy, hyena-like laugh, so intensely galling that his lordship raised his bowed head and found enough spirit to cast an indignant glance. And, as he did so, the hunted look faded from his eyes.

'McAllister!' he cried.

Two new arrivals had just joined the throng, and, being of rugged and knobbly physique, had already shoved themselves through to the ringside seats. One was a tall, handsome, smooth-faced gentleman of authoritative appearance, who, if he had not worn rimless glasses, would have looked like a Roman emperor. The other was a shorter, sturdier man with a bristly red beard.

'McAllister!' moaned his lordship piteously. 'McAllister, my dear fellow, do please tell this man who I am.'

After what had passed between himself and his late employer, a lesser man than Angus McAllister might have seen in Lord Emsworth's predicament merely a judgment. A man of little magnanimity would have felt that here was where he got a bit of his own back.

Not so this splendid Glaswegian.

'Aye,' he said. 'Yon's Lorrud Emsworruth.'

'Who are you?' inquired the constable searchingly.

'I used to be head-gardener at the cassel.'

'Exactly,' bleated Lord Emsworth. 'Precisely. My head-gardener.'

The constable was shaken. Lord Emsworth might not look like an earl, but there was no getting away from the fact that Angus McAllister was supremely head-gardeneresque. A staunch admirer of the aristocracy, the constable perceived that zeal had caused him to make a bit of a bloomer.

In this crisis, however, he comported himself with masterly tact. He scowled blackly upon the interested throng.

'Pass along there, please. Pass along,' he commanded austerely. 'Ought to know better than block up a public thoroughfare like this. Pass along!'

He moved off, shepherding the crowd before him. The Roman emperor with the rimless glasses advanced upon Lord Emsworth, extending a large hand.

'Pleased to meet you at last,' he said. 'My name is Donaldson, Lord Emsworth.'

For a moment the name conveyed nothing to his lordship. Then its significance hit him, and he drew himself up with hauteur.

'You'll excuse us, Angus,' said Mr. Donaldson. 'High time you and I had a little chat, Lord Emsworth.'

Lord Emsworth was about to speak, when he caught the other's eye. It was a strong, keen, level grey eye, with a curious forcefulness about it that made him feel strangely inferior.

There is every reason to suppose that Mr. Donaldson had subscribed for years to those personality courses advertised in the magazines which guarantee to impart to the pupil who takes ten correspondence lessons the ability to look the boss in the eye and make him wilt. Mr. Donaldson looked Lord Emsworth in the eye, and Lord Emsworth wilted.

'How do you do?' he said weakly.

'Now listen, Lord Emsworth,' proceeded Mr. Donaldson. 'No sense in having hard feelings between members of a family. I take it you've heard by this time that your boy and my girl have gone ahead and fixed it up? Personally, I'm delighted. That boy is a fine young fellow.'

Lord Emsworth blinked.

'You are speaking of my son Frederick?' he said incredulously.

'Of your son Frederick. Now, at the moment, no doubt, you are feeling a trifle sore. I don't blame you. You have every right to be sorer than a gumboil. But you must remember – young blood, eh? It will, I am convinced, be a lasting grief to that splendid young man—'

'You are still speaking of my son Frederick?'

'Of Frederick, yes. It will, I say, be a lasting grief to him if he feels he has incurred your resentment. You must forgive him, Lord Emsworth. He must have your support.'

'I suppose he'll have to have it, dash it!' said his lordship unhappily. 'Can't let the boy starve.'

Mr. Donaldson's hand swept round in a wide, grand gesture.

'Don't you worry about that. I'll look after that end of it. I am not a rich man—'

'Ah!' said Lord Emsworth rather bleakly. There had been something about the largeness of the other's manner which had led him to entertain hopes.

'I doubt,' continued Mr. Donaldson frankly, for he was a man who believed in frankness in these matters, 'if, all told, I have as much as ten million dollars in the world.'

Lord Emsworth swayed like a sapling in the breeze.

'Ten million? Ten million? Did you say you had ten million dollars?'

'Between nine and ten, I suppose. Not more. You must remember,' said Mr. Donaldson, with a touch of apology, 'that conditions have changed very much in America of late. We have been through a tough time, a mighty tough time. Many of my friends have been harder hit than I have. But things are coming back. Yes, sir, they're coming right back. I am a firm believer in President Roosevelt and the New Deal. Under the New Deal, the American dog is beginning to eat more biscuits. That, I should have mentioned, is my line. I am Donaldson's Dog-Biscuits.'

'Donaldson's Dog-Biscuits? Indeed? Really! Fancy that!'

'You have heard of Donaldson's Dog-Biscuits?' asked their proprietor eagerly.

'Never,' said Lord Emsworth cordially.

'Oh! Well, that's who I am. And, as I say, the business is beginning to pick up nicely after the slump. All over the country our salesmen are reporting that the American dog is once more becoming biscuit-conscious. And so I am in a position, with your approval, to offer Frederick a steady and possibly a lucrative job. I propose, always with your consent, of course, to send him over to Long Island City to start learning the business. I have no doubt that he will in time prove a most valuable asset to the firm.'

Lord Emsworth could conceive of no way in which Freddie could be of value to a dog-biscuit firm, except possibly as a taster; but he refrained from damping the other's enthusiasm by saying so. In any case, the thought of the young man actually earning his living, and doing so three thousand miles from Blandings Castle, would probably have held him dumb.

'He seems full of keenness. But, in my opinion, to be able to give of his best and push the Donaldson biscuit as it should be pushed, he must feel that he has your moral support, Lord Emsworth – his father's moral support.'

'Yes, yes, yes!' said Lord Emsworth heartily. A feeling of positive adoration for Mr. Donaldson was thrilling him. The getting rid of Freddie, which he himself had been unable to achieve in twenty-six years, this godlike dog-biscuit manufacturer had accomplished in less than a week. What a man! felt Lord Emsworth. 'Oh, yes, yes, yes!' he said. 'Yes, indeed. Most decidedly.'

'They sail on Wednesday.'

'Capital!'

'Early in the morning.'

'Splendid!'

'I may give them a friendly message from you? A forgiving, fatherly message?'

'Certainly, certainly, certainly. Inform Frederick that he has my best wishes.'

'I will.'

'Mention that I shall watch his future progress with considerable interest.'

'Exactly.'

'Say that I hope he will work hard and make a name for himself.'

'Just so.'

'And,' concluded Lord Emsworth, speaking with a paternal

earnestness well in keeping with this solemn moment, 'tell him – er – not to hurry home.'

He pressed Mr. Donaldson's hand with feelings too deep for further speech. Then he galloped swiftly to where Angus McAllister stood brooding over the tulip bed.

'McAllister!'

The head-gardener's beard waggled grimly. He looked at his late employer with cold eyes. It is never difficult to distinguish between a Scotsman with a grievance and a ray of sunshine, and Lord Emsworth, gazing upon the dour man, was able to see at a glance into which category Angus McAllister fell. His tongue seemed to cleave to his palate, but he forced himself to speak.

'McAllister . . . I wish . . . I wonder . . .'

'Weel?'

'I wonder . . . I wish . . . What I want to say,' faltered Lord Emsworth humbly, 'is, have you accepted another situation yet?'

'I am conseederin' twa.'

'Come back to me!' pleaded his lordship, his voice breaking. 'Robert Barker is worse than useless. Come back to me!'

Angus McAllister gazed woodenly at the tulips.

'A' weel—' he said at length.

'You will?' cried Lord Emsworth joyfully. 'Splendid! Capital! Excellent!'

'A' didna say I wud.'

'I thought you said I will,' said his lordship, dashed.

'I didna say "A' weel"; I said "A' weel," said Mr. McAllister stiffly. 'Meanin' mebbe I might, mebbe not.'

Lord Emsworth laid a trembling hand upon his shoulder.

'McAllister, I will raise your salary.'

The beard twitched.

'Dash it, I'll double it!'

The eyebrows flickered.

'McAllister . . . Angus . . .' said Lord Emsworth in a low voice. 'Come back! The pumpkin needs you.'

In an age of rush and hurry like that of to-day, an age in which there are innumerable calls on the time of everyone, it is possible that here and there throughout the ranks of those who have read this chronicle there may be one or two who for various reasons found themselves unable to attend the last Agricultural Show at Shrewsbury. For these a few words must be added.

Sir Gregory Parsloe-Parsloe, of Matchingham Hall, was there, of course, but it would not have escaped the notice of a close observer that his mien lacked something of the haughty arrogance which had characterized it in other years. From time to time, as he paced the tent devoted to the exhibition of vegetables, he might have been seen to bite his lip, and his eye had something of that brooding look which Napoleon's must have worn at Waterloo.

But there was the right stuff in Sir Gregory. He was a gentleman and a sportsman. In the Parsloe tradition there was nothing small or mean. Half-way down the tent he stopped, and with a quick, manly gesture thrust out his hand.

'I congratulate you, Emsworth,' he said huskily.

Lord Emsworth looked up with a start. He had been deep in his thoughts. 'Eh? Oh, thanks. Thanks, my dear fellow, thanks, thanks. Thank you very much' He hesitated. 'Er – can't both win, eh?'

Sir George puzzled it out and saw that he was right.

'No,' he said. 'No. See what you mean. Can't both win. No getting round that.'

He nodded and walked on, with who knows what vultures

gnawing at his broad bosom. And Lord Emsworth – with Angus McAllister, who had been a silent, beard-waggling witness of the scene, at his side – turned once more to stare reverently at that which lay on the strawy bottom of one of the largest packing-cases ever seen in Shrewsbury town.

A card had been attached to the exterior of the packing-case. It bore the simple legend:

PUMPKINS. FIRST PRIZE.

The housekeeper's room at Blandings Castle, G.H.Q. of the domestic staff that ministered to the needs of the Earl of Emsworth, was in normal circumstances a pleasant and cheerful apartment. It caught the afternoon sun; and the paper which covered its walls had been conceived in a jovial spirit by someone who held that the human eye, resting on ninety-seven simultaneous pink birds perched upon ninety-seven blue rose-bushes, could not but be agreeably stimulated and refreshed. Yet, with the entry of Beach, the butler, it was as though there had crept into its atmosphere a chill dreariness; and Mrs. Twemlow, the housekeeper, laying down her knitting, gazed at him in alarm.

'Whatever is the matter, Mr. Beach?'

The butler stared moodily out of the window His face was drawn and he breathed heavily, as a man will who is suffering from a combination of strong emotion and adenoids. A ray of sunshine, which had been advancing jauntily along the carpet, caught sight of his face and slunk out, abashed.

'I have come to a decision, Mrs. Twemlow.'

'What about?'

'Ever since his lordship started to grow it I have seen the writing on the wall plainer and plainer, and now I have made up my mind. The moment his lordship returns from London, I tender my resignation. Eighteen years have I served in his lordship's household, commencing as under-footman and rising to my present position, but now the end has come.'

'You don't mean you're going just because his lordship has grown a beard?'

'It is the only way, Mrs. Twemlow. That beard is weakening his lordship's position throughout the entire country-side. Are you aware that at the recent Sunday school treat I heard cries of "Beaver!"?'

'No!'

'Yes! And this spirit of mockery and disrespect will spread. And, what is more, that beard is alienating the best elements in the County. I saw Sir Gregory Parsloe-Parsloe look very sharp at it when he dined with us last Friday.'

'It is not a handsome beard,' admitted the housekeeper.

'It is not. And his lordship must be informed. As long as I remain in his lordship's service, it is impossible for me to speak. So I shall tender my resignation. Once that is done, my lips will no longer be sealed. Is that buttered toast under that dish, Mrs Twemlow?'

'Yes, Mr. Beach. Take a slice. It will cheer you up.'

'Cheer me up!' said the butler, with a hollow laugh that sounded like a knell.

It was fortunate that Lord Emsworth, seated at the time of this conversation in the smoking-room of the Senior Conservative Club in London, had no suspicion of the supreme calamity that was about to fall upon him; for there was already much upon his mind.

In the last few days, indeed, everything seemed to have gone wrong. Angus McAllister, his head-gardener, had reported an alarming invasion of greenfly among the roses. A favourite and respected cow, strongly fancied for the Milk-Giving Jerseys event at the forthcoming Cattle Show, had contracted a mysterious ailment which was baffling the skill of the local vet. And on top of all this a telegram had arrived from his lordship's younger son, the Hon. Frederick Threepwood, announcing that he was back in England and desirous of seeing his father immediately.

This, felt Lord Emsworth, as he stared bleakly before him at the little groups of happy Senior Conservatives, was the most unkindest cut of all. What on earth was Freddie doing in England? Eight months before he had married the only daughter of Donaldson's Dog-Biscuits, of Long Island City, in the United States of America; and in Long Island City he ought now to have been, sedulously promoting the dog-biscuit industry's best interests. Instead of which, here he was in London – and, according to his telegram, in trouble.

Lord Emsworth passed a hand over his chin, to assist thought, and was vaguely annoyed by some obstacle that intruded itself in the path of his fingers. Concentrating his faculties, such as they were, on this obstacle, he discovered it to be his beard. It irritated him. Hitherto, in moments of stress, he had always derived comfort from the feel of a clean-shaven chin. He felt now as if he were rubbing his hand over seaweed; and most unjustly – for it was certainly not that young man's fault that he had decided to grow a beard – he became aware of an added sense of grievance against the Hon. Freddie.

It was at this moment that he perceived his child approaching him across the smoking-room floor.

'Hullo, guv'nor!' said Freddie.

'Well, Frederick?' said Lord Emsworth.

There followed a silence. Freddie was remembering that he had not met his father since the day when he had slipped into the latter's hand a note announcing his marriage to a girl whom Lord Emsworth had never seen − except once, through a telescope, when he, Freddie, was kissing her in the grounds of Blandings Castle. Lord Emsworth, on his side, was brooding on that phrase 'in trouble', which had formed so significant a part of his son's telegram. For fifteen years he had been reluctantly helping Freddie out of trouble; and now, when it had seemed that he was off his hands for ever, the thing had started all over again.

'Do sit down,' he said testily.

Freddie had been standing on one leg, and his constrained attitude annoyed Lord Emsworth.

'Right-ho,' said Freddie, taking a chair. 'I say, guv'nor, since when the foliage?'

'What?'

'The beard. I hardly recognized you.'

Another spasm of irritation shot through his lordship.

'Never mind my beard!'

'I don't if you don't,' said Freddie agreeably. 'It was dashed good of you, guv'nor, to come bounding up to town so promptly.'

'I came because your telegram said that you were in trouble.'

'British,' said Freddie approvingly. 'Very British.'

'Though what trouble you can be in I cannot imagine. It is surely not money again?'

'Oh, no. Not money. If that had been all, I would have applied to the good old pop-in-law. Old Donaldson's an ace. He thinks the world of me.'

'Indeed? I met Mr. Donaldson only once, but he struck me as a man of sound judgment.'

'That's what I say. He thinks I'm a wonder. If it were simply a question of needing a bit of the ready, I could touch him like a shot. But it isn't money that's the trouble. It's Aggie. My wife, you know.'

'Well?'

'She's left me.'

'Left you!'

'Absolutely flat. Buzzed off, and the note pinned to the pincushion. She's now at the Savoy and won't let me come near her; and I'm at a service-flat in King Street, eating my jolly old heart out, if you know what I mean.'

Lord Emsworth uttered a deep sigh. He gazed drearily at his son, marvelling that it should be in the power of any young man, even a specialist like Freddie, so consistently to make a mess of his affairs. By what amounted to a miracle this offspring of his had contrived to lure a millionaire's daughter into marrying him; and now, it seemed, he had let her get away. Years before, when a boy, and romantic as most boys are, his lordship had sometimes regretted that the Emsworths, though an ancient clan, did not possess a Family Curse. How little he had suspected that he was shortly about to become the father of it.

'The fault,' he said tonelessly, 'was, I suppose, yours?'

'In a way, yes. But—'

'What precisely occurred?'

'Well, it was like this, guv'nor. You know how keen I've always been on the movies. Going to every picture I could manage, and so forth. Well, one night, as I was lying awake, I suddenly got the idea for a scenario of my own. And dashed good it was, too. It was about a poor man who had an accident, and the coves at the hospital said that an operation was the only thing that could save his life. But they wouldn't operate without five hundred dollars down in advance, and he hadn't got five hundred dollars. So his wife got hold of a millionaire.'

'What,' inquired Lord Emsworth, 'is all this drivel?'

'Drivel, guv'nor?' said Freddie, wounded. 'I'm only telling you my scenario.'

'I have no wish to hear it. What I am anxious to learn from you – in as few words as possible – is the reason for the breach between your wife and yourself.'

'Well, I'm telling you. It all started with the scenario. When I'd written it, I naturally wanted to sell it to somebody; and just about then Pauline Petite came East and took a house at Great Neck, and a pal of mine introduced me to her.'

'Who is Pauline Petite?'

'Good heavens, guv'nor!' Freddie stared, amazed. 'You don't mean to sit there and tell me you've never heard of Pauline Petite! The movie star. Didn't you see *Passion's Slaves*?'

'I did not.'

'Nor *Silken Fetters*?'

'Never.'

'Nor *Purple Passion*? Nor *Bonds of Gold*? Nor *Seduction*? Great Scott, guv'nor, you haven't lived!'

'What about this woman?'

'Well, a pal introduced me to her, you see, and I started to pave the way to getting her interested in this scenario of mine. Because, if she liked it, of course it meant everything. Well, this involved seeing a good deal of her, you understand, and one night Jane Yorke happened to come on us having a bite together at an inn.'

'Good God!'

'Oh, it was all perfectly respectable, guv'nor. All strictly on the up-and-up. Purely a business relationship. But the trouble was I had kept the thing from Aggie because I wanted to surprise her. I wanted to be able to come to her with the scenario accepted and tell her I wasn't such a fool as I looked.'

'Any woman capable of believing that—'

'And most unfortunately I had said that I had to go to Chicago that night on business. So, what with one thing and another— Well, as I said just now, she's at the Savoy and I'm—'

'Who is Jane Yorke?'

A scowl marred Freddie's smooth features.

'A pill, guv'nor. One of the worst. A Jebusite and Amalekite. If it hadn't been for her, I believe I could have fixed the thing. But she got hold of Aggie and whisked her away and poisoned her mind. This woman, guv'nor, has got a brother in the background, and she wanted Aggie to marry the brother. And my belief is that she is trying to induce Aggie to pop over to Paris and get a divorce, so as to give the blighted brother another look in, dash him! So now, guv'nor, is the time for action. Now is the moment to rally round as never before. I rely on you.'

'Me? What on earth do you expect me to do?'

'Why, go to her and plead with her. They do it in the movies. I've seen thousands of pictures where the white-haired old father—'

'Stuff and nonsense!' said Lord Emsworth, stung to the quick – for, like so many well-preserved men of ripe years, he was under the impression that he was merely slightly brindled. 'You have made your bed, and you must stew in it.'

'Eh?'

'I mean, you must stew in your own juice. You have brought this trouble on yourself by your own idiotic behaviour, and you must bear the consequences.'

'You mean you won't go and plead?'

'No.'

'You mean yes?'

'I mean no.'

'Not plead?' said Freddie, desiring to get this thing clear.

'I refuse to allow myself to be drawn into the matter.'

'You won't even give her a ring on the telephone?'

'I will not.'

'Oh, come, guv'nor. Be a sport. Her suite's Number Sixty-seven. You can get her in a second and state my case, all for the cost of twopence. Have a pop at it.'

'No.'

Freddie rose with set face.

'Very well,' he said tensely 'Then I may as well tell you, guv'nor, that my life is as good as over. The future holds nothing for me. I am a spent egg. If Aggie goes to Paris and gets that divorce, I shall retire to some quiet spot and there pass the few remaining years of my existence, a blighted wreck. Goodbye, guv'nor.'

'Goodbye.'

'Honk-honk!' said Freddie moodily.

As a general rule, Lord Emsworth was an early and a sound sleeper, one of the few qualities which he shared with Napoleon Bonaparte being the ability to slumber the moment his head touched the pillow. But that night, weighed down with his troubles, he sought unconsciousness in vain. And somewhere in the small hours of the morning he sat up in bed, quaking. A sudden grisly thought had occurred to him.

Freddie had stated that, in the event of his wife obtaining a divorce, he proposed to retire for the rest of his life to some quiet spot. Suppose by 'quiet spot' he meant Blandings Castle! The possibility shook Lord Emsworth like an ague. Freddie had visited Blandings for extended periods before, and it was his lordship's considered opinion that the boy was a worse menace to the happy life of rural England than botts, green-fly or foot-and-mouth disease. The prospect of having him at Blandings indefinitely affected Lord Emsworth like a blow on the base of the skull.

An entirely new line of thought was now opened. Had he in the recent interview, he asked himself, been as kind as he should have been? Had he not been a little harsh? Had he been just a shade lacking in sympathy? Had he played quite the part a father ought to have played?

The answers to the questions, in the order stated, were as follows: No. Yes. Yes. And No.

Waking after a belated sleep and sipping his early tea, Lord Emsworth found himself full of a new resolve. He had changed his mind. It was his intention now to go to this daughter-in-law of his and plead with her as no father-in-law had ever pleaded yet.

A man who has had a disturbed night is not at his best on the following morning. Until after luncheon Lord Emsworth felt much too heavy-headed to do himself justice as a pleader. But a visit to the flowers at Kensington Gardens, followed by a capital chop and half a bottle of claret at the Regent Grill, put him into excellent shape. The heaviness had vanished, and he felt alert and quick-witted.

So much so that, on arriving at the Savoy Hotel, he behaved with a cunning of which he had never hitherto suspected himself capable. On the very verge of giving his name to the desk-clerk, he paused. It might well be, he reflected, that this daughter-in-law of his, including the entire Emsworth family in her feud, would, did she hear that he was waiting below, nip the whole programme in the bud by refusing to see him. Better, he decided, not to risk it. Moving away from the desk, he headed for the lift, and presently found himself outside the door of Suite Sixty-seven.

He tapped on the door. There was no answer. He tapped again, and, once more receiving no reply, felt a little nonplussed. He was not a very farseeing man, and the possibility that his daughter-in-law might not be at home had not occurred to him. He was about to go away when, peering at the door, he perceived that it was ajar. He pushed it open; and, ambling in, found himself in a cosy sitting-room, crowded, as feminine sitting-rooms are apt to be, with flowers of every description.

Flowers were always a magnet to Lord Emsworth, and for some happy minutes he pottered from vase to vase, sniffing.

It was after he had sniffed for perhaps the twentieth time that the impression came to him that the room contained a curious echo. It was almost as though, each time he sniffed, some other person sniffed too. And yet the place was apparently empty. To submit the acoustics to a final test, his lordship sniffed once more. But this time the sound that followed was of a more sinister character. It sounded to Lord Emsworth exactly like a snarl.

It was a snarl. Chancing to glance floorwards, he became immediately aware, in close juxtaposition to his ankles, of what appeared at first sight to be a lady's muff. But, this being one of his bright afternoons, he realized in the next instant that it was no muff, but a toy dog of the kind which women are only too prone to leave lying about their sitting-rooms.

'God bless my soul!' exclaimed Lord Emsworth, piously commending his safety to Heaven, as so many of his rugged

ancestors had done in rather similar circumstances on the battlefields of the Middle Ages.

He backed uneasily. The dog followed him. It appeared to
have no legs, but to move by faith alone.

'Go away, sir!' said Lord Emsworth.

He hated small dogs. They nipped you. Take your eye off
them, and they had you by the ankle before you knew where you
were. Discovering that his manoeuvres had brought him to a
door, he decided to take cover. He opened the door and slipped
through. Blood will tell. An Emsworth had taken cover at
Agincourt.

He was now in a bedroom, and, judging by the look of things,
likely to remain there for some time. The woolly dog, foiled by
superior intelligence, was now making no attempt to conceal its
chagrin. It had cast off all pretence of armed neutrality and was
yapping with a hideous intensity and shrillness. And ever and
anon it scratched with baffled fury at the lower panels.

'Go away, sir!' thundered his lordship.

'Who's there?'

Lord Emsworth leaped like a jumping bean. So convinced
had he been of the emptiness of this suite of rooms that the
voice, speaking where no voice should have been, crashed into
his nerve centres like a shell.

'Who is there?'

The mystery, which had begun to assume an aspect of the
supernatural, was solved. On the other side of the room was a
door, and it was from behind this that the voice had spoken. It
occurred to Lord Emsworth that it was merely part of the
general malignity of Fate that he should have selected for a
formal father-in-lawful call the moment when his daughter-in-
law was taking a bath.

He approached the door, and spoke soothingly.

'Pray do not be alarmed, my dear.'

'Who are you? What are you doing in my room?'

'There is no cause for alarm—'

He broke off abruptly, for his words had suddenly been proved fundamentally untrue. There was very vital cause for alarm. The door of the bedroom had opened, and the muff-like dog, shrilling hate, was scuttling in its peculiar legless manner straight for his ankles.

Peril brings out unsuspected qualities in every man. Lord Emsworth was not a professional acrobat, but the leap he gave in this crisis would have justified his being mistaken for one. He floated through the air like a homing bird. From where he had been standing the bed was a considerable distance away, but he reached it with inches to spare, and stood there quivering. Below him, the woolly dog raged like the ocean at the base of a cliff.

It was at this point that his lordship became aware of a young woman standing in the doorway through which he had just passed.

About this young woman there were many points which would have found little favour in the eyes of a critic of feminine charm. She was too short, too square, and too solid. She had a much too determined chin. And her hair was of an unpleasing gingery hue. But the thing Lord Emsworth liked least about her was the pistol she was pointing at his head.

A plaintive voice filtered through the bathroom door.

'Who's there?'

'It's a man,' said the girl behind the gun.

'I know it's a man. He spoke to me. Who is he?'

'I don't know. A nasty-looking fellow. I saw him hanging

300

about the passage outside your door, and I got my gun and came along. Come on out.'

'I can't. I'm all wet.'

It is not easy for a man who is standing on a bed with his hands up to achieve dignity, but Lord Emsworth did the best he could.

'My dear madam!'

'What are you doing here?'

'I found the door ajar—'

'And walked in to see if there were any jewel-cases ajar, too. I think,' added the young woman, raising her voice so as to make herself audible to the unseen bather, 'it's Dopey Smith.'

'Who?'

'Dopey Smith. The fellow the cops said tried for your jewels in New York. He must have followed you over here.'

'I am not Dopey Smith, madam,' cried his lordship. 'I am the Earl of Emsworth.'

'You are?'

'Yes, I am.'

'Yes, you are!'

'I came to see my daughter-in-law.'

'Well, here she is.'

The bathroom door opened, and there emerged a charming figure draped in a kimono. Even in that tense moment Lord Emsworth was conscious of a bewildered astonishment that such a girl could ever have stooped to mate with his son Frederick.

'Who did you say he was?' she asked, recommending herself still more strongly to his lordship's esteem by scooping up the woolly dog and holding it securely in her arms.

'He says he's the Earl of Emsworth.'

'I *am* the Earl of Emsworth.'

The girl in the kimono looked keenly at him as he descended from the bed.

'You know, Jane,' she said, a note of uncertainty in her voice, 'it might be. He looks very like Freddie.'

The appalling slur on his personal appearance held Lord Emsworth dumb. Like other men, he had had black moments when his looks had not altogether satisfied him, but he had never supposed that he had a face like Freddie's.

The girl with the pistol uttered a stupefying whoop.

'Jiminy Christmas!' she cried. 'Don't you see?'

'See what?'

'Why, it *is* Freddie. Disguised. Trying to get at you this way. It's just the sort of movie stunt he would think clever. Take them off, Ralph Vandeleur – I know you!'

She reached out a clutching hand, seized his lordship's beard in a vice-like grip, and tugged with all the force of a modern girl, trained from infancy at hockey, tennis and Swedish exercises.

It had not occurred to Lord Emsworth a moment before that anything could possibly tend to make his situation more uncomfortable than it already was. He saw now that he had been mistaken in this view. Agony beyond his liveliest dreams flamed through his shrinking frame.

The girl regarded him with a somewhat baffled look.

'H'm!' she said disappointedly. 'It seems to be real. Unless,' she continued, on a more optimistic note, 'he's fixed it on with specially strong fish-glue or something. I'd better try again.'

'No, don't,' said his lordship's daughter-in-law. 'It isn't Freddie. I would have recognized him at once.'

'Then he's a crook after all. Kindly step into that cupboard, George, while I 'phone for the constabulary.'

Lord Emsworth danced a few steps.

'I will not step into cupboards. I insist on being heard. I don't know who this woman is—'

'My name's Jane Yorke, if you're curious.'

'Ah! The woman who poisons my son's wife's mind against him! I know all about you.' He turned to the girl in the kimono. 'Yesterday my son Frederick implored me by telegram to come to London. I saw him at my club. Stop that dog barking!'

'Why shouldn't he bark?' said Miss Yorke. 'He's in his own home.'

'He told me,' proceeded Lord Emsworth, raising his voice, 'that there had been a little misunderstanding between you—'

'Little misunderstanding is good,' said Miss Yorke.

'He dined with that woman for a purpose.'

'And directly I saw them,' said Miss Yorke, 'I knew what the purpose was.'

The Hon. Mrs. Threepwood looked at her friend, wavering.

'I believe it's true,' she said, 'and he really is Lord Emsworth. He seems to know all that happened. How could he know if Freddie hadn't told him?'

'If this fellow is a crook from the other side, of course he would know. The thing was *Broadway Whispers* and *Town Gossip* wasn't it?'

'All the same—'

The telephone bell rang sharply.

'I assure you—' began Lord Emsworth.

'Right!' said the unpleasant Miss Yorke, at the receiver. 'Send him right up.' She regarded his lordship with a brightly triumphant eye. 'You're out of luck, my friend,' she said. 'Lord Emsworth has just arrived, and he's on his way up now.'

There are certain situations in which the human brain may be excused for reeling. Lord Emsworth's did not so much reel as perform a kind of dance, as if it were in danger of coming unstuck. Always a dreamy and absent-minded man, unequal to the rough hurly-burly of life, he had passed this afternoon through an ordeal which might well have unsettled the most practical. And this extraordinary announcement coming on top of all he had been through, was too much for him. He tottered into the sitting-room and sank into a chair. It seemed to him that he was living in a nightmare.

And certainly in the figure that entered a few moments later there was nothing whatever to correct this impression. It might have stepped straight into anybody's nightmare and felt perfectly at home right from the start.

The figure was that of a tall, thin man with white hair and a long and flowing beard of the same venerable hue. Strange as it seemed that a person of such appearance should not have been shot on sight early in his career, he had obviously reached an extremely advanced age. He was either a man of about a hundred and fifty who was rather young for his years or a man of about a hundred and ten who had been aged by trouble.

'My dear child!' piped the figure in a weak, quavering voice.

'Freddie!' cried the girl in the kimono.

'Oh, dash it!' said the figure.

There was a pause, broken by a sort of gasping moan from Lord Emsworth. More and more every minute his lordship was feeling the strain.

'Good God, guv'nor!' said the figure, sighting him.

His wife pointed at Lord Emsworth.

'Freddie, is that your father?'

'Oh, yes. Rather. Of course. Absolutely. But he said he wasn't coming.'

'I changed my mind,' said Lord Emsworth in a low, stricken voice.

'I told you so, Jane,' said the girl. 'I thought he was Lord Emsworth all the time. Surely you can see the likeness now?'

A kind of wail escaped his lordship.

'Do I look like that?' he said brokenly. He gazed at his son once more and shut his eyes.

'Well,' said Miss Yorke, in her detestable managing way, turning her forceful personality on the newcomer, 'now that you are here, Freddie Threepwood, looking like Father Christmas, what's the idea? Aggie told you never to come near her again.'

A young man of his natural limpness of character might well have retired in disorder before this attack, but Love had apparently made Frederick Threepwood a man of steel. Removing his beard and eyebrows, he directed a withering glance at Miss Yorke.

'I don't want to talk to you,' he said. 'You're a serpent in the bosom. I mean a snake in the grass.'

'Oh, am I?'

'Yes, you are. You poisoned Aggie's mind against me. If it hadn't been for you, I could have got her alone and told her my story as man to man.'

'Well, let's hear it now. You've had plenty of time to rehearse it.'

Freddie turned to his wife with a sweeping gesture.

'I—' He paused. 'I say, Aggie, old thing, you look perfectly topping in that kimono.'

'Stick to the point,' said Miss Yorke.

'That is the point,' said Mrs. Freddie, not without a certain softness. 'But if you think I look perfectly topping, why do you go running around with movie-actresses with carroty hair?'

'Red-gold,' suggested Freddie deferentially.

'Carroty!'

'Carroty it is. You're absolutely right. I never liked it all along.'

'Then why were you dining with it?'

'Yes, why?' inquired Miss Yorke.

'I wish you wouldn't butt in,' said Freddie petulantly. 'I'm not talking to you.'

'You might just as well, for all the good it's going to do you.'

'Be quiet, Jane. Well, Freddie?'

'Aggie,' said the Hon. Freddie, 'it was this way.'

'Never believe a man who starts a story like that,' said Miss Yorke.

'Do please be quiet, Jane. Yes, Freddie?'

'I was trying to sell that carroty female a scenario, and I was keeping it from you because I wanted it to be a surprise.'

'Freddie darling! Was that really it?'

'You don't mean to say—' began Miss Yorke incredulously.

'Absolutely it. And, in order to keep in with the woman – whom, I may as well tell you, I disliked rather heartily from the start – I had to lush her up a trifle from time to time.'

'Of course.'

'You have to with these people.'

'Naturally.'

'Makes all the difference in the world if you push a bit of food into them preparatory to talking business.'

'All the difference in the world.'

Miss Yorke, who seemed temporarily to have lost her breath, recovered it.

'You don't mean to tell me,' she cried, turning in a kind of wild despair to the injured wife, 'that you really believe this apple sauce?'

'Of course she does,' said Freddie. 'Don't you, precious?'

'Of course I do, sweetie-pie.'

'And, what's more,' said Freddie, pulling from his breast-pocket a buff-coloured slip of paper with the air of one who draws from his sleeve that extra ace which makes all the difference in a keenly-contested game, 'I can prove it. Here's a cable that came this morning from the Super-Ultra-Art Film Company, offering me a thousand solid dollars for the scenario. So another time, you, will you kindly refrain from judging your – er – fellows by the beastly light of your own – ah – foul imagination?'

'Yes,' said his wife, 'I must say, Jane, that you have made as much mischief as anyone ever did. I wish in future you would stop interfering in other people's concerns.'

'Spoken,' said Freddie, 'with vim and not a little terse good sense. And I may add—'

'If you ask me,' said Miss Yorke, 'I think it's a fake.'

'What's a fake?'

'That cable.'

'What do you mean, a fake?' cried Freddie indignantly. 'Read it for yourself.'

'It's quite easy to get cables cabled you by cabling a friend in New York to cable them.'

'I don't get that,' said Freddie, puzzled.

'I do,' said his wife; and there shone in her eyes the light that shines only in the eyes of wives who, having swallowed their husband's story, resent destructive criticism from outsiders. 'And I never want to see you again, Jane Yorke.'

'Same here,' agreed Freddie. 'In Turkey they'd shove a girl like that in a sack and drop her in the Bosphorus.'

'I might as well go,' said Miss Yorke.

P.G. WODEHOUSE

'And don't come back,' said Freddie. 'The door is behind you.'

The species of trance which had held Lord Emsworth in its grip during the preceding conversational exchanges was wearing off. And now, perceiving that Miss Yorke was apparently as unpopular with the rest of the company as with himself, he came gradually to life again. His recovery was hastened by the slamming of the door and the spectacle of his son Frederick clasping in his arms a wife who, his lordship had never forgotten, was the daughter of probably the only millionaire in existence who had that delightful willingness to take Freddie off his hands which was, in Lord Emsworth's eyes, the noblest quality a millionaire could possess.

He sat up and blinked feebly. Though much better, he was still weak.

'What was your scenario about, sweetness?' asked Mrs. Freddie.

'I'll tell you, angel-face. Or should we stir up the guv'nor? He seems a bit under the weather.'

'Better leave him to rest for awhile. That woman Jane Yorke upset him.'

'She would upset anybody. If there's one person I bar, it's the blister who comes between man and wife. Not right, I mean, coming between man and wife. My scenario's about a man and wife. This fellow, you understand, is a poor cove – no money, if you see what I mean – and he has an accident, and the hospital blokes say they won't operate unless he can chip in with five hundred dollars down in advance. But where to get it? You see the situation?'

'Oh, yes.'

'Strong, what?'

'Awfully strong.'

'Well, it's nothing to how strong it gets later on. The cove's wife gets hold of a millionaire bloke and vamps him and lures him to the flat and gets him to promise he'll cough up the cash. Meanwhile, cut-backs of the doctor at the hospital on the 'phone. And she laughing merrily so as not to let the millionaire bloke guess that her heart is aching. I forgot to tell you the cove had to be operated on immediately or he would hand in his dinner-pail. Dramatic, eh?'

'Frightfully.'

'Well, then the millionaire bloke demands his price. I thought of calling it *A Woman's Price*.'

'Splendid.'

'And now comes the blow-out. They go into the bedroom and— Oh, hullo, guv'nor! Feeling better?'

Lord Emsworth had risen. He was tottering a little as he approached them, but his mind was at rest.

'Much better, thank you.'

'You know my wife, what?'

'Oh, Lord Emsworth,' said Mrs. Freddie, 'I'm so dreadfully sorry. I wouldn't have had anything like this happen for the world. But—'

Lord Emsworth patted her hand paternally. Once more he was overcome with astonishment that his son Frederick should have been able to win the heart of a girl so beautiful, so sympathetic, so extraordinarily rich.

'The fault was entirely mine, my dear child. But—' He paused. Something was plainly troubling him. 'Tell me, when Frederick was wearing that beard – when Frederick was – was – when he was wearing that beard, did he really look like me?'

'Oh, yes. Very like.'

'Thank you, my dear. That was all I wanted to know. I will leave you now. You will wish to be alone. You must come down to Blandings, my dear child, at the very earliest opportunity.'

He walked thoughtfully from the room.

'Does this hotel,' he inquired of the man who took him down in the lift, 'contain a barber's shop?'

'Yes, sir.'

'I wonder if you would direct me to it?' said his lordship.


Lord Emsworth sat in his library at Blandings Castle, drinking that last restful whisky and soda of the day. Through the open window came the scent of flowers and the little noises of the summer night.

He should have been completely at rest, for much had happened since his return to sweeten life for him. Angus McAllister had reported that the green-fly were yielding to treatment with whale-oil solution; and the stricken cow had taken a sudden turn for the better, and at last advices was sitting up and taking nourishment with something of the old appetite. Moreover, as he stroked his shaven chin, his lordship felt a better, lighter man, as if some burden had fallen from him.

And yet, as he sat there, a frown was on his forehead.

He rang the bell.

'M'lord?'

Lord Emsworth looked at his faithful butler with appreciation. Deuce of a long time Beach had been at the Castle, and would, no doubt, be there for many a year to come. A good fellow. Lord Emsworth had liked the way the man's eyes had lighted up on his return, as if the sight of his employer had removed a great weight from his mind.

'Oh, Beach,' said his lordship, 'kindly put in a trunk-call to London on the telephone.'

'Very good, m'lord.'

'Get through to Suite Number Sixty-seven at the Savoy Hotel, and speak to Mr. Frederick.'

'Yes, your lordship.'

'Say that I particularly wish to know how that scenario of his ended.'

'Scenario, your lordship?'

'Scenario.'

'Very good, m'lord.'

Lord Emsworth returned to his reverie. Time passed. The butler returned.

'I have spoken to Mr. Frederick, your lordship.'

'Yes?'

'He instructed me to give your lordship his best wishes, and to tell you that, when the millionaire and Mr. Cove's wife entered the bedroom, there was a black jaguar tied to the foot of the bed.'

'A jaguar?'

'A jaguar, your lordship. Mrs. Cove stated that it was there to protect her honour, whereupon the millionaire, touched by this, gave her the money, and they sang the Theme Song as a duet. Mr. Cove made a satisfactory recovery after his operation, your lordship.'

'Ah!' said Lord Emsworth, expelling a deep breath. 'Thank you, Beach, that is all.'

Thanks to the publicity given to the matter by *The Bridgnorth, Shifnal and Albrighton Argus* (with which is incorporated *The Wheat-Growers' Intelligencer and Stock Breeders' Gazette*), the whole world to-day knows that the silver medal in the Fat Pigs class at the eighty-seventh annual Shropshire Agricultural Show was won by the Earl of Emsworth's black Berkshire sow, Empress of Blandings.

Very few people, however, are aware how near that splendid animal came to missing the coveted honour.

Now it can be told.

This brief chapter of Secret History may be said to have begun on the night of the eighteenth of July, when George Cyril Wellbeloved (twenty-nine), pig-man in the employ of Lord Emsworth, was arrested by Police Constable Evans of Market Blandings for being drunk and disorderly in the tap-room of the Goat and Feathers. On July the nineteenth, after first offering to apologise, then explaining that it had been his birthday, and finally attempting to prove an alibi, George Cyril was very properly jugged for fourteen days without the option of a fine.

On July the twentieth, Empress of Blandings, always hitherto a hearty and even a boisterous feeder, for the first time on record declined all nourishment. And on the morning of July the twenty-first, the veterinary surgeon called in to diagnose and deal with this strange asceticism, was compelled to confess to Lord Emsworth that the thing was beyond his professional skill.

Let us just see, before proceeding, that we have got these dates correct:

July 18. – Birthday Orgy of Cyril Wellbeloved.
July 19. – Incarceration of Ditto.
July 20. – Pig Lays off the Vitamins.
July 21. – Veterinary Surgeon Baffled.
Right.

The effect of the veterinary surgeon's announcement on Lord Emsworth was overwhelming. As a rule, the wear and tear of our complex life left this vague and amiable peer unscathed. So long as he had sunshine, regular meals, and complete freedom from the society of his younger son Frederick, he was placidly happy. But there were chinks in his armour, and one of these had been pierced this morning. Dazed by the news he had received, he stood at the window of the great library of Blandings Castle, looking out with unseeing eyes.

As he stood there, the door opened. Lord Emsworth turned; and having blinked once or twice, as was his habit when confronted suddenly with anything, recognized in the handsome and imperious-looking woman who had entered his sister, Lady Constance Keeble. Her demeanour, like his own, betrayed the deepest agitation.

'Clarence,' she cried, 'an awful thing has happened!'
Lord Emsworth nodded dully.
'I know. He's just told me.'

'What! Has he been here?'

'Only this moment left.'

'Why did you let him go? You must have known I would want to see him.'

'What good would that have done?'

'I could at least have assured him of my sympathy,' said Lady Constance stiffly.

'Yes, I suppose you could,' said Lord Emsworth, having considered the point. 'Not that he deserves any sympathy. The man's an ass.'

'Nothing of the kind. A most intelligent young man, as young men go.'

'Young? Would you call him young? Fifty, I should have said, if a day.'

'Are you out of your senses? Heacham fifty?'

'Not Heacham. Smithers.'

As frequently happened to her when in conversation with her brother, Lady Constance experienced a swimming sensation in the head.

'Will you kindly tell me, Clarence, in a few simple words, what you imagine we are talking about?'

'I'm talking about Smithers. Empress of Blandings is refusing her food, and Smithers says he can't do anything about it. And he calls himself a vet!'

'Then you haven't heard? Clarence, a dreadful thing has happened. Angela has broken off her engagement to Heacham.'

'And the Agricultural Show on Wednesday week!'

'What on earth has that got to do with it?' demanded Lady Constance, feeling a recurrence of the swimming sensation.

'What has it got to do with it?' said Lord Emsworth warmly. 'My champion sow, with less than ten days to prepare herself for a most searching examination in competition with all the finest pigs in the county, starts refusing her food—'

'Will you stop maundering on about your insufferable pig and give your attention to something that really matters? I tell you that Angela – your niece Angela – has broken off her engagement to Lord Heacham and expresses her intention of marrying that hopeless ne'er-do-well, James Belford.'

'The son of old Belford, the parson?'

'Yes.'

'She can't. He's in America.'

'He is not in America. He is in London.'

'No,' said Lord Emsworth, shaking his head sagely. 'You're wrong. I remember meeting his father two years ago out on the road by Meeker's twenty-acre field, and he distinctly told me the boy was sailing for America next day. He must be there by this time.'

'Can't you understand? He's come back.'

'Oh? Come back? I see. Come *back*?'

'You know there was once a silly sentimental sort of affair between him and Angela; but a year after he left she became engaged to Heacham and I thought the whole thing was over and done with. And now it seems that she met this young man Belford when she was in London last week, and it has started all over again. She tells me she has written to Heacham and broken the engagement.'

There was a silence. Brother and sister remained for a space plunged in thought. Lord Emsworth was the first to speak.

'We've tried acorns,' he said. 'We've tried skim milk. And we've tried potato-peel. But, no, she won't touch them.'

Conscious of two eyes raising blisters on his sensitive skin, he came to himself with a start.

'Absurd! Ridiculous! Preposterous!' he said, hurriedly. 'Breaking the engagement? Pooh! Tush! What non-sense! I'll have a word with that young man. If he thinks he can go about the place playing fast and loose with my niece and jilting her without so much as a—'

'Clarence!'

Lord Emsworth blinked. Something appeared to be wrong, but he could not imagine what. It seemed to him that in his last speech he had struck just the right note – strong, forceful, dignified.

'Eh?'

'It is Angela who has broken the engagement.'

'Oh, Angela?'

'She is infatuated with this man Belford. And the point is, what are we to do about it?'

Lord Emsworth reflected.

'Take a strong line,' he said firmly. 'Stand no nonsense. Don't send 'em a wedding-present.'

There is no doubt that, given time, Lady Constance would have found and uttered some adequately corrosive comment on this imbecile suggestion; but even as she was swelling preparatory to giving tongue, the door opened and a girl came in.

She was a pretty girl, with fair hair and blue eyes which in their softer moments probably reminded all sorts of people of twin lagoons slumbering beneath a southern sky. To Lord Emsworth, as they met his, they looked like something out of an oxy-acetylene blowpipe; and, as far as he was capable of being disturbed by anything that was not his younger son Frederick, he was disturbed. Angela, it seemed to him, was upset about something; and he was sorry. He liked Angela.

To ease a tense situation, he said:

'Angela, my dear, do you know anything about pigs?'

The girl laughed. One of those sharp, bitter laughs which are so unpleasant just after breakfast.

'Yes, I do. You're one.'

'Me?'

'Yes, you. Aunt Constance says that, if I marry Jimmy, you won't let me have my money.'

'Money? Money?' Lord Emsworth was mildly puzzled. 'What money? You never lent me any money.'

Lady Constance's feelings found vent in a sound like an overheated radiator.

'I believe this absent-mindedness of yours is nothing but a ridiculous pose, Clarence. You know perfectly well that when poor Jane died she left you Angela's trustee.'

'And I can't touch my money without your consent till I'm twenty-five.'

'Well, how old are you?'

'Twenty-one.'

'Then what are you worrying about?' asked Lord Emsworth, surprised. 'No need to worry about it for another four years. God bless my soul, the money is quite safe. It is in excellent securities.'

Angela stamped her foot. An unladylike action, no doubt, but how much better than kicking an uncle with it, as her lower nature prompted.

'I have told Angela,' explained Lady Constance, 'that, while we naturally cannot force her to marry Lord Heacham, we can at least keep her money from being squandered by this wastrel on whom she proposes to throw herself away.'

'He isn't a wastrel. He's got quite enough money to marry me on, but he wants some capital to buy a partnership in a—'

'He is a wastrel. Wasn't he sent abroad because—'

'That was two years ago. And since then—'

'My dear Angela, you may argue until—'

'I'm not arguing. I'm simply saying that I'm going to marry Jimmy, if we both have to starve in the gutter.'

'What gutter?' asked his lordship, wrenching his errant mind away from thoughts of acorns.

'Any gutter.'

'Now, please listen to me, Angela.'

It seemed to Lord Emsworth that there was a frightful amount of conversation going on. He had the sensation of having become a mere bit of flotsam upon a tossing sea of female voices. Both his sister and his niece appeared to have much to say, and they were saying it simultaneously and fortissimo. He looked wistfully at the door.

It was smoothly done. A twist of the handle, and he was where beyond those voices there was peace. Galloping gaily down the stairs, he charged out into the sunshine.

His gaiety was not long-lived. Free at last to concentrate itself on the really serious issues of life, his mind grew sombre and grim. Once more there descended upon him the cloud which had been oppressing his soul before all this Heacham-Angela-Belford business began. Each step that took him nearer to the sty where the ailing Empress resided seemed a heavier step than the last. He reached the sty; and, draping himself over the rails, peered moodily at the vast expanse of pig within.

For, even though she had been doing a bit of dieting of late, Empress of Blandings was far from being an ill-nourished animal. She resembled a captive balloon with ears and a tail, and was as nearly circular as a pig can be without bursting. Nevertheless, Lord Emsworth, as he regarded her, mourned and would not be comforted. A few more square meals under her belt, and no pig in all Shropshire could have held its head up in the Empress's presence. And now, just for lack of those few meals, the supreme animal would probably be relegated to the mean obscurity of an 'Honourably Mentioned'. It was bitter, bitter.

He became aware that somebody was speaking to him; and, turning, perceived a solemn young man in riding breeches.

'I say,' said the young man.

Lord Emsworth, though he would have preferred solitude, was relieved to find that the intruder was at least one of his own sex. Women are apt to stray off into side-issues, but men are practical and can be relied on to stick to the fundamentals. Besides, young Heacham probably kept pigs himself and might have a useful hint or two up his sleeve.

'I say, I've just ridden over to see if there was anything I could do about this fearful business.'

'Uncommonly kind and thoughtful of you, my dear fellow,' said Lord Emsworth, touched. 'I fear things look very black.'

'It's an absolute mystery to me.'

'To me, too.'

'I mean to say, she was all right last week.'

'She was all right as late as the day before yesterday.'

'Seemed quite cheery and chirpy and all that.'

'Entirely so.'

'And this happens – out of a blue sky, as you might say.'

'Exactly. It is insoluble. We have done everything possible to tempt her appetite.'

'Her appetite? Is Angela ill?'

'Angela? No, I fancy not. She seemed perfectly well a few minutes ago.'

'You've seen her this morning, then? Did she say anything about this fearful business?'

'No. She was speaking about some money.'

'It's all so dashed unexpected.'

'Like a bolt from the blue,' agreed Lord Emsworth. 'Such a thing has never happened before. I fear the worst. According to the Wolff-Lehmann feeding standards, a pig, if in health, should consume daily nourishment amounting to fifty-seven thousand eight hundred calories, these to consist of proteins four pounds five ounces, carbohydrates twenty-five pounds—'

'What has that got to do with Angela?'

'Angela?'

'I came to find out why Angela has broken off our engagement.'

Lord Emsworth marshalled his thoughts. He had a misty idea that he had heard something mentioned about that. It came back to him.

'Ah, yes, of course. She has broken off the engagement, hasn't she? I believe it is because she is in love with someone else. Yes, now that I recollect, that was distinctly stated. The whole thing comes back to me quite clearly. Angela has decided to marry someone else. I knew there was some satisfactory explanation. Tell me, my dear fellow, what are your views on linseed meal.'

'What do you mean, linseed meal?'

'Why, linseed meal,' said Lord Emsworth, not being able to find a better definition. 'As a food for pigs.'

'Oh, curse all pigs!'

'What!' There was a sort of astounded horror in Lord Emsworth's voice. He had never been particularly fond of young

Heacham, for he was not a man who took much to his juniors, but he had not supposed him capable of anarchistic sentiments like this. 'What did you say?'

'I said, "Curse all pigs!" You keep talking about pigs. I'm not interested in pigs. I don't want to discuss pigs. Blast and damn every pig in existence!'

Lord Emsworth watched him, as he strode away, with an emotion that was partly indignation and partly relief – indignation that a landowner and a fellow son of Shropshire could have brought himself to utter such words, and relief that one capable of such utterance was not going to marry into his family. He had always in his woollen-headed way been very fond of his niece Angela, and it was nice to think that the child had such solid good sense and so much cool discernment. Many girls of her age would have been carried away by the glamour of young Heacham's position and wealth; but she, divining with an intuition beyond her years that he was unsound on the subject of pigs, had drawn back while there was still time and refused to marry him.

A pleasant glow suffused Lord Emsworth's bosom, to be frozen out a few moments later as he perceived his sister Constance bearing down upon him. Lady Constance was a beautiful woman, but there were times when the charm of her face was marred by a rather curious expression; and from nursery days onward his lordship had learned that this expression meant trouble. She was wearing it now.

'Clarence,' she said, 'I have had enough of this nonsense of Angela and young Belford. The thing cannot be allowed to go drifting on. You must catch the two o'clock train to London.'

'What! Why?'

'You must see this man Belford and tell him that, if Angela

insists on marrying him, she will not have a penny for four years. I shall be greatly surprised if that piece of information does not put an end to the whole business.'

Lord Emsworth scratched meditatively at the Empress's tank-like back. A mutinous expression was on his mild face.

'Don't see why she shouldn't marry that fellow,' he mumbled.

'Marry James Belford?'

'I don't see why not. Seems fond of him and all that.'

'You never have had a grain of sense in your head, Clarence. Angela is going to marry Heacham.'

'Can't stand that man. All wrong about pigs.'

'Clarence, I don't wish to have any more discussion and argument. You will go to London on the two o'clock train. You will see Mr. Belford. And you will tell him about Angela's money. Is that quite clear?'

'Oh, all right,' said his lordship moodily. 'All right, all right, all right.'

The emotions of the Earl of Emsworth, as he sat next day facing his luncheon-guest, James Batholomew Belford, across a table in the main dining-room of the Senior Conservative Club, were not of the liveliest and most agreeable. It was bad enough to be in London at all on such a day of golden sunshine. To be charged, while there, with the task of blighting the romance of two young people for whom he entertained a warm regard was unpleasant to a degree.

For, now that he had given the matter thought, Lord Emsworth recalled that he had always liked this boy Belford. A pleasant lad, with, he remembered now, a healthy fondness for that rural existence which so appealed to himself. By no means the sort of fellow who, in the very presence and hearing of

Empress of Blandings, would have spoken disparagingly and with oaths of pigs as a class. It occurred to Lord Emsworth, as it has occurred to so many people, that the distribution of money in this world is all wrong. Why should a man like pig-despising Heacham have a rent roll that ran into the tens of thousands, while this very deserving youngster had nothing?

These thoughts not only saddened Lord Emsworth – they embarrassed him. He hated unpleasantness, and it was suddenly borne in upon him that, after he had broken the news that Angela's bit of capital was locked up and not likely to get loose, conversation with his young friend during the remainder of lunch would tend to be somewhat difficult.

He made up his mind to postpone the revelation. During the meal, he decided, he would chat pleasantly of this and that; and then, later, while bidding his guest goodbye, he would spring the thing on him suddenly and dive back into the recesses of the club.

Considerably cheered at having solved a delicate problem with such adroitness, he started to prattle.

'The gardens at Blandings,' he said, 'are looking particularly attractive this summer. My head-gardener, Angus McAllister, is a man with whom I do not always find myself seeing eye to eye, notably in the matter of hollyhocks, on which I consider his views subversive to a degree; but there is no denying that he understands roses. The rose-garden—'

'How well I remember that rose-garden,' said James Belford, sighing slightly and helping himself to brussels sprouts. 'It was there that Angela and I used to meet on summer mornings.'

Lord Emsworth blinked. This was not an encouraging start, but the Emsworths were a fighting clan. He had another try.

'I have seldom seen such a blaze of colour as was to be

witnessed there during the month of June. Both McAllister and I adopted a very strong policy with the slugs and plant lice, with the result that the place was a mass of flourishing Damasks and Ayrshires and—'

'Properly to appreciate roses,' said James Belford, 'You want to see them as a setting for a girl like Angela. With her fair hair gleaming against the green leaves she makes a rose-garden seem a veritable Paradise.'

'No doubt,' said Lord Emsworth. 'No doubt. I am glad you like my rose-garden. At Blandings, of course, we have the natural advantage of loamy soil, rich in plant food and humus; but, as I often say to McAllister, and on this point we have never had the slightest disagreement, loamy soil by itself is not enough. You must have manure. If every autumn a liberal mulch of stable manure is spread upon the beds and the coarser parts removed in the spring before the annual forking—'

'Angela tells me,' said James Belford, 'that you have forbidden our marriage.'

Lord Emsworth choked dismally over his chicken. Directness of this kind, he told himself with a pang of self-pity, was the sort of thing young Englishmen picked up in America. Diplomatic circumlocution flourished only in a more leisurely civilization, and in those energetic and forceful surroundings you learned to Talk Quick and Do It Now, and all sorts of uncomfortable things.

'Er – well, yes, now you mention it, I believe some informal decision of that nature was arrived at. You see, my dear fellow, my sister Constance feels rather strongly—'

'I understand. I suppose she thinks I'm a sort of prodigal.'

'No, no, my dear fellow. She never said that. Wastrel was the term she employed.'

'Well, perhaps I did start out in business on those lines. But you can take it from me that when you find yourself employed on a farm in Nebraska belonging to an applejack-nourished patriarch with strong views on work and a good vocabulary, you soon develop a certain liveliness.'

'Are you employed on a farm?'

'I was employed on a farm.'

'Pigs?' said Lord Emsworth in a low, eager voice.

'Among other things.'

Lord Emsworth gulped. His fingers clutched at the table-cloth.

'Then perhaps, my dear fellow, you can give me some advice. For the last two days my prize sow, Empress of Blandings, has declined all nourishment. And the Agricultural Show is on Wednesday week. I am distracted with anxiety.' James Belford frowned thoughtfully.

'What does your pig-man say about it?'

'My pig-man was sent to prison two days ago. Two days!' For the first time the significance of the coincidence struck him. 'You don't think that can have anything to do with the animal's loss of appetite?'

'Certainly. I imagine she is missing him and pining away because he isn't there.'

Lord Emsworth was surprised. He had only a distant acquaintance with George Cyril Wellbeloved, but from what he had seen of him he had not credited him with this fatal allure.

'She probably misses his afternoon call.'

Again his lordship found himself perplexed. He had had no notion that pigs were such sticklers for the formalities of social life.

'His call?'

'He must have had some special call that he used when he

wanted her to come to dinner. One of the first things you learn on a farm is hog-calling. Pigs are temperamental. Omit to call them, and they'll starve rather than put on the nose-bag. Call them right, and they will follow you to the ends of the earth with their mouths watering.'

'God bless my soul! Fancy that.'

'A fact, I assure you. These calls vary in different parts of America. In Wisconsin, for example, the words "Poig, Poig, Poig" bring home – in both the literal and the figurative sense – the bacon. In Illinois, I believe they call "Burp, Burp, Burp", while in Iowa the phrase "Kus, Kus, Kus" is preferred. Proceeding to Minnesota, we find "Peega, Peega, Peega" or, alternatively, "Oink, Oink, Oink", whereas in Milwaukee, so largely inhabited by those of German descent, you will hear the good old Teuton "Komm Schweine, Komm Schweine". Oh, yes, there are all sorts of pig-calls, from the Massachusetts "Phew, Phew, Phew" to the "Loo-ey, Loo-ey, Loo-ey" of Ohio, not counting various local devices such as beating on tin cans with axes or rattling pebbles in a suit-case. I knew a man out in Nebraska who used to call his pigs by tapping on the edge of the trough with his wooden leg.'

'Did he, indeed?'

'But a most unfortunate thing happened. One evening, hearing a woodpecker at the top of a tree, they started shinning up it; and when the man came out he found them all lying there in a circle with their necks broken.'

'This is no time for joking,' said Lord Emsworth, pained.

'I'm not joking. Solid fact. Ask anybody out there.'

Lord Emsworth placed a hand to his throbbing forehead.

'But if there is this wide variety, we have no means of knowing which call Wellbeloved . . .'

'Ah,' said James Belford, 'but wait. I haven't told you all. There is a master-word.'

'A what?'

'Most people don't know it, but I had it straight from the lips of Fred Patzel, the hog-calling champion of the Western States. What a man! I've known him to bring pork chops leaping from their plates. He informed me that, no matter whether an animal has been trained to answer to the Illinois "Burp" or the Minnesota "Oink", it will always give immediate service in response to this magic combination of syllables. It is to the pig world what the Masonic grip is to the human. "Oink" in Illinois or "Burp" in Minnesota, and the animal merely raises its eyebrows and stares coldly. But go to either state and call "Pig-hoo-oo-ey!" . . .'

The expression on Lord Emsworth's face was that of a drowning man who sees a lifeline.

'Is that the master-word of which you spoke?'

'That's it.'

'Pig-?'

'– hoo-oo-ey.'

'Pig-hoo-o-ey?'

'You haven't got it quite right. The first syllable should be short and staccato, the second long and rising into a falsetto, high but true.'

'Pig-hoo-o-o-ey.'

'Pig-hoo-o-o-ey.'

'Pig-hoo-o-o-ey!' yodelled Lord Emsworth, flinging his head back and giving tongue in a high, penetrating tenor which caused ninety-three Senior Conservatives, lunching in the vicinity, to congeal into living statues of alarm and disapproval.

'More body to the "hoo",' advised James Belford.

'Pig-hoo-o-o-o-ey!'

The Senior Conservative Club is one of the few places in London where lunchers are not accustomed to getting music with their meals. White-whiskered financiers gazed bleakly at bald-headed politicians, as if asking silently what was to be done about this. Bald-headed politicians stared back at white-whiskered financiers, replying in the language of the eye that they did not know. The general sentiment prevailing was a vague determination to write to the Committee about it.

'Pig-hoo-o-o-o-ey!' carolled Lord Emsworth. And, as he did so, his eye fell on the clock over the mantelpiece. Its hands pointed to twenty minutes to two.

He started convulsively. The best train in the day for Market Blandings was the one which left Paddington Station at two sharp. After that there was nothing till the five-five.

He was not a man who often thought; but, when he did, to think was with him to act. A moment later he was scudding over the carpet, making for the door that led to the broad staircase.

Throughout the room which he had left, the decision to write in strong terms to the Committee was now universal; but from the mind, such as it was, of Lord Emsworth the past, with the single exception of the word 'Pig-hoo-o-o-o-ey!' had been completely blotted.

Whispering the magic syllables, he sped to the cloakroom and retrieved his hat. Murmuring them over and over again, he sprang into a cab. He was still repeating them as the train moved out of the station; and he would doubtless have gone on repeating them all the way to Market Blandings, had he not, as was his invariable practice when travelling by rail, fallen asleep after the first ten minutes of the journey.

The stopping of the train at Swindon Junction woke him

with a start. He sat up, wondering, after his usual fashion on these occasions, who and where he was. Memory returned to him, but a memory that was, alas, incomplete. He remembered his name. He remembered that he was on his way home from a visit to London. But what it was that you said to a pig when inviting it to drop in for a bite of dinner he had completely forgotten.

It was the opinion of Lady Constance Keeble, expressed verbally during dinner in the brief intervals when they were alone, and by means of silent telepathy when Beach, the butler, was adding his dignified presence to the proceedings, that her brother Clarence, in his expedition to London to put matters plainly to James Belford, had made an outstanding idiot of himself.

There had been no need whatever to invite the man Belford to lunch; but, having invited him to lunch, to leave him sitting, without having clearly stated that Angela would have no money for four years, was the act of a congenital imbecile. Lady Constance had been aware ever since their childhood days that her brother had about as much sense as a—

Here Beach entered, superintending the bringing-in of the savoury, and she had been obliged to suspend her remarks.

This sort of conversation is never agreeable to a sensitive man, and his lordship had removed himself from the danger zone as soon as he could manage it. He was now seated in the library, sipping port and straining his brain which Nature had never intended for hard exercise in an effort to bring back that word of magic of which his unfortunate habit of sleeping in trains had robbed him.

'Pig—'

He could remember as far as that; but of what avail was a

single syllable? Besides, weak as his memory was, he could recall that the whole gist or nub of the thing lay in the syllable that followed. The 'pig' was a mere preliminary.

Lord Emsworth finished his port and got up. He felt restless, stifled. The summer night seemed to call to him like some silver-voiced swineherd calling to his pig. Possibly, he thought, a breath of fresh air might stimulate his brain-cells. He wandered downstairs; and, having dug a shocking old slouch hat out of the cupboard where he hid it to keep his sister Constance from impounding and burning it, he strode heavily out into the garden.

He was pottering aimlessly to and fro in the parts adjacent to the rear of the castle when there appeared in his path a slender female form. He recognized it without pleasure. Any unbiased judge would have said that his niece Angela, standing there in the soft, pale light, looked like some dainty spirit of the moon. Lord Emsworth was not an unbiased judge. To him Angela merely looked like Trouble. The march of civilization has given the modern girl a vocabulary and an ability to use it which her grandmother never had. Lord Emsworth would not have minded meeting Angela's grandmother a bit.

'Is that you, my dear?' he said nervously.

'Yes.'

'I didn't see you at dinner.'

'I didn't want any dinner. The food would have choked me. I can't eat.'

'It's precisely the same with my pig,' said his lordship. 'Young Belford tells me—'

Into Angela's queenly disdain there flashed a sudden animation.

'Have you seen Jimmy? What did he say?'

'That's just what I can't remember. It began with the word "Pig"—'

'But after he had finished talking about you, I mean. Didn't he say anything about coming down here?'

'Not that I remember.'

'I expect you weren't listening. You've got a very annoying habit, Uncle Clarence,' said Angela maternally, 'of switching your mind off and just going blah when people are talking to you. It gets you very much disliked on all sides. Didn't Jimmy say anything about me?'

'I fancy so. Yes, I am nearly sure he did.'

'Well, what.'

'I cannot remember.'

There was a sharp clicking noise in the darkness. It was caused by Angela's upper front teeth meeting her lower front teeth; and was followed by a sort of wordless exclamation. It seemed only too plain that the love and respect which a niece should have for an uncle were in the present instance at a very low ebb.

'I wish you wouldn't do that,' said Lord Emsworth plaintively.

'Do what?'

'Make clicking noises at me.'

'I will make clicking noises at you. You know perfectly well, Uncle Clarence, that you are behaving like a bohunkus.'

'A what?'

'A bohunkus,' explained his niece, coldly, 'is a very inferior sort of worm. Not the kind of worm that you see on lawns, which you can respect, but a really degraded species.'

'I wish you would go in, my dear,' said Lord Emsworth. 'The night air may give you a chill.'

'I won't go in. I came out here to look at the moon and think of Jimmy. What are you doing out here, if it comes to that?'

'I came here to think. I am greatly exercised about my pig, Empress of Blandings. For two days she has refused her food, and young Belford says she will not eat until she hears the proper call or cry. He very kindly taught it to me, but unfortunately I have forgotten it.'

'I wonder you had the nerve to ask Jimmy to teach you pig-calls, considering the way you're treating him.'

'But—'

'Like a leper, or something. And all I can say is that, if you remember this call of his, and it makes the Empress eat, you ought to be ashamed of yourself if you still refuse to let me marry him.'

'My dear,' said Lord Emsworth earnestly, 'if through young Belford's instrumentality Empress of Blandings is induced to take nourishment once more, there is nothing I will refuse him – nothing.'

'Honour bright?'

'I give you my solemn word.'

'You won't let Aunt Constance bully you out of it?'

Lord Emsworth drew himself up.

'Certainly not,' he said proudly. 'I am always ready to listen to your Aunt Constance's view, but there are certain matters where I claim the right to act according to my own judgment.' He paused and stood musing. 'It began with the word "Pig—".'

From somewhere near at hand music made itself heard. The servants' hall, its day's labours ended, was refreshing itself with the housekeeper's gramophone. To Lord Emsworth the strains were merely an additional annoyance. He was not fond of music. It reminded him of his younger son Frederick, a flat but persevering songster both in and out of the bath.

'Yes, I can distinctly recall as much as that. Pig – Pig—'

'WHO—'

Lord Emsworth leaped in the air. It was as if an electric shock had been applied to his person.

'WHO stole my heart away?' howled the gramophone. 'WHO—?'

The peace of the summer night was shattered by a triumphant shout.

'Pig-HOO-o-o-o-ey!'

A window opened. A large, bald head appeared. A dignified voice spoke.

'Who is there? Who is making that noise?'

'Beach!' cried Lord Emsworth. 'Come out here at once.'

'Very good, your lordship.'

And presently the beautiful night was made still more lovely by the added attraction of the butler's presence.

'Beach, listen to this.'

'Very good, your lordship.'

'Pig-hoo-o-o-o-ey!'

'Very good, your lordship.'

'Now you do it.'

'I, your lordship?'

'Yes. It's a way you call pigs.'

'I do not call pigs, your lordship,' said the butler coldly.

'What do you want Beach to do it for?' asked Angela.

'Two heads are better than one. If we both learn it, it will not matter should I forget it again.'

'By Jove, yes! Come on, Beach. Push it over the thorax,' urged the girl eagerly. 'You don't know it, but this is a matter of life and death. At-a-boy, Beach! Inflate the lungs and go to it.'

It had been the butler's intention, prefacing his remarks with the statement that he had been in service at the Castle for eighteen years, to explain frigidly to Lord Emsworth that it was not his place to stand in the moonlight practising pig-calls. If, he would have gone on to add, his lordship saw the matter from a different angle, then it was his, Beach's, painful duty to tender his resignation, to become effective one month from that day.

But the intervention of Angela made this impossible to a man of chivalry and heart. A paternal fondness for the girl, dating from the days when he had stooped to enacting – and very convincingly, too, for his was a figure that lent itself to the impersonation – the *role* of a hippopotamus for her childish amusement, checked the words he would have uttered. She was looking at him with bright eyes, and even the rendering of pig-noises seemed a small sacrifice to make for her sake.

'Very good, your lordship,' he said in a low voice, his face pale and set in the moonlight. 'I shall endeavour to give satisfaction. I would merely advance the suggestion, your lordship, that we move a few steps farther away from the vicinity of the servants' hall. If I were to be overheard by any of the lower domestics, it would weaken my position as a disciplinary force.'

'What chumps we are!' cried Angela, inspired. 'The place to do it is outside the Empress's sty. Then, if it works, we'll see it working.'

Lord Emsworth found this a little abstruse, but after a moment he got it.

'Angela,' he said, 'You are a very intelligent girl. Where you get your brains from, I don't know. Not from my side of the family.'

The bijou residence of the Empress of Blandings looked very snug and attractive in the moonlight. But beneath even the beautiful things of life there is always an underlying sadness. This was supplied in the present instance by a long, low trough, only too plainly full to the brim of succulent mash and acorns. The fast, obviously, was still in progress.

The sty stood some considerable distance from the Castle walls, so that there had been ample opportunity for Lord Emsworth to rehearse his little company during the journey. By the time they had ranged themselves against the rails, his two assistants were letter-perfect.

'Now,' said his lordship.

There floated out upon the summer night a strange composite sound that sent the birds roosting in the trees above shooting off their perches like rockets. Angela's clear soprano rang out like the voice of the village blacksmith's daughter. Lord Emsworth contributed a reedy tenor. And the bass notes of Beach probably did more to startle the birds than any other one item in the programme.

They paused and listened. Inside the Empress's boudoir there sounded the movement of a heavy body. There was an inquiring grunt. The next moment the sacking that covered the door way was pushed aside, and the noble animal emerged.

'Now!' said Lord Emsworth again.

Once more that musical cry shattered the silence of the night. But it brought no responsive movement from Empress of Blandings. She stood there motionless, her nose elevated, her ears hanging down, her eyes everywhere but on the trough where, by rights, she should now have been digging in and getting hers. A chill disappointment crept over Lord Emsworth, to be succeeded by a gust of petulant anger.

'I might have known it,' he said bitterly. 'That young scoundrel was deceiving me. He was playing a joke on me.'

'He wasn't,' cried Angela indignantly. 'Was he, Beach?'

'Not knowing the circumstances, miss, I cannot venture an opinion.'

'Well, why has it no effect, then?' demanded Lord Emsworth.

'You can't expect it to work right away. We've got her stirred up, haven't we? She's thinking it over, isn't she? Once more will do the trick. Ready, Beach?'

'Quite ready, miss.'

'Then when I say three. And this time, Uncle Clarence, do please for goodness' sake not yowl like you did before. It was enough to put any pig off. Let it come out quite easily and gracefully. Now, then, one, two – three!'

The echoes died away. And as they did so a voice spoke.

'Community singing!'

'Jimmy!' cried Angela, whisking round.

'Hullo, Angela. Hullo, Lord Emsworth. Hullo, Beach.'

'Good evening, sir. Happy to see you once more.'

'Thanks. I'm spending a few days at the Vicarage with my father. I got down here by the five-five.'

Lord Emsworth cut peevishly in upon these civilities.

'Young man,' he said, 'what do you mean by telling me that my pig would respond to that cry? It does nothing of the kind.'

'You can't have done it right.'

'I did it precisely as you instructed me. I have had, moreover, the assistance of Beach here and my niece Angela—'

'Let's hear a sample.'

Lord Emsworth cleared his throat.

'Pig-hoo-o-o-o-ey!'

James Belford shook his head.

'Nothing like it,' he said. 'You want to begin the "Hoo" in a low minor of two quarter notes in four-four time. From this build gradually to a higher note, until at last the voice is soaring in full crescendo, reaching F sharp on the natural scale and dwelling for two retarded half-notes, then breaking into a shower of accidental grace-notes.'

'God bless my soul!' said Lord Emsworth, appalled. 'I shall never be able to do it.'

'Jimmy will do it for you,' said Angela. 'Now that he's engaged to me, he'll be one of the family and always popping about here. He can do it every day till the show is over.'

James Belford nodded.

'I think that would be the wisest plan. It is doubtful if an amateur could ever produce real results. You need a voice that has been trained on the open prairie and that has gathered richness and strength from competing with tornadoes. You need a manly, sunburned, wind-scorched voice with a suggestion in it of the crackling of corn husks and the whisper of evening breezes in the fodder. Like this!'

Resting his hands on the rail before him, James Belford swelled before their eyes like a young balloon. The muscles on his cheekbones stood out, his forehead became corrugated, his ears seemed to shimmer. Then, at the very height of the tension, he let it go like, as the poet beautifully puts it, the sound of a great Amen.

'Pig-HOOOOO-OOO-OOO-O-O-ey!'

They looked at him, awed. Slowly, fading off across hill and dale, the vast bellow died away. And suddenly, as it died, another, softer sound succeeded it. A sort of gulpy, gurgly, ploddy, squishy, woffle-some sound, like a thousand eager men drinking soup in a foreign restaurant. And, as he heard it, Lord Emsworth uttered a cry of rapture.

The Empress was feeding.

## 1. TROUBLE BREWING AT BLANDINGS

### I

Blandings Castle slept in the sunshine. Dancing little ripples of heat-mist played across its smooth lawns and stone-flagged terraces. The air was full of the lulling drone of insects. It was that gracious hour of a summer afternoon, midway between luncheon and tea, when Nature seems to unbutton its waistcoat and put its feet up.

In the shade of a laurel bush outside the back premises of this stately home of England, Beach, butler to Clarence, ninth Earl of Emsworth, its proprietor, sat sipping the contents of a long glass and reading a weekly paper devoted to the doings of Society and the Stage. His attention had just been arrested by a photograph in an oval border on one of the inner pages: and for perhaps a minute he scrutinized this in a slow, thorough, pop-eyed way, absorbing its every detail. Then, with a fruity chuckle, he took a penknife from his pocket, cut out the photograph, and placed it in the recesses of his costume.

At this moment, the laurel bush, which had hitherto not spoken, said 'Psst!'

The butler started violently. A spasm ran through his ample frame.

'Beach!' said the bush.

Something was now peering out of it. This might have been a wood-nymph, but the butler rather thought not, and he was right. It was a tall young man with light hair. He recognised his employer's secretary, Mr. Hugo Carmody, and rose with pained reproach. His heart was still jumping, and he had bitten his tongue.

'Startle you, Beach?'

'Extremely, sir.'

'I'm sorry. Excellent for the liver, though. Beach, do you want to earn a quid?'

The butler's austerity softened. The hard look died out of his eyes.

'Yes, sir.'

'Can you get hold of Miss Millicent alone?'

'Certainly, sir.'

'Then give her this note, and don't let anyone see you do it. Especially – and this is where I want you to follow me very closely, Beach – Lady Constance Keeble.'

'I will attend to the matter immediately, sir.'

He smiled a paternal smile. Hugo smiled back. A perfect understanding prevailed between these two. Beach understood that he ought not to be giving his employer's niece surreptitious notes: and Hugo understood that he ought not to be urging a good man to place such a weight upon his conscience.

'Perhaps you are not aware, sir,' said the butler, having trousered the wages of sin, 'that her ladyship went up to London on the 3.30 train?'

Hugo uttered an exclamation of chagrin.

'You mean that all this Red Indian stuff – creeping from bush to bush and not letting a single twig snap beneath my feet – has simply been a waste of time?' He emerged, dusting his clothes. 'I wish I'd known that before,' he said. 'I've severely injured a good suit, and it's a very moot question whether I haven't got some kind of a beetle down my back. However, nobody ever took a toss through being careful.'

'Very true, sir.'

Relieved by the information that the X-ray eye of the aunt of the girl he loved was operating elsewhere, Mr. Carmody became conversational.

'Nice day, Beach.'

'Yes, sir.'

'You know, Beach, life's rummy. I mean to say, you never can tell what the future holds in store. Here I am at Blandings Castle, loving it. Sing of joy, sing of bliss, home was never like this. And yet, when the project of my coming here was first placed on the agenda, I don't mind telling you the heart was rather bowed down with weight of woe.'

'Indeed, sir?'

'Yes. Noticeably bowed down. If you knew the circumstances, you would understand why.'

Beach did know the circumstances. There were few facts concerning the dwellers in Blandings Castle of which he remained in ignorance for long. He was aware that young Mr. Carmody had been, until a few weeks back, co-proprietor with Mr. Ronald Fish, Lord Emsworth's nephew, of a night-club called the Hot Spot, situated just off Bond Street in the heart of London's pleasure-seeking area; that, despite this favoured position, it had proved a financial failure; that Mr. Ronald had gone off with his mother, Lady Julia Fish, to recuperate at Biarritz; and that Hugo on the insistence of Ronnie that unless some niche was found for his boyhood friend he would not stir a step towards Biarritz or any other blighted place, had come to Blandings as Lord Emsworth's private secretary.

'No doubt you were reluctant to leave London, sir?'

'Exactly. But now, Beach, believe me or believe me not, as far as I am concerned, anyone who likes can have London. Mark you, I'm not saying that just one brief night in the Piccadilly neighbourhood would come amiss. But to dwell in, give me Blandings Castle. What a spot, Beach!'

'Yes, sir.'

'A Garden of Eden, shall I call it?'

'Certainly, sir, if you wish.'

'And now that old Ronnie's coming here, joy, as you might say, will be unconfined.'

'Is Mr. Ronald expected, sir?'

'Coming either to-morrow or the day after. I had a letter from him this morning. Which reminds me. He sends his regards to you, and asks me to tell you to put your shirt on Baby Bones for the Medbury Selling Plate.'

The butler pursed his lips dubiously.

'A long shot, sir. Not generally fancied.'

'Rank outsider. Leave it alone, is my verdict.'

'And yet Mr. Ronald is usually very reliable. It is many years now since he first began to advise me in these matters, and I have done remarkably well by following him. Even as a lad at Eton he was always singularly fortunate in his information.'

'Well, suit yourself,' said Hugo, indifferently. 'What was that thing you were cutting out of the paper just now?'

'A photograph of Mr. Galahad, sir. I keep an album in which I paste items of interest relating to the Family.'

'What that album needs is an eye-witness's description of

Lady Constance Keeble falling out of a window and breaking her neck.'

A nice sense of the proprieties prevented Beach from endorsing this view verbally, but he sighed a little wistfully. He had frequently felt much the same about the chatelaine of Blandings.

'If you would care to see the clipping, sir? There is a reference to Mr. Galahad's literary work.'

Most of the photographs in the weekly paper over which Beach had been relaxing were of peeresses trying to look like chorus-girls and chorus-girls trying to look like peeresses: but this one showed the perky features of a dapper little gentleman in the late 'fifties. Beneath it, in large letters, was the single word:

### 'GALLY'

Under this ran a caption in smaller print.

*The Hon. Galahad Threepwood, brother of the Earl of Emsworth. A little bird tells us that "Gally" is at Blandings Castle, Shropshire, the ancestral seat of the family, busily engaged in writing his Reminiscences. As every member of the Old Brigade will testify, they ought to be as warm as the weather if not warmer.'*

Hugo scanned the exhibit thoughtfully, and handed it back, to be placed in the archives.

'Yes,' he observed, 'I should say that about summed it up. That old bird must have been pretty hot stuff, I imagine, back in the days of Edward the Confessor.'

'Mr. Galahad was somewhat wild as a young man,' agreed the butler with a sort of feudal pride in his voice. It was the opinion of the Servants' Hall that the Hon. Galahad shed lustre on Blandings Castle.

'Has it ever occurred to you, Beach, that that book of his is going to make no small stir when it comes out?'

'Frequently, sir.'

'Well, I'm saving up for my copy. By the way, I knew there was something I wanted to ask you. Can you give me any information on the subject of a bloke named Baxter?'

'Mr. Baxter, sir? He used to be private secretary to his lordship.'

'Yes, so I gathered. Lady Constance was speaking to me about him this morning. She happened upon me as I was taking the air in riding kit and didn't seem overpleased. "You appear to enjoy a great deal of leisure, Mr. Carmody," she said. "Mr. Baxter," she continued, giving me the meaning eye, "never seemed to find time to go riding when he was Lord Emsworth's secretary. Mr. Baxter was always so hard at work. But, then, Mr. Baxter," she added, the old lamp becoming more meaning than ever, "loved his work. Mr. Baxter took a real interest in his duties. Dear me! What a very conscientious man Mr. Baxter was, to be sure!" Or words to that effect. I may be wrong, but I classed it as a dirty dig. And what I want to know is, if Baxter was such a world-beater, why did they ever let him go?'

The butler gazed about him cautiously.

'I fancy, sir, there was some Trouble.'

'Pinched the spoons, eh? Always the way with these zealous workers.'

'I never succeeded in learning the full details, sir, but there was something about some flower-pots.'

'He pinched the flower-pots?'

'Threw them at his lordship, I was given to understand.'

Hugo looked injured. He was a high-spirited young man who chafed at injustice.

'Well, I'm dashed if I see then,' he said, 'where this Baxter can claim to rank so jolly high above me as a secretary. I may be leisurely, I may forget to answer letters, I may occasionally on warm afternoons go in to some extent for the folding of the hands in sleep, but at least I don't throw flower-pots at people. Not so much as a pen-wiper have I ever bunged at Lord Emsworth. Well, I must be getting about my duties. That ride this morning and a slight slumber after lunch have set the schedule back a bit. You won't forget that note, will you?'

'No, sir.'

Hugo reflected.

'On second thoughts,' he said, 'perhaps you'd better hand it back to me. Safer not to have too much written matter circulating about the place. Just tell Miss Millicent that she will find me in the rose-garden at six sharp.'

'In the rose-garden . . .'

'At six sharp.'

'Very good, sir. I will see that she receives the information.'

## II

For two hours after this absolutely nothing happened in the grounds of Blandings Castle. At the end of that period there sounded through the mellow, drowsy stillness a drowsy, mellow chiming. It was the clock over the stables striking five. Simultaneously, a small but noteworthy procession filed out of the house and made its way across the sun-bathed lawn to where the big cedar cast a grateful shade. It was headed by James, a footman, bearing a laden tray. Following him came Thomas, another footman, with a gate-leg table. The rear was brought up by Beach, who carried nothing, but merely lent a tone.

The instinct which warns all good Englishmen when tea is ready immediately began to perform its silent duty. Even as Thomas set gate-leg table to earth there appeared, as if answering a cue, an elderly gentleman in stained tweeds and a hat he should have been ashamed of. Clarence, ninth Earl of Emsworth, in person. He was a long, lean, stringy man of about sixty, slightly speckled at the moment with mud, for he had spent most of the afternoon pottering round pig-styes. He surveyed the preparations for the meal with vague amiability through rimless pince-nez.

'Tea?'

'Yes, your lordship.'

'Oh?' said Lord Emsworth. 'Ah? Tea, eh? Tea? Yes. Tea. Quite so. To be sure, tea. Capital.'

One gathered from his remarks that he realized that the tea-hour had arrived and was glad of it. He proceeded to impart his discovery to his niece, Millicent, who, lured by that same silent call, had just appeared at his side.

'Tea, Millicent.'

'Yes.'

'Er – tea,' said Lord Emsworth, driving home his point.

Millicent sat down, and busied herself with the pot. She was a tall, fair girl with soft blue eyes and a face like the Soul's Awakening. Her whole appearance radiated wholesome innocence. Not even an expert could have told that she had just received a whispered message from a bribed butler and was proposing at six sharp to go and meet a quite ineligible young man among the rose-bushes.

'Been down seeing the Empress, Uncle Clarence?'

'Eh? Oh, yes. Yes, my dear. I have been with her all the afternoon.'

Lord Emsworth's mild eyes beamed. They always did when that noble animal, Empress of Blandings, was mentioned. The ninth Earl was a man of few and simple ambitions. He had never desired to mould the destinies of the State, to frame its laws and make speeches in the House of Lords that would bring all the peers and bishops to their feet, whooping and waving their hats. All he yearned to do, by way of ensuring admittance to England's Hall of Fame, was to tend his prize sow, Empress of Blandings, so sedulously that for the second time in two consecutive years she would win the silver medal in the Fat Pigs class at the Shropshire Agricultural Show. And every day, it seemed to him, the glittering prize was coming more and more within his grasp.

Earlier in the summer there had been one breathless sickening moment of suspense, and disaster had seemed to loom. This was when his neighbour, Sir Gregory Parsloe-Parsloe, of Matchingham Hall, had basely lured away his pig-man, the superbly gifted George Cyril Wellbeloved, by the promise of higher wages. For a while Lord Emsworth had feared lest the Empress, mourning for her old friend and valet, might refuse food and fall from her high standard of obesity. But his apprehensions had proved groundless. The Empress had taken to Pirbright, George Cyril's successor, from the first, and was tucking away her meals with all the old abandon. The Right triumphs in this world far more often than we realize.

'What do you do to her?' asked Millicent, curiously. 'Read her bedtime stories?'

Lord Emsworth pursed his lips. He had a reverent mind, and disliked jesting on serious subjects.

'Whatever I do, my dear, it seems to effect its purpose. She is in wonderful shape.'

'I didn't know she had a shape. She hadn't when I last saw her.'

This time Lord Emsworth smiled indulgently. Gibes at the Empress's rotundity had no sting for him. He did not desire for her that school-girl slimness which is so fashionable nowadays.

'She has never fed more heartily,' he said. 'It is a treat to watch her.'

'I'm so glad. Mr. Carmody,' said Millicent, stooping to tickle a spaniel which had wandered up to take pot-luck, 'told me he had never seen a finer animal in his life.'

'I like that young man,' said Lord Emsworth emphatically. 'He is sound on pigs. He has his head screwed on the right way.'

'Yes, he's an improvement on Baxter, isn't he?'

'Baxter!' His lordship choked over his cup.

'You didn't like Baxter much, did you, Uncle Clarence?'

'Hadn't a peaceful moment while he was in the place. Dreadful feller! Always fussing. Always wanting me to *do* things. Always coming round corners with his infernal spectacles gleaming and making me sign papers when I wanted to be out in the garden. Besides, he was off his head. Thank goodness I've seen the last of Baxter.'

'But have you?'

'What do you mean?'

'If you ask me,' said Millicent, 'Aunt Constance hasn't given up the idea of getting him back.'

Lord Emsworth started with such violence that his pince-nez fell off. She had touched on his favourite nightmare. Sometimes he would wake trembling in the night, fancying that his late secretary had returned to the Castle. And though on these occasions he always dropped off to sleep again with a happy smile of relief, he had never ceased to be haunted by the fear that his sister Constance, in her infernal managing way, was scheming to restore the fellow to office.

'Good God! Has she said anything to you?'

'No. But I have a feeling. I know she doesn't like Mr. Carmody.'

Lord Emsworth exploded.

'Perfect nonsense! Utter, absolute, dashed nonsense. What on earth does she find to object to in young Carmody? Most capable, intelligent boy. Leaves me alone. Doesn't fuss me. I wish to heaven she would . . .'

He broke off, and stared blankly at a handsome woman of middle age who had come out of the house and was crossing the lawn.

'Why, here she is!' said Millicent, equally and just as disagreeably surprised. 'I thought you had gone up to London, Aunt Constance.'

Lady Constance Keeble had arrived at the table. Declining, with a distrait shake of the head, her niece's offer of the seat of honour by the tea-pot, she sank into a chair. She was a woman of still remarkable beauty, with features cast in a commanding mould and fine eyes. These eyes were at the moment dull and brooding.

'I missed my train,' she explained. 'However, I can do all I have to do in London to-morrow. I shall go up by the eleven-fifteen. In a way, it will be more convenient, for Ronald will be able to motor me back. I will look in at Norfolk Street and pick him up there before he starts.'

'What made you miss your train?'

'Yes,' said Lord Emsworth, complainingly. 'You started in good time.'

The brooding look in his sister's eyes deepened.

'I met Sir Gregory Parsloe.' Lord Emsworth stiffened at the name. 'He kept me talking. He is extremely worried.' Lord Emsworth looked pleased. 'He tells me he used to know Galahad very well a number of years ago, and he is very much alarmed about this book of his.'

'And I bet he isn't the only one,' murmured Millicent.

She was right. Once a man of the Hon. Galahad Threepwood's antecedents starts taking pen in hand and being reminded of amusing incidents that happened to my dear old friend So-and-So, you never know where he will stop; and all over England, among the more elderly of the nobility and gentry, something like a panic had been raging ever since the news of his literary activities had got about. From Sir Gregory Parsloe-Parsloe, of Matchingham Hall, to grey-headed pillars of Society in distant Cumberland and Kent, whole droves of respectable men who in their younger days had been rash enough to chum with the Hon. Galahad were recalling past follies committed in his company and speculating agitatedly as to how good the old pest's memory was.

For Galahad in his day had been a notable lad about town. A *beau sabreur* of Romano's. A Pink 'Un. A Pelican. A crony of Hughie Drummond and Fatty Coleman; a brother-in-arms of the Shifter, the Pitcher, Peter Blobbs and the rest of an interesting but not straight-laced circle. Bookmakers had called him by his pet name, barmaids had simpered beneath his gallant chaff. He had heard the chimes at midnight. And when he had looked in at the old Gardenia, commissionaires had fought for the privilege of throwing him out. A man, in a word, who should never have been taught to write and who, if unhappily gifted with that ability, should have been restrained by Act of Parliament from writing Reminiscences.

So thought Lady Constance, his sister. So thought Sir Gregory Parsloe-Parsloe, his neighbour. And so thought the pillars of Society in distant Cumberland and Kent. Widely as they differed on many points, they were unanimous on this.

'He wanted me to try to find out if Galahad was putting anything about him into it.'

'Better ask him now,' said Millicent. 'He's just come out of the house and seems to be heading in this direction.'

Lady Constance turned sharply: and, following her niece's pointing finger, winced. The mere sight of her deplorable brother was generally enough to make her wince. When he began to talk and she had to listen, the wince became a shudder. His conversation had the effect of making her feel as if she had suddenly swallowed something acid.

'It always makes me laugh,' said Millicent, 'when I think what a frightfully bad shot Uncle Gally's godfathers and godmothers made when they christened him.'

She regarded her approaching relative with that tolerant – indeed, admiring – affection which the young of her sex, even when they have Madonna-like faces, are only too prone to lavish on such of their seniors as have had interesting pasts.

'Doesn't he look marvellous?' she said. 'It really is an extraordinary thing that anyone who has had as good a time as he has can be so amazingly healthy. Everywhere you look, you see men leading model lives and pegging out in their prime, while good old Uncle Gally, who apparently never went to bed till he was fifty, is still breezing along as fit and rosy as ever.'

'All our family have had excellent constitutions,' said Lord Emsworth.

'And I'll bet Uncle Gally needed every ounce of his,' said Millicent.

The Author, ambling briskly across the lawn, had now joined the little group at the tea-table. As his photograph had indicated he was a short, trim, dapper little man of the type one associates automatically in one's mind with checked suits, tight trousers, white bowler hats, pink carnations and race-glasses bumping against the left hip. Though bare-headed at the moment and in his shirt-sleeves, and displaying on the tip of his nose the ink-spot of the literary life, he still seemed out of place away from a paddock or an American bar. His bright eyes, puckered at the corners, peered before him as though watching horses rounding into the straight. His neatly-shod foot had about it a suggestion of pawing in search of a brass rail. A jaunty little gentleman, and, as Millicent had said, quite astonishingly fit and rosy. A thoroughly mis-spent life had left the Hon. Galahad Threepwood, contrary to the most elementary justice, in what appeared to be perfect, even exuberantly perfect physical condition. How a man who ought to have had the liver of the century could look and behave as he did was a constant mystery to his associates. His eye was not dimmed nor his natural force abated. And when, skipping blithely across the turf, he tripped over the spaniel, so graceful was the agility with which he recovered his balance that he did not spill a drop of the whisky and soda in his hand. He continued to bear the glass aloft like some brave banner beneath which he had often fought and won. Instead of the blot on the proud family, he might have been a teetotal acrobat.

Having disentangled himself from the spaniel and soothed the animal's wounded feelings by permitting it to sniff the whisky-and-soda, the Hon. Galahad produced a black-rimmed monocle, and, screwing it into his eye, surveyed the table with a frown of distaste.

'Tea?'

Millicent reached for a cup.

'Cream and sugar, Uncle Gally?'

He stopped her with a gesture of shocked loathing.

'You know I never drink tea. Too much respect for my inside. Don't tell me you are ruining your inside with that poison.'

'Sorry, Uncle Gally. I like it.'

'You be careful,' urged the Hon. Galahad, who was fond of his niece and did not like to see her falling into bad habits. 'You be very careful how you fool about with that stuff. Did I ever tell you about poor Buffy Struggles back in 'ninety-three? Some misguided person lured poor old Buffy into one of those temperance lectures illustrated with coloured slides, and he called on me next day ashen, poor old chap – ashen. "Gally," he said. "What would you say the procedure was when a fellow wants to buy tea? How would a fellow set about it?" "Tea?" I said. "What do you want tea for?" "To drink," said Buffy. "Pull yourself together, dear boy," I said. "You're talking wildly. You can't drink tea. Have a brandy and soda." "No more alcohol for me," said Buffy. "Look what it does to the common earthworm." "But you're not a common earthworm," I said, putting my finger on the flaw in his argument right away. "I dashed soon shall be if I go on drinking alcohol," said Buffy. Well, I begged him with tears in my eyes not to do anything rash, but I couldn't move him. He ordered in ten pounds of the muck and was dead inside the year.'

'Good heavens! Really?'

The Hon. Galahad nodded impressively.

'Dead as a door-nail. Got run over by a hansom cab, poor dear old chap, as he was crossing Piccadilly. You'll find the story in my book.'

'How's the book coming along?'

'Magnificently, my dear. Splendidly. I had no notion writing was so easy. The stuff just pours out. Clarence, I wanted to ask you about a date. What year was it there was that terrible row between young Gregory Parsloe and Lord Burper, when Parsloe stole the old chap's false teeth, and pawned them at a shop in the Edgware Road? '96? I should have said later than that – '97 or '98. Perhaps you're right, though. I'll pencil in '96 tentatively.'

Lady Constance uttered a sharp cry. The sunlight had now gone quite definitely out of her life. She felt, as she so often felt in her brother Galahad's society, as if foxes were gnawing her vitals. Not even the thought that she could now give Sir Gregory Parsloe-Parsloe the inside information for which he had asked was able to comfort her.

'Galahad! You are not proposing to print libellous stories like that about our nearest neighbour?'

'Certainly I am.' The Hon. Galahad snorted militantly. 'And, as for libel, let him bring an action if he wants to. I'll fight him to the House of Lords. It's the best documented story in my book. Well, if you insist it was '96, Clarence . . . I'll tell you what,' said the Hon. Galahad, inspired. 'I'll say "towards the end of the 'nineties". After all, the exact date isn't so important. It's the facts that matter.'

And, leaping lightly over the spaniel, he flitted away across the lawn.

Lady Constance sat rigid in her chair. Her fine eyes were now protruding slightly, and her face was drawn. This and not the

Mona Lisa's, you would have said, looking at her, was the head on which all the sorrows of the world had fallen.

'Clarence!'

'My dear?'

'What are you going to do about this?'

'Do?'

'Can't you see that something must be done? Do you realize that if this awful book of Galahad's is published it will alienate half our friends? They will think we are to blame. They will say we ought to have stopped him somehow. Imagine Sir Gregory's feelings when he reads that appalling story!'

Lord Emsworth's amiable face darkened.

'I am not worrying about Parsloe's feelings. Besides, he did steal Burper's false teeth. I remember him showing them to me. He had them packed up in cotton-wool in a small cigar-box.'

The gesture known as wringing the hands is one that is seldom seen in real life, but Lady Constance Keeble at this point did something with hers which might by a liberal interpretation have been described as wringing.

'Oh, if Mr. Baxter were only here!' she moaned.

Lord Emsworth started with such violence that his pince-nez fell off and he dropped a slice of seed-cake.

'What on earth do you want that awful feller here for?'

'He would find a way out of this dreadful business. He was always so efficient.'

'Baxter's off his head.'

Lady Constance uttered a sharp exclamation.

'Clarence, you really can be the most irritating person in the world. You get an idea and you cling to it in spite of whatever anybody says. Mr. Baxter was the most wonderfully capable man I ever met.'

'Yes, capable of anything,' retorted Lord Emsworth with spirit. 'Threw flower-pots at me in the middle of the night. I woke up in the small hours and found flower-pots streaming in at my bedroom window and looked out and there was this feller Baxter standing on the terrace in lemon-coloured pyjamas, hurling the dashed things as if he thought he was a machine-gun, or something. I suppose he's in an asylum by this time.'

Lady Constance had turned a bright scarlet. Even in their nursery days she had never felt quite so hostile towards the head of the family as now.

'You know perfectly well that there was a quite simple explanation. My diamond necklace had been stolen, and Mr. Baxter thought the thief had hidden it in one of the flower-pots. He went to look for it and got locked out and tried to attract attention by . . .'

'Well, I prefer to think the man was crazy, and that's the line Galahad takes in his book.'

'His! . . . ! Galahad is not putting that story in his book?'

'Of course he's putting it in his book. Do you think he's going to waste excellent material like that? And, as I say, the line Galahad takes – and he's a clear-thinking, level-headed man – is that Baxter was a raving, roaring lunatic. Well, I'm going to have another look at the Empress.'

He pottered off pigwards.

III

For some moments after he had gone, there was silence at the tea-table. Millicent lay back in her chair, Lady Constance sat stiffly upright in hers. A little breeze that brought with it a scent of wall-flowers began whispering the first tidings that the cool of evening was on its way.

'Why are you so anxious to get Mr. Baxter back, Aunt Constance?' asked Millicent.

Lady Constance's rigidity had relaxed. She was looking her calm, masterful self again. She had the air of a woman who has just solved a difficult problem.

'I think his presence here essential,' she said.

'Uncle Clarence doesn't seem to agree with you.'

'Your Uncle Clarence has always been completely blind to his best interests. He ought never to have dismissed the only secretary he has ever had who was capable of looking after his affairs.'

'Isn't Mr. Carmody any good?'

'No. He is not. And I shall never feel easy in my mind until Mr. Baxter is back in his old place.'

'What's wrong with Mr. Carmody?'

'He is grossly inefficient. And,' said Lady Constance, unmasking her batteries, 'I consider that he spends far too much of his time mooning around you, my dear. He appears to imagine that he is at Blandings Castle simply to dance attendance on you.'

The charge struck Millicent as unjust. She thought of pointing out that she and Hugo only met occasionally and then on the sly, but it occurred to her that the plea might be injudicious. She bent over the spaniel. A keen observer might have noted a defensiveness in her manner. She looked like a girl preparing to cope with an aunt.

'Do you find him an entertaining companion?'

Millicent yawned.

'Mr. Carmody? No, not particularly.'

'A dull young man, I should have thought.'

'Deadly.'

'Vapid.'

'Vap to a degree.'

'And yet you went riding with him last Tuesday.'

'Anything's better than riding alone.'

'You play tennis with him, too.'

'Well, tennis is a game I defy you to play by yourself.'

Lady Constance's lips tightened.

'I wish Ronald had never persuaded your uncle to employ him. Clarence should have seen by the mere look of him that he was impossible.' She paused.

'It will be nice having Ronald here,' she said.

'Yes.'

'You must try to see something of him. If,' said Lady Constance, in the manner which her intimates found rather less pleasant than some of her other manners, 'Mr. Carmody can spare you for a moment from time to time.'

She eyed her niece narrowly. But Millicent was a match for any number of narrow glances, and had been from her sixteenth birthday. She was also a girl who believed that the best form of defence is attack.

'Do you think I'm in love with Mr. Carmody, Aunt Constance?'

Lady Constance was not a woman who relished the direct methods of the younger generation. She coloured.

'Such a thought never entered my head.'

'That's fine. I was afraid it had.'

'A sensible girl like you would naturally see the utter impossibility of marriage with a man in his position. He has no money and very little prospects. And, of course, your uncle holds your own money in trust for you and would never dream of releasing it if you wished to make an unsuitable marriage.'

'So it does seem lucky I'm not in love with him, doesn't it?'

'Extremely fortunate.'

Lady Constance paused for a moment, then introduced a topic on which she had frequently touched before. Millicent had seen it coming by the look in her eyes.

'Why you won't marry Ronald, I can't think. It would be so suitable in every way. You have been fond of one another since you were children.'

'Oh, I like old Ronnie a lot.'

'It has been a great disappointment to your Aunt Julia.'

'She must cheer up. She'll get him off all right, if she sticks at it.'

Lady Constance bridled.

'It is not a question of . . . If you will forgive my saying so, my dear, I think you have allowed yourself to fall into a way of taking Ronald far too much for granted. I am afraid you have the impression that he will always be there, ready and waiting for you when you at last decide to make up your mind. I don't think you realize what a very attractive young man he is.'

'The longer I wait, the more fascinating it will give him time to become.'

At a moment less tense, Lady Constance would have taken time off to rebuke this flippancy; but she felt it would be unwise to depart from her main theme.

'He is just the sort of young man that girls are drawn to. In fact, I have been meaning to tell you. I had a letter from your Aunt Julia, saying that during their stay at Biarritz they met a most charming American girl, a Miss Schoonmaker, whose father, it seems, used to be a friend of your Uncle Galahad. She appeared to be quite taken with Ronald, and he with her. He travelled back to Paris with her and left her there.'

'How fickle men are!' sighed Millicent.

'She had some shopping to do,' said Lady Constance sharply. 'By this time she is probably in London. Julia invited her to stay at Blandings, and she accepted. She may be here any day now. And I do think, my dear,' proceeded Lady Constance earnestly, 'that before she arrives, you ought to consider very carefully what your feelings towards Ronald really are.'

'You mean, if I don't watch my step, this Miss Doopenhacker may steal my Ronnie away from me?'

It was not quite how Lady Constance would have put it herself, but it conveyed her meaning.

'Exactly.'

Millicent laughed. It was plain that her flesh declined to creep at the prospect.

'Good luck to her,' she said. 'She can count on a fish-slice from me, and I'll be a bridesmaid, too, if wanted. Can't you understand, Aunt Constance, that I haven't the slightest desire to marry Ronnie. We're great pals, and all that, but he's not my style. Too short, for one thing.'

'Short?'

'I'm inches taller than he is. When we went up the aisle, I should look like someone taking her little brother for a walk.'

Lady Constance would undoubtedly have commented on this remark, but before she could do so the procession reappeared, playing an unexpected return date. Footman James bore a dish of fruit, Footman Thomas a salver with a cream-jug on it. Beach, as before, confined himself to a straight ornamental role.

'Oo!' said Millicent welcomingly. And the spaniel, who liked anything involving cream, gave a silent nod of approval.

'Well,' said Lady Constance, as the procession withdrew, giving up the lost cause, 'if you won't marry Ronald, I suppose you won't.'

'That's about it,' agreed Millicent, pouring cream.

'At any rate, I am relieved to hear that there is no nonsense going on between you and this Mr. Carmody. That I could not have endured.'

'He's only moderately popular with you, isn't he?'

'I dislike him extremely.'

'I wonder why. I should have thought he was fairly all right, as young men go. Uncle Clarence likes him. So does Uncle Gally.'

Lady Constance had a high, arched nose, admirably adapted for sniffing. She used it now to the limits of its power.

'Mr. Carmody,' she said, 'is just the sort of young man your Uncle Galahad would like. No doubt he reminds him of the horrible men he used to go about London with in his young days.'

'Mr. Carmody isn't a bit like that.'

'Indeed?' Lady Constance sniffed again. 'Well, I dislike mentioning it to you, Millicent, for I am old-fashioned enough to think that young girls should be shielded from a knowledge of the world, but I happen to know that Mr. Carmody is not at all a nice young man. I have it on the most excellent authority that he is entangled with some impossible chorus girl.'

It is not easy to sit suddenly bolt-upright in a deep garden-chair, but Millicent managed the feat.

'What!'

'Lady Allardyce told me so.'

'And how does she know?'

'Her son Vernon told her. A girl of the name of Brown.

Vernon Allardyce says that he used to see her repeatedly, lunching and dining and dancing with Mr. Carmody.'

There was a long silence.

'Nice boy, Vernon,' said Millicent.

'He tells his mother everything.'

'That's what I meant. I think it's so sweet of him.' Millicent rose. 'Well, I'm going to take a short stroll.'

She wandered off towards the rose-garden.

## IV

A young man who has arranged to meet the girl he loves in the rose-garden at six sharp naturally goes there at five-twenty-five, so as not to be late. Hugo Carmody had done this, with the result that by three minutes to six he was feeling as if he had been marooned among roses since the beginning of the summer.

If anybody had told Hugo Carmody six months before that half-way through the following July he would be lurking in trysting-places like this, his whole being alert for the coming of a girl, he would have scoffed at the idea. He would have laughed lightly. Not that he had not been fond of girls. He had always liked girls. But they had been, as it were, the mere playthings, so to speak, of a financial giant's idle hour. Six months ago he had been the keen, iron-souled man of business, all his energies and thoughts devoted to the management of the Hot Spot.

But now he stood shuffling his feet and starting hopefully at every sound, while the leaden moments passed sluggishly on their way. Then his vigil was enlivened by a wasp, which stung him on the back of the hand. He was leaping to and fro, licking his wounds, when he perceived the girl of his dreams coming down the path.

'Ah!' cried Hugo.

He ceased to leap and, rushing forward, would have clasped her in a fond embrace. Many people advocate the old-fashioned blue-bag for wasp-stings, but Hugo preferred this treatment.

To his astonishment she drew back. And she was not a girl who usually drew back on these occasions.

'What's the matter?' he asked, pained. It seemed to him that a spanner had been bunged into a holy moment.

'Nothing.'

Hugo was concerned. He did not like the way she was looking at him. Her soft blue eyes appeared to have been turned into stone.

'I say,' he said, 'I've just been stung by a beastly great wasp.'

'Good!' said Millicent.

The way she was talking seemed to him worse than the way she was looking.

Hugo's concern increased.

'I say, what's up?'

The granite eye took on an added hardness.

'You want to know what's up?'

'Yes – what's up?'

'I'll tell you what's up.'

'Well, what's up?' asked Hugo.

He waited for enlightenment, but she had fallen into a chilling silence.

'You know,' said Hugo, breaking it, 'I'm getting pretty fed up with all this secrecy and general snakiness. Seeing you for an occasional odd five minutes a day and having to put on false whiskers and hide in bushes to manage that. I know the Keeble looks on me as a sort of cross between a leper and a nosegay of deadly nightshade, but I'm strong with the old boy. I talk pig to him. You might almost say I play on him as on a stringed instrument. So what's wrong with going to him and telling him in a frank and manly way that we love each other and are going to get married?'

The marble of Millicent's face was disturbed by one of those quick, sharp, short, bitter smiles that do nobody any good.

'Why should we lie to Uncle Clarence?'

'Eh?'

'I say, why should we tell him something that isn't true?'

'I don't get your drift.'

'I will continue snowing,' said Millicent coldly. 'I am not quite sure if I am ever going to speak to you again in this world or the next. Much will depend on how good you are as an explainer. I have it on the most excellent authority that you are entangled with a chorus girl. How about it?'

Hugo reeled. But then St. Anthony himself would have reeled if a charge like that had suddenly been hurled at him. The best of men require time to overhaul their consciences on such occasions. A moment and he was himself again.

'It's a lie!'

'Name of Brown.'

'Not a word of truth in it. I haven't set eyes on Sue Brown since I first met you.'

'No. You've been down here all the time.'

'And when I *was* setting eyes on her why, dash it, my attitude from start to finish was one of blameless, innocent, one hundred per cent brotherliness. A wholesome friendship. Brotherly. Nothing more. I liked dancing and she liked dancing and our steps fitted. So occasionally we would go out together and tread the measure. That's all there was to it. Pure brotherliness. Nothing more. I looked on myself as a sort of brother.'

'Brother, eh?'

'Absolutely a brother. Don't,' urged Hugo earnestly, 'go running away, my dear old thing, with any sort of silly notion that Sue Brown was something in the nature of a vamp. She's one of the nicest girls you would ever want to meet.'

'Nice, is she?'

'A sweet girl. A girl in a million. A real good sort. A sound egg.'

'Pretty, I suppose?'

The native good sense of the Carmodys asserted itself at the eleventh hour.

'Not pretty,' said Hugo decidedly. 'Not pretty, no. Not at all pretty. Far from pretty. Totally lacking in sex-appeal, poor girl. But nice. A good sort. No nonsense about her. Sisterly.'

Millicent pondered.

'H'm,' she said.

Nature paused, listening. Birds checked their song, insects their droning. It was as if it had got about that this young man's fate hung in the balance and the returns would be in shortly.

'Well, all right,' she said at length. 'I suppose I'll have to believe you.'

' ''At's the way to talk!'

'But just you bear this in mind, my lad. Any funny business from now on . . .'

'As if . . . !'

'One more attack of that brotherly urge . . .'

'As though . . . !'

'All right, then.'

Hugo inhaled vigorously. He felt like a man who has just dodged a wounded tigress.

'Banzai!' he said. 'Sweethearts still!'

V

Blandings Castle dozed in the twilight. Its various inmates were variously occupied. Clarence, ninth Earl of Emsworth, after many a longing lingering look behind, had dragged himself away from the Empress's boudoir and was reading his well-thumbed copy of *British Pigs*. The Hon. Galahad, having fixed up the Parsloe-Burper passage, was skimming through his day's output with an artist's complacent feeling that this was the stuff to give 'em. Butler Beach was pasting the Hon. Galahad's photograph into his album. Millicent, in her bedroom, was looking a little thoughtfully into her mirror. Hugo, in the billiard-room, was practising pensive canons and thinking loving thoughts of his lady, coupled with an occasional reflection that a short, swift binge in London would be a great wheeze if he could wangle it.

And in her boudoir on the second floor, Lady Constance Keeble had taken pen in hand and was poising it over a sheet of notepaper.

'Dear Mr. Baxter,' she wrote.

## 2. THE COURSE OF TRUE LOVE

### I

The brilliant sunshine which so enhanced the attractions of life at Blandings Castle had brought less pleasure to those of England's workers whose duties compelled them to remain in London. In his offices on top of the Regal Theatre in Shaftesbury Avenue, Mr. Mortimer Mason, the stout senior partner in the firm of Mason and Saxby, Theatrical Enterprises, Ltd., was of opinion that what the country really needed was one of those wedge-shaped depressions off the Coast of Iceland. Apart from making him feel like a gaffed salmon, Flaming July was ruining business. Only last night, to cut down expenses, he had had to dismiss some of the chorus from the show downstairs, and he hated dismissing chorus girls. He was a kind-hearted man, and, having been in the profession himself in his time, knew what it meant to get one's notice in the middle of the summer.

There was a tap on the door. The human watchdog who guarded the outer offices entered.

'Well?' said Mortimer Mason wearily.

'Can you see Miss Brown, sir?'

'Which Miss Brown? Sue?'

'Yes, sir.'

'Of course.' In spite of the heat, Mr. Mason brightened. 'Is she outside?'

'Yes, sir.'

'Then pour her in.'

Mortimer Mason had always felt a fatherly fondness for this girl, Sue Brown. He liked her for her own sake, for her unvarying cheerfulness and the honest way she worked. But what endeared her more particularly to him was the fact that she was Dolly Henderson's daughter. London was full of elderly gentlemen who became pleasantly maudlin when they thought of Dolly Henderson and the dear old days when the heart was young and they had had waists. He heaved himself from his chair: then fell back again, filled with a sense of intolerable injury.

'My God!' he cried. 'Don't look so cool.'

The rebuke was not undeserved. On an afternoon when the asphalt is bubbling in the roadways and theatrical managers melting where they sit, no girl has a right to resemble a dewy rose plucked from some old-world garden. And that, Mr. Mason considered, was just what this girl was deliberately resembling. She was a tiny thing, mostly large eyes and a wide, happy smile. She had a dancer's figure and in every movement of her there was Youth.

'Sorry, Pa.' She laughed, and Mr. Mason moaned faintly. Her laugh had reminded him, for his was a nature not without its poetical side, of ice tinkling in a jug of beer. 'Try not looking at me.'

'Well, Sue, what's on your mind? Come to tell me you're going to be married?'

'Not at the moment, I'm afraid.'

'Hasn't that young man of yours got back from Biarritz yet?'

'He arrived this morning. I had a note during the matinee. I suppose he's outside now, waiting for me. Want to have a look at him?'

'Does it mean walking downstairs?' asked Mr. Mason, guardedly.

'No. He'll be in his car. You can see him from the window.'

Mr. Mason was equal to getting to the window. He peered down at the rakish sports-model two-seater in the little street below. Its occupant was lying on his spine, smoking a cigarette in a long holder and looking austerely at certain children of the neighbourhood whom he seemed to suspect of being about to scratch his paint.

'They're making fiancés very small this season,' said Mr. Mason, concluding his inspection.

'He is small, isn't he? He's sensitive about it, poor darling. Still, I'm small, too, so that's all right.'

'Fond of him?'

'Frightfully.'

'Who is he, anyway? Yes, I know his name's Fish, and it doesn't mean a thing to me. Any money?'

'I believe he's got quite a lot, only his uncle keeps it all. Lord Emsworth. He's Ronnie's trustee, or something.'

'Emsworth? I knew his brother years ago.' Mr. Mason chuckled reminiscently. 'Old Gally! What a lad! I've got a scheme I'd like to interest old Gally in. I wonder where he is now.'

'The *Prattler* this week said he was down at Blandings Castle. That's Lord Emsworth's place in Shropshire. Ronnie's going down there this evening.'

'Deserting you so soon?' Mortimer Mason shook his head. 'I don't like this.'

Sue laughed.

'Well, I don't,' said Mr. Mason. 'You be careful. These lads will all bear watching.'

'Don't worry, Pa. He means to do right by our Nell.'

'Well, don't say I didn't warn you. So old Gally is at Blandings, is he? I must remember that. I'd like to get in touch with him. And now, what was it you wanted to see me about?'

Sue became grave.

'I've come to ask you a favour.'

'Go ahead. You know me.'

'It's about those girls you're getting rid of.'

Mr. Mason's genial face took on a managerial look.

'Got to get rid of them.'

'I know. But one of them's Sally Field.'

'Meaning what?'

'Well, Sally's awfully hard up, Pa. And what I came to ask,' said Sue breathlessly, 'was, will you keep her on and let me go instead?'

Utter amazement caused Mortimer Mason momentarily to forget the heat. He sat up, gaping.

'Do what?'

'Let me go instead.'

'Let you go instead?'

'Yes.'

'You're crazy.'

'No, I'm not. Come on, Pa. Be a dear.'

'Is she a great friend of yours?'

'Not particularly. I'm sorry for her.'

'I won't do it.'

'You must. She's down to her last bean.'

'But I need you in the show.'

'What nonsense! As if I made the slightest difference.'

'You do. You've got – I don't know—' Mr. Mason twiddled his fingers. 'Something. Your mother used to have it. Did you know I was the second juvenile in the first company she was ever in?'

'Yes, you told me. And haven't you got on! There's enough of you now to make two second juveniles. Well, you will do it, won't you?'

Mr. Mason reflected.

'I suppose I'll have to, if you insist,' he said at length. 'If I don't, you'll just hand your notice in anyway. I know you. You're a sportsman, Sue. Your mother was just the same. But are you sure you'll manage all right? I shan't be casting the new show till the end of August, but I may be able to fix you up somewhere if I look round.'

'I don't see how you could look any rounder if you tried, you poor darling. Do you realize, Pa, that if you got up early every morning and did half an hour's Swedish exercises . . .'

'If you don't want to be murdered, stop!'

'It would do you all the good in the world, you know. Well, it's awfully sweet of you to bother about me, Pa, but you mustn't. You've got enough to worry you already. I shall be all right. Goodbye. You've been an angel about Sally. It'll save her life.'

'If she's that cross-eyed girl at the end of the second row who's always out of step, I'm not sure I want to save her life.'

'Well, you're going to do it, anyway. Goodbye.'

'Don't run away.'

'I must. Ronnie's waiting. He's going to take me to tea somewhere. Up the river, I hope. Think how nice it will be there, under the trees, with the water rippling . . .'

'The only thing that stops me hitting you with this ruler,' said Mr. Mason, 'is the thought that I shall soon be getting out of this Turkish Bath myself. I've a show opening at Blackpool next week. Think how nice and cool it will be on the sands there, with the waves splashing . . .'

'. . . And you with your little spade and bucket, paddling! Oh, Pa, do send me a photograph. Well, I can't stand here all day, chatting over your vacation plans. My poor darling Ronnie must be getting slowly fried.'

II

The process of getting slowly fried, especially when you are chafing for a sight of the girl you love after six weeks of exile from her society, is never an agreeable one. After enduring it for some time, the pink faced young man with the long cigarette-holder had left his seat in the car and had gone for shade and comparative coolness to the shelter of the stage entrance, where he now stood reading the notices on the call-board. He read them moodily. The thought that, after having been away from Sue for all these weeks, he was now compelled to leave her again and go to Blandings Castle was weighing on Ronald Overbury Fish's mind sorely.

Mac, the guardian of the stage door, leaned out of his hutch. The matinee over, he had begun to experience that solemn joy which comes to camels approaching an oasis and stage-door men who will soon be at liberty to pop round the corner. He endeavoured to communicate his happiness to Ronnie.

'Won't be long now, Mr. Fish.'

'Eh?'

'Won't be long now, sir.'

'Ah,' said Ronnie.

Mac was concerned at his companion's gloom. He liked smiling faces about him. Reflecting, he fancied he could diagnose its cause.

'I was sorry to hear about that, Mr. Fish.'

'Eh?'

'I say I was sorry to hear about that, sir.'

'About what?'

'About the Hot Spot, sir. That night-club of yours. Busting up that way. Going West so prompt.'

Ronnie Fish winced. He presumed the man meant well, but there are certain subjects one does not want mentioned. When you have contrived with infinite pains to wheedle a portion of your capital out of a reluctant trustee and have gone and started a night-club with it and seen that night-club flash into the receiver's hands like some frail egg-shell engulfed by a whirlpool, silence is best.

'Ah,' he said briefly, to indicate this.

Mac had many admirable qualities, but not tact. He was the sort of man who would have tried to cheer Napoleon up by talking about the Winter Sports at Moscow.

'When I heard that you and Mr. Carmody was starting one of those places, I said to the fireman "I give it two months," I said. And it was six weeks, wasn't it, sir?'

'Seven.'

'Six or seven. Immaterial which. Point is I'm usually pretty right. I said to the fireman "It takes brains to run a night-club," I said. "Brains and a certain what-shall-I-say." Won me half-a-dollar, that did.'

He searched in his mind for other topics to interest and amuse.

'Seen Mr. Carmody lately, sir?'

'No. I've been in Biarritz. He's down in Shropshire. He's got a job as secretary to an uncle of mine.'

'And I shouldn't wonder,' said Mac cordially, 'if he wouldn't make a mess of *that*.'

He began to feel that the conversation was now going with a swing.

'Used to see a lot of Mr. Carmody round here at one time.'

The advance guard of the company appeared, in the shape of a flock of musicians. They passed out of the stage door, first a couple of thirsty-looking flutes, then a group of violins, finally an oboe by himself with a scowl on his face. Oboes are always savage in captivity.

'Yes, sir. Came here a lot, Mr. Carmody did. Asking for Miss Brown. Great friends those two was.'

'Oh?' said Ronnie thickly.

'Used to make me laugh to see them together.'

Ronnie appeared to swallow something large and jagged.

'Why?'

'Well, him so tall and her so small. But there,' said Mac philosophically, 'they say it's opposites that get on best. I know I weigh seventeen stone and my missus looks like a ninepenny rabbit, and yet we're as happy as can be.'

Ronnie's interest in the poundage of the stage-door keeper's domestic circle was slight.

'Ah,' he said.

Mac, having got onto the subject of Sue Brown, stayed there.

'You see the flowers arrived all right, sir.'

'Eh?'

'The flowers you sent Miss Brown, sir,' said Mac, indicating with a stubby thumb a bouquet on the shelf behind him. 'I haven't given her them yet. Thought she'd rather have them after the performance.'

It was a handsome bouquet, but Ronnie Fish stared at it with a sort of dumb horror. His pink face had grown pinker, and his eyes were glassy.

'Give me those flowers, Mac,' he said in a strangled voice.

'Right, sir. Here you are, sir. Now you look just the bride-groom, sir,' said the stage-door keeper, chuckling the sort of chuckle that goes with seventeen stone and a fat head.

This thought had struck Ronnie, also. It was driven home a moment later by the displeasing behaviour of two of the chorus girls who came flitting past. Both looked at him in a way painful to a sensitive young man, and one of them giggled. Ronnie turned to the door.

'When Miss Brown comes, tell her I'm waiting outside in my car.'

'Right, sir. You'll be in again, I suppose, sir?'

'No.' The sombre expression deepened on Ronnie's face. 'I've got to go down to Shropshire this evening.'

'Be away long?'

'Yes. Quite a time.'

'Sorry to hear that, sir. Well, goodbye, sir. Thank you, sir.'

Ronnie, clutching the bouquet, walked with leaden steps to the two-seater. There was a card attached to the flowers. He read it, frowned darkly, and threw the bouquet into the car.

Girls were passing now in shoals. They meant nothing to Ronnie Fish. He eyed them sourly, marvelling why the papers talked about 'beauty choruses'. And then, at last, there appeared one at the sight of whom his heart, parting from its moorings, began to behave like a jumping bean. It had reached his mouth when she ran up with both hands extended.

'Ronnie, you precious angel lambkin!'

'Sue!'

To a young man in love, however great the burden of sorrows beneath which he may be groaning, the spectacle of the only girl in the world, smiling up at him, seldom fails to bring a temporary balm. For the moment, Ronnie's gloom ceased to be. He forgot that he had recently lost several hundred pounds in a disastrous commercial venture. He forgot that he was going off that evening to live in exile. He even forgot that this girl had just been sent a handsome bouquet by a ghastly bargee named P. Frobisher Pilbeam, belonging to the Junior Constitutional Club. These thoughts would return, but for the time being the one that occupied his mind to the exclusion of all others was the thought that after six long weeks of separation he was once more looking upon Sue Brown.

'I'm sorry I kept you waiting, precious. I had to see Mr. Mason.'

Ronnie started.

'What about?'

A student of the motion-pictures, he knew what theatrical managers were.

'Just business.'

'Did he ask you to lunch, or anything?'

'No. He just fired me.'

'Fired you!'

'Yes, I've lost my job,' said Sue happily.

Ronnie quivered.

'I'll go and break his neck.'

'No, you won't. It isn't his fault. It's the weather. They have to cut down expenses when there's a heat-wave. It's all the fault of people like you for going abroad instead of staying in London and coming to the theatre.' She saw the flowers and uttered a delightful squeal. 'For me?'

A moment before, Ronnie had been all chivalrous concern – a knight prepared to battle to the death for lady-love. He now froze.

'Apparently,' he said coldly.

'How do you mean, apparently?'

'I mean they are.'

'You pet!'

'Leap in.'

Ronnie's gloom was now dense and froglike once more. He gestured fiercely at the clustering children and trod on the self-starter. The car moved smoothly round the corner into Shaftesbury Avenue.

Opposite the Monico, there was a traffic-block, and he unloaded his soul.

'In re those blooms.'

'They're lovely.'

'Yes, but I didn't send them.'

'You brought them. Much nicer.'

'What I'm driving at,' said Ronnie heavily, 'is that they aren't from me at all. They're from a blighter named P. Frobisher Pilbeam.'

Sue's smile had faded. She knew her Ronald's jealousy so well. It was the one thing about him which she could have wished changed.

'Oh?' she said dismally.

The crust of calm detachment from all human emotion, built up by years of Eton and Cambridge, cracked abruptly, and there peeped forth a primitive Ronald Overbury Fish.

'Who is this Pilbeam?' he demanded. 'Pretty much the Boy Friend, I take it, what?'

'I've never even met him!'

'But he sends you flowers.'

'I know he does,' wailed Sue, mourning for a golden afternoon now probably spoiled beyond repair. 'He keeps sending me his beastly flowers and writing me his beastly letters . . .'

Ronnie gritted his teeth.

'And I tell you I've never set eyes on him in my life.'

'You don't know who he is?'

'One of the girls told me that he used to edit that paper *Society Spice*. I don't know what he does now.'

'When he isn't sending flowers, you mean?'

'I can't help him sending me flowers.'

'I don't suppose you want to.'

Sue's eyes flickered. Realizing, however, that her Ronnie in certain moods resembled a child of six, she made a pathetic attempt to lighten the atmosphere.

'It's not my fault if I get persecuted with loathsome addresses, is it? I suppose, when you go to the movies, you blame Lilian Gish for being pursued by the heavy.'

Ronnie was not to be diverted.

'Sometimes I ask myself,' he said darkly, 'if you really care a hang for me.'

'Oh, Ronnie!'

'Yes, I do – repeatedly. I look at you and I look at myself and that's what I ask myself. What on earth is there about me to make a girl like you fond of a fellow? I'm a failure. Can't even run a night-club. No brains. No looks.'

'You've got a lovely complexion.'

'Too pink. Much too pink. And I'm so damned short.'

'You're not a bit too short.'

'I am. My Uncle Gally once told me I looked like the protoplasm of a minor jockey.'

'He ought to have been ashamed of himself.'

'Why the dickens,' said Ronnie, laying bare his secret dreams, 'I couldn't have been born a decent height, like Hugo . . .' He paused. His hand shook on the steering-wheel. 'That reminds me. That fellow Mac at the stage-door was saying that you and Hugo used to be as thick as thieves. Always together, he said.'

Sue sighed. Things were being difficult to-day.

'That was before I met you,' she explained patiently. 'I used to like dancing with him. He's a beautiful dancer. You surely don't suppose for a minute that I could ever be in love with Hugo?'

'I don't see why not.'

'Hugo!' Sue laughed. There was something about Hugo Carmody that always made her want to laugh.

'Well, I don't see why not. He's better looking than I am. Taller. Not so pink. Plays the saxophone.'

'Will you stop being silly about Hugo.'

'Well, I fear that bird. He's my best pal and I know his work. He's practically handsome. And lissom, to boot.' A hideous thought smote Ronnie like a blow. 'Did he ever . . .' He choked. 'Did he ever hold your hand?'

'Which hand?'

'Either hand.'

'How can you suggest such a thing!' cried Sue, shocked.

'Well, will you swear there's nothing between him and you?'

'Of course there isn't.'

'And nothing between this fellow Pilbeam and you?'

'Of course not.'

'Ah!' said Ronnie. 'Then I can go ahead, as planned.'

His was a mercurial temperament, and it had lifted him in an instant from the depths to the heights. The cloud had passed his face, the look of Byronic despair from his eyes. He beamed.

'Do you know why I'm going down to Blandings to-night?' he asked.

'No. I only wish you weren't.'

'Well, I'll tell you. I've got to get round my uncle.'

'Do what?'

'Make myself solid with my Uncle Clarence. If you've ever had anything to do with trustees you'll know that the one thing they bar like poison is parting with money. And I've simply got to have another chunk of my capital, and a good big one, too. Without money, how on earth can I marry you? Let me get hold of funds, and we'll dash off to the registrar's the moment you say the word. So now you understand why I've got to get to Blandings at the earliest possible moment and stay there till further notice.'

'Yes. I see. And you're a darling. Tell me about Blandings, Ronnie.'

'How do you mean?'

'Well, what sort of a place is it? I want to imagine you there while you're away.'

Ronnie pondered. He was not at his best as a word painter.

'Oh, you know the kind of thing. Parks and gardens and terraces and immemorial elms and all that. All the usual stuff.'

'Any girls there?'

'My cousin Millicent. She's my Uncle Lancelot's daughter. He's dead. The family want Millicent and me to get married.'

'To each other, you mean? What a perfectly horrible idea!'

'Oh, it's all right. We're both against the scheme.'

'Well, that's some comfort. What other girls will there be at Blandings?'

'Only one that I know of. My mother met a female called Schoonmaker at Biarritz. American. Pots of money, I believe. One of those beastly tall girls. Looked like something left over from Dana Gibson. I couldn't stand her myself, but my mother was all for her, and I didn't at all like the way she seemed to be trying to shove her off onto me. You know – "Why don't you ring up Myra Schoonmaker, Ronnie? I'm sure she would like to go to the Casino to-night. And then you could dance afterwards." Sinister, it seemed to me.'

'And she's going to Blandings? H'm!'

'There's nothing to h'm about.'

'I'm not so sure. Oh, well, I suppose your family are quite right. I suppose you ought really to marry some nice girl in your own set.'

Ronnie uttered a wordless cry, and in his emotion allowed the mudguard of the two-seater to glide so closely past an Austin Seven that Sue gave a frightened squeak and the Austin Seven went on its way thinking black thoughts.

'Do be careful, Ronnie, you old chump!'

'Well, what do you want to go saying things like that for? I get enough of that from the family, without having *you* start.'

'Poor old Ronnie! I'm sorry. Still, you must admit that they'd be quite within their rights, objecting to me. I'm not so hot, you know. Only a chorus girl. Just one of the Ensemble!'

Ronnie said something between his teeth that sounded like 'Juk!' What he meant was, Be her station never so humble, a pure, sweet girl is a fitting mate for the highest in the land.

'And my mother was a music-hall singer.'

'A what!'

'A music-hall singer. What they used to call a Serio. You know – pink tights and rather risky songs.'

This time Ronnie did not say 'Juk!'. He merely swallowed painfully. The information had come as a shock to him. Somehow or other, he had never thought of Sue as having encumbrances in the shape of relatives; and he could not hide from himself the fact that a pink-tighted Serio might stir the Family up quite a little. He pictured something with peroxide hair who would call his Uncle Clarence 'dearie'.

'English, do you mean? On the Halls here in London?'

'Yes. Her stage name was Dolly Henderson.'

'Never heard of her.'

'I daresay not. But she was the rage of London twenty years ago.'

'I always thought you were American,' said Ronnie, aggrieved. 'I distinctly recollect Hugo, when he introduced us, telling me that you had just come over from New York.'

'So I had. Father took me to America soon after Mother died.'

'Oh, your mother is – er – no longer with us?'

'No.'

'Too bad,' said Ronnie, brightening.

'My father's name was Cotterleigh. He was in the Irish Guards.'

'What!'

Ronnie's ecstatic cry seriously inconvenienced a traffic policeman in the exercise of his duties.

'But this is fine! This is the goods! It doesn't matter to me, of course, one way or the other. I'd love you just the same if your father had sold jellied eels. But think what an enormous difference this will make to my blasted family!'

'I doubt it.'

'But it will. We must get him over at once and spring him on them. Or is he in London?'

Sue's brown eyes clouded.

'He's dead.'

'Eh? Oh? Sorry!' said Ronnie.

He was dashed for a moment.

'Well, at least let me tell the family about him,' he urged, recovering. 'Let me dangle him before their eyes a bit.'

'If you like. But they'll still object to me because I'm in the chorus.'

Ronnie scowled. He thought of his mother, he thought of his Aunt Constance, and reason told him that her words were true.

'Dash all this rot people talk about chorus girls!' he said. 'They seem to think that just because a girl works in the chorus she must be a sort of animated champagne-vat. . . .'

'Ugh!'

'Spending her life dancing on supper-tables with tight stockbrokers. . . .'

'And not a bad way of passing an evening,' said Sue meditatively. 'I must try it some time.'

'. . . with the result that when it's a question of her marrying anybody, fellow's people look down their noses and kick like mules. It's happened in our family before. My Uncle Gally was in love with some girl on the stage back in the dark ages, and they formed a wedge and bust the thing up and shipped him off to South Africa or somewhere to forget her. And look at him! Drew three sober breaths in the year nineteen-hundred and then decided that was enough. I expect I shall be the same. If I don't take to drink, cooped up at Blandings a hundred miles away from you, I shall be vastly surprised. It's all a lot of silly nonsense. I haven't any patience with it. I've a jolly good mind to go to Uncle Clarence to-night and simply tell him that I'm in love with you and intend to marry you and that if the family don't like it they can lump it.'

'I wouldn't.'

Ronnie simmered down.

'Perhaps you're right.'

'I'm sure I am. If he hears about me, he certainly won't give you your money. Whereas, if he doesn't, he may. What sort of a man is he?'

'Uncle Clarence? Oh, a mild, dreamy old boy. Mad about gardening and all that. At the moment, I hear, he's wrapped up in his pig.'

'That sounds cosy.'

'I'd feel a lot easier in my mind, I can tell you, going down there to tackle him, if I were a pig. I'd expect a much warmer welcome.'

'You were rather a pig just now, weren't you?'

Ronnie quivered. Remorse gnawed the throbbing heart beneath his beautifully cut waistcoat.

'I'm sorry. I'm frightfully sorry. The fact is, I'm so crazy about you, I get jealous of everybody you meet. Do you know, Sue, if you ever let me down, I'd . . . I don't know what I'd do. Er – Sue!'

'Hullo?'

'Swear something.'

'What?'

'Swear that, while I'm at Blandings, you won't go out with a soul. Not even to dance.'

'Not even to dance?'

'No.'

'All right.'

'Especially this man Pilbeam.'

'I thought you were going to say Hugo.'

'I'm not worrying about Hugo. He's safe at Blandings.'

'Hugo at Blandings?'

'Yes. He's secretarying for my Uncle Clarence. I made my mother get him the job when the Hot Spot conked.'

'So you'll have him *and* Millicent *and* Miss Schoonmaker there to keep you company! How nice for you.'

'Millicent!'

'It's all very well to say "Millicent!" like that. If you ask me, I think she's a menace. She sounds coy and droopy. I can see her taking you for walks by moonlight under those immemorial elms and looking up at you with big, dreamy eyes . . .'

'Looking down at me, you mean. She's about a foot taller than I am. And, anyway, if you imagine there's a girl on earth who could extract so much as a kindly glance from me when I've got you to think about, you're very much mistaken. I give you my honest word . . .'

He became lyrical. Sue, leaning back, listened contentedly. The cloud had been a threatening cloud, blackening the skies for awhile, but it had passed. The afternoon was being golden, after all.

III

'By the way,' said Ronnie, the flood of eloquence subsiding. 'A thought occurs. Have you any notion where we're headed for?'

'Heaven.'

'I mean at the moment.'

'I supposed you were taking me to tea somewhere.'

'But where? We've got right out of the tea zone. What with one thing and another, I've just been driving at random – to and fro, as it were – and we seem to have worked round to somewhere in the Swiss Cottage neighbourhood. We'd better switch back and set a course for the Carlton or some place. How do you feel about the Carlton?'

'All right.'

'Or the Ritz?'

'Whichever you like.'

'Or – Gosh!'

'What's the matter?'

'Sue! I've got an idea.'

'Beginner's luck.'

'Why not go to Norfolk Street?'

'To your home?'

'Yes. There's nobody there. And our butler is a staunch bird. He'll get us tea and say nothing.'

'I'd like to meet a staunch butler.'

'Then shall we?'

'I'd love it. You can show me all your little treasures and belongings and the photographs of you as a small boy.'

Ronnie shook his head. It irked him to discourage her pretty enthusiasm, but a man cannot afford to take risks.

'Not those. No love could stand up against the sight of me in a sailor suit at the age of ten. I don't mind,' he said, making a concession, 'letting you see the one of me and Hugo, just before the Public Schools Rackets Competition, my last year at school. We were the Eton pair.'

'Did you win?'

'No. At a critical moment in the semi-final that ass Hugo foozled a shot a one-armed cripple ought to have taken with his eyes shut. It dished us.'

'Awful!' said Sue. 'Well, if I ever had any impulse to love Hugo, that's killed it.' She looked about her. 'I don't know this aristocratic neighbourhood at all. How far is it to Norfolk Street?'

'Next turning.'

'You're sure there's nobody in the house? None of the dear old Family?'

'Not a soul.'

He was right. Lady Constance Keeble was not actually in the house. At the moment when he spoke she had just closed the front door behind her. After waiting half an hour in the hope of her nephew's return, she had left a note for him on the hall table, and was going to Claridge's to get a cup of tea.

It was not until he had drawn up immediately opposite the house that Ronnie perceived what stood upon the steps. Having done so, he blenched visibly.

'Oh, my sainted aunt!' he said.

And seldom can the familiar phrase have been used with more appropriateness.

The sainted aunt was inspecting the two-seater and its contents with a frozen stare. Her eyebrows were two marks of interrogation. As she had told Millicent, she was old-fashioned, and when she saw her flesh and blood snuggled up to girls of attractive appearance in two-seaters, she suspected the worst.

'Good afternoon, Ronald.'

'Er – hullo, Aunt Constance.'

'Will you introduce me?'

There is no doubt that peril sharpens the intellect. His masters at school and his tutors at the University, having had to do with Ronald Overbury Fish almost entirely at times when his soul was at rest, had classed him among the less keen-witted of their charges. Had they seen him now in this crisis they would have pointed at him with pride. And, being the sportsmen and gentlemen that they were, they would have hastened to acknowledge that they had grossly underestimated his ingenuity and initiative.

For, after turning a rather pretty geranium tint and running a finger round the inside of his collar for an instant, as if he found it too tight, Ronnie Fish spoke the only two words in the language which could have averted disaster.

'Miss Schoonmaker,' he said, huskily.

Sue, at his side, gave a little gasp. These were unsuspected depths.

'Miss Schoonmaker!'

Lady Constance's resemblance to Apollyon straddling right across the way had vanished abruptly. Remorse came upon her that she should have wronged her blameless nephew with unfounded suspicions.

'Miss Schoonmaker, my aunt, Lady Constance Keeble,' said Ronnie, going from strength to strength, and speaking now quite easily and articulately.

Sue was not the girl to sit dumbly by and fail a partner in his hour of need. She smiled brightly.

'How do you do, Lady Constance?' she said. She smiled again, if possible even more brightly than before. 'I feel I know you already. Lady Julia told me so much about you at Biarritz.'

A momentary qualm lest, in the endeavour to achieve an easy cordiality, she had made her manner a shade too patronising, melted in the sunshine of the older woman's smile. Lady Constance had become charming, almost effusive. She had always hoped that Ronald and Millicent would make a match of it: but, failing that, this rich Miss Schoonmaker was certainly the next best thing. And driving chummily about London together like this must surely, she thought, mean something, even in these days when chummy driving is so prevalent between the sexes. At any rate, she hoped so.

'So here you are in London!'

'Yes.'

'You did not stay long in Paris.'

'No.'

'When can you come down to Blandings?'

'Oh very soon, I hope.'

'I am going there this evening. I only ran up for the day. I want you to drive me back, Ronald.'

Ronnie nodded silently. The crisis passed, a weakness had come upon him. He preferred not to speak, if speech could be avoided.

'Do try to come soon. The gardens are looking delightful. My brother will be so glad to see you. I was just on my way to Claridge's for a cup of tea. Won't you come too?'

'I'd love to,' said Sue, 'but I really must be getting on. Ronnie was taking me shopping.'

'I thought you stayed in Paris to do your shopping.'

'Not all of it.'

'Well, I shall hope to see you soon.'

'Oh, yes.'

'At Blandings.'

'Thank you so much. Ronnie, I think we ought to be getting along.'

'Yes.' Ronnie's mind was blurred, but he was clear on that point. 'Yes, getting along. Pushing off.'

'Well, I'm so delighted to have seen you. My sister told me so much about you in her letters. After you have put your luggage on the car, Ronald, will you come and pick me up at Claridge's?'

'Right ho.'

'I would like to make an early start, if possible.'

'Right ho.'

'Well, goodbye for the present, then.'

'Right ho.'

'Goodbye, Lady Constance.'

'Goodbye.'

The two-seater moved off, and Ronnie, taking his right hand from the wheel as it turned the corner, groped for a handkerchief, found it, and passed it over his throbbing brow.

'So that was Aunt Constance!' said Sue.

Ronnie breathed deeply.

'Nice meeting one of whom I have heard so much.'

Ronnie replaced his hand on the wheel and twiddled it feebly to avoid a dog. Reaction had made him limp.

Sue was gazing at him almost reverently.

'What genius, Ronnie! What ready wit! What presence of mind! If I hadn't heard it with my own ears, I wouldn't have believed it. Why didn't you ever tell me you were one of those swift thinkers?'

'I didn't know it myself.'

'Of course, I'm afraid it has complicated things a little.'

'Eh?' Ronnie started. This aspect of the matter had not struck him. 'How do you mean?'

'When I was a child, they taught me a poem . . .'

Ronnie raised a suffering face to hers.

'Don't let's talk about your childhood now, old thing,' he pleaded. 'Feeling rather shaken. Any other time . . .'

'It's all right. I'm not wandering from the subject. I can only remember two lines of the poem. They were, "Oh, what a tangled web we weave when first we practise to deceive." You do see the web is a bit tangled, don't you, Ronnie, darling?'

'Eh? Why? Everything looks pretty smooth to me. Aunt Constance swallowed you without a yip.'

'And when the real Miss Schoonmaker arrives at Blandings with her jewels and her twenty-four trunks?' said Sue gently.

The two-seater swerved madly across Grosvenor Street.

'Gosh!' said Ronnie.

Sue's eyes were sparkling.

'There's only one thing to do,' she said. 'Now you're in, you'll have to go in deeper. You'll have to put her off.'

'How?'

'Send her a wire saying she mustn't come to Blandings, because scarlet fever or something has broken out.'

'I couldn't!'

'You must. Sign it in Lady Constance's name.'

'But suppose . . .'

'Well, suppose they do find out? You won't be in any worse hole than you will be if she comes sailing up to the front door, all ready to stay a couple of weeks. And she will unless you wire.'

'That's true.'

'What it means,' said Sue, 'is that instead of having plenty of time to get that money out of Lord Emsworth you'll have to work quick.' She touched his arm. 'Here's a post-office,' she said. 'Go in and send that wire before you weaken.'

Ronnie stopped the car.

'You will have to do the most rapid bit of trustee-touching in the history of the world, I should think,' said Sue reflectively. 'Do you think you can manage it?'

'I'll have a jolly good prod.'

'Remember what it means.'

'I'll do that all right. The only trouble is that in the matter of biting Uncle Clarence's ear I've nothing to rely on but my natural charm. And as far as I've been able to make out,' said Ronnie, 'he hasn't noticed yet that I have any.'

He strode into the post-office, thinking deeply.

## 3. SENSATIONAL THEFT OF A PIG

I

It was the opinion of the poet Calverley, expressed in his immortal 'Ode to Tobacco', that there is no heaviness of the soul which will not vanish beneath the influence of a quiet smoke. Ronnie Fish would have disputed this theory. It was the third morning of his sojourn at Blandings Castle; and, taking with him a tennis-ball which he proposed to bounce before him in order to assist thought, he had wandered out into the grounds, smoking hard. And tobacco, though Turkish and costly, was not lightening his despondency at all. It seemed to Ronnie that the present was bleak and the future grey. Roaming through the sun-flooded park, he bounced his tennis-ball and groaned in spirit.

On the credit side of the ledger one single item could be inscribed. Hugo was at the Castle. He had the consolation, therefore, of knowing that that tall and lissom young man was not in London, exercising his fatal fascination on Sue. But, when you had said this, you had said everything. After all, even eliminating Hugo, there still remained in the metropolis a vast population of adult males, all either acquainted with Sue or trying to make her acquaintance. The poison-sac Pilbeam, for instance. By now it might well be that that bacillus had succeeded in obtaining an introduction to her. A devastating thought.

And even supposing he hadn't, even supposing that Sue, as she had promised, was virtuously handing the mitten to all the young thugs who surged around her with invitations to lunch and supper; where did that get a chap? What, in other words, of the future?

In coming to Blandings Castle, Ronnie was only too well aware, he had embarked on an expedition, the success or failure of which would determine whether his life through the years was to be roses, roses all the way or a dreary desert. And so far, in his efforts to win the favour and esteem of his Uncle Clarence, he seemed to have made no progress whatsoever. On the occasions when he had found himself in Lord Emsworth's society, the latter had looked at him sometimes as if he did not know he was there, more often as if he wished he wasn't. It was only too plain that the collapse of the Hot Spot had left his stock in bad shape. There had been a general sagging of the market. Fish Preferred, taking the most sanguine estimate, could scarcely be quoted at more than about thirty to thirty-five.

Plunged in thought, and trying without any success to conjure up a picture of a benevolent uncle patting him on the head with one hand while writing cheques with the other, he had wandered some distance from the house and was passing a small spinney, when he observed in a little dell to his left a peculiar object.

It was a large yellow caravan. And what, he asked himself, was a caravan doing in the grounds of Blandings Castle?

To aid him in grappling with the problem, he flung the tennis ball at it. Upon which, the door opened and a spectacled head appeared.

'Hullo!' said the head.

'Hullo!' said Ronnie.

'Hullo!'

'Hullo!'

The thing threatened to become a hunting-chorus. At this moment, however, the sun went behind a cloud and Ronnie was enabled to recognise the head's proprietor. Until now, the light, shining on the other's glasses, had dazzled him.

'Baxter!' he exclaimed.

The last person he would have expected to meet in the park of Blandings. He had heard all about that row a couple of years ago. He knew that, if his own stock with Lord Emsworth was low, that of the Efficient Baxter was down in the cellar, with no takers. Yet here the fellow was, shoving his head out of caravans as if nothing had ever happened.

'Ah, Fish!'

Rupert Baxter descended the steps, a swarthy-complexioned young man with a supercilious expression which had always been displeasing to Ronnie.

'What are you doing here?' asked Ronnie.

'I happened to be taking a caravan holiday in the neighbourhood. And, finding myself at Market Blandings last night, I thought I would pay a visit to the place where I had spent so many happy days.'

'I see.'

'Perhaps you could tell me where I could find Lady Constance?'

'I haven't seen her since breakfast. She's probably about somewhere.'

'I will go and inquire. If you meet her, perhaps you would not mind mentioning that I am here.'

The Efficient Baxter strode off, purposeful as ever; and Ronnie, having speculated for a moment as to how his Uncle Clarence would comport himself if he came suddenly round a corner and ran into this bit of the dead past, and having registered an idle hope that, when this happened, he might be present with a camera, inserted another cigarette in its holder and passed on his way.

II

Five minutes later, Lord Emsworth, leaning pensively out of the library window and sniffing the morning air, received an unpleasant shock. He could have sworn he had seen his late secretary, Rupert Baxter, cross the gravel and go in at the front door.

'Bless my soul!' said Lord Emsworth.

The only explanation that occurred to him was that Baxter, having met with some fatal accident, had come back to haunt the place. To suppose the fellow could be here in person was absurd. When you shoot a secretary out for throwing flower-pots at you in the small hours, he does not return to pay social calls. A frown furrowed his lordship's brow. The spectre of one of his ancestors he could have put up with, but the idea of a Blandings Castle haunted by Baxter he did not relish at all. He decided to visit his sister Constance in her boudoir and see what she had to say about it.

'Constance, my dear.'

Lady Constance looked up from the letter she was writing. She clicked her tongue, for it annoyed her to be interrupted at her correspondence.

'Well, Clarence?'

'I say, Constance, a most extraordinary thing happened just now, I was looking out of the library window and – you remember Baxter?'

'Of course I remember Mr. Baxter.'

'Well, his ghost has just walked across the gravel.'

'What *are* you talking about, Clarence?'

'I'm telling you. I was looking out of the library window and I suddenly saw—'

'Mr. Baxter,' announced Beach, flinging open the door.

'Mr. Baxter!'

'Good morning, Lady Constance.'

Rupert Baxter advanced with joyous camaraderie glinting from both lenses. Then he perceived his former employer and his exuberance diminished. 'Er – good morning, Lord Emsworth,' he said, flashing his spectacles austerely upon him.

There was a pause. Lord Emsworth adjusted his pince-nez and regarded the visitor dumbly. Of the relief which was presumably flooding his soul at the discovery that Rupert Baxter was still on this side of the veil, he gave no outward sign.

Baxter was the first to break an uncomfortable silence.

'I happened to be taking a caravan holiday in this neighbourhood, Lady Constance, and finding myself near Market Blandings last night, I thought I would . . .'

'Why, of course! We should never have forgiven you if you had not come to see us. Should we, Clarence?'

'Eh?'

'I said, should we?'

'Should we what?' said Lord Emsworth, who was still adjusting his mind.

Lady Constance's lips tightened, and a moment passed during which it seemed always a fifty-fifty chance that a handsome silver ink-pot would fly through the air in the direction of her brother's head. But she was a strong woman. She fought down the impulse.

'Did you say you were travelling in a caravan, Mr. Baxter?'

'In a caravan. I left it in the park.'

'Well, of course you must come and stay with us. The Castle,' she continued, raising her voice a little, to compete with a sort of wordless bubbling which had begun to proceed from her brother's lips, 'is almost empty now. We shall not be having our first big house-party till the middle of next month. You must make quite a long visit. I will send somebody over to fetch your things.'

'It is exceedingly kind of you.'

'It will be delightful having you here again. Won't it, Clarence?'

'Eh?'

'I said won't it?'

'Won't it what?'

Lady Constance's hand trembled above the ink-pot like a hovering butterfly. She withdrew it.

'Will it not be delightful,' she said, catching her brother's eye and holding it like a female Ancient Mariner, 'having Mr. Baxter back at the Castle again?'

'I'm going down to see my pig,' said Lord Emsworth.

A silence followed his departure, such as would have fallen had a coffin just been carried out. Then Lady Constance shook off gloom.

'Oh Baxter, I'm so glad you were able to come. And how clever of you to come in a caravan. It prevented your arrival seeming pre-arranged.'

'I thought of that.'

'You think of everything.'

Rupert Baxter stepped to the door, opened it, satisfied himself that no listeners lurked in the passage, and returned to his seat.

'Are you in any trouble, Lady Constance? Your letter seemed so very urgent.'

'I am in dreadful trouble, Mr. Baxter.'

If Rupert Baxter had been a different type of man and Lady Constance Keeble a different type of woman he would probably at this point have patted her hand. As it was, he merely hitched his chair an inch closer to hers.

'If there is anything I can do?'

'There is nobody except you who can do anything. But I hardly like to ask you.'

'Ask me whatever you please. And if it is in my power . . .'

'Oh, it is.'

Rupert Baxter gave his chair another hitch.

'Tell me.'

Lady Constance hesitated.

'It seems such an impossible thing to ask of anyone.'

'Please!'

'Well. . . you know my brother?'

Baxter seemed puzzled. Then an explanation of the peculiar question presented itself.

'Oh, you mean Mr . . . . ?'

'Yes, yes, yes. Of course I wasn't referring to Lord Emsworth. My brother Galahad.'

'I have never met him. Oddly enough, though he visited the castle twice during the period when I was Lord Emsworth's secretary, I was away both times on my holiday. Is he here now?'

'Yes. Finishing his Reminiscences.'

'I saw in some paper that he was writing the history of his life.'

'And if you know what a life his has been you will understand why I am distracted.'

'Certainly I have heard stories,' said Baxter guardedly.

Lady Constance performed that movement with her hands which came so close to wringing.

'The book is full from beginning to end of libellous anecdotes, Mr. Baxter. About all our best friends. If it is published we shall not have a friend left. Galahad seems to have known everybody in England when they were young and foolish, and to remember everything particularly foolish and disgraceful that they did. So . . .'

'So you want me to get hold of the manuscript and destroy it?'

Lady Constance stared, stunned by this penetration. She told herself that she might have known that she would not have to make long explanations to Rupert Baxter. His mind was like a searchlight, darting hither and thither, lighting up whatever it touched.

'Yes,' she gasped. She hurried on: 'It does seem, I know, an extraordinary thing to . . .'

'Not at all.'

'. . . but Lord Emsworth refuses to do anything.'

'I see.'

'You know how he is in the face of an emergency.'

'Yes, I do, indeed.'

'So supine. So helpless. So vague and altogether incompetent.'

'Precisely.'

'Mr. Baxter, you are my only hope.'

Baxter removed his spectacles, polished them, and put them back again.

'I shall be delighted, Lady Constance, to do anything to help you that lies in my power. And to obtain possession of this manuscript should be an easy task. But is there only one copy of it in existence?'

'Yes, yes, yes. I am sure of that. Galahad told me that he was waiting till it was finished before sending it to the typist.'

'Then you need have no further anxiety.'

It was a moment when Lady Constance Keeble would have given much for eloquence. She sought for words that should adequately express her feelings, but could find none.

'Oh, Mr. Baxter!' she said.

### III

Ronnie Fish's aimlessly wandering feet had taken him westward. It was not long, accordingly, before there came to his nostrils a familiar and penetrating odour, and he found that he was within a short distance of the detached residence employed by Empress of Blandings as a combined bedroom and restaurant. A few steps, and he was enabled to observe that celebrated animal in person. With her head tucked well down and her tail wiggling with pure *joie de vivre*, the Empress was hoisting in a spot of lunch.

Everybody likes to see somebody eating. Ronnie leaned over the rail, absorbed. He poised the tennis-ball and with an absentminded flick of the wrist bounced it on the silver medallist's back. Finding the pleasant, ponging sound which resulted soothing to harassed nerves, he did it again. The Empress made excellent bouncing. She was not one of your razor-backs. She presented a wide and resistant surface. For some minutes, therefore, the pair carried on according to plan – she eating, he bouncing, until presently Ronnie was thrilled to discover that this outdoor sport of his was assisting thought. Gradually – mistily at first, then assuming shape – a plan of action was beginning to emerge from the murk of his mind.

How would this be, for instance?

If there was one thing calculated to appeal to his Uncle Clarence, to induce in his Uncle Clarence a really melting mood, it was the announcement that somebody desired to return to the Land. He loved to hear of people returning to the Land. How, then, would this be? Go to the old boy, state that one had seen the light and was in complete agreement with him that England's future depended on checking the Drift to the Towns, and then ask for a good fat slice of capital with which to start a farm.

The project of starting a farm was one which was bound to . . . Half a minute. Another idea on the way. Yes, here it came, and it was a pippin. Not merely just an ordinary farm, but a pig-farm! Wouldn't Uncle Clarence leap in the air and shower gold on anybody who wanted to live in the country and breed pigs? You bet your Sunday cuffs he would. And, once the money was safely deposited to the account of Ronald Overbury Fish in Cox's Bank, then ho! for the registrar's hand in hand with Sue.

There was a musical *plonk* as Ronnie bounced the ball for the last time on the Empress's complacent back. Then, no longer with dragging steps but treading on air, he wandered away to sketch out the last details of the scheme before going indoors and springing it.

IV

Too often it happens that, when you get these brain-waves, you take another look at them after a short interval and suddenly detect some fatal flaw. No such disappointment came to mar the happiness of Ronnie Fish.

'I say, Uncle Clarence,' he said, prancing into the library, some half-hour later.

Lord Emsworth was deep in the current issue of a weekly paper of porcine interest. It seemed to Ronnie, as he looked up, that his eye was not any too chummy. This, however, did not disturb him. That eye, he was confident, would melt anon. If, at the moment, Lord Emsworth could hardly have sat for his portrait in the role of a benevolent uncle, there would, Ronnie felt, be a swift change of demeanour in the very near future.

'I say, Uncle Clarence, you know that capital of mine.'

'That what?'

'My capital. My money. The money you're trustee of. And a jolly good trustee,' said Ronnie handsomely. 'Well, I've been thinking things over and I want you, if you will, to disgorge a segment of it for a sort of venture I've got in mind.'

He had not expected the eye to melt yet, and it did not. Seen through the glass of his uncle's pince-nez, it looked like an oyster in an aquarium.

'You wish to start another night-club?'

Lord Emsworth's voice was cold, and Ronnie hastened to disabuse him of the idea.

'No, no. Nothing like that. Night-clubs are a mug's game. I ought never to have touched them. As a matter of fact, Uncle Clarence, London as a whole seems to me a bit of a washout these days. I'm all for the country. What I feel is that the drift to the towns should be checked. What England wants is more blokes going back to the land. That's the way it looks to me.'

Ronnie Fish began to experience the first definite twinges of uneasiness. This was the point at which he had been confident that the melting process would set in. Yet, watching the eye, he was dismayed to find it as oysterlike as ever. He felt like an actor who has been counting on a round of applause and goes off after his speech without a hand. The idea occurred to him that his uncle might possibly have grown a little hard of hearing.

'To the Land,' he repeated, raising his voice. 'More blokes going back to the Land. So I want a dollop of capital to start a farm.'

He braced himself for the supreme revelation.

'I want to breed pigs,' he said reverently.

Something was wrong. There was no blinking the fact any longer. So far from leaping in the air and showering gold, his uncle merely stared at him in an increasingly unpleasant manner. Lord Emsworth had removed his pince-nez and was wiping them; and Ronnie thought that his eye looked rather less agreeable in the nude than it had done through glass.

'Pigs!' he cried, fighting against a growing alarm.

'Pigs?'

'Pigs.'

'You wish to breed pigs?'

'That's right,' bellowed Ronnie. 'Pigs!' And from somewhere in his system he contrived to dig up and fasten on his face an ingratiating smile.

Lord Emsworth replaced his pince-nez.

'And I suppose,' he said throatily, quivering from his bald head to his roomy shoes, 'that when you've got 'em you'll spend the whole day bouncing tennis-balls on their backs?'

Ronnie gulped. The shock had been severe. The ingratiating smile lingered on his lips, as if fastened there with pins, but his eyes were round and horrified.

'Eh?' he said feebly.

Lord Emsworth rose. So long as he insisted on wearing an old shooting jacket with holes in the elbows and letting his tie slip down and show the head of a brass stud, he could never hope to be completely satisfactory as a figure of outraged majesty; but he achieved as imposing an effect as his upholstery would permit. He drew himself up to his full height, which was considerable, and from this eminence glared balefully down on his nephew.

'I saw you! I was on my way to the piggery and I saw you there bouncing your infernal tennis-balls on my pig's back. Tennis-balls!' Fire seemed to steam from the pince-nez. 'Are you aware that Empress of Blandings is an excessively nervous, highly-strung animal, only too ready on the lightest provocation to refuse her meals? You might have undone the work of months with your idiotic tennis-ball.'

'I'm sorry. . . .'

'What's the good of being sorry?'

'I never thought. . . .'

'You never do. That's what's the trouble with you. Pig-farm!' said Lord Emsworth vehemently, his voice soaring into the upper register. 'You couldn't manage a pig-farm. You aren't fit to manage a pig-farm. You aren't worthy to manage a pig-farm. If I had to select somebody out of the whole world to manage a pig-farm, I would choose you last.'

Ronnie Fish groped his way to the table and supported himself on it. He had a sensation of dizziness. On one point he was reasonably clear, viz. that his Uncle Clarence did not consider him ideally fitted to manage a pig-farm, but apart from that his mind was in a whirl. He felt as if he had stepped on something and it had gone off with a bang.

'Here! What *is* all this?'

It was the Hon. Galahad who had spoken, and he had spoken

peevishly. Working in the small library with the door ajar, he had found the babble of voices interfering with literary composition and, justifiably annoyed, had come to investigate.

'Can't you do your reciting some time when I'm not working, Clarence?' he said. 'What's all the trouble about?'

Lord Emsworth was still full of his grievance.

'He bounced tennis-balls on my pig!'

The Hon. Galahad was not impressed. He did not register horror.

'Do you mean to tell me,' he said sternly, 'that all this fuss, ruining my morning's work, was simply about that blasted pig of yours?'

'I refuse to allow you to call the Empress a blasted pig! Good heavens!' cried Lord Emsworth passionately. 'Can none of my family appreciate the fact that she is the most remarkable animal in Great Britain? No pig in the whole annals of the Shropshire Agricultural Show has ever won the silver medal two years in succession. And that, if only people will leave her alone and refrain from incessantly pelting her with tennis-balls, is what the Empress is quite certain to do. It is an unheard-of feat.'

The Hon. Galahad frowned. He shook his head reprovingly. It was all very well, he felt, a stable being optimistic about its nominee, but he was a man who could face facts. In a long and checkered life he had seen so many good things unstuck. Besides, he had his superstitions, and one of them was that counting your chickens in advance brought bad luck.

'Don't you be too cocksure, my boy,' he said gravely. 'I looked in at the Emsworth Arms the other day for a glass of beer, and there was a fellow in there offering three to one on an animal called Pride of Matchingham. Offering it freely. Tall, red-haired fellow with a squint. Slightly bottled.'

Lord Emsworth forgot Ronnie, forgot tennis-balls, forgot, in the shock of this announcement, everything except that deeper wrong which so long had been poisoning his peace.

'Pride of Matchingham belongs to Sir Gregory Parsloe,' he said, 'and I have no doubt that the man offering such ridiculous odds was his pig-man, Wellbeloved. As you know, the fellow used to be in my employment, but Parsloe lured him away from me by the promise of higher wages.' Lord Emsworth's expression had now become positively ferocious. The thought of George Cyril Wellbeloved, that perjured pig-man, always made the iron enter into his soul. 'It was a most abominable and unneighbourly thing to do.'

The Hon. Galahad whistled.

'So that's it, is it? Parsloe's pig-man going about offering three to one – against the form-book, I take it?'

'Most decidedly. Pride of Matchingham was awarded second prize last year, but it is a quite inferior animal to the Empress.'

'Then you look after that pig of yours, Clarence.' The Hon. Galahad spoke earnestly. 'I see what this means. Parsloe's up to his old games, and intends to queer the Empress somehow.'

'Queer her?'

'Nobble her. Or, if he can't do that, steal her.'

'You don't mean that.'

'I do mean it. The man's as slippery as a greased eel. He would nobble his grandmother if it suited his book. Let me tell you I've known young Parsloe for thirty years and I solemnly state that if his grandmother was entered in a competition for fat pigs and his commitments made it desirable for him to get her out of the way, he would dope her bran-mash and acorns without a moment's hesitation.'

'God bless my soul!' said Lord Emsworth, deeply impressed.

'Let me tell you a little story about young Parsloe. One or two of us used to meet at the Black Footman in Gossiter Street in the old days – they've pulled it down now – and match our dogs against rats in the room behind the bar. Well, I put my Towser, an admirable beast, up against young Parsloe's Banjo on one occasion for a hundred pounds a side. And when the night came and he was shown the rats, I'm dashed if he didn't just give a long yawn and roll over and go to sleep. I whistled him . . . called him . . . Towser, Towser . . . No good. . . . Fast asleep. And my firm belief has always been that young Parsloe took him aside just before the contest was to start and gave him about six pounds of steak and onions. Couldn't prove anything, of course, but I sniffed the dog's breath and it was like opening the kitchen door of a Soho chophouse on a summer night. That's the sort of man young Parsloe is.'

'Galahad!'

'Fact. You'll find the story in my book.'

Lord Emsworth was tottering to the door.

'God bless my soul! I never realized . . . I must see Pirbright at once. I didn't suspect . . . It never occurred . . .'

The door closed behind him. The Hon. Galahad, preparing to return to his labours, was arrested by the voice of his nephew Ronald.

'Uncle Gally!'

The young man's pink face had flamed to a bright crimson. His eyes gleamed strangely.

'Well?'

'You don't really think Sir Gregory will try to steal the Empress?'

'I certainly do. Known him for thirty years, I tell you.'

'But how could he?'

'Go to her stye at night, of course, and take her away.'

'And hide her somewhere?'

'Yes.'

'But an animal that size. Rather like looking in at the Zoo and pocketing one of the elephants, what?'

'Don't talk like an idiot. She's got a ring through her nose, hasn't she?'

'You mean, Sir Gregory could catch hold of the ring and she would breeze along quite calmly?'

'Certainly. Puffy Benger and I stole old Wivenhoe's pig the night of the Bachelors' Ball at Hammer's Easton in the year '95. We put it in Plug Basham's bedroom. There was no difficulty about the thing whatsoever. A little child could have led it.'

He withdrew into the small library, and Ronnie slid limply into the chair which Lord Emsworth had risen from so majestically. He felt the need of sitting. The inspiration which had just come to him had had a stunning effect. The brilliance of it almost frightened him. That idea about starting a pig-farm had shown that this was one of his bright mornings, but he had never foreseen that he would be as bright as this.

'Golly!' said Ronnie.

Could he . . . ?

Well, why not?

Suppose . . . ?

No, the thing was impossible.

Was it? Why? Why was it impossible? Suppose he had a stab at it. Suppose, following his Uncle Galahad's expert hints, he were to creep out to-night, abstract the Empress from her home, hide her somewhere for a day or two and then spectacularly restore her to her bereaved owner? What would be the result? Would Uncle Clarence sob on his neck, or would he not?

Would he feel that no reward was too good for his benefactor or wouldn't he? Most decidedly he would. Fish Preferred would soar immediately. That little matter of the advance of capital would solve itself. Money would stream automatically from the Emsworth coffers.

But could it be done? Ronnie forced himself to examine the scheme dispassionately, with a mind alert for snags.

He could detect none. A suitable hiding place occurred to him immediately – that disused gamekeeper's cottage in the west wood. Nobody ever went there. It would be as good as a Safe Deposit.

Risk of Detection? Why should there be any risk of detection? Who would think of connecting Ronald Fish with the affair?

Feeding the animal . . . ?

Ronnie's face clouded. Yes, here at last was the snag. This did present difficulties. He was vague as to what pigs ate, but he knew that they needed a lot of whatever it was. It would be no use restoring to Lord Emsworth a skeleton Empress. The cuisine must be maintained at its existing level, or the thing might just as well be left undone.

For the first time he began to doubt the quality of his recent inspiration. Scanning the desk with knitted brows, he took from the book-rest the volume entitled *Pigs, and How to Make Them Pay*. A glance at page 61, and his misgivings were confirmed.

''Myes,' said Ronnie, having skimmed through all the stuff about barley meal and maize meal and linseed meal and potatoes and separated milk or buttermilk. This, he now saw clearly, was no-one man job. It called not only for a dashing principal but a zealous assistant.

And what assistant?

Hugo?

No. In many respects the ideal accomplice for an undertaking of this nature, Hugo Carmody had certain defects which automatically disqualified him. To enrol Hugo as his lieutenant would mean revealing to him the motives that lay at the back of the venture. And if Hugo knew that he, Ronnie, was endeavouring to collect funds in order to get married, the thing would be all over Shropshire in a couple of days. Short of putting it on the front page of the *Daily Mail* or having it broadcasted over the wireless, the surest way of obtaining publicity for anything you wanted kept dark was to confide it to Hugo Carmody. A splendid chap, but the real, genuine human colander. No, not Hugo.

Then who? . . .

Ah!

Ronnie Fish sprang from his chair, threw his head back and uttered a yodel of joy so loud and penetrating that the door of the small library flew open as if he had touched a spring.

A tousled literary man emerged.

'Stop that damned noise! How the devil can I write with a row like that going on?'

'Sorry, uncle. I was just thinking of something.'

'Well, think of something else. How do you spell "intoxicated"?'

'One "x".'

'Thanks,' said the Hon. Galahad, and vanished again.

V

In his pantry, in shirt-sleeved ease, Beach, the butler, sat taking the well-earned rest of a man whose silver is all done and who has no further duties to perform till lunch-time. A bullfinch sang gaily in a cage on the window-sill, but it did not disturb him, for he was absorbed in the Racing Intelligence page of the *Morning Post*.

Suddenly he rose, palpitating. A sharp rap had sounded on the door, and he was a man who reacted nervously to sudden noises. There entered his employer's nephew, Mr. Ronald Fish.

'Hullo, Beach.'

'Sir?'

'Busy?'

'No, sir.'

'Just thought I'd look in.'

'Yes, sir.'

'For a chat.'

'Very good, sir.'

Although the butler spoke with his usual smooth courtesy, he was far from feeling easy in his mind. He did not like Ronnie's looks. It seemed to him that his young visitor was feverish. The limbs twitched, the eyes gleamed, the blood-pressure appeared heightened, and there was a super-normal pinkness in the epidermis of the cheek.

'Long time since we had a real, cosy talk, Beach.'

'Yes, sir.'

'When I was a kid, I used to be in and out of this pantry of yours all day long.'

'Yes, sir.'

A mood of extreme sentimentality now appeared to grip the young man. He sighed like a centenarian recalling far off, happy things.

'Those were the days, Beach.'

'Yes, sir.'

'No problems then. No worries. And even if I had worries, I could always bring them to you, couldn't I?'

'Yes, sir.'

'Remember the time I hid in here when my Uncle Gally was after me with a whangee for putting tintacks on his chair?'

'Yes, sir.'

'It was a close call, but you saved me. You were staunch and true. A man in a million. I've always thought that if there were more people like you in the world, it would be a better place.'

'I do my best to give you satisfaction, sir.'

'And how you succeed! I shall never forget your kindness in those dear old days, Beach.'

'Extremely good of you to say so, sir.'

'Later, as the years went by, I did my best to repay you, by sharing with you such snips as came my way. Remember the time I gave you Blackbird for the Manchester November Handicap?'

'Yes, sir.'

'You collected a packet.'

'It did prove a remarkably sound investment, sir.'

'Yes. And so it went on. I look back through the years, and I seem to see you and me standing side by side, each helping each, each doing the square thing by the other. You certainly always did the square thing by me.'

'I trust I shall always continue to do so, sir.'

'I know you will, Beach. It isn't in you to do otherwise. And that,' said Ronnie, beaming on him lovingly, 'is why I feel so sure that, when I have stolen my uncle's pig, you will be there helping to feed it till I give it back.'

The butler's was not a face that registered nimbly. It took some time for a look of utter astonishment to cover its full acreage. Such a look had spread to perhaps two-thirds of its surface when Ronnie went on.

'You see, Beach, strictly between ourselves, I have made up my mind to sneak the Empress away and keep her hidden in that gamekeeper's cottage in the west wood and then, when Uncle Clarence is sending out S.O.S.'s and offering large rewards, I shall find it there and return it, thus winning his undying gratitude and putting him in the right frame of mind to yield up a bit of money that I want to dig out of him. You get the idea?'

The butler blinked. He was plainly endeavouring to conquer a suspicion that his mind was darkening. Ronnie nodded kindly at him as he fought for speech.

'It's the scheme of a lifetime, you were going to say? You're quite right. It is. But it's one of those schemes that call for a sympathetic fellow-worker. You see, pigs like the Empress, Beach, require large quantities of food at frequent intervals. I can't possibly handle the entire commissariat department myself. That's where you're going to help me, like the splendid fellow you are and always have been.'

The butler had now begun to gargle slightly. He cast a look of agonized entreaty at the bullfinch, but the bird had no comfort to offer. It continued to chirp reflectively to itself, like a man trying to remember a tune in his bath.

'An enormous quantity of food they need,' proceeded Ronnie. 'You'd be surprised. Here it is in this book I took from my uncle's desk. At least six pounds of meal a day, not to mention milk or buttermilk and bran made sloppy with swill.'

Speech at last returned to the butler. It took the form at first of a faint sound like the cry of a frightened infant. Then words came.

'But, Mr. Ronald . . . !'

Ronnie stared at him incredulously. He seemed to be wrestling with an unbelievable suspicion.

'Don't tell me you're thinking of throwing me down, Beach? You? My friend since I was so high?' He laughed. He could see now how ridiculous the idea was. 'Of course you aren't! You couldn't. Apart from wanting to do a good turn, you've gathered by this time with that quick intelligence of yours, that there's money in the thing. Ten quid down, Beach, the moment you give the nod. And nobody knows better than yourself that ten quid, invested on Baby Bones for the Medbury Selling Plate at the current odds, means considerably more than a hundred in your sock on settling-day.'

'But, sir. . . . It's impossible. . . . I couldn't dream. . . . If ever it was found out. . . . Really, I don't think you ought to ask me, Mr. Ronald. . . .'

'Beach!'

'Yes, but, really, sir. . . .'

Ronnie fixed him with a compelling eye.

'Think well, Beach. Who gave you Creole Queen for the Lincolnshire?'

'But, Mr. Ronald . . . .'

'Who gave you Mazzawattee for the Jubilee Stakes, Beach? What a beauty!'

A tense silence fell upon the pantry. Even the bullfinch was hushed.

'And it may interest you to know,' said Ronnie, 'that just before I left London I heard of something really hot for the Goodwood Cup.'

A low gasp escaped Beach. All butlers are sportsmen, and Beach had been a butler for eighteen years. Mere gratitude for past favours might not have been enough in itself to turn the scale, but this was different. On the subject of form for the Goodwood Cup he had been quite unable to reach a satisfying decision. It had baffled him. For days he had been groping in the darkness.

'Jujube, sir?' he whispered.

'Not Jujube.'

'Ginger George?'

'Not Ginger George. It's no use your trying to guess, for you'll never do it. Only two touts and the stable-cat know this one. But you shall know it, Beach, the minute I give that pig back and claim my reward. And that pig needs to be fed. Beach, how about it?'

For a long minute the butler stared before him. Then, as if he felt that some simple, symbolic act of the sort was what this moment demanded, he went to the bullfinch's cage and put a green baize cloth over it.

'Tell me just what it is you wish me to do, Mr. Ronald,' he said.

VI

The dawn of another day crept upon Blandings Castle. Hour by hour the light grew stronger till, piercing the curtains of Ronnie's bedroom, it woke him from a disturbed slumber. He turned sleepily on the pillow. He was dimly conscious of having had the most extraordinary dream, all about stealing pigs. In this dream . . .

He sat up with a jerk. Like cold water dashed in his face had come the realisation that it had been no dream.

'Gosh!' said Ronnie, blinking.

Few things have such a tonic effect on a young man

accustomed to be a little heavy on waking in the morning as the discovery that he has stolen a prize pig overnight. Usually, at this hour, Ronnie was more or less of an inanimate mass till kindly hands brought him his early cup of tea: but to-day he thrilled all down his pyjama-clad form with a novel alertness. Not since he had left school had he 'sprung out of bed', but he did so now. Bed, generally so attractive to him, had lost its fascination. He wanted to be up and about.

He had bathed, shaved, and was slipping into his trousers when his toilet was interrupted by the arrival of his old friend Hugo Carmody. On Hugo's face there was an expression which it was impossible to misread. It indicated as plainly as a label that he had come bearing news, and Ronnie, guessing the nature of this news, braced himself to be suitably startled.

'Ronnie!'

'Well?'

'Heard what's happened?'

'What?'

'You know that pig of your uncle's?'

'What about it?'

'It's gone.'

'Gone!'

'Gone!' said Hugo, rolling the word round his tongue. 'I met the old boy half a minute ago, and he told me. It seems he went down to the pig-bin for a before-breakfast look at the animal, and it wasn't there.'

'Wasn't there?'

'Wasn't there.'

'How do you mean, wasn't there?'

'Well, it wasn't. Wasn't there at all. It had gone.'

'Gone?'

'Gone! Its room was empty and its bed had not been slept in.'

'Well, I'm dashed!' said Ronnie.

He was feeling pleased with himself. He felt he had played his part well. Just the right incredulous amazement, changing just soon enough into stunned belief.

'You don't seem very surprised,' said Hugo.

Ronnie was stung. The charge was monstrous.

'Yes, I do,' he cried. 'I seem frightfully surprised. I *am* surprised. Why shouldn't I be surprised?'

'All right. Just as you say. Spring about a bit more, though, another time when I bring you these sensational items. Well, I'll tell you one thing,' said Hugo with satisfaction. 'Out of evil cometh good. It's an ill wind that has no turning. For me this startling occurrence has been a life-saver. I've got thirty-six hours' leave out of it. The old boy is sending me up to London to get a detective.'

'A what?'

'A detective.'

'A detective!'

Ronnie was conscious of a marked spasm of uneasiness. He had not bargained for detectives.

'From a place called the Argus Enquiry Agency.'

Ronnie's uneasiness increased. This thing was not going to be so simple after all. He had never actually met a detective, but he had read a lot about them. They nosed about and found clues. For all he knew, he might have left a hundred clues.

'Naturally I shall have to stay the night in town. And, much as I like this place,' said Hugo, 'there's no denying that a night in town won't hurt. I've got fidgety feet, and a spot of dancing will do me all the good in the world. Bring back the roses to my cheeks.'

'Whose idea was it, getting down this blighted detective?' demanded Ronnie. He knew he was not being nonchalant, but he was disturbed.

'Mine.'

'Yours, eh?'

'All mine. I suggested it.'

'You did, did you?' said Ronnie.

He directed at his companion a swift glance of a kind that no one should have directed at an old friend.

'Oh?' he said morosely. 'Well, buzz off. I want to dress.'

## VII

A morning spent in solitary wrestling with a guilty conscience had left Ronnie Fish thoroughly unstrung. By the time the clock over the stable struck the hour of one, his mental condition had begun to resemble that of the late Eugene Aram. He paced the lower terrace with bent head, starting occasionally at the sudden chirp of a bird, and longed for Sue. Five minutes of Sue, he felt, would make him a new man.

It was perfectly foul, mused Ronnie, this being separated from the girl he loved. There was something about Sue . . . he couldn't describe it, but something that always seemed to act on a fellow's whole system like a powerful pick-me-up. She was the human equivalent of those pink drinks you went and got – or, rather, which you used to go and get before a good woman's love had made you give up all that sort of thing – at that chemist's at the top of the Haymarket after a wild night on the moors. It must have been with a girl like Sue in mind, he felt, that the poet had written those lines 'When something something something brow, a ministering angel thou!'

At this point in his meditations, a voice from immediately behind him spoke his name.

'I say, Ronnie.'

It was only his cousin Millicent. He became calmer. For an instant, so deep always is a criminal's need for a confidant, he had a sort of idea of sharing his hideous secret with this girl, between whom and himself there had long existed a pleasant friendship. Then he abandoned the notion. His secret was not one that could be lightly shared. Momentary relief of mind was not worth purchasing at the cost of endless anxiety.

'Ronnie, have you seen Mr. Carmody anywhere?'

'Hugo? He went up to London on the ten-thirty.'

'Went up to London? What for?'

'He's gone to a place called the Argus Enquiry Agency to get a detective.'

'What, to investigate this business of the Empress?'

'Yes.'

Millicent laughed. The idea tickled her.

'I'd like to be there to see old man Argus's face when he finds that all he's wanted for is to track down missing pigs. I should think he would beat Hugo over the head with a bloodstain.'

Her laughter trailed away. There had come into her face the look of one suddenly visited by a displeasing thought.

'Ronnie!'

'Hullo?'

'Do you know what?'

'What?'

'This looks fishy to me.'

'How do you mean?'

'Well, I don't know how it strikes you, but this Argus

Enquiry Agency is presumably on the 'phone. Why didn't Uncle Clarence just ring them up and ask them to send down a man?'

'Probably didn't think of it.'

'Whose idea was it, anyway, getting down a man?'

'Hugo's.'

'He suggested that he should run up to town?'

'Yes.'

'I thought as much,' said Millicent darkly.

'What do you mean?'

Millicent's eyes narrowed. She kicked moodily at a passing worm.

'I don't like it,' she said. 'It's fishy. Too much zeal. It looks very much to me as if our Mr. Carmody had a special reason for wanting to get up to London for the night. And I think I know what the reason was. Did you ever hear of a girl named Sue Brown?'

The start which Ronnie gave eclipsed in magnitude all the other starts he had given that morning. And they had been many and severe.

'It isn't true!'

'What isn't true?'

'That there's anything whatever between Hugo and Sue Brown.'

'Oh? Well, I had it from an authoritative source.'

It was not the worm's lucky morning. It had now reached Ronnie, and he kicked at it, too. The worm had the illusion that it had begun to rain shoes.

'I've got to go in and make a 'phone call,' said Millicent, abruptly.

Ronnie scarcely noticed her departure. He had supposed himself to have been doing some pretty tense thinking all the morning, but, compared with its activity now, his brain hitherto had been stagnant.

It couldn't be true, he told himself. Sue had said definitely that it wasn't, and she couldn't have been lying to him. Girls like Sue didn't lie. And yet . . .

The sound of the luncheon gong floated over the garden.

Well, one thing was certain. It was simply impossible to remain here at Blandings Castle, getting his mind poisoned with doubts and speculations which for the life of him he could not keep out of it. If he took the two-seater and drove off in it the moment this infernal meal was over, he could be in London before eight. He could call at Sue's flat; receive her assurance once more that Hugo Carmody, tall and lissom though he might be, expert on the saxophone though he admittedly was, meant nothing to her; take her out to dinner and, while dining, ease his mind of that which weighed upon it. Then, fortified with comfort and advice, he could pop into the car and be back at the Castle by lunch-time on the following day.

It wasn't, of course, that he didn't trust her implicitly. Nevertheless . . .

Ronnie went into lunch.

I

If you go up Beeston Street in the south-western postal division of London and follow the pavement on the right-hand side, you come to a blind alley called Hayling Court. If you enter the first building on the left of this blind alley and mount a flight of stairs, you find yourself facing a door, on the ground-glass of which is the legend:

ARGUS
ENQUIRY
AGENCY
LTD.

and below it, to one side, the smaller legend

P. FROBISHER PILBEAM, MGR.

And if, at about the hour when Ronnie Fish had stepped into his two-seater in the garage of Blandings Castle, you had opened this door and gone in and succeeded in convincing the gentlemanly office-boy that yours was a *bona fide* visit, having nothing to do with the sale of life insurance, proprietary medicines or handsomely bound sets of Dumas, you would have been admitted to the august presence of the Mgr. himself. P. Frobisher Pilbeam was seated at his desk, reading a telegram which had arrived during his absence at lunch.

This is peculiarly an age of young men starting out in business for themselves; of rare, unfettered spirits chafing at the bonds of employment and refusing to spend their lives working forty-eight weeks in the year for a salary. Quite early in his career Pilbeam had seen where the big money lay, and decided to go after it.

As editor of that celebrated weekly scandal-sheet, *Society Spice*, Percy Pilbeam had had exceptional opportunities of discovering in good time the true bent of his genius: with the result that, after three years of nosing out people's discreditable secrets on behalf of the Mammoth Publishing Company, his employers, he had come to the conclusion that a man of his gifts would be doing far better for himself nosing out such secrets on his own behalf. Considerably to the indignation of Lord Tilbury, the Mammoth's guiding spirit, he had borrowed some capital, handed in his portfolio, and was now in an extremely agreeable financial position.

The telegram over which he sat brooding with wrinkled forehead was just the sort of telegram an Enquiry agent ought to have been delighted to receive, being thoroughly cryptic and consequently a pleasing challenge to his astuteness as a detective, but Percy Pilbeam, in his ten minutes' acquaintance with it, had come to dislike it heartily. He preferred his telegrams easier.

It ran as follows:

*Be sure send best man investigate big robbery.*

It was unsigned.

What made the thing particularly annoying was that it was so tantalizing. A big robbery probably meant jewels, with a correspondingly big fee attached to their recovery. But you cannot scour England at random, asking people if they have had a big robbery in their neighbourhood.

Reluctantly, he gave the problem up; and, producing a pocket mirror, began with the aid of a pen nib to curl his small and revolting moustache. His thoughts had drifted now to Sue. They were not altogether sunny thoughts, for the difficulty of making Sue's acquaintance was beginning to irk Percy Pilbeam. He had written her notes. He had sent her flowers. And nothing had happened. She ignored the notes, and what she did with the flowers he did not know. She certainly never thanked him for them.

Brooding upon these matters, he was interrupted by the opening of the door. The gentlemanly office-boy entered. Pilbeam looked up, annoyed.

'How many times have I told you not to come in here without knocking?' he asked sternly.

The office-boy reflected.

'Seven,' he replied.

'What would you have done if I had been in conference with an important client?'

'Gone out again,' said the office-boy. Working in a Private Enquiry Agency, you drop into the knack of solving problems.

'Well, go out now.'

'Very good, sir. I merely wished to say that, while you were absent at lunch, a gentleman called.'

'Eh? Who was he?'

The office-boy, who liked atmosphere, and hoped some day to be promoted to the company of Mr. Murphy and Mr. Jones, the two active assistants who had their lair on the ground floor, thought for a moment of saying that, beyond the obvious facts that the caller was a Freemason, left-handed, a vegetarian and a traveller in the East, he had made no deductions from his appearance. He perceived, however, that his employer was not in the vein for that sort of thing.

'A Mr. Carmody, sir. Mr. Hugo Carmody.'

'Ah!' Pilbeam displayed interest. 'Did he say he would call again?'

'He mentioned the possibility, sir.'

'Well, if he does, inform Mr. Murphy and tell him to be ready when I ring.'

The office-boy retired, and Pilbeam returned to his thoughts of Sue. He was quite certain now that he did not like her attitude. Her attitude wounded him. Another thing he deplored was the reluctance of stage-door keepers to reveal the private addresses of the personnel of the company. Really, there seemed to be no way of getting to know the girl at all.

Eight respectful knocks sounded on the door. The office-boy, though occasionally forgetful, was conscientious. He had restored the average.

'Well?'

'Mr. Carmody to see you, sir.'

Pilbeam once more relegated Sue to the hinterland of his mind. Business was business.

'Show him in.'

'This way, sir,' said the office-boy with a graceful courtliness which, even taking into account the fact that he suffered from adenoids, had an old-world flavour, and Hugo sauntered across the threshold.

Hugo felt, and was looking, quietly happy. He seemed to

bring the sunshine with him. Nobody could have been more whole-heartedly attached than he to Blandings Castle and the society of his Millicent but he was finding London, revisited, singularly attractive.

'And this, if I mistake not, Watson, is our client now,' said Hugo genially.

Such was his feeling of universal benevolence that he embraced with his goodwill even the repellent-looking young man who had risen from the desk. Percy Pilbeam's eyes were too small and too close together and he marcelled his hair in a manner distressing to right-thinking people, but to-day he had to be lumped in with the rest of the species as a man and a brother, so Hugo bestowed a dazzling smile upon him. He still thought Pilbeam should not have been wearing pimples with a red tie. One or the other if he liked. But not both. Nevertheless he smiled upon him.

'Fine day,' he said.

'Quite,' said Pilbeam.

'Very jolly, the smell of the asphalt and carbonic gas.'

'Quite.'

'Some people might call London a shade on the stuffy side on an afternoon like this. But not Hugo Carmody.'

'No?'

'No. H. Carmody finds it just what the doctor ordered.' He sat down. 'Well, sleuth,' he said, 'to business. I called before lunch, but you were out.'

'Yes.'

'But here I am again. And I suppose you want to know what I've come about?'

'When you're quite ready to get round to it,' said Pilbeam patiently.

Hugo stretched his long legs comfortably.

'Well, I know you detective blokes always want a fellow to begin at the beginning and omit no detail, for there is no saying how important some seemingly trivial fact may be. Omitting birth and early education then, I am at the moment private secretary to Lord Emsworth at Blandings Castle, in Shropshire. And,' said Hugo, 'I maintain, a jolly good secretary. Others may think differently, but that is my view.'

'Blandings Castle?'

A thought had struck the proprietor of the Argus Enquiry Agency. He fumbled in his desk and produced the mysterious telegram. Yes, as he had fancied, it had been handed in at a place called Market Blandings.

'Do you know anything about this?' he asked, pushing it across the desk.

Hugo glanced at the document.

'The old boy must have sent that after I left,' he said. 'The absence of signature is, no doubt, due to mental stress. Lord Emsworth is greatly perturbed. A-twitter. Shaken to the core, you might say.'

'About this robbery?'

'Exactly. It has got right in amongst him.'

Pilbeam reached for pen and paper. There was a stern, set, bloodhound sort of look in his eyes.

'Kindly give me the details.'

Hugo pondered a moment.

'It was a dark and stormy night . . . No, I'm a liar. The moon was riding serenely in the sky. . . .'

'This big robbery? Tell me about it.'

Hugo raised his eyebrows.

'Big?'

'The telegram says "big".'

'These telegraph-operators will try to make sense. You can't stop them editing. The word should be "pig". Lord Emsworth's pig has been stolen!'

'Pig!' cried Percy Pilbeam.

Hugo looked at him a little anxiously.

'You know what a pig is, surely? If not, I'm afraid there is a good deal of tedious spade work ahead of us.'

The roseate dreams which the proprietor of the Argus had had of missing jewels broke like bubbles. He was deeply affronted. A man of few ideals, the one deep love of his life was for this Enquiry Agency which he had created and nursed to prosperity through all the dangers and vicissitudes which beset Enquiry Agencies in their infancy. And the thought of being expected to apply its complex machinery to a search for lost pigs cut him, as Millicent had predicted, to the quick.

'Does Lord Emsworth seriously suppose that I have time to waste looking for stolen pigs?' he demanded shrilly. 'I never heard such nonsense in my life.'

'Almost the exact words which all the other Hawkshaws used. Finding you not at home,' explained Hugo, 'I spent the morning going round to other Agencies. I think I visited six in all, and every one of them took the attitude you do.'

'I am not surprised.'

'Nevertheless, it seemed to me that they, like you, lacked vision. This, you see, is a prize pig. Don't picture to yourself something with a kink in its tail sporting idly in the mud. Imagine, rather, a favourite daughter kidnapped from her ancestral home. This is heavy stuff, I assure you. Restore the animal in time for the Agricultural Show, and you may ask of Lord Emsworth what you will, even unto half his kingdom.'

Percy Pilbeam rose. He had heard enough.

'I will not trouble Lord Emsworth. The Argus Enquiry Agency . . .'

'. . . does not detect pigs? I feared as much. Well, well, so be it. And now,' said Hugo, affably, 'may I take advantage of the beautiful friendship which has sprung up between us to use your telephone?'

Without waiting for permission – for which, indeed, he would have had to wait some time – he drew the instrument to him and gave a number. He then began to chat again.

'You seem a knowledgeable sort of bloke,' he said. 'Perhaps you can tell me where the village swains go these days when they want to dance upon the green? I have been absent for some little time from the centre of the vortex, and I have become as a child in these matters. What is the best that London has to offer to a young man with his blood up and the vine leaves more or less in his hair?'

Pilbeam was a man of business. He had no wish to converse with this client who had disappointed him and wounded his finest feelings, but it so happened that he had recently bought shares in a rising restaurant.

'Mario's,' he replied promptly. 'It's the only place.'

Hugo sighed. Once he had dreamed that the answer to a question like that would have been 'The Hot Spot'. But where was the Hot Spot now? Gone like the flowers that wither in the first frost. The lion and the lizard kept the courts where Jamshyd gloried and – after hours, unfortunately, which had started all the trouble – drank deep. Ah well, life was pretty complex.

A voice from the other end of the wire broke in on his reverie. He recognized it as that of the porter of the block of flats where Sue had her tiny abode.

'Hullo? Bashford? Mr. Carmody speaking. Will you make a long arm and haul Miss Brown to the instrument. Eh? Miss Sue Brown, of course. No other Browns are any use to me whatsoever. Right ho, I'll wait.'

The astute detective never permits himself to exhibit emotion. Pilbeam turned his start of surprise into a grave, distrait nod, as if he were thinking out deep problems. He took up his pen and drew three crosses and a squiggle on the blotting-paper. He was glad that no gentlemanly instinct had urged him to leave his visitor alone to do his telephoning.

'Mario's, eh?' said Hugo. 'What's the band like?'

'It's Leopold's.'

'Good enough for me,' said Hugo with enthusiasm. He hummed a bar or two, and slid his feet dreamily about the carpet. 'I'm shockingly out of practice, dash it. Well, that's that. Touching this other matter, you're sure you won't come to Blandings?'

'Quite.'

'Nice place. Gravel soil, spreading views, well laid-out pleasure grounds, Company's own water. . . . I would strongly advise you to bring your magnifying-glass and spend the summer. However, if you really feel . . . Sue! Hullo-ullo-ullo! This is Hugo. Yes, just up in town for the night on a mission of extraordinary secrecy and delicacy which I am not empowered to reveal. Speaking from the Argus Enquiry Agency, by courtesy of proprietor. I was wondering if you would care to come out and help me restore my lost youth, starting at about eight-thirty. Eh?'

A silence had fallen at the other end of the wire. What was happening was that in the hall of the block of flats Sue's conscience was fighting a grim battle against heavy odds.

Ranged in opposition to it were her loneliness, her love of dancing and her desire once more to see Hugo, who, though he was not a man one could take seriously, always cheered her up and made her laugh. And she had been needing a laugh for days.

Hugo thought he had been cut off.

'Hullo-ullo-ullo-ullo-ullo-ullo!' he barked peevishly.

'Don't yodel like that,' said Sue. 'You've nearly made me deaf.'

'Sorry, dear heart. I thought the machine had conked. Well, how do you react? Is it a bet?'

'I do want to see you again,' said Sue, hesitatingly.

'You shall. In person. Clean shirt, white waist-coat, the Carmody studs, and everything.'

'Well . . . !'

A psychically gifted bystander, standing in the hall of the block of flats, would have heard at this moment a faint moan. It was Sue's conscience collapsing beneath an unexpected flank attack. She had just remembered that if she went to dine with Hugo she would learn all the latest news about Ronnie. It put the whole thing in an entirely different light. Surely Ronnie himself could have no objection to the proposed feast if he knew that all she was going for was to talk about him? She might dance a little, of course, but purely by the way. Her real motive in accepting the invitation, she now realized quite clearly, was to hear all about Ronnie.

'All right,' she said. 'Where?'

'Mario's. They tell me it's the posh spot these days.'

'Mario's?'

'Yes. M. for mange, A. for asthma, R. for rheumatism . . . oh, you've got it? All right, then. At eight-thirty.'

Hugo put the receiver back. Once more he allowed his dazzling smile to play upon the Argus' proprietor.

'Much obliged for use of instrument,' he said. 'Thank you.'

'Thank *you*,' said Pilbeam.

'Well, I'll be pushing along. Ring us up if you change your mind. Market Blandings 32X. If you don't take on the job no one will. I suppose there are other sleuths in London besides the bevy I've interviewed to-day, but I'm not going to see them. I consider that I have done my bit and am through.' He looked about him. 'Make a good thing out of this business?' he asked, for he was curious on these points and was never restrained by delicacy from seeking information.

'Quite.'

'What does the work consist of? I've often wondered. Measuring footprints and putting the tips of your fingers together, and all that, I suppose?'

'We are frequently asked to follow people and report on their movements.'

Hugo laughed amusedly.

'Well, don't go following me and reporting on my movements. Much trouble might ensue. Bung-ho.'

'Goodbye,' said Percy Pilbeam.

He pressed a bell on the desk, and moved to the door to show his visitor out.

II

Leopold's justly famous band, its cheeks puffed out and its eyeballs rolling, was playing a popular melody with lots of stomp in it, and for the first time since she had accepted Hugo's invitation to the dance, Sue, gliding round the floor, was conscious of a spiritual calm. Her conscience, quieted by the moaning of the saxophones, seemed to have retired from business. It realized, no doubt, the futility of trying to pretend that there was anything wrong in a girl enjoying this delightful exercise.

How absurd, she felt, Ronnie's objections were. It was, considered Sue, becoming analytical, as if she were to make a tremendous fuss because he played tennis and golf with girls. Dancing was just a game like those two pastimes, and it so happened that you had to have a man with you or you couldn't play it. To get all jealous and throaty just because one went out dancing was simply ridiculous.

On the other hand, placid though her conscience now was, she had to admit that it was a relief to feel that he would never know of this little outing.

Men were such children when they were in love. Sue found herself sighing over the opposite sex's eccentricities. If they were only sensible, how simple life would be. It amazed her that Ronnie could ever have any possible doubt, however she might spend her leisure hours, that her heart belonged to him alone. She marvelled that he should suppose for a moment that even if she danced all night and every night with every other man in the world it would make any difference to her feelings towards him.

All the same, holding the peculiar views he did, he must undoubtedly be humoured.

'You won't breathe a word to Ronnie about our coming here, will you, Hugo?' she said, repeating an injunction which had been her opening speech on arriving at the restaurant.

'Not a syllable.'

'I can trust you?'

'Implicitly. Telegraphic address, Discretion, Market Blandings.'

'Ronnie's funny, you see.'

'One long scream.'

'I mean, he wouldn't understand.'

'No. Great surprise it was to me,' said Hugo, doing complicated things with his feet, 'to hear that you and the old hound had decided to team up. You could have knocked me down with a feather. Odd he never confided in his boyhood friend.'

'Well, it wouldn't do for it to get about.'

'Are you suggesting that Hugo Carmody is a babbler?'

'You do like gossiping. You know you do.'

'I know nothing of the sort,' said Hugo with dignity. 'If I were asked to give my opinion, I should say that I was essentially a strong, silent man.'

He made a complete circle of the floor in that capacity. His taciturnity surprised Sue.

'What's the matter?' she asked.

'Dudgeon,' said Hugo.

'What?'

'I'm sulking. That remark of yours rankles. That totally unfounded accusation that I cannot keep a secret. It may interest you to know that I, too, am secretly engaged and have never so much as mentioned it to a soul.'

'Hugo!'

'Yes. Betrothed. And so at long last came a day when Love wound his silken fetters about Hugo Carmody.'

'Who's the unfortunate girl?'

'There is no unfortunate girl. The lucky girl . . . Was that your foot?'

'Yes.'

'Sorry. I haven't got the hang of these new steps yet. The lucky girl, I was saying, is Miss Millicent Threepwood.'

As if stunned by the momentousness of the announcement, the band stopped playing; and, chancing to be immediately opposite their table, the man who never revealed secrets led his partner to her chair. She was gazing at him ecstatically.

'You don't mean that?'

'I do mean that. What did you think I meant?'

'I never heard anything so wonderful in my life!'

'Good news?'

'I'm simply delighted.'

'I'm pleased, too,' said Hugo.

'I've been trying not to admit it to myself, but I was very scared about Millicent. Ronnie told me the family wanted him and her to marry, and you never know what may happen when families throw their weight about. And now it's all right!'

'Quite all right.'

The music had started again, but Sue remained in her seat.

'Not?' said Hugo, astonished.

'Not just yet. I want to talk. You don't realize what this means to me. Besides, your dancing's gone off, Hugo. You're not the man you were.'

'I need practice.' He lit a cigarette and tapped a philosophical vein of thought, eyeing the gyrating couples meditatively. 'It's the way they're always introducing new steps that bothers the man who has been living out in the woods. I have become a rusty rustic.'

'I didn't mean you were bad. Only you used to be such a marvel. Dancing with you was like floating on a pink cloud above an ocean of bliss.'

'A very accurate description, I should imagine,' agreed Hugo. 'But don't blame me. Blame these Amalgamated Professors of the Dance, or whatever they call themselves – the birds who get together every couple of weeks or so to decide how they can make things more difficult. Amazing thing that they won't leave well alone.'

'You must have change.'

'I disagree with you,' said Hugo. 'No other walk in life is afflicted by a gang of thugs who are perpetually altering the rules of the game. When you learn to play golf, the professional doesn't tell you to bring the club up slowly and keep the head steady and roll the forearms and bend the left knee and raise the left heel and keep your eye on the ball and not sway back and a few more things, and then, after you've sweated yourself to the bone learning all that, suddenly add, "Of course, you understand that this is merely intended to see you through till about three weeks from next Thursday. After that the Supreme Grand Council of Consolidated Divot-Shifters will scrap these methods and invent an entirely new set!"'

'Is this more dudgeon?'

'No. Not dudgeon.'

'It sounds like dudgeon. I believe your little feelings are hurt because I said your dancing wasn't as good as it used to be.'

'Not at all. We welcome criticism.'

'Well, get your mind off it and tell me all about you and Millicent and . . .'

'When I was about five,' resumed Hugo, removing his cigarette from the holder and inserting another, 'I attended my first dancing-school. I'm a bit shaky on some of the incidents of the days when I was trailing clouds of glory, but I do remember that dancing-school. At great trouble and expense I was taught to throw up a rubber ball with my left hand and catch it with my right, keeping the small of the back rigid and generally behaving in a graceful and attractive manner. It doesn't sound a likely sort of thing to learn at a dancing-school, but I swear to you that that's what the curriculum was. Now, the point I am making . . .'

'Did you fall in love with Millicent right away, or was it gradual?'

'The point I am making is this. I became very good at throwing and catching that rubber ball. I dislike boasting, but I stood out conspicuously among a pretty hot bunch. People would nudge each other and say "Who is he?" behind their hands. I don't suppose, when I was feeling right, I missed the rubber ball more than once in twenty goes. But what good does it do me now? Absolutely none. Long before I got a chance of exhibiting my accomplishment in public and having beautiful women fawn on me for my skill, the Society of Amalgamated Professors of the Dance decided that the Rubber-Ball Glide, or whatever it was called, was out of date.'

'Is she very pretty?'

'And what I say is that all this chopping and changing handicaps a chap. I am perfectly prepared at this moment to step out on that floor and heave a rubber ball about, but it simply isn't being done nowadays. People wouldn't understand what I was driving at. In other words, all the time and money and trouble that I spent on mastering the Rubber-Ball Shimmy is a dead loss. I tell you, if the Amalgamated Professors want to make people cynics, they're going the right way to work.'

'I wish you would tell me all about Millicent.'

'In a moment. Dancing, they taught me at school, dates back to the early Egyptians, who ascribed the invention to the god Thoth. The Phrygian Corybantes danced in honour of somebody whose name I've forgotten, and every time the festival of Rhea Silvia came round the ancient Roman hoofers were there with their hair in a braid. But what was good enough for the god Thoth isn't good enough for these blighted Amalgamated Professors! Oh no! And it's been the same all through the ages. I don't suppose there has been a moment in history when some poor, well-meaning devil, with ambition at one end of him and two left feet at the other, wasn't getting it in the neck.'

'And all this,' said Sue, 'because you trod on my foot for just one half-second.'

'Hugo Carmody dislikes to tread on women's feet, even for half a second. He has his pride. Ever hear of Father Mariana?'

'No.'

'Mariana, George. Born twelve hundred and something. Educated privately and at Leipsic University. Hobbies, fishing, illuminating vellum and mangling the wurzel. You must have heard of old Pop Mariana?'

'I haven't, and I don't want to. I want to hear about Millicent.'

'It was the opinion of Father Mariana that dancing was a deadly sin. He was particularly down, I may mention, on the saraband. He said the saraband did more harm than the Plague. I know just how he felt. I'll bet he had worked like a dog at twenty-five pazazas the complete course of twelve lessons, guaranteed to teach the fandango: and, just when his instructor had finally told him that he was fit to do it at the next Saturday Night Social, along came the Amalgamated Brothers with their new-fangled saraband, and where was Pop? Leaning against the wall with the other foot-and-mouth diseasers, trying to pretend dancing bored him. Did I hear you say you wanted a few facts about Millicent?'

'You did.'

'Sweetest girl on earth.'

'Really?'

'Absolutely. It's well known. All over Shropshire.'

'And she really loves you?'

'Between you and me,' said Hugo confidentially, 'I don't wonder you speak in that amazed tone. If you saw her, you'd be still more surprised. I am a man who thinks before he speaks. I weigh my words. And I tell you solemnly that that girl is too good for me.'

'But you're a sweet darling precious pet.'

'I know I'm a sweet darling precious pet. Nevertheless, I still maintain that she is too good for me. She is the nearest thing to an angel that ever came glimmering through the laurels in the quiet evenfall in the garden by the turrets of the old manorial hall.'

'Hugo! I'd no idea you were so poetical.'

'Enough to make a chap poetical, loving a girl like that.'

'And you really do love her?'

Hugo took a feverish gulp of champagne and rolled his eyeballs as if he had been a member of Leopold's justly famous band.

'Madly. Devotedly. And when I think how I have deceived her my soul sickens.'

'Have you deceived her?'

'Not yet. But I'm going to in about five minutes. I put in a 'phone call to Blandings just now, and when I get through I shall tell her I'm speaking from my hotel bedroom, where I am on the point of going to bed. You see,' said Hugo confidentially, 'Millicent, though practically perfect in every other respect, is one of those girls who might misunderstand this little night out of mine, did it but come to her ears. Speaking of which, you ought to see them. Like alabaster shells.'

'I know what you mean. Ronnie's like that.'

Hugo stared.

'Ronnie?'

'Yes.'

'You mean to sit there and tell me that Ronnie's ears are like alabaster shells?'

'No, I meant that he would be furious if he knew that I had come out dancing. And, oh, I do love dancing so,' sighed Sue.

'He must never know!'

'No. That's why I asked you just now not to tell him.'

'I won't. Secrecy and silence. Thank goodness there's nobody who could tell Millicent, even if they wanted to. Ah! this must be the bringer of glad tidings, come to say my call is through. All set?' he asked the page-boy who had threaded his way through the crowd to their table.

'Yes, sir.'

Hugo rose.

'Amuse yourself somehow till I return.'

'I shan't be dull,' said Sue.

She watched him disappear, then leaned back in her seat, watching the dancers. Her eyes were bright, and Hugo's news had brought a flush to her cheeks. Percy Pilbeam, who had been hovering in the background, hoping for such an opportunity ever since his arrival at the restaurant, thought he had never seen her looking prettier. He edged between the tables, and took Hugo's vacated chair. There are men who, approaching a member of the other sex, wait for permission before sitting down, and men who sit down without permission. Pilbeam was one of the latter.

'Good evening,' he said.

She turned, and was aware of a nasty-looking little man at her elbow. He seemed to have materialised from nowhere.

'May I introduce myself, Miss Brown?' said this blot. 'My name is Pilbeam.'

At the same moment there appeared in the doorway and stood there raking the restaurant with burning eyes the flannel-suited figure of Ronald Overbury Fish.

### III

Ronnie Fish's estimate of the time necessary for reaching London from Blandings Castle in a sports-model two-seater had been thrown out of gear by two mishaps. Half-way down the drive the car had developed some mysterious engine-trouble, which had necessitated taking it back to the stables and having it overhauled by Lord Emsworth's chauffeur. It was not until nearly an hour later that he had been able to resume his journey, and a blowout near Oxford had delayed him still further. He arrived at Sue's flat just as Sue and Hugo were entering Mario's.

Ringing Sue's front-door bell produced no result. Ronnie regretted that in the stress of all the other matters that occupied his mind he had forgotten to send her a telegram. He was about to creep away and have a bite of dinner at the Drones Club – a prospect which pleased him not at all, for the Drones at dinner-time was always full of hearty eggs who talked much too loud for a worried man's nerves, and might even go so far as to throw bread at him – when, descending the stairs into the hall, he came upon Bashford, the porter.

Bashford, who knew Ronnie well, said "Ullo, Mr. Fish,' and Ronnie said 'Hullo, Bashford,' and Bashford said the weather seemed to keep up, and Ronnie said, 'Yes, that's right, it did,' and it was at this point that the porter uttered these memorable – and, as events proved, epoch-making – words:

'If you're looking for Miss Brown, Mr. Fish, I've an idea she's gone to a place called Mario's.'

He poured further details into Ronnie's throbbing ear. Mr. Carmody had rung up on the 'phone, might have been ar-parse four, and he, Bashford, not listening but happening to hear, had thought he had caught something said about this place Mario's.

'Mario's?' said Ronnie. 'Thanks, Bashford. Mario's eh? Right!'

The porter, for Eton and Cambridge train their sons well, found nothing in the way Mr. Fish spoke to cause a thrill. Totally unaware that he had been conversing with Othello's younger brother, he went back to his den in the basement and sat down with a good appetite to steak and chips. And Ronnie, quivering from head to foot, started the car and drove off.

Jealousy, said Shakespeare, and he was about right, is the green-eyed monster which doth mock the meat he feeds on. By the time Ronald Overbury Fish pushed through the swinging-door that guards the revelry at Mario's from the gaze of the passer-by, he was, like the Othello he so much resembled, perplexed in the extreme. He felt hot all over, then cold all over, then hot again, and the waiter who stopped him on the threshold of the dining-room to inform him that evening dress was indispensable on the dancing-floor, and that flannel suits must go up to the balcony, was running a risk which would have caused his insurance company to purse its lips and shake its head.

Fortunately for him, Ronnie did not hear. He was scanning the crowd before him in an effort to find Sue.

'Plenty of room in the balcony, sir,' urged the waiter, continuing to play with fire.

This time Ronnie did become dimly aware that somebody was addressing him, and he was about to turn and give the man one look, when half-way down a grove of black coats and gaily-coloured frocks he suddenly saw what he was searching for. The next moment he was pushing a path through the throng, treading on toes of brave men and causing fair women to murmur bitterly that this sort of thing ought to be prevented by the management.

Five yards from Sue's table, Ronnie Fish would have said that his cup was full and could not possibly be made any fuller. But when he had covered another two and pushed aside a fat man who was standing in the fairway, he realized his mistake. It was not Hugo who was Sue's companion, but a reptilian-looking squirt with narrow eyes and his hair done in ridges. And, as he saw him, something seemed to go off in Ronnie's brain like a released spring.

A waiter, pausing with a tray of glasses, pointed out to him that on the dancing-floor evening dress was indispensable.

Gentlemen in flannel suits, he added, could be accommodated in the balcony.

'Plenty of room in the balcony, sir,' said the waiter.

Ronnie reached the table. Pilbeam at the moment was saying that he had wanted for a long time to meet Sue. He hoped she had got his flowers all right.

It was perhaps a natural desire to look at anything but this odious and thrusting individual who had forced his society upon her, that caused Sue to raise her eyes.

Raising them, she met Ronnie's. And, as she saw him, her conscience, which she had supposed lulled for the night, sprang to life more vociferous than ever. It had but been crouching, the better to spring.

'Ronnie!'

She started up. Pilbeam also rose. The waiter with the glasses pressed the edge of the tray against Ronnie's elbow in a firm but respectful manner and told him that on the dancing-floor evening dress was indispensable. Gentlemen in flannel suits, however, would find ample accommodation in the balcony.

Ronnie did not speak. And it would have been better if Sue had not done so. For, at this crisis, some subconscious instinct, of the kind which is always waiting to undo us at critical moments, suggested to her dazed mind that when two men who do not know each other are standing side by side in a restaurant one ought to introduce them.

'Mr. Fish, Mr. Pilbeam,' murmured Sue.

Only the ringing of the bell that heralds the first round of a heavy-weight championship fight could have produced more instant and violent results. Through Ronnie's flannel-clad body a sort of galvanic shock seemed to pass. Pilbeam! He had come expecting Hugo, and Hugo would have been bad enough. But Pilbeam! The man she had said she didn't even know. The man she hadn't met. The man whose gifts of flowers she had professed to resent. In person! In the flesh! Hobnobbing with her in a restaurant! By Gad, he meant to say. By George! Good Gosh!

His fists clenched. Eton was forgotten, Cambridge not even a memory. He inhaled so sharply that a man at the next table who was eating a mousse of chicken stabbed himself in the chin with his fork. He turned on Pilbeam with a hungry look. And at this moment, the waiter, raising his voice a little, for he was beginning to think that Ronnie's hearing was slightly affected, mentioned as an interesting piece of information that the management of Mario's preferred to reserve the dancing-floor exclusively for clients in evening dress. But there was a bright side. Gentlemen in flannel suits could be accommodated in the balcony.

It was the waiter who saved Percy Pilbeam. Just as a mosquito may divert for an instant a hunter who is about to spring at and bite in the neck a tiger of the jungle, so did this importunate waiter divert Ronnie Fish. What it was all about, he was too overwrought to ascertain, but he knew that the man was annoying him, pestering him, trying to chat with him when he had business elsewhere. With all the force of a generous nature, sorely tried, he plugged the waiter in the stomach with his elbow. There was a crash which even Leopold's band could not drown. The man who had stabbed himself with the fork had his meal still further spoiled by the fact that it suddenly began to rain glass. And, as regards the other occupants of the restaurant, the word 'Sensation' about sums the situation up.

Ronnie and the management of Mario's now formed two sharply contrasted schools of thought. To Ronnie the only thing that seemed to matter was this Pilbeam – this creeping, slinking, cuckoo-in-the-nest Pilbeam, the Lothario who had lowered all speed records in underhand villany by breaking up his home before he had got one. He concentrated all his faculties to the task of getting round the table, to the other side of which the object of his dislike had prudently withdrawn, and showing him in no uncertain manner where he got off.

To the management, on the other hand, the vital issue was all this broken glassware. The waiter had risen from the floor, but the glasses were still there, and scarcely one of them was in a condition ever to be used again for the refreshment of Mario's customers. The head-waiter, swooping down on the fray like some god in the *Iliad* descending from a cloud, was endeavouring to place his point of view before Ronnie. Assisting him with word and gesture were two inferior waiters – Waiter A. and Waiter B.

Ronnie was in no mood for abstract debate. He hit the head-waiter in the abdomen, Waiter A. in the ribs, and was just about to dispose of Waiter B., when his activities were hampered by the sudden arrival of reinforcements. From all parts of the room other waiters had assembled – to name but a few, Waiters C., D., E., F., G. and H. – and he found himself hard pressed. It seemed to him that he had dropped into a Waiters' Convention. As far as the eye could reach, the area was crammed with waiters, and more coming. Pilbeam had disappeared altogether, and so busy was Ronnie now that he did not even miss him. He had reached that condition of mind which the old Vikings used to call Berserk and which among modern Malays is termed running amok.

Ronnie Fish in the course of his life had had many ambitions. As a child, he had yearned some day to become an engine-driver. At school, it had seemed to him that the most attractive career the world had to offer was that of the professional cricketer. Later, he had hoped to run a prosperous night-club. But now, in his twenty-sixth year, all these desires were cast aside and forgotten. The only thing in life that seemed really worth while was to massacre waiters; and to this task he addressed himself with all the energy and strength at his disposal.

Matters now began to move briskly. Waiter C., who rashly clutched the sleeve of Ronnie's coat, reeled back with a hand pressed to his right eye. Waiter D., a married man, contented himself with standing on the outskirts and talking Italian. But waiter E., made of sterner stuff, hit Ronnie rather hard with a dish containing *omelette aux champignons*, and it was as the latter reeled beneath this buffet that there suddenly appeared in the forefront of the battle a figure wearing a gay uniform and almost completely concealed behind a vast moustache, waxed at the ends. It was the commissionaire from the street-door; and anybody who has ever been bounced from a restaurant knows that commissionaires are heavy metal.

This one, whose name was McTeague, and who had spent many lively years in the army before retiring to take up his present duties, had a grim face made of some hard kind of wood and the muscles of a village blacksmith. A man of action rather than words, he clove his way through the press in silence. Only when he reached the centre of the maelstrom did he speak. This was when Ronnie, leaping upon a chair the better to perform the operation, hit him on the nose. On receipt of this blow, he uttered the brief monosyllable 'Ho!' and then, without more delay, scooped Ronnie into an embrace of steel and bore him towards the door, through which was now moving a long, large leisurely policeman.

IV

It was some few minutes later that Hugo Carmody, emerging from the telephone-booth on the lower floor where the cocktail bars is, sauntered back into the dancing-room and was interested to find waiters massaging bruised limbs, other waiters replacing fallen tables, and Leopold's band playing in a sort of hushed undertone like a band that has seen strange things.

'Hullo!' said Hugo. 'Anything up?'

He eyed Sue inquiringly. She looked to him like a girl who has had some sort of a shock. Not, or his eyes deceived him, at all her old bright self.

'What's up?' he asked.

'Take me home, Hugo!'

Hugo stared.

'Home? Already? With the night yet young?'

'Oh, Hugo, take me home, quick.'

'Just as you say,' assented Hugo agreeably. He was now pretty certain that something was up. 'One second to settle the bill, and then homeward ho. And on the way you shall tell me all about it. For I jolly well know,' said Hugo, who prided himself on his keenness of observation, 'that something is – or has been – up.'

The law of Great Britain is a remorseless machine, which, once set in motion, ignores first causes and takes into account only results. It will not accept shattered dreams as an excuse for shattering glass-ware: nor will you get far by pleading a broken heart in extenuation of your behaviour in breaking waiters. Haled on the morrow before the awful majesty of Justice at Bosher Street Police Court and charged with disorderly conduct in a public place – to wit, Mario's Restaurant, and resisting an officer – to wit, P.C. Murgatroyd, in the execution of his duties, Ronald Fish made no impassioned speeches. He did not raise clenched fists aloft and call upon Heaven to witness that he was a good man wronged. Experience, dearly bought in the days of his residence at the University, had taught him that when the Law gripped you with its talons the only thing to do was to give a false name, say nothing and hope for the best.

Shortly before noon, accordingly, on the day following the painful scene just described, Edwin Jones, of 7 Nasturtium Villas, Cricklewood, poorer by the sum of five pounds, was being conveyed in a swift taxi-cab to his friend Hugo Carmody's hotel, there to piece together his broken life and try to make a new start.

On the part of the man Jones himself during the ride there was a disposition toward silence. He gazed before him bleakly and gnawed his lower lip. Hugo Carmody, on the other hand, was inclined to be rather jubilant. It seemed to Hugo that after a rocky start things had panned out pretty well.

'A nice, smooth job,' he said approvingly. 'I was scanning the beak's face closely during the summing up and I couldn't help fearing for a moment that it was going to be a case of fourteen days without the option. As it is, here you are, a free man, and no chance of your name being in the papers. A moral victory, I call it.'

Ronnie released his lower lip in order to bare his teeth in a bitter sneer.

'I wouldn't care if my name were in every paper in London.'

'Oh, come, old loofah! The honoured name of Fish?'

'What do I care about anything now?'

Hugo was concerned. This morbid strain, he felt, was unworthy of a Nasturtium Villas Jones.

'Aren't you rather tending to make a bit too much heavy weather over this?'

'Heavy weather!'

'I think you are. After all, when you come right down to it, what has happened? You find poor little Sue . . .'

'Don't call her "poor little Sue"!'

'You find the party of the second part,' amended Hugo, 'at a dance place. Well, why not? What, if you follow me, of it? Where's the harm in her going out to dance?'

'With a man she swore she didn't know!'

'Well, at the time when you asked her, probably she didn't know him. Things move quickly in a great city. I wish I had a quid for every girl I've been out dancing with, whom

I hadn't known from Eve a couple of days before.'

'She promised me she wouldn't go out with a soul.'

'Ah, but with a merry twinkle in her eye, no doubt? I mean to say, you can't expect a girl nowadays to treat a promise like that seriously. I mean, dash it, be reasonable!'

'And with that little worm of all people!'

Hugo cleared his throat. He was conscious of a slight embarrassment. He had not wished to touch on this aspect of the affair, but Ronnie's last words gave a Carmody and a gentleman no choice.

'As a matter of fact, Ronnie, old man,' he said, 'you are wrong in supposing that she went to Mario's with the above Pilbeam. She went with me. Blameless Hugo, what. I mean, more like a brother than anything.'

Ronnie declined to be comforted.

'I don't believe you.'

'My dear chap!'

'I suppose you think you're damned clever, trying to smooth things over. She was at Mario's with Pilbeam.'

'I took her there.'

'You may have taken her. But she was dining with Pilbeam.'

'Nothing of the kind.'

'Do you think I can't believe my own eyes? It's no use your saying anything, Hugo, I'm through with her. She's let me down. Less than a week I've been away,' said Ronnie, his voice trembling 'and she lets me down. Well, it serves me right for being such a fool as to think she ever cared a curse for me.'

He relapsed into silence. And Hugo, after turning over in his mind a few specimen remarks, decided not to make them. The cab drew up before the hotel, and Ronnie, getting out, uttered a wordless exclamation.

'No, let me,' said Hugo considerately. A bit rough on a man, he felt, after coughing up five quid to the hell-hounds of the Law, to be expected to pay the cab. He produced money and turned to the driver. It was some moments before he turned back again, for the driver, by the rules of the taxi-chauffeurs Union, kept his petty cash tucked into his underclothing. When he did so, he was considerably astonished to find that Ronnie, while his back was turned, had, in some unaccountable manner, become Sue. The changeling was staring unhappily at him from the exact spot where he had left his old friend.

'Hullo!' he said.

'Ronnie's gone,' said Sue.

'Gone?'

'Yes. He walked off as quick as he could round the corner when he saw me. He . . .' Sue's voice broke. 'He didn't say a word.'

'How did you get here?' asked Hugo. There were other matters, of course, to be discussed later, but he felt he must get this point cleared up first.

'I thought you would bring him back to your hotel, and I thought that if I could see him I could . . . say something.'

Hugo was alarmed. He was now practically certain that this girl was going to cry, and if there was one thing he disliked it was being with crying girls in a public spot. He would not readily forget the time when a female named Yvonne Something had given way to a sudden twinge of neuralgia in his company not far from Piccadilly Circus, and an old lady had stopped and said that it was brutes like him who caused all the misery in the world.

'Come inside,' he urged quickly. 'Come and have a cocktail or a cup of tea or a bun or something. I say,' he said, as he led the way into the hotel lobby and found two seats in a distant corner, 'I'm frightfully sorry about all this. I can't help feeling it's my fault.'

'Oh, no.'

'If I hadn't asked you to dinner. . . .'

'It isn't that that's the trouble. Ronnie might have been a little cross for a minute or two if he had found you and me together, but he would soon have got over it. It was finding me with that horrid little man Pilbeam. You see, I told him – and it was quite true – that I didn't know him.'

'Yes, so he was saying to me in the cab.'

'Did he— What did he say?'

'Well, he plainly resented the Pilbeam, I'm afraid. His manner, when touching on the Pilbeam, was austere. I tried to drive into his head that that was just an accidental meeting and that you had come to Mario's with me, but he would have none of it. I fear, old thing, there's nothing to be done but leave the whole bilge to Time, the Great Healer.'

A page-boy was making a tour of the lobby. He seemed to be seeking a Mr. Gargery.

'If only I could get hold of him and make him listen. I haven't been given a chance to explain.'

'You think you could explain, even if given a chance?'

'I could try. Surely he couldn't help seeing that I really loved him, if we had a real talk?'

'And the trouble is, you're here and he'll be back at Blandings in a few hours. Difficult,' said Hugo, shaking his head. 'Complex.'

'Mr. Carmody,' chanted the page-boy, coming nearer. 'Mr. Carmody.'

'Hi!' cried Hugo.

'Mr. Carmody? Wanted on the telephone, sir.'

Hugo's face became devout and saint-like.

'Awfully sorry to leave you for an instant,' he said, 'but do you mind if I rush? It must be Millicent. She's the only person who knows I'm here.'

He sped away, and Sue, watching him, found herself choking with sudden tears. It seemed to emphasise her forlornness so, this untimely evidence of another love-story that had not gone awry. She seemed to be listening to that telephone-conversation, hearing Hugo's delighted yelps as the voice of the girl he loved floated to him over the wire.

She pulled herself together. Beastly of her to be jealous of Hugo just because he was happy. . . .

Sue sat up abruptly. She had had an idea.

It was a breath-taking idea, but simple. It called for courage, for audacity, for a reckless disregard of consequences, but nevertheless it was simple.

'Hugo,' she cried, as that lucky young man returned and dropped into the chair at her side. 'Hugo, listen!'

'I say,' said Hugo.

'I've suddenly thought . . .'

'I say,' said Hugo.

'Do listen!'

'I say,' said Hugo, 'that was Millicent on the 'phone.'

'Was it? How nice. Listen, Hugo . . .'

'Speaking from Blandings.'

'Yes. But . . .'

'And she has broken off the engagement!'

'What!'

'Broken off the bally engagement,' repeated Hugo. He signalled urgently to a passing waiter. 'Get me a brandy-and-

454

soda, will you?' he said. His face was pale and set. 'A stiffish brandy-and-soda, please.'

'Brandy-and-soda, sir?'

'Yes,' said Hugo. 'Stiffish.'

S ue stared at him, bewildered.

'Broken off the engagement?'

'Broken off the engagement.'

In moments of stress, the foolish question is always the one that comes uppermost in the mind.

'Are you sure?'

Hugo emitted a sound which resembled the bursting of a paper bag. He would have said himself, if asked, that he was laughing mirthlessly.

'Sure? Not much doubt about it.'

'But why?'

'She knows all.'

'All what?'

'Everything, you poor fish,' said Hugo, forgetting in a strong man's agony the polish of the Carmodys. 'She's found out that I took you to dinner last night.'

'What!'

'She has.'

'But how?'

The paper bag exploded again. A look of intense bitterness came into Hugo's face.

'If ever I meet that slimy, slinking, marcelle-waved-by-product Pilbeam again,' he said, 'let him commend his soul to God! If he has time,' he added.

He took the brandy-and-soda from the waiter, and eyed Sue dully.

'Anything on similar lines for you?'

'No, thanks.'

'Just as you like. It's not easy for a man in my position to realize,' said Hugo, drinking deeply, 'that refusing a brandy-and-soda is possible. I shouldn't have said, off-hand, that it could be done.'

Sue was a warm-hearted girl. In the tragedy of this announcement she had almost forgotten that she had troubles herself.

'Tell me all about it, Hugo.'

He put down the empty glass.

'I came up from Blandings yesterday,' he said, 'to interview the Argus Enquiry Agency on the subject of sending a man down to investigate the theft of Lord Emsworth's pig.'

Sue would have liked to hear more about this pig, but she knew that this was no time for questions.

'I went to the Argus and saw this wen Pilbeam, who runs it.'

Again Sue would have liked to speak. Once more she refrained. She felt as if she were at a sick-bed, hearing a dying man's last words. On such occasions one does not interrupt.

'Meanwhile,' proceeded Hugo tonelessly, 'Millicent, suspecting – and I am surprised at her having a mind like that. I always looked on her as a pure, white soul – suspecting that I might be up to something in London, got the Argus on the long-distance telephone and told them to follow my movements and report to her. And, apparently, just before she called me up, she had been talking to them on the wire and getting their statement. All this she revealed to me in short, burning sentences, and then she said that if I thought we were still engaged, I could have three more guesses. But, to save me trouble, she would tell me the answer – viz.: No wedding-bells for me. And to think,' said Hugo, picking up the glass and putting it down again, after inspection, with a hurt and disappointed look, 'that I actually rallied this growth Pilbeam on the subject of following people and reporting on their movements. Yes, I assure you. Rallied him blithely. Just as I was leaving his office, we kidded merrily back and forth. And then I went out into the world, happy and carefree, little knowing that my every step was dogged by a blasted bloodhound. Well, all I can say is that, if Ronnie wants this Pilbeam's gore, and I gather that he does, he will jolly well have to wait till I've helped myself.'

Sue, womanlike, blamed the woman.

'I don't think Millicent can be a very nice girl,' she said, primly.

'An angel,' said Hugo. 'Always was. Celebrated for it. I don't blame her.'

'I do.'

'I don't.'

'I do.'

'Well, have it your own way,' said Hugo handsomely. He beckoned to the waiter. 'Another of the same, please.'

'This settles it,' said Sue.

Her eyes were sparkling. Her chin had a resolute tilt.

'Settles what?'

'While you were at the telephone, I had an idea.'

'I have had ideas in my time,' said Hugo. 'Many of them. At the moment, I have but one. To get within arm's length of the yam Pilbeam and twist his greasy neck till it comes apart in my hands. "What do you do here?" I said. "Measure footprints?" "We follow people and report on their movements," said he. "Ha, ha!" I laughed carelessly. "Ha, ha!" laughed he. General mirth and jollity. And all the while—'

'Hugo, will you listen?'

'And this is the bitter thought that now strikes me. What chance have I of scooping out the man's inside with my bare hands? I've got to go back to Blandings on the two-fifteen, or I lose my job. Leaving him unscathed in his bally lair, chuckling over my downfall and following some other poor devil's movements.'

'Hugo!'

The broken man passed a weary hand over his forehead.

'You spoke?'

'I've been speaking for the last ten minutes, only you won't listen.'

'Say on,' said Hugo, listlessly starting on the second restorative.

'Have you ever heard of a Miss Schoonmaker?'

'I seem to know the name. Who is she?'

'Me.'

Hugo lowered his glass, pained.

'Don't talk drip to a broken-hearted man,' he begged. 'What do you mean?'

'When Ronnie was driving me in his car, we met Lady Constance Keeble.'

'A blister,' said Hugo. 'Always was. Generally admitted all over Shropshire.'

'She thought I was this Miss Schoonmaker.'

'Why?'

'Because Ronnie said I was.'

Hugo sighed hopelessly.

'Complex. Complex. My God! How complex.'

'It was quite simple and natural. Ronnie had just been telling me about this girl – how he had met her at Biarritz and that she was coming to Blandings and so on, and when he saw Lady Constance looking at me with frightful suspicion it suddenly occurred to him to say that I was her.'

'That you were Lady Constance?'

'No, idiot. Miss Schoonmaker. And now I'm going to wire her – Lady Constance, not Miss Schoonmaker, in case you were going to ask – saying that I'm coming to Blandings right away.'

'Pretending to be this Miss Schoonmaker?'

'Yes.'

Hugo shook his head.

'Imposs.'

'Why?'

'Absolutely out of the q.'

'Why? Lady Constance is expecting me. Do be sensible.'

'I'm being sensible all right. But somebody is gibbering and, naming no names, it's you. Don't you realize that, just as you reach the front door, this Miss Schoonmaker will arrive in person, dishing the whole thing?'

'No, she won't.'

'Why won't she?'

'Because Ronnie sent her a telegram, in Lady Constance's name, saying that there's scarlet fever or something at Blandings and she wasn't to come.'

Hugo's air of the superior critic fell from him like a garment. He sat up in his chair. So moved was he that he spilled his brandy-and-soda and did not give it so much as a look of regret.

He let it soak into the carpet, unheeded.

'Sue!'

'Once I'm at Blandings, I shall be able to see Ronnie and make him be sensible.'

'That's right.'

'And then you'll be able to tell Millicent that there couldn't have been much harm in my being out with you last night because I'm engaged to Ronnie.'

'That's right, too.'

'Can you see any flaws?'

'Not a flaw.'

'I suppose as a matter of fact, you'll give the whole thing away in the first five minutes by calling me Sue.'

Hugo waved an arm buoyantly.

'Don't give the possibility another thought,' he said. 'If I do, I'll cover it up adroitly by saying I meant, "Schoo." Short for Schoonmaker. And now go send her another telegram. Keep on sending telegrams. Leave nothing to chance. Send a dozen and pitch it strong. Say that Blandings Castle is ravaged with disease. Not merely scarlet fever *and* mumps. Not to mention housemaid's knee, diabetes, measles, shingles, and the botts. We're onto a big thing, my Susan. Let us push it along.'

## 7. A JOB FOR PERCY PILBEAM

I

Sunshine, calling to all right-thinking men to come out and revel in its heartening warmth, poured in at the windows of the great library of Blandings Castle. But to Clarence, ninth Earl of Emsworth, much as he liked sunshine as a rule, it brought no cheer. His face drawn, his pince-nez askew, his tie drooping away from its stud like a languorous lily, he sat staring sightlessly before him. He looked like something that had just been prepared for stuffing by a taxidermist.

A moralist, watching Lord Emsworth in his travail, would have reflected smugly that it cuts both ways, this business of being a peer of the realm with large private means and a good digestion. Unalloyed prosperity, he would have pointed out in his offensive way, tends to enervate; and in this world of ours, full of alarms and uncertainties, where almost anything is apt to drop suddenly on top of your head without warning at almost any moment, what one needs is to be tough and alert.

When some outstanding disaster happens to the ordinary man, it finds him prepared. Years of missing the eight-forty-five, taking the dog for a run on rainy nights endeavouring to abate smoky chimneys, and coming down to breakfast and discovering that they have burned the bacon again, have given his soul a protective hardness, so that by the time his wife's relations arrive for a long visit he is ready for them.

Lord Emsworth had had none of this salutary training. Fate, hitherto, had seemed to spend its time thinking up ways of pampering him. He ate well, slept well and had no money troubles. He grew the best roses in Shropshire. He had won a first prize for pumpkins at that county's Agricultural Show, a thing no Earl of Emsworth had ever done before. And, just previous to the point at which this chronicle opens, his younger son, Frederick, had married the daughter of an American millionaire and had gone to live three thousand miles away from Blandings Castle with lots of good, deep water in between him and it. He had come to look on himself as Fate's spoiled darling.

Can we wonder, then, that in the agony of this sudden, treacherous blow he felt stunned and looked eviscerated? Is it surprising that the sunshine made no appeal to him? May we not consider him justified, as he sat there, in swallowing a lump in his throat like an ostrich gulping down a brass door-knob?

The answer to these questions, in the order given, is No, No, and Yes.

The door of the library opened, revealing the natty person of his brother Galahad. Lord Emsworth straightened his pince-nez and looked at him apprehensively. Knowing how little reverence there was in the Hon. Galahad's composition, and how tepid was his interest in the honourable struggles for supremacy of Fat Pigs, he feared that the other was about to wound him in his bereavement with some jarring flippancy. Then his gaze softened and he was conscious of a soothing feeling of relief. There was no frivolity in his brother's face, only a gravity which became him well. The Hon. Galahad sat down, hitched up the knees of his trousers, cleared his throat, and spoke in a tone that could not have been more sympathetic or in better taste.

'Bad business, this, Clarence.'

'Appalling, my dear fellow.'

'What are you going to do about it?'

Lord Emsworth shrugged his shoulders hopelessly. He generally did when people asked him what he was going to do about things.

'I am at a loss,' he confessed. 'I do not know how to act. What young Carmody tells me has completely upset all my plans.'

'Carmody?'

'I sent him to the Argus Enquiry Agency in London to engage the services of a detective. It is a firm that Sir Gregory Parsloe once mentioned to me, in the days when we were on better terms. He said, in rather a meaning way, I thought, that if ever I had any trouble of any sort that needed expert and tactful handling, these were the people to go to. I gathered that they had assisted him in some matter the details of which he did not confide to me, and had given complete satisfaction.'

'Parsloe!' said the Hon. Galahad, and sniffed.

'So I sent young Carmody to London to approach them about finding the Empress. And now he tells me that his errand proved fruitless. They were firm in their refusal to trace missing pigs.'

'Just as well.'

'What do you mean?'

'Save you a lot of unnecessary expense. There's no need for you to waste money employing detectives.'

'I thought that possibly the trained mind. . . .'

'I can tell you who's got the Empress. I've known it all along.'

'What!'

'Certainly.'

'Galahad!'

'It's as plain as the nose on your face.'

Lord Emsworth felt his nose.

'Is it?' he said doubtfully.

'I've just been talking to Constance. . . .'

'Constance?' Lord Emsworth opened his mouth feebly.

'She hasn't got my pig?'

'I've just been talking to Constance,' repeated the Hon. Galahad, 'and she called me some very unpleasant names.'

'She does, sometimes. Even as a child, I remember . . .'

'Most unpleasant names. A senile mischief-maker, among others, and a meddling old penguin. And all because I told her that the man who had stolen Empress of Blandings was young Gregory Parsloe.'

'Parsloe!'

'Parsloe. Surely it's obvious? I should have thought it would have been clear to the meanest intelligence.'

From boyhood up, Lord Emsworth had possessed an intelligence about as mean as an intelligence can be without actually being placed under restraint. Nevertheless, he found his brother's theory incredible.

'Parsloe?'

'Don't keep saying "Parsloe".'

'But, my dear Galahad . . .'

'It stands to reason.'

'You don't really think so?'

'Of course I think so. Have you forgotten what I told you the other day?'

'Yes,' said Lord Emsworth. He always forgot what people told him the other day.

'About young Parsloe,' said the Hon. Galahad impatiently. 'About his nobbling my dog Towser.'

Lord Emsworth started. It all came back to him. A hard expression crept into the eyes behind the pince-nez, which emotion had just jerked crooked again.

'To be sure. Towser. Your dog. I remember.'

'He nobbled Towser, and he's nobbled the Empress. Dash it. Clarence, use your intelligence. Who else except young Parsloe had any interest in getting the Empress out of the way? And, if he hadn't known there was some dirty work being planned, would that pig-man of his, Brotherhood or whatever his name is, have been going about offering three to one on Pride of Matchingham? I told you at the time it was fishy.'

The evidence was damning, and yet Lord Emsworth found himself once more a prey to doubt. Of the blackness of Sir Gregory Parsloe-Parsloe's soul he had, of course, long been aware. But could the man actually be capable of the Crime of the Century? A fellow-landowner? A Justice of the Peace? A man who grew pumpkins? A Baronet?

'But Galahad . . . A man in Parsloe's position . . .'

'What do you mean a man in his position? Do you suppose a fellow changes his nature just because a cousin of his dies and he comes into a baronetcy? Haven't I told you a dozen times that I've known young Parsloe all his life? Known him intimately. He was always as hot as mustard and as wide as Leicester Square. Ask anybody who used to go around Town in those days. When they saw young Parsloe coming, strong men winced and hid their valuables. He hadn't a penny except what he could get by telling the tale, and he always did himself like a prince. When I knew him first, he was living down on the river at Shepperton. His old father, the Dean, had made an arrangement with the keeper of the pub there to give him breakfast and bed and nothing else. "If he wants dinner, he must earn it," the old boy said. And do you know how he used to earn it? He trained that mongrel of his, Banjo, to go and do tricks in front of parties that came to the place in steam-launches. And then he would stroll up and hope his dog was not annoying them and stand talking till they went in to dinner and then go in with them and pick up the wine-list, and before they knew what was happening he would be bursting with their champagne and cigars. That's the sort of fellow young Parsloe was.'

'But even so —'

'I remember him running up to me outside that pub one afternoon – the Jolly Miller it was called – his face shining with positive ecstasy. "Come in, quick!" he said. "There's a new barmaid, and she hasn't found out yet I'm not allowed credit."'

'But, Galahad. . . .'

'And if young Parsloe thinks I've forgotten a certain incident that occurred in the early summer of the year '95, he's very much mistaken. He met me in the Haymarket and took me into the Two Goslings for a drink – there's a hat-shop now where it used to be – and after we'd had it he pulls a sort of dashed little top affair out of his pocket, a thing with numbers written round it. Said he'd found it in the street and wondered who thought of these ingenious little toys and insisted on our spinning it for half-crowns. "You take the odd numbers, I'll take the even," says young Parsloe. And before I could fight my way out into the fresh air, I was ten pounds seven and sixpence in the hole. And I discovered next morning that they make those beastly things so that if you push the stem through and spin them the wrong way up you're bound to get an even number. And when I asked him the following afternoon to show me that top again, he said he'd lost it. That's the sort of fellow young Parsloe was. And you expect me to believe that inheriting a baronetcy and settling down in the country has made him so dashed pure and high-minded that he wouldn't stoop to nobbling a pig.'

Lord Emsworth uncoiled himself. Cumulative evidence had done its work. His eyes glittered, and he breathed stertorously.

'The scoundrel!'

'Tough nut, always was.'

'What shall I do?'

'Do? Why, go to him right away and tax him.'

'Tax him?'

'Yes. Look him squarely in the eye and tax him with his crime.'

'I will! Immediately.'

'I'll come with you.'

'Look him squarely in the eye!'

'And tax him!'

'And tax him.' Lord Emsworth had reached the hall and was peering agitatedly to right and left. 'Where the devil's my hat? I can't find my hat. Somebody's always hiding my hat. I will not have my hats hidden.'

'You don't need a hat to tax a man with stealing a pig,' said the Hon. Galahad, who was well versed in the manners and rules of good society.

II

In his study at Matchingham Hall in the neighbouring village of Much Matchingham, Sir Gregory Parsloe-Parsloe sat gazing at the current number of a weekly paper. We have seen that weekly paper before. On that occasion it was in the plump hands of Beach. And, oddly enough, what had attracted Sir Gregory's attention was the very item which had interested the butler.

*'The Hon. Galahad Threepwood, brother of the Earl of Emsworth. A little bird tells us that "Gally" is at Blandings Castle, Shropshire, the ancestral seat of the family, busily engaged in writing his reminiscences. As every member of the Old Brigade will testify, they ought to be as warm as the weather, if not warmer!'*

But whereas Beach, perusing this, had chuckled, Sir Gregory Parsloe-Parsloe shivered, like one who on a country ramble suddenly perceives a snake in his path.

Sir Gregory Parsloe-Parsloe, of Matchingham Hall, seventh baronet of his line, was one of those men who start their lives well, skid for awhile, and then slide back onto the straight and narrow path and stay there. That is to say, he had been up to the age of twenty a blameless boy and from the age of thirty-one, when he had succeeded to the title, a practically blameless Bart. So much so that now, in his fifty-second year, he was on the eve of being accepted by the local Unionist Committee as their accredited candidate for the forthcoming by-election in the Bridgeford and Shifley Parliamentary Division of Shropshire.

But there had been a decade in his life, that dangerous decade of the twenties, when he had accumulated a past so substantial that a less able man would have been compelled to spread it over a far longer period. It was an epoch in his life to which he did not enjoy looking back, and years of irreproachable Barthood had enabled him, as far as he personally was concerned, to bury the past. And now, it seemed, this pestilential companion of his youth was about to dig it up again.

The years had turned Sir Gregory into a man of portly habit; and, as portly men do in moments of stress, he puffed. But, puff he never so shrewdly, he could not blow away that paragraph. It was still there, looking up at him, when the door opened and the butler announced Lord Emsworth and Mr. Galahad Threepwood.

Sir Gregory's first emotion on seeing the taxing party file into the room was one of pardonable surprise. Aware of the hard feelings which George Cyril Wellbeloved's transference of his allegiance had aroused in the bosom of that gifted pig-man's former employer, he had not expected to receive a morning call from the Earl of Emsworth. As for the Hon. Galahad, he had ceased to be on cordial terms with him as long ago as the Winter of the year nineteen hundred and six.

Then, following quickly on the heels of surprise, came indignation. That the author of the Reminiscences should be writing scurrilous stories about him with one hand and strolling calmly into his private study with, so to speak, the other occasioned him the keenest resentment. He drew himself up and was in the very act of staring haughtily, when the Hon. Galahad broke the silence.

'Young Parsloe,' said the Hon. Galahad, speaking in a sharp, unpleasant voice, 'your sins have found you out!'

It had been the baronet's intention to inquire to what he was indebted for the pleasure of this visit, and to inquire it icily; but at this remarkable speech the words halted on his lips.

'Eh?' he said blankly.

The Hon. Galahad was regarding him through his monocle rather as a cook eyes a black-beetle in discovering it in the kitchen sink. It was a look which would have aroused pique in a slug, and once more the Squire of Matchingham's bewilderment gave way to wrath.

'What the devil do you mean?' he demanded.

'See his face?' asked the Hon. Galahad in a rasping aside.

'I'm looking at it now,' said Lord Emsworth.

'Guilt written upon it.'

'Plainly,' agreed Lord Emsworth.

The Hon. Galahad, who had folded his arms in a menacing manner, unfolded them and struck the desk a smart blow.

'Be very careful, Parsloe! Think before you speak. And, when you speak, speak the truth. I may say, by way of a start, that we know all.'

How low an estimate Sir Gregory Parsloe had formed of his visitors' collective sanity was revealed by the act that it was actually to Lord Emsworth that he now turned as the more intelligent of the pair.

'Emsworth! Explain! What the deuce are you doing here? And what the devil is that old image talking about?'

Lord Emsworth had been watching his brother with growing admiration. The latter's spirited opening of the case for the prosecution had won his hearty approval.

'You know,' he said curtly.

'I should say he dashed well does know,' said the Hon. Galahad. 'Parsloe, produce that pig!'

Sir Gregory pushed his eyes back into their sockets a split second before they would have bulged out of his head beyond recovery. He did his best to think calm, soothing thoughts. He had just remembered that he was a man who had to be careful about his blood-pressure.

'Pig?'

'Pig.'

'Did you say pig?'

'Pig.'

'What pig?'

'He says "What pig?"'

'I heard him,' said Lord Emsworth.

Sir Gregory Parsloe again had trouble with his eyes.

'I don't know what you are talking about.'

The Hon. Galahad unfolded his arms again and smote the desk a blow that unshipped the cover of the ink-pot.

'Parsloe, you sheep-faced, shambling exile from Hell,' he cried. 'Disgorge that pig immediately!'

'My Empress,' added Lord Emsworth.

'Precisely. Empress of Blandings. The pig you stole last night.'

Sir Gregory Parsloe-Parsloe rose slowly from his chair. The Hon. Galahad pointed an imperious finger at him, but he ignored the gesture. His blood-pressure was now hovering around the hundred-and-fifty mark.

'Do you mean to tell me that you seriously accuse . . .'

'Parsloe, sit down!'

Sir Gregory choked.

'I always knew, Emsworth, that you were as mad as a coot.'

'As a what?' whispered his lordship.

'Coot,' said the Hon. Galahad curtly. 'Sort of duck.' He turned to the defendant again. 'Vituperation will do you no good, young Parsloe. We *know* that you have stolen that pig.'

'I haven't stolen any damned pig. What would I want to steal a pig for?'

The Hon. Galahad snorted.

'What did you want to nobble my dog Towser for in the back

room of the Black Footman in the Spring of the year '97?' he said. 'To queer the favourite, that's why you did it. And that's what you're after now, trying to queer the favourite again. Oh, we can see through you all right, young Parsloe. We read you like a book.'

Sir Gregory had stopped worrying about his blood-pressure. No amount of calm, soothing thoughts could do it any good now.

'You're crazy! Both of you. Stark, staring mad.'

'Parsloe, will you or will you not cough up that pig?'

'I have not got your pig.'

'That is your last word, is it?'

'I haven't seen the creature.'

'Why a coot?' asked Lord Emsworth, who had been brooding for some time in silence.

'Very well,' said the Hon. Galahad. 'If that is the attitude you propose to adopt, there is no course before me but to take steps. And I'll tell you the steps I'm going to take, young Parsloe. I see now that I have been foolishly indulgent. I have allowed my kind heart to get the better of me. Often and often, when I've been sitting at my desk, I've remembered a good story that simply cried out to be put into my Reminiscences, and every time I've said to myself, "No," I've said. "That would wound young Parsloe. Good as it is, I can't use it. I must respect young Parsloe's feelings." Well, from now on there will be no more forbearance. Unless you restore that pig, I shall insert in my book every dashed thing I can remember about you – starting with our first meeting, when I came into Romano's and was introduced to you while you were walking round the supper-table with a soup tureen on your head and stick of celery in your hand, saying that you were a sentry outside Buckingham Palace.

The world shall know you for what you are – the only man who was ever thrown out of the Café de l'Europe for trying to raise the price of a bottle of champagne by raffling his trousers at the main bar. And, what's more, I'll tell the full story of the prawns.'

A sharp cry escaped Sir Gregory. His face had turned a deep magenta. In these affluent days of his middle age, he always looked rather like a Regency buck who has done himself well for years among the flesh-pots. He now resembled a Regency buck who, in addition to being on the verge of apoplexy, has been stung in the leg by a hornet.

'I will,' said the Hon. Galahad firmly. 'The full, true and complete story of the prawns, omitting nothing.'

'What was the story of the prawns, my dear fellow?' asked Lord Emsworth, interested.

'Never mind. I know. And young Parsloe knows. And if Empress of Blandings is not back in her sty this afternoon, you will find it in my book.'

'But I keep telling you,' cried the suffering baronet, 'that I know nothing whatever about your pig.'

'Ha!'

'I've not seen the animal since last year's Agricultural Show.'

'Ho!'

'I didn't know it had disappeared till you told me.'

The Hon. Galahad stared fixedly at him through the black-rimmed monocle. Then, with a gesture of loathing, he turned to the door.

'Come, Clarence!' he said.

'Are we going?'

'Yes,' said the Hon. Galahad with quiet dignity. 'There is nothing more that we can do here. Let us get away from this house before it is struck by a thunderbolt.'

III

The gentlemanly office-boy who sat in the outer room of the Argus Enquiry Agency read the card which the stout visitor had handed to him and gazed at the stout visitor with respect and admiration. A polished lad, he loved the aristocracy. He tapped on the door of the inner office.

'A gentleman to see me?' asked Percy Pilbeam.

'A *baronet* to see you, sir,' corrected the office-boy. 'Sir Gregory Parsloe-Parsloe, Matchingham Hall, Salop.'

'Show him in immediately,' said Pilbeam with enthusiasm.

He rose and pulled down the lapels of his coat. Things, he felt, were looking up. He remembered Sir Gregory Parsloe. One of his first cases. He had been able to recover for him some letters which had fallen into the wrong hands. He wondered, as he heard the footsteps outside, if his client had been indulging in correspondence again.

From the baronet's sandbagged expression, as he entered, such might well have been the case. It is the fate of Sir Gregory Parsloe-Parsloe to come into this chronicle puffing and looking purple. He puffed and looked purple now.

'I have called to see you, Mr. Pilbeam,' he said, after the preliminary civilities had been exchanged and he had lowered his impressive bulk into a chair, 'because I am in a position of serious difficulty.'

'I am sorry to hear that, Sir Gregory.'

'And because I remember with what discretion and resource you once acted on my behalf.'

Pilbeam glanced at the door. It was closed. He was now convinced that his visitor's little trouble was the same as on the previous occasion, and he looked at the indefatigable man with frank astonishment.

Didn't these old bucks, he was asking himself, ever stop writing compromising letters? You would have thought they would have got writer's cramp.

'If there is any way in which I can assist you, Sir Gregory . . . Perhaps you will tell me the facts from the beginning?'

'The beginning?' Sir Gregory pondered. 'Well, let me put it this way. At one time, Mr. Pilbeam, I was younger than I am to-day.'

'Quite.'

'Poorer.'

'No doubt.'

'And less respectable. And during that period of my life I unfortunately went about a good deal with a man named Threepwood.'

'Galahad Threepwood?'

'You know him?' said Sir Gregory, surprised.

Pilbeam chuckled reminiscently.

'I know his name. I wrote an article about him once, when I was editing a paper called *Society Spice.* Number One of the Thriftless Aristocrats series. The snappiest thing I ever did in my life. They tell me he called twice at the office with a horse-whip, wanting to see me.'

Sir Gregory exhibited concern.

'You have met him, then?'

'I have not. You are probably not familiar with the inner workings of a paper like *Society Spice*, Sir Gregory, but I may tell you that it is foreign to the editorial policy ever to meet visitors who call with horsewhips.'

'Would he have heard your name?'

'No. There was a very strict rule in the *Spice* office that the names of the editorial staff were not to be divulged.'

'Ah!' said Sir Gregory, relieved.

His relief gave place to indignation. There was an inconsistency about the Hon. Galahad's behaviour which revolted him.

'He cut up rough, did he, because you wrote things about him in your paper? And yet he doesn't seem to mind writing things himself about other people, damn him. That's quite another matter. A different thing altogether. Oh yes!'

'Does he write? I didn't know.'

'He's writing his reminiscences at this very moment. He's down at Blandings Castle, finishing them now. And the book's going to be full of stories about me. That's why I've come to see you. Dashed, infernal, damaging stories, which'll ruin my reputation in the country. There's one about some prawns. . . .'

Words failed Sir Gregory. He sat puffing. Pilbeam nodded gravely. He understood the position now. As to what his client expected him to do about it, however, he remained hazy.

'But if these stories you speak of are libellous . . .'

'What has that got to do with it? They're true.'

'The greater the truth, the greater the . . .'

'Oh, I know all about that,' interrupted Sir Gregory impatiently. 'And a lot of help it's going to be to me. A jury could give me the heaviest damages on record and it wouldn't do me a bit of good. What about my reputation in the county? What about knowing that every damned fool I met was laughing at me behind my back? What about the Unionist Committee? I may tell you, Mr. Pilbeam, apart from any other consideration, that I am on the point of being accepted by our local Unionist Committee as their candidate at the next election. And if that old pest's book is published, they will drop me like a hot coal. Now do you understand?'

Pilbeam picked up a pen, and with it scratched his chin thoughtfully. He liked to take an optimistic view with regard to his clients' affairs, but he could not conceal from himself that Sir Gregory appeared to be out of luck.

'He is determined to publish this book?'

'It's the only object he's got in life, the miserable old fossil.'

'And he is resolved to include the stories?'

'He called on me this morning expressly to tell me so. And I caught the next train to London to put the matter in your hands.'

Pilbeam scratched his left cheekbone.

'Hm!' he said. 'Well, in the circumstances, I really don't see what is to be done except . . .'

'. . . get hold of the manuscript and destroy it, you were about to say? Exactly. That's precisely what I've come to ask you to do for me.'

Pilbeam opened his mouth, startled. He had not been about to say anything of the kind. What he had been intending to remark was that, the situation being as described, there appeared no course to pursue but to fold the hands, set the teeth, and await the inevitable disaster like a man and a Briton. He gazed blankly at this lawless Bart. Baronets are proverbially bad, but surely, felt Percy Pilbeam, there was no excuse for them to be as bad as all that.

'Steal the manuscript?'

'Only possible way.'

'But that's rather a tall order, isn't it, Sir Gregory?'

'Not,' replied the baronet ingratiatingly, 'for a clever young fellow like you.'

The flattery left Pilbeam cold. His distant, unenthusiastic manner underwent no change. However clever a man is, he was thinking, he cannot very well abstract the manuscript of a book of Reminiscences from a house unless he is first able to enter that house.

'How could I get into the place?'

'I should have thought you would have found a dozen or so ways.'

'Not even one,' Pilbeam assured him.

'Look how you recovered those letters of mine.'

'That was easy.'

'You told them you had come to inspect the gas meter.'

'I could scarcely go to Blandings Castle and say I had come to inspect the gas meter and hope to be invited to make a long visit on the strength of it. You do not appear to realize, Sir Gregory, that the undertaking you suggest would not be a matter of a few minutes. I might have to remain in the house for quite a considerable time.'

Sir Gregory found his companion's attitude damping. He was a man, who, since his accession to the baronetcy and its accompanying wealth, had grown accustomed to seeing people jump smartly to it when he issued instructions. He became peevish.

'Why couldn't you go there as a butler or something?'

Percy Pilbeam's only reply to this was a tolerant smile. He raised the pen and scratched his head with it.

'Scarcely feasible,' he said. And again that rather pitying smile flitted across his face.

The sight of it brought Sir Gregory to the boil. He felt an irresistible desire to say something to wipe it away. It reminded him of the smiles he had seen on the faces of bookmakers in his younger days when he had suggested backing horses with them on credit and in a spirit of mutual trust.

'Well, have it your own way,' he snapped. 'But it may interest you to know that to get that manuscript into my possession I am willing to pay a thousand pounds.'

It did, as he had foreseen, interest Pilbeam extremely. So much so that in his emotion he jerked the pen wildly, inflicting a nasty scalp wound.

'A thuth?' he stammered.

Sir Gregory, a prudent man in money matters, perceived that he had allowed his sense of the dramatic to carry him away.

'Well, five hundred,' he said, rather quickly. 'And five hundred pounds is a lot of money, Mr. Pilbeam.'

The point was one which he had no need to stress. Percy Pilbeam had grasped it without assistance, and his face grew wan with thought. The day might come when the proprietor of the Argus Enquiry Agency would remain unmoved by the prospect of adding five hundred pounds to his bank balance, but it had not come yet.

'A cheque for five hundred the moment that old weasel's manuscript is in my hands,' said Sir Gregory, insinuatingly.

Nature had so arranged it that in no circumstances could Percy Pilbeam's face ever become really beautiful; but at this moment there stole into it an expression which did do something to relieve, to a certain extent, its normal unpleasantness. It was an expression of rapture, of joy, of almost beatific happiness – the look, in short, of a man who sees his way clear to laying his hands on five hundred pounds.

There is about the mention of any substantial sum of money something that seems to exercise a quickening effect on the human intelligence. A moment before, Pilbeam's mind had been an inert mass. Now abruptly, it began to function like a dynamo.

Get into Blandings Castle? Why, of course he could get into Blandings Castle. And not sneak in, either, with a trousers-seat itching in apprehension of the kick that should send him out again, but bowl proudly up to the front door in his two-seater and hand his suit-case to the butler and be welcomed as the honoured guest. Until now he had forgotten, for he had deliberately set himself to forget, the outrageous suggestion of that young idiot whose name escaped him that he should come to Blandings and hunt about for lost pigs. It had wounded his self-respect so deeply at the time that he had driven it from his thoughts. When he found himself thinking about Hugo, he had immediately pulled himself together and started thinking about something else. Now it all came back to him. And Hugo's parting words, he recalled, had been that if ever he changed his mind the commission would still be open.

'I will take this case, Sir Gregory,' he said.

'Woof?'

'You may rely on my being at Blandings Castle by to-morrow evening at the latest. I have thought of a way of getting there.'

He rose from his desk, and paced the room with knitted brows. That agile brain had begun to work under its own steam. He paused once to look in a distrait manner out of the window; and when Sir Gregory cleared his throat to speak, jerked an impatient shoulder at him. He could not have baronets, even with hyphens in their names, interrupting him at a moment like this.

'Sir Gregory,' he said at length. 'The great thing in matters like this is to be prepared with a plan. I have a plan.'

'Woof!' said Sir Gregory.

This time he meant that he had thought all along that his companion would get one after pacing like that.

'When you arrive home, I want you to invite Mr. Galahad Threepwood to dinner to-morrow night.'

The baronet shook like a jelly. Wrath and amazement fought within him. Ask the man to dinner? After what had occurred?

'As many others of the Blandings Castle party as you think fit, of course, but Mr. Threepwood without fail. Once he is out of the house, my path will be clear.'

Wrath and amazement died away. The baronet had grasped the idea. The beauty and simplicity of the stratagem stirred his admiration. But was it not, he felt, a simpler matter to issue such an invitation than to get it accepted? A vivid picture rose before his eyes of the Hon. Galahad as he had just seen him.

Then there came to him the blessed, healing thought of Lady Constance Keeble. He would send the invitation to her and – yes, dash it! – he would tell her the full facts, put his cards on the table and trust to her sympathy and proper feeling to enlist her in the cause. He had been long aware that her attitude towards the Reminiscences resembled his own. He could rely on her to help him. He could also rely on her somehow – by what strange feminine modes of coercion he, being a bachelor, could only guess at – to deliver the Hon. Galahad Threepwood at Matchingham Hall in time for dinner. Women, he knew, had this strange power over their near relations.

'Splendid!' he said. 'Excellent! Capital. Woof! I'll see it's done.'

'Then you can leave the rest to me.'

'You think, if I can get him out of the house, you will be able to secure the manuscript?'

'Certainly.'

Sir Gregory rose and extended a trembling hand.

'Mr. Pilbeam,' he said, with deep feeling, 'coming to see you was the wisest thing I ever did in my life.'

'Quite,' said Percy Pilbeam.

## 8. THE STORM CLOUDS HOVER OVER BLANDINGS

Having re-read the half-dozen pages which he had written since luncheon, the Hon. Galahad Threepwood attached them with a brass paper-fastener to the main body of his monumental work and placed the manuscript in its drawer – lovingly like a young mother putting her first-born to bed. The day's work was done. Rising from the desk, he yawned and stretched himself.

He was ink-stained but cheerful. Happiness, as solid thinkers have often pointed out, comes from giving pleasure to others; and the little anecdote which he had just committed to paper would, he knew, give great pleasure to a considerable number of his fellowmen. All over England they would be rolling out of their seats when they read it. True, their enjoyment might possibly not be shared to its fullest extent by Sir Gregory Parsloe-Parsloe, of Matchingham Hall, for what the Hon. Galahad had just written was the story of the prawns: but the first lesson an author has to learn is that he cannot please everybody.

He left the small library which he had commandeered as a private study and, descending the broad staircase, observed Beach in the hall below. The butler was standing mountainously beside the tea-table, staring in a sort of trance at a plateful of anchovy sandwiches: and it struck the Hon. Galahad, not for the first time in the last few days, that he appeared to have something on his mind. A strained, haunted look he seemed to have, as if he had done a murder and was afraid somebody was going to find the body. A more practised physiognomist would have been able to interpret that look. It was the one that butlers always wear when they have allowed themselves to be persuaded against their better judgment into becoming accessories before the fact in the theft of their employers' pigs.

'Beach,' he said, speaking over the banisters, for he had just remembered there was a question he wanted to ask the man about the somewhat eccentric Major-General Magnus in whose employment he had once been.

'What's the matter with you?' he added with some irritation. For the butler, jerked from his reverie, had jumped a couple of inches and shaken all over in a manner that was most trying to watch. A butler, felt the Hon. Galahad, is a butler, and a startled fawn is a startled fawn. He disliked the blend of the two in a single body.

'I beg your pardon, sir?'

'Why on earth do you spring like that when anyone speaks to you? I've noticed it before. He leaps,' he said complainingly to his niece Millicent, who now came down the stairs with slow, listless steps. 'When addressed, he quivers like a harpooned whale.'

'Oh?' said Millicent dully. She had dropped into a chair and picked up a book. She looked like something that might have occurred to Ibsen in one of his less frivolous moments.

'I am extremely sorry, Mr. Galahad.'

'No use being sorry. Thing is not to do it. If you are practising the Shimmy for the Servants' Ball, be advised by an old friend and give it up. You haven't the build.'

'I think I may have caught a chill, sir.'

'Take a stiff whisky toddy. Put you right in no time. What's the car doing out there?'

'Her ladyship ordered it, sir. I understand that she and Mr. Baxter are going to Market Blandings to meet the train arriving at four-forty.'

'Somebody expected?'

'The American young lady, sir. Miss Schoonmaker.'

'Of course, yes. I remember. She arrives to-day, does she?'

'Yes, sir.'

The Hon. Galahad mused.

'Schoonmaker. I used to know old Johnny Schoonmaker well. A great fellow. Mixed the finest mint-juleps in America. Have you ever tasted a mint-julep, Beach?'

'Not to my recollection, sir.'

'Oh, you'd remember all right if you had. Insidious things. They creep up to you like a baby sister and slide their little hands into yours and the next thing you know the Judge is telling you to pay the clerk of the court fifty dollars. Seen Lord Emsworth anywhere?'

'His lordship is at the telephone, sir.'

'Don't do it, I tell you!' said the Hon. Galahad petulantly. For once again the butler had been affected by what appeared to be a kind of palsy.

'I beg your pardon, Mr. Galahad. It was something I was suddenly reminded of. There was a gentleman just after luncheon who desired to communicate with you on the telephone. I understood him to say he was speaking from Oxford, being on his way from London to Blackpool in his automobile.

Knowing that you were occupied with your literary work, I refrained from disturbing you. And till I mentioned the word "telephone", the matter slipped my mind.'

'Who was he?'

'I did not get the gentleman's name, sir. The wire was faulty. But he desired me to inform you that his business had to do with a dramatic entertainment.'

'A play?'

'Yes, sir,' said Beach, plainly impressed by his happy way of putting it. 'I took the liberty of advising him that you might be able to see him later in the afternoon. He said that he would call after tea.'

The butler passed from the hall with heavy, haunted steps, and the Hon. Galahad turned to his niece.

'I know who it is,' he said. 'He wrote to me yesterday. It's a theatrical manager fellow I used to go about with years ago. Man named Mason. He's got a play, adapted from the French, and he's had the idea of changing it into the period of the 'nineties and getting me to put my name to it.'

'Oh?'

'On the strength of my book coming out at the same time. Not a bad notion, either. Galahad Threepwood's a name that's going to have box-office value pretty soon. The house'll be sold out for weeks to all the old buffers who'll come flocking up to London to see if I've put anything about them into it.'

'Oh?' said Millicent.

The Hon. Galahad frowned. He sensed a lack of interest and sympathy.

'What's the matter with you?' he demanded.

'Nothing.'

'Then why are you looking like that?'

'Like what?'

'Pale and tragic, as if you'd just gone into Tattersall's and met a bookie you owed money to.'

'I am perfectly happy.'

The Hon. Galahad snorted.

'Yes, radiant. I've seen fogs that were cheerier. What's that book you're reading?'

'It belongs to Aunt Constance.' Millicent glanced wanly at the cover. 'It seems to be about Theosophy.'

'Theosophy! Fancy a young girl in the springtime of life . . . What the devil has happened to everybody in this house? There's some excuse, perhaps, for Clarence. If you admit the possibility of a sane man getting so attached to a beastly pig, he has a right to be upset. But what's wrong with all the rest of you? Ronald! Goes about behaving like a bereaved tomato. Beach! Springs up and down when you speak to him. And that young fellow Carmody . . . .'

'I am not interested in Mr. Carmody.'

'This morning,' said the Hon., aggrieved, 'I told the boy one of the most humorous limericks I ever heard in my life – about an Old Man Of – however, that is neither here nor there – and he just gaped at me with his jaw dropped, like a spavined horse looking over a fence. There are mysteries afoot in this house, and I don't like 'em. The atmosphere of Blandings Castle has changed all of a sudden from that of a normal, happy English home into something Edgar Allan Poe might have written on a rainy Sunday. It's getting on my nerves. Let's hope this girl of Johnny Schoonmaker's will cheer us up. If she's anything like her father, she ought to be a nice, lively girl. But I suppose, when she arrives, it'll turn out that she's in mourning for a great-aunt or brooding over the situation in Russia or something. I don't know what young people are coming to nowadays. Gloomy. Introspective. The old gay spirit seems to have died out altogether. In my young days a girl of your age would have been upstairs making an apple-pie bed for somebody instead of lolling on chairs reading books about Theosophy.'

Snorting once more, the Hon. Galahad disappeared into the smoking-room, and Millicent, tight-lipped, returned to her book. She had been reading for some minutes when she became aware of a long, limp, drooping figure at her side.

'Hullo,' said Hugo, for this ruin of a fine young man was he.

Millicent's ear twitched, but she did not reply.

'Reading?'

He had been standing on his left leg. With a sudden change of policy, he now shifted, and stood on his right.

'Interesting book?'

Millicent looked up.

'I beg your pardon?'

'Only said – is that an interesting book?'

'Very,' said Millicent.

Hugo decided that his right leg was not a success. He stood on his left again.

'What's it about?'

'Transmigration of Souls.'

'A thing I'm not very well up on.'

'One of the many, I should imagine,' said the haughty girl. 'Every day you seem to know less and less about more and more.' She rose, and made for the stairs. Her manner suggested that she was disappointed in the hall of Blandings Castle. She had supposed it a nice place for a girl to sit and study the best literature, and now, it appeared, it was over-run by the Underworld. 'If you're really anxious to know what Transmigration means, it's simply that some people believe that when you die your soul goes into something else.'

'Rum idea,' said Hugo, becoming more buoyant. He began to draw hope from her chattiness. She had not said as many consecutive words as this to him for quite a time. 'Into something else, eh? Odd notion. What do you suppose made them think of that?'

'Yours, for instance, would probably go into a pig. And then I would come along and look into your sty and I'd say, "Good gracious! Why, there's Hugo Carmody. He hasn't changed a bit!"'

The spirit of the Carmodys had been a good deal crushed by recent happenings, but at this it flickered into feeble life.

'I call that a beastly thing to say.'

'Do you?'

'Yes, I do.'

'I oughtn't to have said it?'

'No, you oughtn't.'

'Well, I wouldn't have, if I could have thought of anything worse.'

'And when you let a little thing like what happened the other night rot up a great love like ours, I – well, I call it a bit rotten. You know perfectly well that you're the only girl in the world I ever . . .'

'Shall I tell you something?'

'What?'

'You make me sick.'

Hugo breathed passionately through his nose.

'So all is over, is it?'

'You can jolly well bet all is over. And if you're interested in my future plans, I may mention I intend to marry the first man who comes along and asks me. And you can be a page at the wedding if you like. You couldn't look any sillier than you do now, even in a frilly shirt and satin knickerbockers.'

Hugo laughed raspingly.

'Is that so?'

'It is.'

'And once you said there wasn't another man like me in the world.'

'Well, I should hate to think there was,' said Millicent. And as the celebrated James-Thomas-Beach procession had entered with cakes and gate-leg tables and her last word seemed about as good a last word as a girl might reasonably consider herself entitled to, she passed proudly up the stairs.

James withdrew. Thomas withdrew. Beach remained gazing with a hypnotised eye at the cake.

'Beach!' said Hugo.

'Sir?'

'Curse all women!'

'Very good, sir,' said Beach.

He watched the young man disappear through the open front door, heard his footsteps crunch on the gravel, and gave himself up to meditation again. How gladly, he was thinking, if it had not been for upsetting Mr. Ronald's plans, would he have breathed in his employer's ear as he filled his glass at dinner, "The pig is in the gamekeeper's cottage in the west wood, your lordship. Thank you, your lordship." But it was not to be. His face twisted, as if with sudden pain, and he was aware of the Hon. Galahad emerging from the smoking-room.

'Just remembered something I wanted to ask you, Beach. You were with old General Magnus, weren't you, some years ago, before you came here?'

'Yes, Mr. Galahad.'

'Then perhaps you can tell me the exact facts about that trouble in 1912. I know the old chap chased young Mandeville three times round the lawn in his pyjamas, but did he merely try to stab him with the bread-knife or did he actually get home?'

'I could not say, sir. He did not honour me with his confidence.'

'Infernal nuisance,' said the Hon. Galahad. 'I like to get these things right.' He eyed the butler discontentedly as he retired. More than ever was he convinced that the fellow had something on his mind. The very way he walked showed it. He was about to return to the smoking-room when his brother Clarence came into the hall. And there was in Lord Emsworth's bearing so strange a gaiety that he stood transfixed. It seemed to the Hon. Galahad years since he had seen anyone looking cheerful in Blandings Castle. 'Good God, Clarence! What's happened?'

'What, my dear fellow?'

'You're wreathed in smiles, dash it, and skipping like the high hills. Found that pig under the drawing-room sofa or something?'

Lord Emsworth beamed.

'I have had the most cheering piece of news, Galahad. That detective – the one I sent young Carmody to see – the Argus man, you know – he has come after all. He drove down in his car and is at this moment in Market Blandings, at the Emsworth Arms. I have been speaking to him on the telephone. He rang up to ask if I still required his services.'

'Well, you don't.'

'Certainly I do, Galahad. I consider his presence vital.'

'He can't tell you any more than you know already. There's only one man who can have stolen that pig, and that's young Parsloe.'

'Precisely. Yes. Quite true. But this man will be able to collect evidence and bring the thing home and – er – bring it home. He has the trained mind. I consider it most important that the case should be in the hands of a man with a trained mind. We should be seeing him very shortly. He is having what he describes as a bit of a snack at the Emsworth Arms. When he has finished, he will drive over. I am delighted. Ah, Constance, my dear.'

Lady Constance Keeble, attended by the Efficient Baxter, had appeared at the foot of the stairs. His lordship eyed her a little warily. The chatelaine of Blandings was apt sometimes to react unpleasantly to the information that visitors not invited by herself were expected at the Castle.

'Constance, my dear, a friend of mine is arriving this evening, to spend a few days. I forgot to tell you.'

'Well, we have plenty of room for him,' replied Lady Constance, with surprising amiability. 'There is something I forgot to tell you, too. We are dining at Matchingham to-night.'

'Matchingham?' Lord Emsworth was puzzled. He could think of no one who lived in the village of Matchingham except Sir Gregory Parsloe-Parsloe. 'With whom?'

'Sir Gregory, of course. Who else do you suppose it could be?' 'What!'

'I had a note from him after luncheon. It is short notice, of course, but that doesn't matter in the country. He took it for granted that we would not be engaged.'

'Constance!' Lord Emsworth swelled slightly. 'Constance, I will not – dash it, I will not – dine with that man. And that's final.'

Lady Constance smiled a sort of lion-tamer's smile. She had foreseen a reaction of this kind. She had expected sales-resistance, and was prepared to cope with it. Not readily, she knew, would her brother become Parsloe-conscious.

'Please do not be absurd, Clarence. I thought you would say that. I have already accepted for you, Galahad, myself and Millicent. You may as well understand at once that I do not intend to be on bad terms with our nearest neighbour, even if a hundred of your pig-men leave you and go to him. Your attitude in the matter has been perfectly childish from the very start. If Sir Gregory realizes that there has been a coolness, and has most sensibly decided to make the first move towards a reconciliation, we cannot possibly refuse the overture.'

'Indeed? And what about my friend? Arriving this evening.'

'He can look after himself for a few hours, I should imagine.'

'Abominable rudeness he'll think it.' This line of attack had occurred to Lord Emsworth quite suddenly. He found it good. Almost an inspiration, it seemed to him. 'I invite my friend Pilbeam here to pay us a visit, and the moment he arrives we meet him at the front door, dash it, and say, "Ah, here you are, Pilbeam! Well amuse yourself, Pilbeam. We're off." And this Miss – er – . . . this American girl. What will she think?'

'Did you say Pilbeam?' asked the Hon. Galahad.

'It is no use talking, Clarence. Dinner is at eight. And please see that your dress clothes are nicely pressed. Ring for Beach and tell him now. Last night you looked like a scarecrow.'

'Once and for all, I tell you . . .'

At this moment an unexpected ally took the arena on Lady Constance's side.

'Of course we must go, Clarence,' said the Hon. Galahad, and Lord Emsworth, spinning round to face this flank attack, was surprised to see a swift, meaning wink come and go on his brother's face. 'Nothing gained by having unpleasantness with your neighbours in the country. Always a mistake. Never pays.'

'Exactly,' said Lady Constance, a little dazed at finding this Saul among the prophets, but glad of the helping hand. 'In the country one is quite dependent on one's neighbours.'

'And young Parsloe – not such a bad chap, Clarence. Lots of good in Parsloe. We shall have a pleasant evening.'

'I am relieved to find that you, at any rate, have sense, Galahad,' said Lady Constance handsomely. 'I will leave you to try and drive some of it into Clarence's head. Come, Mr. Baxter, we shall be late.'

The sound of the car's engine had died away before Lord Emsworth's feelings found relief in speech.

'But, Galahad, my dear fellow!'

The Hon. Galahad patted his shoulder reassuringly.

'It's all right, Clarence, my boy. I know what I'm doing. I have the situation well in hand.'

'Dine with Parsloe after what has occurred? After what occurred yesterday? It's impossible. Why on earth the man is inviting us, I can't understand.'

'I suppose he thinks that if he gives us a dinner I shall relent and omit the prawn story. Oh, I see Parsloe's motive all right. A clever move. Not that it'll work.'

'But what do you want to go for?'

The Hon. Galahad raked the hall with a conspiratorial monocle. It appeared to be empty. Nevertheless, he looked under a settee and, going to the front door, swiftly scanned the gravel.

'Shall I tell you something, Clarence?' he said, coming back. 'Something that'll interest you?'

'Certainly, my dear fellow. Certainly. Most decidedly.'

'Something that'll bring the sparkle to your eyes?'

'By all means. I should enjoy it.'

'You know what we're going to do? To-night? After dining with Parsloe and sending Constance back in the car?'

'No.'

The Hon. Galahad placed his lips to his brother's ear.

'We're going to steal his pig, my boy.'

'What!'

'It came to me in a flash while Constance was talking. Parsloe stole the Empress. Very well, we'll steal Pride of Matchingham. Then we'll be in a position to look young Parsloe squarely in the eye and say, "What about it?"'

Lord Emsworth swayed gently. His brain, never a strong one, had tottered perceptibly on its throne.

'Galahad!'

'Only thing to do. Reprisals. Recognized military manoeuvre.'

'But how? Galahad, how can it be done?'

'Easily. If young Parsloe stole the Empress, why should we have any difficulty in stealing his animal? You show me where he keeps it, my boy, and I'll do the rest. Puffy Benger and I stole old Wivenhoe's pig at Hammer's Easton in the year '95. We put it in Plug Basham's bedroom. And we'll put Parsloe's pig in a bedroom, too.'

'In a bedroom?'

'Well, a sort of bedroom. Where are we to hide the animal – that's what you've been asking yourself, isn't it? I'll tell you. We're going to put it in that caravan that your flower-pot-throwing friend Baxter arrived in. Nobody's going to think of looking there. Then we'll be in a position to talk terms to young Parsloe, and I think he will very soon see the game is up.'

Lord Emsworth was looking at his brother almost devoutly. He had always known that Galahad's intelligence was superior to his own, but he had never realized it could soar to quite such lofty heights as this. It was, he supposed, the result of the life his brother had lived. He himself, sheltered through the peaceful, uneventful years at Blandings Castle, had allowed his brain to become comparatively atrophied. But Galahad, battling through these same years with hostile skittle-sharps and the sort of man that used to be a member of the old Pelican Club, had kept his clear and vigorous.

'You really think it would be feasible?'

'Trust me. By the way, Clarence, this man Pilbeam of yours. Do you know if he was ever anything except a detective?'

'I have no idea, my dear fellow. I know nothing of him. I have merely spoken to him on the telephone. Why?'

'Oh, nothing. I'll ask him when he arrives. Where are you going?'

'Into the garden.'

'It's raining.'

'I have my macintosh. I really – feel I really must walk about after what you have told me. I am in a state of considerable excitement.'

'Well, work it off before you see Constance again. It won't do to have her start suspecting there's something up. If there's anything you want to ask me about, you'll find me in the smoking-room.'

For some twenty minutes the hall of Blandings Castle remained empty. Then Beach appeared. At the same moment, from the gravel outside there came the purring of a high-powered car and the sound of voices. Beach posed himself in the doorway, looking, as he always did on these occasions, like the Spirit of Blandings welcoming the lucky guest.

'Leave the door open, Beach,' said Lady Constance.
'Very good, your ladyship.'

'I think the smell of the wet earth and the flowers is so refreshing, don't you?'

The butler did not. He was not one of your fresh-air men. Rightly conjecturing, however, that the question had been addressed not to him but to the girl in the beige suit who had accompanied the speaker up the steps, he forbore to reply. He cast an appraising bulging-eyed look at this girl and decided that she met with his approval. Smaller and slighter than the type of woman he usually admired, he found her, nevertheless, even by his own exacting standards of criticism, noticeably attractive. He liked her face and he liked the way she was dressed. Her frock was right, her shoes were right, her stockings were right, and her hat was right. As far as Beach was concerned, Sue had passed the Censor.

Her demeanour pleased him, too. From the flush on her face and the sparkle in her eyes, she seemed to be taking her first entry into Blandings Castle in quite the proper spirit of reverential excitement. To be at Blandings plainly meant something to her, was an event in her life: and Beach who, after many years of residence within its walls had come to look on the Castle as a piece of personal property, felt flattered and gratified.

'I don't think this shower will last long,' said Lady Constance.

'No,' said Sue, smiling brightly.

'And now you must be wanting some tea after your journey.'

'Yes,' said Sue, smiling brightly.

It seemed as if she had been smiling brightly for centuries. The moment she had alighted from the train and found her formidable hostess and this strangely sinister Mr. Baxter waiting to meet her on the platform, she had begun to smile brightly and had been doing it ever since.

'Usually we have tea on the lawn. It is so nice there.'

'It must be.'

'When the rain is over, Mr. Baxter, you must show Miss Schoonmaker the rose-garden.'

'I shall be delighted,' said the Efficient Baxter.

He flashed gleaming spectacles in her direction, and a momentary panic gripped Sue. She feared that already this man had probed her secret. In his glance, it seemed to her, there shone suspicion.

Such, however, was not the case. It was only the combination of large spectacles and heavy eyebrows that had created the illusion. Although Rupert Baxter was a man who generally suspected everybody on principle, it so happened that he had accepted Sue without question. The glance was an admiring, almost a loving glance. It would be too much to say that Baxter had already fallen a victim to Sue's charms, but the good looks which he saw and the wealth which he had been told about were undeniably beginning to fan the hidden fire.

'My brother is a great rose-grower.'

'Yes, isn't he? I mean, I think roses are so lovely.' The

spectacles were beginning to sap Sue's morale. They seemed to be eating into her soul like some sort of corrosive acid. 'How nice and old everything is here,' she went on hurriedly. 'What is that funny-looking gargoyle thing over there?'

What she actually referred to was a Japanese mask which hung from the wall, and it was unfortunate that the Hon. Galahad should have chosen this moment to come out of the smoking-room. It made the question seem personal.

'My brother Galahad,' said Lady Constance. Her voice lost some of the kindly warmth of the hostess putting the guest at her ease and took on the cold disapproval which the author of the Reminiscences always induced in her. 'Galahad, this is Miss Schoonmaker.'

'Really?' The Hon. Galahad trotted briskly up. 'Is it? Bless my soul! Well, well, well!'

'How do you do?' said Sue, smiling brightly.

'How are you, my dear? I know your father intimately.'

The bright smile faded. Sue had tried to plan this venture of hers carefully, looking ahead for all possible pitfalls, but that she would encounter people who knew Mr. Schoonmaker intimately she had not foreseen.

'Haven't seen him lately, of course. Let me see. . . . Must be twenty-five years since we met. Yes, quite twenty-five years.'

A warm and lasting friendship was destined to spring up between Sue and the Hon. Galahad Threepwood, but never in the whole course of it did she experience again quite the gush of whole-hearted affection which surged over her at these words.

'I wasn't born then,' she said.

The Hon. Galahad was babbling on happily.

'A great fellow, old Johnny. You'll find some stories about him in my book. I'm writing my Reminiscences, you know.

Fine sportsman, old Johnny. Great grief to him, I remember, when he broke his leg and had to go into a nursing-home in the middle of the racing season. However, he made the best of it. Got the nurses interested in current form, and used to make a book with them in fruit and cigarettes and things. I recollect coming to see him one day and finding him quite worried. He was a most conscientious man, with a horror of not settling up when he lost, and apparently one of the girls had had a suet dumpling on the winner of the three o'clock race at fifteen to eight and he couldn't figure out what he had got to pay her.'

Sue, laughing gratefully, was aware of a dropping presence at her side.

'My niece Millicent,' said Lady Constance. 'Millicent, my dear, this is Miss Schoonmaker.'

'How do you do?' said Sue, smiling brightly.

'How do you do?' said Millicent, like the silent tomb breaking its silence.

Sue regarded her with interest. So this was Hugo's Millicent. The sight of her caused Sue to wonder at the ardent nature of that young man's devotion. Millicent was pretty, but she would have thought that one of Hugo's exuberant disposition would have preferred something a little livelier.

She was startled to observe in the girl's eye a look of surprise. In a situation as delicate as hers was, Sue had no wish to occasion surprise to anyone.

'Ronnie's friend?' asked Millicent. 'The Miss Schoonmaker Ronnie met at Biarritz?'

'Yes,' said Sue faintly.

'But I had the impression that you were very tall. I'm sure Ronnie told me so.'

'I suppose almost anyone seems tall to that boy,' said the Hon. Galahad.

Sue breathed again. She had had a return of the unpleasant feeling of being boneless which had come upon her when the Hon. Galahad had spoken of knowing Mr. Schoonmaker intimately. But, though she breathed, she was still shaken. Life at Blandings Castle was plainly going to be a series of shocks. She sat back with a sensation of dizziness. Baxter's spectacles seemed to her to be glittering more suspiciously than ever.

'Have you seen Ronald anywhere, Millicent?' asked Lady Constance.

'Not since lunch. I suppose he's out in the grounds somewhere.'

'I saw him half an hour ago,' said the Hon. Galahad. 'He came mooning along under my window while I was polishing up some stuff I wrote this afternoon. I called to him, but he just grunted and wandered off.'

'He will be surprised to find you here,' said Lady Constance, turning to Sue. 'Your telegram did not arrive till after lunch, so he does not know that you were planning to come to-day. Unless you told him, Galahad.'

'I didn't tell him. Never occurred to me that he knew Miss Schoonmaker. Forgot you'd met him at Biarritz. What was he like then? Reasonably cheerful?'

'Yes, I think so.'

'Didn't scowl and jump and gasp and quiver all over the place?'

'No.'

'Then something must have happened when he went up to London. It was after he came back that I remember noticing that he seemed upset about something. Ah, the rain's stopped.'

Lady Constance looked over her shoulder.

'The sky still looks very threatening,' she said, 'but you might be able to get out for a few minutes. Mr. Baxter,' she explained, 'is going to show Miss Schoonmaker the rose-garden.'

'No, he isn't,' said Hon. Galahad, who had been scrutinising Sue through his monocle with growing appreciation. 'I am. Old Johnny Schoonmaker's little girl . . . why, there are a hundred things I want to discuss.'

The last thing Sue desired was to be left alone with the intimidating Baxter. She rose quickly.

'I should love to come,' she said.

The prospect of discussing the intimate affairs of the Schoonmaker family was not an agreeable one, but anything was better than the society of the spectacles.

'Perhaps,' said the Hon. Galahad, as he led her to the door, 'you'll be able to put me right about that business of old Johnny and the mysterious woman at the New Year's Eve party. As I got the story Johnny suddenly found this female – a perfect stranger, mind you – with her arms round his neck, telling him in a confidential undertone that she had made up her mind to go straight back to Des Moines, Iowa, and stick a knife into Fred. What he had done to win her confidence and who Fred was and whether she ever did stick a knife into him, your father hadn't found out by the time I left for home.'

His voice died away, and a moment later the Efficient Baxter, starting as if a sudden thought had entered his powerful brain, rose abruptly and made quickly for the stairs.

The rose-garden of Blandings Castle was a famous beauty-spot. Most people who visited it considered it deserving of a long and leisurely inspection. Enthusiastic horticulturists frequently went pottering and sniffing about it for hours on end. The tour through its fragrant groves personally conducted by the Hon. Galahad Threepwood lasted some six minutes.

'Well, that's what it is, you see,' he said, as they emerged, waving a hand vaguely. 'Roses and – er – roses, and all that sort of thing. You get the idea. And now, if you don't mind, I ought to be getting back. I want to keep in touch with the house. It slipped my mind, but I'm expecting a man to call to see me at any moment on some rather important business.'

Sue was quite willing to return. She liked her companion, but she had found his company embarrassing. The subject of the Schoonmaker family history showed a tendency to bulk too largely in his conversation for comfort. Fortunately, his practice of asking a question and answering it himself and then rambling off into some anecdote of the person or persons involved had enabled her so far to avoid disaster: but there was no saying how long this happy state would last. She was glad of the opportunity of being alone.

Besides, Ronnie was somewhere out in these grounds. At any moment, if she went wandering through them, she might come upon him. And then, she told herself, all would be well. Surely he would not preserve his sullen hostility in the face of the fact that she had come all this way, pretending dangerously to be Miss Schoonmaker, of New York, simply in order to see him?

Her companion, she found, was still talking.

'He wants to see me about a play. This book of mine is going to make a stir, you see, and he thinks that if he can get me to put my name to the play . . .'

Sue's thoughts wandered again. She gathered that the caller he was expecting had to do with the theatrical industry, and wondered for a moment if it was anyone she had ever heard of. She was not sufficiently interested to make inquiries. She was too busy thinking of Ronnie.

'I shall be quite happy,' she said, as the voice beside her ceased. 'It's such a lovely place. I shall enjoy just wandering about by myself.'

The Hon. Galahad seemed shocked at the idea.

'Wouldn't dream of leaving you alone. Clarence will look after you, and I shall be back in a few minutes.'

The name seemed to Sue to strike a familiar chord. Then she remembered. Lord Emsworth. Ronnie's Uncle Clarence. The man who held Ronnie's destinies in the hollow of his hand.

'Hi! Clarence!' called the Hon. Galahad.

Sue perceived pottering towards them a long, stringy man of mild benevolent aspect. She was conscious of something of a shock. In Ronnie's conversation, the Earl of Emsworth had always appeared in the light of a sort of latter-day ogre, a man to whom the stoutest nephew might well shudder. She saw nothing formidable in this newcomer.

'Is that Lord Emsworth?' she asked, surprised.

'Yes. Clarence, this is Miss Schoonmaker.'

His lordship had pottered up and was beaming amiably.

'Is it, indeed? Oh, ah, yes, to be sure. Delighted. How are you? Miss Who?'

'Schoonmaker. Daughter of my old friend Johnny Schoonmaker. You knew she was arriving. Considering that you were in the hall when Constance went to meet her . . .'

'Oh, yes.' The cloud was passing from what, for want of a better word, must be called Lord Emsworth's mind. 'Yes, yes, yes. Yes, to be sure.'

'I've got to leave you to look after her for a few minutes, Clarence.'

'Certainly, certainly.'

'Take her about and show her things. I wouldn't go too far from the house, if I were you. There's a storm coming up.'

'Exactly. Precisely. Yes, I will take her about and show her things. Are you fond of pigs?'

Sue had never considered this point before. Hers had been an urban life, and she could not remember ever having come into contact with a pig on what might be termed a social footing. But, remembering that this was the man whom Ronnie had described as being wrapped up in one of these animals, she smiled her bright smile.

'Oh, yes. Very.'

'Mine has been stolen.'

'I'm so sorry.'

Lord Emsworth was visibly pleased at this womanly sympathy.

'But I now have strong hopes that she may be recovered. The trained mind is everything. What I always say . . .'

What it was that Lord Emsworth always said was unfortunately destined to remain unrevealed. It would probably have been something good, but the world was not to hear it; for at this moment, completely breaking his train of thought, there came from above, from the direction of the window of the small library, an odd, scrabbling sound. Something shot through the air. And the next instant there appeared in the middle of a flower-bed containing lobelias something that was so manifestly not a lobelia that he stared at it in stunned amazement, speech wiped from his lips as with a sponge.

It was the Efficient Baxter. He was on all fours, and seemed to be groping about for his spectacles, which had fallen off and got hidden in the undergrowth.

II

Properly considered, there is no such thing as an insoluble mystery. It may seem puzzling at first sight when ex-secretaries start falling as the gentle rain from heaven upon the lobelia beneath, but there is always a reason for it. That Baxter did not immediately give the reason was due to the fact that he had private and personal motives for not doing so.

We have called Rupert Baxter efficient, and efficient he was. The word, as we interpret it, implies not only a capacity for performing the ordinary tasks of life with a smooth firmness of touch but in addition a certain alertness of mind, a genius for opportunism, a gift for seeing clearly, thinking swiftly, and Doing It Now. With these qualities Rupert Baxter was pre-eminently equipped; and it had been with him the work of a moment to perceive, directly the Hon. Galahad had left the house with Sue, that here was his chance of popping upstairs, nipping into the small library, and abstracting the manuscript of the Reminiscences. Having popped and nipped, as planned, he was in the very act of searching the desk when the sound of a footstep outside froze him from his spectacles to the soles of his feet. The next moment, fingers began to turn the door-handle.

You may freeze a Baxter's body, but you cannot numb his active brain. With one masterful, lightning-like flash of clear thinking he took in the situation and saw the only possible way out. To reach the door leading to the large library, he would have to circumnavigate the desk. The window, on the other hand, was at his elbow. So he jumped out of it.

All these things Baxter could have explained in a few words. Refraining from doing so, he rose to his feet and began to brush the mould from his knees.

'Baxter! What on earth?'

The ex-secretary found the gaze of his late employer trying to nerves which had been considerably shaken by his fall. The occasions on which he disliked Lord Emsworth most intensely were just these occasions when the other gaped at him open-mouthed like a surprised halibut.

'I overbalanced,' he said curtly.

'Overbalanced?'

'Slipped.'

'Slipped?'

'Yes. Slipped.'

'How? Where?'

It now occurred to Baxter that by a most fortunate chance the window of the small library was not the only one that looked out onto this arena into which he had precipitated himself. He might equally well have descended from the larger library which adjoined it.

'I was leaning out of the library window . . .'

'Why?'

'Inhaling the air . . .'

'What for?'

'And I lost my balance.'

'Lost your balance?'

'I slipped.'

'Slipped?'

Baxter had the feeling – it was one which he had often had in the old days when conversing with Lord Emsworth – that an exchange of remarks had begun which might go on for ever. A keen desire swept over him to be – and that right speedily – in some other place. He did not care where it was. So long as Lord Emsworth was not there, it would be Paradise enow.

'I think I will go indoors and wash my hands,' he said.

'And face,' suggested the Hon. Galahad.

'My face, also,' said Rupert Baxter coldly.

He started to move round the angle of the house, but long before he had got out of hearing Lord Emsworth's high and penetrating tenor was dealing with the situation. His lordship, as so often happened on these occasions, was under the impression that he spoke in a hushed whisper.

'Mad as a coot!' he said. And the words rang out through the still summer air like a public oration.

They cut Baxter to the quick. They were not the sort of words to which a man with an inch and a quarter of skin off his left shinbone ought ever to have been called upon to listen. With flushed ears and glowing spectacles, the Efficient Baxter passed on his way. Statistics relating to madness among coots are not to hand, but we may safely doubt whether even in the ranks of these notoriously unbalanced birds there could have been found at this moment one who was feeling half as mad as he did.

Lord Emsworth continued to gaze at the spot where his late secretary had passed from sight.

'Mad as a coot,' he repeated.

In his brother Galahad he found a ready supporter.

'Madder,' said the Hon. Galahad.

'Upon my word, I think he's actually worse than he was two years ago. Then, at least, he never fell out of windows.'

'Why on earth do you have the fellow here?'

Lord Emsworth sighed.

'It's Constance, my dear Galahad. You know what she is. She insisted on inviting him.'

'Well, if you take my advice, you'll hide the flower-pots. One of the things this fellow does when he gets these attacks,' explained the Hon. Galahad, taking Sue into the family confidence, 'is to go about hurling flower-pots at people.'

'Really?'

'I assure you. Looking for me, Beach?'

The careworn figure of the butler had appeared, walking as one pacing behind the coffin of an old friend.

'Yes, sir. The gentleman has arrived, Mr. Galahad. I looked in the small library, thinking that you might possibly be there, but you were not.'

'No, I was out here.'

'Yes, sir.'

'That's why you couldn't find me. Show him up to the small library, Beach, and tell him I'll be with him in a moment.'

'Very good, sir.'

The Hon. Galahad's temporary delay in going to see his visitor was due to his desire to linger long enough to tell Sue, to whom he had taken a warm fancy and whom he wished to shield as far as it was in his power from the perils of life, what every girl ought to know about the Efficient Baxter.

'Never let yourself be alone with that fellow in a deserted spot, my dear,' he counselled. 'If he suggests a walk in the woods, call for help. Been off his head for years. Ask Clarence.'

Lord Emsworth nodded solemnly.

'And it looks to me,' went on the Hon. Galahad, 'as if his mania had now taken a suicidal turn. Overbalanced, indeed! How the deuce could he have overbalanced? Flung himself out bodily, that's what he did. I couldn't think who it was he reminded me of till this moment. He's the living image of a man I used to know in the 'nineties. The first intimation any of us had that this chap had anything wrong with him was when he turned up to supper at the house of a friend of mine – George Pallant. You remember George, Clarence? – with a couple of days' beard on him. And when Mrs. George, who had known him all her life, asked him why he hadn't shaved – "Shaved?" says this fellow, surprised. Packleby, his name was. One of the Leicestershire Packlebys. "Shaved, dear lady?" he says. "Well, considering that they even hide the butter-knife when I come down to breakfast for fear I'll try to cut my throat with it, is it reasonable to suppose they'd trust me with a razor?" Quite stuffy about it, he was, and it spoiled the party. Look after Miss Schoonmaker, Clarence. I shan't be long.'

Lord Emsworth had little experience in the art of providing diversion for young girls. Left thus to his native inspiration, he pondered awhile. If the Empress had not been stolen, his task would, of course, have been simple. He could have given this Miss Schoonmaker a half-hour of sheer entertainment by taking her down to the piggeries to watch that superb animal feed. As it was, he was at something of a loss.

'Perhaps you would care to see the rose-garden?' he hazarded.

'I should love it,' said Sue.

'Are you fond of roses?'

'Tremendously.'

Lord Emsworth found himself warming to this girl. Her personality pleased him. He seemed dimly to recall something his sister Constance had said about her – something about wishing that her nephew Ronald would settle down with some nice girl with money like that Miss Schoonmaker whom Julia had met at Biarritz. Feeling so kindly towards her, it occurred to him that a word in season, opening her eyes to his nephew's true character, might prevent the girl making a mistake which she would regret for ever when it was too late.

'I think you know my nephew Ronald?' he said.

'Yes.'

Lord Emsworth paused to smell a rose. He gave Sue a brief biography of it before returning to the theme.

'That boy's an ass,' he said.

'Why?' said Sue sharply. She began to feel less amiable towards this stringy old man. A moment before, she had been thinking that it was rather charming, that funny, vague manner of his. Now she saw him clearly for what he was – a dodderer, and a Class A dodderer at that.

'Why?' His lordship considered the point. 'Well, heredity, probably, I should say. His father, old Miles Fish, was the biggest fool in the Brigade of Guards.' He looked at her impressively through slanting pince-nez, as if to call her attention to the fact that this was something of an achievement. 'The boy bounces tennis-balls on pigs,' he went on, getting down to the ghastly facts.

Sue was surprised. The words, if she had caught them correctly, seemed to present a side of Ronnie's character of which she had been unaware.

'Does what?'

'I saw him with my own eyes. He bounced a tennis-ball on Empress of Blandings. And not once but repeatedly.'

The mother instinct which all girls feel towards the men they love urged Sue to say something in Ronnie's defence. But, apart from suggesting that the pig had probably started it, she could not think of anything. They left the rose-garden and began to walk back to the lawn, Lord Emsworth still exercised by the thought of his nephew's shortcomings. For one reason and another, Ronnie had always been a source of vague annoyance to him since boyhood. There had even been times when he had felt that he would almost have preferred the society of his younger son, Frederick.

'Aggravating boy,' he said. 'Most aggravating. Always up to something or other. Started a night-club the other day. Lost a lot of money over it. Just the sort of thing he would do. My brother Galahad started some kind of club many years ago. It cost my old father nearly a thousand pounds, I recollect. There is something about Ronald that reminds me very much of Galahad at the same age.'

Although Sue had found much in the author of the Reminiscences to attract her, she was able to form a very fair estimate of the sort of young man he must have been in the middle 'twenties. This charge, accordingly, struck her as positively libellous.

'I don't agree with you, Lord Emsworth.'

'But you never knew my brother Galahad as a young man,' his lordship pointed out cleverly.

'What is the name of that hill over there?' asked Sue in a cold voice, changing the unpleasant subject.

'What hill? Oh, that one?' It was the only one in sight. 'It is called the Wrekin.'

'Oh?' said Sue.

'Yes,' said Lord Emsworth.

'Ah,' said Sue.

They had crossed the lawn and were on the broad terrace that looked out over the park. Sue leaned on the low stone wall that bordered it and gazed before her into the gathering dusk.

The Castle had been built on a knoll of rising ground, and on this terrace one had the illusion of being perched up at a great height. From where she stood, Sue got a sweeping view of the park and of the dim, misty Vale of Blandings that dreamed beyond. In the park, rabbits were scuttling to and fro. In the shrubberies birds called sleepily. From somewhere out across the fields there came the faint tinkling of sheep-bells. The lake shone like old silver, and there was a river in the distance, dull grey between the dull green of the trees.

It was a lovely sight, age-old, orderly and English, but it was spoiled by the sky. The sky was overcast and looked bruised. It seemed to be made of dough, and one could fancy it pressing down on the world like a heavy blanket. And it was muttering to itself. A single heavy drop of rain splashed on the stone beside Sue, and there was a low growl far away as if some powerful and unfriendly beast had spied her.

She shivered. She had been gripped by a sudden depression, a strange foreboding that chilled the spirit. That muttering seemed to say that there was no happiness anywhere and never could be any. The air was growing close and clammy. Another drop of rain fell, squashily like a toad, and spread itself over her hand.

Lord Emsworth was finding his companion unresponsive. His stream of prattle slackened and died away. He began to wonder how he was to escape from a girl who, though undeniably pleasing to the eye, was proving singularly difficult to talk to. Raking the horizon in search of aid, he perceived Beach approaching, a silver salver in his hand. The salver had a card in it, and an envelope.

'For me, Beach?'

'The card, your lordship. The gentleman is in the hall.'

Lord Emsworth breathed a sigh of relief.

'You will excuse me, my dear? It is most important that I should see this fellow immediately. My brother Galahad will be back very shortly, I have no doubt. He will entertain you. You don't mind?'

He bustled away, glad to go, and Sue became conscious of the salver, thrust deferentially towards her.

'For you, miss.'

'For me?'

'Yes, miss,' moaned Beach, like a winter wind wailing through dead trees.

He inclined his head sombrely, and was gone. Sue tore open the envelope. For one breath-taking instant she had thought it might be from Ronnie. But the writing was not Ronnie's familiar scrawl. It was bold, clear, decisive writing, the writing of an efficient man.

She looked at the last page.

*Yours sincerely,*
*R. J. BAXTER.*

Sue's heart was beating faster as she turned back to the

beginning. When a girl in the position in which she had placed herself has been stared at through steel-rimmed spectacles in the way this R. J. Baxter had stared at her through his spectacles, her initial reaction to mysterious notes from the man behind the lenses cannot but be a panic fear that all has been discovered.

The opening sentence dispelled her alarm. Purely personal motives, it appeared, had caused Rupert Baxter to write these few lines. The mere fact that the letter began with the words,

*'Dear Miss Schoonmaker,'*

was enough in itself to bring comfort.

*'At the risk of annoying you by the intrusion of my private affairs* (wrote the Efficient Baxter), *I feel that I must give you an explanation of the incident which occurred in the garden in your presence this afternoon. From the observation – in the grossest taste – which Lord Emsworth let fall in my hearing, I fear you may have placed a wrong construction on what took place. (I allude to the expression "Mad as a coot", which I distinctly heard Lord Emsworth utter as I moved away.)*

*'The facts were precisely as I stated. I was leaning out of the library window, and, chancing to lean too far, I lost my balance and fell. That I might have received serious injuries and was entitled to expect sympathy, I overlook. But the words "Mad as a coot" I resent extremely.*

*'Had this incident not occurred, I would not have dreamed of saying anything to prejudice you against your host. As it is, I feel that in justice to myself I must tell you that Lord Emsworth is a man to whose utterances no attention should be paid. He is to all intents and purposes half-witted. Life in the country,*

*with its lack of intellectual stimulus, has caused his natural feebleness of mind to reach a stage which borders closely on insanity. His relatives look on him as virtually an imbecile and have, in my opinion, every cause to do so.*

*'In these circumstances, I think I may rely on you to attach no importance to his remarks this afternoon.*

*'Yours sincerely,*

*'R. J. BAXTER.'*

*'P.S. You will, of course, treat this as entirely confidential.*

*'P.P.S. If you are fond of chess and would care for a game after dinner, I am a good player.*

*'P.P.S.S. Or Bezique.'*

Sue thought it a good letter, neat and well-expressed. Why it had been written, she could not imagine. It had not occurred to her that love – or, at any rate, a human desire to marry a wealthy heiress – had begun to burgeon in R. J. Baxter's bosom. With no particular emotions, other than the feeling that if he was counting on playing Bezique with her after dinner he was due for a disappointment, she put the letter in her pocket, and looked out over the park again.

The object of all good literature is to purge the soul of its petty troubles. This, she was pleased to discover, Baxter's letter had succeeded in doing. Recalling its polished phrases, she found herself smiling appreciatively.

That muttering sky did not look so menacing now. Everything, she told herself, was going to be all right. After all, she did not ask much from Fate – just an uninterrupted five minutes with Ronnie. And if Fate so far had denied her this very moderate demand . . .

'All alone?'

Sue turned, her heart beating quickly. The voice, speaking close behind her, had had something of the effect of a douche of iced water down her back. For, restorative though Baxter's letter had been, it had not left her in quite the frame of mind to enjoy anything so sudden and jumpy as an unexpected voice.

It was the Hon. Galahad, back from his interview with the gentleman, and the sight of him did nothing to calm her agitation. He was eyeing her, she thought, with a strange and sinister intentness. And though his manner, as he planted himself beside her and began to talk, seemed all that was cordial and friendly, she could not rid herself of a feeling of uneasiness. That look still lingered in her mind's eye. With the air all heavy and woolly and the sky growling pessimistic prophecies, it had been a look to alarm the bravest girl.

Chattering amiably, the Hon. Galahad spoke of this and that; of scenery and the weather; of birds and rabbits; of friends of his who had served terms in prison and of other friends who, one would have said on the evidence, had been lucky to escape. Then his monacle was up again, and that look was back on his face.

The air was more breathless than ever.

'You know,' said the Hon. Galahad, 'it's been a great treat to me, meeting you, my dear. I haven't seen any of your people for a number of years, but your father and I correspond pretty regularly. He tells me all the news. Did you leave your family well?'

'Quite well.'

'How was your Aunt Edna?'

'Fine,' said Sue feebly.

'Ah,' said the Hon. Galahad. 'Then your father must have been mistaken when he told me she was dead. But perhaps you thought I meant your Aunt Edith?'

'Yes,' said Sue gratefully.

'She's all right, I hope?'

'Oh, yes.'

'What a lovely woman!'

'Yes.'

'You mean she still is?'

'Oh, yes.'

'Remarkable! She must be well over seventy by now. No doubt you mean beautiful considering she is over seventy?'

'Yes.'

'Pretty active?'

'Oh, yes.'

'When did you see her last?'

'Oh – just before I sailed.'

'And you say she's active? Curious! I heard two years ago that she was paralysed. I suppose you mean active for a paralytic.'

The little puckers at the corner of his eyes deepened into wrinkles. The monocle gleamed like the eye of a dragon. He smiled genially.

'Confide in me, Miss Brown,' he said. 'What's the game?'

I

Sue did not answer. When the solid world melts abruptly beneath the feet, one feels disinclined for speech. Avoiding the monocle, she stood looking with wide, blank eyes at a thrush which hopped fussily about the lawn. Behind her, the sky gave a low chuckle, as if this was what it had been waiting for.

'Up there,' proceeded the Hon. Galahad, pointing to the small library, 'is the room where I work. And sometimes, when I'm not working, I look out of the window. I was looking out a short while back when you were down here talking to my brother Clarence. There was a fellow with me. He looked out, too.' His voice sounded blurred and far-away. 'A theatrical manager fellow whom I used to know very well in the old days. A man named Mason.'

The thrush had flown away. Sue continued to gaze at the spot where it had been. Across the years, for the mind works oddly in times of stress, there had come to her a vivid recollection of herself at the age of ten, taken by her mother to the Isle of Man on her first steamer trip and just beginning to feel the motion of the vessel. There had been a moment then, just before the supreme catastrophe, when she had felt exactly as she was feeling now.

'We saw you, and he said "Why, there's Sue!" – I said "Sue? Sue Who?" "Sue Brown," said this fellow Mason. He said you were one of the girls at his theatre. He didn't seem particularly surprised to see you here. He said he took it that everything had been fixed up all right and he was glad, because you were one of the best. He wanted to come and have a chat with you, but I headed him off. I thought you might prefer to talk over this little matter of your being Miss Sue Brown alone with me. Which brings me back to my original question. What, Miss Brown, is the game?'

Sue felt dizzy, helpless, hopeless.

'I can't explain,' she said.

The Hon. Galahad tut-tutted protestingly.

'You don't mean to say you propose to leave the thing as just another of those historic mysteries? Don't you want me ever to get a good night's sleep again?'

'Oh, it's so long.'

'We have the evening before us. Take it bit by bit, a little at a time. To begin with, what did Mason mean by saying that everything was all right?'

'I told him about Ronnie.'

'Ronnie? My nephew Ronald?'

'Yes. And, seeing me here, he naturally took it for granted that Lord Emsworth and the rest of you had consented to the engagement and invited me to the Castle.'

'Engagement?'

'I used to be engaged to Ronnie.'

'What! That young Fish?'

'Yes.'

'Good God!' said the Hon. Galahad.

Suddenly Sue began to feel conscious of a slackening of the

tension. Mysteriously, the conversation was seeming less difficult. In spite of the fact that Reason scoffed at the absurdity of such an idea, she felt just as if she were talking to a potential friend and ally. The thought had come to her at the moment when, looking up, she caught sight of her companion's face. It is an unpleasant thing to say of any man, but there is no denying that the Hon. Galahad's face, when he was listening to the confessions of those who had behaved as they ought not to have behaved, very frequently lacked the austerity and disapproval which one likes to see in faces on such occasions.

'But however did Pa Mason come to be here?' asked Sue.

'He came to discuss some business in connection with. . . . Never mind about that,' said the Hon. Galahad, calling the meeting to order. 'Kindly refrain from wandering from the point. I'm beginning to see daylight. You are engaged to Ronald, you say?'

'I was.'

'But you broke it off?'

'He broke it off.'

'He did?'

'Yes. That's why I came here. You see, Ronnie was here and I was in London and you can't put things properly in letters, so I thought that if I could get down to Blandings I could see him and explain and put everything right . . . and I'd met Lady Constance in London one day when I was with Ronnie and he had introduced me as Miss Schoonmaker, so that part of it was all right . . . so . . . Well, so I came.'

If this chronicle has proved anything, it has proved by now that the moral outlook of the Hon. Galahad Threepwood was fundamentally unsound. A man to shake the head at. A man to view with concern. So felt his sister, Lady Constance Keeble, and she was undoubtedly right. If final evidence were needed, his next words supplied it.

'I never heard,' said the Hon. Galahad, beaming like one listening to a tale of virtue triumphant, 'anything so dashed sporting in my life.'

Sue's heart leaped. She had felt all along that Reason, in denying the possibility that this man could ever approve of what she had done, had been mistaken. These pessimists always are.

'You mean,' she cried, 'you won't give me away?'

'Me?' said the Hon. Galahad, aghast at the idea. 'Of course I won't. What do you take me for?'

'I think you're an angel.'

The Hon. Galahad seemed pleased at the compliment, but it was plain that there was something that worried him. He frowned a little.

'What I can't make out,' he said, 'is why you want to marry my nephew Ronald.'

'I love him, bless his heart.'

'No, seriously!' protested the Hon. Galahad. 'Do you know that he once put tin-tacks on my chair?'

'And he bounces tennis-balls on pigs. All the same, I love him.'

'You can't!'

'I do.'

'How can you possibly love a fellow like that?'

'That's just what he always used to say,' said Sue softly. 'And I think that's why I love him.'

The Hon. Galahad sighed. Fifty years' experience had taught him that it was no use arguing with women on this particular point but he had conceived a warm affection for this girl, and it shocked him to think of her madly throwing herself away.

'Don't you go doing anything in a hurry, my dear. Think it over carefully. I've seen enough of you to know that you're a very exceptional girl.'

'I don't believe you like Ronnie.'

'I don't dislike him. He's improved since he was a boy. I'll admit that. But he isn't worthy of you.'

'Why not?'

'Well, he isn't.'

She laughed.

'It's funny that you of all people should say that. Lord Emsworth was telling me just now that Ronnie is exactly like what you used to be at his age.'

'What!'

'That's what he said.'

The Hon. Galahad stared incredulously.

'That boy like me?' He spoke with indignation, for his pride had been sorely touched. 'Ronald like me? Why, I was twice the man he is. How many policemen do you think it used to take to shift me from the Alhambra to Vine Street when I was in my prime? Two! Sometimes three. And one walking behind carrying my hat. Clarence ought to be more careful what he says, dash it. It's just this kind of loose talk that makes trouble. The fact of the matter is, he's gone and got his brain so addled with pigs he doesn't know what he is saying half the time.'

He pulled himself together with a strong effort. He became calmer.

'What did you and that young poop quarrel about?' he asked.

'He is not a poop!'

'He is. It's astonishing to me that one individual can be such a poop. You'd have thought it would have required a large syndicate. How long have you known him?'

'About nine months.'

'Well, I've known him all his life. And I say he's a poop. If he wasn't, he wouldn't have quarrelled with you. However, we won't split straws. What did you quarrel about?'

'He found me dancing.'

'What's wrong with that?'

'I had promised I wouldn't.'

'And is that all the trouble?'

'It's quite enough for me.'

The Hon. Galahad made light of the tragedy.

'I don't see what you're worrying about. If you can't smooth a little thing like that over, you're not the girl I take you for.'

'I thought I might be able to.'

'Of course you'll be able to. Girls were always doing that sort of thing to me in my young days, and I never held out for five minutes, once the crying started. Go and sob on the boy's waistcoat. How are you as a sobber?'

'Not very good, I'm afraid.'

'Well, there are all sorts of other tricks you can try. Every girl knows a dozen. Falling on your knees, fainting, laughing hysterically, going rigid all over . . . scores of them.'

'I think it will be all right if I can just talk to him. The difficulty is to get an opportunity.'

The Hon. Galahad waved a hand spaciously.

'Make an opportunity! Why, I knew a girl years ago – she's a grandmother now – who had a quarrel with the fellow she was engaged to, and a week or so later she found herself staying at the same country-house with him – Heron's Hill it was. The Matchelows' place in Sussex – and she got him into her room one night and locked the door and said she was going to keep him there all night and ruin both their reputations unless he handed back the ring and agreed that the engagement was on again. And she'd have done it, too. Her name was Frederica Something. Redhaired girl.'

'I suppose you have to have red hair to do a thing like that. I was thinking of a quiet meeting in the rose-garden.'

The Hon. Galahad seemed to consider this tame, but he let it pass.

'Well, whatever you do, you'll have to be quick about it, my dear. Suppose old Johnny Schoonmaker's girl really turns up? She said she was going to.'

'Yes, but I made Ronnie send her a telegram, signed with Lady Constance's name, saying that there was scarlet fever at the Castle and she wasn't to come.'

One dislikes the necessity of perpetually piling up the evidence against the Hon. Galahad Threepwood, to show ever more and more clearly how warped was his moral outlook. Nevertheless the fact must be stated that at these words he threw his head up and uttered a high, piercing laugh that sent the thrush, which had just returned to the lawn, starting back as if a bullet had hit it. It was a laugh which, when it had rung out in days of yore in London's more lively night-resorts, had caused commissionaires to leap like war-horses at the note of the bugle, to spit on their hands, feel their muscles and prepare for action.

'It's the finest thing I ever heard!' cried the Hon. Galahad. 'It restores my faith in the younger generation. And a girl like you seriously contemplates marrying a boy like . . . Oh, well!' he said resignedly, seeming to brace himself to make the best of a distasteful state of affairs. 'It's your business, I suppose. You know your own mind best. After all, the great thing is to get you into the family. A girl like you is what this family has been needing for years.'

He patted her kindly on the shoulder, and they started to walk towards the house. As they did so, two men came out of it. One was Lord Emsworth. The other was Percy Pilbeam.

## II

There is about a place like Blandings Castle something which, if you are not in the habit of visiting country-houses planned on the grand scale, tends to sap the morale. At the moment when Sue caught sight of him, the proprietor of the Argus Enquiry Agency was not feeling his brightest and best.

Beach, ushering him through the front door, had started the trouble. He had merely let his eye rest upon Pilbeam, but it had been enough. The butler's eye, through years of insufficient exercise and too hearty feeding, had acquired in the process of time a sort of glaze which many people found trying when they saw it. In Pilbeam it created an inferiority complex of the severest kind.

He could not know that to this godlike man he was merely a blur. To Beach, tortured by the pangs of a guilty conscience, almost everything nowadays was merely a blur. Misinterpreting his gaze, Pilbeam had read into it a shocked contempt, a kind of wincing agony at the thought that things like himself should be creeping into Blandings Castle. He felt as if he had crawled out from under a flat stone.

And it was at this moment that somebody in the dimness of the hall had stepped forward and revealed himself as the young man, name unknown, who had showed such a lively disposition to murder him on the dancing-floor of Mario's restaurant. And from the violent start which he gave, it was plain that the young man's memory was as good as his own.

So far, things had not broken well for Percy Pilbeam. But now his luck had turned. There had appeared in the nick of time an angel from heaven, effectively disguised in a shabby shootingcoat and an old hat. He had introduced himself as Lord Emsworth, and he had taken Pilbeam off with him into the garden. Looking back over his shoulder, Pilbeam saw that the young man was still standing there, staring after him – wistfully, it seemed to him; and he was glad, as he followed his host out into the fresh air, to be beyond the range of his eye. Between it and the eye of Beach, the butler, there seemed little to choose.

Relief, however, by the time he arrived on the terrace, had not completely restored his composure. That inferiority complex was still at work, and his surroundings intimidated him. At any moment, he felt, on a terrace like this, there might suddenly appear to confront him and complete his humiliation some brilliant shattering creature indigenous to this strange and disturbing world – a Duchess, perhaps – a haughty hunting woman it might be – the dashing daughter of a hundred Earls, possibly, who would look at him as Beach had looked at him and, raising beautifully pencilled eyebrows in aristocratic disdain, turn away with a murmured 'Most extraordinary!' He was prepared for almost anything.

One of the few things he was not prepared for was Sue. And at the sight of her he leaped three clear inches and nearly broke a collar stud.

'Gaw!' he said.

'I beg your pardon?' said Lord Emsworth. He had not caught his companion's remark and hoped he would repeat it. The lightest utterance of a detective with the trained mind is something not to be missed. 'What did you say, my dear fellow?'

He, too, perceived Sue; and with a prodigious effort of the memory, working by swift stages through Schofield, Maybury, Coolidge and Spooner, recalled her name.

'Mr. Pilbeam, Miss Schoonmaker,' he said. 'Galahad, this is Mr. Pilbeam. Of the Argus, you remember.'

'Pilbeam?'

'How do you do?'

'Pilbeam?'

'My brother,' said Lord Emsworth, exerting himself to complete the introduction. 'This is my brother Galahad.'

'Pilbeam?' said the Hon. Galahad, looking intently at the proprietor of the Argus. 'Were you ever connected with a paper called *Society Spice*, Mr Pilbeam?'

The gardens of Blandings Castle seemed to the detective to rock gently. There had, he knew, been a rigid rule in the office of that bright, but frequently offensive paper that the editor's name was never to be revealed to callers: but it now appeared only too sickeningly evident that a leakage had occurred. Underlings, he realized too late, can be bribed.

He swallowed painfully. Force of habit had come within a hair's-breadth of making him say 'Quite'.

'Never,' he gasped. 'Certainly not. No! Never.'

'A fellow of your name used to edit it. Uncommon name, too.'

'Relation, perhaps. Distant.'

'Well, I'm sorry you're not the man,' said the Hon. Galahad regretfully. 'I've been wanting to meet him. He wrote a very offensive thing about me once. Most offensive thing.'

Lord Emsworth, who had been according the conversation the rather meagre interest which he gave to all conversations that did not deal with pigs, created a diversion.

'I wonder,' he said, 'if you would like to see some photographs?'

It seemed to Pilbeam, in his disordered state, strange that anyone should suppose that he was in a frame of mind to enjoy the Family Album, but he uttered a strangled sound which his host took for acquiescence.

'Of the Empress, I mean, of course. They will give you some idea of what a magnificent animal she is. They will . . .' He sought for the *mot juste*. '. . . Stimulate you. I'll go to the library and get them out.'

The Hon. Galahad was now his old, affable self again.

'You doing anything after dinner?' he asked Sue.

'There was some talk,' said Sue, 'of a game of Bezique with Mr. Baxter.'

'Don't dream of it,' said the Hon. Galahad vehemently. 'The fellow would probably try to brain you with the mallet. I was thinking that if I hadn't got to go out to dinner I'd like to read you some of my book. I think you would appreciate it. I wouldn't read it to anybody except you. I somehow feel you've got the right sort of outlook. I let my sister Constance see a couple of pages once, and she was too depressing for words. An author can't work if people depress him. I'll tell you what I'll do. I'll give you the thing to read. Which is your room?'

'The Garden Room, I think it's called.'

'Oh yes. Well, I'll bring the manuscript to you before I leave.'

He sauntered off. There was a moment's pause. Then Sue turned to Pilbeam. Her chin was tilted. There was defiance in her eye.

'Well?' she said.

## III

Percy Pilbeam breathed a sigh of relief. At the first moment of their meeting, all that he had ever read about doubles had raced through his mind. This question clarified the situation. It put matters on a firm basis. His head ceased to swim. It was Sue Brown and no other who stood before him.

'What on earth are you doing here?' he asked.

'Never mind.'

'What's the game?'

'Never mind.'

'There's no need to be so dashed unfriendly.'

'Well, if you must know, I came here to see Ronnie and try to explain about that night at Mario's.'

There was a pause.

'What was that name the old boy called you?'

'Schoonmaker.'

'Why did he call you that?'

'Because that's who he thinks I am.'

'What on earth made you choose a name like that?'

'Oh, don't keep on asking questions.'

'I don't believe there is such a name. And when it comes to asking questions,' said Pilbeam warmly, 'what do you expect me to do? I never got such a shock in my life as when I met you just now. I thought I was seeing things. Do you mean to say you're here under a false name, pretending to be somebody else?'

'Yes.'

'Well, I'm hanged! And as friendly as you please with everybody.'

'Yes.'

'Everybody except me.'

'Why should I be friendly with you? You've done your best to ruin my life.'

'Eh?'

'Oh, never mind,' said Sue impatiently.

There was another pause.

'Chatty!' said Pilbeam, wounded again.

He fidgeted his fingers along the wall.

'That Galahad fellow seems to look on you as a daughter or something.'

'We are great friends.'

'So I see. And he's going to give you his book to read.'

'Yes.'

A keen, purposeful, Argus-Enquiry-Agency sort of look shot into Pilbeam's face.

'Well, this is where you and I get together,' he said.

'What do you mean?'

'I'll tell you what I mean. Do you want to make some money?'

'No,' said Sue.

'What! Of course you do. Everybody does. Now listen. Do you know why I'm here?'

'I've stopped wondering why you're anywhere. You just seem to pop up.'

She started to move away. A sudden, disturbing thought had come to her. At any moment Ronnie might appear on the terrace. If he found her here, closeted, so to speak, with the abominable Pilbeam, what would he think? What, rather, would he not think?

'Where are you going?'

'Into the house.'

'Come back,' said Pilbeam urgently.

'I'm going.'

'But I've got something important to say.'

'Well?'

She stopped.

'That's right,' said Pilbeam approvingly. 'Now listen. You'll admit that, if I liked, I could give you away and spoil whatever game it is that you're up to in this place?'

'Well?'

'But I'm not going to do it. If you'll be sensible.'

'Sensible?'

Pilbeam looked cautiously up and down the terrace.

'Now listen,' he said. 'I want your help. I'll tell you why I'm here. The old boy thinks I've come down to find his pig, but I haven't. I've come to get that book your friend Galahad is writing.'

'What!'

'I thought you'd be surprised. Yes, that's what I'm after. There's a man living near here who's scared stiff that there's going to be a lot of stories about him in that book, and he came to see me at my office yesterday and offered me . . .' he hesitated a moment. '. . . Offered me,' he went on, 'a hundred pounds if I'd get into the house somehow and snitch the manuscript. And you being friendly with the old buster has made everything simple.'

'You think so?'

'Easy,' he assured her. 'Especially now he's going to give you the thing to read. All you have to do is hand it over to me, and there's fifty quid for you. For doing practically nothing.'

Sue's eyes lit up. Pilbeam had expected that they would. He could not conceive of a girl whose eyes would not light up at such an offer.

'Oh?' said Sue.

'Fifty quid,' said Pilbeam. 'I'm going halves with you.'

'And if I don't do what you want I suppose you will tell them who I really am?'

'That's it,' said Pilbeam, pleased at her ready intelligence.

'Well, I'm not going to do anything of the kind.'

'What!'

'And if,' said Sue, 'you want to tell these people who I am, go ahead and tell them.'

'I will.'

'Do. But just bear in mind that the moment you do I shall tell Mr. Threepwood that it was you who wrote that thing about him in *Society Spice*.'

Percy Pilbeam swayed like a sapling in the breeze. The blow had unmanned him. He found no words with which to reply.

'I will,' said Sue.

Pilbeam continued speechless. He was still trying to recover from this deadly thrust through an unexpected chink in his armour when the opportunity for speech passed. Millicent had appeared, and was walking along the terrace towards them. She wore her customary air of settled gloom. On reaching them, she paused.

'Hullo,' said Millicent, from the depths.

'Hullo,' said Sue.

The library window framed the head and shoulders of Lord Emsworth.

'Pilbeam, my dear fellow, will you come up to the library. I have found the photographs.'

Millicent eyed the detective's retreating back with a mournful curiosity.

'Who's he?'

'A man named Pilbeam.'

'Pill, I should say, is right. What makes him waddle like that?'

Sue was unable to supply a solution to this problem. Millicent came and stood beside her, and, leaning on the stone parapet, gazed disparagingly at the park. She gave the impression of disliking all parks, but this one particularly.

'Ever read Schopenhauer?' she asked, after a silence.

'No.'

'You should. Great stuff.'

She fell into a heavy silence again, her eyes peering into the gathering gloom. Somewhere in the twilight world a cow had begun to emit long, nerve-racking bellows. The sound seemed to sum up and underline the general sadness.

'Schopenhauer says that all the suffering in the world can't be mere chance. Must be meant. He says life's a mixture of suffering and boredom. You've got to have one or the other. His stuff's full of snappy cracks like that. You'd enjoy it. Well, I'm going for a walk. You coming?'

'I don't think I will, thanks.'

'Just as you like. Schopenhauer says suicide's absolutely O.K. He says Hindoos do it instead of going to church. They bung themselves into the Ganges and get eaten by crocodiles and call it a well-spent day.'

'What a lot you seem to know about Schopenhauer.'

'I've been reading him up lately. Found a copy in the library. Schopenhauer says we are like lambs in a field, disporting themselves under the eye of the butcher, who chooses first one and then another for his prey. Sure you won't come for a walk?'

'No thanks, really. I think I'll go in.'

'Just as you like,' said Millicent. 'Liberty Hall.'

She moved off a few steps, then returned.

'Sorry if I seem loopy,' she said. 'Something on my mind.

Been giving it a spot of thought. The fact is, I've just got engaged to be married to my cousin Ronnie.'

The trees that stood out against the banking clouds seemed to swim before Sue's eyes. An unseen hand had clutched her by the throat and was crushing the life out of her.

'Ronnie!'

'Yes,' said Millicent, rather in the tone of voice which Schopenhauer would have used when announcing the discovery of a caterpillar in his salad. 'We fixed it up just now.'

She wandered away, and Sue clung to the terrace wall. That at least was solid in a world that rocked and crashed.

'I say!'

It was Hugo. She was looking at him through a mist, but there was never any mistaking Hugo Carmody.

'I say! Did she tell you?'

Sue nodded.

'She's engaged.'

Sue nodded.

'She's going to marry Ronnie.'

Sue nodded.

'Death, where is thy sting?' said Hugo, and vanished in the direction taken by Millicent.

The firm and dignified note in which Rupert Baxter had expressed his considered opinion of the Earl of Emsworth had been written in the morning-room immediately upon the ex-secretary's return to the house and delivered into Beach's charge with hands still stained with garden-mould. Only when this urgent task had been performed did he start to go upstairs in quest of the wash and brush-up which he so greatly needed. He was mounting the stairs to his bedroom and had reached the first floor when a door opened and his progress was arrested by what in a lesser woman would have been a yelp. Proceeding as it did, from the lips of Lady Constance Keeble, we must call it an exclamation of surprise.

'Mr. Baxter!'

She was standing in the doorway of her boudoir, and she eyed his dishevelled form with such open-mouthed astonishment that for an instant the ex-secretary came near to including her with the head of the family in the impromptu Commination Service which was taking shape in his mind. He was in no mood for wide-eyed looks of wonder.

'May I come in?' he said curtly. He could explain all, but he did not wish to do so on the first-floor landing of a house where almost anybody might be listening with flapping ears.

'But, Mr. Baxter!' said Lady Constance.

He paused for a moment to grit his teeth, then closed the door.

'What *have* you been doing, Mr. Baxter?'

'Jumping out of window.'

'Jumping out of *win*-dow?'

He gave a brief synopsis of the events which had led up to his spirited act. Lady Constance drew in her breath with a remorseful hiss.

'Oh, dear!' she said. 'How foolish of me. I should have told you.'

'I beg your pardon?'

Even though she was in the safe retirement of her boudoir Lady Constance Keeble looked cautiously over her shoulder. In the stirring and complicated state into which life had got itself at Blandings Castle, practically everybody in the place, except Lord Emsworth, had fallen into the habit nowadays of looking cautiously over his or her shoulder before he or she spoke.

'Sir Gregory Parsloe said in his note,' she explained, 'that this man Pilbeam who is coming here this evening is acting for him.'

'Acting for him?'

'Yes. Apparently Sir Gregory went to see him yesterday and has promised him a large sum of money if he will obtain possession of my brother Galahad's manuscript. That is why he has invited us to dinner to-night, to get Galahad out of the house. So there was no need for you to have troubled.'

There was a silence.

'So there was no need,' repeated the Efficient Baxter slowly, wiping from his eye the remains of a fragment of mould which had been causing him some inconvenience, 'for me to have troubled.'

'I am so sorry, Mr. Baxter.'

'Pray do not mention it, Lady Constance.'

His eye, now that the mould was out of it, was able to work again with its customary keenness. His spectacles, as he surveyed the remorseful woman before him, had a cold, steely look.

'I see,' he said. 'Well, it might perhaps have spared me some little inconvenience had you informed me of this earlier, Lady Constance. I have bruised my left shin somewhat severely and, as you see, made myself rather dirty.'

'I am so sorry.'

'Furthermore, I gathered from the remark he let fall that the impression my actions have made upon Lord Emsworth is that I am insane.'

'Oh, dear.'

'He even specified the precise degree of insanity. As mad as a coot, were his words.'

He softened a little. He reminded himself that this woman before him, who was so nearly doing what is described as wringing her hands, had always been his friend, had always wished him well, had never slackened her efforts to restore to him the secretarial duties which he had once enjoyed.

'Well, it cannot be helped,' he said. 'The thing now is to think of some way of recovering the lost ground.'

'You mean, if you could find the Empress?'

'Exactly.'

'Oh, Mr. Baxter, if you only could!'

'I can.'

Lady Constance stared at his dark, purposeful efficient face in dumb admiration. To another man who had spoken those words she would have replied "How?" or even "How on earth?" But, as they had proceeded from Rupert Baxter, she merely waited silently for enlightenment.

'Have you given this matter any consideration, Lady Constance?'

'Yes.'

'To what conclusions have you come?'

Lady Constance felt dull and foolish. She felt like Doctor Watson – almost like a Scotland Yard Bungler.

'I don't think I have come to any,' she said, avoiding the spectacles guiltily. 'Of course,' she added, 'I think it is absurd to suppose that Sir Gregory . . .'

Baxter waved aside the notion. It was not even worth a 'Tchah!'

'In any matter of this kind,' he said, 'the first thing to do is to seek motive. Who is there in Blandings Castle who could have had a motive for stealing Lord Emsworth's pig?'

Lady Constance would have given a year's income to have been able to make some reasonably intelligent reply, but all she could do was look and listen. Baxter was not annoyed. He would not have had it otherwise. He preferred his audiences dumb and expectant.

'Carmody.'

'Mr. Carmody!'

'Precisely. He is Lord Emsworth's secretary, and a most inefficient secretary, a secretary who stands hourly in danger of losing his position. He sees me arrive at the Castle, a man who formerly held the post he holds. He is alarmed. He suspects. He searches wildly about in his mind for means of consolidating himself in Lord Emsworth's regard. Then he has an idea, the sort of wild, motion-picture-bred idea which would come to a man of his stamp. He thinks to himself that if he removes the pig and conceals it somewhere and then pretends to have found it and restores it to its owner, Lord Emsworth's gratitude will be so intense that all danger of his dismissal will be at an end.'

He removed his spectacles and wiped them. Lady Constance uttered a low cry. In anybody else it would have been a squeak. Baxter replaced his spectacles.

'I have no doubt the pig is somewhere in the grounds at this moment,' he said.

'But, Mr. Baxter . . . !'

The ex-secretary raised a compelling hand.

'But he would not have undertaken a thing like this single-handed. A secretary's time is not his own, and it would be necessary to feed the pig at regular intervals. He would require an accomplice. And I think I know who that accomplice is. Beach!'

This time not even the chronicler's desire to place Lady Constance's utterances in the best and most attractive light can hide the truth. She bleated.

'Be-ee-ee-ee-ech!'

The spectacles raked her keenly.

'Have you observed Beach closely of late?'

She shook her head. She was not a woman who observed butlers closely.

'He has something on his mind. He is nervous. Guilty. Conscience-stricken. He jumps when you speak to him.'

'Does he?'

'Jumps,' repeated the Efficient Baxter. 'Just now I gave him a – I happened to address him, and he sprang in the air.' He paused. 'I have half a mind to go and question him.'

'Oh, Mr. Baxter! Would that be wise?'

Rupert Baxter's intention of interrogating the butler had been merely a nebulous one, a sort of idle dream, but these words crystallised it into a resolve. He was not going to have people asking him if things would be wise.

'A few searching questions should force him to reveal the truth.'

'But he'll give notice!'

This interview had been dotted with occasions on which Baxter might reasonably have said 'Tchah!' but, as we have seen, until this moment he had refrained. He now said it.

'Tchah!' said the Efficient Baxter. 'There are plenty of other butlers.'

And with this undeniable truth he stalked from the room. The wash and brush-up were still as necessary as they had been ten minutes before, but he was too intent on the chase to think about washes and brushes-up. He hurried down the stairs. He crossed the hall. He passed through the green baize door that led to the quarters of the Blandings Castle staff. And he was making his way along the dim passage to the pantry where at this hour Beach might be supposed to be, when its door opened abruptly and a vast form emerged.

It was the butler. And from the fact that he was wearing a bowler hat it was plain that he was seeking the great outdoors.

Baxter stopped in mid-stride and remained on one leg, watching. Then, as his quarry disappeared in the direction of the back-entrance, he followed quickly.

Out in the open it was almost as dark as it had been in the passage. That grey, threatening sky had turned black by now. It was a swollen mass of inky clouds, heavy with the thunder, lightning and rain which so often come in the course of an

English Summer to remind the island race that they are hardly Nordics and must not be allowed to get their fibre all sapped by eternal sunshine like the less favoured dwellers in more southerly climes. It bayed at Baxter like a bloodhound.

But it took more than dirty weather to quell the Efficient Baxter when duty called. Like the character in Tennyson's poem who followed the gleam, he followed the butler. There was but one point about Beach which even remotely resembled a gleam, but it happened to be the only one which at this moment really mattered. He was easy to follow.

The shrubbery swallowed the butler. A few seconds later, it had swallowed the Efficient Baxter.

## II

There are those who maintain – and make a nice income by doing so in the evening papers – that in these degenerate days the old, hardy spirit of the Briton has died out. They represent themselves as seeking vainly for evidence of the survival of those qualities of toughness and endurance which once made Englishmen what they were. To such, the spectacle of Rupert Baxter braving the elements could not have failed to bring cheer and consolation. They would have been further stimulated by the conduct of Hugo Carmody.

It had not escaped Hugo's notice, as he left Sue on the terrace and started out in the wake of Millicent, that the weather was hotting up for a storm. He saw the clouds. He heard the fast-approaching thunder. For neither did he give a hoot. Let it rain, was Hugo's verdict. Let it jolly well rain as much as it dashed well wanted to. As if encouraged, the sky sent down a fat, wet drop which insinuated itself just between his neck and collar.

He hardly noticed it. The information confided to him by his friend Ronald Fish had numbed his senses so thoroughly that water down the back of his neck was merely an incident. He was feeling as he had not felt since the evening some years ago when, boxing for his University in the light-weight division, he had incautiously placed the point of his jaw in the exact spot at the moment occupied by his opponent's right fist. When you have done this or – equally – when you have just been told that the girl you love is definitely betrothed to another, you begin to understand how Anarchists must feel when the bomb goes off too soon.

In all the black days through which he had been living recently, Hugo had never really lost hope. It had been dim sometimes, but it had always been there. It was his opinion that he knew women, just as it was Sue's idea that she knew men. Like Sue, he had placed his trust in the thought that true love conquers all obstacles; that coldness melts; that sundered hearts may at long last be brought together again by a little judicious pleading and reasoning. Even the fact that Millicent stared at him, when they met, with large, scornful eyes that went through him like stilettos, unpleasant though it was, had not caused him to despair. He had looked forward to the moment when he should contrive to get her alone and do a bit of snappy talking along the right lines.

But this was final. This was the end. This put the tin hat on it. She was engaged to Ronnie. Soon she would be married to Ronnie. Like a gad-fly the hideous thought sent Hugo Carmody reeling on through the gloom.

It was so dark now that he could scarcely see before him. And, looking about him, he discovered that the reason for this was that he had made his way into a wood of sorts. The west wood, he deduced dully, taking into consideration the fact that there was no other in this particular part of the estate. Well, he might just as well be in the west wood as anywhere. He trudged on.

The ground beneath his feet was spongy, and equipped with low-lying brambles which pricked through his thin flannels and would have caused him discomfort if he had been in the frame of mind to notice brambles. There were trees against which he bumped, and logs over which he tripped. And ahead of him, in a small clearing, there was a dilapidated-looking cottage. He noticed this because it seemed the sort of place where a man, now that a warm gusty wind had sprung up, might shelter and light a cigarette. The need for tobacco had become imperative.

He was surprised to find that it was raining, and had apparently, from the state of his clothes, been raining for quite some time. It was also thundering. The storm had broken, and the boom of it seemed to be all round him. A flash of lightning reminded him that he was in just the kind of place, among all these trees, where blokes get struck. At dinner-time they are missed, and later on search-parties come out with lanterns. Somebody stumbles over something soft, and the rays of the lantern fall on a charred and blackened form. Here, quickly, we have found him! Where? Over here. Is *that* Hugo Carmody? Well, well! Pick him up, boys, and bring him along. He was a good chap once. Moody, though, of late. Some trouble about a girl, wasn't it? She will be sorry when she hears of this. Drove him to it, you might almost say. Steady with that stretcher. Now, when I say '*To* me.' Right!

There was something about this picture which quite cheered Hugo up. Ajax defied the lightning. Hugo Carmody rather encouraged it than otherwise. He looked approvingly at a more than usually vivid flash that seemed to dart among the tree-tops like a snake. All the same, he was forced to reflect, he was getting dashed wet. No sense, when you came right down to it, in getting dashed wet. After all, a man could be struck by lightning just as well in that cottage sort of place over there. Ho! for the cottage, felt Hugo, and headed for it at a gallop.

He had just reached the door, when it was flung open. There was a noise rather like that made by a rising pheasant, and the next moment something white had flung itself into his arms and was weeping emotionally on his chest.

'Hugo! Hugo, darling!'

Reason told Hugo it could scarcely be Millicent who was clinging to him like this and speaking to him like this. And yet Millicent it most certainly appeared to be. She continued to speak, still in the same friendly, even chatty strain.

'Hugo! Save me!'

'Right ho!'

'I wur-wur-went in thur-thur-there to shush-shush-shelter from the rain and it's all pitch dark.'

Hugo squeezed her fondly and with the sort of relief that comes to men who find themselves squeezing where they had not thought to squeeze. No need for that snappy bit of talking now. No need for arguments and explanations, for pleadings and entreaties. No need for anything but good biceps.

He was bewildered. But mixed with his bewilderment had come a certain feeling of complacency. There was no denying that it was enjoyable, this exhibition of tremulous weakness in one who, if she had had the shadow of a fault, had always been inclined to matter-of-factness and the display of that rather hard, bright self-sufficiency which is so characteristic of the modern girl. If this melting mood was due to the fact that

Millicent, while in the cottage, had seen a ghost, Hugo wanted to meet that ghost and shake its hand. Every man likes to be in a position to say 'There, there, little woman!' to the girl of his heart, particularly if for the last few days she has been treating him like a more than ordinarily unpleasant worm, and Hugo Carmody felt that he was in that position now.

'There, there!' he said, not quite feeling up to risking the 'little woman'.

'It's all right.'

'But it tut-tut-tut . . .'

'It what?' said Hugo, puzzled.

'It tut-tut-tut-tisn't. There's a man in there!'

'A man?'

'Yes. I didn't know there was anyone there, and it was pitch dark and I heard something move and I said "Who's that?" and then he suddenly spoke to me in German.'

'In German?'

'Yes.'

Hugo released her gently. His face was determined.

'I'm going in to have a look.'

'Hugo! Stop! You'll be killed.'

She stood there, rigid. The rain lashed about her, but she did not need it. The lightning gleamed. She paid it no attention. For the minute that lasts an hour she waited, straining her ears for sounds of the death-struggle. Then a dim form appeared.

'I say, Millicent.'

'Hugo! Are you all right?'

'Yes. I'm all right. I say, Millicent, do you know what?'

'No, what?'

A chuckle came to her through the darkness. 'It's the pig.'

'It's what?'

'The pig?'

'Who's a pig?'

'This is. Your friend in here. It's Empress of Blandings, as large as life. Come and have a look.'

### III

Millicent had a look. She came to the door of the cottage and peered in. Yes, just as he had said, there was the Empress. In the feeble light of the match which Hugo was holding, the noble animal's attractive face was peering up at her – questioningly, as if wondering if she might be the bearer of the evening snack which would be so exceedingly welcome. The picture was one which would have set Lord Emsworth screaming with joy. Millicent merely gaped.

'How on earth did she get here?'

'That's what I'm going to find out,' said Hugo. 'One always knew she must be cached somewhere, of course. What is this place, anyway?'

'It used to be a gamekeeper's cottage, I believe.'

'Well, there seems to be a room up above,' said Hugo, striking another match. 'I'm going to go up there and wait. It's quite likely that somebody will be along soon to feed the animal, and I'm going to see who it is.'

'Yes, that's what we'll do. How clever of you!'

'Not you. You get back home.'

'I won't.'

There was a pause. A strong man would, no doubt, have asserted himself. But Hugo, though feeling better than he had done for days, was not feeling quite so strong as all that.

'Just as you like.' He shut the door. 'Well, come on. We'd

better be making a move. The fellow may be here at any moment.'

They climbed the crazy stairs and lowered themselves cautiously to a floor which smelled of mice and mildew. Below, all was in darkness, but there were holes through which it would be possible to look when the time should come for looking. Millicent could feel one near her face.

'You don't think this floor will give way?' she asked rather nervously.

'I shouldn't think so. Why?'

'Well, I don't want to break my neck.'

'You don't, don't you? Well, I would jolly well like to break mine,' said Hugo, speaking tensely in the darkness. It had just occurred to him that now would be a good time for a heart-to-heart talk. 'If you suppose I'm keen on going on living with you and Ronnie doing the Wedding Glide all over the place, you're dashed well mistaken. I take it you're aware that you've broken my bally heart, what?'

'Oh, Hugo!' said Millicent.

Silence fell. Below, the Empress rustled. Aloft, something scuttered.

'Oo!' cried Millicent. 'Was that a rat?'

'I hope so.'

'What!'

'Rats gnaw you,' explained Hugo. 'They cluster round and chew you to the bone and put an end to your misery.'

There was silence again. Then Millicent spoke in a small voice.

'You're being beastly,' she said.

Remorse poured over Hugo in a flood.

'I'm frightfully sorry. Yes, I know I am, dash it. But, look here, you know . . . I mean, all this getting engaged to Ronnie. A bit thick, what? You don't expect me to give three hearty cheers, do you? Wouldn't want me to break into a few care-free dance-steps?'

'I can't believe it's really happened.'

'Well, how did it happen?'

'It sort of happened all of a sudden. I was feeling miserable and very angry with you and . . . and all that. And I met Ronnie and he took me for a stroll and we went down by the lake and started throwing little bits of stick at the swans, and suddenly Ronnie sort of grunted and said "I say!" and I said "Hullo?" and he said "Will you marry me?" and I said "All right," and he said "I ought to warn you, I despise all women," and I said "And I loathe all men" and he said "Right-ho, I think we shall be very happy."'

'I see.'

'I only did it to score off you.'

'You succeeded.'

A trace of spirit crept into Millicent's voice.

'You never really loved me,' she said. 'You know jolly well you didn't.'

'Is that so?'

'Well, what did you want to go sneaking off to London for, then, and stuffing that beastly girl of yours with food?'

'She isn't my girl. And she isn't beastly.'

'She is.'

'Well, you seem to get on with her all right. I saw you chatting on the terrace together as cosily as dammit.'

'What!'

'Miss Schoonmaker.'

'I don't know what you're talking about. What's Miss Schoonmaker got to do with it?'

'Miss Schoonmaker isn't Miss Schoonmaker. She's Sue Brown.'

For a moment it seemed to Millicent that the crack in her companion's heart had spread to his head. Futile though the action was, she stared in the direction from which his voice had proceeded. Then, suddenly, his words took on a meaning. She gasped.

'She's followed you down here!'

'She hasn't followed me down here. She's followed Ronnie down here. Can't you get it into your nut,' said Hugo with justifiable exasperation, 'that you've been making floaters and bloomers and getting everything mixed up all along? Sue Brown has never cared a curse for me, and I've never thought anything about her, except that she's a jolly girl and nice to dance with. That's absolutely and positively the only reason I went out with her. I hadn't had a dance for six weeks and my feet had begun to itch so that I couldn't sleep at night. So I went to London and took her out and Ronnie found her talking to that pestilence Pilbeam and thought he had taken her out and she had told him she didn't even know the man, which was quite true, but Ronnie cut up rough and said he was through with her and came down here and she wanted to get a word with him, so she came down here pretending to be Miss Schoonmaker, and the moment she gets here she finds Ronnie is engaged to you. A nice surprise for the poor girl!'

Millicent's head had begun to swim long before the conclusion of this recital.

'But what is Pilbeam doing down here?'

'Pilbeam?'

'He was on the terrace talking to her.'

A low snarl came through the darkness.

'Pilbeam here? Ah! So he came, after all, did he? He's the fellow Lord Emsworth sent me to, about the Empress. He runs the Argus Enquiry Agency. It was Pilbeam's minions that dogged my steps that night, at your request. So he's here, is he? Well, let him enjoy himself while he can. Let him sniff the country air while the sniffing is good. A bitter reckoning awaits that bloke.'

From the disorder of Millicent's mind another point emerged insistently demanding explanation.

'You said she wasn't pretty!'

'Who?'

'Sue Brown.'

'Nor she is.'

'You don't call her pretty? She's fascinating.'

'Not to me,' said Hugo doggedly. 'There's only one girl in the world that I call pretty, and she's going to marry Ronnie.' He paused. 'If you haven't realized by this time that I love you, and always shall love you, and have never loved anybody else, and never shall love anybody else, you're a fathead. If you brought me Sue Brown or any other girl in the world on a plate with watercress round her, I wouldn't so much as touch her hand.'

Another rat – unless it was an exceptionally large mouse – had begun to make its presence felt in the darkness. It seemed to be enjoying an early dinner off a piece of wood. Millicent did not even notice it. She had reached out, and her hand had touched Hugo's arm. Her fingers closed on it desperately.

'Oh, Hugo!' she said.

The arm became animated. It clutched her, drew her along the mouse-and-mildew scented floor. And time stood still.

Hugo was the first to break the silence.

'And to think that not so long ago I was wishing that a flash of lightning would strike me amidships!' he said.

The aroma of mouse and mildew had passed away. Violets seemed to be spreading their fragrance through the cottage. Violets and roses. The rat, a noisy feeder, had changed into an orchestra of harps, dulcimers and sackbuts that played soft music.

And then, jarring upon these sweet strains, there came the sound of the cottage door opening. And a moment later light shone through the holes in the floor.

Millicent gave Hugo's arm a warning pinch. They looked down. On the floor below stood a lantern, and beside it a man of massive build who, from the galloping noises that floated upwards, appeared to be giving the Empress those calories and proteins which a pig of her dimensions requires so often and in such large quantities.

This Good Samaritan had been stooping. Now he straightened himself and looked about him with an apprehensive eye. He raised the lantern, and its light fell upon his face.

And, as she saw that face, Millicent, forgetting prudence, uttered in a high, startled voice a single word.

'Beach!' cried Millicent.

Down below, the butler stood congealed. It seemed to him that the voice of Conscience had spoken.

IV

Conscience, besides having a musical voice, appeared also to be equipped with feet. Beach could hear them clattering down the stairs, and the volume of noise was so great that it seemed as if

Conscience must be a centipede. But he did not stir. It would have required at that moment a derrick to move him, and there was no derrick in the gamekeeper's cottage in the west wood. He was still standing like a statue when Hugo and Millicent arrived. Only when the identity of the newcomers impressed itself on his numbed senses did his limbs begin to twinge and show some signs of relaxing. For he looked on Hugo as a friend. Hugo, he felt, was one of the few people in his world who, finding him in his present questionable position, might be expected to take the broad and sympathetic view.

He nerved himself to speak.

'Good evening, sir. Good evening, miss.'

'What's all this?' said Hugo.

Years ago, in his hot and reckless youth, Beach had once heard that question from the lips of a policeman. It had disconcerted him then. It disconcerted him now.

'Well, sir,' he replied.

Millicent was staring at the Empress, who, after one courteous look of inquiry at the intruders, had given a brief grunt of welcome and returned to the agenda.

'*You* stole her, Beach? *You!*'

The butler quivered. He had known this girl since her long hair and rompers days. She had sported in his pantry. He had cut elephants out of paper for her and taught her tricks with bits of string. The shocked note in her voice seared him like vitriol. To her, he felt, niece to the Earl of Emsworth and trained by his lordship from infancy in the best traditions of pig-worship, the theft of the Empress must seem the vilest of crimes. He burned to re-establish himself in her eyes.

There comes in the life of every conspirator a moment when loyalty to his accomplices wavers before the urge to make things right for himself. We can advance no more impressive proof of the nobility of the butler's soul than that he did not obey this impulse. Millicent's accusing eyes were piercing him, but he remained true to his trust. Mr. Ronald had sworn him to secrecy: and even to square himself he could not betray him.

And, as if by way of a direct reward from Providence for this sterling conduct, inspiration descended upon Beach.

'Yes, miss,' he replied.

'Oh, Beach!'

'Yes, miss. It was I who stole the animal. I did it for your sake, miss.'

Hugo eyed him sternly.

'Beach,' he said. 'This is pure apple-sauce.'

'Sir?'

'Apple-sauce, I repeat. Why endeavour to swing the lead, Beach? What do you mean, you stole the pig for her sake?'

'Yes,' said Millicent. 'Why for my sake?'

The butler was calm now. He had constructed his story, and he was going to stick to it.

'In order to remove the obstacles in your path, miss.'

'Obstacles?'

'Owing to the fact that you and Mr. Carmody have frequently entrusted me with your – may I say surreptitious correspondence, I have long been cognisant of your sentiments towards one another, miss. I am aware that it is your desire to contract a union with Mr. Carmody, and I knew that there would be objections raised on the part of certain members of the family.'

'So far,' said Hugo critically, 'this sounds to me like drivel of the purest water. But go on.'

'Thank you, sir. And then it occurred to me that, were his lordship's pig to disappear, his lordship would, on recovering the animal, be extremely grateful to whoever restored it. It was my intention to apprise you of the animal's whereabouts, and suggest that you should inform his lordship that you had discovered it. In his gratitude, I fancied, his lordship would consent to the union.'

There could never be complete silence in any spot where Empress of Blandings was partaking of food; but something as near silence was possible followed this speech. In the rays of the lantern Hugo's eyes met Millicent's. In hers, as in his, there was a look of stunned awe. They had heard of faithful old servitors. They read about faithful old servitors. They had seen faithful old servitors on the stage. But never had they dreamed that faithful old servitors could be as faithful as this.

'Oh, Beach!' said Millicent.

She had used the words before. But how different this 'Oh, Beach!' was from that other, earlier 'Oh, Beach!' On that occasion, the exclamation had been vibrant with reproach, pain, disillusionment. Now, it contained gratitude, admiration, and affection almost too deep for speech.

And the same may be said of Hugo's 'Gosh!'

'Beach,' cried Millicent, 'you're an angel!'

'Thank you, miss.'

'A topper!' agreed Hugo.

'Thank you, sir.'

'However did you get such a corking idea?'

'It came to me, miss.'

'I'll tell you what it is, Beach,' said Hugo earnestly. 'When you hand in your dinner-pail in due course of time – and may the moment be long distant! – you've got to leave your brain to the nation. You've simply got to. Have it pickled and put in the British Museum, because it's the outstanding brain of the century. I never heard of anything so brilliant in my puff. Of course the old boy will be all over us.'

'He'll do anything for us,' said Millicent.

'This is not merely a scheme. It is more. It is an egg. Pray silence for your chairman. I want to think.'

Outside, the storm had passed. Birds were singing. Far away, the thunder still rumbled. It might have been the sound of Hugo's thoughts, leaping and jostling one another.

'I've worked it all out,' said Hugo at length. 'Some people might say, Rush to the old boy now and tell him we've found his pig. I say, No. In my opinion we ought to hold this pig for a rising market. The longer we wait, the more grateful he will be. Give him another forty-eight hours, I suggest, and he will have reached the stage where he will deny us nothing.'

'But . . .'

'No! Act precipitately and we are undone. Don't forget that it is not merely a question of getting your uncle's consent to our union. We've got to break it to him that you aren't going to marry Ronnie. And the family have always been pretty keen on your marrying Ronnie. To my mind, another forty-eight hours at the very least is essential.'

'Perhaps you're right.'

'I know I'm right.'

'Then we'll simply leave the Empress here?'

'No,' said Hugo decidedly. 'This place doesn't strike me as safe. If we found her here, anybody might. We require a new safe-deposit, and I know the very one. It's . . .'

Beach came out of the silence. His manner betrayed agitation.

'If it is all the same to you, sir, I would much prefer not to hear it.'

'Eh?'

'It would be a great relief to me, sir, to be able to expunge the entire matter from my mind. I have been under a considerable mental strain of late, sir, and I really don't think I could bear any more of it. Besides, supposing I were questioned, sir. It may be my imagination, but I have rather fancied from the way he has looked at me occasionally that Mr. Baxter harbours suspicions.'

'Baxter always harbours suspicions about something,' said Millicent.

'Yes, miss. But in this case they are well-grounded, and if it is all the same to you and Mr. Carmody, I would greatly prefer that he was not in a position to go on harbouring them.'

'All right, Beach,' said Hugo. 'After what you have done for us, your lightest wish is law. You can be out of this, if you want to. Though I was going to suggest that, if you cared to go on feeding the animal . . .'

'No, sir . . . really . . . if you please . . .'

'Right ho, then. Come along, Millicent. We must be shifting.'

'Are you going to take her away now?'

'This very moment. I pass this handkerchief through the handy ring which you observe in the nose and . . . Ho! Allez-oop! Goodbye, Beach. It is a far, far better thing that I do than I have ever done, I think.'

'Goodbye, Beach,' said Millicent. 'I can't tell you how grateful we are.'

'I am glad to have given satisfaction, miss. I wish you every success and happiness, sir.'

Left alone the butler drew in his breath till he swelled like a balloon, then poured it out again in a long, sighing puff. He picked up the lantern and left the cottage. His walk was the walk of a butler from whose shoulders a great weight has rolled.

V

It is a fact not generally known, for a nice sense of the dignity of his position restrained him from exercising it, that Beach possessed a rather attractive singing-voice. It was a mellow baritone, in timbre not unlike that which might have proceeded from a cask of very old, dry sherry, had it had vocal cords; and we cannot advance a more striking proof of the lightness of heart which had now come upon him than by mentioning that, as he walked home through the wood, he broke his rigid rule and definitely warbled.

*'There's a light in thy bow-er,'*

sang Beach,

*'a light in thy BOW-er ...'*

He felt more like a gay young second footman than a butler of years standing. He listened to the birds with an uplifted heart. Upon the rabbits that sported about his path he bestowed a series of indulgent smiles. The shadow that had darkened his life had passed away. His conscience was at rest.

So completely was this so that when, on reaching the house, he was informed by Footman James that Lord Emsworth had been inquiring for him and desired his immediate presence in the library, he did not even tremble. A brief hour ago, and what menace this announcement would have seemed to him to hold.

But now it left him calm. It was with some little difficulty that, as he mounted the stairs, he kept himself from resuming his song.

'Er – Beach.'

'Your lordship?'

The butler now became aware that his employer was not alone. Dripping in an unpleasant manner on the carpet, for he seemed somehow to have got himself extremely wet, stood the Efficient Baxter. Beach regarded him with a placid eye. What was Baxter to him or he to Baxter now?

'Your lordship?' he said again, for Lord Emsworth appeared to be experiencing some difficulty in continuing the conversation.

'Eh? What? What? Oh, yes.'

The ninth Earl braced himself with a visible effort.

'Er – Beach.'

'Your lordship?'

'I – er – I sent for you, Beach . . .'

'Yes, your lordship?'

At this moment Lord Emsworth's eye fell on a volume on the desk dealing with Diseases in Pigs. He seemed to draw strength from it.

'Beach,' he said, in quite a crisp, masterful voice, 'I sent for you because Mr. Baxter has made a remarkable charge against you. Most extraordinary.'

'I shall be glad to be acquainted with the gravamen of the accusation, your lordship.'

'The what?' asked Lord Emsworth, starting.

'If your lordship would be kind enough to inform me of the substance of Mr. Baxter's charge?'

'Oh, the substance? Yes. You mean the substance? Precisely. Quite so. The substance. Yes, to be sure. Quite so. Quite so. Yes, exactly. No doubt.'

It was plain to the butler that his employer had begun to dodder. Left to himself this human cuckoo-clock would go maundering on like this indefinitely. Respectfully, but with the necessary firmness, he called him to order.

'What is it that Mr. Baxter says, your lordship?'

'Eh? Oh, tell him, Baxter. Yes, tell him, dash it.'

The Efficient Baxter moved a step closer and began to drip on another part of the carpet. His spectacles gleamed determinedly. Here was no stammering, embarrassed Peer of the Realm, but a man who knew his own mind and could speak it.

'I followed you to the gamekeeper's cottage in the west wood just now, Beach.'

'Sir?'

'You heard what I said.'

'Undoubtedly, sir. But I fancied I must be mistaken. I have not been to the spot you mention, sir.'

'I saw you with my own eyes.'

'I can only repeat my asseveration, sir,' said the butler with a saintly meekness.

Lord Emsworth, who had taken another look at *Diseases in Pigs*, became brisk again.

'He says he peeped through the window, dash it.'

Beach raised a respectful eyebrow. It was as if he had said that it was not his place to comment on the pastimes of the Castle's guests, however childish. If Mr. Baxter wished to go out into the woods in the rain and play solitary games of Peep-Bo, that, said the eyebrow, was a matter that concerned Mr. Baxter alone.

'And you were in there, he says, feeding the Empress.'

'Your lordship?'

'And you were in there . . . Dash it, you heard.'

'I beg your pardon, your lordship, but I really fail to comprehend.'

'Well, if you want it in a nutshell, Mr. Baxter says it was you who stole my pig.'

There were few things in the world that the butler considered worth raising both eyebrows at. This was one of the few. He stood for a moment, exhibiting them to Lord Emsworth; then turned to Baxter, so that he could see them, too. This done, he lowered them and permitted about three-eighths of a smile to play for a moment about his lips.

'Might I speak frankly, your lordship?'

'Dash it, man, we want you to speak frankly. That's the whole idea. That's why I sent for you. We want a full confession and the name of your accomplice and all that sort of thing.'

'I hesitate only because what I should like to say may possibly give offence to Mr. Baxter, your lordship, which would be the last thing I should desire.'

The prospect of offending the Efficient Baxter which caused such concern to Beach appeared to disturb his lordship not at all.

'Get on. Say what you like.'

'Well, then, your lordship, I think it possible that Mr. Baxter, if he will pardon my saying so, may have been suffering from a hallucination.'

'Tchah!' said the Efficient Baxter.

'You mean he's potty?' said Lord Emsworth, struck with the idea. In the excitement of his late secretary's information, he had overlooked this simple explanation. Now there came surging back to him all the evidence that went to support such a theory. Those flower-pots. . . . That leap from the library window. He looked at Baxter keenly. There *was* a sort of wild gleam in his eyes. The old coot glitter.

'Really, Lord Emsworth!'

'Oh, I'm not saying you are, my dear fellow. Only . . .'

'It is quite obvious to me,' said Baxter stiffly, 'that this man is lying. Wait!' he continued, raising a hand. 'Are you prepared to come with his lordship and me to the cottage now, at this very moment, and let his lordship see for himself?'

'No, sir.'

'Ha!'

'I should first,' said Beach, 'wish to go downstairs and get my hat.'

'Quite right,' agreed Lord Emsworth cordially. 'Very sensible. Might catch a nasty cold in the head. Certainly get your hat, Beach, and meet us at the front door.'

'Very good, your lordship.'

A bystander, observing the little party that was gathered some five minutes later on the gravel outside the great door of Blandings Castle, would have noticed about it a touch of chill, a certain restraint. None of its three members seemed really in the mood for a ramble through the woods. Beach, though courtly, was not cordial. The face under his bowler hat was the face of a good man misjudged. Baxter was eyeing the sullen sky as though he suspected it of something. As for Lord Emsworth, he had just become conscious that he was about to accompany through dark and deserted ways one who, though on this afternoon's evidence the trend of his tastes seemed to be towards suicide, might quite possibly become homicidal.

'One moment,' said Lord Emsworth.

He scuttled into the house again, and came out looking happier. He was carrying a stout walking stick with an ivory knob on it.

I

Blandings Castle basked in the afterglow of a golden summer evening. Only a memory now was the storm which, two hours since, had raged with such violence through its parks, pleasure grounds and messuages. It had passed, leaving behind it peace and bird-song and a sunset of pink and green and orange and opal and amethyst. The air was cool and sweet, and the earth sent up a healing fragrance. Little stars were peeping down from a rain-washed sky.

To Ronnie Fish, slumped in an armchair in his bedroom on the second floor, the improved weather conditions brought no spiritual uplift. He could see the sunset, but it left him cold. He could hear the thrushes calling in the shrubberies, but did not think much of them. It is, in short, in no sunny mood that we re-introduce Ronald Overbury Fish to the reader of this chronicle.

The meditations of a man who has recently proposed to and been accepted by a girl, some inches taller than himself, for whom he entertains no warmer sentiment than a casual feeling that, take her for all in all, she isn't a bad sort of egg, must of necessity tend towards the sombre: and the surroundings in which Ronnie had spent the latter part of the afternoon had not been of a kind to encourage optimism. At the moment when the skies suddenly burst asunder and the world became a shower-bath, he had been walking along the path that skirted the wall of the kitchen-garden: and the only shelter that offered itself was a gloomy cave or dug-out that led to the heating apparatus of the hothouses. Into this he had dived like a homing rabbit, and here, sitting on a heap of bricks, he had remained for the space of fifty minutes with no company but one small green frog and his thoughts.

The place was a sort of Sargasso Sea into which had drifted all the flotsam and jetsam of the kitchen-garden which it adjoined. There was a wheelbarrow, lacking its wheel and lying drunkenly on its side. There were broken pots in great profusion. There was a heap of withered flowers, a punctured watering can, a rake with large gaps in its front teeth, some potatoes unfit for human consumption and half a dead blackbird. The whole effect was extraordinarily like Hell, and Ronnie's spirits, not high at the start, had sunk lower and lower.

Sobered by rain, wheelbarrows, watering cans, rakes, potatoes and dead blackbirds, not to mention the steady, supercilious eye of a frog which resembled that of a Bishop at the Athenaeum inspecting a shy new member, Ronnie had begun definitely to repent of the impulse which had led him to ask Millicent to be his wife. And now, in the cosier environment of his bedroom, he was regretting it more than ever.

Like most people who have made a defiant and dramatic gesture and then have leisure to reflect, he was oppressed by a feeling that he had gone considerably farther than was prudent. Samson, as he heard the pillars of the temple begin to crack, must have felt the same. Gestures are all very well while the intoxication lasts. The trouble is that it lasts such a very little while.

In asking Millicent to marry him, he had gone, he now definitely realized, too far. He had overdone it. It was not that he had any objection to Millicent as a wife. He had none whatever – provided she were somebody else's wife. What was so unpleasant was the prospect of being married to her himself.

He groaned in spirit, and became aware that he was no longer alone. The door had opened, and his friend Hugo Carmody was in the room. He noted with a dull surprise that Hugo was in the conventional costume of the English gentleman about to dine. He had not supposed the hour so late.

'Hullo,' said Hugo. 'Not dressed? The gong's gone.'

It now became clear to Ronnie that he simply was not equal to facing his infernal family at the dinner-table. He supposed that Millicent had spread the news of their engagement by this time, and that meant discussions, wearisome congratulations, embraces from his Aunt Constance, chaff of the vintage of 1895 from his Uncle Galahad – in short, fuss and gabble. And he was in no mood for fuss and gabble. Pot-luck with a tableful of Trappist monks he might just have endured, but not a hearty feed with the family.

'I don't want any dinner.'

'No dinner?'

'No.'

'Ill or something?'

'No.'

'But you don't want any dinner? I see. Rummy! However, your affair, of course. It begins to look as if I should have to don the nose-bag alone. Beach tells me that Baxter also will be absent from the trough. He's upset about something, it seems, and has asked for a snort and sandwiches in the smoking-room. And as for the pustule Pilbeam,' said Hugo grimly, 'I propose to interview him at the earliest possible date. And after that he won't want any dinner, either.'

'Where are the rest of them?'

'Didn't you know?' said Hugo, surprised. 'They're dining over at old Parsloe's. Your aunt, Lord Emsworth, old Galahad and Millicent.' He coughed. A moment of some slight embarrassment impended. 'I say, Ronnie, old man, while on the subject of Millicent . . .'

'Well?'

'You know that engagement of yours?'

'What about it?'

'It's off.'

'Off?'

'Right off. A wash-out. She's changed her mind.'

'What!'

'Yes. She's going to marry me. I may tell you we have been engaged for weeks – one of those secret betrothals – but we had a row. Row now over. Complete reconciliation. So she asked me to break it to you gently that in the circs, she proposes to return you to store.'

A thrill of ecstasy shot through Ronnie. He felt as men on the scaffold feel when the messenger bounds in with the reprieve.

'Well, that's the first bit of good news I've had for a long time,' he said.

'You mean you didn't want to marry Millicent?'

'Of course I didn't.'

'Not so much of the "of course", laddie,' said Hugo, offended. 'She's an awfully nice girl . . .'

'An angel. Shropshire's leading seraph.'

'. . . but I'm not in love with her any more than she's in love with me.'

'In that case,' said Hugo, with justifiable censure, 'why propose to her? A goofy proceeding, it seems to me.' He clicked his tongue. 'Of course! I see what happened. You grabbed Millicent to score off Sue, and she grabbed you to score off me. And now, I suppose, you've fixed it up with Sue again. Very sound. Couldn't have made a wiser move. She's obviously the girl for you.'

Ronnie winced. The words had touched a nerve. He had been trying not to think of Sue, but without success. Her picture insisted on rising before him. Not being able to exclude her from his thoughts, he had tried to think of her bitterly.

'I haven't,' he cried.

Extraordinary how difficult it was, even now, to think bitterly of Sue. Sue was Sue. That was the fundamental fact that hampered him. Try as he might to concentrate it on the tragedy of Mario's restaurant, his mind insisted on slipping back to earlier scenes of sunshine and happiness.

'You haven't?' said Hugo, damped.

That Ronnie could possibly be in ignorance of Sue's arrival at the Castle never occurred to him. Long ere this, he took it for granted, they must have met. And he assumed, from the equanimity with which his friend had received the news of the loss of Millicent, that Sue and he must have had just such another heart-to-heart talk as had taken place in the room above the gamekeeper's cottage. The dour sullenness of Ronnie's face made his kindly heart sink.

'You mean you haven't fixed things up?'

'No.'

Ronnie writhed. Sue in his car. Sue up the river. Sue in his arms to the music of sweet saxophones. Sue laughing. Sue smiling. Sue in the Springtime, with the little breezes ruffling her hair. . . .

He forced his mind away from these weakening visions. Sue at Mario's . . . . That was better. . . . Sue letting him down. . . . Sue hobnobbing with the blister Pilbeam. . . . That was much better.

'I think you're being very hard on that poor little girl, Ronnie.'

'Don't call her a poor little girl.'

'I will call her a poor little girl,' said Hugo firmly. 'To me, she is a poor little girl, and I don't care who knows it. I don't mind telling you that my heart bleeds for her. Bleeds profusely. And I must say I should have thought . . .'

'I don't want to talk about her.'

'. . . after her doing what she has done . . .'

'I don't want to talk about her, I tell you.'

Hugo sighed. He gave it up. The situation was what they called an *impasse*.

Too bad. His best friend and a dear little girl like that parted for ever. Two jolly good eggs sundered for all eternity. Oh, well, that was Life.

'If you want to talk about anything,' said Ronnie, 'you had much better talk about this engagement of yours.'

'Only too glad, old man. Was afraid it might bore you, or would have touched more freely on subject.'

'I suppose you realize the Family will squash it flat?'

'Oh, no, they won't.'

'You think my Aunt Constance is going to leap about and bang the cymbals?'

'The Keeble, I admit,' said Hugo, with a faint shiver, 'may

make her presence felt to some extent. But I rely on the ninth earl's support and patronage. Before long, I shall be causing the ninth to look on me as a son.'

'How?'

For a moment Hugo almost yielded to the temptation to confide in this friend of his youth. Then he realized the unwisdom of such a course. By an odd coincidence, he was thinking exactly the same of Ronnie as Ronnie at an earlier stage of this history had thought of him. Ronnie, he considered, though a splendid chap, was not fitted to be a repository of secrets. A blabber. A sieve. The sort of fellow who would spread a secret hither and thither all over the place before nightfall.

'Never mind,' he said. 'I have my methods.'

'What are they?'

'Just methods,' said Hugo, 'and jolly good ones. Well, I'll be pushing off. I'm late. Sure you won't come down to dinner? Then I'll be going. It is imperative that I get hold of Pilbeam with all possible speed. Don't want the sun to go down on my wrath. All has ended happily in spite of him, but that's no reason why he shouldn't be massacred. I look on myself as a man with a public duty.'

For some minutes after the door had closed, Ronnie remained humped up in the chair. Then, in spite of everything, there began to creep upon him a desire for food, too strong to be resisted. Perfect health and a tealess afternoon in the open had given him a compelling appetite. He still shrank from the thought of the dining-room. Fond as he was of Hugo, he simply could not stand his conversation to-night. A chop at the Emsworth Arms would meet the case. He could get down there in five minutes in his two-seater.

He rose. His mind, as he moved to the door, was not entirely occupied with thoughts of food. Hugo's parting words had turned it in the direction of Pilbeam again.

What had brought Pilbeam to the Castle, he did not know. But now that he was here, let him look out for himself! A couple of minutes alone with P. Frobisher Pilbeam was just the medicine his bruised soul required. Apparently, from what he had said, Hugo also entertained some grievance against the man. It could be nothing compared with his own.

Pilbeam! The cause of all his troubles. Pilbeam! The snake in the grass. Pilbeam . . . ! Yes . . . ! His heart might be broken, his life a wreck, but he could still enjoy the faint consolation of dealing faithfully with Pilbeam.

He went out into the corridor. And, as he did so, Percy Pilbeam came out of the room opposite.

## II

Pilbeam had dressed for dinner with considerable care. Owing to the fact that Lord Emsworth, in his woollen-headed way, had completely forgotten to inform him of the exodus to Matchingham Hall, he was expecting to meet a gay and glittering company at the meal, and had prepared himself accordingly. Looking at the result in the mirror, he had felt a glow of contentment. This glow was still warming him as he passed into the corridor. As his eyes fell on Ronnie, it faded abruptly.

In the days of his editorship of *Society Spice*, that frank and fearless journal, P. Frobisher Pilbeam had once or twice had personal encounters with people having no cause to wish him well. They had not appealed to him. He was a man who found no pleasure in physical violence. And that physical violence threatened now was only too sickeningly plain. It was foreshadowed in the very manner in which this small but sturdy young man confronting him had begun to creep forward. Pilbeam, who was an F.R.Z.S., had seen leopards at the Zoo creep just like that.

Years of conducting a weekly scandal-sheet, followed by a long period of activity as a private enquiry agent, undoubtedly train a man well for the exhibition of presence-of-mind in sudden emergencies. One finds it difficult in the present instance to overpraise Percy Pilbeam's ready resource. Had a great military strategist been present, he would have nodded approval. With the grim menace of Ronnie Fish coming closer and closer, Percy Pilbeam did exactly what Napoleon, Hannibal or the great Duke of Marlborough would have done. Reaching behind him for the handle and twisting it sharply, he slipped through the door of his bedroom, banged it, and was gone. Many an eel has disappeared into the mud with less smoothness and celerity.

If the leopard which he resembled had seen its prey vanish into the undergrowth just before dinner-time, it would probably have expressed its feelings in exactly the same kind of short, rasping cry as proceeded from Ronnie Fish, witnessing this masterly withdrawal. For an instant he was completely taken aback. Then he plunged for the door and plunged into the room.

He stood, baffled. Pilbeam had vanished. To Ronnie's astonished eyes the apartment appeared entirely free from detectives in any shape or form whatsoever. There was the bed. There were the chairs. There were the carpet, the dressing-table and the book-shelf. But of private enquiry agents there was a complete shortage.

How long this miracle would have continued to afflict him

one cannot say. His mind was still dealing dazedly with it, when there came to his ears a sharp click, as of a key being turned in the lock. It seemed to proceed from a hanging-cupboard at the other side of the room.

Old Miles Fish, Ronnie's father, might as Lord Emsworth had asserted, have been the biggest fool in the Brigade of Guards, but his son could reason and deduce. Springing forward, he tugged at the handle of the cupboard. The door stood fast.

At the same moment there filtered through it the sound of muffled breathing.

Ronnie was already looking grim. He now looked grimmer. He placed his lips to the panel.

'Come out of that!'

The breathing stopped.

'All right,' said Ronnie, with a hideous calm. 'Right jolly ho! I can wait.'

For some moments there was silence. Then from the beyond a voice spoke in reply.

'Be reasonable!' said the voice.

'Reasonable?' said Ronnie thickly. 'Reasonable, eh?' He choked. 'Come out! I only want to pull your head off,' he added, with a note of appeal.

The voice became conciliatory.

'I know what you're upset about,' it said.

'You do, eh?'

'Yes, I quite understand. But I can explain everything.'

'What?'

'I say I can explain everything.'

'You can, can you?'

'Quite,' said the voice.

Up till now Ronnie had been pulling. It now occurred to him

that pushing might possibly produce more satisfactory results. So he pushed. Nothing, however, happened. Blandings Castle was a house which rather prided itself on its solidity. Its wall, were walls and its doors doors. No jimcrack work here. The cupboard creaked, but did not yield.

'I say!'

'Well?'

'I wish you'd listen. I tell you I can explain everything. About that night at Mario's I mean. I know exactly how it is. You think Miss Brown is fond of me. I give you my solemn word she can't stand the sight of me. She told me so herself.'

A pleasing thought came to Ronnie.

'You can't stay in there all night,' he said.

'I don't want to stay in here all night.'

'Well, come on out then.'

The voice became plaintive.

'I tell you she had never set eyes on me before that night at Mario's. She was dining with that fellow Carmody, and he went out and I came over and introduced myself. No harm in that, was there?'

Ronnie wondered if kicking would do any good. A tender feeling for his toes, coupled with the reflection that his Uncle Clarence might have something to say if he started breaking up cupboard doors, caused him to abandon the scheme. He stood, breathing tensely.

'Just a friendly word, that's all I came over to say. Why shouldn't a fellow introduce himself to a girl and say a friendly word?'

'I wish I'd got there earlier.'

'I'd have been glad to see you,' said Pilbeam courteously.

'Would you?'

'Quite.'

'I shall be glad to see *you*,' said Ronnie, 'when I can get this damned door open.'

Pilbeam began to fear asphyxiation. The air inside the cupboard was growing closer. Peril lent him the inspiration which it so often does.

'Look here,' he said, 'are you Ronnie?'

Ronnie turned pinker.

'I don't want any of your dashed cheek.'

'No, but listen. Is your name Ronnie?'

Silence without.

'Because, if it is,' said Pilbeam, 'you're the fellow she's come here to see.'

More silence.

'She told me so. In the garden this evening. She came here calling herself Miss Schoonmaker or some such name, just to see you. That ought to show you that I'm not the man she's keen on.'

The silence was broken by a sharp exclamation.

'What's that?'

Pilbeam repeated his remark. A growing hopefulness lent an almost finicky clearness to his diction.

'Come out!' cried Ronnie.

'That's all very well, but . . .'

'Come out, I want to talk to you.'

'You are talking to me.'

'I don't want to bellow this through a door. Come on out. I swear I won't touch you.'

It was not so much Pilbeam's faith in the knightly word of the Fishes that caused him to obey the request as a feeling that, if he stayed cooped up in this cupboard much longer, he would get a rush of blood to the head. Already he was beginning to feel as if he were breathing a solution of dust and moth-balls. He emerged. His hair was rumpled, and he regarded his companion warily. He had the air of a man who has taken his life in his hands. But the word of the Fishes held good. As far as Ronnie was concerned, the war appeared to be over.

'What did you say? She's here?'

'Quite.'

'What do you mean, quite?'

'Certainly. Quite. She got here just before I did. Haven't you seen her?'

'No.'

'Well, she's here. She's in the room they call the Garden Room. I heard her tell that old bird Galahad so. If you go there now,' said Pilbeam insinuatingly, 'you could have a quiet word with her before she goes down to dinner.'

'And she said she had come here to see me?'

'Yes. To explain about that night at Mario's. And what I say,' proceeded Pilbeam warmly, 'is if a girl didn't love a fellow, would she come to a place like this, calling herself Miss Schoolbred or something, simply to see him? I ask you!' said Pilbeam.

Ronnie did not answer. His feelings held him speechless. He was too deep in a morass of remorse to be able to articulate. Indeed, he was in a frame of mind so abased that he almost asked Pilbeam to kick him. The thought of how he had wronged his blameless Sue was almost too bitter to be borne. It bit like a serpent and stung like an adder.

From the surge and riot of his reflections one thought now emerged clearly, shining like a beacon on a dark night. The Garden Room!

Turning without a word, he shot out of the door as quickly as Percy Pilbeam a short while ago had shot in. And Percy Pilbeam, with a deep sigh, went to the dressing-table, took up the brush, and started to restore his hair to a state fit for the eyes of the nobility and gentry. This done, he smoothed his moustache and went downstairs to the drawing-room.

### III

The drawing-room was empty. And, to Pilbeam's surprise, it continued to be empty for quite a considerable time. He felt puzzled. He had expected to meet a reproachful host with an eye on the clock and a haughty hostess clicking her tongue. As the minutes crept by and his solitude remained unbroken, he began to grow restless.

He wandered about the room staring at the pictures, straightening his tie and examining the photographs on the little tables. The last of these was one of Lord Emsworth, taken apparently at about the age of thirty, in long whiskers and the uniform of the Shropshire Yeomanry. He was gazing at this with the fascinated horror which it induced in everyone who saw it suddenly for the first time, when the door at last opened; and with a sinking sensation of apprehension Pilbeam beheld the majestic form of Beach.

For an instant he stood eyeing the butler with that natural alarm which comes to all of us when in the presence of a man who a few short hours earlier has given us one look and made us feel like a condemned food product. Then, his tension relaxed.

It has been well said that for every evil in this world Nature supplies an antidote. If butlers come, can cocktails be far behind? Beach was carrying a tray with glasses and a massive shaker on it; and Pilbeam, seeing these, found himself regarding their formidable bearer almost with equanimity.

'A cocktail, sir?'

'Thanks.'

He accepted a brimming glass. The darkness of its contents suggested a welcome strength. He drank. And instantaneously all through his system beacon-fires seemed to burst into being.

He drained the glass. His whole outlook on life was now magically different. Quite suddenly he had begun to feel equal to a dozen butlers, however glazed their eyes might be.

And it might have been an illusion caused by gin and vermouth, but this butler seemed to have changed considerably for the better since their last meeting. His eyes, though still glassy, had lost the old basilisk quality. There appeared now, in fact, to be something so positively lighthearted about Beach's whole demeanour that the proprietor of the Argus Enquiry Agency was emboldened to plunge into conversation.

'Nice evening.'

'Yes, sir.'

'Nice after the storm.'

'Yes, sir.'

'Came down a bit, didn't it?'

'The rain was extremely heavy, sir. Another cocktail?'

'Thanks.'

The re-lighting of the beacons had the effect of removing from Pilbeam the last trace of diffidence and shyness. He saw now that he had been entirely mistaken in this butler. Encountering him in the hall at the moment of his arrival, he had supposed him supercilious and hostile. He now perceived that he was a butler and a brother. More like Old King Cole, that jolly old soul, indeed, than anybody Pilbeam had met for months.

'I got caught in it,' he said affably.

'Indeed, sir?'

'Yes. Lord Emsworth had been showing me some photographs of that pig of his . . . By the way, in strict confidence . . . what's your name?'

'Beach, sir.'

'In strict confidence, Beach, I know something about that pig.'

'Indeed, sir?'

'Yes. Well, after I had seen the photographs, I went for a walk in the park and the rain came on and I got pretty wet. In fact, I don't mind telling you I had to get under cover and take my trousers off to dry.'

He laughed merrily.

'Another cocktail, sir?'

'Making three in all?'

'Yes, sir.'

'Perhaps you're right,' said Pilbeam.

For some moments he sat, pensive and distrait, listening to the strains of a brass band which seemed to have started playing somewhere in the vicinity. Then his idly floating thoughts drifted back to the mystery which had been vexing him before this delightful butler's entry.

'I say, Beach, I've been waiting here hours and hours. Where's this dinner I heard you beating gongs about?'

'Dinner is ready, sir, but I put it back some little while, as gentlemen aren't punctual in the summer time.'

Pilbeam considered this statement. It sounded to him as if it would make rather a good song-title. Gentlemen aren't punctual in the summertime, in the summertime (I said, In the summertime), So take me back to that old Kentucky shack . . . He tried to fit it to the music which the brass band was playing, but it did not go very well and he gave it up.

'Where is everybody?' he asked.

'His lordship and her ladyship and Mr. Galahad and Miss Threepwood are dining at Matchingham Hall.'

'What! With old Pop Parsloe?'

'With Sir Gregory Parsloe-Parsloe, yes, sir.'

Pilbeam chuckled.

'Well, well, well! Quick worker, old Parsloe. Don't you think so, Beach? I mean, you advise him to do a thing, to act in a certain way, to adopt a certain course of action, and he does it right away. You agree with me, Beach?'

'I fear my limited acquaintance with Sir Gregory scarcely entitles me to offer an opinion, sir.'

'Talking of old Parsloe, Beach . . . you did say your name was Beach?'

'Yes, sir.'

'With a capital B?'

'Yes, sir.'

'Well, talking of old Parsloe, Beach, I could tell you something about him. Something he's up to.'

'Indeed, sir?'

'But I'm not going to. Respect client's confidence. Lips sealed. Professional secret.'

'Yes, sir.'

'As you rightly say, yes. Any more of that stuff in the shaker, Beach?'

'A little, sir, if you consider it judicious.'

'That's just what I do consider it. Start pouring.'

The detective sipped luxuriously, fuller and fuller every moment of an uplifting sense of well-being. If the friendship which had sprung up between himself and the butler was possibly a little one-sided, on the one side on which it did exist it was warm, even fervent. It seemed to Pilbeam that for the first time since he had arrived at Blandings Castle he had found a real chum, a kindred soul in whom he might confide. And he was filled with an overwhelming desire to confide in somebody.

'As a matter of fact, Beach,' he said, 'I could tell you all sorts of things about all sorts of people. Practically everybody in this house I could tell you something about. What's the name of that chap with the light hair, for instance? The old boy's secretary?'

'Mr. Carmody, sir.'

'Carmody! That's the name. I've been trying to remember it. Well, I could tell you something about Carmody.'

'Indeed, sir?'

'Yes. Something about Carmody that would interest you very much. I saw Carmody this afternoon when Carmody didn't see me.'

'Indeed, sir?'

'Yes. Where is Carmody?'

'I imagine he will be down shortly, sir. Mr. Ronald also.'

'Ronald!' Pilbeam drew in his breath sharply. 'There's a tough baby, Beach. That Ronnie. Do you know what he wanted to do just now? Murder me!'

In Beach's opinion, for he did not look on Percy Pilbeam as a very necessary member of society, this would have been a commendable act, and he regretted that its consummation had been prevented. He was also feeling that the conscientious butler he had always prided himself on being would long ere this have withdrawn and left this man to talk to himself. But even the best of butlers have human emotions, and the magic of Pilbeam's small-talk held Beach like a spell. It reminded him of the Gossip page of *Society Spice*, a paper to which he was a regular subscriber. He was piqued and curious. So far, it was true, his companion had merely hinted, but something seemed to tell him that, if he lingered on, a really sensational news-item would shortly emerge.

He had never been more right in his life. Pilbeam by this time had finished the fourth cocktail, and the urge to confide had become over powering. He looked at Beach, and it nearly made him cry to think that he was holding anything back from such a splendid fellow.

'And do you know why he wanted to murder me, Beach?'

It scarcely seemed to the butler that the action required anything in the nature of a reasoned explanation, but he murmured the necessary response.

'I could not say, sir.'

'Of course you couldn't. How could you? You don't know. That's why I'm telling you. Well, listen. He's in love with a girl in the chorus at the Regal, a girl named Sue Brown, and he thought I had been taking her out to dinner. That's why he wanted to murder me, Beach.'

'Indeed, sir?'

The butler spoke calmly, but he was deeply stirred. He had always flattered himself that the inmates of Blandings Castle kept few secrets from him, but this was something new.

'Yes. That was why. I had the dickens of a job holding him off, I can tell you. Do you know what saved me, Beach?'

'No, sir.'

'Presence of mind. I put it to him – to Ronnie – I put it to Ronnie as a reasonable man that, if this girl loved me, would she have come to this place, pretending to be Miss Shoemaker, simply so as to see him?'

'Sir!'

'Yes, that's who Miss Shoemaker is, Beach. She's a chorus girl called Sue Brown, and she's come here to see Ronnie.'

Beach stood transfixed. His eyes swelled bulbously from their sockets. He was incapable of even an 'Indeed, sir?'

He was still endeavouring to assimilate this extraordinary revelation when Hugo Carmody entered the room.

'Ah!' said Hugo, his eye falling on Pilbeam. He stiffened. He stood looking at the detective like Schopenhauer's butcher at the selected lamb.

'Leave us, Beach,' he said, in a grave, deep voice.

The butler came out of his trance.

'Sir?'

'Pop off.'

'Very good, sir.'

The door closed.

'I've been looking for you, viper,' said Hugo.

'Have you, Carmody?' said Percy Pilbeam effervescently. 'I've been looking for you, too. Got something I want to talk to you about. Each looking for each. Or am I thinking of a couple of other fellows? Come right in, Carmody, and sit down. Good old Carmody! Jolly old Carmody! Splendid old Carmody! Well, well, well, well, well!'

If the lamb mentioned above had suddenly accosted the above-mentioned butcher in a similar strain of hearty camaraderie, it could have hardly disconcerted him more than Pilbeam with these cheery words disconcerted Hugo. His stern, set gaze became a gaping stare.

Then he pulled himself together. What did words matter? He

had no time to bother about words. Action was what he was after. Action!

'I don't know if you're aware of it, worm,' he said, 'but you came jolly near to blighting my life.'

'Doing what, Carmody?'

'Blighting my life.'

'Listen to me while I tell you of the Spaniard who blighted my life,' sang Percy Pilbeam, letting it go like a lark in the Springtime. He had never felt happier or in more congenial society. 'How did I blight your life, Carmody?'

'You didn't.'

'You said I did.'

'I said you tried to.'

'Make up your mind, Carmody.'

'Don't keep calling me Carmody.'

'But, Carmody,' protested Pilbeam, 'it's your name, isn't it? Certainly it is. Then why try to hush it up, Carmody? Be frank and open. I don't mind people knowing my name. I glory in it. It's Pilbeam – Pilbeam – Pilbeam – that's what it is – Pilbeam!'

'In about thirty seconds,' said Hugo, 'it will be Mud.'

It struck Percy Pilbeam for the first time that in his companion's manner there was a certain peevishness.

'Something the matter?' he asked, concerned.

'I'll tell you what's the matter.'

'Do, Carmody, do,' said Pilbeam. 'Do, do, do. Confide in me. I like your face.'

He settled himself in a deep arm-chair, and putting the tips of his fingers together after a little preliminary difficulty in making them meet, leaned back, all readiness to listen to whatever trouble it was that was disturbing this new friend of his.

'Some days ago, insect . . .'

Pilbeam opened his eyes.

'Speak up, Carmody,' he said. 'Don't mumble.'

Hugo's fingers twitched. He regarded his companion with a burning eye, and wondered why he was wasting time talking instead of at once proceeding to the main business of the day and knocking the fellow's head off at the roots. What saved Pilbeam was the reclining position he had assumed. If you are a Carmody and a sportsman, you cannot attack even a viper, if it persists in lying back on its spine and keeping its eyes shut.

'Some days ago,' he began again, 'I called at your office. And after we had talked of this and that, I left. I discovered later that immediately upon my departure you had set your foul spies on my trail and had instructed them to take notes of my movements and report on them. The result being that I came jolly close to having my bally life ruined. And, if you want to know what I'm going to do, I'm going to haul you out of that chair and turn you round and kick you hard and go on kicking till I kick you out of the house. And if you dare to shove your beastly little nose back inside the place, I'll disembowel you.'

Pilbeam unclosed his eyes.

'Nothing,' he said, 'could be fairer than that. Nevertheless, that's no reason why you should go about stealing pigs.'

Hugo had often read stories in which people reeled and would have fallen, had they not clutched at whatever it was that they clutched at. He had never expected to undergo that experience himself. But it is undoubtedly the fact that, if he had not at this moment gripped the back of a chair, he would have been hard put to it to remain perpendicular.

'Pig-pincher!' said Pilbeam austerely, and closed his eyes again.

Hugo, having established his equilibrium by means of the

chair, had now moved away. He was making a strong effort to recover his morale. He picked up the photograph of Lord Emsworth in his Yeomanry uniform and looked at it absently; then, as if it had just dawned upon him, put it down with a shudder like a man who finds that he had been handling a snake.

'What do you mean?' he said thickly.

Pilbeam's eyes opened.

'What do I mean? What do you think I mean? I mean you're a pig-pincher. That's what I mean. You go to and fro, sneaking pigs and hiding them in caravans.'

Hugo took up Lord Emsworth's photograph again, saw what he was doing, and dropped it quickly. Pilbeam had closed his eyes once more, and, looking at him, Hugo could not repress a reluctant thrill of awe. He had often read about the superhuman intuition of detectives, but he had never before been privileged to observe it in operation. Then an idea occurred to him.

'Did you see me?'

'What say, Carmody?'

'Did you see me?'

'Yes, I see you, Carmody,' said Pilbeam playfully. 'Peep-bo!'

'Did you see me put that pig in the caravan?'

Pilbeam nodded eleven times in rapid succession.

'Certainly I saw you, Carmody. Why shouldn't I see you, considering I'd been caught in the rain and taken shelter in the caravan and was in there with my trousers off, trying to dry them because I'm subject to lumbago?'

'I didn't see you.'

'No, Carmody, you did not. And I'll tell you why, Carmody. Because I heard a girl's voice outside saying "Be quick, or somebody will come along!" and I hid. You don't suppose I would let a sweet girl see me in knee-length mesh-knit underwear, do you? Not done, Carmody,' said Pilbeam, severely. 'Not cricket.'

Hugo was experiencing the bitterness which comes to all criminals who discover, too late, that they have undone themselves by trying to be clever. It had seemed at the time such a good idea to remove the Empress from the gamekeeper's cottage in the west wood and place her in Baxter's caravan, where nobody would think of looking. How could he have anticipated that the caravan would be bulging with blighted detectives?

At this tense moment, the door opened and Beach appeared.

'I beg your pardon, sir, but do you propose to wait any longer for Mr. Ronald?'

'Eh?'

'Certainly not,' said Pilbeam. 'Who the devil's Mr. Ronald, I should like to know? I didn't come to this place to do a fast-cure. I want my dinner, and I want it now. And if Mr. Ronald doesn't like it, he can do the other thing.' He strode in a dominating manner to the door. 'Come along, Carmody. Din-dins.'

Hugo had sunk into a chair.

'I don't want any dinner,' he said, dully.

'You don't want any dinner?'

'No.'

'No dinner?'

'No.'

Pilbeam shrugged his shoulders impatiently.

'The man's an ass,' he said.

He headed for the stairs. His manner seemed to indicate that he washed his hands of Hugo.

Beach lingered.

'Shall I bring you some sandwiches, sir?'

'No thanks. What's that?'

A loud crash had sounded. The butler went to the door and looked out.

'It is Mr. Pilbeam, sir. He appears to have fallen downstairs.'

For an instant a look of hope crept into Hugo's careworn face.

'Has he broken his neck?'

'Apparently not, sir.'

'Ah,' said Hugo regretfully.

I

The Efficient Baxter had retired to the smoking-room shortly before half-past seven. He desired silence and solitude, and in this cosy haven he got both. For a few minutes nothing broke the stillness but the slow ticking of a clock on the mantelpiece. Then from the direction of the hall there came a new sound, faint at first but swelling and swelling to a frenzied blare, seeming to throb through the air with a note of passionate appeal like a woman wailing for her demon lover. It was that tocsin of the soul, that muezzin of the country-house, the dressing-for-dinner gong.

Baxter did not stir. The summons left him unmoved. He had heard it, of course. Butler Beach was a man who swung a pretty gong-stick. He had that quick fore-arm flick and wristy follow-through which stamped the master. If you were anywhere within a quarter of a mile or so, you could not help hearing him. But the sound had no appeal for Baxter. He did not propose to go in to dinner. He wanted to be alone with his thoughts.

They were not the sort of thoughts with which most men would have wished to be left alone, being both dark and bitter. That expedition to the gamekeeper's cottage in the west wood had not proved a pleasure-trip for Rupert Baxter. Reviewing it in his mind, he burned with baffled rage.

And yet everybody had been very nice to him – very nice and tactful. True, at the moment of the discovery that the cottage contained no pig and appeared to have been pigless from its foundation, there had been perhaps just the slightest suspicion of constraint. Lord Emsworth had grasped his ivory-knobbed stick a little more tightly, and had edged behind Beach in a rather noticeable way, his manner saying more plainly than was agreeable, 'If he springs, be ready!' And there had come into the butler's face a look, hard to bear, which was a blend of censure and pity. But after that both of them had been charming.

Lord Emsworth had talked soothingly about light and shade effects. He had said – and Beach agreed with him – that in the darkness of a thunderstorm anybody might have been deceived into supposing that he had seen a butler feeding a pig in the gamekeeper's cottage. It was probably, said Lord Emsworth – and Beach thought so, too – a bit of wood sticking out of the wall or something. He went on to tell a longish story of how he himself, when a boy, had fancied he had seen a cat with flaming eyes. He had concluded by advising Baxter – and Beach said the suggestion was a good one – to hurry home and have a nice cup of hot tea and go to bed.

His attitude, in short, could not have been pleasanter or more considerate. Yet Baxter, as he sat in the smoking-room, burned, as stated, with baffled rage.

The door handle turned. Beach stood on the threshold.

'If you have changed your mind, sir, about dinner, the meal is quite ready.'

He spoke as friend to friend. There was nothing in his manner to suggest that the man he addressed had ever accused him of stealing pigs. As far as Beach was concerned, all was forgotten and forgiven.

But the milk of human kindness, of which the butler was so full, had not yet been delivered on Baxter's doorstep. The hostility in his eye, as he fixed it on his visitor, was so marked that a lesser man than Beach might have been disconcerted.

'I don't want any dinner.'

'Very good, sir.'

'Bring me that whisky and soda quick.'

'Yes, sir.'

The door closed as softly as it had opened, but not before a pang like a red-hot needle had pierced the ex-secretary's bosom. It was caused by the fact that he had distinctly heard the butler, as he withdrew, utter a pitying sigh.

It was the sort of sigh which a kind-hearted man would have given on peeping into a padded cell in which some old friend was connected, and Baxter resented it with all force of an imperious nature. He had not ceased to wonder what, if anything, could be done about it when the refreshments arrived, carried by James the footman. James placed them gently on the table, shot a swift glance of respectful commiseration at the patient, and passed away.

The sigh had cut Baxter like a knife. The look stabbed him like a dagger. For a moment he thought of calling the man back and asking him what the devil he meant by staring at him like that, but wiser counsels prevailed. He contented himself with draining a glass of whisky and soda and swallowing two sandwiches. This done, he felt a little – not much, but a little – better. Before, he would gladly have murdered Beach and James and danced on their graves. Now, he would have been satisfied with straight murder.

However, he was alone at last. That was some slight consolation. Beach had come and gone. Footman James had come and gone. Everybody else must by now be either at Matchingham Hall or assembled in the dining-room. On the solitude which he so greatly desired there could be no further intrusion. He resumed his meditations.

For a time these dealt exclusively with the recent past, and were, in consequence, of a morbid character. Then, as the grateful glow of the whisky began to make itself felt, a softer mood came to Rupert Baxter. His mind turned to thoughts of Sue.

Men as efficient as Rupert Baxter do not fall in love in the generally accepted sense of the term. Their attitude towards the tender passion is more restrained than that of the ordinary feckless young man who loses his heart at first sight with a whoop and a shiver. Baxter approved of Sue. We cannot say more. But this approval, added to the fact that he had been informed by Lady Constance that the girl was the only daughter of a man who possessed sixty million dollars, had been enough to cause him to ear-mark her in his mind as the future Mrs. Baxter. In that capacity he had docketed her and filed her away at the first moment of their meeting.

Naturally, therefore, the remarks which Lord Emsworth had let fall in her hearing had caused him grave concern. It hampers a man in his wooing if the girl he has selected for his bride starts with the idea that he is as mad as a coot. He congratulated himself on the promptitude with which he had handled the situation. That letter which he had written her could not fail to put him right in her eyes.

Rupert Baxter was a man in whose lexicon there was no such word as failure. An heiress like this Miss Schoonmaker would not, he was aware, lack for suitors: but he did not fear them. If only she were making a reasonably long stay at the castle, he felt that he could rely on his force of character to win the day. In fact, it seemed to him that he could almost hear the wedding bells ringing already. Then, coming out of his dreams, he realized that it was the telephone.

He reached for the instrument with a frown, annoyed at the interruption, and spoke with an irritated sharpness.

'Hullo?'

A ghostly voice replied. The storm seemed to have affected the wires.

'Speak up!' barked Baxter.

He banged the telephone violently on the table. The treatment, as is so often the case, proved effective.

'Blandings Castle?' said the voice, no longer ghostly.

'Yes.'

'Post Office, Market Blandings, speaking. Telegram for Lady Constance Keeble.'

'I will take it.'

The voice became faint again. Baxter went through the movements as before.

'Lady Constance Keeble, Blandings Castle, Market Blandings, Shropshire, England,' said the voice, recovering strength, as if it had shaken off a wasting sickness. 'Handed in at Paris.'

'Where?'

'Paris, France.'

'Oh? Well?'

The voice gathered volume.

'"Terribly sorry hear news . . ."'

'What?'

'"News".'

'Yes?'

'"Terribly sorry hear news stop Quite understand stop So disappointed shall be unable come to you later as going back America at end of month stop Do hope we shall be able arrange something when I return next year stop Regards stop!"'

'Yes?'

'Signed "Myra Schoonmaker".'

'Signed – *what?*'

'Myra Schoonmaker.'

Baxter's mouth had fallen open. The forehead above the spectacles was wrinkled, the eyes behind them staring blankly and with a growing horror.

'Shall I repeat?'

'What?'

'Do you wish the message repeated?'

'No,' said Baxter in a choking voice.

He hung up the receiver. There seemed to be something crawling down his back. His brain was numbed.

Myra Schoonmaker! Telegraphing from Paris!

Then who was this girl who was at the Castle calling herself by that preposterous name? An imposter, an adventuress. She must be.

And if he made a move to expose her she would revenge herself by showing Lord Emsworth that letter of his.

In his agitation of the moment he had risen to his feet. He now sat down heavily.

That letter . . . !

He must recover it. He must recover it at once. As long as it remained in the girl's possession, it was a pistol pointed at his head. Once let Lord Emsworth become acquainted with those very frank criticisms of himself which it contained, and not even his ally, Lady Constance, would be able to restore him to his lost secretaryship. The ninth Earl was a mild man, accustomed to bowing to his sister's decrees, but there were limits beyond which he could not be pushed.

And Baxter yearned to be back at Blandings Castle in the position he had once enjoyed. Blandings was his spiritual home. He had held other secretaryships – he held one now, at a salary far higher than that which Lord Emsworth had paid him – but never had he succeeded in recapturing that fascinating sense of power, of importance, of being the man who directed the destinies of one of the largest houses in England.

At all costs he must recover that letter. And the present moment, he perceived, was ideal for the venture. The girl must have the thing in her room somewhere, and for the next hour at least she would be in the dining-room. He would have ample opportunity for a search.

He did not delay. Thirty seconds later he was mounting the stairs, his face set, his spectacles gleaming grimly. A minute later, he reached his destination. No good angel, aware of what the future held, stood on the threshold to bar his entry. The door was ajar. He pushed it open and went in.

II

Blandings Castle, like most places of its size and importance, contained bedrooms so magnificent that they were never used. With their four-poster beds and their superb but rather oppressive tapestries, they had remained untenanted since the time when Queen Elizabeth, dodging from country-house to country-house in that restless, snipe-like way of hers, had last slept in them. Of the guest-rooms still in commission, the most luxurious was that which had been given to Sue.

At the moment when Baxter stole cautiously in, it was looking its best in the gentle evening light. But Baxter was not in sight-seeing mood. He ignored the carved bedstead, the cosy arm-chairs, the pictures, the decorations, and the soft carpet into which his feet sank. The beauty of the sky through the French windows that gave onto the balcony drew but a single brief glance from him. Without delay, he made for the writing-desk which stood against the wall near the bed. It seemed to him a good point of departure for his search.

There were several pigeon-holes in the desk. They contained single sheets of notepaper, double sheets of notepaper, post-cards, envelopes, telegraph-forms, and even a little pad on which the room's occupant was presumably expected to jot down any stray thoughts and reflections on Life which might occur to him or her before turning in for the night. But not one of them contained the fatal letter.

He straightened himself and looked about the room. The drawer of the dressing-table now suggested itself as a possibility. He left the desk and made his way towards it.

The primary requisite of dressing-tables being a good supply of light, they are usually placed in a position to get as much of it as possible. This one was no exception. It stood so near to the open windows that the breeze was ruffling the tassels on its lamp-shades: and Baxter, arriving in front of it, was enabled for the first time to see the balcony in its entirety.

And, as he saw it, his heart seemed to side-slip. Leaning upon the parapet and looking out over the sea of gravel that swept up to the front door from the rhododendron-fringed drive, stood a girl. And not even the fact that her back was turned could prevent Baxter identifying her.

For an instant he remained frozen. Even the greatest men

congeal beneath the chill breath of the totally unexpected. He had assumed as a matter of course that Sue was down in the dining-room, and it took him several seconds to adjust his mind to the unpleasing fact that she was up on her balcony. When he recovered his presence of mind sufficiently to draw noiselessly away from the line of vision, his first emotion was one of irritation. This chopping and changing, this eleventh hour alteration of plans, these sudden decisions to remain upstairs when they ought to be downstairs, were what made women as a sex so unsatisfactory.

To irritation succeeded a sense of defeat. There was nothing for it, he realized, but to give up his quest and go. He started to tip-toe silently to the door, agreeably conscious now of the softness and thickness of the Axminster pile that made it possible to move unheard, and had just reached it, when from the other side there came to his ears a sound of chinking and clattering – the sound, in fact, which is made by plates and dishes when they are carried on a tray to a guest who, after a long railway journey, has asked her hostess if she may take dinner in her room.

Practice makes perfect. This was the second time in the last three hours that Baxter had found himself trapped in a room in which it was vitally urgent that he should not be discovered: and he was getting the technique of the thing. On the previous occasion, in the small library, he had taken to himself wings like a bird and sailed out of the window. In the present crisis, such a course, he perceived immediately, was not feasible. The way of an eagle would profit him nothing. Soaring over the balcony, he would be observed by Sue and would, in addition, unquestionably break his neck. What was needed here was the way of a diving-duck.

And so, as the door-handle turned, Rupert Baxter, even in this black hour efficient, dropped on all-fours and slid under the bed as smoothly as if he had been practising for weeks.

### III

Owing to the restricted nature of his position and the limited range of vision which he enjoys, virtually the only way in which a man who is hiding under a bed can entertain himself is by listening to what is going on outside. He may hear something of interest, or he may hear only the draught sighing along the floor: but, for better or for worse, that is all he is able to do.

The first sound that came to Rupert Baxter was that made by the placing of the tray on the table. Then, after a pause, a pair of squeaking shoes passed over the carpet and squeaked out of hearing. Baxter recognized them as those of Footman Thomas, a confirmed squeaker.

After this somebody puffed, causing him to deduce the presence of Beach.

'Your dinner is quite ready, miss.'

'Oh, thank you.'

The girl had apparently come in from the balcony. A chair scraped to the table. A savoury scent floated to Baxter's nostrils, causing him acute discomfort. He had just begun to realize how extremely hungry he was and how rash he had been, firstly to attempt to dine off a couple of sandwiches, and secondly to undertake a mission like his present one without a square meal inside him.

'That is chicken, miss. *En casserole.*'

Baxter had deduced as much, and was trying not to let his

mind dwell on it. He uttered a silent groan. In addition to the agony of having to smell food, he was beginning to be conscious of a growing cramp in his left leg. He turned on one side and did his best to emulate the easy nonchalance of those Indian fakirs who, doubtless from the best motives, spend the formative years of their lives lying on iron spikes.

'It looks very good.'

'I trust you will enjoy it, miss. Is there anything further that I can do for you?'

'No, thank you. Oh, yes. Would you mind fetching that manuscript from the balcony. I was reading it out there, and I left in on the chair. It's Mr. Threepwood's book.'

'Indeed, miss? An exceedingly interesting compilation, I should imagine?'

'Yes, very.'

'I wonder if it would be taking a liberty, miss, to ask you to inform me later, at your leisure, if I make any appearance in its pages.'

'You?'

'Yes, miss. From what Mr. Galahad has let fall from time to time, I fancy it was his intention to give me printed credit as his authority for certain of the stories which appear in the book.'

'Do you want to be in it?'

'Most decidedly, miss. I should consider it an honour. And it would please my mother.'

'Have you a mother?'

'Yes, miss. She lives at Eastbourne.'

The butler moved majestically onto the balcony, and Sue's mind had turned to speculation about his mother and whether she looked anything like him, when there was a sound of hurrying feet without, the door flew open, and Beach's mother passed from her mind like the unsubstantial fabric of a dream. With a little choking cry she rose to her feet. Ronnie was standing before her.

And meanwhile, if we may borrow an expression from a sister art, what of Hugo Carmody?

It is a defect unfortunately inseparable from any such document as this faithful record of events in and about Blandings Castle that the chronicler, in order to give a square deal to each of the individuals whose fortunes he has undertaken to narrate, is compelled to flit abruptly from one to the other in a manner popularized by the chamois of the Alps leaping from crag to crag. The activities of the Efficient Baxter seeming to him to demand immediate attention, he was reluctantly compelled some little while back to leave Hugo in the very act of reeling beneath a crushing blow. The moment has now come to return to him.

The first effect on a young man of sensibility and gentle upbringing of the discovery that an unfriendly detective has seen him placing stolen pigs in caravans is to induce a stunned condition of mind, a sort of mental coma. The face lengthens. The limbs grow rigid. The tie slips sideways and the cuffs recede into the coat-sleeves. The subject becomes temporarily, in short, a total loss.

It is perhaps as well, therefore, that we did not waste valuable time watching Hugo in the process of digesting Percy Pilbeam's sensational announcement, for it would have been like looking at a statue. If the reader will endeavour to picture Rodin's Thinker in a dinner-jacket and trousers with braid down the sides, he will have got the general idea. At the instant when Hugo Carmody makes his reappearance, life has just begun to return to the stiffened frame.

And with life came the dawning of intelligence. This ghastly snag which had popped up in his path was too big, reflected Hugo, for any man to tackle. It called for a woman's keener wit. His first act on emerging from the depths, therefore, was to leave the drawing-room and totter downstairs to the telephone. He got the number of Matchingham Hall and, establishing communication with Sir Gregory Parsloe-Parsloe's butler, urged him to summon Miss Millicent Threepwood from the dinner-table. The butler said in rather a reproving way that Miss Threepwood was at the moment busy drinking soup. Hugo, with the first flash of spirit he had shown for a quarter of an hour, replied that he didn't care if she was bathing in it. Fetch her, said Hugo, and almost added the words 'You scurvy knave'. He then clung weakly to the receiver, waiting, and in a short while a sweet, but agitated, voice floated to him across the wire.

'Hugo?'

'Millicent?'

'Is that you?'

'Yes. Is that you?'

'Yes.'

Anything in the nature of misunderstanding was cleared away. It was both of them.

'What's up?'

'Everything's up.'

'How do you mean?'

'I'll tell you,' said Hugo, and did so. It was not a difficult story to tell. Its plot was so clear that a few whispered words sufficed.

'You don't mean that?' said Millicent, the tale concluded.

'I do mean that.'

'Oh, golly!' said Millicent.

Silence followed. Hugo waited palpitatingly. The outlook seemed to him black. He wondered if he had placed too much reliance in woman's wit. That 'Golly!' had not been hopeful.

'Hugo!'

'Hullo?'

'This is a bit thick.'

'Yes,' agreed Hugo. The thickness had not escaped him.

'Well, there's only one thing to do.'

A faint thrill passed through Hugo Carmody. One would be enough. Woman's wit was going to bring home the bacon after all.

'Listen!'

'Well?'

'The only thing to do is for me to go back to the dining-room and tell Uncle Clarence you've found the Empress.'

'Eh?'

'Found her, fathead.'

'How do you mean?'

'Found her in the caravan.'

'But weren't you listening to what I was saying?' There were tears in Hugo's voice. 'Pilbeam saw us putting her there.'

'I know.'

'Well, what's our move when he says so?'

'Stout denial.'

'Eh?'

'We stoutly deny it,' said Millicent.

The thrill passed through Hugo again, stronger than before. It might work. Yes, properly handled, it would work. He poured broken words of love and praise into the receiver.

'That's right,' he cried. 'I see daylight. I will go to Pilbeam and tell him privately that if he opens his mouth I'll strangle him.'

'Well, hold on. I'll go and tell Uncle Clarence. I expect he'll be out in a moment to have a word with you.'

'Half a minute! Millicent!'

'Well?'

'When am I supposed to have found this ghastly pig?'

'Ten minutes ago, when you were taking a stroll before your dinner. You happened to pass the caravan and you heard an odd noise inside, and you looked to see what it was, and there was the Empress and you then raced back to the house to telephone.'

'But, Millicent! Half a minute!'

'Well?'

'The old boy will think Baxter stole her.'

'So he will! Isn't that splendid! Well, hold on.'

Hugo resumed his vigil. It was some moments later that a noise like the clucking of fowls broke out at the Matchingham Hall end of the wire. He deduced correctly that this was caused by the ninth Earl of Emsworth endeavouring to clothe his thoughts in speech.

'Kuk-kuk-kuk . . .'

'Yes, Lord Emsworth?'

'Kuk-Carmody!'

'Yes, Lord Emsworth?'

'Is this true?'

'Yes, Lord Emsworth.'

'You've found the Empress?'

'Yes, Lord Emsworth.'

'In that feller Baxter's caravan?'

'Yes, Lord Emsworth.'

'Well, I'll be damned!'

'Yes, Lord Emsworth.'

So far Hugo Carmody had found his share of the dialogue delightfully easy. On these lines he would have been prepared to continue it all night. But there was something else besides, 'Yes, Lord Emsworth' that he must now endeavour to say. There is a tide in the affairs of men which, taken at the flood, leads on to fortune: and that tide, he knew, would never rise higher than at the present moment. He swallowed twice to unlimber his vocal cords.

'Lord Emsworth,' he said, and, though his heart was beating fast, his voice was steady, 'there is something I would like to take this opportunity of saying. It will come as a surprise to you, but I hope not as an unpleasant surprise. I love your niece Millicent, and she loves me, Lord Emsworth. We have loved each other for many weeks and it is my hope that you will give your consent to our marriage. I am not a rich man, Lord Emsworth. In fact, strictly speaking, except for my salary I haven't a bean in the world. But my Uncle Lester owns Rudge Hall, in Worcestershire – I daresay you have heard of the place? You turn to the left off the main road to Birmingham and go about a couple of miles . . . well, anyway, it's a biggish sort of place in Worcestershire and my Uncle Lester owns it and the property is entailed and I'm next in succession. . . . I don't pretend that my Uncle Lester shows any indications of passing in his checks, he was extremely fit last time I saw him, but, after all, he's getting on and all flesh is as grass and, as I say, I'm next man in, so I shall eventually succeed to quite a fairish bit of the stuff and a house and park and rentroll and all that, so what I mean is, it isn't as if I wasn't in a position to support Millicent later on, and if you realized, Lord Emsworth, how we love one another I'm sure you would see that it wouldn't be playing the game to put any obstacles in the way of our happiness, so what I'm driving at, if you follow me, is, may we charge ahead?'

There was dead silence at the other end of the wire. It seemed as if the revelation of a good man's love had struck Lord Emsworth dumb. It was only some moments later, after he had said 'Hullo!' six times and 'I say, are you there?' twice that it was borne upon Hugo that he had wasted two hundred and eighty words of the finest eloquence on empty space.

His natural chagrin at this discovery was sensibly diminished by the sudden sound of Millicent's voice in his ear.

'Hullo!'

'Hullo!'

'Hullo!'

'Hullo?'

'Hugo!'

'Hullo!'

'I say, Hugo!' She spoke with the joyous excitement of a girl who has just emerged from the centre of a family dog-fight. 'I say, Hugo, things are hotting up here properly. I sprung it on Uncle Clarence just now that I want to marry you!'

'So did I. Only he wasn't there.'

'I said "Uncle Clarence, aren't you grateful to Mr. Carmody for finding the Empress?" and he said "Yes, yes, yes, yes, yes, to be sure. Capital boy! Capital boy! Always liked him." And I said "I suppose you wouldn't by any chance let me marry him?" and he said "Eh, what? Marry him?" "Yes," I said. "Marry him." And he said "Certainly, certainly, certainly, certainly, by all means." And then Aunt Constance had a fit, and Uncle Gally said she was a kill-joy and ought to be ashamed of herself for throwing the gaff into love's young dream, and Uncle Clarence kept on saying "Certainly, certainly, certainly." I don't know what old Parsloe thinks of it all. He's sitting in his chair, looking at the ceiling and drinking hock. The butler left at the end of round one. I'm going back to see how it's all coming out. Hold the line.'

A man for whom Happiness and Misery are swaying in the scales three miles away, and whose only medium of learning the result of the contest is a telephone wire, is not likely to ring off impatiently. Hugo sat tense and breathless, like one listening in on the radio to a championship fight in which he has a financial interest. It was only when a cheery voice spoke at his elbow that he realized that his solitude had been invaded, and by Percy Pilbeam at that.

Percy Pilbeam was looking rosy and replete. He swayed slightly and his smile was rather wider and more pebble-beached than a total abstainer's would have been.

'Hullo, Carmody,' said Percy Pilbeam. 'What ho, Carmody. So here you are, Carmody.'

It came to Hugo that he had something to say to this man.

'Here, you!' he cried.

'Yes, Carmody?'

'Do you want to be battered to a pulp?'

'No, Carmody.'

'Then listen. You didn't see me put that pig in the caravan. Understand?'

'But I did, Carmody.'

'You didn't – not if you want to go on living.'

Percy Pilbeam appeared to be in a mood not only of keen intelligence but of the utmost reasonableness and amiability.

'Say no more, Carmody,' he said agreeably. 'I take your point. You want me not to tell anybody I saw you put that caravan in the pig. Quite, Carmody, quite.'

'Well, bear it in mind.'

'I will, Carmody. Oh yes, Carmody, I will. I'm going for a stroll outside, Carmody. Care to join me?'

'Go to hell!'

'Quite,' said Percy Pilbeam.

He tacked unsteadily to the door, aimed himself at it and passed through. And a moment later Millicent's voice spoke.

'Hugo?'

'Hullo?'

'Oh, Hugo, darling, the battle's over. We've won. Uncle Clarence has said "Certainly" sixty-five times, and he's just told Aunt Constance that if she thinks she can bully him she's very much mistaken. It's a walk-over. They're all coming back right away in the car. Uncle Clarence is an angel.'

'So are you.'

'Me?'

'Yes, you.'

'Not such an angel as you are.'

'Much more of an angel than I am,' said Hugo, in the voice of one trained to the appraising and classifying of angels.

'Well, anyway, you precious old thing, I'm going to give them the slip and walk home along the road. Get out Ronnie's two-seater and come and pick me up and we'll go for a drive together, miles and miles through the country. It's the most perfect evening.'

'You bet it is!' said Hugo fervently. 'What I call something like an evening. Give me two minutes to get the car out and five to make the trip and I'll be with you.'

''At-a-boy!' said Millicent.

''At-a-baby!' said Hugo.

Sue stood staring, wide-eyed. This was the moment which she had tried to picture to herself a hundred times. And always her imagination had proved unequal to the task. Sometimes she had seen Ronnie in her mind's eye cold, aloof, hostile; sometimes gasping and tottering, dumb with amazement; sometimes pointing a finger at her like a character in a melodrama and denouncing her as an imposter. The one thing for which she had not been prepared was what happened now.

Eton and Cambridge train their sons well. Once they have grasped the fundamental fact of life that all exhibitions of emotion are bad form, bomb-shells cannot disturb their poise and earthquakes are lucky if they get so much as an 'Eh, what?' from them. But Cambridge has its limitations, and so has Eton. And remorse had goaded Ronnie Fish to a point where their iron discipline had ceased to operate. He was stirred to his depths, and his scarlet face, his rumpled hair, his starting eyes and his twitching fingers all proclaimed the fact.

'Ronnie!' cried Sue.

It was all she had time to say. The thought of what she had done for his sake; the thought that for love of him she had come to Blandings Castle under false colours – an imposter – faced at every turn by the risk of detection – liable at any moment to be ignominiously exposed and looked at through a lorgnette by his Aunt Constance; the thought of the shameful way he had treated her . . . all these thoughts were racking Ronald Fish with a searing anguish. They had brought the hot blood of the Fishes to the boil, and now, face to face with her, he did not hesitate.

He sprang forward, clasped her in his arms, hugged her to him. To Baxter's revolted ears, though he tried not to listen, there came in a husky cataract the sound of a Fish's self-reproaches. Ronnie was saying what he thought of himself, and his opinion appeared not to be high. He said he was a beast, a brute, a swine, a cad, a hound and a worm. If he had been speaking of Percy Pilbeam, he could scarcely have been less complimentary.

Even up to this point, Baxter had not liked the dialogue. It now became perfectly nauseating. Sue said it had all been her fault. Ronnie said, No, his. No, hers, said Sue. No, his, said Ronnie. No, hers, said Sue. No, altogether his, said Ronnie. It must have been his, he pointed out, because, as she had observed before, he was a hound and a worm. He now went further. He revealed himself as a blister, a trick and a perishing outsider.

'You're not!'

'I am!'

'You're not!'

'I am!'

'Of course you're not!'

'I certainly am!'

'Well, I love you anyway.'

'You can't.'

'I do.'

'You can't.'

'I do.'

Baxter writhed in silent anguish.

'How long?' said Baxter to his immortal soul. 'How long?'

The question was answered with a startling promptitude. From the neighbourhood of the French windows there sounded a discreet cough. The debaters sprang apart, two minds with but a single thought.

'Your manuscript, miss,' said Beach sedately.

Sue looked at him. Ronnie looked at him. Sue until this moment had forgotten his existence. Ronnie had supposed him downstairs, busy about his butlerine duties. Neither seemed very glad to see him.

Ronnie was the first to speak.

'Oh – hullo, Beach!'

There being no answer to this except 'Hullo, sir!' which is a thing that butlers do not say, Beach contented himself with a benignant smile. It had the unfortunate effect of making Ronnie think that the man was laughing at him, and the Fishes were men at whom butlers may not lightly laugh. He was about to utter a heated speech, indicating this, when the injudiciousness of such a course presented itself to his mind. Beach must be placated. He forced his voice to a note of geniality.

'So there you are, Beach?'

'Yes, sir.'

'I suppose all this must seem tolerably rummy to you?'

'No, sir.'

'No?'

'I had already been informed, Mr. Ronald, of the nature of your feelings towards this lady.'

'What!'

'Yes, sir.'

'Who told you?'

'Mr. Pilbeam, sir.'

Ronnie uttered a gasp. Then he became calmer. He had suddenly remembered that this man was his ally, his accomplice, linked to him not only by a friendship dating back to his boyhood but by the even stronger bond of mutual crime. Between them there need be no reserves. Delicate though the situation was, he now felt equal to it.

'Beach,' he said. 'How much do you know?'

'All, sir.'

'All?'

'Yes, sir.'

'Such as—?'

Beach coughed.

'I am aware that this lady is a Miss Sue Brown. And, according to my informant, she is employed in the chorus of the Regal Theatre.'

'Quite the Encyclopaedia, aren't you?'

'Yes, sir.'

'I want to marry Miss Brown, Beach.'

'I can readily appreciate such a desire on your part, Mr. Ronald,' said the butler with a paternal smile.

Sue caught at the smile.

'Ronnie! He's all right. I believe he's a friend.'

'Of course he's a friend! Old Beach. One of my earliest and stoutest pals.'

'I mean, he isn't going to give us away.'

'Me, miss?' said Beach, shocked. 'Certainly not.'

'Splendid fellow, Beach!'

'Thank you, sir.'

'Beach,' said Ronnie, 'the time has come to act. No more

delay. I've got to make myself solid with Uncle Clarence at once. Directly he gets back to-night, I shall go to him and tell him that Empress of Blandings is in the gamekeeper's cottage in the west wood, and then, while he's still weak, I shall spring on him the announcement of my engagement.'

'Unfortunately, Mr. Ronald, the animal is no longer in the cottage.'

'You've moved it?'

'Not I, sir. Mr. Carmody. By a most regrettable chance Mr. Carmody found me feeding it this afternoon. He took it away and deposited it in some place of which I am not cognizant, sir.'

'But, good heavens, he'll dish the whole scheme. Where is he?'

'You wish me to find him, sir?'

'Of course I wish you to find him. Go at once and ask him where that pig is. Tell him it's vital.'

'Very good, sir.'

Sue had listened with bewilderment to this talk of pigs.

'I don't understand, Ronnie.'

Ronnie was pacing the room in agitation. Once he came so close to where Baxter lay in his snug harbour that the ex-secretary had a flashing glimpse of a sock with a lavender clock. It was the first object of beauty that he had seen for a long time, and he should have appreciated it more than he did.

'I can't explain now,' said Ronnie. 'It's too long. But I can tell you this. If we don't get that pig back, we're in the soup.'

'Ronnie!'

Ronnie had ceased to pace the room. He was standing in a listening attitude.

'What's that?'

He sprang quickly to the balcony, looked over the parapet and came softly back.

'Sue!'

'What!'

'It's that blighter Pilbeam,' said Ronnie in a guarded undertone. 'He's climbing up the water-spout!'

From the moment when it left the door of Matchingham Hall and started on its journey back to Blandings Castle, a silence as of the tomb had reigned in the Antelope car which was bringing Lord Emsworth, his sister Lady Constance Keeble, and his brother, the Hon. Galahad Threepwood, home from their interrupted dinner-party. Not so much as a syllable proceeded from one of them.

In the light of what Millicent, an eyewitness at the Front, had told Hugo over the telephone of the family battle which had been raging at Sir Gregory Parsloe's table, this will appear strange. If ever three people with plenty to say to one another were assembled together in a small space, these three, one would have thought, were those three. Lady Constance alone might have been expected to provide enough conversation to keep the historian busy for hours.

The explanation, like all explanations, is simple. It is supplied by that one word Antelope.

Owing to the fact that some trifling internal ailment had removed from the active list the Hispano-Suiza in which Blandings Castle usually went out to dinner, Voules, the chauffeur, had had to fall back upon this secondary and inferior car; and anybody who has ever owned an Antelope is aware that there is no glass partition inside it shutting off the driver from the cash customers. He is right there in their midst, ready and eager to hear everything that is said and to hand it on in due course to the Servants' Hall.

In these circumstances, though the choice seemed one between speech and spontaneous combustion, the little company kept their thoughts to themselves. They suffered, but they did it. It would be difficult to find a better illustration of all that is implied in the fine old phrase *Noblesse oblige*. At Lady Constance we point with particular pride. She was a woman, and silence weighed hardest on her.

There were times during the drive when even the sight of Voules' large, red ears, all pricked up to learn the reason for this sudden and sensational return, was scarcely sufficient to restrain Lady Constance Keeble from telling her brother Clarence just what she thought of him. From boyhood up, he had not once come near to being her ideal man; but never had he sunk so low in her estimation as at the moment when she heard him giving his consent to the union of her niece Millicent with a young man who, besides being penniless, had always afflicted her with a nervous complaint for which she could find no name, but which is known to Scientists as the heeby-jeebies.

Nor had he re-established himself in any way by his outspoken remarks on the subject of the Efficient Baxter. He had said things about Baxter which no admirer of that energetic man could forgive. The adjectives mad, crazy, insane, gibbering – and, worse, potty – had played in and out of his conversation like flashes of lightning. And from the look in his eye she gathered that he was still saying them all over again to himself.

Her surmise was correct. To Lord Emsworth the events of

this day had come as a stunning revelation. On the strength of that flower-pot incident two years ago, he had always looked on Baxter as mentally unbalanced; but, being a fair-minded man, he had recognized the possibility that a quiet, regular life and freedom from worries might, in the interval which had elapsed since his late secretary's departure from the Castle, have effected a cure. Certainly the man had appeared quite normal on the day of his arrival. And now into the space of a few hours he had crammed enough variegated lunacy to equip all the March Hares in England and leave some over for the Mad Hatters.

The ninth Earl of Emsworth was not a man who was easily disturbed. His was a calm which, as a rule, only his younger son Frederick could shatter. But it was not proof against the sort of thing that had been going on to-day. No matter how placid you may be, if you find yourself in close juxtaposition with a man who, when he is not hurling himself out of windows, is stealing pigs and trying to make you believe they were stolen by your butler, you begin to think a bit. Lord Emsworth was thoroughly upset. As the car bowled up the drive, he was saying to himself that nothing could surprise him now.

And yet something did. As the car turned the corner by the rhododendrons and wheeled into the broad strip of gravel that faced the front door, he beheld a sight which brought the first sound he had uttered since the journey began bursting from his lips.

'Good God!'

The words were spoken in a high, penetrating tenor, and they made Lady Constance jump as if they had been pins running into her. This unexpected breaking of the great silence was agony to her taut nerves.

'What *is* the matter?'

'Matter? Look! Look at that fellow!'

Voules took it upon himself to explain. Never having met Lady Constance socially, as it were, he ought perhaps not to have spoken. He considered, however, that the importance of the occasion justified the solecism.

'A man is climbing the water-spout, m'lady.'

'What! Where? I don't see him.'

'He has just got into the balcony outside one of the bedrooms,' said the Hon. Galahad.

Lord Emsworth went straight to the heart of the matter.

'It's that fellow Baxter!' he exclaimed.

The summer day, for all the artificial aid lent by daylight saving, was now definitely over, and gathering night had spread its mantle of dusk over the world. The visibility, therefore, was not good: and the figure which had just vanished over the parapet of the balcony of the Garden Room had been unrecognizable except to the eye of intuition. This, however, was precisely the sort of eye that Lord Emsworth possessed.

He reasoned closely. There were, he knew, on the premises of Blandings Castle other male adults besides Rupert Baxter: but none of these would climb up water-spouts and disappear over balconies. To Baxter, on the other hand, such a pursuit would seem the normal, ordinary way of passing an evening. It would be his idea of wholesome relaxation. Soon, no doubt, he would come out onto the balcony again and throw himself to the ground. That was the sort of fellow Baxter was – a man of strange pleasures.

And so, going as we say, straight to the heart of the matter, Lord Emsworth, jerking the pince-nez off his face in his emotion, exclaimed:

'It's that fellow Baxter!'

Not since a certain day in their mutual nursery many years ago had Lady Constance gone to the length of actually hauling off and smiting her elder brother on the head with the flat of an outraged hand: but she came very near to doing it now. Perhaps it was the presence of Voules that caused her to confine herself to words.

'Clarence, you're an idiot!'

Even Voules could not prevent her saying that. After all, she was revealing no secrets. The chauffeur had been in service at the Castle quite long enough to have formed the same impression for himself.

Lord Emsworth did not argue the point. The car had drawn up now outside the front door. The front door was open, as always of a summer evening, and the ninth Earl, accompanied by his brother Galahad, hurried up the steps and entered the hall. And, as they did so, there came to their ears the sound of running feet. The next moment, the flying figure of Percy Pilbeam came into view, taking the stairs four at a time.

'God bless my soul!' said Lord Emsworth.

If Pilbeam heard the words or saw the speaker, he gave no sign of having done so. He was plainly in a hurry. He shot through the hall and, more like a startled gazelle than a private enquiry agent, vanished down the steps. His shirt front was dark with dirt-stains, his collar had burst from its stud, and it seemed to Lord Emsworth, in the brief moment during which he was able to focus him, that he had a black eye. The next instant, there descended the stairs and flitted past with equal speed the form of Ronnie Fish.

Lord Emsworth got an entirely wrong conception of the affair. He had no means of knowing what had taken place in the Garden Room when Pilbeam, inspired by alcohol and flushed with the thought that now was the time to get into that apartment and possess himself of the manuscript of the Hon. Galahad's reminiscences, had climbed the water-spout to put the plan into operation. He knew nothing of the detective's sharp dismay at finding himself unexpectedly confronted with the menacing form of Ronnie Fish. He was ignorant of the lively and promising mix-up which had been concluded by Pilbeam's tempestuous dash for life. All he saw was two men fleeing madly for the open spaces, and he placed the obvious interpretation upon this phenomenon.

Baxter, he assumed, had run amok and had done it with such uncompromising thoroughness that strong men ran panic-stricken before him.

Mild though the ninth Earl was by nature, a lover of rural peace and the quiet life, he had, like all Britain's aristocracy, the right stuff in him. It so chanced that during the years when he had held his commission in the Shropshire Yeomanry the motherland had not called to him to save her. But, had that call been made, Clarence, ninth Earl of Emsworth, would have answered it with as prompt a 'Bless my Soul! Of course. Certainly!' as any of his Crusader ancestors. And in his sixtieth year the ancient fire still lingered. The Hon. Galahad, who had turned to watch the procession through the front door with a surprised monocle, turned back and found that he was alone. Lord Emsworth had disappeared. He now beheld him coming back again. On his amiable face was a look of determination. In his hand was a gun.

'Eh? What?' said the Hon. Galahad, blinking.

The head of the family did not reply. He was moving towards the stairs. In just that same silent purposeful way had an Emsworth advanced on the foe at Agincourt.

A sound as of disturbed hens made the Hon. Galahad turn again.

'Galahad! What is all this? What is happening?'

The Hon. Galahad placed his sister in possession of the facts as known to himself.

'Clarence has just gone upstairs with a gun.'

'With a gun!'

'Yes. Looked like mine too. I hope he takes care of it.'

He perceived that Lady Constance had also been seized with the urge to Climb. She was making excellent time up the broad staircase. So nimbly did she move that she was on the second landing before he came up with her.

And, as they stood there, a voice made itself heard from a room down the corridor.

'Baxter! Come out! Come out, Baxter, my dear fellow, immediately.'

In the race for the room which the words had appeared to proceed, Lady Constance, getting off to a good start, beat her brother by a matter of two lengths. She was thus the first to see a sight unusual even at Blandings Castle, though strange things had happened there from time to time.

Her young guest, Miss Schoonmaker, was standing by the window, looking excited and alarmed. Her brother Clarence, pointing a gun expertly from his hip, was staring fixedly at the bed. And from under the bed, a little like a tortoise protruding from its shell, there was coming into view the spectacled head of the Efficient Baxter.

A man who has been lying under a bed for a matter of some thirty minutes and, while there, has been compelled to listen to the sort of dialogue which accompanied a lovers' reconciliation seldom appears at his best or feels his brightest. There was fluff in Baxter's hair, dust on his clothes, and on Baxter's face a scowl of concentrated hatred of all humanity. Lord Emsworth, prepared for something pretty wild-looking, found his expectations exceeded. He tightened his grasp on the gun, and to ensure a more accurate aim raised the butt of it to his shoulder, closing one eye and allowing the other to gleam along the barrel.

'I have you covered, my dear fellow,' he said mildly.

Rupert Baxter had not yet begun to stick straws in his hair, but he seemed on the verge of that final piece of self-expression.

'Don't point that damned thing at me!'

'I shall point it at you,' replied Lord Emsworth with spirit. He was not a man to be dictated to in his own house. 'And at the slightest sign of violence . . .'

'Clarence!' It was Lady Constance who spoke. 'Put that gun down.'

'Certainly not.'

'Clarence!'

'Oh, all right.'

'And now, Mr. Baxter,' said Lady Constance, proceeding to dominate the scene in her masterly way. 'I am sure you can explain.'

Her agitation had passed. It was not in this strong woman to remain agitated long. She had been badly shaken, but her faith in her idol held good. Remarkable as his behaviour might appear, she was sure that he could account for it in a perfectly satisfactory manner.

Baxter did not speak. His silence gave Lord Emsworth the opportunity of advancing his own views.

'Explain?' He spoke petulantly, for he resented the way in which his sister had thrust him from the centre of the stage. 'What on earth is there to explain? The thing's obvious.'

'Can't say I've quite got to the bottom of it,' murmured the Hon. Galahad. 'Fellow under bed. Why? Why under bed? Why here at all?'

Lord Emsworth hesitated. He was a kind-hearted man, and he felt that what he had to say would be better said in Baxter's absence. However, there seemed no way out of it, so he proceeded.

'My dear Galahad, think!'

'Eh?'

'That flower-pot affair. You remember?'

'Oh!' Understanding shone in the Hon. Galahad's monocle. 'You mean . . . ?'

'Exactly.'

'Yes, yes. Of course. Subject to these attacks, you mean?'

'Precisely.'

This was not the first time Lady Constance Keeble had had

the opportunity of hearing a theory ventilated by her brothers which she found detestable. She flushed brightly.

'Clarence!'

'My dear?'

'Kindly stop talking in that offensive way.'

'God bless my soul!' Lord Emsworth was stung. 'I like that. What have I said that is offensive?'

'You know perfectly well.'

'If you mean that I was reminding Galahad in the most delicate way that poor Baxter here is not quite . . .'

'Clarence!'

'All very well to say "Clarence!" like that. You know yourself he isn't right in the head. Didn't he throw flower-pots at me? Didn't he leap out of the window this very afternoon? Didn't he try to make me think that Beach . . .'

Baxter interrupted. There were certain matters on which he considered silence best, but this was one on which he could speak freely.

'Lord Emsworth!'

'Eh?'

'It has now come to my knowledge that Beach was not the prime mover in the theft of your pig. But I have ascertained that he was an accessory.'

'A what?'

'He helped,' said Baxter, grinding his teeth a little. 'The man who committed the actual theft was your nephew Ronald.'

Lord Emsworth turned to his sister with a triumphant gesture, like one who has been vindicated.

'There! Now perhaps you'll say he's not potty? It won't do, Baxter, my dear fellow,' he went on, waggling a reproachful gun at his late employee. 'You really mustn't excite yourself by making up these stories.'

'Bad for the blood-pressure,' agreed the Hon. Galahad.

'The Empress was found this evening in your caravan,' said Lord Emsworth.

'What!'

'In your caravan. Where you put her when you stole her. And bless my soul,' said Lord Emsworth, with a start, 'I must be going and seeing that she is put back in her sty. I must find Pirbright. I must . . .'

'In my caravan?' Baxter passed a feverish hand across his dust-stained forehead. Illumination came to him. 'Then that's what that fellow Carmody did with the animal!'

Lord Emsworth had had enough of this. Empress of Blandings was waiting for him. Counting the minutes to that holy reunion, he chafed at having to stand here listening to these wild ravings.

'First Beach, then Ronald, then Carmody! You'll be saying I stole her next, or Galahad here, or my sister Constance. Baxter, my dear fellow, we aren't blaming you. Please don't think that. We quite see how it is. You will overwork yourself, and, of course, nature demands the penalty. I wish you would go quietly to your room, my dear fellow, and lie down. All this must be very bad for you.'

Lady Constance intervened. Her eye was aflame, and she spoke like Cleopatra telling an Ethiopian slave where he got off.

'Clarence, will you kindly use whatever slight intelligence you may possess? The theft of your pig is one of the most trivial and unimportant things that ever happened in this world, and I consider the fuss that has been made about it quite revolting. But whoever stole the wretched animal . . .'

Lord Emsworth blanched. He stared as if wondering if he had heard aright.

'. . . and wherever it has been found, it was certainly not Mr. Baxter who stole it. It is, as Mr. Baxter says, much more likely to have been a young man like Mr. Carmody. There is a certain type of young man, I believe, to which Mr. Carmody belongs, which considers practical joking amusing. Do ask yourself, Clarence, and try to answer the question as reasonably as is possible for a man of your mental calibre: What earthly motive would Mr. Baxter have for coming to Blandings Castle and stealing pigs?'

It may have been the feel of the gun in his hand which awoke in Lord Emsworth old memories of dashing days with the Shropshire Yeomanry and lent him some of the hot spirit of his vanished youth. The fact remains that he did not wilt beneath his sister's dominating eye. He met it boldly, and boldly answered back.

'And ask yourself, Constance,' he said, 'what earthly motive Mr. Baxter has for anything he does.'

'Yes,' said the Hon. Galahad loyally. 'What motive had our friend Baxter for coming to Blandings Castle and scaring girls stiff by hiding under beds?'

Lady Constance gulped. They had found the weak spot in her defences. She turned to the man who she still hoped could deal efficiently with this attack.

'Mr. Baxter!' she said, as if she were calling on him for an after-dinner speech.

But Rupert Baxter had had no dinner. And it was perhaps this that turned the scale. Quite suddenly there descended on him a frenzied desire to be out of this, cost what it might. An hour before, half an hour before, even five minutes before, his tongue had been tied by a still lingering hope that he might yet find his way back to Blandings Castle in the capacity of private secretary to the Earl of Emsworth. Now, he felt that he would not accept that post, were it offered to him on bended knee.

A sudden overpowering hatred of Blandings Castle and all it contained gripped the Efficient Baxter. He marvelled that he had ever wanted to come back. He held the present moment the well, paid responsible position of secretary and adviser to J. Horace Jevons, the American millionaire, a man who not only treated him with an obsequiousness and respect which were balm to his soul, but also gave him such sound advice on the investment of money that already he had trebled his savings. And it was this golden-hearted Chicagoan whom he had been thinking of deserting, purely to satisfy some obscure sentiment which urged him to return to a house which, he now saw, he loathed as few houses have been loathed since human beings left off living in caves.

His eyes flashed through their lenses. His mouth tightened.

'I will explain!'

'I knew you would have an explanation,' cried Lady Constance.

'I have. A very simple one.'

'And short, I hope?' asked Lord Emsworth, restlessly. He was aching to have done with all this talk and discussion and to be with his pig once more. To think of the Empress languishing in a beastly caravan was agony to him.

'Quite short,' said Rupert Baxter.

The only person in the room who so far had remained entirely outside this rather painful scene was Sue. She had looked on from her place by the window, an innocent bystander. She now found herself drawn abruptly into the maelstrom of the debate. Baxter's spectacles were raking her from head to foot, and he had pointed at her with an accusing forefinger.

'I came to this room,' he said, 'to try to recover a letter which I had written to this lady who calls herself Miss Schoonmaker.'

'Of course she calls herself Miss Schoonmaker,' said Lord Emsworth, reluctantly dragging his thoughts from the Empress. 'It's her name, my dear fellow. That,' he explained gently, 'is why she calls herself Miss Schoonmaker. God bless my soul!' he said, unable to restrain a sudden spurt of irritability. 'If a girl's name is Schoonmaker, naturally she calls herself Miss Schoonmaker.'

'Yes, if it is. But hers is not. It is Brown.'

'Listen, my dear fellow,' said Lord Emsworth soothingly. 'You are only exciting yourself by going on like this. Probably doing yourself a great deal of harm. Now, what I suggest is, that you go to your room and put a cool compress on your forehead and lie down and take a good rest. I will send Beach up to you with some nice bread-and-milk.'

'Rum-and-milk,' amended the Hon. Galahad. 'It's the only thing. I knew a fellow in the year '97 who was subject to these spells – you probably remember him, Clarence. Bellamy. Barmy Bellamy we used to call him – and whenever . . .'

'Her name is Brown!' repeated Baxter, his voice soaring in a hysterical crescendo. 'Sue Brown. She is a chorus girl at the Regal Theatre in London. And she is apparently engaged to be married to your nephew Ronald.'

Lady Constance uttered a cry. Lord Emsworth expressed his feelings with a couple of tuts. The Hon. Galahad alone was silent. He caught Sue's eye, and there was concern in his gaze.

'I overheard Beach saying so in this very room. He said he had had the information from Mr. Pilbeam. I imagine it to be accurate. But in any case, I can tell you this much. Whoever she is, she is an imposter who has come here under a false name. While I was in the smoking-room some time back a telegram came through on the telephone from Market Blandings. It was signed Myra Schoonmaker, and it had been handed in in Paris this afternoon. That is all I have to say,' concluded Baxter. 'I will now leave you, and I sincerely hope I shall never set eyes on any of you again. Good evening!'

His spectacles glinting coldly, he strode from the room and in the doorway collided with Ronnie, who was entering.

'Can't you look where you're going?' he asked.

'Eh?' said Ronnie.

'Clumsy idiot!' said the Efficient Baxter, and was gone.

In the room he had left, Lady Constance Keeble had become a stony figure of menace. She was not at ordinary times a particularly tall woman, but she seemed now to tower like something vast and awful: and Sue quailed before her.

'Ronnie!' cried Sue weakly.

It was the cry of the female in distress, calling to her mate. Just so in prehistoric days must Sue's cave-woman ancestress have cried to the man behind the club when suddenly cornered by the sabre-toothed tiger which Lady Constance Keeble so closely resembled.

'Ronnie!'

'What's all this?' asked the last of the Fishes.

He was breathing rather quickly for the going had been fast. Pilbeam, once out in the open, had shown astonishing form at the short sprint. He had shaken off Ronnie's challenge twenty yards down the drive, and plunged into a convenient shrubbery, and Ronnie, giving up the pursuit, had come back to Sue's room to report. It occasioned him some surprise to find that in his absence it had become the scene of some sort of public meeting.

'What's all this?' he said, addressing that meeting.

Lady Constance wheeled round upon him.

'Ronald, who is this girl?'

'Eh?' Ronnie was conscious of a certain uneasiness, but he did his best. He did not like his aunt's looks, but then he never had. Something was evidently up, but it might be that airy nonchalance would save the day. 'You know her, don't you? Miss Schoonmaker? Met her with me in London.'

'Is her name Brown? And is she a chorus girl?'

'Why, yes,' admitted Ronnie. It was a bomb-shell, but Eton and Cambridge stood it well. 'Why, yes,' he said, 'as a matter of fact, that's right.'

Words seemed to fail Lady Constance. Judging from the expression on her face this was just as well.

'I'd been meaning to tell you about that,' said Ronnie. 'We're engaged.'

Lady Constance recovered herself sufficiently to find one word.

'Clarence!'

'Eh?' said Lord Emsworth. His thoughts had been wandering.

'You heard?'

'Heard what?'

Beyond the stage of turbulent emotion, Lady Constance had become suddenly calm and icy.

'If you have not been sufficiently interested to listen,' she said, 'I may inform you that Ronald has just announced his intention of marrying a chorus girl.'

'Oh, ah?' said Lord Emsworth. Would a man of Baxter's outstandingly unbalanced intellect, he was wondering, have remembered to feed the Empress regularly? The thought was like a spear quivering in his heart. He edged in agitation towards the door, and had reached it when he perceived that his sister had not yet finished talking to him.

'So that is all the comment you have to make, is it?'

'Eh? What about?'

'The point I have been endeavouring to make you understand,' went on Lady Constance, with laborious politeness, 'is that your nephew Ronald has announced his intention of marrying into the Regal Theatre chorus.'

'Who?'

'Ronald. This is Ronald. He is anxious to marry Miss Brown, a chorus girl. This is Miss Brown.'

'How do you do?' said Lord Emsworth. He might be vague, but he had the manners of the old school.

Ronnie interposed. The time had come to place the ace of trumps.

'She isn't an ordinary chorus girl.'

'From the fact of her coming to Blandings Castle under a false name,' said Lady Constance, 'I imagine not. It shows unusual enterprise.'

'What I mean,' continued Ronnie, 'is, I know what a bally snob you are, Aunt Constance – no offence, but you know what I mean – keen on birth and family and all that sort of rot . . . well, what I'm driving at is that Sue's father was in the Guards.'

'A private? Or a corporal?'

'Captain. A fellow named . . .'

'Cotterleigh,' said Sue in a small voice.

'Cotterleigh,' said Ronnie.

'Cotterleigh!'

It was the Hon. Galahad who had spoken. He was staring at Sue open-mouthed.

'Cotterleigh? Not Jack Cotterleigh?'

'I don't know whether it was Jack Cotterleigh,' said Ronnie. 'The point I'm making is that it was Cotterleigh and that he was in the Irish Guards.'

The Hon. Galahad was still staring at Sue.

'My dear,' he cried, and there was an odd sharpness in his voice. 'Was your mother Dolly Henderson, who used to be a Serio at the old Oxford and the Tivoli?'

Not for the first time Ronald Fish was conscious of a feeling that his Uncle Galahad ought to be in some kind of a home. He would drag in Dolly Henderson! He would stress the Dolly Henderson note at just this point in the proceedings! He would spoil the whole thing by calling attention to the Dolly Henderson aspect of the matter, just when it was vital to stick to the Cotterleigh, the whole Cotterleigh, and nothing but the Cotterleigh. Ronnie sighed wearily. Padded cells, he felt, had been invented specially for the Uncle Galahads of this world, and the Uncle Galahads, he considered, ought never to be permitted to roam about outside them.

'Yes,' said Sue. 'She was.'

The Hon. Galahad was advancing on her with outstretched hands. He looked like some father in melodrama welcoming the prodigal daughter.

'Well, I'm dashed!' he said. He repeated three times that he was in this condition. He seized Sue's limp paws and squeezed them fondly. 'I've been trying to think all this while who it was that you reminded me of, my dear girl. Do you know that in the years '96, '97 and '98, I was madly in love with your mother myself? Do you know that if my infernal family hadn't shipped me off to South Africa I would certainly have married her? Fact, I assure you. But they got behind me and shoved me on to the boat and when I came back I found that young Cotterleigh had cut me out. Well!'

It was a scene which some people would have considered touching. Lady Constance Keeble was not one of them.

'Never mind about that now, Galahad,' she said. 'The point is . . .'

'The point is,' retorted the Hon. Galahad warmly, 'that that young Fish there wants to marry Dolly Henderson's daughter, and I'm for it. And I hope, Clarence, that you'll have some sense for once in your life and back them up like a sportsman.'

'Eh?' said the ninth Earl. His thought had once more been wandering. Even assuming that Baxter had fed the Empress, would he have given her the right sort of food and enough of it?

'You see for yourself what a splendid girl she is.'

'Who?'

'This girl.'

'Charming,' agreed Lord Emsworth courteously, and returned to his meditations.

'Clarence!' cried Lady Constance, jerking him out of them.

'Eh?'

'You are not to consent to this marriage.'

'Who says so?'

'I say so. And think what Julia will say.'

She could not have advanced a more impressive argument. In this chronicle the Lady Julia Fish, relict of the late Major-General Sir Miles Fish, C.B.O., of the Brigade of Guards, has made no appearance. We, therefore, know nothing of her compelling eye, her dominant chin, her determined mouth, and her voice, which, at certain times – as, for example, when rebuking a brother – could raise blisters on a sensitive skin. Lord Emsworth was aware of all these things. He had had experience of them from boyhood. His idea of happiness was to be where Lady Julia Fish was not. And the thought of her coming down to Blandings Castle and tackling him in his library about this business froze him to the marrow. It had been his amiable intention until this moment to do whatever the majority of those present wanted him to do. But now he hesitated.

'You think Julia wouldn't like it?'

'Of course Julia would not like it.'

'Julia's an ass,' said the Hon. Galahad.

Lord Emsworth considered this statement, and was inclined to agree with it. But it did not alter the main point.

'You think she would make herself unpleasant about it?'

'I do.'

'In that case . . .' Lord Emsworth paused. Then a strange soft light came into his eyes. 'Well, see you all later,' he said. 'I'm going down to look at my pig.'

His departure was so abrupt that it took Lady Constance momentarily by surprise, and he was out of the room and well down the corridor before she could recover herself sufficiently to act. Then, she too hurried out. They could hear her voice diminishing down the stairs. It was calling 'Clarence!'

The Hon. Galahad turned to Sue. His manner was brisk, yet soothing.

'A shame to inflict these fine old English family rows on a visitor,' he said, patting her shoulder as one who, if things had broken right and there had not been a regular service of boats to South Africa in the 'nineties, might have been her father. 'What you need, my dear, is a little rest and quiet. Come along, Ronald, we'll leave you. The place to continue this discussion is somewhere outside this room. Cheer up, my dear. Everything may come out all right yet.'

Sue shook her head.

'It's no good,' she said hopelessly.

'Don't you be too sure,' said the Hon. Galahad.

'I'll jolly well tell you one thing,' said Ronnie. 'I'm going to marry you, whatever happens. And that's that. Good heavens! I can work, can't I?'

'What at?' asked the Hon. Galahad.

'What at? Why – er – why, at anything.'

'The market value of any member of this family,' said the Hon. Galahad, who harboured no illusions about his nearest and dearest, 'is about threepence-ha'-penny per annum. No! What we've got to do is get round old Clarence somehow, and that means talk and argument, which had better take place elsewhere. Come along, my boy. You never know your luck. I've seen stickier things than this come out right in my time.'

Sue stood on the balcony, looking out into the night. Velvet darkness shrouded the world, and from the heart of it came the murmur of rustling trees and the clean, sweet smell of earth and flowers. A little breeze had sprung up, stirring the ivy at her side. Somewhere in it a bird was chirping drowsily, and in the distance sounded the tinkle of running water.

She sighed. It was a night made for happiness. And she was quite sure now that happiness was not for her.

A footstep sounded behind her, and she turned eagerly.

'Ronnie?'

It was the voice of the Hon. Galahad Threepwood that answered.

'Only me, I'm afraid, my dear. May I come on to your balcony? God bless my soul, as Clarence would say, what a wonderful night!'

'Yes,' said Sue doubtfully.

'You don't think so.'

'Oh, yes.'

'I bet you don't. I know I didn't, that night when my old father put his foot down and told me I was leaving for South Africa on the next boat. Just such a night as this it was, I remember.' He rested his arms on the parapet. 'I never saw your mother after she was married,' he said.

'No?'

'No. She left the stage and . . . Oh, well, I was rather busy at the time – lot of heavy drinking to do, and so forth – and somehow we never met. The next thing I heard – two or three years ago – was that she was dead. You're very like her, my dear. Can't think why I didn't spot the resemblance right away.'

He became silent. Sue did not speak. She slid her hand under his arm. It was all that there seemed to do. A corncrake began to call monotonously in the darkness.

'That means rain,' said the Hon. Galahad. 'Or not. I forget which. Did you ever hear your mother sing that song . . . ? No, you wouldn't. Before your time. About young Ronald,' he said, abruptly.

'What about him?'

'Fond of him?'

'Yes.'

'I mean really fond?'

'Yes.'

'How fond?'

Sue leaned out over the parapet. At the foot of the wall beneath her Percy Pilbeam, who had been peering out of a bush, popped his head back again. For the detective, possibly remembering with his sub-conscious mind stories heard in childhood of Bruce and the spider, had refused to admit defeat and had returned by devious ways to the scene of his disaster. Five hundred pounds is a lot of money, and Percy Pilbeam was not going to be deterred from attempting to earn it by the fact that at his last essay he had only just succeeded in escaping with his life. The influence of his potations had worn off to some extent, and he was his calm, keen self again. It was his intention to lurk in these bushes till the small hours, if need be, and then to attack the water-spout again and so to the Garden Room where the manuscript of the Hon. Galahad's Reminiscences lay. You cannot be a good detective if you are easily discouraged.

'I can't put it into words,' said Sue.

'Try.'

'No. Everything you say straight out about the way you feel about anybody always sounds silly. Besides, to you Ronnie isn't the sort of man you could understand anyone raving about. You look on him just as something quite ordinary.'

'If that,' said the Hon. Galahad critically.

'Yes, if that. Whereas to me he's something . . . rather special. In fact, if you really want to know how I feel about Ronnie, he's the whole world to me. There! I told you it would sound silly. It's like something out of a song, isn't it? I've worked in the chorus of that sort of song a hundred times. Two steps left, two steps right, kick, smile, both hands on heart – because he's all the wo-orld to me-ee! You can laugh if you like.'

There was a momentary pause.

'I'm not laughing,' said the Hon. Galahad. 'My dear, I only wanted to find out if you really cared for that young Fish . . .'

'I wish you wouldn't call him "that young Fish".'

'I'm sorry, my dear. It seems to describe him so neatly. Well, I just wanted to be quite sure you really were fond of him, because . . .'

'Well?'

'Well, because I've just fixed it all up.'

She clutched at the parapet.

'What!'

'Oh, yes,' said the Hon. Galahad. 'It's all settled. I don't say

638

that you can actually count on an aunt-in-law's embrace from my sister Constance – in fact, if I were you, I wouldn't risk it. She might bite you – but, apart from that, everything's all right. The wedding bells will ring out. Your young man's in the garden somewhere. You had better go and find him and tell him the news. He'll be interested.'

'But . . . but . . .'

Sue was clutching his arm. A wild impulse was upon her to shout and sob. She had no doubts now as to the beauty of the night.

'But . . . how? Why? What has happened?'

'Well . . . . You'll admit I might have married your mother?'

'Yes.'

'Which makes me a sort of honorary father to you.'

'Yes.'

'In which capacity, my dear, your interests are mine. More than mine, in fact. So what I did was to make your happiness the *Price of the Papers*. Ever see that play? No, before your time. It ran at the Adelphi before you were born. There was a scene where . . .'

'What do you mean?'

The Hon. Galahad hesitated a moment.

'Well, the fact of the matter is, my dear, knowing how strongly my sister Constance has always felt on the subject of those Reminiscences of mine, I went to her and put it to her squarely. "Clarence," I said to her, "is not the sort of man to make any objection to anyone marrying anybody, so long as he isn't expected to attend the wedding. You're the real obstacle," I said. "You and Julia. And if you come round, you can talk Julia over in five minutes. You know she relies on your judgment." And then I said that, if she gave up acting like a barbed-wire entanglement in the path of true love, I would undertake not to publish the Reminiscences.'

Sue clung to his arm. She could find no words.

Percy Pilbeam, who, for the night was very still, had heard all, could have found many. Nothing but the delicate nature of his present situation kept him from uttering them, and that only just. To Percy Pilbeam it was as if he had seen five hundred pounds flutter from his grasp like a vanishing blue bird. He raged dumbly. In all London and the Home Counties there were few men who liked five hundred pounds better than P. Frobisher Pilbeam.

'Oh!' said Sue. Nothing more. Her feelings were too deep. She hugged his arm. 'Oh!' she said, and again 'Oh!'

She found herself crying, and was not ashamed.

'Now, come!' said the Hon. Galahad protestingly. 'Nothing so very extraordinary in that, was there? Nothing so exceedingly remarkable in one pal helping another?'

'I don't know what to say.'

'Then don't say it,' said the Hon. Galahad, much relieved. 'Why, bless you, I don't care whether the damned things are published or not. At least. . . . No, certainly I don't. . . . Only cause a lot of unpleasantness. Besides, I'll leave the dashed book to the Nation and have it published in a hundred years and become the Pepys of the future, what? Best thing that could have happened. Homage of Posterity and all that.'

'Oh!' said Sue.

The Hon. Galahad chuckled.

'It is a shame, though, that the world will have to wait a hundred years before it hears the story of young Gregory Parsloe and the prawns. Did you get to that when you were reading the thing this evening?'

'I'm afraid I didn't read very much,' said Sue. 'I was thinking of Ronnie rather a lot.'

'Oh? Well, I can tell you. You needn't wait a hundred years. It was at Ascot, the year Martingale won the Gold Cup . . .'

Down below, Percy Pilbeam rose from his bush. He did not care now if he were seen. He was still a guest in this hole of a castle, and if a guest cannot pop in and out of bushes if he likes, where does British hospitality come in? It was his intention to shake the dust of Blandings off his feet, to pass the night at the Emsworth Arms, and on the morrow to return to London, where he was appreciated.

'Well, my dear, it was like this. Young Parsloe . . .'

Percy Pilbeam did not linger. The story of the prawns meant nothing to him. He turned away, and the summer night swallowed him. Somewhere in the darkness an owl hooted. It seemed to Pilbeam that there was derision in the sound. He frowned. His teeth came together with a click.

If he could have found it, he would have had a word with that owl.

Also available in Arrow

# *Leave it to Psmith*

## P.G. Wodehouse

*A Blandings novel*

Lady Constance Keeble, sister of Lord Emsworth of Blandings
Castle, has both an imperious manner and a valuable diamond
necklace. The precarious peace of Blandings is shattered when
her necklace becomes the object of dark plottings, for within the
castle lurk some well-connected jewel thieves – among them the
Honourable Freddie Threepwood, Lord Emsworth's younger
son, who wants the reward money to set up a bookmaking
business. Psmith, the elegant socialist, is also after it for his
newly married chum Mike. And on patrol with the impossible
task of bringing management to Blandings is the Efficient
Baxter, whose strivings for order lead to a memorable encounter
with the castle flowerpots.

Will peace ever return to Blandings Castle. . . ?

arrow books

Also available in Arrow

# *Uncle Fred in the Springtime*

## P.G. Wodehouse

*A Blandings novel*

Uncle Fred is one of the hottest earls that ever donned a coronet. Or as he crisply said, 'There are no limits, literally none, to what I can achieve in the springtime.'

Even so, his gifts are stretched to the limit when he is urged by Lord Emsworth to save his prize pig, the Empress of Blandings, from the enforced slimming cure of the haughty Duke of Dunstable. Pongo Twistleton knows his debonair but wild uncle shouldn't really be allowed at large – especially when disguised as a brain surgeon. He fears the worst. And his fears are amply justified.

arrow books

Also available in Arrow

## *Full Moon*

### P.G. Wodehouse

*A Blandings novel*

When the moon is full at Blandings, strange things happen:
among them the painting of a portrait of The Empress, twice in
succession winner in the Fat Pigs Class at the Shropshire
Agricultural Show. What better choice of artist, in Lord
Emsworth's opinion, than Landseer. The renowned painter of
The Stag at Bay may have been dead for decades, but that doesn't
prevent Galahad Threepwood from introducing him to the castle
– or rather introducing Bill Lister, Gally's godson, so desperately
in love with Prudence that he's determined to enter Blandings in
yet another imposture. Add a gaggle of fearsome aunts, uncles
and millionaires, mix in Freddie Threepwood, Beach the Butler
and the gardener McAllister, and the moon is full indeed.

arrow books

Also available in Arrow

# *Service with a Smile*

## P.G. Wodehouse

*A Blandings novel*

As a peer of the realm, Clarence, Ninth Earl of Emsworth, has an occasional duty to leave the Empress of Blandings, surely the most considerable pig in the whole world, and travel to London for the opening of parliament. It comes hard to him, for he has a proper sense of the priorities in life, which rate pigs and flowerbeds higher than politicians.

But no sooner has he returned to Blandings than his real problems begin: the dastardly Duke of Dunstable is out to steal the Empress. His sister Lady Constance has inflicted on him a particularly nasty new secretary. And the Church Lads' Brigade are camped all over his lawns.

Thank God for the Earl of Ickenham, better known as Uncle Fred, whose own particularly devious brand of sweetness and light aims to banish blackmailers and pig-stealers and restore true love all over the castle grounds.

arrow books

Also available in Arrow

# A Pelican at Blandings

## P.G. Wodehouse

*A Blandings novel*

Unwelcome guests are descending on Blandings Castle –
particularly the overbearing Duke of Dunstable, who settles in
the Garden Suite with no intention of leaving, and Lady
Constance, Lord Emsworth's sister and a lady of firm
disposition, who arrives unexpectedly from New York.
Skulduggery is also afoot involving the sale of a modern nude
painting (mistaken by Lord Emsworth for a pig). It's enough to
take the noble earl on the short journey to the end of his wits.

Luckily Clarence's brother Galahad Threepwood, cheery
survivor of the raffish Pelican Club, is on hand to set things
right, restore sundered lovers and even solve all the mysteries.

arrow books

Also available in Arrow

# The World of Jeeves

## P.G. Wodehouse

*A Jeeves and Wooster omnibus*

'Jeeves knows his place, and it is between the covers of a book.'

This is an omnibus of wonderful Jeeves and Wooster stories, specially selected and introduced by Wodehouse himself, who was struck by the size of his selection and described it as almost the ideal paperweight. As he wrote:

'I find it curious, now that I have written so much about him, to recall how softly and undramatically Jeeves first entered my little world. Characteristically, he did not thrust himself forward. On that occasion, he spoke just two lines.
The first was:
"Mrs Gregson to see you, sir."
The second:
"Very good, sir, which suit will you wear?"
It was only some time later that the man's qualities dawned upon me. I still blush to think of the off-hand way I treated him at our first encounter . . .'.

arrow books

Also available in Arrow

# The Code of the Woosters

## P.G. Wodehouse

*A Jeeves and Wooster novel*

When Bertie Wooster goes to Totleigh Towers to pour oil on
the troubled waters of a lovers' breach between Madeline
Bassett and Gussie Fink-Nottle, he isn't expecting to see Aunt
Dahlia there – nor to be instructed by her to steal some silver.
But purloining the antique cow creamer from under the baleful
nose of Sir Watkyn Bassett is the least of Bertie's tasks. He has
to restore true love to both Madeline and Gussie and to the
Revd Stinker Pinker and Stiffy Byng – and confound the insane
ambitions of would-be Dictator Roderick Spode and his Black
Shorts. It's a situation that only Jeeves can unravel . . .

arrow books

Also available in Arrow

# *Joy in the Morning*

## P.G. Wodehouse

*A Jeeves and Wooster novel*

Trapped in rural Steeple Bumpleigh, a man less stalwart than
Bertie Wooster would probably give way at the knees.

For among those present were Florence Craye, to whom Bertie
had once been engaged and her new fiancé 'Stilton'
Cheesewright, who sees Bertie as a snake in the grass. And that
biggest blot on the landscape, Edwin the Boy Scout, who is busy
doing acts of kindness out of sheer malevolence.

All Bertie's forebodings are fully justified. For in his efforts to
oil the wheels of commerce, promote the course of true love
and avoid the consequences of a vendetta, he becomes the prey
of all and sundry. In fact only Jeeves can save him...

arrow books

Also available in Arrow

# *Thank You, Jeeves*

## P.G. Wodehouse

*A Jeeves and Wooster novel*

*Thank You, Jeeves* is the first novel to feature the incomparable
valet Jeeves and his hapless charge Bertie Wooster – and
you've hardly started to turn the pages when Jeeves resigns
over Bertie's dedicated but somewhat untuneful playing of the
banjo. In high dudgeon, Bertie disappears to the country as a
guest of his chum Chuffy – only to find his peace shattered by
the arrival of his ex-fiancée Pauline Stoker, her formidable
father and the eminent loony-doctor Sir Roderick Glossop.
When Chuffy falls in love with Pauline and Bertie seems to be
caught in flagrante, a situation boils up which only Jeeves
(whether employed or not) can simmer down . . .

arrow books

Also available in Arrow

# *Cocktail Time*

## P.G. Wodehouse

*An Uncle Fred novel*

Frederick, Earl of Ickenham, remains young at heart. So it is for
him the act of a moment to lean out of the Drones Club
window with a catapult and ping the silk top-hat off his grumpy
in-law, the distinguished barrister Sir Raymond Bastable.

Unfortunately things don't end there.

The sprightly earl finds that his action has inspired a scandalous
bestseller and a film script – but this is as nothing compared
with the entangled fates of the couples that surround him and
which only his fabled sweetness and light can unravel.

arrow books

Also available in Arrow

# The Heart of a Goof

## P.G. Wodehouse

*A Golf collection*

From his favourite chair on the terrace above the ninth hole,
The Oldest Member tells a series of hilarious golfing stories.
From Evangeline, Bradbury Fisher's fifth wife and a notorious
'golfing giggler', to poor Rollo Podmarsh whose game was so
unquestionably inept that 'he began to lose his appetite and
would moan feebly at the sight of a poached egg', the game of
golf, its players and their friends and enemies are here shown in
all their comic glory.

arrow books

Also available in Arrow

# *Ukridge*

## P.G. Wodehouse

*A Ukridge collection*

Money makes the world go round for Stanley
Featherstonehaugh Ukridge – and when there isn't enough of
it, the world just has to spin a bit faster.

Ever on the lookout for a quick buck, a solid gold fortune, or at
least a plausible little scrounge, the irrepressible Ukridge gives
con men a bad name. Looking like an animated blob of mustard
in his bright yellow raincoat, he invests time, passion and
energy (but seldom actual cash) in a series of increasingly
bizarre money-making schemes. Finance for a dog college? It's
yours. Shares in an accident syndicate? Easily arranged.
Promoting a kind-hearted heavyweight boxer? A snip.

Poor Corky Corcoran, Ukridge's old school chum and
confidant, trails through these pages in the ebullient wake of
Wodehouse's most disreputable but endearing hero and hopes
to escape with his shirt at least.

arrow books

Also available in Arrow

# *Mulliner Nights*

## P.G. Wodehouse

*A Mulliner collection*

A private detective who can make the guilty confess simply by
smiling at them. An artist so intimidated by his morally
impeccable cat that he feels compelled to wear formal attire at
dinner. A devotee of Proust whose life is turned upside down
when he inadvertently subscribes to a correspondence course on
How to Acquire Complete Self-Confidence and an Iron Will.
These are just a few of the many members of the eccentric
Mulliner clan whose lives and exploits are laid before the
regulars of the Angler's Rest by that doyen of raconteurs, Mr
Mulliner, in a series of tall stories where lunacy and comic
exuberance reign supreme.

arrow books

# The P G Wodehouse Society (UK)

The P G Wodehouse Society (UK) was formed in 1997 to promote the enjoyment of the writings of the twentieth century's greatest humorist. The Society publishes a quarterly magazine, *Wooster Sauce*, which includes articles, features, reviews, and current Society news. Occasional special papers are also published. Society events include regular meetings in central London, cricket matches and a formal biennial dinner, along with other activities. The Society actively supports the preservation of the Berkshire pig, a rare breed, in honour of the incomparable Empress of Blandings.

## MEMBERSHIP ENQUIRIES

Membership of the Society is open to applicants from all parts of the world. The cost of a year's membership in 2013 is £22. Enquiries and requests for membership forms should be made to the Membership Secretary, The P G Wodehouse Society (UK), 26 Radcliffe Rd, Croydon, Surrey, CRO 5QE, or alternatively from info@pgwodehousesociety.org.uk

The Society's website can be viewed at
www.pgwodehousesociety.org.uk